A GUIDE TO THE STAR WARS UNIVERSE

The Star Wars Library Published by Del Rey Books

Star Wars: The Essential Guide to Droids
Star Wars: The Essential Guide to Alien Species
Star Wars: The Essential Guide to Planets and Moons
Star Wars: The New Essential Chronology
Star Wars: The New Essential Guide to Characters
Star Wars: The New Essential Guide to Vehicles and Vessels
Star Wars: The New Essential Guide to Weapons and Technology

Star Wars Encyclopedia
A Guide to the Star Wars Universe
Star Wars: Diplomatic Corps Entrance Exam
Star Wars: Galactic Phrase Book and Travel Guide
I'd Just As Soon Kiss A Wookiee: The Quotable Star Wars
The Secrets of Star Wars: Shadows of the Empire

The Art of Star Wars: A New Hope
The Art of Star Wars: The Empire Strikes Back
The Art of Star Wars: Return of the Jedi
The Art of Star Wars: Episode I: The Phantom Menace
The Art of Star Wars: Episode II: Attack of the Clones
The Art of Star Wars: Episode III: Revenge of the Sith

Script Facsimile: Star Wars: A New Hope
Script Facsimile: Star Wars: The Empire Strikes Back
Script Facsimile: Star Wars: Return of the Jedi
Script Facsimile: Star Wars: Episode I: The Phantom Menace

Star Wars: The Annotated Screenplays
Illustrated Screenplay: Star Wars: A New Hope
Illustrated Screenplay: Star Wars: The Empire Strikes Back
Illustrated Screenplay: Star Wars: Return of the Jedi
Illustrated Screenplay: Star Wars: Episode I: The Phantom Menace

The Making of Star Wars: Episode I: The Phantom Menace
Mythmaking: Behind the Scenes of Star Wars: Episode II: Attack of the Clones
The Making of Star Wars: Episode III: Revenge of the Sith

A GUIDE TO THE STAR WARS UNIVERSE

THIRD EDITION, REVISED AND EXPANDED

BILL SLAVICSEK

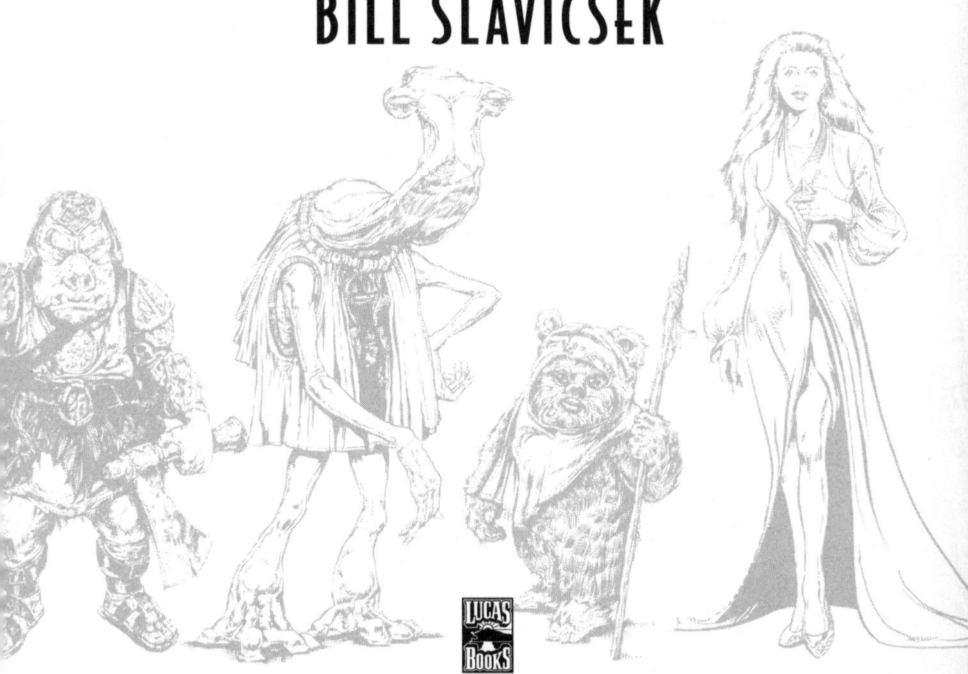

DEL REY THE BALLANTINE PUBLISHING GROUP • NEW YORK

A Del Rey® Book
Published by The Random House Publishing Group

Published in the United States by Del Rey Books, an imprint of The Random House Publishing Group, a division of Random House, Inc., New York, and simultaneously in Canada by Random House of Canada Limited, Toronto.

Del Rey is a registered trademark and the Del Rey colophon is a trademark of Random House, Inc.

www.starwars.com
www.delreybooks.com

Library of Congress Catalog Card Number: 00-104015

ISBN 0-345-42066-7

Edited by Allan Kausch (Lucasfilm) and Steve Saffel (Del Rey)

Cover design by Min Choi
Cover art: Ralph McQuarrie production painting
Interior design by Michaelis/Carpelis Design Assoc., Inc.

Manufactured in the United States of America

First Edition: October 2000

9 8 7 6 5 4

Dedication

For Michele, who loves this stuff as much as I do.
I couldn't have done this without you.

Acknowledgments

Special thanks to George Lucas for creating this faraway galaxy; to all the authors whose collected works contributed to this guide; to Steve Saffel, Alexandra Krijgsman, and Lisa Collins at Del Rey Books; and to Lucy Autrey Wilson and Allan Kausch at Lucas Licensing for asking me to revise this guide one more time.

A long time ago
in a galaxy far, far away. . . .

A Few Notes about What Follows

This is the newest revision to a guide I first revised six years ago. At the time, about ten years had passed since the original guide had been published. The original included a handful of novels, a scattering of sketchbooks and art volumes, a couple of radio plays, a TV special, and the original *Star Wars* movie trilogy. When my turn came to expand the guide, the mythos had grown to include comics, a bunch of sourcebooks from West End Games, and a new trilogy of novels by Timothy Zahn that were set after *Return of the Jedi*.

Since then, the wealth of material has become enormous. This third edition has been expanded to include all of the novels and comics and other new material produced from 1994 through 1999. It features some material pertaining to Episode I *The Phantom Menace* and the New Jedi Order series.

The entries are presented in alphabetical order. They give a brief explanation of each person, place, and thing, but they are far from complete. There are many details that simply could not fit in the space allotted to each topic. Interested readers are encouraged to track down the original sources for a complete view of a topic that captures your attention. An extensive bibliography is included for that purpose.

Be aware that time plays an important role in the *Star Wars* universe. Stories have been told throughout the ages, and when it is relevant an entry provides a time frame in which to view it. Time frames fall into these categories:

- Four thousand years before the Galactic Civil War: time of the Sith Wars.
- The Galactic Civil War: the period of Rebellion against the Empire, generally considered to start with the Battle of Yavin and end with the Battle of Endor.
- The New Republic: events that occur after the Alliance victory at Endor.

Even though this guide has been revised and expanded, space wasn't available to cover every single topic in depth. I'm sure I had to leave something out that some reader will want to know about. I apologize for that in advance, and hope that most of the highlights from twenty-plus years of *Star Wars* stories have been touched upon. I love this universe, and I loved gathering the details between these covers. So turn to any page, start reading, and let the wonders engulf you for the first time or all over again. I guarantee you'll discover some new secret or detail waiting for you inside.

—Bill Slavicsek, October 1999

Entry Codes and Sources

AC—*Ambush at Corellia,* volume 1 of The Corellian Trilogy, Roger MacBride Allen, Bantam Books, 1995.

AS—*Assault at Selonia,* volume 2 of The Corellian Trilogy, Roger MacBride Allen, Bantam Books, 1995.

BF—*Boba Fett,* one-shot and limited-series comics, Dark Horse Comics, 1995–1997.

BFE—*Ewoks: The Battle for Endor,* MGM/UA, 1986.

BFEE—*Boba Fett: Enemy of the Empire,* 4-issue series, John Wagner, Dark Horse Comics, 1999.

BGS—*Battle for the Golden Sun,* Douglas Kaufman, West End Games, 1988.

BI—*Black Ice,* Paul Murphy and Bill Slavicsek, West End Games, 1990.

BTS—*Before the Storm,* volume 1 of The Black Fleet Crisis Trilogy, Michael P. Kube-McDowell, Bantam Books, 1996.

BW—*The Bacta War,* volume 4 of The X-Wing series, Michael A. Stackpole, Bantam Books, 1997.

CCC—*Crisis on Cloud City,* Christopher Kubasik, West End Games, 1989.

CE—*Crimson Empire I & II,* Mike Richardson and Randy Stradley, Dark Horse Comics, 1997–1999.

CHR—*The Essential Star Wars Chronology,* Kevin J. Anderson and Daniel Wallace, Del Rey Books, 2000.

COF—*Champions of the Force,* volume 3 of The Jedi Academy Trilogy, Kevin J. Anderson, Bantam Books, 1994.

COJ—*Children of the Jedi,* Barbara Hambly, Bantam Books, 1995.

CPL—*The Courtship of Princess Leia,* Dave Wolverton, Bantam Books, 1994.

CRFG—*Cracken's Rebel Field Guide,* Christopher Kubasik, West End Games, 1991.

CS—*The Crystal Star,* Vonda McIntyre, Bantam Books, 1994.

CSSB—*Han Solo & the Corporate Sector Sourcebook,* Michael Allen Horne, West End Games, 1993.

CSW—*Classic Star Wars,* 20-issue series, Archie Goodwin and Al Williamson, Dark Horse Comics, 1992–1994.

D—*Droids,* series and specials, Dark Horse Comics, 1994–1995.

DA—*Dark Apprentice,* volume 2 of The Jedi Academy Trilogy, Kevin J. Anderson, Bantam Books, 1994.

DE—*Star Wars: Dark Empire,* 6-issue series, Tom Veitch and Cam Kennedy, Dark Horse Comics, 1991–1992.

DE2—*Star Wars: Dark Empire II,* 6-issue series, Tom Veitch and Cam Kennedy, Dark Horse Comics, 1994–1995.

DESB—*Star Wars: Dark Empire Sourcebook,* Michael Allen Horne, West End Games, 1993.

DF—Dark Forces, volumes 1–3, *Soldier for the Empire, Rebel Agent, Jedi Knight,* William C. Dietz, Dark Horse Comics and Boulevard/Putnam, 1997–1998.

DFR—*Dark Force Rising,* volume 2 of The Thrawn Trilogy, Timothy Zahn, Bantam Books, 1992.

DFRSB—*Dark Force Rising Sourcebook,* Bill Slavicsek, West End Games, 1992.

DLS—*Tales of the Jedi: Dark Lords of the Sith,* 6-issue series, Tom Veitch and Kevin J. Anderson, Dark Horse Comics, 1994–1995.

DS—*Darksaber,* Kevin J. Anderson, Bantam Books, 1995.

DSC—*The DarkStryder Campaign,* Peter Schweighofer et al., West End Games, 1995.

DSTC—*Death Star Technical Companion,* Bill Slavicsek, West End Games, 1991, 1993.

DTV—*Droids,* animated television show, episodes 1–13, Nelvana, 1985.

EA—*The Ewok Adventure (Caravan of Courage),* MGM/UA, 1984.

EE—*Empire's End,* 2-issue series, Tom Veitch, Dark Horse Comics, 1995.

ESB, ESBN—*Star Wars V: The Empire Strikes Back* film, Twentieth Century Fox, 1980; novelization, Donald F. Glut, Del Rey Books, 1980.

ESBR—*The Empire Strikes Back,* National Public Radio dramatization, Brian Daley, 1981; published by Del Rey Books, 1995.

ETV—*Ewoks,* animated television show, episodes 1–26, Nelvana, 1985–1986.

FNU—*The Freedon Nadd Uprising,* 2-issue series, Tom Veitch et al., Dark Horse Comics, 1994.

FP—*Farlander Papers,* as reprinted and continued in *X-Wing: The Official Strategy Guide*, Rusel DeMaria, Prima Publishing, 1993.

FSE—*Tales of the Jedi: The Fall of the Sith Empire,* 5-issue series, Kevin J. Anderson, Dark Horse Comics, 1997.

FT—*Fantastic Technology,* Rick D. Stuart, West End Games, 1995.

GA—*Graveyard of Alderaan,* Bill Slavicsek, West End Games, 1991.

GAS—*Tales of the Jedi: The Golden Age of the Sith,* 6-issue series, Kevin J. Anderson, Dark Horse Comics, 1996–1997.

GDV—*The Glove of Darth Vader,* Paul and Hollace Davids, Bantam Skylark Books, 1992.

GF—Galaxy of Fear, volumes 1–12, *Eaten Alive, City of the Dead, Planet Plague, The Nightmare Machine, Ghost of the Jedi, Army of Terror, The Brain Spiders, The Swarm, Spore, The Doomsday Ship, Clones, The Hunger,* John Whitman, Bantam Books, 1997–1998.

GG1—*Galaxy Guide 1: A New Hope,* Grant Boucher, West End Games, 1989.

GG2—*Galaxy Guide 2: Yavin and Bespin,* Jonatha Caspian and Bill Slavicsek et al., West End Games, 1989.

GG3—*Galaxy Guide 3: The Empire Strikes Back,* Michael Stern, West End Games, 1989.

GG4—*Galaxy Guide 4: Alien Races,* Troy Denning, West End Games, 1989.

GG5—*Galaxy Guide 5: Return of the Jedi,* Michael Stern, West End Games, 1990.

GG6—*Galaxy Guide 6: Tramp Freighters,* Mark Rein-Hagen and Stewart Wieck, West End Games, 1990.

GG7—*Galaxy Guide 7: Mos Eisley,* Martin Wixted, West End Games, 1993.

GG9—*Galaxy Guide 9: Fragments from the Rim,* Simon Smith and Eric S. Trautmann, West End Games, 1993.

GG10—*Galaxy Guide 10: Bounty Hunters,* Rick D. Stuart, West End Games, 1993.

GG11—*Galaxy Guide 11: Criminal Organizations,* Rick D. Stuart, West End Games, 1994.

GG12—*Galaxy Guide 12: Aliens: Enemies and Allies,* Bill Smith, editor, West End Games, 1995.

HE—*Heir to the Empire,* volume 1 of The Thrawn Trilogy, Timothy Zahn, Bantam Books, 1991.

HESB—*Heir to the Empire Sourcebook,* Bill Slavicsek, West End Games, 1992.

HG—*The Hutt Gambit,* volume 2 of The Han Solo Trilogy, A. C. Crispin, Bantam Books, 1997.

HLL—*Han Solo and the Lost Legacy,* Brian Daley, Del Rey Books, 1980.

HSE—*Han Solo at Stars' End,* Brian Daley, Del Rey Books, 1979.

HSR—*Han Solo's Revenge,* Brian Daley, Del Rey Books, 1979.

HT—*Hero's Trial,* Book 1 of The New Jedi Order: Agents of Chaos, Jim Luceno, Del Rey Books, 2000.

IC—*The Isis Coordinates,* Christopher Kubasik, West End Games, 1990.

IF—*Iron Fist,* volume 6 of The X-Wing series, Aaron Allston, Bantam Books, 1998.

IJ—*I, Jedi,* Michael A. Stackpole, Bantam Books, 1998.

IR—*Isard's Revenge,* volume 8 of The X-Wing series, Michael A. Stackpole, Bantam Books, 1999.

ISB—*Imperial Sourcebook,* Greg Gorden, West End Games, 1989.

ISWU—*The Illustrated Star Wars Universe,* Kevin J. Anderson and Ralph McQuarrie, Bantam Books, 1995.

JAB—*Jabba the Hutt,* specials, Jim Woodring, Dark Horse Comics, 1995.

JAL—*Jedi Academy: Leviathan,* 4-issue series, Kevin J. Anderson, Dark Horse Comics, 1998–1999.

JASB—*Jedi Academy Sourcebook,* Paul Sudlow, West End Games, 1996.

JJK—Junior Jedi Knights, volumes 1–3, *The Golden Globe, Lyric's World, Promises,* Nancy Richardson; volumes 4–6, *Anakin's Quest, Vader's Fortress, Kenobi's Blade,* Rebecca Moesta; Berkley Books, 1995–1996.

JS—*Jedi Search,* volume 1 of The Jedi Academy Trilogy, Kevin J. Anderson, Bantam Books, 1994.

JT—*The Jabba Tape,* John Wagner, Dark Horse Comics, 1998.

KK—*Bounty Hunters: Kenix Kil,* Randy Stradley, Dark Horse Comics, 1999.

KT—*The Krytos Trap,* volume 3 of The X-Wing series, Michael A. Stackpole, Bantam Books, 1996.

LC—*The Last Command,* volume 3 of The Thrawn Trilogy, Timothy Zahn, Bantam Books, 1993.

LCF—*Lando Calrissian and the Flamewind of Oseon,* L. Neil Smith, Del Rey Books, 1983.

LCJ—*The Lost City of the Jedi,* Paul and Hollace Davids, Bantam Skylark Books, 1992.

LCM—*Lando Calrissian and the Mindharp of Sharu,* L. Neil Smith, Del Rey Books, 1983.

LCS—*Lando Calrissian and the StarCave of ThonBoka,* L. Neil Smith, Del Rey Books, 1983.

LCSB—*The Last Command Sourcebook,* Eric S. Trautmann, West End Games, 1994.

MJ—*Mara Jade: By the Emperor's Hand,* 6-issue series, Timothy Zahn and Michael A. Stackpole, Dark Horse Comics, 1998–1999.

ML—*Mission to Lianna,* Joanne E. Wyrick, West End Games, 1992.

MMY—*Mission from Mount Yoda,* Paul and Hollace Davids, Bantam Skylark Books, 1993.

MTS—*Movie Trilogy Sourcebook,* Grant Boucher and Michael Stern et al., West End Games, 1993.

NR—*The New Rebellion,* Kristine Kathryn Rusch, Bantam Books, 1996.

OS—*Otherspace,* Bill Slavicsek, West End Games, 1989.

OS2—*Otherspace II: Invasion,* Douglas Kaufman, West End Games, 1989.

PDS—*Prophets of the Dark Side,* Paul and Hollace Davids, Bantam Skylark Books, 1993.

POG—*Planets of the Galaxy, Volume One,* Grant Boucher et al., West End Games, 1991; *Volume Two,* John Terra, West End Games, 1992; *Volume Three,* Bill Smith, West End Games, 1993.

POT—*Planet of Twilight,* Barbara Hambly, Bantam Books, 1997.

PS—*The Paradise Snare,* volume 1 of The Han Solo Trilogy, A. C. Crispin, Bantam Books, 1997.

PSG—*Platt's Starport Guide,* Peter Schweighofer, West End Games, 1995.

QE—*Queen of the Empire,* Paul and Hollace Davids, Bantam Skylark Books, 1993.

RD—*Rebel Dawn,* volume 3 of The Han Solo Trilogy, A. C. Crispin, Bantam Books, 1998.

RJ, RJN—*Star Wars VI: Return of the Jedi* film, Twentieth Century Fox, 1983; novelization, James Kahn, Del Rey Books, 1983.

RJSE—*Star Wars VI: Return of the Jedi Special Edition* film, Twentieth Century Fox, 1997.

RM—*Riders of the Maelstrom,* Ray Winninger, West End Games, 1989.

ROC—*River of Chaos,* 4-issue series, Louise Simonson, Dark Horse Comics, 1995.

RP—*Rogue Planet,* Greg Bear, Del Rey Books, 2000.

RS—*Rogue Squadron,* volume 1 of The X-Wing series, Michael A. Stackpole, Bantam Books, 1996.

RSB—*The Rebel Alliance Sourcebook,* Paul Murphy, West End Games, 1990.

SAC—*Showdown at Centerpoint,* volume 3 of The Corellian Trilogy, Roger MacBride Allen, Bantam Books, 1995.

SEE—*Shadows of the Empire: Evolution,* 5-issue series, Steve Perry, Dark Horse Comics, 1998.

SESB—*Shadows of the Empire Sourcebook,* Peter Schweighofer, West End Games, 1996.

SF—*Starfall,* Rob Jenkins and Michael Stern, West End Games, 1989.

SFS—*Strike Force: Shantipole,* Ken Rolston and Steve Gilbert, West End Games, 1988.

SH—*Scavenger Hunt,* Brad Freeman, West End Games, 1989.

SME—*Splinter of the Mind's Eye,* Alan Dean Foster, Del Rey Books, 1978.

SOL—*Shield of Lies,* volume 2 of The Black Fleet Crisis Trilogy, Michael P. Kube-McDowell, Bantam Books, 1996.

SOTE—*Shadows of the Empire,* Steve Perry, Bantam Books, 1996.

SOTEALB—*Shadows of the Empire* CD liner notes, Varese Saraband, 1996.

SP—*Specter of the Past,* Timothy Zahn, Bantam Books, 1997.

SS—*Shadow Stalker,* Ryder Windham, Dark Horse Comics, 1997.

SW, SWN—*Star Wars IV: A New Hope* film, Twentieth Century Fox, 1977; novelization, George Lucas, Del Rey Books, 1976.

SWCG—*Star Wars: The Essential Guide to Characters,* Andy Mangels, Del Rey Books, 1995.

SWHS—"Star Wars Holiday Special," television show, Nelvana, 1978.

SWR—*Star Wars* National Public Radio dramatizations, Brian Daley, episodes 1–13, 1981; published by Del Rey Books, 1994.

SWRPG—*Star Wars: The Roleplaying Game,* Greg Costikyan, West End Games, 1987.

SWRPG2—*Star Wars: The Roleplaying Game, Second Edition,* Bill Smith, West End Games, 1992.

SWSB—*Star Wars Sourcebook,* Bill Slavicsek and Curtis Smith, West End Games, 1987.

SWSE—*Star Wars IV: A New Hope Special Edition* film, Twentieth Century Fox, 1997.

SWTPM, SWTPMN—*Star Wars I: The Phantom Menace* film, Twentieth Century Fox, 1999; novelization, Terry Brooks, Del Rey Books, 1999.

SWVG—*Star Wars: The Essential Guide to Vehicles and Vessels,* Bill Smith, Del Rey Books, 1996.

SWWS—*Star Wars: The Wookiee Storybook,* Random House, 1979.

TAB—*The Truce at Bakura,* Kathy Tyers, Bantam Books, 1994.

TBH—*Tales of the Bounty Hunters,* Kevin J. Anderson, editor, Bantam Books, 1996.

TBSB—*The Truce at Bakura Sourcebook,* Kathy Tyers and Eric S. Trautmann, West End Games, 1996.

TGH—*The Great Heep,* animated television special, Nelvana, 1986.

TJP—*Tales from Jabba's Palace,* Kevin J. Anderson, editor, Bantam Books, 1996.

TM—*Tatooine Manhunt,* Bill Slavicsek and Daniel Greenberg, West End Games, 1988.

TMEC—*Tales from the Mos Eisley Cantina,* Kevin J. Anderson, editor, Bantam Books, 1995.

TOJ—*Tales of the Jedi,* 5-issue series, Tom Veitch, Dark Horse Comics, 1993–1994.

TOJR—*Tales of the Jedi: Redemption,* 6-issue series, Kevin J. Anderson, Dark Horse Comics, 1998.

TRG—*The Red Ghost,* Melinda Luke, Random House, 1986.

TSC—*The Stele Chronicles* and its continuation in *TIE Fighter: The Official Strategy Guide,* Rusel DeMaria, David Wessman, and David Maxwell, Prima Publishing, 1994. Supplemented by *TIE Fighter: The Collector's CD-ROM* game by Lucas Arts, 1995.

TSW—*The Sith War,* 6-issue series, Kevin J. Anderson, Dark Horse Comics, 1993–1994.

TT—*Tyrant's Test,* volume 3 of The Black Fleet Crisis Trilogy, Michael P. Kube-McDowell, Bantam Books, 1997.

VF—*Vision of the Future,* Timothy Zahn, Bantam Books, 1998.

VP—*Vector Prime,* R. A. Salvatore, Del Rey Books, 1999.

VQ—*Vader's Quest,* 4-issue series, Darko Macan, Dark Horse Comics, 1999.

WG—*Wedge's Gamble,* volume 2 of The X-Wing series, Michael A. Stackpole, Bantam Books, 1996.

XW—*X-Wing Rogue Squadron,* 35-issue series, Dark Horse Comics, 1995–1998.

YJK—Young Jedi Knights, volumes 1–14, *Heirs of the Force, Shadow Academy, The Lost Ones, Lightsabers, Darkest Knight, Jedi under Siege, Shards of Alderaan, Diversity Alliance, Delusions of Grandeur, Jedi Bounty, The Emperor's Plague, Return to Ord Mantell, Trouble on Cloud City, Crisis at Crystal Reef,* Kevin J. Anderson and Rebecca Moesta, Berkley Books, 1995–1998.

ZHR—*Zorba the Hutt's Revenge,* Paul and Hollace Davids, Bantam Skylark Books, 1992.

A GUIDE TO THE STAR WARS UNIVERSE

A-3DO (ThreeDee)

This multitalented service droid was in the service of Jedi Andur Sunrider when Sunrider died at the hands of Great Bogga the Hutt's gang of criminals. Programmed as a mechanic and pilot, A-3DO later served Andur's wife, Nomi, while she trained to take her husband's place among the Jedi. [TOJ]

A-9 Vigilance Interceptor

An Imperial starfighter that first saw action against New Republic forces during the events that led to the return of the Emperor six years after the Battle of Endor. It was designed as an answer to the Republic's A-wing fighters, but has limited maneuverability and a weak hull. [DE, SWVG]

Aalun, Syron

One of three famous Gand ruetsavii, or observers, who were assigned to Rogue Squadron pilot Ooryl Qrygg. They were sent to observe Qrygg's activities and determine his worthiness to become janwuine, the highest possible honor in the communal Gand society. In addition to watching Qrygg, Aalun and the other ruetsavii served as pilots and undercover operatives for the squadron. [BW]

Aar'aa

Members of a reptilian species of skin-changers, they are able to change the color of their pebbly textured skin to match their surroundings. The Ylesian priests used Aar'aa to guard their spice-processing plants. [PS]

Aba

A Wookiee doll, named by its owner, young Jacen Solo. [CS]

A'baht, General Etahn

Commander of the New Republic's Fifth Fleet. A'baht led from aboard his flagship, the fleet carrier *Intrepid.* His disregard for orders and the defeat of the fleet at the Koornacht

Cluster led Princess Leia Organa Solo to relieve him of command and place the fleet under the authority of her husband, Han Solo. [BTS]

Abbaji

This planet is home to the Irugian Rain Forest, where one-hundred-meter-tall firethorn trees grow in a single grove. Prince Xizor, leader of the Black Sun criminal organization, counted a 600-year-old dwarf firethorn tree among his most prized possessions. [SOTE]

abo

An old Imperial slang word for the native inhabitants of a planet, often used in a derogatory manner. [SME]

Abregado-rae

This manufacturing and trade-oriented planet within the Abregado star system was part of the New Republic some five years after the Battle of Endor. During the time of the Empire, the spaceport was considered on par with the worst places in the Rim Territories. Since the birth of the New Republic, the place has cleaned up its act. A bright, painfully clean cityscape towers over its landing pits, but the wild air of all spaceports, created by the mix of cultures and species, cannot be washed from the place. A repressive bureaucracy that struggled to bring outlying clans into line rules the world. [DFR, HE, HESB]

Abregado system

This planetary system is located in the Borderland Regions, a militarized zone that separates the New Republic from the remnants of the Empire. A vast manufacturing infrastructure links the system's planets, and the goods produced there are vitally important to the New Republic. [HE, HESB]

Abrion sector

The location of the planet Ukio, one of the top-five food-producing worlds in the New Republic. [LC]

Abyssin

A primitive and violent species that inhabits the planet Byss, located in the binary star system of Byss and Abyss. Averaging about two meters tall, each humanoid Abyssin has long limbs and a single eye in its forehead. [GG4]

Academy, the

During the time of the Old Republic, this elite educational institution produced highly trained personnel to fill posts in Exploration, Military, and Merchant Services. Under the rule of the Emperor, the Academy slowly turned into the training ground for Imperial officers, especially the Raithal Academy in the Core region. All of its numerous campuses, spread across the galaxy, had a reputation for a competitive selection process and a rigorous curriculum. [ISB, SW, SWR]

acceleration compensator

This device provides artificial gravity and neutralizes the effects of high-speed maneuvering for crew and cargo aboard space vessels. The *Millennium Falcon*, for example, is equipped with such a device. [HSE]

acceleration straps

These passenger safety harnesses, usually built into seats, serve to restrain passengers during takeoffs, landings, and adverse traveling conditions. [SW]

Access Chute

This kilometers-long tunnel snakes through the decaying buildings and docking towers of the spaceport moon Nar Shaddaa, leading to Shug Ninx's repair facility. An advertising holoscreen hides the entrance to the Chute. [DE]

Accuser

See *Emancipator*.

Ackbar, Admiral

A respected and highly regarded member of the Mon Calamari species, Ackbar overcame hardship and adversity to take a pivotal role in the Rebel Alliance and later the New Republic. His public life began when he served as the leader of Coral Depths City on the Mon Calamari homeworld. The Empire attacked the watery planet and enslaved many of its citizens, including Ackbar. He eventually became Grand Moff Tarkin's interpreter, and while in the Imperial's service he heard about the Rebellion and learned of a new superweapon. Ackbar made a study of Imperial tactics and defenses while serving the grand moff. Rebel agents released him from servitude during a failed attempt to assassinate Tarkin. Ackbar returned to his homeworld and convinced the normally peaceful Mon Calamari to join the Rebels, bringing a much-needed fleet of capital ships into the Alliance arsenal.

Admiral Ackbar

Shortly after the Battle of Yavin, the newly ranked Commander Ackbar proposed a plan for dealing with Imperial escort frigates. He argued that a specially designed starfighter was the Alliance's best hope—at least until more funds became available or the number of Rebel capital ships dramatically increased. With the aid of the Verpine, a renowned species of shipbuilders, Ackbar developed the B-wing starfighter.

Ackbar then became one of Mon Mothma's two senior Rebel Alliance advisers. He was promoted to admiral and helped develop the plans for the Alliance surprise attack on the second Death Star battle station. He led the assault from the bridge of his personal flagship during the Battle of Endor. With the rise of the New Republic, Ackbar was named commander in chief of Republic military operations. As a member of both the Provisional Council and the ruling Inner Council, he helped forge the new galactic government.

During the events surrounding the return of Grand Admiral Thrawn, Ackbar was falsely accused of embezzling New Republic funds thanks to fake evidence planted by Thrawn. Ackbar was later cleared, through the efforts of Luke Skywalker and his companions, and the Mon Calamari led the New Republic fleet to victory over Thrawn's forces at the Bilbringi Shipyards.

A few days after Thrawn's defeat, survivors of the Emperor's ruling circle and a handful of Imperial fleet commanders attacked and recaptured Coruscant. Ackbar and other New Republic leaders planned a counterstrike, and their forces regained Coruscant a few months later.

Later, on a diplomatic mission to Vortex, Ackbar's personal B-wing starfighter crashed into the Cathedral of Winds. This towering crystalline structure was considered to be the world's greatest artistic treasure, and Ackbar was once again accused of a serious crime. His chief mechanic was discovered to have been an Imperial operative who had sabotaged the B-wing, and Ackbar was cleared of any wrongdoing.

After he resumed his role in the New Republic, Ackbar returned to Vortex to attend the ceremony dedicating the rebuilt Cathedral of Winds. Winter, Princess Leia's aide, accompanied him on the trip, and the two developed a close relationship. [DA, DE, DFR, DS, HE, LC, RJ, SFS, SWCG, SWSB]

Adamant

Admiral Ackbar commanded this New Republic bulk space cruiser. Some nineteen years after the Battle of Endor, the *Adamant* was attacked while transporting a cargo of hyperdrive cores and turbolaser battery emplacements to the Kuat Drive Yards. It was boarded and captured by onetime Imperial TIE fighter pilot Qorl and his troops, who set the crew adrift in escape pods and made off with the cruiser and its cargo. [YJK]

Adamantine

This New Republic escort cruiser visited the planet Nam Chorios. The ship and its crew were lost when the Death Seed plague was unleashed on the surrounding sector of space. [POT]

Adega

This star system located in the Outer Rim Territories was the site of an important Jedi stronghold in ancient times. [DE]

Adegan crystals

These crystals were the types most commonly used in ancient times in the construction of lightsabers. They spontaneously emit powerful bursts of light and energy when resonant frequencies are transmitted through them. These crystals are also known as Ilum crystals. [DE]

Adin

This former Imperial stronghold was the homeworld of Senator Meido. [NR]

Adjudicator

One of two Imperial Star Destroyers captured by the Alliance during the Battle of Endor, the *Adjudicator* was renamed the *Liberator* and placed under the command of Luke Skywalker. After the Empire recaptured Coruscant, *Liberator* crashed into Imperial City as the result of damage sustained during combat. Skywalker's skillful deployment of the Star Destroyer's shields and repulsorlifts prevented the death of the crew. [DE, DESB]

Adriana

This gas giant, the third planet in the Tatoo system, has rings of ice. The rings are periodically mined to provide the planet Tatooine with water. [GG7]

Af'El

The homeworld of the Defels, or Wraiths, this high-gravity world orbiting Ka'Dedus specializes in the export of meleenium, a metal used to build durasteel. Af'El is the only known source of the metal. [GG4]

affect mind

A Jedi Knight can use this Force technique to tamper with the perceptions of a person or creature. It creates illusions or blocks the senses so that the target can't understand what's really happening. It can also be used to alter a person's memories, replace them with false memories, or totally wipe out memories of a particular event. [DFRSB, SWRPG, SWRPG2]

Affytechan

A sentient form of plant life that originated on the Outer Rim world of Dom-Bradden. Each Affytechan appears beautiful, with a high musical voice and a body composed of thousands of colorful petals, tendrils, and stalks. However, it also smells of ammonia and musk. [COJ]

Afyon, Captain

Native of Alderaan and New Republic captain at the helm of the escort frigate *Larkhess*, Afyon grew bitter over the years, believing that men like him were doing the real work of the new government, while the credit was going to hotshot starfighter pilots. Right before the appearance of Grand Admiral Thrawn, his warship was relegated to cargo transport duty. During the Battle of Sluis Van, he proved himself to be an excellent commander. [HE, HESB]

Agamar

Home to the famous Rebel pilot Keyan Farlander, this planet is located in the Lahara sector of the Outer Rim Territories. Sites of interest include the large city Calna Muun and the backwater town Tondatha. The Empire wiped out the latter for harboring Rebel collaborators. [FP]

Aggregator

This Imperial Interdictor cruiser was the property of High Admiral Teradoc. He leased it to Ysanne Isard to aid her quest to destroy Rogue Squadron. The cruiser was badly damaged during a battle in the section of space known as the Graveyard of Alderaan. [BW]

Agrilat

A region on the planet Corellia known for its crystal swamps. The swamps contain hot springs, geysers of boiling water, and sharp blades of crystalline brush. The bounty hunter Dengar suffered serious injuries here during a swoop bike race against Han Solo that took place long before Solo became an infamous bounty hunter. [MTS, TBH]

agrirobot

This primitive droid is programmed to tend the land and harvest foodstuffs. Such droids come in a variety of forms, each designed to fulfill a primary function. Models include harvesters, sowers, sprayers, and packagers. [HSE]

Aquarl 3

During the Rebellion, this ocean-covered planet contained a submerged Rebel base. A Quarren spy revealed the location of the base to the Empire, leading to an attack by a wing of TIE bombers. [ROC]

Ahazi

This New Republic fleet tender was destroyed during the Fifth Fleet's live-fire training exercise code-named Hammerblow. All six on board were killed. [BTS]

Aikhibba

A planet in a system of the same name, it was the home of crimelord Spadda the Hutt and a minor stopping point for smugglers on the Gamor Run. [DESB]

Aing-Tii

Alien monks who spend most of their lives near the Kathol Rift. Aing-Tii monks hate slavers and believe that while not all events are predetermined, they are all somehow guided. The Aing-Tii have an understanding of the Force, but a different one from the Jedi. They also have a different type of technology, one that includes a star drive that does not employ hyperspace. Instead, their ship makes instantaneous jumps to whatever point in space they want to go. [VF]

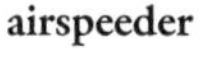

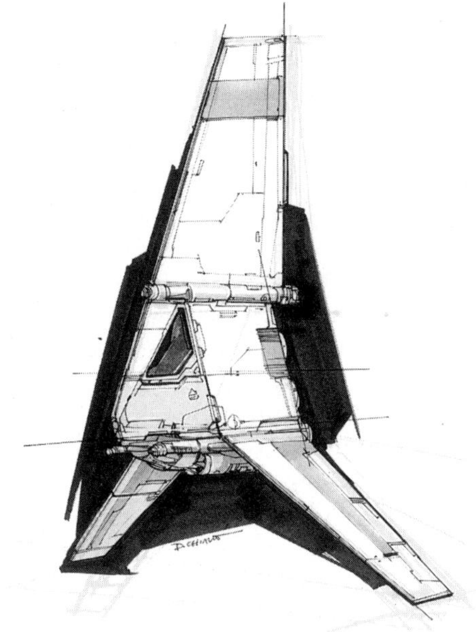

airspeeder

Any type of airship designed to operate within a planet's atmosphere. The term is usually applied to repulsorlift vehicles that operate high above the ground. [HLL, SWSB]

Ak-Buz

A Weequay, he commanded Jabba the Hutt's sail barge until Anzati Dannik Jerriko murdered him. [TJP]

A'Kla, Elegos

A Caamasi, he was the trustant for the Caamasi Remnant. Seven years after the Battle of Endor, he met Corran Horn and helped the pilot rescue his wife from the clutches of ex-Moff Leonia Tavira. Nine years later, he helped the New Republic survive the crisis instigated by the impostor of Grand Admiral Thrawn. [IJ, SP, VF]

Akrit'tar

One of the galaxy's many penal colony worlds. The Empire imprisoned Tycho Celchu of Rogue Squadron here. He escaped after three months. [HSR, WG]

Alderaan

The adopted homeworld of Leia Organa Solo, Alderaan was once a shining star in the Old Republic. It spawned such heroes as Bail Organa, Leia's adoptive father, who fought beside Obi-Wan Kenobi during the Clone Wars. The horrors of the Clone Wars convinced Alderaan to take a new stance once peace was restored. The planetary government instituted a philosophy of pacifism and banned all weapons from the planet.

Alderaan was known for its high culture and education. It was famous for its artists, its cuisine, and its people, who loved the land. There were no oceans, but the planet had an ice-rimmed polar sea and thousands of lakes and waterways.

When Alderaan dismantled its massive war machine, its government decided to hide the weapons where no one would be able to find them. At the same time, the weapons would be readily available should the planet ever need to protect itself or its beliefs. The weapons were stored aboard a massive armory ship named *Another Chance*, which was programmed to continually jump through hyperspace until the Council of Elders called it home. Sightings of a ghost ship in the asteroid ruins of Alderaan's orbit, called the Graveyard, have been attributed to this legendary vessel.

Due to the tyrannical acts and unchallenged injustices of the Emperor's New Order, many young people, including

Senator Leia Organa, began to question Alderaan's pacifistic policies. As the New Order became more open in its tyranny, Alderaan became more supportive of the growing Rebellion. Some believe that the Alliance was born on this world. Before Alderaan could officially join the Alliance, the Empire destroyed the entire planet as a demonstration of the original Death Star's destructive capabilities. [GA, ISWU, SW, SWR, SWSB]

Aleema

A direct descendant of Empress Teta, she was the heir to the throne of the Empress Teta system some 4,000 years before the Galactic Civil War. Her cousin, Satal Keto, shared the role of heir with her. Spoiled, rich, and bored with life, she turned to the dark-side illusions of Sith magicians for amusement. Later, her interest turned to a lust for power. Eventually, she became powerful enough to help stage a coup and take over the system. Aleema and Satal jointly led the Krath dark-side cult. The spirit of Freedon Nadd, a dark-side Jedi, bestowed additional powers upon Aleema. [DLS, TSW]

Algar

This planet is the source for Algarine torve weed, a mood-enhancing drug. Wing Tip Theel, an expert computer slicer and former associate of Han Solo and Lando Calrissian, had a base of operations here. [POT]

Alien Combine

This secret organization of nonhumanoid species was formed to protest unfair treatment and misconduct by Imperial forces on Coruscant after the Battle of Endor. Also known as the Alien League, the organization later joined the Alliance and helped liberate Coruscant. [BW]

Alien League

See Alien Combine.

Alima, Captain

This Imperial officer commanded the Star Destroyer *Conquest* during an attack against a herd ship on the planet Ithor. He forced the High Priest Momaw Nadon to reveal secrets of Ithorian technology to the Empire. [TMEC]

Alkhara

Centuries before the time of the Galactic Civil War, this bandit took control of Tatooine's B'omarr monastery. (Later, the place became Jabba the Hutt's palace.) It was Alkhara who started the blood feud between the Tusken Raiders and Tatooine's human settlers by butchering the Sand People he had earlier allied with. [ISWU]

Alk'Lellish III

The homeworld of a dangerous carnivore called the ketrann. [TAB]

Allegiance

This Super Star Destroyer was the Imperial command ship at the Battle of Calamari. [DE]

Alliance High Command

The top military component of the Rebel Alliance, and later of the New Republic. In the early days of the New Republic, the High Command consisted of General Jan Dodonna, General Carlist Rieekan, General Crix Madine, Admiral Ackbar, and Senator Garm Bel Iblis. [JS, RSB]

Alliance masternav

A computer system developed to track the orbits of planets within known star systems. The quality of the software and the ability to constantly update the data determines the reliability of the system. [TAB]

All Terrain Armored Transport (AT-AT)

This four-legged combat vehicle, sometimes called a walker, serves as both a troop transport and an assault craft. It provides high-powered support to ground forces. An individual walker is over fifteen meters tall with blaster-impervious armor plating. It resembles a mechanical beast as it strides across the battlefield. The moveable "head" contains the crew deck, with a pilot station, gunner station, and a commanding-officer–combat-coordination station. A walker's armament consists of heavy blaster cannons mounted on each side of the head and under the chin.

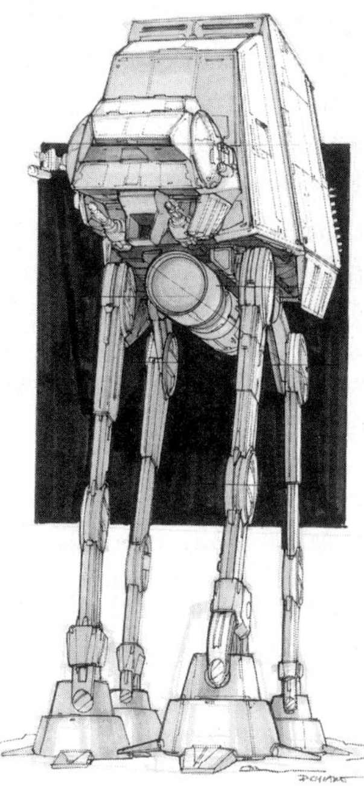

All Terrain Armored Transport

When the Empire began to design its military war machine, it sought weapons to match the terror inspired by Star Destroyers and unending hordes of stormtroopers. The AT-AT fit in well with the Imperial doctrine of "rule by terror." A walker could carry troops and light vehicles into combat areas, marching relentlessly through most defenses. The massive AT-AT knelt to unload its troops, lowering assault ramps from the rear portion of its armored body. These vehicles played important roles in the Battles of Hoth and Endor, among others. [ESB, SWSB, SWVG]

All Terrain Personal Transport (AT-PT)

This was the ancestor of the modern Imperial walker. The Old Republic developed this experimental weapon as a personal weapons platform for ground soldiers. It was supposed to turn a common soldier into a walking fortress. The majority of AT-PTs were installed aboard the legendary *Katana* fleet, and when that fleet was lost the project was abandoned. In this scaled-down version of the scout walker, a soldier crowded into a cramped control pod nestled between two multijointed legs. In the armored pod, slightly raised above the battlefield, the soldier operated a powerful array of weaponry, including a twin blaster cannon, a concussion grenade launcher, and a primitive combat sensor package. [DFR, DFRSB, SWVG]

All Terrain Scout Transport (AT-ST)

Modeled after the larger AT-AT, this reconnaissance or defense vehicle is lightweight and built for speed. The "chicken" or "scout walker" moves on two metal legs, its two-man crew stationed in a small, armored command pod atop the multijointed limbs. Its maneuverability and quickness allow a scout walker to provide covering fire for ground troops or to defend the flanks and undersides of AT-ATs. The seven-meter-tall AT-ST has chin- and side-mounted blaster cannons, a concussion grenade launcher, and feet claws for cutting through fixed defenses. [ESB, RJ, SWSB, SWVG]

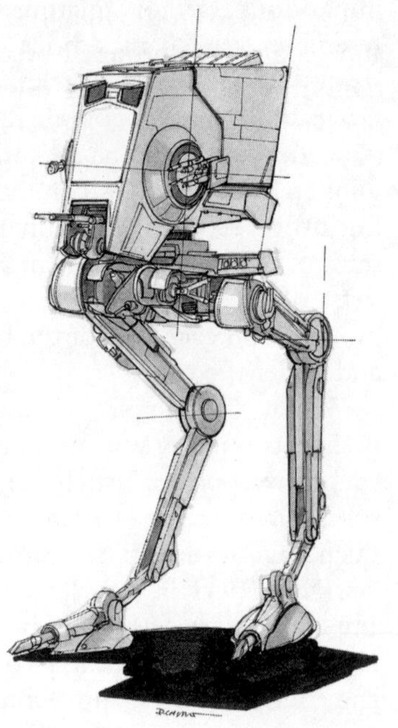

All Terrain Scout Transport

alluvial damper

A subsystem of a starship's hyperdrive unit, an alluvial damper blocks the emission of ion particles by moving a servo-controlled plate, thus regulating the amount of thrust. [ESB]

Allyuen

Darth Vader ordered this planet to be searched by recalibrated probe droids in an effort to locate the hidden Rebel base. The planets Hoth and Tokmia were also subjected to such searches. [ESBR]

Almania system

This planetary system on the far reaches of the galaxy never became part of the Old Republic, due to the great distance that separated it from the Republic's center. Almania, a large white and blue world shrouded by clouds, was loosely aligned with the Rebel Alliance during the Galactic Civil War and was part of the fledgling New Republic until its leadership changed shortly after the defeat of Grand Admiral Thrawn. [NR]

Alole

A loyal aide to Princess Leia Organa Solo. [BTS, SOL]

Alpha Blue

A mysterious covert intelligence group within the New Republic's military and security hierarchy. Admiral Hiram Drayson was in charge of Alpha Blue. [BTS, SOL]

Alpheridies

The homeworld of the Miraluka. [FNU]

Alsakan

Colonists on the *Kuat Explorer* settled this heavily populated planet in the Galactic Core millennia before the foundation of the New Republic. Imperial Commander Titus Klev and Corporate Sector Viceprex Mirkovig Hirken were born on Alsakan. [CSSB, DESB]

Altis, Djinn

This Jedi Master lived and taught on a training platform hidden in the clouds of the planet Bespin. His students included Geith and Callista. [DS]

Altorian

Two intelligent species inhabit the hot, dry planet Altor 14. The Avogwi, or Altorian Birds, are large, two-meter-tall predatory birds with three opposable fingers on the apex of their wings. The Nuiwit, or Altorian Lizards, are bipedal reptiles about 1.5 meters tall. While the Avogwi are primitive and lawless, the Nuiwit possess a highly structured and harmonious society. Both species hate each other, each constantly attempting to eliminate or subjugate the other. [GG4]

Alzoc III

The homeworld of the Talz and the source of the Alzoc pearl. Frozen plains cover this planet, located in the Alzoc system of the Outer Rim Territories. [CO, GG4, TAB]

Amanaman

This long-armed alien with big hands carried a three-headed staff and spent time in Jabba the Hutt's court. His species is more commonly known as the Head Hunters, for it is believed that the skulls dangling from the staves are obtained firsthand. The proper name of the species is Amanin. [GG12, RJ]

Amanin

See Amanaman.

Amanoa

The queen of Onderon, she ruled more than 4,000 years before the Galactic Civil War. She dabbled in Sith magic, which earned her the title Dark Queen. [FNU, TOJ]

Ambria

A desolate, ringed planet in the Stenness system. Jedi Master Thon's training compound was located here, in a desert known as the Ambrian wastes. Thon cleansed the planet, driving the great dark-side forces that once occupied the world into Lake Natth. [TOJ]

Amfar

A popular recreation world known for its beaches. [SOL]

Amidala, Queen

The fourteen-year-old elected ruler of the planet Naboo during the Trade Federation blockade. Her attempts to seek aid in ending the blockade led her to Coruscant, the Republic capital. When the senate became mired in endless political discussions, she was forced to initiate a vote of no confidence against the chancellor of the Republic. Amidala periodically chose to disguise herself as a handmaiden, Padmé Naberrie, in order to walk unnoticed among the general populace. [SWTPM]

ammonia bomb

Typically used by the ammonia-breathing Gands, these explosives distribute lethal amounts of ammonia to the atmosphere of oxygen-rich worlds. [TBH]

Ammuud

A planet governed by a feudal coalition of seven clans, under a contract from the Corporate Sector Authority. Its rigid code of honor is known throughout Authority space. [HSR]

Ammuud clans

These feudal families govern the planet Ammuud. The Corporate Sector Authority demanded that each clan provide forces for port security. Two of the more prominent clans are House Reesbon and House Glayyd. [HSR]

amphibion

Amphibious assault vessels used by New Republic Sea Commandos in the Battle of Calamari. This moderately armored hovercraft carries twenty troops and can operate over water or any flat terrain. [DE, DESB, SWVG]

Ampliquen

A planet in the Meridian sector. [POT]

Analysis Bureau

A division of Imperial Intelligence charged with gathering data from tens of millions of sources to watch for enemy activity. Its branches included Media, which listened in on every comlink transmission and holocast in the known galaxy; Signal, which studied the channels through which information flowed; Crypt-analysis, which worked to break enemy codes; Tech, which studied enemy hardware and provided improved versions for Imperial Intelligence use; and Interrogation, which specialized in questioning and reprogramming Rebel agents. [ISB]

Anchorhead

A small moisture farming community located on the desert flats of the planet Tatooine. Luke Skywalker grew up on a farm outside of Anchorhead, spending much of his free time in the sleepy town with his friends at the Tosche Station water and power distribution complex. [ISWU, SW]

Anchoron

The world where Corellian hero Garm Bel Iblis was believed to have been killed. [DFR, LC]

Ando

A watery planet that mainly exports foodstuffs and is the homeworld of the Aqualish species. [DFR, GG4, LC, TMEC]

Andona, Mari'ha

An old friend of Han Solo, she ran flight control for a sector of the planet Coruscant. She would bend the rules and occasionally authorize his unorthodox flight plans. [TBH]

Andur

This Coruscant bureaucrat was vice chair of the orbital debris committee. [JS]

angler

This spiderlike crustacean native to Yavin 4 lives in the dangling aerial roots of the great Massassi trees. [ISWU]

animated metal sealant

A special paste found in a spacer's tool kit. When applied, the paste crawls across a spacecraft's damaged area, smooths itself out, then forms a seal even stronger than the original hull. [YJK]

Annihilator

When the droid Bollux participated in Han Solo's ploy to deceive Viceprex Mirkovig Hirken, Bollux pretended to be the gladiator droid Annihilator, a member of Madam Atuarre's Roving Performers. In this guise, Bollux hoped to help Solo and his companions infiltrate the Corporate Sector Authority penal colony known as Stars' End. [HSE]

Annoo

During the early days of the Empire the gangster Sise Fromm maintained a stronghold on this agricultural world. Demma Moll and her daughter also had a farm complex there. [DTV]

Annoo-dat

A species of reptilian humanoids that originated on the planet Annoo. Members of this species boast heavy-lidded eyes, flat noses, and spotted faces. [DTV]

Anoat system

Located in the backwater Ison Corridor, the system includes the planets Anoat, Gentes (homeworld of the Ugnaughts), and the colony world Deyer. It was in this largely deserted star system that Han Solo managed to evade the Imperial Star Destroyers that chased his *Millennium Falcon* from the Rebel base on Hoth. [DA, DF, ESB, GG2, JS, MTS]

Anomid

A humanoid species native to the Yablari system, they are born without vocal cords. They wear elaborate vocalizer masks to produce synthesized sounds so they can communicate with other species. The technologically advanced Anomids dress in long, hooded robes and like to travel the galaxy as tourists. [RM]

Anor, Nom

A mysterious alien who masterminded the assassinations of the Imperial Interim Ruling Council members some eleven years after the Battle of Endor. He planted evidence to make it appear that Kir Kanos had committed the crimes, then gave orders to the newly elected Xandel Carivus. When Carivus dismissed Anor, refusing further assistance, the alien left him to his own demise at the council's hands.

Nom Anor surfaced again ten years later. This time, he was the leader of a religious movement, a cult figure stirring up trouble on the planet Rhommamool. His fanatical followers, the Red Knights of Life, hated all things mechanical and technological—from landspeeders to droids. Especially droids. Nom Anor also raged against the New Republic and the Jedi Knights, demonstrating a deep hatred for the government and its most visible symbols.

Nom Anor dressed in an outfit that was reminiscent of Darth Vader's and thoroughly masked his true features. A blank within the Force, as though the Force had no connection to him, he loved the chaos he inflicted upon the order of the galaxy. He was actually an executor, part of an advance force for aliens from beyond the galactic rim. He was a member of the Yuuzhan Vong species, sent to prepare the way for invasion. A gifted alchemist, he bred spores for a variety of purposes, including developing a method for killing Jedi Knights. He infected Mara Jade Skywalker with one of his spore diseases. He hoped to rise to the exalted position of high prefect of his people, but that would depend on the success of his mission.

As the first invasion force, the Praetorite Vong, entered the galaxy, Nom Anor kept the bulk of enemy warships occupied in the Core by fanning the flames of unrest. Still, the invasion force failed and was defeated at the planet Helska 4, forcing Anor to wait, and to continue stirring the brew of chaos. [CE, VP]

Anoth

This multiple planet orbited a small white sun, unrecorded on any charts. Its three parts were destined to eventually collide and become space dust. Luke Skywalker and Admiral Ackbar chose Anoth as the primary hiding place for Han and Leia Organa Solo's children—Jacen, Jaina, and Anakin. The third chunk of the planet housed the stronghold where Leia's aide Winter cared for the children. [COF, DA, JS, NR]

Another Chance

In keeping with Alderaan's new philosophy following the Clone Wars, all of the planet's weapons were placed aboard this huge armory ship. The ship, controlled only by droids and computers, was programmed to continually jump through hyperspace until called home by the Alderaanian Council of Elders. [GA]

Antar 4

The fourth of six moons orbiting the gas giant Antar in the Prindaar system, it is home to the Gotal species. [GG4, POT, ROC, TMEC]

Antares sapphire

A jewel believed to have remarkable healing powers. It was stolen from Dom Princina by the droid 4-LOM while the two were aboard the *Kuari Princess* passenger liner. [TBH]

Antares Six

One of two New Republic escort frigates that accompanied the *Millennium Falcon* to Coruscant to rescue the crew of the *Liberator*. [DE]

Anteevy

This remote, lifeless world was the site of an Imperial robotics facility. On ice-covered Anteevy, phrik alloy was refined and treated for use in armoring Dark Troopers. Shortly after the Battle of Yavin, Alliance agent Kyle Katarn disabled the facility. [DF]

Antemeridian sector

An Imperial satrapy, this sector of space is known for its heavy industry and a trade artery known as the Antemeridian Route. Moff Getelles ruled the sector after the Emperor's death and was still in power nine years after the Battle of Endor. [POT]

Antemeridias

This planet in the Antemeridian sector was the site of a Loronar Corporation manufacturing facility that turned out synthdroids and CCIR Needle fighters. Siefax, a Loronar dummy corporation, operated the facility. [POT]

anticoncussion field

A magnetic shield used in buildings, fortifications, space stations, and space outposts to protect such structures from damage by solid objects. This type of field works best in preventing small objects from colliding with structures. Anticoncussion fields are practically useless against combat-rated projectiles or energy weapons. [HSE]

antigrav

Any machine or device that counters the normal effects of gravity. The most common antigrav is the repulsorlift engine. [SW]

Antilles, Captain

An Alderaanian officer, he was the commander of the consular ship *Tantive IV*. C-3PO claimed that he and R2-D2 belonged to the captain prior to the Empire's capture of the ship. [SW, SWR]

Antilles, Wedge

This pilot is one of the true aces of the Rebellion and the New Republic. Born and raised in Gus Treta, a Corellian spaceport, Wedge was orphaned as a teenager when pirates killed his parents. He bought a stock light freighter when he was sixteen in the hope of starting a legitimate shipping business. It wasn't long before he was smuggling weapons for the Rebellion, and when the call went out for pilots, he took the controls of an Alliance X-wing.

Wedge Antilles

Antilles met Luke Skywalker at the Rebel base on Yavin 4 just prior to the arrival of the Death Star battle station. They were both assigned to Red Squadron, but during the fight Wedge's X-wing was damaged and he had to withdraw. He became an integral member of the renamed Rogue Squadron and flew a snowspeeder in the Battle of Hoth. He eventually took Luke's place as commander of the squadron, and he worked closely with Lando Calrissian and Admiral Ackbar to plan the attack on the second Death Star. During the conflict that came to be known as the Battle of Endor, Wedge's X-wing followed Calrissian—who was at the controls of the *Millennium Falcon*—into the superstructure of the Death Star. The two ships fired missiles and torpedoes at the reactor core, starting the series of explosions that destroyed the battle station.

As the New Republic began to establish itself, Wedge and his Rogue Squadron played an integral part. They helped defeat the invading Ssi-ruuk at Bakura. They performed an undercover mission to Coruscant that led to the successful Alliance invasion. They engaged the forces of Grand Admiral Thrawn, and at that point Antilles accepted the rank of general, though he also retained command of Rogue Squadron. He demonstrated brilliant military tactics at the second Battle of Coruscant, and he continues to display heroic service to the Alliance and the Republic.

His life hasn't been without tragedy. He has lost members of Rogue Squadron, family, friends, and even his true love, the scientist Qwi Xux, who lost nearly all of her memories due to the actions of a dark Jedi. [BW, DA, DE, DFR, DS, ESB, GG1, GG3, GG5, HE, JS, KT, LC, POT, RJ, RS, SW, SWCG, WG, etc.]

Anzati

This species closely resembles humans, with one major difference. The Anzati hide a prehensile proboscis in fleshy pockets beside their nostrils. It can be uncoiled and inserted through a victim's nostrils to reach the brain and suck out the life essence—or "soup," as the Anzati call it. [TMEC]

A-OIC ("Doc")

This unique medical droid built by Massad Thrumble had the ability to override and reprogram any droid. It was kidnapped by the Pikkel sisters and forced to work for the rogue scientist Spinda Caveel. [SEE]

Aparo sector

One of the inner borders of the Corporate Sector, ruled by Moff Wyrrhem. [CSSB]

approach vector

A trajectory generated by a nav computer, placing a ship on an intercept course with another ship or other target for purpose of attack or rendezvous. [ESBR]

Aqualish

The species name of the walrus-faced humanoids from the planet Ando, a world covered by water, swampy islands, and rocky outcroppings. Ponda Baba, one of the aliens who picked a fight with Luke Skywalker at the Mos Eisley cantina, was an Aqualish. [GDV, GG1, GG4, SW, TMEC]

Aqualish

Aquaris

A water-covered world allied with the Rebel Alliance, and home to Silver Fyre and her Freeholders. [CSW]

arachnor

A giant, spiderlike creature, native to the planet Arzid, that spins very sticky webs. [PDS]

Arakkus, Dr.

The onetime director of an Imperial weapons development complex, Arakkus was contaminated in a radiation experiment. He took up residence in an abandoned Imperial transport—one of many derelict ships orbiting a collapsing star. He died when Han Solo ignited a neutron charge to free the *Millennium Falcon* from the star's gravitational pull. [CSW]

Arakyd Viper probot

Probe droids manufactured under the direction of Imperial Supervisor Gurdun. The assassin droid IG-88 programmed these probots to possess sentience and, without the knowledge of the Empire, used them as scouts for his own purposes. One Viper located the Rebel base on Hoth. It self-destructed when Han Solo and Chewbacca attacked it. [GG3, SWSB, TBH]

Aralia

This small, tropical world in the Andron system is home to the Project Aralia amusement park and the troublesome, semi-intelligent Ranat species. Though Ranats developed on Rydar II, they arrived on Aralia aboard a spice-smuggling ship. [COJ, GG4]

Aramadia

A consular ship that belonged to the Duskhan League. [BTS]

Arastide, Senator

A New Republic Senate Defense Council member from the planet Gantho. [POT]

Arat Fraca

A planet separated from Motexx by the Black Nebula in Parfadi. [SOL]

Arbo Maze

The Arbo Maze on the forest moon of Endor is a thicket of trees so dense and convoluted that most beings and creatures that wander into it become hopelessly lost—including Ewoks. Arbo is also the name of a wise old Ewok legend-keeper. [ETV]

Archimar, Dr.

A surgeon, he served aboard the *Intrepid*, flagship of the New Republic's Fifth Fleet. [BTS]

Arcona

Reptiles without scales, these humanoid snakes have flat, anvil-shaped heads and clear, marblelike eyes. They are natives of the hot world Cona, in the Teke Ro system. [GG4, TMEC]

Ardax

This Imperial colonel led the assault team intent on kidnapping Anakin Solo on Anoth. [COF]

Ardele, Feylis

A beautiful woman with a dazzling smile, she is one of the most recent additions to Rogue Squadron, joining about four and a half years after the Battle of Yavin. Although she has kept her background private, she came from an upper-middle-class family on Commenor. Her family was wiped out after a business rival accused her father of being a Rebel sympathizer. The Imperials hoped to recruit her into Imperial Intelligence, but she joined the Alliance instead. [XW]

Ardiff, Captain

An Imperial officer, he was the captain of the Star Destroyer *Chimaera* and served Supreme Commander Gilad Pellaeon some sixteen years after the Battle of Endor. [SP, VF]

Ardos

A white dwarf star orbited by the Hutt homeworld, Varl. [GG4]

Argazda

This planet in the Kanz sector was the site of a revolt against the Old Republic 4,000 years before the Galactic Civil War. This period, known as the Kanz Disorders, lasted for 300 years. [CSSB]

Argon, Grand Moff

This Imperial sector chief was conned out of 25,000 credits by the notorious Tonnika sisters. [GG1, TMEC]

Arica

The name used by Mara Jade when she went undercover into Jabba's palace as the Emperor's Hand. [TJP]

Aridus

A harsh desert world where Darth Vader set a trap for Luke Skywalker after the Battle of Yavin. [CSW]

Ariela

An Alderaan native who settled on Tatooine, she worked hard to build relations between human moisture farmers and Tatooine's Jawa tribes. [TMEC]

Arkania

This tundra world in the Colonies region was covered with diamond pits. Four thousand years before the Galactic Civil War it housed the training compound of Jedi Master Arca Jeth. [DESB, DLS, FNU, TOJ]

armament rating

A weapons rating assigned to all spacecraft. This classification specifies the level of defensive and offensive weaponry a particular ship carries. A ship's armament rating is contained within its ID profile. The classifications range from "0" (no weaponry), to "1" (light defensive weapons only), to "2" (light defensive and offensive capabilities), to "3" (medium defensive and offensive weapons), to "4" (heavy defensive and offensive weaponry). Specific classifications are determined by the number and type of weapons, the maximum range of those weapons, the associated fire control computers, and the maximum output of the ship's power plants. Armament ratings are also called weapons ratings. [HSR, SWR]

armored defense platform

Many star systems protect themselves from outside threats with strategically placed armored defense platforms. These battle stations have little maneuverability but are heavily armed with multiple turbolaser batteries, proton torpedo launch ports, and tractor beam projectors. While these battle stations could not stand alone against a full-scale fleet offensive, they are perfect for dealing with pirate raids and smuggling ships trying to flee a system. [HE, HESB]

Arranda, Tash

An Alderaan native, she was off planet with her brother, Zak, when her homeworld was destroyed and her parents killed. Thirteen years old at the time of the Galactic Civil War, she and her younger brother had a series of dark adventures before joining up with the Rebel Alliance, through which she hoped to gain revenge against the Empire. Force-sensitive, she gained some minor Force abilities along the way. [GF]

Arranda, Zak

An Alderaan native, he was off planet with his sister, Tash, when his homeworld was destroyed and his parents killed. Twelve years old at the time of the Galactic Civil War, he and his sister had a series of dark adventures before joining up with the Rebel Alliance. [GF]

Artoo-Detoo

See R2-D2.

Aruza

A peaceful forest planet with five moons. Its major city is Bukeen. The native inhabitants are a small, gentle species with blue skin and dark blue hair. Using neural interface jacks called Attanni, they feel the emotions of others. They possess tech-empathic abilities and share a limited group mind. [TBH]

Aryon, Governor Tour

A key Imperial official and the governor of the planet Tatooine. She was stationed at Bestine. [GG7, TJP]

asaari tree

Native to the planet Bimmisaari, these trees can move their leafy branches of their own accord, though their roots are firmly anchored in the ground. [HE, HESB]

Asha

A red-furred Ewok huntress who, separated from her mother and her little sister Kneesaa, was raised by a family of wolflike creatures called korrina. Years later, she was known as the savage Red Ghost and was tracked down by Kneesaa and Wicket W. Warrick. She returned to her village and was reunited with her father, Chief Chirpa. [ETV, TRG]

Ashern

These members of the Vratix species formed the Black-Claw Rebels of Thyferra. They renounced their peaceful nature to fight the tyranny of their human masters. By painting their normally gray bodies black and sharpening their claws, they demonstrated their membership in the rebel organization. [BW]

Ashgad, Seti

A top hyperdrive engineer and a political foe of Senator Palpatine in the Old Republic. Palpatine exiled Seti to the prison planet Nam Chorios. Chief of State Leia Organa Solo traveled to the planet during the time of the New Republic, nine years after the Battle of Endor, and met with the apparent son of the exiled engineer—a young man with the same name. It turned out that he was actually Seti Ashgad, who had been kept alive and young by Dzym, a mutated droch. The drochs were the source of the Death Seed plague, and Dzym and his slave planned to unleash the disease across three-quarters of the sector. [POT]

Askaj

This dry desert world is home to the near-human Askajians, who can absorb and store water. The females of the species have six breasts. Yarna d'al'Gargan, daughter of a tribal chieftain, was captured by slavers and sold to Jabba the Hutt. In the Hutt's court, she served as one of Jabba's dancing girls. [TJP]

ASP-7 labor droid

A general all-purpose labor droid built by Industrial Automaton. These humanoid droids boast a practical and sturdy framework designed for heavy lifting and other menial tasks. With only basic programming, the ASP-7s appear to be limited and somewhat simpleminded, but they are dependable, reliable, and always polite. [SESB, SOTE, SWSE]

assassin droid

This intelligent killing machine could be programmed to hunt down specific targets and destroy them. Assassin droids have been illegal for several decades, but many nonetheless covertly served the Empire and other criminal organizations. Some free-roaming automatons broke their programming or continue to follow orders given in the distant past. These droids were originally designed by the Old Republic to locate and eliminate escaped criminals or other outlaws, and were employed in the corrupt competitions of the decaying senate. Ironically, it was the Emperor himself who banned the use of assassin droids during the rise of his New Order. He did this because the droids were being used against his own forces. [SWSB]

Assassins' Guild

A secret society of professional mercenaries, its members specialize in contract terminations. Different subguilds were established to provide specialized service, including the feared bounty hunter division. The best mercs formed their own subguild, called the Elite Circle, whose members are voted on by their peers. The Circle services the most prominent clients. Most members of the Assassins' Guild are wanted criminals, so the guild operates in secret. Even its headquarters are hidden, and members have to contact the guild via covert means. [HLL]

assault frigate

When the Alliance needed capital ships to fill the ranks of its growing fleet, it commissioned the design of the assault frigate. Using the framework of the Old Republic Dreadnaught, Alliance engineers modified the vessel to create a combat starship. By stripping away huge portions of the superstructure to lower fuel consumption and increase engine capacity, and by adding two aft solar fins, techs made the vessel faster and more maneuverable. To meet the demands of limited crew complements, workstations were retooled to allow for droid and computer control. Once all of the modifications were completed, the barest hint of the original structure remained. Assault frigates have no docking bays. However, twenty umbilical docking tubes are scattered about the hull to accommodate transports, light freighters, and starfighters. After the Battle of Endor, the New Republic continued to use these vessels. Assault frigates patrolled the Borderland Regions as the New Republic's first line of defense against Imperial aggression. [HESB, RSB]

assault shuttle

A heavily armored, thirty-meter-long Imperial spacecraft equipped with tractor beam generators and projectors, full sensor suites, power harpoon guns, concussion missile launchers, and automatic blaster cannons. Its five-person crew was trained to engage enemy ships and serve as field support for the zero-g stormtroopers they carried into battle. Assault shuttles were designed to serve as launch platforms, carrying forty of the armored space warriors within their main holds. Assault shuttles were among the best-shielded vehicles in the Imperial fleet. They could operate in space and in planetary atmospheres. Their limited nav computers could handle up to three hyperspace jumps before needing base-assisted reprogramming. [ISB]

Astarta, Captain

The personal guard of Prince Isolder, she was statuesque, with dark red hair and dark blue eyes. She loved the prince, but above all else she was extremely loyal and an excellent soldier. [CPL]

astrogation computer

See nav computer.

Astrolabe

A New Republic astrographic probe ship that was reportedly operated by the civilian Astrographic Survey Institute but was actually a front for a military intelligence mission. It was destroyed at Doornik-1142 by Yevethan ships, its entire crew lost. [BTS]

astromech droid

Astromech droids specialize in starship maintenance and repair. Some models also assist with piloting and navigation.

Luke Skywalker's droid, R2-D2, is an astromech droid. These droids interface with starship computers to monitor and diagnose flight performance, initiate repairs when necessary, and augment navigational, astrogational, and piloting capacity. The popular R2 unit, designed by Industrial Automaton, includes an extensive sensor package and a variety of tools that assist its jack-of-all-trades programming. [RJ, SW, SWSB]

AT3 Directive

An order that allowed Mara Jade, the Emperor's Hand, to commandeer Imperial troops and resources at will. [MJ]

AT-AT

See All Terrain Armored Transport.

Atedeate

See 8D8.

Athega

The Athega star system has no life-bearing worlds, but its lifeless rocks are great sources of raw material and resources. The intense heat given off by the system's sun had always hindered potential entrepreneurs, for even shielded starships could not long stand the pounding rays of heat and radiation. With the creation of shieldships, Lando Calrissian was able to set up a mining operation on the planet Nkllon, located in the Athega system. [HE, HESB]

AT-PT

See All Terrain Personal Transport.

Atraken

Callista sent Luke Skywalker a message in a music box from this planet. The message warned him to stay away from the Meridian sector. [POT]

Atravis sector

Home to the Atravis star systems, whose planets were devastated by Imperial attacks. Grand Admiral Harrsk's troops gathered in the sector eight years after the Battle of Endor. [COJ]

Atrivis sector

Located in the Outer Rim, this sector contains the Mantooine and Fest star systems and the planet Generis. Mon Mothma helped unite various insurgent organizations during the early days of the Rebellion, including the Atrivis resistance groups. Five years after the Battle of Endor, New Republic pilot Pash Cracken was stationed in this sector. [DESB, FP, LC, RSB]

AT-ST

See All Terrain Scout Transport.

Attanni

A cybernetic device used by the Aruzans to share thoughts, emotions, and memories. [TBH]

Attichitcuk

A Wookiee elder and Chewbacca's father, he resided on the planet Kashyyyk. Friends and family called him Itchy. [SWHS]

Atuarre

The female Trianii who sought to locate political prisoners held by the Corporate Sector Authority. Prior to her meeting with Han Solo, Atuarre worked as an apprentice agronomist on the planet Orron III. [HSE]

Atzerri

A Free Trader world with only a minimal government. Almost anything can be found on Atzerri—for the right price. Visitors have to pay a hefty fee to the Traders' Coalition for every service, especially at the gauntlet of stores known as Trader's Plaza. [BTS, SOL, TT]

Augwynne, Mother

The leader of the Singing Mountain clan of the Witches of Dathomir, she was given the deed to the planet by Han Solo, who won it in a sabacc game. [CPL]

Auril systems

A distant group of nine star systems in the Auril sector of space, which includes the Adega system and the Cron drift. Three of the star systems were destroyed during the Great Sith War, when the Cron Cluster ignited in multiple supernovas. [DE2, TOJ]

Authority Cash Voucher

Corporate Sector Authority worlds would not accept Imperial or Republic credits, so cash vouchers were needed to pay for goods and services. These could be obtained and redeemed at any Corporate Sector Authority Currency Exchange Center. When entering Corporate Sector space, travelers had to exchange other moneys for cash vouchers or risk legal ramifications. [HSE]

Authority Data Center

Authority Data Centers stored computer-processed information for the Corporate Sector Authority. These well-guarded centers could be found throughout Corporate Sector space. [HSE]

autohopper

A self-propelled, unmanned "smart" vehicle that follows a preprogrammed course without the need for a driver or pilot. A central instruction processor, or CIP, controls routing for such vehicles. CIPs can be programmed to remember time and locations of specific job assignments. Certain variables may also be programmed into the CIP, including geography and weather fluctuations. [HLL]

automatic sealup

Many starfighters, capital ships, and deep-space facilities are equipped with emergency automatic sealup features. The system uses pressure sensors, located throughout the ship and hull, to measure air pressure and warn of decompression or exposure to hard vacuum. Besides providing immediate warning, the system seals bulkheads to isolate areas where rapid decompression is occurring. [HSR]

Auyemesh

One of three moons orbiting the planet Almania. Kueller, a dark-side Force user, destroyed the population of Auyemesh about thirteen years after the Battle of Endor. [NR]

avabush spice

This spice causes sleepiness and is used as a truth serum. Imperials frequently served the spice in liquid refreshments or baked it into sweets. [GG4, PDS, ZHR]

Avarice

An Imperial II Star Destroyer commanded by Sair Yonka. The captain and his crew defected, joined the New Republic, and renamed the vessel *Freedom.* [BW]

Avenger

An Imperial Star Destroyer that was part of the task force assigned to locate Rebel forces after the Battle of Yavin. *Avenger* was temporarily incapacitated during the Battle of Hoth. [ESB]

Averam

The planet where Leia Organa Solo's aide Winter, operating under the code name Targeter, worked with a Rebel Alliance cell. [LC]

Aves

One of Talon Karrde's ranking associates, he served with the smuggler chief from the earliest days of Karrde's operation. Aves's role was to stay close to Karrde, serving as an adviser and comm officer. In this capacity, he coordinated the activities of field operatives. [DFR, HE, HESB, LC]

AVVA

The Alliance Veterans' Victory Association, a retirees' club with the ambition to become a militia or the fleet's ready reserve. [TT]

A-wing starfighter

A lightweight, wedge-shaped military starfighter that made its first appearance late in the Galactic Civil War on the side of the Rebel Alliance. Designed for high speed and maneuverability, the A-wing carries two wing-mounted pivoting blaster cannons, a sophisticated targeting computer and sensor array, and light combat shields. It was the Alliance's answer to the Empire's newer TIE fighter models. The A-wing was built for ship-to-ship combat and to serve as escort craft for larger starships. Two extralarge realspace power plants and low total mass made this the fastest combat starfighter in either arsenal, beating out even the TIE interceptor for pure speed in normal space.

The A-wing was developed secretly during the early days of the Rebellion. It has excellent sensor and communications countermeasures, including a power-jamming package designed to blind targets before it attacked. Since this starfighter was introduced, its mission profile has undergone some significant modifications. It was determined through trial and error that the high-speed craft is best suited to hit-and-fade operations. [DFR, SWSB, SWVG]

A-wing starfighter

Azool

A Falleen antique dealer on Coruscant who also bartered information, he was actually Prince Xizor's niece in disguise. After the Battle of Endor, she planned to take control of the Black Sun criminal organization. Her plan hinged on finding the human replica droid Guri, once Xizor's second in command, and acquiring Guri's help through the use of a preprogrammed command. Guri, however, had that programming wiped from her memory. Instead of aiding Xizor's niece, Guri captured her and turned her over to the authorities. [SEE]

Azure Dianoga cantina

A bar used by members of Rogue Squadron as a meeting place while on an undercover mission on Coruscant. [BW]

Azur-Jamin, Daye

Fiancé of the bounty hunter Tinian I'att. Daye helped I'att escape when Imperials took control of her grandparents' armament factory. [TBH]

Baas, Bodo

The gatekeeper of the Jedi Holocron. Baas lived about 600 years before the Galactic Civil War, and he appeared as a cross between an insect and a crustacean. Only someone imbued with the Force could activate the Holocron, and many of its secrets were reserved for those who followed the light side. When it was activated, a holographic Baas would guide the user in the operation of this legendary source of knowledge and wisdom. [DE]

Baas, Master Vodo-Siosk

This Jedi Master and expert lightsaber crafter lived more than 4,000 years before the Galactic Civil War. His students included the powerful Exar Kun. When Kun turned to the dark side, he betrayed and murdered Baas. Vodo-Siosk returned to the Force and became the gatekeeper to a Holocron, an interactive repository of Jedi history and knowledge. Sometime after the birth of the New Republic, the spirit of Vodo-Siosk, with the help of Luke Skywalker and his Jedi-in-training, destroyed Kun forever. [DA, DLS, TSW]

Baba, Ponda

An Aqualish pirate and smuggler, he kept company with the thug Dr. Evazan, also known as Roofoo or Dr. Cornelius. In the Mos Eisley cantina, a drunken Baba shoved Luke Skywalker and subsequently lost his right arm to Ben Kenobi's lightsaber. [GG1, SW, SWCG, TMEC]

Babali

A tropical planet whose archaeological sites draw the interest of scholars from around the galaxy, including those from the Obroan Institute. [SOL]

bacta

This chemical compound will treat and heal all but the most serious wounds. Bacta is applied in a solution of clear synthetic fluid that mimics the body's own vital liquids. A patient is fully immersed in this fluid within specially designed rejuvenation tanks, also called bacta tanks. The gelatinous, translucent red bacta is added to the clear fluid, where it interacts to form a bacterial medium. This bacterial medium adheres to traumatized flesh, promoting regeneration and tissue growth to rapidly heal wounds without causing scarring.

Emperor Palpatine saw bacta as a source of power and control. He limited bacta production to two corporations, Zaltin and Xucphra. The healing medium then fell under the control of a cartel on Thyferra. Later, a war was fought to control the healing substance.

On Hoth, after Luke Skywalker suffered injuries fighting a wampa ice creature, he was treated within a bacta rejuvenation tank. [BW, ESB]

Bacta War

This civil war rocked the planet Thyferra approximately three years after the Battle of Endor. The conflict was instigated by

Ysanne Isard, director of Imperial Intelligence, and the Xucphra Corporation in an effort to destroy the Zaltin Corporation and gain complete control of the Bacta Cartel. Rogue Squadron's pilots temporarily resigned their positions to help the Ashern rebels overthrow Isard's government and defeat her forces. [BW]

Badlands

A flat, desolate area near the arid equator of the planet Kamar. Inhabitants of this region are commonly called Badlanders. Han Solo and Chewbacca spent some time hiding in this region after the Corporate Sector Authority became overly interested in finding them. [HSR]

Badure

One of Han Solo's military mentors. Badure, who also went by the nickname Trooper, taught Solo almost everything he knew about flying. Han Solo, in turn, saved Badure when a training mission turned bad. After leaving the Imperial military, Badure crossed paths with Solo a number of times. He even saved Solo and the Wookiee Chewbacca after an aborted spice run to Kessel. Just prior to Solo's connection with the Rebel Alliance, Badure enlisted Han and Chewbacca in his quest to find the lost treasure of the cargo vessel *Queen of Ranroon*. [HLL]

bafforr tree

These semi-intelligent crystalline trees are found on the planet Ithor. The bark of these trees is as smooth as glass. The more trees in an area, the more intelligent the collective forest. [DA, GF, TMEC]

Baga

This horselike baby bordok was the pet of the Ewok named Wicket W. Warrick. [ETV]

Baji

A Ho'Din healer and medicine man who lived on Yavin 4 and spoke in rhyme. On Yavin 4, Baji spent much of his time gathering roots and plants necessary to make his medicines. He also collected rare plants that he feared were nearing extinction. These he transported to his home planet Moltok for further study by his botanist colleagues. The Empire captured him and forced him to cure the blindness that afflicted Trioculus. Afterwards, he was kept as an Imperial staff physician until the Rebel Alliance rescued him. He then moved to Dagobah to tend medicinal plants grown in an Alliance greenhouse. [LCJ, QE]

Bajic sector

This sector in the Outer Rim contains the Lybeya system, home to a secret Rebel shipyard built on a large asteroid in the Vergesso belt. It was also home to Ororo Transportation, a company that directly competed with Prince Xizor's profitable shipping interests. Xizor convinced the Emperor to send Darth Vader to destroy the Rebel base during the period following the Battle of Yavin. An added benefit, as far as Xizor was concerned, was the destruction of Ororo Transportation. [GG11, SESB, SOTE]

Baker, Mayor

The mayor of the town Dying Slowly, located on the planet Jubilar. Before her marriage, she was known as Incavi Larado. [TBH]

Bakura

A remote world annexed by the Empire three years before the Battle of Endor. The planetary government is situated in the capital city of Salis D'aar. In addition to its repulsor coil industry and agricultural exports, Bakura provided raw materials mined from the planet's two moons for the second Death Star project. While humans make up the majority of Bakura's population, the Kurtzen are indigenous to the planet.

In the days following the victory at Endor, the Alliance intercepted a distress call from the Imperial governor of Bakura. The governor, seeking aid from an Empire that was now shattered and in disarray, reported that his world was under attack by aliens from outside the Emperor's sphere of control. Luke Skywalker led a military task force to Bakura to provide humanitarian aid and to demonstrate that the Alliance wasn't the "band of thieves and murderers" that Imperial propaganda portrayed them to be. Skywalker's task force included the converter cruiser *Flurry*, the *Millennium Falcon*, the Corellian corvette *Ullet*, and the Corellian gunships *Ensaiav*, *Ghorman's Honor*, *Mastala*, *Telsor*, and *Walerv*.

The truce of Bakura provided the means by which the Alliance task force and the Imperial starships could work together to repel the alien invaders. The hostile aliens, called the Ssi-ruuk, had actually been in secret contact with the Emperor for several years. The Emperor wanted Ssi-ruuk technology and was willing to trade the lives of his subjects for it. Fortunately, Skywalker and the heroes of Yavin were able to help drive off the invaders and free Bakura from Imperial rule.

Fourteen years after the truce, Luke Skywalker returned to Bakura to borrow battle cruisers from its powerful defensive fleet. Though his mission was completed successfully, half of the Bakuran cruisers were destroyed. [AS, SAC, TAB, TBSB]

Kurtzen

Balmorra

A factory world located at the fringe of the Galactic Core. Balmorrans were forced to manufacture weapons for the Imperial military and were the primary builders of the AT-ST walker. Though liberated by the New Republic following the Battle of Endor, it again fell under Imperial rule by the time the first clone of Emperor Palpatine appeared. [DE2]

bantha

A large four-legged beast of burden with long, thick fur and bright, inquisitive eyes. Found on Tatooine and throughout the galaxy, banthas have adapted to a variety of climates and terrain types. Wild herds thunder across some worlds, while on others they have been domesticated. Males grow as large as three meters at the shoulders and can be identified by the pair of large spiral horns that grow from the sides of their heads; females are slightly smaller and possess no horns.

The bantha's world of origin has been lost in the distant past. Banthas serve many purposes throughout the galaxy. Herders raise the huge beasts for food and clothing. Some of the finest restaurants serve bantha steaks, and bantha-skin boots and cloaks are popular among the upper classes.

Priests of the Dim-U religion are devoted to the mystery of the bantha. These priests and their followers believe that a great message of universal importance has been hidden in the simple bantha. Once the message is interpreted, they believe, an incredible age of peace and bounty will begin. [SW, SWSB, TM]

"bantha four five six"

An instruction code given by the droid TDL3.5 as proof that it was authorized to replace C-3PO as nanny for Leia and Han Solo's children. Young Anakin Solo provided the code as a prank when he got angry at C-3PO for not reading him his favorite bedtime story, "The Little Lost Bantha Cub." [NR]

Baobab, Mungo

This treasure hunter and adventurer from Manda was a member of the family that owned the Baobab Merchant Fleet during the early days of the Empire. He frequently disregarded safety precautions while recklessly pursuing adventure. He was sent to the planet Biitu to establish a trading post and fuel ore mining operation. His greatest accomplishment was locating and preserving the Roonstones, a crystal structure that contained an encoded version of *Dha Werda Verda*, an epic poem of the conquest of Coruscant by the warrior race, the Taungs. [DTV, SOTEALB, TGH]

Barab I

This dark, humid world orbits the red dwarf Barab. The heat of the day causes standing water to evaporate into haze, but during the cool night, animal life is active and the haze condenses to fall as rain upon the planet's surface. The intelligent Barabels live beneath the surface. When the Empire took control of the world, the Alater-ka underground spaceport was constructed. It was a crude facility by Core standards, but sporting hunters filled the tourist lodges to hunt the terrible beasts that inhabit the world. [CPL, DFR, DFRSB, GG4]

Barabel

These reptilelike humanoids range from 1.75 to 2.5 meters tall. Horny black scales cover their bodies, and long, sharp teeth fill their mouths. They inhabit the dark, humid world of Barab I. Though spice smugglers and other criminals have often used the world as a refuge, it rarely receives open galactic traffic. Thus, the Barabel species is not widely known and few have found their way off planet. Some Barabels have taken jobs as porters and guides for the tourists who come to the planet to hunt the dangerous game that roam the night. A few were even able to leave the world with bounty hunter commissions, but the majority have remained untamed and uncivilized. Barabels hold a deep respect for Jedi Knights, and a few have tried to emulate the Jedi tradition despite little aptitude in the Force. This respect goes back to the time of the Barabel War, when the primitive species split into two factions over access to choice hunting grounds. Passing Jedi Knights intervened and negotiated a peaceful solution, keeping the Barabels from killing themselves needlessly.

Prior to the Battle of Endor, Skahtul, a female Barabel bounty hunter, captured Luke Skywalker on the planet Kothlis. He escaped before she could sell him to the highest bidder. After the Battle of Endor, the Barabels and the Verpine nearly went to war over a shipbuilding contract. [DFR, DFRSB, GG4, SOTE]

Baraboo

Home planet of the Institute for Sentient Studies. [BTS]

Barada

A native of the planet Klatooine, Barada was sold into indentured servitude as punishment for a crime he committed in his youth. The crimelord Jabba the Hutt won Barada's contract and put him to work in the repulsor pool. Barada quickly took charge, becoming responsible for the procurement, modification, crewing, and care of all of Jabba's repulsorlift vehicles. He took his job to heart, serving as captain of the skiffs when they went into battle or when Jabba wanted to travel. He died when Luke Skywalker and his companions freed Han Solo from Jabba's clutches in the Tatooine wilderness. [GG5, RJ, SWCG]

Barak, Koth

This male midshipman on the New Republic escort cruiser *Adamantine*, was one of the first victims of the Death Seed plague. [POT]

Barhu

A boiling-hot lifeless planet in the Churba star system. [DFR, DFRSB]

Baritha

This older woman with graying hair and glittering green eyes was a leading figure among the dark-side Nightsisters of the Witches of Dathomir. She tried to claim Han Solo as her slave, according to the traditions of her society. [CPL]

Baros

This large, arid planet orbits the star Bari. Homeworld of the reptilian Brubb, Baros has high gravity and is wracked by intense windstorms. [GG4, HE, HESB]

Barth

This New Republic flight engineer was captured by Yevethan forces during the same attack in which Han Solo was taken hostage. Nil Spaar, commander of the Yevethan forces, killed the engineer. [TT]

Bartokk

Known for their relentless assassin squads, the Bartokk are insectoid creatures with black shells, tough exoskeletons, and razor-edged claws. They utilize a hive mind. About twenty years after the Battle of Endor, the young Jedi Knights stopped a Bartokk squad from assassinating Queen Mother Ta'a Chume, the grandmother of Jedi academy student Tenel Ka. [YJK]

Barukka

One of the Witches of Dathomir, she was the sister of the evil Gethzerion and was cast out of the Singing Mountain clan after succumbing to her evil urges. After a period of cleansing in the Rivers of Stone caverns, she was recruited to lead Luke Skywalker and Han Solo into an Imperial prison complex to find parts needed to repair the *Millennium Falcon.* [CPL]

Basic

The common language of the galaxy, based on the language of the human civilizations of the Core Worlds. It became the standard trade and diplomatic language during the time of the Old Republic. [HESB, SWRPG, SWRPG2, SWSB]

Basilisk

One of four Star Destroyers under the command of Imperial Admiral Daala, it had to be repaired after receiving severe damage during a battle with Moruth Doole's forces near Kessel. Later, it was destroyed in the Cauldron Nebula as it prepared to make a suicide attack against Coruscant. [DA, JS]

Basilisk, Battle of

Jedi Master Sidrona Diath was killed in this clash. [DLS]

Bast Castle

Darth Vader's stronghold and private retreat, located on the planet Vjun. Dark-side executor Sedriss and the Emperor's elite force of Dark Jedi later used this remote and heavily defended structure as a headquarters. [DE2]

Bastion

This planet was the political center of the Empire at the time of Grand Admiral Thrawn's reported return about sixteen years after the Battle of Endor. [SP, VF]

Bastra, Gil

This former Corellian Security Force officer worked with Corran Horn and Corran's father, Hal. He later assisted Corran and two other members of Rogue Squadron by providing them with false identities, helping them escape from Imperials. He died after being interrogated by Kirtan Loor aboard the *Expeditious.* [BW]

Batcheela

An old Ewok, she was the mother of Teebo and Malani. [ETV]

battle analysis computer (BAC)

Developed by General Jan Dodonna for the Alliance, this computer system analyzes variables of enemy vessels to project the course of a battle. By analyzing speed, firepower, current position, shield strength, and maneuverability, it suggests courses of action. Luke Skywalker tested the battle analysis computer (BAC) at Bakura. [TAB]

battle dog

See nek.

battle droid

The foot soldiers of the Trade Federation army, these droids served as security, ground troops, and pilots of Trade Federation battleships. Armed with blaster rifles, they can be deployed anywhere and derive their strength from their overwhelming numbers and automated discipline. They are not programmed for independent thinking, instead relying on a central data source usually located aboard a control ship. Each battle droid has an identification number printed on its back.

Specialized battle droids are distinguished by color: yellow markings for commanders, blue for pilots, and maroon for security guards. [SWTPM]

battle meditation

This Jedi Force technique strengthens the hopes of a Jedi's allies while heightening the fear of his or her enemies. [GAS]

Battle of Yavin

A modified Imperial customs frigate used by the New Republic in covert missions. [BW]

battle wagon

A massive Ewok war machine originally designed by Erpham Warrick and restored by his great-grandson Wicket. The wagon has four huge wheels and features a large battering ram topped by a bantha skull. [ETV]

Bavo Six

A truth drug primarily used by Imperial agents as part of a normal interrogation procedure. [CRFG]

Bdu, T'nun

A Corellian captain. His supply ship *Sullustan* was intercepted by Imperial Admiral Daala while en route to Dantooine. After raiding the ship's data banks, Daala destroyed the vessel. [DA]

beamdrill

A heavy tool used for mining, employing a high-intensity pulse to disintegrate rock. [HLL]

beam tube

An antiquated handheld weapon powered by a backpack generator. [HLL]

Bearus
Leader of the once-powerful carbonite mining guild in the Empress Teta system, about 4,000 years prior to the Galactic Civil War. [DLS]

Beast-Lord
An honorific title granted to the traditional leader of a group of Onderonian beast-riders. [TOJ]

beast-rider
Onderonians in ancient times who, cast out of the walled fortress called Iziz, learned to tame and ride the great beasts of Dxun's moon. [TOJ]

Beauty of Yevetha
A corvette in Nil Spaar's Black Eleven Fleet. New Republic forces destroyed the vessel during the blockade of Doornik-319. [BTS, SOL]

Bebo, Kevreb
The captain and only survivor from the ship *Misanthrope*, he was the first to find—and crash on—the planet D'vouran. He was killed by a Gank. [GF]

Beedo
A relative of the deceased bounty hunter Greedo, he took his kin's place in Jabba the Hutt's organization after Greedo was killed by Han Solo. [RJ]

Beggar's Canyon
This valley on Tatooine served as the training ground for Luke Skywalker's aerial skills. Luke and his childhood friends raced skyhoppers and engaged in mock dogfights within its twisting confines. One of Luke's favorite pastimes was to fly his T-16 skyhopper at full throttle while hunting womp rats in the canyon.

Three mighty rivers that flowed here in millennia past formed Beggar's Canyon. Features of the canyon include the two-kilometer-long Main Avenue, Dead Man's Turn, and the Stone Needle. Here Luke engaged in a chase and battle with swoop bikers hired to assassinate him just prior to his mission to rescue Han Solo from Jabba the Hutt. [SESB, SOTE, SW, SWR]

Behn-kihl-nahm, Chairman

The chairman of the Defense Council of the New Republic Senate, he was a staunch ally of Chief of State Leia Organa Solo. [BTS, SOL]

Beidlo, Brother

A young B'omarr monk whose brain was removed and put into a brain spider as part of Jabba the Hutt's plan to provide criminals with new identities by giving them new bodies. [GF]

Belden, Eppie

By the time of the truce at Bakura, between the Alliance and the Empire, Eppie Belden was a small, wizened woman of 132 years of age. Once a major operative in the Bakuran underground, where she constantly made trouble for the Empire, she used her expertise in computer programming and electronics to assist in covert operations. She was eventually arrested and subsequently incapacitated by the mistreatments of Imperial Governor Wilek Nereus. She was able to retain a great deal of wit and intelligence, despite Nereus's parasite treatments that damaged her brain. [TAB, TBSB]

Belden, Orn

A senior senator on the planet Bakura, he served his constituents well—usually at a great cost. He hated Imperial rule and opposed Imperial Governor Wilek Nereus at every opportunity. Belden came to openly support the Rebel Alliance despite Nereus's retaliatory tactics. The governor taxed Belden until he was nearly destitute, had his son, Roviden, killed in a purge, and infected

Belden's wife, Eppie, with a brain-damaging parasite. Shortly after the Battle of Endor, Belden provided aid to Princess Leia. He was subsequently arrested, interrogated, and died of a cerebral hemorrhage instigated by Nereus. [TAB, TBSB]

beldon

A giant gas bag that metabolizes the natural chemicals in Bespin's atmosphere, giving off Tibanna gas as a waste product. It is illegal to hunt these creatures. [GG2, ISWU]

Beldorian the Hutt

A massive, twelve-meter-long Hutt who ran Nam Chorios until he was forcibly replaced by Seti Ashgad. He had some Jedi training, but was killed by Leia Organa Solo in a lightsaber duel. [POT]

Bel Iblis, Garm

A senator from the Corellian system who helped start the Rebellion as the threat of the Empire first surfaced. When the Alliance emerged to fight the Empire, Bel Iblis went into hiding and began his own private war against the New Order. Bel Iblis and Mon Mothma never got along. He had worked with her and Bail Organa in the Rebellion's formative years. It was Bel Iblis who convinced three of the biggest resistance groups to join forces and form the Alliance. The results of that meeting became known as the Corellian Treaty, but what should have been Bel Iblis's finest hour turned out to be Mon Mothma's. For she possessed the gift of inspiration and became the symbol of the Alliance. When Bail Organa died in

Garm Bel Iblis

Alderaan's destruction, Bel Iblis left to form his own private army. He feared that Mon Mothma was seeking to overthrow the Emperor in order to set herself up in his place. He waited for that to happen, but it never did. In the subsequent years, pride kept him away. Bel Iblis hoped to build a fleet and return with dignity and respect, but the best he could create was a strike force. Still, after he provided badly needed assistance to Han Solo at the hidden location of the *Katana* fleet, Princess Leia officially invited Bel Iblis and his strike force to join the New Republic. He accepted her offer. [DFR, DFRSB, LC]

Belkadan

A planet located in the Dalonbian sector, near the galactic rim. It was the site of ExGal-4, a solitary outpost of the ExGal Society devoted to watching for signs of life beyond the galaxy. The Yuuzhan Vong started their invasion of the galaxy on this world. Their agent, Yomin Carr, sabotaged the outpost to prevent the scientists from noticing the approach of the invasion force, then murdered the outpost personnel. He used the biological expertise of the Yuuzhan Vong to change the planet's atmosphere into a toxic brew, preparing it so that his people could plant yorik coral—the basis of many of their living ships and weapons. [VP]

Belsavis

Kilometers of icy glaciers separate volcanic rift valleys on this planet located in the Ninth quadrant near the Senex sector. Cities are located within the rifts, and the planet is known for its vine-coffee and vine-silk exports. [COJ, TJP]

Bendone

Home planet of the Howler Tree People. [YJK]

Bengat

A planet covered in water. [TBH]

Ber'asco

Leader of the Charon death cult and commander of the biologically engineered spacecraft *Desolate*. Ber'asco and the Charon came from the strange dimension known as otherspace. [OS]

Berchest

A planet in the Borderland Regions, best known for its major city, Calius saj Leeloo, the City of Glowing Crystal. This city, a spectacular wonder since the earliest days of the Old Republic, was crafted from a single gigantic crystal. The salty spray of the dark red-orange waters of the Leefari Sea created the crystal over the eons, while Berchestian artisans painstakingly sculpted it and nurtured its slow growth, crafting buildings, walkways, and roads directly from the massive crystal. This planet and its crystal city were once a major galactic tourist attraction, but the Clone Wars and the rise of the Empire caused business to slack off over time. The planet achieved modest success as an Imperial trading center during the Galactic Civil War. Grand Admiral Thrawn used Berchest as a troop transfer point for his newly cloned ship crews as he prepared to launch a massive assault on the New Republic. [LC]

Beruss, Avan

The son of an Imperial senator, he tried to join the Rebellion when his childhood friend, Princess Leia Organa, began to act as a Rebel courier. His father forbade it. Later, he disobeyed his father and joined Rogue Squadron. [XW]

Beruss, Doman

A senator from Illodia, he was the chairman of the Ministry Council of the New Republic. He submitted a petition of no confidence in Chief of State Leia Organa Solo during the Yevethan crisis, hoping to keep her from committing the New Republic to war in order to rescue the captured Han Solo.

Also, a flaxen-haired female who represented the Corellian exiles at the New Republic's Provisional Council and signed the Declaration of the New Republic. [BTS, SOL, TT, WG]

Bespin

This gaseous planet in the star system of the same name is the location of the Cloud City mining colony once run by Lando Calrissian. Other planets in the Bespin system include Miser, a small, metal-rich world orbiting close to the sun, and Orin, a hostile world with a violent environment.

The gas giant's many moons include H'gaard and Drudonna, "the Twins." The system is also home to a massive asteroid field known as Velser's Ring. The asteroids are actually chunks of frozen gases and liquids, not metal or stone, leading to the speculation that the field was once a second gas-giant planet.

After the Empire established a presence on Bespin, a giant Imperial floating factory barge was put in place. The barge's factories collected raw materials from the Rethin Sea to produce more war machines. [ESB, GG2, ZHR]

Bessimir

A planet located fifteen parsecs from Coruscant. A dozen years after the Battle of Endor, the newly commissioned Fifth Fleet conducted a live-fire training mission code-named Hammerblow here. [BTS]

Bestine IV

This planet in the Bestine system allied with the Rebellion and housed a secret Rebel base. Biggs Darklighter defected to the Alliance while on a mission to Bestine.

Bestine is also the name of a small farming community on the planet Tatooine, located west of the Mos Eisley spaceport. Imperial control of the planet was situated in this community. [GG1, MTS, RJ, SW, TMEC]

BG-J38

A thin, mantis-headed droid who was in much demand in Jabba the Hutt's court. The droid was an expert hologame player, often serving as an opponent for Jabba or one of his associates. [RJ]

Big L

Spacer slang for the speed of light. To "cross the Big L" is to jump to light speed. [HSE]

Biitu

A beautiful and peaceful planet once covered with lush farmland and inhabited by contented farmers until disaster struck. During the earliest days of the Empire, a droid called the Great Heep installed a fuel ore processing plant equipped with a moisture eater that turned the planet into a barren wasteland. The green-skinned, bald Biituians were saved when R2-D2 destroyed the Great Heep. [TGH]

Bilar

A meter-tall species whose members resemble hairless teddy bears with long arms, short legs, dark eyes, and thin lips that are formed into perpetual grins. They inhabit the tropical world Mima II in the Lar star system. Due to the effects of the Bilar group minds, or claqas, single members of this species possess no more intelligence than a rodent. But when Bilars join together to form a group mind, their intelligence doubles with every new member. Seven-member claqas reach genius-level intelligence, and ten-member claqas have been achieved. These claqas result in group personalities that can be unnerving and unpredictable. [GG4]

Bilbringi

A star system famous for the Bilbringi Shipyards. The New Republic's last battle with the Imperial forces under the command of Grand Admiral Thrawn occurred here. During the conflict, an armada of smuggling ships led by Aves, Mazzic, and Gillespee aided the New Republic. [LC]

Bildor's Canyon

A canyon located in the Dune Sea on the planet Tatooine. [TMEC]

Bille, Dar

Second in command of the Yevethan raiders under Nil Spaar during the attack on the Empire's shipyards at N'zoth. Later, he was primate, or proctor, of the command vessel *Pride of Yevetha*. Dar Bille ordered the attack on Koornacht settlements. [BTS, TT]

Bimm

The diminutive inhabitants of the planet Bimmisaari. The half-furred Bimms are a friendly, peaceful people, with singing voices and a love of stories—especially heroic stories. One of their favorites is the tale of the Battle of Endor, and they are particularly fascinated with the heroic acts of Luke Skywalker. They love to haggle, and discover bargains at the many markets scattered among their planet's forests. They abhor stealing—so much so that shoplifting is considered a capital offense. [HE, HESB]

Bimmisaari

This temperate world is home to the Bimms. Due to the planet's distance from the Core Worlds, the planet escaped most of the horrors inflicted by the Empire during its reign. Bimmisaari entered into negotiations with the New Republic five years after the Battle of Endor. The planet offers a number of impressive marketplaces, including one located next to the Tower of Law. Noghri commandos ambushed Princess Leia and her party during her diplomatic mission to this world. [HE, HESB]

binary loadlifter

A primitive labor droid designed to move heavy objects in spaceports and warehouses, utilizing powerful mechanical claws and either a wheeled or repulsorlift propulsion system. [SW]

Binks, Jar Jar

A member of the amphibious species known as Gungans living on the planet Naboo, Jar Jar Binks was one of the heroes who helped overcome the Trade Federation blockade of his planet. During that campaign, he was saved from certain death by the Jedi Master Qui-Gon Jinn, and Jar Jar swore a life debt to the Jedi. He helped Qui-Gon and his apprentice, Obi-Wan Kenobi, as they sought to end the blockade, and proved helpful in persuading the Gungan leader, Boss Nass, to join the liberation efforts. [SWTPM]

Jar Jar Binks

bioscan

A scanner and diagnostic package designed to identify and analyze the biological composition and medical status of living beings. Not a portable unit, the dedicated sensor array is built into a sturdy framework that is lowered onto a patient. The array includes a medtox detector, vapro-sampler, and doppraymagno scanner, all connected to an analysis computer. In addition to medical applications, the bioscan can be used to identify more than 1,000 alien species. It can be recalibrated to serve as a surveillance device, detecting and analyzing power sources, comm transmissions, and weapon signatures within an extremely limited range. [SESB, SOTE]

Bith

Craniopods—highly evolved humanoids with enlarged craniums—with large, lidless black eyes, receding noses, and baggy epidermal folds beneath their jaws. They originated on the world of Clak'dor VII in the Colu system of the Mayagil sector. A cantina band that regularly played at the Mos Eisley cantina consisted of Bith. [GG4, SW, TMEC]

Bithabus the Mystifier

A Bith stage magician whose performances were famous throughout the galaxy. His act was regularly seen at Hologram Fun World's Asteroid Theater. [QE]

Bix

A sleek droid that teamed with Auren Yomm in the Colonial Games that took place during the early days of the Empire. [DTV]

Bjornsons

A family of Tatooine moisture farmers who opposed Ariq Joanson's plans to establish peace with the Jawas and Tusken Raiders. Their resistance was due to the death of their son, presumably at the hands of the Sand People. [TMEC]

BL-17

A droid owned by the bounty hunter Boba Fett during the early days of the Empire. BL-17 looked like C-3PO but had the olive-drab and yellow coloration of Fett's armor. It carried a rectangular blaster. [DTV]

Black Asp

This Imperial *Interdictor*-class cruiser was involved in a fast and furious skirmish with Rogue Squadron at Chorax. Uwlla Iillor commanded the vessel. [BW]

Black Ice

This cargo train consisted of two engine pods set on each end of connected force spheres, and it was five times the length of an *Imperial*-class Star Destroyer. It carried the equivalent of more than a year's power supply for an Imperial battle fleet. [BI]

Blackmoon

A moon of the planet Borleias, supporting no native life-forms. It was also the code name for Rogue Squadron's assault on Borleias's Imperial stronghold. [BW]

Black Nebula

This nebula in the Parfadi region of space separates the planets Arat Fraca and Motexx. The nebula contains two immense neutron stars and is considered unnavigable. [SOL]

Black Nine

The Imperial shipyard at ILC-905 that was taken over by Yevethan forces. [TT]

Black Sun

The criminal organization known as Black Sun lurked in the shadows of the Empire, employing tens of thousands of operatives throughout the galaxy. Free traders, politicians, newsnet reporters, Imperial bureaucrats, smugglers, assassins, spies, and criminals of all sorts could be found on the payroll of Black Sun or one of its many subsidiaries. Many of those working for Black Sun didn't even know it—in fact, few knew of Black Sun's existence, as it was concealed beneath layers of front organizations, covert operations, and Imperial officials on the take. Black Sun spanned the galaxy, dealing in blackmail, espionage, gambling, smuggling, slaving, spicerunning, racketeering, and a multitude of other activities.

The alien Prince Xizor sat in the center of Black Sun's intricate web of shadow corporations and legitimate businesses. He allowed the alluring human replica droid Guri to serve as the syndicate's public face, and many believed that she led Black Sun. Nine lieutenants, or Vigos, coordinated the criminal activities of tens of thousands of minions in different sectors of the galaxy.

Eleven years after the death of Prince Xizor and the Alliance victory at Endor, Black Sun fell under the leadership of Y'ull Acib. With the help of Grappa the Hutt, he plotted to take control of the Imperial Interim Ruling Council by assassinating council head Xandel Carivus and replacing him with a clone. The plan failed, but Acib remained in charge of the galaxy's underworld. [CE, SESB, SOTE]

blasé tree goat

These lethargic, goatlike creatures live in the great trees that cover Endor's forest moon. [ETV]

blaster

blaster

Common weapons that fire coherent packets of intense light energy called bolts. A blaster's level of intensity can be adjusted to fire stun or killing bolts. When a blaster discharges an energy bolt, a smell similar to ozone fills the air. A variety of different models is available, ranging in size from small holdout blasters, to standard blaster pistols, to heavy blaster pistols and blaster rifles. Larger models require targeting computers and crews to operate them. These include various field artillery and ship-mounted blaster cannons. [ESB, RJ, SW, SWRPG, SWRPG2, SWSB]

blastonecrosis

An allergy to bacta marked by fatigue and loss of appetite. [BW]

blast-rifle

A weapon favored in ancient times by the beast-riders of Onderon. It fired bolts of laser energy. [TOJ]

blba tree

A broad-trunked, jagged-branched tree that grows on the savannas of Dantooine. [DA]

Blessings

A Dreadnaught in Nil Spaar's Black Eleven Fleet. [BTS]

Blissex, Walex

An Old Republic engineer, he designed the *Victory*-class Star Destroyer near the end of the Clone Wars. Later, as the Empire was on the rise, Blissex disappeared from public life and joined the Rebel Alliance. [SWSB]

blob race

A major betting sport in Umgul City on the planet Umgul. This bizarre race features gelatinous blobs moving through a complicated obstacle course. Cheating is punishable by death. [JS]

Blockade Runner

Any Corellian corvette utilized by smugglers and others attempting to circumvent galactic authorities. The Alderaanian consular ship *Tantive IV*, commanded by Captain Antilles, was one such vessel. [SW, SWSB, SWVG]

Bloor, Melvosh

A Kalkal professor of investigative politico-sociology at Beshka University, he went to Jabba's palace to locate a missing colleague and was fed to the rancor. [TJP]

Blue, Sinewy Ana

A beautiful smuggler, she ran the sabacc games on Skip 1 in the Smuggler's Run asteroid field. She sold former Imperial goods to the dark-sider Kueller, who used them in his reign of terror against the New Republic. Later, Kueller ordered her to bring Han Solo to Almania. She eventually told Solo everything she knew, and he rushed to Almania despite the fact that Kueller was waiting for him. [NR]

Blue Desert People

The members of this reptilelike species on the planet Dathomir possess bloodred eyes and sharp black teeth. [CPL]

Blue Leader

At the Battle of Endor, Rebel Captain Merrick Simm commanded one of four Alliance battle wings taking part in the assault against the second Death Star. Simm died when his fighter was caught in the explosion that destroyed an Imperial communications ship. [RJ]

Blue Max

An experimental cube-shaped computer droid packed with more memory and capabilities than that of most shipboard computer systems. Stolen from the Empire, Blue Max eventually wound up in the possession of an outlaw tech named Doc. Doc and his daughter Jessa reprogrammed Max's miniature computer and provided it with a chirpy personality. The deep blue droid's primary function was to process and interpret data. It was equipped with a speech synthesizer, folded appendages, and a glowing red monocular photoreceptor. Doc and Jessa mounted Blue Max inside the chest cavity of the labor droid Bollux. Together, the two droids traveled with Han Solo and Chewbacca throughout the Corporate Sector, prior to Solo's involvement with the Rebellion. [HLL, HSE, HSR]

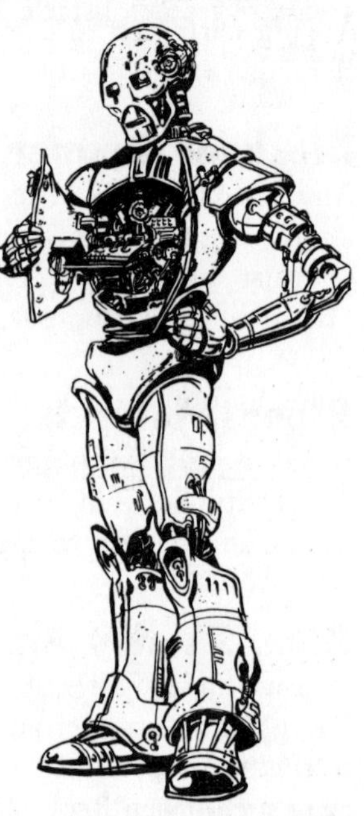

Blue Max

Blue Nebula

An extremely seedy tavern and dining establishment in the Manda spaceport. [DTV]

Bluescale

See Sh'tk'ith, Elder.

Blue Squad

Luke Skywalker awarded the title of Blue Squad to the twenty-four Bothans who took part in the attack on the Imperial freighter *Suprosa*. The squad flew twelve two-man Y-wings, seeking to intercept the secret plans for the second Death Star that were hidden within the freighter. *Suprosa*, although unescorted, was armed with surprisingly powerful cannons and shields. The Bothans captured the plans, but twelve of the Blue Squad Bothans were lost in the terrible battle.

During the Battle of Endor, Blue Squad was one of many A-wing starfighter squadrons in the Alliance's Blue Wing attack element. [RJ, SESB, SOTE]

Blue Squadron

One of the New Republic X-wing battle groups that participated in the Battle of Calamari. [DE]

Blue Wing

The comm unit designation for Blue Leader's second in command at the Battle of Endor. He was responsible for coordinating several of the Blue Wing battle groups. [RJ]

blumfruit

A large, red, egg-shaped berry that grew on Endor's forest moon and was considered by the Ewoks to be a delicacy. [ETV]

blurrg

Beast of burden used by the Marauders of Endor for transportation and to pull carts. [ISWU]

Bnach

This scorched, cracked world was the site of an Imperial prison camp where prisoners labored in rock quarries. [PDS]

Bnar, Master Ood

This ancient Jedi, who some believe evolved from a treelike species on the planet Myrkr, was the gatekeeper of a Jedi Holocron that had belonged to Master Arca Jeth. He proclaimed that Nomi Sunrider would be a powerful Jedi. Thousands of years later, he reawakened on the planet Ossus to help Jem, a young woman with Force powers. He sacrificed himself to destroy the evil Imperial military executor Sedriss. [DE2, TOJ]

boarding craft

Any small spacecraft used to ferry personnel and cargo between space vessels or between vessels and planets or space stations. [HSR]

Bocce

One of many languages used on Tatooine, it was also spoken on the planet Aris, capital world of the Albarrio sector. [RM, SW]

Boda, Ashka

An ancient Jedi who was captured and murdered by the Emperor during the Jedi extermination that marked the start of the New Order. Ashka possessed the Jedi Holocron at the time of his capture. [DE]

Bodgen

A swampy moon that orbits an unnamed planet. During the early days of the Empire, R2-D2 and C-3PO visited the bog moon. At the time, the pirate captain Kybo Ren was holding Princess Gerin of Tammuz-an on a freighter hidden on the moon. [DTV]

body-wood

This incredible wood from the tree of the same name resembles the flesh of the forest dwellers of the planet Firrerre. Many consider it to be the finest wood in the galaxy. The wood's polished surface is pale pink, shot through with streaks of scarlet and a gleaming light similar to precious stones. Some believe that the body-wood trees possess a degree of intelligence and "cry" when chopped down. The cut wood bleeds a scarlet liquid. [CS]

bofa

A sweet, dried fruit considered to be a delicacy. [TSW]

Bogen, Senator

A human from the planet Ralltiir, he served as a New Republic senator and a member of the Senate Defense Council. [BTS, SOL]

bogey

A glittering, formless creature that inhabits the spice mines of Kessel and is the main source of nourishment for Kessel energy spiders. [JS]

Bok, Aidan

A Jedi ghost. He was the guardian of the library of Nespis VIII. [GF]

BolBol the Hutt

A Hutt crimelord who controlled much of the Stenness system. [TMEC]

Boldheart

The New Republic frigate that encountered the mysterious ghost ship called the Teljkon vagabond. [BTS]

Bollux

A battered, heavily modified BLX-5 labor droid who traveled with Han Solo and Chewbacca during their adventures in the Corporate Sector. Bollux was altered by the outlaw tech Jessa to carry a miniature computer named Blue Max inside his chest cavity. The labor droid was more than one hundred years old, and his length of service dated back to his first activation at the great Fondor shipyards. As his model was replaced by newer droids, Bollux took on different jobs in order to avoid deactivation. Over the years, Bollux worked as a construction gang assistant surveyor, a roustabout, and a maintenance assistant, until he fell in with a band of outlaw techs. Bollux was a stocky, dent-covered droid, with long arms and hands that hung nearly to his knees. A flat brown primer was all that remained of his once-bright finish. Two unblinking red photoreceptors stared from Bollux's head, and his outdated speech synthesizer gave him a low, slow voice that matched his pleasant, low-key personality. [HLL, HSE, HSR]

boma beast

A species of wingless monsters that thrived in the Onderon forests some 4,000 years before the Galactic Civil War. [TOJ]

B'omarr monks

Members of this mysterious religious order built a large monastery on Tatooine many centuries ago. They believed that by cutting themselves off from all sensation they could enhance the powers of their minds and journey through inner space. Monks rarely spoke to one another, and even lectures were reduced to a single phrase or word. Committed monks eventually reached a point where they rarely moved. During the final stage of enlightenment, a monk was assisted in shedding his or her body through a surgical procedure. A monk's brain was removed and placed in a nutrient-filled jar. There, it was meant to spend eternity in perpetual thought. In those instances when an enlightened brain had business to attend to, it made use of a spiderlike mechanical walking apparatus. The B'omarr monastery eventually became the palace of crimelord Jabba the Hutt, but some monks continued to inhabit the lower levels of the place during and after Jabba's destruction. [ISWU]

bomat

A small carnivorous pest native to the planet Aruza. [TBH]

Bombaasa, Crev

This crimelord was a vicious yet cultured Corellian who ran most of the illegal operations in the Kathol sector. [VF]

Bômlas

A three-armed Ychthytonian bartender on Skip 1, he reportedly lost his fourth arm in a savage game of sabacc. [NR]

Bonadan

A barren, parched planet that was one of the Corporate Sector Authority's most important factory worlds. Bonadan is a yellow sphere covered with rust-red strips. The planet looks barren, for whatever plant life wasn't deliberately destroyed has died due to careless mining operations, abundant pollutants, and simple neglect. Factories, refineries, docks, and spaceports cover the world. The largest of the ten spaceports is Bonadan Spaceport Southeast II, a sprawling city composed of low permacite buildings constructed on fusion-formed soil.

The highly industrialized and densely populated planet houses many different intelligent species from all over the galaxy, and interspecies rivalries are common. In an effort to keep peace and order, weapons were outlawed on the planet. Bonadan authorities use a vast and advanced network of weapon detectors to enforce the ban.

Even with the complicated array of weapon detectors, C-3PX, a modified protocol droid, was able to utilize concealed internal weaponry to assassinate the brother of Vojak. [CSSB, D, DE, HSR]

Bondo

A jovial, portly Ewok, he served as chieftain of the nomadic Jinda tribe. [ETV]

Bonearm, Dace

An unsavory human bounty hunter, he traveled with an IG-model assassin droid. [TMEC]

bonegnawer

A flying carnivorous creature that lives in the desert wastelands of Tatooine. Its tooth-filled jaws are strong enough to crush rock. [SW]

bongo

A Gungan submarine used on the planet Naboo, organically grown and propelled by rotating tentacles powered by electromagnetic field motors. [SWTPM]

Booldrum

Cousin of Gerney Caslo, he was the owner of a library in Hweg Shul on Nam Chorios. [POT]

Boonda

A "reformed" Hutt who was the target of a droid rebellion led by C-3PO. [D]

Boonta

A planet famous for its speeder races. The speeder courses are oval-shaped tunnels about sixteen kilometers long. Large viewing screens and a comfortable enclosed viewing area are set aside for spectators. The planet also has a gigantic scrap yard that serves as a graveyard for damaged spaceships. [DTV]

Borderland Regions

A militarized zone between New Republic and Imperial space, claimed by both sides but controlled by neither. Major battles in the continuing Galactic Civil War often took place in this area. Systems within the Borderlands took great pains to stay neutral until a clear winner emerged from the ongoing fray. [HE, HESB]

bordok

A medium-sized ponylike creature. Ewoks use them as beasts of burden. [ETV]

Borealis

The flagship used by Chief of State Leia Organa Solo on her mission to Nam Chorios. [POT]

Borealis, Rima

A name used by Princess Leia's trusted aide Winter when she performed as an Alliance intelligence agent who assisted Rogue Squadron during an undercover mission to Coruscant. [BW]

Borgo Prime
A hollowed-out, honeycombed asteroid that features a seedy spaceport and a disreputable trade center. Lando Calrissian's Corusca gem broker operated from this location. Luke Skywalker and Tenel Ka contacted the broker to find out who had purchased an important shipment. [YJK]

Borleias (Blackmoon)
The fourth planet in the Pyria system, it is a steamy, blue-green world with a single dark moon. This feature provided the system with its Alliance code name, Blackmoon. Though this inhabited world lacks valuable resources and passes through a meteor shower once each year, it is located at an important hyperspace crossroads. When the Rebel Alliance planned its attack on Coruscant three years after the Battle of Endor, Borleias was captured to be used as a staging area for the attack. It took two attempts, but Borleias eventually became the operations base for Rogue Squadron. [BW]

borrat
A fearsome, two-meter-long rodent native to Coruscant, distinguished by its tusks, spines, armored flesh, and powerful claws. [BW]

Bortras
This planet in the Reithcas sector was the birthplace of Jedi Master Jorus C'baoth. [DFR]

Bortrek, Captain
The commander of the ship *Pure Sabacc*, he was gruff, swaggering, and frequently drunk. Bortrek rescued R2-D2 and C-3PO after the droids were set adrift in an escape pod during the Nam Chorios crisis. Instead of simply returning them to Princess Leia, he held the droids hostage. [POT]

Bos, Lieutenant

Flight leader of the ferry operation to transfer hostage Han Solo during the Yevethan crisis. [TT]

BoShek

A human smuggler and starship technician, he referred Ben Kenobi to Chewbacca at the Mos Eisley cantina. [TMEC]

Bossk

The Trandoshan bounty hunter contracted by Darth Vader to find the *Millennium Falcon* and her crew after the Battle of Hoth. He specialized in hunting down Wookiees and had many run-ins with Han Solo and Chewbacca. His light freighter, *Hound's Tooth,* was modified for Wookiee hunting. He tried to steal the carbonite block containing Han Solo from Boba Fett, but failed. Much later, Bossk teamed up with the Wookiee bounty hunter Chenlambec and traveled to Lomabu III. The planet contained an Imperial Wookiee prison camp. There, Chenlambec betrayed Bossk and handed him over to Imperial Governor Io Desnand, who wanted to turn Bossk into a reptile-skin dress for his wife. [ESB, GG3, TBH]

Bossk

Bot

The cloaked and mute henchman of Captain-Supervisor Grammel on the planet Circarpous V. [SME]

Bothan

A species from the planet Bothawui and its colony worlds, Bothans are renowned for their extensive spy network. Bothan spies were instrumental in locating the site of the second Death Star and discovering that the Emperor was scheduled to supervise the battle station's final stages of construction. Due to the efforts of the Bothan spies, the Alliance decided to launch the assault that came to be known as the Battle of Endor. [DFR, DFRSB, HE, LC, RJ]

Bothan spynet

A vast, galaxywide intelligence-gathering network, second to none. During the darkest days of the Empire, the Bothan spynet utilized agents, moles, bribes, surveillance devices, and other methods to uncover secrets and turn a tidy profit. Though primarily used in support of the Rebel Alliance, both the Empire and various underworld organizations sometimes used the spynet for their own purposes. [SESB, SOTE]

Bothawui

This high-tech, industrial planet is the homeworld of the Bothans and the headquarters of the Bothan spynet. The planet gained status as neutral ground for trade and diplomatic negotiations long ago, and intrigues of all sorts occur regularly on Bothawui. Pilot Peshk Vri'syk graduated from the Bothan Martial Academy before joining Rogue Squadron. After his death another Bothan, Asyr Sei'lar, took his place in Rogue Squadron. [KT, SESB, SOTE, WG]

Botor Enclave

A group of worlds that formed a protective federation during the six years following the Battle of Endor. The frozen planet Kerensik was among the members of this federation. [DESB]

bounce

A casino game that consists of a moving target suspended within an enclosed space and a gun. The only hits to score are those that are reflected, or "bounced." Direct hits don't count. [HSR]

Bounty Hunters' Creed

The code adhered to by even the most unethical bounty hunters. It states that no hunter should interfere with another's hunt, and no hunter should kill another hunter. [TBH]

Bounty Hunters' Guild

A loosely organized group that monitors the activities of bounty hunters, puts them in touch with clients and other hunters, and upholds the Bounty Hunters' Creed. [TBH]

Boushh

A bounty hunter and contract employee of the Black Sun criminal syndicate. The hunter made the mistake of withholding credits from the syndicate and was eliminated for the insult. Guri, Prince Xizor's assassin, provided Leia Organa with Boushh's helmet and outfit so she could sneak into the Imperial Center. Organa later used the disguise to gain access to Jabba the Hutt's palace. [RJ, SOTE]

Bovo Yagen

This star system was the third to be targeted for destruction during the starbuster crisis about fourteen years after the Battle of Endor. [AS, SAC]

bowcaster

A handcrafted Wookiee weapon that fires energy quarrels. [ESB, RJ, SW, SWSB]

Bozzie

An old Ewok widow who was Paploo's pushy, overbearing mother and Princess Kneesaa's aunt. [ETV]

Bpfassh

A double planet with a complex system of moons, located in the star system of the same name. During the Clone Wars, a group of Bpfasshi Dark Jedi spread terror throughout the Sluis sector before being stopped by an unknown person, or persons, on Dagobah. Because of this incident, most Bpfasshi dislike all Jedi. Later, Bpfassh was one of the targets of a three-system attack launched by Imperial forces as a diversion before their true target, Sluis Van, was to be hit. The attack was designed to frighten and injure, not destroy. The plan was to force Bpfassh and its neighboring systems to call to Sluis Van for aid, which they did. The Empire sought to steal the rescue ships in order to bolster the war-reduced Imperial fleet. [HE, HESB, LC]

Brachnis Chorios

An ice-green and lavender planet located in the outermost orbit of the Chorios systems in the Meridian sector. Leia Organa Solo made a secret rendezvous with hyperdrive engineer Seti Ashgad there, about nine years after the Battle of Endor. [POT]

brachno-jag

Small, carnivorous animals used for torture and painful executions. [TJP]

Bragkis

This planet is the site of a million-credit betting parlor. [SOL]

Brakiss

An Imperial who tried to infiltrate Luke Skywalker's Jedi academy. He was a physically stunning man, endowed with blond hair, blue eyes, flawless skin, and thin lips. Princess Leia referred to him as one of the most handsome men she had ever seen. As an infant, Brakiss was taken from his mother because of his nascent Force powers. Skywalker, believing he had turned Brakiss from the dark side, made him a student at the academy, but a training session in which Brakiss was to confront himself left Brakiss terrified and angry. He left the Jedi academy.

Later, he helped the dark-sider known as Kueller install explosives inside New Republic droids. Luke faced Brakiss in battle on the planet Telti. Six years after that, the Second Imperium put Brakiss in charge of the Shadow Academy aboard a large space station, where he was to train a new army of Dark Jedi. When Jaina Solo revealed the hidden location of the Shadow Academy by disabling its cloaking device, the mysterious leaders of the Second Imperium destroyed the station. [NR, YJK]

Brand, Commander

Commander of Task Force Aster, part of the New Republic's Fifth Fleet deployed at Doornik-319. Brand was stationed aboard the *Indomitable*. [SOL, TT]

Brand, King Empatojayos

A Jedi and the ruler of the Ganathans, Brand was severely injured in a battle with Darth Vader. To survive, he was forced to wear a prosthetic suit of his own design. When he heard that Vader had been vanquished, he joined the Alliance and helped fight against the second clone of Emperor Palpatine. Brand sacrificed himself to keep the Emperor's essence from entering the body of baby Anakin Solo, using his own death to eliminate the Emperor's will. [DE2, EE]

Brandei, Captain

The commander of the Imperial Star Destroyer *Judicator*, a vessel in Grand Admiral Thrawn's personal armada, was one of the few senior officers to survive the Battle of Endor. He hated the Rebellion and the aliens it treated as equals. Confident and daring, but never reckless, he believed it was more important to live to fight than to die spectacularly in a lost cause. [DFR, DFRSB]

Brasck

This smuggling chief was one of the major players operating in the Borderland Regions between New Republic and Imperial space. Brasck was a Brubb from the planet Baros. The humanoid reptile had worked as a mercenary for Jabba the Hutt. When Jabba died, Brasck grabbed as many followers as he could and set up his own smuggling operation, which included kidnapping and slavery. The starship *Green Palace* served as his headquarters, a vessel he kept in constant motion in order to avoid the fate that befell Jabba. Fearful of ambush and assassination, he always wore body armor and kept several weapons hidden on his person. [DFR, HE, HESB]

Brashaa

A humanoid follower of Lord Hethrir. [CS]

Brathis, Moff Tragg

Commander of the Imperial battle fleet reportedly stationed at the planet N'zoth, and an ally of the Duskhan League. The alliance was actually a Yevethan ruse implemented to frighten the New Republic. [TT]

Brattakin, Movo

An acquaintance and victim of the villainous Olag Greck. After he was murdered by Greck, Movo's mind was merged with his droid aide, B-9D7. Later, he reprogrammed C-3PO and turned the protocol droid into a fierce leader who spearheaded the droid rebellion that was designed to destroy Movo's enemy, Boonda the Hutt. R2-D2 foiled the plot and reverted C-3PO back to his old self. [D]

breath mask

Part of a portable system that supplies life-sustaining gases to a user. The mask portion fits over the nose and mouth and is connected to a miniature life-support pack worn on the belt or carried on the back. Breath masks can also be built into environment suits and body armor, such as that worn by Darth Vader. [ESB, RJ, SWSB]

Brebishem

These dancers have long snouts and wide, leaf-shaped ears that are able to flap. When Brebishems touch each other, their soft, wrinkled mauve flesh seems to meld together. [CS]

Breil'lya, Tav

This Bothan served as a top aide to the New Republic's Councilor Borsk Fey'lya. He always wore an ornate neck-piece—his family's lineage crest. As a council-aide, he was extremely loyal to Fey'lya and was often assigned to the most important fact-finding missions. Like most Bothans, Breil'lya played games of politics in such a way that the game was more important than the outcome. He did not possess Fey'lya's subtlety and acted with a heavy, obvious hand. As part of his regular duties, Breil'lya traveled to the planet New Cov to meet with Garm Bel Iblis. The Bothan hoped to convince the one-time Old Republic senator to join the New Republic as an ally of Fey'lya's political faction. [DFR, DFRSB]

bright

This slang term was used by X-wing pilots to refer to Imperial TIE Advanced fighters. [BW]

Bright Hope

This Rebel transport was one of the last to depart during the evacuation of the planet Hoth. It was attacked and severely damaged by the bounty hunters Zuckuss and 4-LOM as it attempted to lift off. The bounty hunters had a change of heart, however, and rescued the *Bright Hope*'s ninety passengers and crew. The pair safely transported them to the planet Darlyn Boda. [TBH]

Brigia

A poor, backward planet in the Tion Hegemony. The University of Rudrig provided guidance and aid to the planet's development and modernization initiative, even though the planet's rulers objected. About two years before the Battle of Yavin, a small group of colonists left Brigia and founded New Brigia, a chromite mining operation located in the Koornacht Cluster. [HLL]

Briil twins

Former associates of Han Solo who were killed while battling an Imperial cruiser on patrol near the Tion Hegemony. [HSR]

Brill, Governor Foga

An Imperial warlord and ruler of the planet Prakith. [BTS, SOL]

Brilliant

This New Republic Star Destroyer was part of the Home Fleet. It shadowed the Yevethan Duskhan League's embassy ship *Aramadia* while it orbited Coruscant. [BTS]

B'rknaa

Living rock creatures from the moon Indobok. High-energy crystals on the moon animate the B'rknaa and give them a group mind. [D]

Brubb

Humanoid reptiles from the planet Baros, they average about 1.6 meters tall, with dusty yellow, pitted, knobby hides, ridged eyes, and flat noses. Males usually possess a single tuft of coarse black hair jutting from the tops of their heads. Social beings, they treat visitors to their world as honored guests. [GG4]

Brusc, Captain

The captain of the Imperial Star Destroyer *Manticore* served under Admiral Daala until he died when the *Manticore* was destroyed during the Battle of Calamari. [DA]

Bubo (BUBOICULLAAR)

A creature that looked like a cross between a dog and a frog, with bulging eyes and a protruding lower jaw. Bubo was a spy and assassin in Jabba's palace on Tatooine. He often consulted with the B'omarr monks and plotted to kill Jabba the Hutt. Few suspected that Bubo was even intelligent, and many believed he was simply a pet to a Jawa tribe. After Jabba's death, the B'omarr monks removed Bubo's brain and freed him to contemplate the mysteries of the universe without the hampering influence of his physical form. [RJ, TJP]

Budpock

This planet in the Meridian sector was a longtime supporter of the Rebel Alliance. Dimmit Station is one of the planet's main ports. [POT]

bulk freighter

These vessels that haul cargo throughout the galaxy come in a variety of different models, though all bulk freighters are basically boxes with hyperdrive engines. These vessels are small to mid-sized to keep fuel costs down and to allow access to almost all space docks and ports. Most of these craft have little or no armament, and they depend on the safety of well-traveled space lanes and the ships that patrol them. While some large companies maintain their own fleets of freighters, most bulk freighters are independently owned. [SWSB]

Bunji, Big

An associate of Han Solo's, he got on the smuggler's bad side for not repaying a debt in a timely fashion. To demonstrate his displeasure, Solo strafed Bunji's pressure dome with blaster fire. Bunji barely escaped with his life. [HSE]

Bur

A commander in dark-sider Kueller's army on Almania, he was Kueller's favorite. [NR]

Bureau of Operations

A division of Imperial Intelligence, it handled all major covert operations. Its missions included surveillance and infiltration operations, counterintelligence, and assassinations. [ISB]

burnout

Spacer jargon referring to the loss of power in a ship's engines. [ESBR]

Burren, Tal

A computer tech, he helped Ysanne Isard, director of Imperial Intelligence, attempt to recapture Mara Jade after her escape from her cell. [MJ]

Burrk

A stormtrooper who deserted from the Imperial military in the confusion that followed the Battle of Endor. He survived thereafter through a variety of illegal activities. [DS]

butcherbug

A multilegged armored creature on Dagobah that spins a tough, microfine cord between the roots of gnarltrees. Flying creatures are sliced into pieces when they fly into the trap. The butcherbug then feasts on the pieces. [ISWU]

Butcher of Montellian Serat

The name given to the Devaronian spy Kardue'sai'Malloc, after he indiscriminately shelled the city of Montellian Serat. [TMEC]

B-wing starfighter

A primary airfoil combined with four power plants and a command pod creates one of the most heavily armed starfighters in the Alliance arsenal. Two movable secondary airfoils form a cross between the command pod and the primary airfoil wingtip. These can change their position during flight. They extend fully to bring the starfighter's maximum concentration of firepower to bear and tuck into the primary airfoil when the fighter is in cruise mode. The command pod employs a radical design. It uses an automatic gyroscopically stabilized suspension system to keep the pod in a fixed position. The airfoil rotates around the stabilized pod, creating a flexible firing platform while the pilot experiences none of the effects of rapid spins, twists, or turns. The primary and two secondary wingtips sport ion cannons, while the command pod features a mounted laser cannon. Other weapons include two internally mounted proton torpedo launchers and two small blaster cannons.

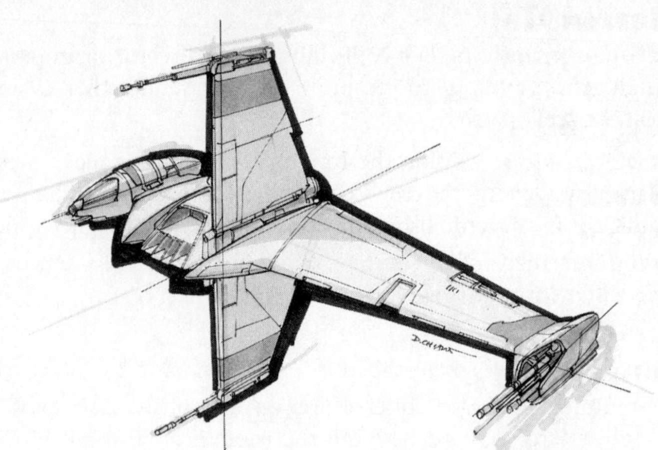

B-wing starfighter

These starfighters played a key role in the Alliance victory at the Battle of Endor. In response to the growing success of Imperial escort warships, Admiral Ackbar conceived and headed the Shantipole Project. With the aid of the Verpine colonies Slayn and Korpil, Ackbar designed the B-wing. The ship combined speed with armor and armament, thus creating a formidable starfighter to aid the Rebel Alliance. Designed as a pure starfighter, the B-wing originally had no hyperdrive capability. Hyperdrives were added to the design prior to the Battle of Endor. [RJ, SFS, SWSB, SWVG]

Byss

The primary planet in the binary star system of Byss and Abyss. The Abyssin species originated on this arid world. [GG4]

Byss

This planet hidden deep within the Galactic Core was Emperor Palpatine's private world and the center of his reborn Empire six years after the Battle of Endor. The planet could be reached only by navigating through encoded routes and past formidable natural defenses. The place was home to almost twenty billion humans, whose life energies fed the Emperor and his Dark

Side Adepts. The planet was eventually destroyed by its own superweapon, the Galaxy Gun. [DE, DE2, DESB, EE]

Byss Bistro

A cantina located within the Imperial Freight Complex on the planet Byss. Freighter crews could find food, drink, and entertainment in this establishment while they waited for their ships to be unloaded. [DE]

C2-R4 (Ceetoo-Arfour)

This household droid escaped from the Jawas on Tatooine and was adopted by Wuher, a Mos Eisley cantina bartender. C2-R4 prepared an especially potent drink using pheromones from the dead bounty hunter Greedo. [TMEC]

C-3PO (See-Threepio)

A golden protocol droid with specialized programming in human-droid relations, language translation, and language interpretation. Human in shape and mannerisms, C-3PO has long been teamed with R2-D2, an astromech droid. While the two appear to argue constantly, they are true friends who depend upon each other to survive the challenges and dangers of the galaxy at large.

C-3PO is fluent in more than six million galactic languages, including those spoken by living beings as well as by machines. With more than thirty secondary functions complementing his protocol programming, C-3PO has experienced many adventures without undergoing the regular memory wipes applied to other droids. This has allowed C-3PO—and R2-D2—to learn by experience and to develop personalities on par with sentient beings.

Over the years, C-3PO has programmed converters, run heavy-duty industrial tools including a shovel loader, and led a brief droid rebellion utilizing programming he wasn't even aware of. He has served smugglers and crimelords, racers and bar owners, and an assortment of heroes and rogues. C-3PO's standard equipment includes visual, auditory, olfactory, and sensory receptors; a broadband antenna for receiving droid transmissions; and a speech vocabulator. Design specifications for this model droid call for limited creativity circuits to keep embellishment to a minimum. Over the long period since C-3PO's last memory wipe—if he ever even had one—he has developed a talent for telling stories, as evidenced by his dramatic re-creation of the events of the Galactic Civil War for the Ewoks of the forest moon of Endor.

C-3PO

C-3PO and R2-D2 were in the service of the Royal House of Alderaan and were aboard the *Tantive IV* during Princess Leia's secret mission to intercept stolen Imperial data. When the ship was boarded, R2-D2 took an escape pod down to the planet Tatooine, carrying the stolen plans for the Death Star in his memory. C-3PO reluctantly followed, and the pair wound up in the possession of Luke Skywalker. They became integral members of the Rebel Alliance and the New Republic that followed it, helping to save the galaxy many times. In later years, C-3PO has also taken on the role of part-time nanny and protector of Han and Leia Organa Solo's three children. [ESB, RJ, SW, SWCG, SWSB]

C-3PX

A modified protocol droid reprogrammed to act as an assassin droid for crimelord Olag Greck. This droid looked just like C-3PO, except for the *X* marked on its forehead. [D]

C4-CZN ion field gun

A large Imperial weapon that moved on rollers. [TMEC]

C-9PO (See-Ninepio)

A newer-model protocol droid that was memory-wiped and modified to serve Brakiss at the droid manufacturing facility on Telti. [NR]

Caamas

A planet destroyed shortly after the end of the Clone Wars. Bothans assisted in the deed; a group of them lowered the planetary shields and allowed destruction to rain down upon the planet. The outrage at the time was great, more so even than when Alderaan was destroyed. The Caamas Document, hidden in Imperial data banks, identified the Bothans responsible for the crime. [SP, VF]

Caamasi

The inhabitants of the planet Caamas. They were considered a good and noble people, with an artistic bent and a gentle wisdom. They believed in peace through moral strength and were firm supporters of the principles of the Old Republic. Caamasi legends claimed that the first Jedi Knights came to Caamas to learn the moral use of their power. A few Caamasi survived the destruction of their homeworld and found shelter on other worlds, including Alderaan. [SP, VF]

Cai

A Mistryl Shadow Guard who was involved in the botched transfer of the Hammertong device to the Empire for use in the second Death Star. [TMEC]

Calamari, Battle of

The watery planet Mon Calamari was the first planet attacked by the reborn Emperor's World Devastators in a conflict that occurred six years after the Battle of Endor. The homeworld of the Mon Calamari suffered great damage, but the new Imperial war machines were eventually stopped, thanks to the actions of Luke Skywalker. [DE]

Calamarian

See Mon Calamari.

Calius saj Leeloo

See Berchest.

caller

A small handheld transmitter that summons droids by sending signals to their restraining bolts. These devices also turn restraining bolts on and off and are sometimes called restraining bolt activators. [SW, SWR]

Callista

A beautiful young woman, she became one of the loves of Luke Skywalker's life. She was strong in the Force, from her earliest days with her family on the water world Chad III. She teamed up with another powerful Force user, Geith, and the pair attempted to destroy the Imperial space station and experimental weapon known as *Eye of Palpatine*. The two died on the station, but Callista's spirit remained behind, held by the Force and a strange power called the Will. She took control of the station's computer, keeping the weapon off-line and forcing the Empire to abandon the project.

Thirty years later, Luke Skywalker and two of his students, Nichos Marr and Cray Mingla, sought to destroy the *Eye*. Callista communicated with Luke through the station's computers and helped the trio complete their mission. The mission was not without cost, however. Both Nichos and Cray would have to sacrifice themselves. Before the end, however, Cray and Callista utilized the last of their Force abilities to transfer Callista into Cray's body. Once again corporeal, but bereft of her Force powers, Callista said good-bye to Luke and set out to regain what she had lost.

Nine years after the Battle of Endor, Callista appeared again and warned Chief of State Leia Organa Solo to avoid a meeting with Seti Ashgad. She helped Leia hone her lightsaber skills, preparing her for a battle with Beldorian the Hutt. [COJ, DS, POT]

Calrissian, Lando

Soldier of fortune and master gambler, Lando Calrissian was the owner of the *Millennium Falcon*, and while at the helm of the *Falcon* he participated in many adventures, including a visit to the planets of the Rafa system in search of ancient alien treasure. Along the way he was stalked by a series of enemies—essentially because of his habit of winning high-stakes games of chance—and he helped a persecuted alien species called the Oswaft. During this period, Lando was accompanied by the five-armed astrogation/pilot droid named Vuffi Raa.

Lando met Han Solo on Nar Shaddaa, where he was looking to hire Solo as a pilot and flight instructor for the *Falcon*. After saving Han from the bounty hunter Boba Fett, he convinced the Corellian to give him a few flying lessons. Solo fell in love with the ship from the moment he saw it, and vowed to own it someday.

Shortly after losing the *Falcon* to Solo in an intense game of sabacc, Lando turned "respectable" when he won stewardship of Bespin's Cloud City in yet another game. As baron administrator of Cloud City and its Tibanna gas mining operation, he proved to be adept at keeping the outpost on an even keel and turning a handsome profit.

Shortly after the Battle of Hoth, Imperial forces under the command of Lord Darth Vader arrived at Cloud City and "persuaded" Calrissian to assist them in setting a trap for Luke Skywalker. Promising to help fix up the *Falcon*, Lando convinced Han Solo, Chewbacca, Princess Leia, and C-3PO they would be safe aboard Cloud City. But the four were nothing more than bait in Vader's trap. When Lando discovered that Vader was changing the terms of their agreement to suit his own purposes and that Cloud City was about to become an armed camp, he finally decided to help Han. He ordered the evacuation of the city but was too late to rescue Han Solo from

Lando Calrissian

Boba Fett. Instead, he helped Leia and Chewbacca escape in the *Falcon* and even managed to help save Luke Skywalker from certain death at the bottom of the floating city.

Although an early attempt to free Han from the bounty hunter failed, Lando *was* able to help rescue Leia from Prince Xizor, head of the Black Sun crime syndicate. Later, Lando took part in the mission that did rescue Solo from the clutches of Jabba the Hutt. He disguised himself as one of Jabba's guards and worked his way into Jabba's court, so he could watch, listen, and wait for an opportunity to make a move.

After saving Solo and helping to destroy Jabba the Hutt, Lando decided to take a commission in the Rebel Alliance. Due to his reputation as a soldier of fortune, especially for his role in the Battle of Taanab, Lando was given the rank of general. He volunteered to lead the starfighter assault on the second Death Star, a job that was made much easier by Solo's generous offer to allow him use of the *Millennium Falcon*. Lando's daring, expertise, and quick thinking were pivotal in the great space battle that took place above Endor's forest moon. In fact, he accompanied Wedge Antilles on the run to destroy the Death Star's power core.

After the Battle of Endor, Lando resigned his commission and went back to the private sector. His dealings with the Alliance led to the New Republic's offer to finance a new venture in the Athega system. Without realizing it, Lando became an upstanding citizen—war hero, honest businessman, and responsible administrator. He established a mining company on the planet Nkllon and supplied a steady flow of raw materials to the New Republic. He was drawn back into the ongoing galactic conflict when the mechanical mole miners used in his operation were stolen by Grand Admiral Thrawn for use in the Imperial assault on Sluis Van. He wound up suspending his business dealings to help Solo and the New Republic deal with this threat.

After the defeat of Thrawn, Lando rejoined the Republic to assist in its continuing struggle against the Empire. He helped command the Republic forces at the Battle of Calamari. Switching easily between businessman and soldier, he became a leading member of SPIN (the Senate Planetary Intelligence Network) for the New Republic and took on the post of baron administrator of Hologram Fun World, a domed floating amusement park. He has helped Luke Skywalker locate recruits for Skywalker's Jedi academy, spearheaded several dubious credit-making schemes, and crashed at least two converted Imperial Star Destroyers.

At the time of the first Yuuzhan Vong incursion, Calrissian was running a mining and processing operation on Destrillion and Dubrillion, and his headquarters is located on Dubrillion. He also oversees the running-the-belt game. [COF, DFR, ESB, HE, HG, LC, LCF, LCM, LCS, RJ, SWCG, etc.]

Camie

A young woman who lived in Tatooine's Anchorhead community. She was a close friend of Luke Skywalker, hanging out at the Tosche Station with Luke and her boyfriend, Fixer. Her family cultivated underground gardens, purchasing water from Luke's uncle, Owen Lars. [DS, SW, SWR]

cannonade

An exploding projectile fired by a crossbow. [TJP]

cantina

See Mos Eisley cantina.

CAP

An acronym for Combat Aerospace Patrol, a unit that consisted of Rogue Squadron Flights One, Two, and Three. [BW]

capital ship

Any class of huge combat starships designed for deep-space warfare, such as Imperial Star Destroyers and Mon Calamari star cruisers. These vessels normally require large crews, are equipped with large numbers of weapons batteries and shield projectors, and often carry smaller ships, such as shuttles and starfighters, in their great docking bays. [SWRPG2, SWSB]

Caprioril

A planet located in the Galactic Core. An assassin droid massacred 20,000 people at a swoop arena here, in order to murder

Governor Amel Bakli. Among the dead was the famous racer, Ignar Ominaz.

Mara Jade, using the name Marellis, worked for a swoop gang on Caprioril following the death of the Emperor. During the time of the New Republic, Imperial forces loyal to the Emperor's clone besieged the planet. [DESB, DFR, SWSB]

Captison, Gaeriel

This slender, intense woman served as an Imperial senator from Bakura during the final years of the Rebellion. Her parents were killed in the uprising that followed the Imperial invasion of Bakura, and her aunt and uncle, Tiree and Yeorg Captison, raised her. She spent a year at Imperial Center before returning to her post on Bakura, just in time to become embroiled in the events surrounding the Ssi-ruuk invasion.

Gaeriel Captison

Despite the differences in their belief systems, Gaeriel became friends with Luke Skywalker, the commander of the Alliance task force sent to aid Bakura. Indeed, the two were attracted to each other, but eventually agreed to part on amicable terms. After the incidents and the Imperial-Alliance truce at Bakura, Gaeriel was offered a place in the Alliance. She decided to remain on Bakura and help her uncle, Prime Minister Yeorg Captison, restore her world to its pre-Imperial splendor.

Gaeriel married former Imperial officer Pter Thanas and was elected prime minister, though she lost the succeeding election. About fourteen years after the truce, Luke Skywalker borrowed Bakura's fleet for a mission in the Corellian system. Although the mission succeeded, half of the Bakuran cruisers were destroyed and Gaeriel was killed. [AS, SAC, SWCG, TAB, TBSB]

Captison, Yeorg

Prime minister of Bakura, he was elected to his post eight years before the Battle of Endor, having served in the Bakuran

Senate for some thirty years. After his brother Dol was killed, Yeorg and his wife, Tiree, raised Dol's children, Gaeriel and Ylanda. As a popular and respected leader, Yeorg did his best to protect the Bakurans—even in the face of increased Imperial domination. After the Ssi-ruuk invasion was repelled and the Imperial forces in the Bakura region surrendered, Yeorg pledged to support the Alliance as it worked to restore the former glory of the Republic. [TAB, TBSB]

Carbanti signal-augmented sensor jammer

A device for jamming sensors. Lando Calrissian discovered it among cargo aboard the *Spicy Lady*, the ship that had been owned by the murdered smuggler Jarril. [NR]

carbon-freezing chamber

An integral device used in the process of storing Tibanna gas. The gas is stored in carbonite to preserve it during transportation to far-off trade centers. This preservation process, called freezing, is accomplished by pumping gas into the chamber, where it is mixed with molten carbonite, then flash-frozen to cool the carbonite into a solid block. The gas remains trapped within the carbonite block until released at a processing center or market. One of the chambers on Bespin's Cloud City was modified for use on a human, so that Darth Vader could safely capture and transport Luke Skywalker back to the Emperor. Before Vader would allow it to be used on Skywalker, it was successfully tested on Han Solo. [ESB]

carbonite

A strong but highly volatile metal alloy used in the manufacturing of hyperdrive engines and to preserve materials such as Tibanna gas. [DLS, ESB]

carbonite guild

This ruthless group controlled the mining of unprocessed carbonite in the Empress Teta system some 4,000 years before the Galactic Civil War. [DLS]

Carconth

This red supergiant star was the second largest and seventh brightest in the known galaxy. It was placed on the supernova watch 600 years before the Battle of Endor. [TT]

Car'das, Jorj

This smuggler started his career during the Clone Wars era and created one of the better organizations. Knowledge and information were his passions, and he passed that passion on to his successor, Talon Karrde. During the Bpfasshi Dark Jedi incident, Car'das's ship was commandeered and he was kidnapped by the Dark Jedi. Half-mad with rage and possessing all of Darth Vader's power but none of his self-control, one of the Dark Jedi rampaged throughout the Bpfasshi sector with Car'das as an unwilling witness to his deeds. Car'das was on Dagobah when the Dark Jedi battled the Jedi Master Yoda for a day and a half. Yoda won, and nursed Car'das back to health. A latent Force sensitivity was triggered during his time with Yoda, but Yoda did not have time to heal him fully. The Jedi Master sent him to the Aing-Tii to learn their ways in the Force. Sixteen years after the Battle of Endor, Karrde visited Car'das in the Kathol sector and received information that would help end the threat of the impostor Grand Admiral Thrawn. [SP, VF]

Cardooine

The world where the fragrant Fijisi wood was harvested for use in the Imperial Palace on Coruscant and even in some space vessels. The Cardooine Chills, a virus whose symptoms included congestion, coughing, fatigue, and body pain, was first diagnosed on this planet. [BW, LC]

cargo lifter

Large utility airships operated by a single pilot. Usually found in spaceports, these crafts are used to load and unload cargo containers and to make short-distance hauls from loading zones to storage facilities in other parts of the port. Older models employ mechanical claws to handle cargo, while newer models use tractor beam and repulsor technology. [HSR]

Carida

A large, high-gravity world located in the Carida system. An important Imperial Academy and stormtrooper training center were located on this planet. The varied terrain, ranging from mountains to ice fields to arid deserts, provided the perfect conditions for combat training in harsh environments.

Han Solo graduated from the Caridan Academy with honors, before he subsequently received a dishonorable discharge from the Imperial Navy. Later, Admiral Daala attended the Caridan Academy before joining Grand Moff Tarkin's staff. Dash Rendar attended the Academy until he was dishonorably discharged after his older brother crashed a freighter into the Emperor's private museum. Terpfen, aide to Admiral Ackbar, underwent torture and reconditioning at the hands of the Empire on this world. Carida was destroyed when Jedi Kyp Durron used the Imperial superweapon, the Sun Crusher, on the system's star. [COF, COJ, DA, HG, JS, SOTE, TJP, TMEC]

Caridan combat arachnid

Spiderlike creatures from the planet Carida, with huge, powerful jaws and crimson body armor. Jabba the Hutt pitted several of the twelve-legged creatures against his rancor, which was injured in the battle. [TJP]

Carkoon, Great Pit of

Located within the Dune Sea on the planet Tatooine, this large depression serves as the resting place for the creature known as the Sarlacc. [RJ]

Carosi

A planet known for its busy spaceport and many pleasure domes. Carosi's larger moon housed a synthdroid factory operated by the Loronar Corporation. These droids were utilized in some of the pleasure domes for the enjoyment of the guests. [POG, POT]

Carr, Yomin

This Yuuzhan Vong warrior infiltrated the ExGal Society outpost on Belkadan in the guise of a human scientist. It was his job to make sure that none of the other scientists noticed the telltale signals coming when the invasion force entered the galaxy at sector L30—Vector Prime. Like other members of his species, Carr painted his flesh and mutilated his body to show his devotion to the dark gods of the Yuuzhan Vong. He hated technology but learned to control his revulsion in order to accomplish his mission. He wore a suit of living flesh—an ooglith masquer—to mask his true features and wielded a variety of deadly living weapons. These included vonduun-crab-shell-plated armor, explosive thud bugs, sentient and binding blorash jelly, and an amphistaff, a vicious serpent that could harden all or part of its body and be used as a staff, a whip, or a missile weapon.

Carr used the biological mastery of the Yuuzhan Vong to metamorphose Belkadan's atmosphere into a toxic brew perfect for raising yorik coral. He murdered the ExGal scientists, then faced off against Mara Jade Skywalker when she and Luke Skywalker arrived to investigate the planet. Weakened by the Yuuzhan Vong disease spores ravaging her body, Mara nonetheless engaged Yomin Carr in a vicious battle. She killed him after a worthy fight, driving her lightsaber blade through his armor and into his heart. [VP]

Carrack-class light cruiser

This small combat star cruiser, approximately 350 meters in length, carries an optimum crew of 1,092. The Carrack has a high proportion of weaponry as compared to its size. This vessel's primary mission profile was to serve as the Empire's answer to the Corellian corvette. The Carrack possesses no internal docking bay. Instead, it carries up to four TIE fighters on an external rack. Though not originally designed for front-line combat duty, in the period after the Battle of Endor the Empire was forced to place more and more of these vessels into harm's way. [HESB, ISB, SWVG]

Carratos

A planet located about forty parsecs from Coruscant, it became a refuge for the Fallanassi religious group, whose youngest members were sent there to escape persecution on Lucazec. Akanah Norand Pell attended a school in the Chofin settlement. The Empire constructed a garrison on the planet and instituted stiff taxes levied against anyone attempting to leave Carratos. [BTS, SOL]

Cartariun

This Devaronian had a lust for power. He discovered a Sith temple on the planet Malrev Four, but the corrupting influence of its power drove him insane. He planned to take the throne of the Empire after Palpatine's death, but a Bothan agent named Girov destroyed Cartariun with the very magic he hoped to master. [XW]

Caslo, Gerney

A loudmouthed merchant who sold precious water on Nam Chorios. He was instrumental in making old pump stations functional after they were allowed to rot. [POT]

Cass

An Imperial officer and adjutant to Grand Moff Tarkin aboard the original Death Star battle station. [SWN]

Cathar

The homeworld of the proud and powerful feline species of the same name. Members of the species sport flowing manes. Males have two tusks protruding downward from their mouths; females possess fangs. Jedi Knights Sylvar and Crado, from Cathar, trained under Master Vodo-Siosk Baas about 4,000 years before the Galactic Civil War. [DLS]

Cathedral of Winds

A magnificent, delicate, and extremely intricate structure located on the planet Vortex, the centuries-old cathedral hosted the Vors' annual Concert of the Winds, a cultural festival to celebrate the planet's dramatic change of seasons. On a diplomatic mission to the planet, Admiral Ackbar crashed his personal B-wing fighter into the cathedral, destroying it and killing hundreds of Vors. Once it was proven that Ackbar's ship had been sabotaged and he was not at fault, the Vors began the painstaking task of rebuilding the monument. [COF, DA]

Cathor Hills

One of many sentient forests on the planet Ithor. Imperial Captain Alima destroyed this forest when he was trying to force Momaw Nadon to provide the Empire with Ithorian technology. [TMEC]

Cauldron Nebula

An interplanetary light show produced by seven blue supergiant stars in close orbit. The inhabitants of Eol Sha, the nearest habitable world, unsuccessfully tried to mine the nebula's gases. The nebula made a perfect hiding place for Admiral Daala's Star Destroyers until Jedi student Kyp Durron used the Imperial superweapon, the Sun Crusher, to cause all seven stars to go nova. [DA, JS, YJK]

Caveel, Spinda

This rogue scientist hired the Pikkel sisters to capture the unique medical droid, A-OIC ("Doc"). He forced Doc to reprogram droids, turning them into soldiers skilled in martial arts. When Caveel refused to accept their resignation, the Pikkel sisters killed him. [SEE]

Cavrilhu Pirates

A gang of marauders who plundered and pillaged merchant ships along the various space lanes of the galaxy. Led by Captain Zothip, who commanded the gang from his gunship *Void Cutter*, the pirates were the scourge of the Amorris star system. His first mate was a Togorian female named Keta. Niles Ferrier stole three patrol ships from the pirates to sell to Grand Admiral Thrawn, shortly after the failed Imperial action at Sluis Van. [DFR, DFRSB]

CB-99

An old, battered, barrel-shaped droid who once belonged to Jabba the Hutt. After the crimelord died, the droid emerged from its secret hiding place in Jabba's desert palace to present Jabba's hologram will to his beneficiaries. [ZHR]

C'baoth, Jorus

This human Jedi Master was born on the planet Bortras in Reithcas sector, back in the days of the Old Republic. His interests in the Jedi Knighthood and his innate abilities in the Force led him to join the Jedi training center on Kamparas. After four years and a period of private training with an unknown Jedi Master, he became a Jedi Knight. Twelve years later, he assumed the title of Jedi Master. He served the Republic as the leader of the demilitarization observation group sent to Ando, as a member of the Senate Interspecies Advisory Committee, and as personal adviser to Senator Palpatine on matters pertaining to the Jedi. He was part of the Jedi Knight task force sent to Bpfassh to deal with the Dark Jedi insurrection. He led the delegation sent to Alderaan to determine which royal family should receive the title of viceroy and helped rule in favor of the Organa family. He assisted Jedi Master Tra's M'ins to mediate a peaceful end to the Duinuogwuin-Gotal conflict. When the Outbound Flight Project to search for life outside the known galaxy was proposed, Jorus was one of six Jedi Masters on the exploration ship launched from Yaga Minor. The exploration ship was presumed lost, but it was really destroyed on Palpatine's orders—by a young officer named Thrawn. [DFR, DFRSB, HE, LC]

C'baoth, Joruus

A clone of the famed Jedi Master Jorus C'baoth. Grand Admiral Thrawn found Joruus on the planet Wayland, where he was guarding one of the Emperor's hidden storehouses. Confused about his origin and past, and hindered by shattered memories and periods of insanity brought on by clone madness—a malady that afflicts clones grown too quickly—Joruus appeared as an old, white-haired man with a long beard. Insane, he nonetheless wielded great powers forged in the dark side of the Force. He believed that all lesser beings hate the Jedi because of their power and knowledge, and that it was the duty of the Jedi to rule over the lesser beings to keep the galaxy safe. Thrawn entered into an uneasy alliance with Joruus in order to reestablish the New Order, promising to turn Luke Skywalker, Leia Organa Solo, and Leia's unborn twins over to the mad Jedi Master. For his part, Joruus planned to reshape the Force users into his own image, starting a new society of Dark Jedi with which to rule the galaxy. Joruus eventually turned on Thrawn to advance his own plans. Although Luke Skywalker tried to heal the madness that corrupted Joruus, in the end he was forced to destroy him. [DFR, DFRSB, HE, LC]

Joruus C'baoth

C'borp

Chief gunner on the pirate ship *Starjacker*. Some 4,000 years before the Galactic Civil War, he destroyed the attacking spacecraft piloted by Dreebo, an employee of Great Bogga the Hutt. [TOJ]

CCIR

An acronym for Centrally Controlled Independent Replicant. [POT]

Celanon

A planet located in the Outer Rim star system of the same name. Celanon is famous for its multicolored skyline and numerous holographic advertising boards. Agriculture and commerce are the planet's main industries. The planet's native sentients are called the Nalroni. [COJ, CSSB, POG]

Celchu, Colonel Tycho

This superior pilot flew an Imperial TIE fighter until he defected to the Alliance after the Empire destroyed his homeworld, Alderaan. He became a member of Rogue Squadron, participating in the Battle of Hoth and the Battle of Endor. He also fought at Bakura and led a covert mission to Coruscant. When Wedge Antilles became leader of the squadron, Celchu became his second. Later, he was named executive officer of Rogue Squadron, in charge of training new recruits. [BW, XW]

Celchu, Skoloc

Brother of Captain Tycho Celchu, he was killed when Alderaan was destroyed. [BW]

Cell 2187

The cell where Princess Leia Organa was held captive during her imprisonment aboard the original Death Star battle station. It was located in Detention Block AA-23. [SW]

Centerpoint Station

An ancient space station in the Corellian system, located at the balance point between the twin worlds of Talus and Tralus. Built before the invention of artificial gravity, the station spins on its axis to provide gravity. Approximately 350 kilometers long, Centerpoint is even larger than the Death Star. Hollowtown, the open sphere at the center of the station, receives heat and light from the Glowpoint, an artificial sun suspended in the center of the sphere. Its light falls upon countless homes, parks, lakes, and farms that cover the interior walls of the sphere.

Many believed that Centerpoint was a hyperspace repulsor that was used in ancient times to transport the five inhabited Corellian planets into their current orbits. When the Sacorrian

Triad discovered that the station could destroy stars, two stars were targeted and destroyed. The resulting flare-ups in the Glowpoint incinerated most of the inhabitants of Hollowtown. The Triad's fleet was later defeated by New Republic and Bakuran forces, who helped stop Centerpoint before it could destroy the Bovo Yagen star. [AC, AS, SAC]

Ceousa, General

A New Republic general, he commanded the *Calamari* in the Battle of Almania. [NR]

C-Gosf

A Gosfambling who served on the New Republic Senate's Inner Council. She risked much running for the senate, as all other Gosfamblings forever ridicule losers on her world. [NR]

Chad III

A beautiful, civilized world in a star system of the same name. The watery planet is home to the Chadra-Fan species. In addition to the rodentlike Chadra-Fan that inhabit the bayous, other life-forms include long-necked cetaceans called tsaelkes, wystohs hunters, phosphorescent tubular eels, and fish-lizards known as cy'een. The human Jedi Callista was from Chad III. [COJ, DS, GG4, QE, TMEC]

Chadra-Fan

These small, quick-witted inhabitants of Chad III resemble humanoid rodents. With large ears, dark eyes, and flat, circular noses sporting four nostrils, the fur-covered Chadra-Fan possess seven senses. In addition to the five shared by most intelligent species, they also are blessed with infrared sight and an advanced chemoreceptive sense of smell. These small, one-meter-tall beings love to have fun, though they have short attention spans, and they enjoy tinkering with technological items. [GG4, QE, TBH]

chak-root

This flavorful red plant grows in the marshlands on the planet Erysthes. High taxes on the plant gave rise to a profitable business for smugglers. They avoid the normal channels of distribution and offer the plant at reduced prices on the Invisible Market. [HLL, HSR]

Chalcedon

A rocky, volcanic world that is a key hub in the galactic slave trade, the inhospitable planet has a barely breathable atmosphere, violent storms, frequent groundquakes, and no indigenous life-forms. Two colonies and one way station were established on the planet, where traders and peasants mingle in the bazaars, and the bureaucrats—boneless creatures with trunks—live in cities of volcanic-glass buildings from which they control the slave trade. [CS]

Chalmun

A beige-and-gray-furred Wookiee, he owned the infamous Mos Eisley cantina. [GG7, TMEC]

Chamma, Master

This Jedi Master instructed Andur Sunrider in the ways of the Force some 4,000 years before the Galactic Civil War. [TOJ]

Chandrila

The homeworld of Mon Mothma, leader of the Alliance to Restore the Republic. This agricultural planet, located in the Bormea sector of the Core, has two primary continents that are covered in rolling, grassy plains. Mon Mothma grew up on the shores of the Silver Sea, where her mother served as the area's governor. Other notable natives have included Jedi Master Avan Post, who served in the Clone Wars and was later killed by Emperor Palpatine, and the New Republic's Admiral Hiram Drayson, who once commanded the Chandrila Defense Fleet. [COJ, DESB, KT, SWSB, TAB]

Chanzari

These Selonian rebels were allied with the Hunchuzuc. Together, the two groups sought to free themselves from oppressive rule. [AS]

Chaos fighter

A type of small, maneuverable fighter used by the Krath in their attempt to overthrow the Empress Teta system about 4,000 years before the Galactic Civil War. [DLS]

Charal

An evil witch who tormented the Ewoks and others on the forest moon of Endor. Charal had a magical ring that gave her the power to change form at will. Some believed that she had escaped from the planet Dathomir and was stranded on the forest moon. The cohort of Terak, king of the Marauders, Charal was an imposing figure with raven-black hair, angular features, and a slender shape. She often wore a cloak of black feathers, and she rode a wild black stallion that also had the ability to change form. [BFE, ISWU]

Chardaan Shipyards

An Alliance space facility where workers constructed space vehicles in zero gravity. The facility turned out many types of starfighters, including Y-wings and E-wings, until it was destroyed by Colonel Cronus's fleet eight years after the Battle of Endor. [DS]

Chariot LAV

A modified military landspeeder used almost exclusively by Imperial forces. These light assault vehicles, LAVs, served as command speeders for officers during routine planet occupations and other assignments where heavy combat was not expected. More heavily armored than a normal landspeeder, but also slower and less armed than combat landspeeders, these vehicles featured battle-assistance computers that provided holographic schematics and constant situational updates to the officers on board. With dedicated sensor and communications arrays, they could coordinate the activities of more than a dozen combat units. Combat speeders carried a crew of three—the unit's commander, a driver, and a bodyguard/gunner. [HESB, ISB, SWVG]

Charon

Humanoid arachnids from a dimension termed otherspace that seems to exist beyond the confines of the known galaxy. The Charon were divided into at least two distinct classes: bioscientists and warriors. The bioscientists were the more intelligent of the two, working to keep the Charon's biologically based technology and constructs in operating condition. The warriors were more single-minded and aggressive. The Charon's homeworld was being devoured by a black hole. This condition led to the development of a death cult that believed that the Void was the only constant in the universe and that everything would eventually return to it. The death cult thought its duty was to help life along on its unavoidable journey to the Void. When the Charon developed space travel, the death cult set out in their biologically engineered vessels to spread its dark doctrine of swift death to all life throughout the galaxy. [GG4, OS, OS2]

Charubah

A technological world in the Hapes Cluster, known for manufacturing the Hapan Gun of Command. [CPL]

Chattza clan

A powerful, warlike clan of Rodians led by Navik the Red. After conquering Rodia, Chattzas hunted and killed the more peaceful clans who had left the homeworld. [TMEC]

Chazwa

This planet in the Chazwa system of the Orus sector orbits a white dwarf star. Heavy freight traffic regularly passes through the system and visits the planet. [LC]

Chenlambec

A Wookiee bounty hunter with deep brown, silver-tipped fur who was known to his friends as Chen. Others knew him as the Raging Wookiee. Despite his reputation, Chen and his human partner Tinian I'att often helped their bounties escape to the Rebellion. Chen's ship was called the *Wroshyr*. [GG10, TBH]

Chevin

From the planet Vinsoth, each of these hunters and farmers stand over two meters tall and have thick arms and long faces. [GG12, TJP]

Chewbacca

This loyal, powerful, two-meter-tall Wookiee served as first mate and copilot on the *Millennium Falcon*. Born on the tree-covered planet Kashyyyk more than two hundred years before the Galactic Civil War, Chewbacca had been a slave, a smuggler, a rebel, a pilot, and a top-notch mechanic over the course of his life. Like all Wookiees, Chewbacca was covered in shaggy fur and communicated in a series of grunts, growls, and terrifying roars. He was extremely strong, even for a Wookiee. Chewbacca's weapons of choice were his massive fists and his bowcaster. Though he was formidable when angered, his terrifying roars sometimes masked his own fear of the unknown.

Chewie, as his friends referred to him, left Kashyyyk when he was about fifty standard years. About 140 years later he was captured by slavers and sold to the Empire. During his absence, Chewbacca's homeworld had been subjugated by Imperial forces and turned into a slave labor planet. Wookiees were declared a slave species, and it became illegal for free Wookiees to travel the space lanes.

The hard-labor camp where Chewbacca was enslaved would have been the death of him, if not for the actions of a young Han Solo. Solo, an Imperial officer at the time, sacrificed his military career to free the Wookiee, and Chewbacca immediately decided he owed the Corellian a life debt. He followed Solo around for a long time before the Corellian decided to accept his Wookiee shadow. Chewbacca became Solo's protector, and his best friend. Solo taught him how to fly a ship and use gunner weapons. Together, the pair embarked on a smuggling career that became extremely profitable after Solo won the *Millennium Falcon* in a game of sabacc.

Chewbacca

During a spice run for the crimelord Jabba the Hutt, the pair were chased down by an Imperial blockade and had to dump their cargo. In need of money to pay off Jabba, the pair accepted a job from Ben Kenobi. Before long, Chewbacca and Solo had helped rescue a princess, blow up an Imperial battle station, and were declared heroes by the Rebel Alliance. Chewbacca added Luke Skywalker and Princess Leia to his honor family, and after Han married Leia, Chewbacca helped raise and protect their three children.

Twenty years after their first meeting, Chewbacca brought a new student to Luke Skywalker's Jedi academy—his nineteen-year-old nephew, Lowbacca.

Twenty-one years after the Battle of Endor, Chewbacca died saving Anakin Solo. As a moon spiraled down toward the planet Sernpidal, caught in the inexorable pull of a Yuuzhan Vong living weapon, Chewbacca tossed Anakin into the hovering *Millennium Falcon.* The ship, packed full of refugees from the doomed planet, was forced to blast away as the moon crashed into the surface of the world—before Han Solo could find a way to get his friend onto the ship. [ESB, HG, HLL, HSE, HSR, RJ, SW, SWCG, SWHS, SWSB, SWWS, TT, VP, etc.]

ch'hala tree

These greenish-purple trees with slender trunks and leafy tops exhibit a unique property. When a noise occurs near the trees, bursts of red ripple across the trunks in time to the sound. The Grand Corridor in the Imperial Palace on Coruscant was lined with these beautiful, colorful trees. Unfortunately, the Emperor set them up as a complex spying system called Delta Source. For once the New Republic established its governmental center on Coruscant, Delta Source was responsible for providing Grand Admiral Thrawn with detailed intelligence about New Republic activities. By using the natural properties of the ch'hala trees, the Emperor developed living circuits for his intelligence-gathering system. When pressure, including sound waves, impacted the tree trunks, small chemical changes in the inner layers of bark produced the bursts of color. Tubes implanted in the trunks continuously sampled the chemicals and shunted the information into a module in the taproot. The module took the chemical data and converted it back into sound, which was then sent on to another module for sorting, encrypting, and transmission. Delta Source was nothing less than a series of organic microphones. This system had been in place since the earliest days of the Empire, giving the Emperor an edge in all senate proceedings. [DFR, HE, LC]

Chief

Chief Technician Viera Cheran, affectionately called Chief, oversaw the technicians who serviced Rogue Squadron shortly after the Battle of Hoth. Though good at her job, she resented the fact that, in her eyes, the pilots received all the glory, while all she got was the hard work of keeping the squadron's X-wings in good repair. Thus, when an unknown operative offered the Chief 10,000 credits and an unspecified bonus to sabotage Luke Skywalker's ship and kill the aspiring Jedi Knight, she accepted—and failed. [SESB, SOTE]

Child of Winds

This Qom Qae youth helped Luke Skywalker and Mara Jade during their mission to find the Hand of Thrawn. Jade suggested that his adult name should be Friend of Jedi. [VF]

Chimaera

Chimaera

This Imperial Star Destroyer was commanded by Captain Gilad Pellaeon. The veteran ship was involved in the Battle of Endor and led the remnants of the Imperial fleet to safety after the battle was lost. When Grand Admiral Thrawn returned from the Unknown Regions, he selected *Chimaera* to serve as his flagship, leaving Pellaeon at its helm. [DFR, HE, LC]

Chin

A chief associate of Talon Karrde, he was from the planet Myrkr and used his knowledge of the planet's indigenous life to aid Karrde. Chin's primary responsibility was to care for and train Karrde's pet vornskrs. He domesticated the creatures and trained them to serve as guards. His understanding of the mysterious ysalamiri led him to develop a method for safely removing them from their tree-branch homes. His other duties included maintaining the security of Karrde's base of operations and overseeing the smooth running of base facilities. [DFR, HE, HESB, LC]

Chip

This droid, whose name was short for Microchip, was the personal property of the Jedi Prince Ken. The size and shape of a twelve-year-old boy, Chip kept young Ken company during his stay in the Lost City of the Jedi. [LCJ, MMY, PDS, ZHR]

Chirpa, Chief

A strong-willed Ewok, he was head of his tribe's Council of Elders. After some initial confusion and hostility, Chirpa decided to befriend the Rebel strike force sent to the forest moon of Endor to clear the way for the Alliance fleet. He even sent his tribe into battle against the Imperial forces, and his warriors proved to be courageous in the face of a superior fighting force. The gray-furred Chief Chirpa carried a reptilian staff of office and wore the teeth, horns, and bones of animals he had bested in the hunt. [RJ]

Chiss

Blue-skinned humanoids with glowing red eyes, they controlled territory in an area of space that the Empire called the Unknown Regions. They came in contact with the Outbound Flight Project, which led to one of their members rising to power in the Empire. That Chiss was Grand Admiral Thrawn. [VF]

Ch'no

An H'drachi scrap scavenger from the planet M'haeli. Ch'no saved the human infant Mora and became her adoptive father. He didn't know that she was of M'haeli royal descent. [ROC]

Choco

The small, battered, and uncoordinated R2 unit that befriended R2-D2 during the famous droid's encounters with the Great Heep years before the start of the Galactic Civil War. [TGH]

ChoFi

A New Republic senator, he was a loyal supporter of Leia Organa Solo. [NR]

Chorax system

This system in the Rachuk sector is known for smuggler and pirate activity. The system contains a single planet, Chorax.

Three years after the Battle of Endor, Rogue Squadron was accidentally dumped out of hyperspace in this system by the Interdictor cruiser *Black Asp*. Rogue Squadron rescued the *Asp*'s true target, the smuggling ship *Pulsar Skate*, and forced the *Asp* to flee. [BW, RS]

Chorios systems

Located in the Meridian sector and consisting of several star systems with the name Chorios, including Nam Chorios, Pedducis Chorios, and Brachnis Chorios. Most of the worlds in the systems are barren and lifeless. The few inhabitants of the area are called Chorians. Nine years after the Battle of Endor, Leia Organa Solo secretly met with Seti Ashgad near Brachnis Chorios's largest moon. [POT]

chromasheath

An iridescent material similar to leather. [HSE]

chrono

A time-measuring device. [HLL, SWSB]

chrysalis

A creature mutated by the dark side of the Force. The second cloned Emperor unleashed chrysalides against Lando Calrissian's war-droid attack force to defend the Emperor's citadel on the planet Byss. [DE2]

Chubb

A small, burrowing reptile that was the pet and constant companion of the young boy Fidge, who met R2-D2 and C-3PO during the early days of the Empire. [TGH]

Chubbit

A small reptilian desert dweller. Chubbits are native to the planet Aridus. [CSW]

Chukha-Trok

A brave Ewok woodsman known for his forest skills and lore. [ETV]

Churba

A star system located in the Mid Rim, containing eight planets, including Churba and New Cov. Churba, the fourth world in the system and the one that gave it its name, is a high-tech planet inhabited by humans and assorted nonhuman species. It is a cosmopolitan metropolis and home to the Sencil Corporation, a major manufacturer of illegal assassin droid components. New Cov, the third world orbiting the sun, boasts vast jungles filled with natural resources. [DFR, DFRSB, RS]

Chusker, Vu

A business associate of the gangster Cabrool Nuum. Nuum and his son and daughter asked Jabba to kill Chusker. The Hutt refused, but did eliminate the Nuum family one by one. Jabba finally encountered Chusker as he was escaping from the Nuum family dungeon. He killed Vu with one swipe of his powerful tail. [JAB]

Chu'unthor

A wrecked spacecraft that Luke Skywalker found half-submerged in a river on the planet Dathomir. The ship had crashed there at least 400 years earlier. It was a huge vessel, two kilometers long, one kilometer wide, and eight levels high. The ship, under the command of Jedi Masters, had served as a mobile training academy for thousands of Jedi apprentices. Luke used records stored within the ship to develop programs for his Jedi academy. [CPL, DA]

Cilghal

A Force-sensitive Calamarian who was recruited by Leia Organa Solo for Luke Skywalker's Jedi academy. Also an ambassador from Mon Calamari, Cilghal used her diplomatic skills to hold the twelve Jedi students together after the spirit of dark-sider Exar Kun attacked Luke. She helped defeat Kun, then healed Mon Mothma. The former chief of state had been infected with nano-destroyers, artificial viruses that were dismantling her cells one nucleus at a time. Cilghal used her considerable Force abilities to instead destroy the billions of nano-destroyers. [COF, DA, DS]

Cilpar

This planet, covered with mountains, jungles, and forests, was once held by the Empire. Rogue Squadron set up a base in the mountains west of the capital, Kiidan, after the Battle of Endor. A simple mission turned deadly when they ran into a TIE fighter ambush. After a long battle, the planet's moff and governor were overthrown. [XW]

Cinnagar

The largest city of the seven worlds of the Empress Teta star system. [DE]

Circarpous IV

The fourth and primary planet in the Circarpous Major star system was to be the site of Princess Leia's diplomatic meeting with Circarpousian resistance groups. Her mission, undertaken shortly after the Battle of Yavin, was to persuade the groups to join the Alliance. Luke Skywalker accompanied her on this important mission, and her prime directive was to convince the Circarpousians that the Alliance could withstand the might of the Empire. [SME]

Circarpous V

See Mimban.

Circarpous XIV

The fourteenth and outermost planet in the Circarpous Major star system was the location of a hidden Rebel base during the initial stages of the Galactic Civil War. [SME]

Circarpous Major

A populous star system made up of fourteen planets. While many of the system's inhabitants were sympathetic to the cause of the Rebellion, they were afraid to become involved and risk the wrath of the Empire. To gain their support and convince the system to join the Alliance, Princess Leia traveled to Circarpous Major on a diplomatic mission. [SME]

Circus Horrificus

A traveling alien-monstrosity show that terrified audiences in system after system. Malakili, the main rancor keeper at Jabba's palace, once worked for the circus. [TJP]

Clak'dor VII

This small planet in the Mayagil sector orbits the large white star Colu and is the homeworld of the highly evolved Bith. Once a lush world, the planet became an ecological wasteland after two Bith cities, Nozho and Weogar, went to war. The biological weapons they unleashed on each other mutated the planet's surface and forced the Bith to live within domed cities. Many Bith sold their great intellectual abilities to purchase the basic necessities their world could no longer produce. Others made their way as entertainers, including Figrin D'an and the Modal Nodes, who played at the Mos Eisley cantina. [COJ, GG4, TMEC]

Clays

A family of moisture farmers on Tatooine, they opposed Ariq Joanson's plans to negotiate peace with the Tusken Raiders and Jawas. [TMEC]

Clezo

A member of the fierce Chattza clan of Rodians, he served as a Black Sun Vigo and controlled many of the criminal activities on Rodia. He always wore conservative but finely tailored suits, demonstrating his desire to run his activities more like a business executive instead of a crimelord. [SESB, SOTE]

cliffborer worm

Long, armored worms that dwell among the rocks on Tatooine, feeding on razor moss. [ISWU]

cloaking device

A defensive antidetection system that reached the development stages but was never mass-produced. A cloaking device disrupted all electromagnetic waves emanating or reflecting from the ship it was installed in, rendering the ship electronically invisible to all sensors. During the Galactic Civil War, these devices were too costly and power-prohibitive to install on anything larger than a starfighter. Even then, the defensive properties rendered the pilot of a cloaked craft as blind to the galaxy around him as his ship was invisible to other vessels.

The Emperor made development of cloak technology a priority during the building of the second Death Star. The project yielded a working prototype that absorbed sensor radiation, thus disguising the device and anything under its cloak as empty space. Before it could be mass-produced, the Emperor was killed and the Empire shattered. Years later, Grand Admiral Thrawn discovered the prototype in one of the Emperor's hidden storehouses and employed it in his bid to destroy the New Republic. [DFR, ESB, HE, HESB, LC]

Cloak of the Sith

A region of space occupied by a huge dark cloud of dangerous meteors, asteroids, and planetoids, blocks the only known path to the Roon system. [DTV]

CloakShape fighter

An outdated starfighter designed for atmospheric and short-range space combat. By the time of the Galactic Civil War, mostly bounty hunters, pirates, and other small-time operators in need of assault starships utilized the fighter. [DE, DESB]

Clone Keepers

The scientists and attendants responsible for the Emperor's clone vats on the planet Byss. [DE]

Clone Wars

A terrible series of conflicts that erupted during the time of the Old Republic, some years prior to the start of the Galactic Civil War. The wars produced such heroes as Bail Organa, Anakin Skywalker, and General Obi-Wan Kenobi. [ESB, RJ, SW]

cloud car, combat

Built upon the standard cloud car design, extra hull plating and enhanced weapon systems allow it to take on fighters and freighters. [DFR, LC, SWVG]

cloud car, twin-pod

An atmospheric flying vehicle that employs both repulsorlifts and ion engines. Typical models utilize twin pods for pilots and passengers. Cloud cars serve as patrol craft, traffic control vehicles, cars for hire, and pleasure craft. [ESB, SWSB]

Cloud City

A mining outpost and trading station that floats within the atmosphere of the gas-giant planet Bespin. The facility is actually a small city of landing platforms, delicate spires, jutting towers, and airy plazas—all held aloft atop a long repulsorlift unipod. Cloud City's major industry is the mining and exporting of Tibanna gas, but it also serves as a merchant outpost and recreational center. Though off the main space lanes, many come from far and wide to enjoy its casinos, restaurants, and shop-

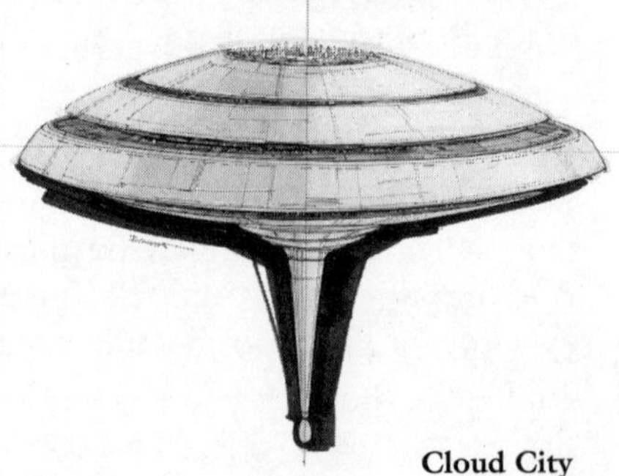

Cloud City

ping plazas. In addition to the many spacers who frequent its ports, Cloud City boasts a diverse citizenry of humans, droids, and assorted species. Lord Ecclessis Figg of Corellia founded Cloud City. Later, Lando Calrissian won the entire operation in a game of sabacc. [CCC, ESB, GG2]

Cnorec, Lord

A slave trader and follower of Lord Hethrir. Hethrir murdered Cnorec after Cnorec challenged him. [CS]

Cobak

The Bith bounty hunter hired by Zorba the Hutt to capture Princess Leia. To accomplish this mission, Cobak impersonated Bithabus the Mystifier to lure the princess into a trap. [QE]

Coby

The son of Lord Toda of Tammuz-an, he met the droids R2-D2 and C-3PO when he was nine years old, in the early days of the Empire. [DTV]

Codru-Ji

A four-armed humanoid species native to Munto Codru. Their language is made up of whistles and warbles, some beyond the range of human hearing. [CS]

Colonial Games

A series of athletic competitions pitting champions from the various colonies of the Roon star system against one another for fun and glory. The main event is the drainsweeper, a no-holds-barred relay race. [DTV]

Colonies, the

One of the first settled areas outside the Galactic Core, this region was heavily populated and industrialized by the time of the Galactic Civil War. The Empire ruthlessly controlled this area before the birth of the New Republic. Thereafter, much of the area decided to support the new government. [SWRPG2]

colossus wasp of Ithull

A huge flying insect native to Ithull. The insect's strong exoskeleton carapace can be used as the framework for ore-hauling spaceships. [TOJ]

Colton, Captain

See Antilles, Captain.

Columi

These craniopods from the planet Columus are devoted to the pursuits of mental activities. Their huge, hairless heads are fully a third of their size, with throbbing veins twining around the cerebrum and huge black eyes. The rest of their bodies are puny, with thin, nonfunctioning arms and legs. Droids and other machines, with which the Columi communicate via brain-wave transmissions, perform all physical work for the species. They are a peaceful species, often hired as advisers and soothsayers. [CPL, GG4]

Columus

This small, low-gravity planet is the homeworld of the Columi species. [GG4]

combat sense

This Force technique allows a Jedi Knight to focus his or her attention on the battle at hand. Opponents appear as bright images in an otherwise dull landscape. [DFR, DFRSB]

comlink

A personal communications transceiver. Produced in a wide variety of handheld and headset-mounted models, it consists of a transmitter, a receiver, and a power source. Comlinks are also built into stormtrooper helmets and provide shipwide communications aboard large space vessels. [ESB, RJ, SW]

command control voice
A method for controlling droids via voice-pattern recognition. [SWR]

Commenor
A planet in the system of the same name, just outside the Core and near Corellia. This trading outpost and spaceport houses an Alliance starfighter training center on its largest moon, Folor. [SWN]

comm unit
A shipboard communications device that allows a ship to transmit and receive communications signals from outside sources. [SWSB]

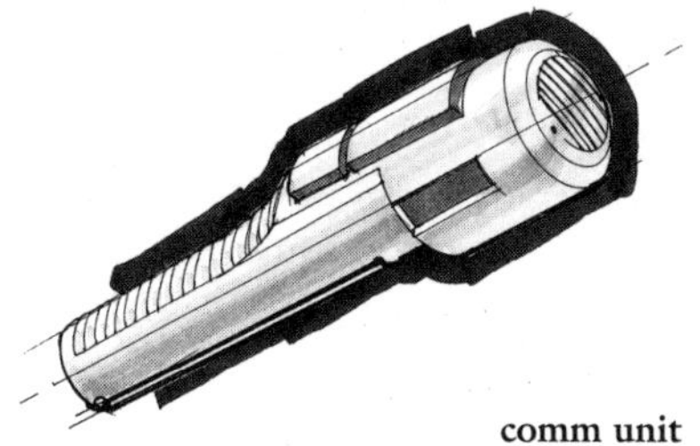
comm unit

compact assault vehicle (CAV)
A small, single-operator vehicle equipped with a medium blaster cannon. The CAV was supposed to transform a single Imperial trooper into a formidable assault force, but the tracked-wheeled vehicle, while fast, proved highly susceptible to sensor jamming. [ISB]

COMPNOR
The Commission for the Preservation of the New Order was formed as one of Emperor Palpatine's first official actions. It started as a populist movement against the chaos of the final days of the Old Republic but was quickly molded into a powerful political tool of the New Order. Through its subtle

manipulations, COMPNOR taught the galaxy the everyday ethics of the New Order and worked to turn the structure of the Old Republic into a relic of the past. [ISB, TBH]

computer probe

A device for accessing a computer network. The most common probes—or scomp links—are the appendages droids use to tap into computers and the portable consoles used by computer technicians. [HSE]

com-scan

Specialized sensor sweeps designed to detect the energy that results from the transmission and reception of communication signals. [ESB]

Cona

A hot, dense planet that orbits the blue giant Teke Ro, it is the homeworld of the Arcona. Many companies established mining colonies on Cona. [GG4, TMEC]

Concert of the Winds

This annual cultural festival celebrates the change of seasons on the planet Vortex. Winds rushing through the Cathedral of Winds, a crystalline structure, produce the concert. [DA]

Concord Dawn

Birthplace of Journeyman Protector Jaster Mereel, who later changed his name to Boba Fett. [TBH]

concussion missile

A sublightspeed projectile that causes shock waves on impact. The concussive waves penetrate and destroy heavily armored targets, though they work best against stationary targets. Concussion missiles were used to destroy the second Death Star during the Battle of Endor. [RJ]

concussion shield
A strong energy field that protects ships from space debris. [TBH]

condor dragon
A cave-dwelling predator from Endor's forest moon, it flies on large leathery wings. [ISWU]

Conquest
This *Imperial*-class Star Destroyer was among those that chased the *Millennium Falcon* when it departed from Tatooine. [TMEC]

construction droid
A huge factory on wheels that can be used to demolish and rebuild structures. Its internal furnaces recycle debris and extrude new girders and transparisteel sheets. The droid then assembles a new building based on preprogrammed blueprints. [BW, ISWU]

consular ship
Any vessel officially registered to a member of the Imperial Senate. On diplomatic missions, a consular ship was supposed to be immune to inspection. [SW, SWR]

container ship
These super transports are among the largest commercial vessels. Big, slow, and expensive, they often prove the most efficient way to transport huge amounts of cargo between star systems. By using standardized cargo containers, sealed and loaded by automated barges, the ships are extremely efficient. Some containers have even been designed to carry passengers. Too large to land on a planet or approach a space dock, container ships rely on stock light freighters and other small craft to collect and transfer their cargo to orbital ports within a system. [SWSB]

control mind

This Force technique allows a user to take direct control of another person's mind. A person subjected to this technique becomes an automaton who must obey the Force user's will. This technique is considered a corruption of the Force, a product of the dark side. [DFR, DFRSB, HE, LC]

Contruum

Birthplace of Alliance General Airen Cracken and his son, fighter pilot Pash. [WG]

Convarion, Ait

This Imperial captain was given command of the *Corrupter* and a mission to suppress systems in the Outer Rim and assigned to protect the bacta convoys leaving Thyferra. When Rogue Squadron hijacked one of the convoys, Convarion destroyed the last tanker in the convoy, as well as three Rogue Squadron ships. *Corrupter* and *Aggregator* went to the Graveyard of Alderaan to annihilate Rogue Squadron, but Convarion was killed when Wedge Antilles targeted his bridge with proton torpedoes. [BW]

Coome, R'yet

A junior New Republic senator from Exodeen, he replaced M'yet Luure after Luure was killed in the bombing of Senate Hall on Coruscant. Coome was later elected to the Inner Council. [NR]

Coral Depths City

One of the floating cities of Mon Calamari. [DA]

Coral Vanda

A subocean cruise ship operating in the ocean depths of the vacation world Pantolomin. It explores the huge network of coral reefs off the coast of the Tralla continent. Vacationers mostly utilize its impressive casino, complete with eight ornate gambling halls. Full-wall transparisteel hulls separate each hall from the ocean, giving tourists breathtaking views of sea life and the fabulous reefs. [DFR, DFRSB]

Corbantis

Loronar Corporation tested its new Needle smart missiles on this cruiser. Han Solo rescued fifteen injured beings from the damaged cruiser and transported them to Nim Drovis. [POT]

Corbos

This experimental mining colony was a prefabricated industrial city erected in the bowels of a planetary crater. Corbos miners uncovered a huge creature that attacked the colony. Chief of State Leia Organa Solo requested that Luke Skywalker send one of his Jedi trainees to investigate the situation. Luke sent Kyp Durron, who asked to take Dorsk 82 along. The pair eventually discovered the truth of the creatures and released the miners' spirits that were trapped within them. [JAL]

Corellia

Located in the Corellian sector and system, this planet and four other habitable worlds orbit the star Corell. All were among the first members of the Old Republic. The system is known for its fast ships, skilled traders, and pirates who regularly raid the local space lanes.

Corellia is referred to as the Elder Brother of the Five Brothers, the inhabited worlds of the system. It is a beautiful planet, covered in farms and small towns situated between rolling hills and fields. The capital city, Coronet, boasts plenty of open space due to its small buildings and trading stalls that are separated by parks and plazas. The three native species are humans, Selonians, and Drall.

The Selonians live beneath the planet's surface, in a vast network of tunnels that date back to before the Republic. A planetary repulsor was discovered in this ancient complex. It apparently moved the world into its current orbit from an unknown location.

Once ruled by a royal family, Corellia became a republic 300 years before the Galactic Civil War, when Berethon e Solo introduced democracy to the system. [AC, AS, CPL, RS, SAC, SWRPG2, TJP]

Corellian

A human race that inhabits the Corellian star system. Han Solo is Corellian. [SW]

Corellian Bloodstripe

Red piping that adorns the trousers of those Corellians who have distinguished themselves through brave and heroic acts. Han Solo wears the Bloodstripe on his trousers, his only nod toward his time of military service. [HG, HLL]

Corellian corvette

An older multipurpose capital ship model, this mid-sized vessel is 150 meters long and functions as a troop carrier, light escort vessel, cargo transport, or passenger liner. Like most Corellian-built ships, the corvette has a fast sublight drive and a quick hyperjump calculator for fast exits into hyperspace. Because this vessel type has seen a lot of duty among the Corellian pirates, authorities nicknamed it the Blockade Runner. Princess Leia's consular ship *Tantive IV* was a Corellian corvette. [SWSB]

Corellian grass snake

This creature resembles an ysalamiri but has neither claws nor fur. [NR]

Corellian gunship

A dedicated combat capital ship designed to be fast and deadly, it measures 120 meters in length and is typically mounted with eight double turbolaser cannons, six quad laser cannons, and four concussion missile launch tubes. Engines fill more than half of its interior, while weaponry, computers, and shield generators take up most of the rest of the ship. With a small command crew and tech staff, but lots of gunners, the gunship makes an excellent antistarfighter platform. The Alliance—and later the New Republic—made extensive use of these vessels, and some can even be found in private defense fleets and independent armies. [DFRSB, RSB]

Corellian Port Control

A security force that tries to maintain law and order on the smugglers' moon Nar Shaddaa. [TMEC]

Corellian sector

A sector of space that consists of several dozen star systems located in the most heavily populated portion of the galaxy. The Corellian system is considered the most important in the sector. Five inhabited worlds orbit its star: Selonia, Drall, Talus, Tralus, and Corellia. Moff Fliry Vorru controlled the sector during the last days of the Old Republic, allowing smugglers to come and go as they pleased. With the coming of the Empire, the three dominant species—humans, Selonians, and Drall—were forced to coexist. With the collapse of the Empire, the three turned toward their own self-interests as each attempted to assert their dominance in the region. [AC, AS, RS, SAC]

Corellian system

A star system that contains five inhabited worlds: Corellia, Selonia, Drall, Talus, and Tralus. The worlds are collectively referred to as the Five Brothers, due to their close orbits. It is believed that the ancient Centerpoint Station transported the five planets through hyperspace to their Corellian orbits. Both the Corellian Defense Force and the Corellian Security Force (CorSec) defend the system. Famed for the Corellian Engineering Corporation's extensive shipyards and notorious for its many smugglers and pirates, the system was also the place where Mon Mothma convinced three major resistance groups to join forces and form the Rebel Alliance. [AC, AS, COJ, DFR, HLL, MTS, RS, SAC, SW]

Core Worlds, the

See Galactic Core.

Corgan, Colonel

General Etahn A'baht's staff tactical officer, he served aboard the fleet carrier *Intrepid.* [SOL, TT]

Cornelius, Dr.

See Evazan, Dr.

Corporate Sector, the

A portion of the known galaxy set aside for the exclusive use of the Corporate Sector Authority. The sector consists of tens of thousands of star systems that apparently maintain no native sentient life-forms. Many of the resources mined from the planets of the Corporate Sector went into the construction of the Imperial war machine. [CSSB, DESB, HLL, HSE, HSR]

Corporate Sector Authority, the

A vast private corporation made up of dozens of contributing companies, granted a charter by the Old Republic—and later sanctioned by the Empire—to control that portion of the galaxy known as the Corporate Sector. According to the terms of the charter, the Authority has the right to exploit the resources of the region to the fullest extent. It rules the region in much the same way as the Empire ruled the rest of the galaxy, as its charter empowers the Authority to act as owner, employer, landlord, government, police, and military to all persons, places, and things within the Corporate Sector. A fifty-five-member board of directors, headed by the ExO, runs the CSA.

Originally established hundreds of years ago, the corporations were allowed to operate under the watchful eye of the Republic. Later, Emperor Palpatine permitted the sector to expand to nearly 30,000 stars. Eleven native intelligent species were discovered in the expanded region, though this fact was hidden from the general public. When the cloned Emperor reappeared six years after the Battle of Endor, the CSA declared its neutrality and supplied both sides with weapons. [CSSB, DESB, HLL, HSE, HSR]

Corridan

A planet located in the center of the Rim Territories and defended by the Black Sword Command. [BTS]

corridor ghoul

A meter-high quadruped native to Coruscant's lowest levels. These fast and deadly creatures are believed to be mammals. They have stark white skin, big ears, and sharp teeth. [AS]

Corrupter

A *Victory*-class Star Destroyer under the command of Imperial Captain Ait Convarion, it destroyed the colony on Halanit as part of its campaign of terror after Rogue Squadron hijacked a bacta convoy. The vessel was destroyed in the Graveyard of Alderaan while engaged in a fierce battle with Rogue Squadron. [BW]

Corsair

An ancient ship used by the dark-side sorcerer Naga Sadow to flee across the galaxy. [DLS]

Cort, Farl

The former administrator of the colony on Halanit, he placed the distress call to the New Republic requesting bacta to aid his dying people. Rogue Squadron liberated a shipment from the Bacta Cartel and delivered it to the colony. Ysanne Isard, head of the Bacta Cartel, decided to destroy the colony as an example to other worlds. Cort was believed to have died in the massacre. [BW]

Cortina

A planet that, along with the world Jandur, petitioned for membership in the New Republic. At first prideful and arrogant, both planets eventually signed the standard articles of confederation. [BTS]

cortosis ore

This rare material exhibits a property that shuts down lightsabers when the blade touches it. Some Force users have made sets of body armor out of woven cortosis fibers, and Emperor Palpatine inserted it between the double walls of his private residence on Coruscant. When a lightsaber blade hits the rock, a feedback crash starts in the weapon's activation loop. [VF]

Corulag

This planet in the Bormea sector of the Core was devoted to Emperor Palpatine and considered to be a model world of Imperial behavior. [HESB]

Corusca gem

An extremely rare mineral found only in the lower levels of the gas giant Yavin. The hardest known substance in the galaxy, a Corusca gem can even cut through transparisteel. [YJK]

Coruscant

The jewel of the Core Worlds and the center of the known galaxy, this planet has been the seat of galactic government for as long as records exist. An enormous multileveled city covers most of the planet's land mass. Kilometer-high skyscrapers and numerous spaceports decorate Imperial City. The Old Republic built the Senate Hall on this beautiful world, among the majestic spires and dazzling lights of the capital city. When the Emperor took power, he created the Imperial Palace, a structure that loomed over Senate Hall from that day forward. By Imperial decree, the Emperor changed the name of the planet to Imperial Center. Later, after the fall of the Empire and the rise of the New Republic, Coruscant regained its original name and has remained the seat of the galactic government.

It is said that Coruscant sets the tone for the entire galaxy.

Styles and fads start on this capital world and slowly spread out into the galaxy. The level of culture is unsurpassed anywhere else in the Core or beyond, and all of the "standard" measurements used throughout the galaxy are based upon the norms of this planet.

Throughout the collapse of the Old Republic, the time of the Empire, and the rise of the New Republic, the people of Coruscant knew war and hardship only by the news they received. Most viewed the shift of governments as others considered the changing of the seasons. They didn't care who occupied the seats of power, for Coruscant was considered eternal. Those who were particularly loyal to the Empire fled or were expelled once the New Republic took charge.

Between the end of Grand Admiral Thrawn's threat and the return of the reborn Emperor, the Empire launched a successful attack on Coruscant. The New Republic leadership was forced to flee from the capital planet, which was left in ruins by the Imperial onslaught. The New Republic government eventually recaptured the planet and quickly went about restoring Imperial City.

Coruscant's attractions included the snow-covered Manarai Mountains, the Skydome Botanical Gardens, the Grand Towers, the pyramidal Imperial Palace, the underground city of Dometown, the Holographic Zoo of Extinct Animals, and the Galactic Museum, which houses ancient Sith artifacts. The lowest, darkest levels of Imperial City were abandoned long ago. Discarded equipment, wrecked starships, spider-roaches, armored rats, wild gangs like the Lost Ones, and other nameless subhumans roam the shadows of the deep.

Twelve years after the Battle of Endor, Luke Skywalker built a hidden retreat atop the stones of Darth Vader's former refuge. Mon Mothma built her own private estate surrounded by gardens and a tree moat. [DE, DFR, DFRSB, HE, HESB, ISWU, LC, SESB]

Coruscant Guards

The highly trained peacekeepers of Imperial City and the rest of the capital planet, they were also referred to as Imperial

Guards and elite stormtroopers. Utilizing provisions of martial law, the Coruscant Guards were empowered to search any facility or dwelling, arrest any citizen, and otherwise locate and detain suspected Rebel operatives and others who threatened the Empire. Coruscant Guards were equipped with crimson body armor, blaster rifles, and force pikes. [SESB, SOTE]

Coruscant Guard

Corusca Rainbow

Formerly the *Black Asp*, the ship was renamed when its captain and crew defected to the Alliance. It led the invasion fleet to liberate Coruscant. [BW]

Cosmic Balance

The predominant faith of the people of Bakura, the religion originated on Hemei IV. This form of extreme dualism holds the primary belief that for every rise in power there is a corresponding decline elsewhere. The followers of the Cosmic Balance opposed the Jedi Knights in earlier times, claiming that a Jedi's increased abilities diminished someone else in another part of the galaxy. When Emperor Palpatine began the persecution of the Jedi, the Cosmic Balance adherents felt that the action was timely and well deserved. The faith's sacred text, the *Fulcrum*, outlines its chief tenets, including the belief that in the afterlife all inequities will be redressed. [TAB, TBSB]

Cosmic Egg

The deity of the Kitonak species. [TJP]

Council of Elders

The ruling body of the Ewoks of Endor's forest moon. Chief Chirpa led the council during the time of the Battle of Endor. [RJ]

Courage of Sullust

A reconfigured Rebel transport that carried ten X-wings from Rogue Squadron to the planet Ryloth on a secret mission. It returned to Coruscant loaded with the addictive ryll kor that was to be used in a secret Alliance Intelligence project. [BW]

Court of the Fountain

An eatery and tourist trap owned by Jabba the Hutt on Tatooine, it was the closest thing to a high-class restaurant that the planet had. [TMEC]

Covell, General

A young Imperial officer who was placed in charge of the Empire's ground troops upon the return of Grand Admiral Thrawn. Covell was among the most experienced of the remaining Imperial officers, and he had learned from the legendary General Maximilian Veers—he had served as Veers's first officer during the Battle of Hoth. Captain Gilad Pellaeon promoted Covell to major general in charge of *Chimaera*'s ground troops after the Battle of Endor. Thrawn gave Covell the rank of general and ordered him to immediately begin training his troops for real battle. General Covell died on the planet Wayland after Joruus C'baoth destroyed his mind. [DFR, DFRSB, LC]

Coway

A troglodyte race of bipedal humanoids who inhabit Circarpous V. Covered by a fine gray down, these tribal beings live in caves and wells that were built by the now-extinct Thrella. Coway have an intense dislike of surface dwellers. A triumvirate of leaders rule the tribes. [SME]

Cracken, General Airen

The head of Alliance Intelligence and a decorated hero of the Rebellion and New Republic, he was placed in charge of Rogue Squadron's mission to Coruscant in advance of the invasion fleet. [BW, CRFG]

Cracken, Pash

Son of General Airen Cracken, a member of Rogue Squadron. Pash entered the Imperial Naval Academy with fabricated identity files. When he graduated, he led his entire TIE wing to defect to the Alliance. The wing became known as Cracken's Flight Group, building their reputation by destroying a *Victory*-class Star Destroyer. He then took over an A-wing unit stationed on the Rim, before joining Rogue Squadron. [BW, LC]

Crado

A Cathar Jedi, he lived 4,000 years before the Galactic Civil War. This humanoid feline learned from Master Vodo-Siosk Baas and later became a follower of Exar Kun. Crado and dark-sider Aleema were killed in the multiple supernova they triggered. [DLS, TSW]

credit standard

The basic monetary unit used throughout the Empire. Based upon the Old Republic credit, it stayed in use during the time of the New Republic, though both the New Republic and the Imperial remnants produced their own currency. Most credits are stored and exchanged via computer transactions, but there is credit currency that can be carried and physically exchanged. [HESB, SME, SWRPG]

Creed, the

A popular and benign Tarrick cult founded on the principles of joy and service. [TT]

Creel, Pleader Irving

The famous pleader who defended Journeyman Protector Jaster Mereel—who later became Boba Fett—in his trial for killing another protector. [TBH]

Crondre

The site of a diversionary battle that took place during Grand Admiral Thrawn's multipronged attack. The true target of the attack was the planet Ukio. [LC]

Cron drift

This charted sector of the known galaxy is the remnant of a trinary system supernova that exploded in the distant past. During the Sith War, it was a densely packed group of stars known as the Cron Cluster, located in the Cron system.

Alliance listening post Ax-235 was located within the drift's large asteroid belt. This post intercepted the Death Star's technical plans prior to the Battle of Yavin and relayed them to Alliance High Command. [DA, DE2, HLL, HSE, TSW]

Cronus, Colonel

This low-ranking Imperial officer teamed up with Admiral Daala. The colonel was aboard his flagship, *Victory*, when it was destroyed. [DS]

Crseih Research Station

An artificial planetoid and former Imperial research station formed by a cluster of asteroids joined by gravity fields and connecting airlink tunnels. Also known as Asylum Station, the secret facility served as a headquarters for Lord Hethrir, the former Imperial Procurator of Justice. He also used it as a prison for his enemies. A strange being called Waru started a cult on Crseih. [CS]

Crumb, Salacious

This Kowakian monkey-lizard held a favored position in Jabba the Hutt's court. He usually sat close to his bloated lord and master, catching and consuming food and drink that Jabba spilled. Known for his taunting cackle and his habit of mimicking everything said around him, Salacious Crumb was considered an annoying and disgusting being. He was Jabba's court jester, hired to make his boss laugh day in and day out. He died along with many of Jabba's associates during Han Solo's rescue and escape. [GG5, RJ, SWCG]

crystal fern

A primitive silicon-based life-form found in the asteroid belt near Hoth. [ISWU]

Crystal Jewel

The seedy casino on Coruscant where Han Solo won the deed to the planet Dathomir and later met a former smuggling contact, Jarril. [CPL, NR]

crystalline vertex

Currency used throughout the Corporate Sector to supplement Authority Cash Vouchers. Vertex is made from a crystal mineral found on the planet Kir, deep within the heart of the Corporate Sector. On this planet, Authority mining outposts refine the crystals into a standard size and color. When individuals enter the Corporate Sector, they are required to exchange all other forms of currency for vertex crystals or Cash Vouchers. [HSE]

Crystal Moon

A highly regarded restaurant in Mos Eisley that was opened by two of Jabba the Hutt's employees after the crimelord's death. The owners are Malakili, the former rancor keeper, and Porcellus, Jabba's former chef. [TJP]

crystal oscillator

A standard part of the mechanical systems of many star cruisers. One was stolen from the Towani family's star cruiser after it crashed on the forest moon of Endor. [BFE]

crystal snake

A transparent reptile native to Yavin 4. Its painful bite sends its victim into a deep sleep. Jacen Solo kept one as a pet. [YJK]

Culroon III

A remote, violence-plagued planet ignored by the Old Republic. When the Empire decided to construct a garrison here, the Imperial general in charge of the operation agreed to a ceremonial surrender to Kloff, leader of the Culroon people. It was a trap, however, and then-Lieutenant Maximilian Veers charged to the rescue in his AT-AT. [GG3, MTS, SWSB]

Culu, Shoaneb

A Jedi Knight who lived about 4,000 years before the Galactic Civil War, she was a Miraluka from the planet Alpheridies. Like others of her species, she was born without eyes and could "see" only through the Force. [DLS]

Cundertol, Senator

A senator from Bakura and a member of the New Republic Senate Defense Council, he was prejudiced against nonhumans. The traitorous Senator Tig Peramis stole a drunk Cundertol's voting key and used it to provide top secret information to Yevethan leader Nil Spaar. [SOL]

Cuthus, Naroon

The talent scout for crimelord Jabba the Hutt, he signed the Max Rebo Band to play at Jabba's palace. [GG5, TJP]

Cyax

An uncharted, unexplored star system far from the galactic trade routes. The system contains the planet Da Soocha and Da Soocha's uncharted fifth moon. The Alliance established Pinnacle Base on the moon during the Emperor's return. [DE, DESB]

cyberostasis

A condition that affects droids that have received a traumatic, external shock, have experienced an internal systems defect, or have induced the state as a function of a protective reflex system. In this state, all of a droid's cybernetic functions are impaired or halted, usually resulting in shutdown. [HSE]

Cybloc XII

This small, lifeless moon in the Meridian sector orbits the glowing, green-gold planet Cybloc. Cybloc, in turn, orbits the star Erg Es 992. A New Republic fleet installation was put in place on the moon, and the area served as a trade hub. Nine years after the Battle of Endor, all personnel assigned to the installation were killed by the Death Seed plague. [POT]

Cyborg Operations

A department in Jabba the Hutt's court controlled by the droid EV-9D9. Located deep within the dungeons of Jabba's palace, Cyborg Operations was concerned with breaking the programming and personalities of droids through torture and other means before assigning them to tasks and duties in Jabba's organization. [RJ]

Cyborrea

A high-gravity planet in a star system of the same name. Nek battle dogs are bred and trained here. [DE, DESB]

D-89

This pilotless ferret ship was part of Colonel Pakkpekatt's armada. It chased the mysterious ghost ship called the Teljkon vagabond, in order to breach its defenses and provoke it to make the jump to light speed. The vagabond destroyed the ferret before it could accomplish its mission. [BTS]

Daala, Admiral

The highest-ranking female fleet officer to ever serve the Emperor, Admiral Daala was equally brilliant, ruthless, and beautiful. Hidden and out of touch throughout most of the Galactic Civil War and the earliest years of the New Republic, she reappeared to become one of the New Republic's primary military opponents.

As a young woman, Daala weathered the sexist Imperial culture to excel at the Academy on Carida. Moff Tarkin noticed Daala, making her his protégée and lover. Tarkin placed Daala in charge of the Maw Installation, his top secret weapons research facility located in the black-hole fields outside Kessel. The admiral commanded four Star Destroyers—including her flagship *Gorgon*—180,000 researchers and staff, and the entire Maw Installation. Under her command, the Installation produced plans and a prototype for the Death Star battle stations, the World Devastators, and the Sun Crusher.

After eleven years of isolation, the Maw Installation was discovered when an Imperial shuttle carrying Han Solo, Chewbacca, and Kyp Durron arrived. Under interrogation, the trio revealed the news of the galaxy—including Tarkin's death, the destruction of both Death Stars, and the fall of the Empire. Obsessed with a need for revenge, Daala unleashed the power of her ultimate weapon—the Sun Crusher. She destroyed much of the Kessel fleet and a Dantooine colony and laid waste to Mon Calamari before Admiral Ackbar employed a brilliant tactic and gained the upper hand.

Admiral Daala

Daala's plan to strike the New Republic capital on Coruscant was also overturned, and she made her next stand at the Maw Installation. She destroyed the complex, then slipped away. The next time she surfaced, she killed thirteen of the leading warlords, who were all that remained of Imperial authority, and took control of all Imperial forces. From the bridge of the Super Star Destroyer *Knight Hammer*, she once again sought to destroy the New Republic, and again she failed.

Years later, she reappeared as the president of the Independent Company of Settlers. This group, some 3,000 beings strong, purchased 1.5 billion acres on the planet Pedducis Chorios. Daala was eventually reunited with her long-lost love Liegeus Vorn, and Daala and her people were allowed to go their own way. [COF, POT, SWCG]

Dack

See Ralter, Dack.

Dadeferron, Torm

A tall, brawny man with red hair and blue eyes, born to a wealthy family on the planet Kail, he was part of the secret civilian group, organized by Rekkon, the Kalla university professor, that located missing friends and relatives who were suspected prisoners of the Corporate Sector Authority. Torm served as second in command of the group's mission to infiltrate an Authority Data Center on Orron III. The group hoped to learn the location of the Authority's illegal detention center in order to rescue the political prisoners. [HSE]

Da'Gara

The huge and powerful prefect of the Praetorite Vong—the first invasion force of the extragalactic Yuuzhan Vong—he commanded the living worldship that had breached the galactic rim and settled at the planet Helska 4. The greater mission was under the command of the yammosk, a creature genetically engineered to serve the Yuuzhan Vong and help them conquer their enemies. Da'Gara served as the yammosk's adviser. He died when New Republic forces led by Luke Skywalker destroyed Helska 4 and the powerful, deadly yammosk. [VP]

Dagobah

A mist-shrouded, mysterious swamp planet in the Dagobah system of the Sluis sector. With no cities or advanced technology, Dagobah teems with a wide variety of life. It was the home and hiding place of Yoda, the Jedi Master, who had instructed both Obi-Wan Kenobi and Luke Skywalker before his death, prior to the Battle of Endor. Dagobah was considered to be a haunted place due to its connection to the Dark Jedi of Bpfassh. The evil rampage of the Dark Jedi came to an end on the swamp planet, after the group terrorized the systems of the Sluis sector some years before the Galactic Civil War. [DS, ESB, ESBR, ESBN, HE, ISWU]

Dahai, Tedn

A member of Figrin D'an's jizz band, he played the fanfar. [TMEC]

Dalla the Hutt

Han Solo borrowed money from Dalla to buy Princess Leia a planet for the refugees who were off world when Alderaan was destroyed. [CPL]

Dalron Five

A planet devastated during an infamous Imperial siege. [GG1, MTS]

Daluuj

This fog-shrouded, watery world served as home to an Imperial training center. When the Imperials attacked Mon Calamari shortly after the destruction of the first Death Star, Admiral Ackbar and his troops fled to Daluuj in life pods and were rescued by the *Millennium Falcon.* [CSW]

Damaya

A member of the Singing Mountain clan of the Witches of Dathomir. [CPL]

Damonite Yors-B

An uninhabited ice-covered world in the Meridian sector. Han Solo and Lando Calrissian came to this planet in search of the missing Leia Organa Solo, nine years after the Battle of Endor. [POT]

D'an, Figrin

The Bith musician who was the leader of the jizz band Figrin D'an and the Modal Nodes. D'an played the kloo horn. Figrin, who loved sabacc and glitterstim spice, brought the band to Tatooine to play for Jabba the Hutt, but after incurring the crimelord's wrath he got the band a job at the Mos Eisley cantina. [GG1, SW, SWCG, TMEC,]

Dandalas

A planet in the Farlax sector, near the Koornacht Cluster. [SOL]

Dan'kre, Liska

A wealthy Bothan and old school friend of Asyr Sei'lar. She invited Sei'lar and Rogue Squadron pilot Gavin Darklighter to a party in a skyhook above Coruscant. [BW]

Dantooine

A remote planet far from the centers of civilization, it has no industrial settlements or advanced technology. Two moons orbit the planet. The Dantari, primitive nomadic tribesmen, live along the coasts, though they are few in number. About 4,000 years before the Galactic Civil War, Jedi Master Vodo-Siosk Baas established a training center among Dantooine's ruins. Four millennia later, it served as the primary base for the Rebel Alliance until it was evacuated after an Imperial tracking device was discovered in a shipment of cargo. Eleven years after that, Admiral Daala's AT-AT walkers wiped out colonists who had relocated to Dantooine from Eol Sha. [DA, DLS, ISWU, JASB, JS, LC, SW]

Danuta

The planet where the technical plans for the first Death Star were hidden within a secret Imperial base. Rebel agent Kyle Katarn infiltrated the facility and stole the plans, which were later given to Princess Leia for transport back to Alliance High Command. [DFRSB, SWR]

Daragon, Gav

A hyperspace explorer who lived some 5,000 years before the Galactic Civil War, he and his sister, Jori, mapped new hyperspace paths in their ship, *Starbreaker 12*. Gav had strong Force potential but no training. When Gav and his sister made a blind hyperspace jump to escape assassins, they discovered the Sith planet, Korriban. Captured by Sith Lords, Gav was forced to tell Naga Sadow everything he knew about the Republic's defenses. When Sadow invaded Republic space, Gav damaged his meditation pod and disrupted the illusions he was using in the attack. Gav died when Sadow triggered solar flares in an unstable star and destroyed his own ship. [FSE, GAS]

Daragon, Jori

A hyperspace explorer who lived some 5,000 years before the Galactic Civil War, she and her brother, Gav, mapped new hyperspace paths in their ship, *Starbreaker 12.* Like her brother, she had strong Force potential but no training. When *Starbreaker 12* was forced to make a blind hyperspace jump to escape assassins, Jori and Gav discovered the Sith planet, Korriban. Captured by the Sith, Jori was sent back to the Republic by Naga Sadow. She carried a tracking beacon the Sith could follow. Upon returning, she was arrested and sent to the prison world Ronika. Jori escaped and set out to find Empress Teta to warn her of the impending Sith invasion. [FSE, GAS]

Darek system

A star system located near the Hensara and Morobe systems, where Rogue Squadron made a hyperspace transit jump in order to disguise its origin point and protect its hidden base. [RS]

Darepp

The planet where the starliner *Star Morning*, owned by the Fallanassi religious order, traveled after it departed from Teyr. [SOL]

Dargul

The sister world of the planet Umgul and location of Duchess Mistal's Palace Dargul. [JS]

Dark Force

See *Katana* fleet.

Dark Jedi

Evil Jedi Knights operating during the Clone Wars were called Dark Jedi, and a group of them threatened the Bpfassh system. The reborn clone Emperor Palpatine later envisioned a new breed of Jedi Knights, trained under the tenets of the dark side of the Force and loyal to him for the thousand years he expected to rule. Nineteen years after the Battle of Endor, the Second Imperium attempted to train a new legion of Dark Jedi at the Shadow Academy, in an effort to retake the galaxy and reestablish the Empire. [DE, DFR, YJK]

Darklighter, Biggs

A childhood friend of and role model for Luke Skywalker. The two grew up together on Tatooine, dreaming of adventures beyond the endless dunes. Biggs finally found a way off Tatooine when he was accepted into the Imperial Space Academy. While studying at the Academy, Biggs and some of his classmates made contact with the Rebel Alliance and planned to defect to the Alliance at the first opportunity. Upon graduation, Biggs received a post as first mate on the merchant ship *Rand Ecliptic.* Along with his executive officer, Biggs staged a mutiny and turned the ship and its cargo of ore over to the Alliance. Biggs was reunited with Luke Skywalker during the Battle of Yavin, where both piloted Rebel X-wings against the Empire's Death Star. Biggs lost his life during this battle, destroyed by a blast from Darth Vader's TIE fighter. [SW, SWN]

Biggs Darklighter

Darklighter, Gavin

Cousin of Rogue Squadron legend Biggs Darklighter, Gavin was a sixteen-year-old Tatooine farm boy when Wedge Antilles offered him a spot in Rogue Squadron. Gavin was part of the reconnaissance mission to Coruscant prior to the Alliance invasion. After insulting Asyr Sei'lar, a female Bothan, and narrowly escaping death twice, he and the other Rogues convinced

Sei'lar and her Alien Combine to join the Alliance against the Empire. With their help—and Gavin's idea to use a thunderstorm to short out the planetary shields—the Alliance invasion fleet took the planet. [BW]

Darklighter, Huff "Huk"

Biggs Darklighter's father, and one of the wealthiest residents of Tatooine, he trafficked Imperial armor, weapons, and fighter craft on the black market. Later, he became a source of weapons and munitions when Rogue Squadron needed arms to use against former Director of Imperial Intelligence Ysanne Isard. [BW, XW]

Darklighter, Jula

Brother of Huff Darklighter and father of Gavin Darklighter, he was a hardworking moisture farmer on Tatooine. [BW]

Darklighter, Lanal

Huff Darklighter's third wife, she was Silya Darklighter's sister. [BW]

Darklighter, Silya

Gavin Darklighter's mother, she kept busy raising her younger children and running the farm on Tatooine. [BW]

Dark Lord of the Sith

Originally, powerful Jedi Knights who used the dark side of the Force. The title passed down from generation to generation, with only one or two Dark Lords existing at a time. Many Dark Lords were mummified, and their remains were preserved in the temples on Korriban. Darth Vader and Emperor Palpatine were the Dark Lords active during the Galactic Civil War. [DLS, SWN, TOJ]

Darksaber Project

Code name for the secret weapon that Durga and his Hutt crimelords ordered built using modified and improved plans for the original Death Star's superlaser. [DS]

dark side, the

See Force, the.

Dark Side Adepts

Members of the reborn Emperor's New Imperial Council, drawn from the ranks of the Emperor's cohorts in the dark side of the Force. In the years prior to the Battle of Yavin, the Emperor used Byss as his private retreat. On this hidden world, he began to train men of great intelligence who demonstrated some ability to use the Force. He twisted them to the dark side, turning them into powerful Force users. These adepts served the Emperor's will, and he planned to eventually disperse them throughout the galaxy, to replace the planetary governors. [DE]

Dark Side Compendium

An encyclopedia of dark-side lore written by the reborn clone Emperor Palpatine. He completed three volumes of his proposed several-hundred-volume set before Luke Skywalker and Princess Leia defeated him. These completed books were *The Book of Anger*, *The Weakness of Inferiors*, and *The Creation of Monsters.* Luke Skywalker read all three. [DE]

DarkStryder

A powerful and sentient alien force, it provided technology to a rogue Imperial moff, Kentor Sarne. [DSC]

Darlyn Boda

A steamy, muddy Imperial planet near Hoth that supported a thriving criminal underground and an active network of Rebel contacts. [TBH]

Darm, Umolly

A Nam Chorios trader, she could acquire many off-world items. She exported Spook-crystals, which she thought were used to help flowers grow on K-class worlds, but were really being used as components in long-distance smart missiles called Needles. [POT]

D'armon, Pav

A Mistryl Shadow Guard who served as second in command of the Hammertong operation. She was killed in an Imperial raid. [TMEC]

Dar'Or

A low-gravity forested planet, home to the Ri'Dar species of intelligent flying mammals. The planet was declared a Species Preservation Zone, but that hasn't stopped hunters from operating within the thick forests. [GG4]

Darsk, Ris

On the surface, a wealthy Kuati traveling with her telbun to Coruscant to conceive a child. In reality, this was Erisi Dlarit of Rogue Squadron, undercover during the reconnaissance mission to Imperial Center. [BW]

Dartibek system

This system contains the planet Moltok, home of the Ho'Din species. [GG4]

Da Soocha

A watery world, also called Gla Soocha, located in the Cyax system. The name means "Waking Planet" in Huttese, and Hutt legends claim that the great, planet-covering ocean is a single, intelligent entity. The Mon Calamari evacuees hoped to reach this world and find a safe haven from Imperial forces during the attack of the World Devastators. [DE, DESB]

D'Asta, Baron Ragez

A powerful shipping magnate, he supplied the Empire with most of its cargo ships and controlled a strategically located sector of the Empire about eleven years after the Battle of Endor. He had the largest privately owned fleet of starfighters in the galaxy. When the New Republic apprehended the Imperial Interim Ruling Council, D'Asta withdrew his sector from the Empire and proclaimed it an independent territory. [CE]

data card

Thin, flat plastic rectangles used to store information and programs for use in datapads and computers. [HE, HESB, TM]

datapad

A palm-sized personal computer consisting of a readout screen, input touch pad, data card slot, internal power source, and ports for coupling with droids or larger computer terminals. [HE, HESB, TM]

Datar

This planet was the site of the massacre of Rebels by Imperial troops who disobeyed Darth Vader's order that he wanted prisoners to interrogate. [TMEC]

Dathomir

This low-gravity world with four small moons, located in the Quelii sector, was home to the Witches of Dathomir, a group of Force-sensitive women, as well as to fearsome rancors. Semi-intelligent humanoid reptiles called the Blue Desert People also live on the planet. The Jedi Knights exiled a group of illegal arms manufacturers to Dathomir. Several generations later, a rogue Jedi named Allya was also exiled to the planet. She taught the ways of the Force to the inhabitants and her descendants, who learned to tame the wild rancors into riding animals. About 400 years before the Galactic Civil War, the Jedi academy ship *Chu'unthor* crashed into a Dathomir tar pit.

As time passed, the female Force users divided into different clans, including the Singing Mountain, Frenzied River, and Misty Falls clans. There was even a clan, called the Nightsisters, dedicated to the dark side and led by a witch named Gethzerion. Females remained dominant in the clans, and males were used as slaves and for breeding.

The Empire built orbital shipyards and a surface penal colony on Dathomir. When the Emperor discovered the extent of Gethzerion's power, he ordered the destruction of all prison ships to prevent the Nightsisters' leader from leaving the planet. Imperials who were also stranded in the process became Gethzerion and the Nightsisters' slaves. Han Solo won the planet in a game of sabacc four years after the Battle of Endor, beginning a series of events that led to the defeat of Warlord Zsinj and the destruction of the Nightsisters. Eleven years later, a new group of Nightsisters appeared, founded by Luke Skywalker's former student Brakiss. This group, based in Dathomir's Great Canyon, teamed with the remnants of the Empire. They treated males as equals and sent their best Force users to learn at the Empire's Shadow Academy. [COJ, CPL, DS, ISWU, YJK]

Dauren, Lieutenant

Comm officer on Carida, stationed in the main citadel of the Imperial military training center. He escorted the stormtrooper Zeth Durron to meet his brother, Kyp. Dauren then attacked Zeth, forcing Zeth to fight back and kill him. [COF]

Davis

A smuggler from Fwatna who saved Han Solo from a gang of Glottalphibs on Skip 5. He was later killed in one of dark-sider Kueller's bombings. [NR]

Dawferm Selfhood States

A group of worlds that formed their own protective organization during the chaotic times following the Battle of Endor. [DESB]

Daykim

"King" of the feral bureaucrats who lived in Imperial City's lowest levels. [DA]

Deak

A childhood friend of Luke Skywalker, he lived in Anchorhead, on the desert world of Tatooine. As teens, Luke and Deak often flew their skyhoppers in mock aerial duels and raced through the many twisting canyons near their homes. [SW]

Death

A town on the penal planet Jubilar. It used to be called Dying Slowly. [TBH]

death engine

This crab-shaped Imperial weapon was massive, heavily shielded, covered with blast weapons, and moved via repulsors. [TMEC]

Deathseed

Lethal TIE fighter variant built for use by Twi'lek pilots. [BW]

Death Seed plague

This infestation, thought to be a disease, was undetectable and 100 percent lethal to all species. Bacta, instead of curing the plague, accelerated its horrific attack. It was actually an invasion of a host by drochs, small insects that bury themselves in the flesh and drink out the life fluids of a victim. After an outbreak more than 700 years before the Galactic Civil War, the drochs were relocated to Nam Chorios. On that world, peculiar geology and filtered sunlight held the insects in check. Seti Ashgad and Dzym, a mutated droch, reintroduced the plague to the galaxy when they starting planting drochs aboard New Republic ships. [POT]

Death's Head

This Imperial Star Destroyer, commanded by Captain Harbid, served as part of Grand Admiral Thrawn's armada. [DFR, HE, LC]

Death Star

The ultimate weapon in the Empire's arsenal, it was a top secret battle station the size of a small moon and armed with more destructive power than the combined Imperial fleet. It was designed to end any remaining opposition to the Emperor and his New Order. Once it was fully operational, the Emperor ordered the Imperial Senate disbanded and declared that the Empire would keep local star systems in line.

Death Star

The Death Star was the culmination of the Tarkin Doctrine, a plan and course of action proposed by Grand Moff Tarkin. It called for rule through the fear of force, using a battle station of such destructive magnitude that fear alone would keep the member worlds of the Empire in line. Imperial space station designer Bevel Lemelisk was charged with bringing Tarkin's terrible vision to fruition.

Measuring 120 kilometers in diameter, the battle station was constructed over the penal colony world Despayre in the remote Horuz star system. The completed Death Star's personnel complement included more than a million officers, troops, pilots, support personnel, and stormtroopers. It carried assault shuttles, blastboats, Strike cruisers, drop ships, land vehicles, and various support ships in its massive holds, and seven thousand TIE fighters. Its surface was protected by thousands of turbolaser batteries, laser cannons, ion cannons, tractor beam projectors, and its primary weapon—a planet-destroying superlaser. In addition, the outer shell was covered with navigation trenches, docking bays, and turbolaser emplacements to fend off capital ship attacks. Artificial mountains and canyons were formed from rising docking ports and command complexes. Though the Death Star showed its relentless power by destroying the planet Alderaan, Rebel agents were able to discover a weakness when they stole the technical readouts for the battle station. The Battle of Yavin ended with the destruction of the Death Star.

Three years later, as the second Death Star neared completion, another battle was waged to keep the massive weapon from being activated. Though never finished, the second Death Star was larger than the original—160 kilometers in diameter—and armed with a more powerful and accurate superlaser that could be trained upon capital ships. The Rebels were able to destroy it at the Battle of Endor. [DSTC, RJ, SW, SWVG]

decicred

A monetary unit equal to one-tenth of a credit. [SOTE]

Declaration of a New Republic

A text-file document that set forth the principles, goals, and ideals of the new galactic government formed by the Alliance after the Battle of Endor. The document was released one month after the battle ended. It was signed by Mon Mothma of Chandrila, Princess Leia Organa of Alderaan, Borsk Fey'lya of Kothlis, Admiral Ackbar of Mon Calamari, Sian Tevv of Sullust, Doman Beruss of Corellia, Kerrithrarr of Kashyyyk, and Verrinnefra B'thog Indriummsegh of Elom. [HESB]

Deega, Senator

A Bith senator from Clak'dor VII, he served on the New Republic Senate Defense Council. He was committed to pacifism and ecological preservation. He replaced the traitorous Senator Tig Peramis. [SOL]

Deegan, Lieutenant

A top-rated Corellian pilot and a member of Team Orange who worked with Wedge Antilles on the Imperial City reconstruction crews. [JS, RS]

Deej

An Ewok warrior married to Shodu and father of Weechee, Willy, Wicket, and Winda. [ETV]

Deep Core hauler

A type of freighter licensed by the Empire to haul cargo to the Imperial systems in the Deep Core. [DE]

Deep Core Security Zone

An area formed by sealed-off sectors of the inner Galactic Core. The throneworld Byss was hidden within the zone. [DE]

Deep Galactic Core

A region located between the perimeter of the Galactic Core and the very center of the galaxy. At the Core's center is a black hole surrounded by masses of antimatter and dense stars. The reborn clone Emperor consolidated his forces in this region in order to launch a final strike against the Rebellion. [DE]

Defeen

A cunning, sharp-clawed Defel who served as an interrogator first class at the Imperial Reprogramming Institute located in the Valley of Royalty on the planet Duro. His work helped him get promoted to the rank of supreme interrogator for the Prophets of the Dark Side on Space Station Scardia. [MMY, PDS]

Defel

Stocky, fur-covered humanoids commonly called Wraiths. A Defel stands about 1.3 meters tall, with shoulders as wide as 1.2 meters across, protruding snouts, and long, clawed, triple-jointed fingers. In most light, a Defel appears as a large, red-eyed shadow. Under ultraviolet light, a Defel can be seen in its natural form. This species lives in underground cities on the planet Af'El, where most inhabitants make their living through mining and metallurgy. In the galaxy at large, due to their shadowy appearance, Defels often find employment as hired muscle, spies, and assassins. [DFRSB, GG4]

Defender

A destroyer in the Bakuran task force. [TAB]

Defiance

The Mon Calamari warship that replaced *Home One* as the flagship of the New Republic fleet and served as Admiral Ackbar's personal vessel. [DE]

deflection tower

The cornerstone of most planetary defense systems, these towers generate high-intensity deflection fields. [SW]

deflector shield

A force field that repulses solid objects or absorbs energy. Ray shielding defends against energy such as radiation and blaster bolts; particle shielding prevents matter from penetrating the field. [ESB, RJ, SW, SWSB]

dejarik

A classic board game that requires skill and strategy to play, it consists of a hologram generator in a circular housing topped by a checkered surface. The game is played with holographic pieces that look like living creatures and battle each other with every move a player makes. [FT]

Delaya

Sister world to Alderaan. [MTS]

Dellalt

A planet located in the Outer Rim, in the Tion Hegemony star group. It held strategic importance in the pre-Republic time known as the Expansionist Period, when Xim the Despot built colossal vaults to hold the treasures he plundered from surrounding star systems. Dellalt's two moons orbit its watery surface. Three main land masses extend far enough above the waterline to provide living space for its human and Sauropteroid inhabitants, called the Survivors and the Swimming People, respectively. [HLL]

Delrian

A prison planet for dangerous criminals. The infamous Dr. Evazan was imprisoned there. [MTS]

Delta Source

See ch'hala tree.

Delvardus, Superior General

One of thirteen feuding warlords that Admiral Daala tried to unite against the New Republic. He died, along with the others, when Daala's plan failed and she inflicted nerve gas upon the warlords. [DS]

Denab

This planet was the site of the Battle of Denab, a major Rebel Alliance victory over the Imperial Fourth Attack Squadron. [SWR]

Denarii Nova

This rare double star was the site of a battle between Old Republic forces and the dark Jedi Naga Sadow thousands of years before the Galactic Civil War. The entire star system was destroyed in the clash. [DLS]

Dendo, Kapp

A Devaronian intelligence agent, he worked with Winter, Leia Organa Solo's personal assistant. He was a fierce fighter with a grim sense of humor who often pretended to be a criminal and blended in with underworld figures. He sometimes worked with Rogue Squadron and was a fast friend to pilot Plourr Ilo. [XW]

Deneba

A desert world that was the site of a historic meeting of thousands of Jedi Knights and Jedi Masters on Mount Meru 4,000 years before the Galactic Civil War. The discussion covered such topics as the takeover of the Empress Teta system by the evil Krath sect and a failed mission to save Koros Major. [DE, TOJ]

Dengar

One of the bounty hunters hired by the Empire to find and capture the *Millennium Falcon* and her crew immediately following the Battle of Hoth. This human was once a successful swoop jockey on the professional circuit. As a young man, he challenged a hot-rodder named Han Solo to a race. As the two neared the finish line, Dengar crashed into Solo's swoop. He suffered severe head injuries and was barred from professional racing. He blamed his fate on Solo and became obsessed with evening the score.

Dengar

The Empire re-built Dengar into an assassin, but he later went freelance. He took up Jabba the Hutt's bounty on Solo and almost captured the smuggler on Ord Mantell. Then he accepted a bounty from Darth Vader to locate and capture the *Millennium Falcon* and its crew. Boba Fett beat him to the prize.

Later, Dengar rescued Boba Fett from the Sarlacc's pit and nursed him back to health. Fett was the best man at Dengar's wedding to Manaroo, a former dancing girl in Jabba's court. Six years later, Dengar and Fett tried to capture Solo again—this time on Nar Shaddaa. They failed again. [ESB, GG3, SWCG, TBH]

Deppo

A calibration engineer serving in an onboard factory within an Imperial World Devastator. [DE]

Dequc

A Jeodu, he was the leader of the Black Nebula criminal cartel who sought to revive Black Sun after the death of the Emperor. Mara Jade killed a decoy on the planet Svivren, thinking it was Dequc. Later, she tracked him to his base on Qiaxx and finished the job. [MJ]

Derlin, Major Bren

An Alliance field officer, he was in charge of security at Echo Base on Hoth at the time of the Imperial invasion. [ESB]

Derra IV

The site of a significant Rebel defeat prior to the Battle of Hoth. An Alliance convoy, on its way to Hoth with desperately needed supplies, was ambushed by several squadrons of TIE fighters in the vicinity of the fourth planet in the Derra star system. The attack was brutal and swift. The convoy was destroyed and all Alliance personnel were killed. [ESBR]

Derricote, General Evir

This Imperial general was in charge of the small Borleias base in the Pyria system. Derricote used his post to smuggle black market goods. After Rogue Squadron and other Alliance forces attacked the base, the Empire became aware of Derricote's sideline endeavors. He was ordered back to Imperial Center to work under Ysanne Isard, the director of Imperial Intelligence. There, he developed the Krytos virus. Later, Derricote died in a battle against Corran Horn and Jan Dodonna. [BW]

Desnand, Io

Imperial governor of the Aida system, he planned to ship Wookiee females and their cubs to the prison camp on Lomabu III and use them as bait in a trap for Rebel forces. He also took the captured Bossk off the hands of bounty hunters Chenlambec and Tinian I'att. [TBH]

Despayre

A prison planet in the Horuz system, located deep within the Outer Rim. The original Death Star was constructed there. The penal colony, surrounded by thick jungles and countless predators, provided many of the laborers needed to build the battle station. When it was completed, the Death Star superlaser was tested by destroying the planet. [DS, DSTC, MTS]

Destiny of Yevetha

This ship, formerly known as the *Redoubtable*, was seized by Nil Spaar during a raid on the Imperial shipyards at N'zoth. It was part of the Yevethan mobilization at Doornik-13. [BTS]

destroyer droid

Also known as wheel droids, these elite units of the Trade Federation army were engineered to roll at high speeds when in wheel configuration, then transform into two-meter-tall, three-legged walking battle droids. When in battle configuration, each destroyer droid wields a laser gun of immense firepower and generates its own deflector shield. [SWTPM]

detainment droid

Imperial detention centers made extensive use of these droids. Floating atop repulsorlift-generated fields, they secured and guarded prisoners, using the binders on the ends of their four limbs to grasp and hold them. [DE]

Detention Block AA-23

The location deep within the Death Star battle station where Princess Leia Organa was held captive by the Imperials. She was imprisoned in Cell 2187. [SW]

Devaron

Homeworld of the horned Devaronians, or Devish, this sparsely populated world near the Core has multiple suns and a temperate climate. Mountain ranges and deep valleys cover the planet. [GG4]

Devaronian

Humanoids that originate on the planet Devaron. A male Devaronian, or Devish, is hairless, with a pair of horns springing from the top of his head and sharp incisors filling his mouth. Many species feel uncomfortable in their presence, for they resemble the devils of a thousand myths. The females are larger, with thick fur and no horns. The males experience a constant wanderlust and can be found in spaceports throughout the galaxy, seeking passage to someplace else. The females prefer to remain at home and keep the advanced Devaronian industries running. [GG1, GG4]

Devastator

The Imperial Star Destroyer that subjugated and terrorized the planet Ralltiir, then captured Princess Leia's consular ship over the planet Tatooine. This was Lord Tion's flagship until his death. [SWR, SWSB]

Devist, Carib

A clone of Baron Soontir Fel created by Grand Admiral Thrawn, he was part of Imperial Sleeper Cell Jenth-44. He was called back to duty by the impostor Grand Admiral Thrawn about sixteen years after the Battle of Endor. He believed in stability more than war and led his fellow clones to help the New Republic expose the impostor. [SP, VF]

Devlia, Admiral

An Imperial officer, he was in charge of the forces at Vladet. Thanks to Intelligence Agent Kirtan Loor, Devlia was made aware of Rogue Squadron's base on Talasea. The admiral sent only one squadron of stormtroopers to attack the base. The troopers died and their shuttle was captured. Later, the Alliance returned the favor and attacked Vladet, presumably killing Devlia. [BW]

Devotion

One of the vessels captured by Nil Spaar during a raid on the Imperial shipyards at N'zoth. It was formerly called the *Valorous.* [BTS]

dewback

A large four-legged reptile native to the desert planet Tatooine. These herbivores are used as beasts of burden by moisture farmers and as patrol animals by the local authorities. The reptiles are often used in place of mechanized vehicles, due to their ability to withstand extremely high temperatures and the wear and tear of sandstorms. [SW, SWR]

Dewlannamapia (DEWLANNA)

A Wookiee and a widow, she was Han Solo's closest friend when he was growing up on *Trader's Luck*. She was nearly 600 years old when Garris Shrike killed her while she was protecting Han. As she was dying, she made Han promise to leave Shrike's band and be happy. [PS]

Deyer Colony

A colony world in the Anoat system featuring floating raft cities, terraformed lakes, and abundant sea life. The peaceful political climate of the Deyer Colony changed after the colonists spoke out against the destruction of Alderaan. In response, the Empire staged a brutal military takeover. [COF, DA, JS]

dianoga

This omnivorous creature lives in shallow, stagnant pools and murky swamps, growing to an average length of ten meters, with seven tentacles that it uses to move around and grab prey. An eyestalk attached to the dianoga's trunk can be raised above the surface of the water to help the creature locate nearby prey. A dianoga made its way into the waste disposal system of the original Death Star battle station. It lived off the station's refuse and almost made a meal of Luke Skywalker when he fell into its watery, garbage-filled lair. [SW]

Diath, Dace

A Jedi Knight from Tatooine, he lived some 4,000 years before the Galactic Civil War. [DLS, FNU, TSW]

Diath, Sidrona

A Jedi Master killed in the Battle of Basilisk about 4,000 years before the Galactic Civil War. He was the father of Jedi Knight Dace Diath. [DLS]

digworm

A small creature native to the planet Kamar. These worms burrow through solid rock by excreting acidic digestive juices. [HSR]

diktat

The title given to the Corellian chief of state. [AC]

Dimok

One of two primary worlds located in the Sepan system. The second world, Ripoblus, had been involved in a long war with Dimok until the conflict was forcibly ended by Imperial forces after the Battle of Hoth. [TSC]

Dim-U monks

A religious order in Mos Eisley on the planet Tatooine. Its members worship banthas. [GG7, ISWU, TM]

dinko

A venomous, palm-sized creature known for its nasty disposition. With powerful rear legs covered with serrated spurs, twin pairs of grasping extremities jutting from its chest, and sharp, needlelike fangs, the dinko is especially formidable for its size. [HSE]

directional landing beacon

A device that transmits fixed signals for ships to use to orient themselves. Landing beacons located at official ports of call are listed in galactic navigation charts. [SME]

Disra, Moff

Chief administrator of the Braxant sector and ruler of the Imperial capital planet code-named Bastion, he was one of eight remaining moffs who Supreme Commander Gilad Pellaeon tried to convince to discuss peace with the New Republic about sixteen years after the Battle of Endor. Disra had other ideas, including forming a partnership with Major Grodin Tierce and the con artist Flim to foist an impostor Grand Admiral Thrawn on the galaxy for his own gain. [SP, VF]

disruption bubble generator

A small electronic device that creates a localized bubble impervious to sonic scanning. [TAB]

disruptor

A weapon that fires a visible blast of energy. The blast can shatter objects and kills in a painful, inhumane manner. Disruptors are illegal in most sectors of the galaxy. [HLL, HSE, HSR]

disruptor

divto

A fearsome three-headed snake, as large as three meters long, native to Endor's forest moon. A divto hunts at night, striking and delivering numbing poison to its prey. [DFRSB]

DJ-88 (DEE-JAY)

A powerful droid who served as the caretaker and teacher in the Lost City of the Jedi, DJ-88 was white, with ruby eyes and a metal "beard." He raised young Ken from the time the Jedi prince was a small child, and Ken looked up to the droid as a father figure. [LCJ, PDS]

Djo, Teneniel

One of the Witches of Dathomir and a member of the Singing Mountain clan. She has red-gold hair and brown eyes flecked with orange. Her mother, Allaya Djo, led the clan until her death. Teneniel was being groomed for the position by her grandmother Augwynne. She fell in love with the Hapan Prince Isolder. The couple married and had a daughter, Tenel Ka, who was accepted into Luke Skywalker's Jedi academy. [CPL, SWCG]

DL-44

This heavy blaster pistol made by BlasTech is illegal or restricted in most systems. [RSB]

Dlarit, Aerin

Father of former Rogue Squadron member Erisi Dlarit and one of the leaders of the bacta monopoly in the Xucphra Corporation. Originally scheduled for termination because of his position in the company and his connection to Ysanne Isard, instead he was discredited. [BW]

Dlarit, Erisi

A wealthy, beautiful former member of Rogue Squadron, she betrayed the Rebel Alliance. Her family made its money in the Xucphra Corporation, the bacta monopoly. She twice tried to seduce fellow Rogue Corran Horn but was rebuffed both times. She eventually attained a post in the Thyferran Home Defense Corps. Her TIE fighter unit was sent to defend Ysanne Isard's Super Star Destroyer *Lusankya* during the final moments of the Bacta War. Corran Horn fired on and destroyed Erisi's TIE fighter as it attempted to protect Isard's escaping shuttle. [BW]

Doallyn

A humanoid bounty hunter from the planet Geran, he had a huge scar on his face from a Corellian sand panther attack. After Jabba the Hutt's death on the planet Tatooine, he helped the Askajian dancer Yarna d'al' Gargan escape across the desert to Mos Eisley. [TJP]

Dobah

A female Phlog on the forest moon of Endor, she was the mate of Zut and the mother of Hoom and Nahkee. [ETV]

Doc

Leader of a band of outlaw techs wanted throughout Imperial space, his real name was Klaus Vandanganten. Doc and his elusive techs specialized in making modifications, usually of an illegal nature, to space vehicles. They had a hidden asteroid base in the Corporate Sector. Doc's daughter Jessa was a member of the band. [CSSB, HSE]

Docking Bay 94

The holding bay in Tatooine's Mos Eisley spaceport where the *Millennium Falcon* waited while Han Solo met with Ben Kenobi, Luke Skywalker, and the droids R2-D2 and C-3PO. Docking Bay 94, like the rest of the bays at Mos Eisley, consists of an entrance ramp and a restraining wall that surrounds a shallow pit. [SW]

Dodonna

This monstrous assault frigate was a modified Imperial Dreadnaught that served as the cornerstone of General Wedge Antilles's fleet. [DS]

Dodonna, General Jan

The Alliance officer who planned and coordinated the assault on the first Death Star at the Battle of Yavin. Dodonna has always looked more like a professor than a warrior, but he was a brilliant tactician who specialized in logistics and sieges. He was one of the first Star Destroyer captains for the Old Republic. When the Empire decided he was too old to learn the ways of the New Order, and called for his termination, Dodonna joined the Rebellion and became one of its top leaders.

General Dodonna was presumed to have died on Yavin 4. He had remained behind to set off concussion charges in the main buildings after the Rebel fleet left. This stopped a wave of Imperial bombers that was attacking the base and gave the Alliance more time to evacuate. He was critically wounded, captured, and imprisoned in the buried Super Star Destroyer *Lusankya*. He helped Rogue Squadron member Corran Horn escape from the prison and was later rescued himself by a Rebel assault team. Six years after the Battle of Endor, he helped plan the battle against the new Imperial World Devastators. [BW, DESB, GG1, SW, SWCG]

Dodonna, Vrad

Son of Jan Dodonna, he was an Alliance pilot who initially retreated from an encounter with the Super Star Destroyer *Executor*. He redeemed himself by ramming his ship into the *Executor*, destroying a section of its defensive shields so that Han Solo could disable the vessel. Dodonna died in the effort. [CSW]

Dodt, Parin

A false identity used by Pash Cracken during an undercover mission to Coruscant. Dodt was supposed to be an Imperial prefect. [XW]

Dogot, Captain Ors

Commander of the Prakith raider *Bloodprice*. [BTS]

Dokrett, Captain Voba

Commander of the Prakith light cruiser *Gorath*. Dokrett attempted to capture the Teljkon vagabond ghost ship, but instead his own ship was destroyed. [TT]

Dolomar sector

A major target in an offensive by Grand Admiral Thrawn. [LC, LCSB]

Dolph

The birth name of the dark-sider known as Kueller. As Dolph, Kueller was an extremely talented student of Luke Skywalker. He left the Jedi academy after a short time, accepted his dark side, and took the name Kueller. [NR]

Dom-Bradden

This Outer Rim world is home to a sentient form of plant life known as the Affytechans. [COJ]

Domed City of Aquarius

Located in a giant bubble far below the Mon Calamari oceans, the Domed City of Aquarius was designed for use by both air- and water-breathing beings. Watery canals feature underwater dwellings, while markets and other structures are located in the air-filled areas above the canals. [GDV]

Dometown

A hollow dome a kilometer across that Lando Calrissian and other investors built in a huge cavern underneath Coruscant, to house an underground city of low stone buildings and cool green parks. [AC]

Dominis

A Jedi Master from ancient times whose favorite apprentice was Zona Luka. Luka assassinated Dominis. [TSW]

Doneeta, Tott

A Jedi Twi'lek trained by Master Arca Jeth on the planet Arkania about 4,000 years before the Galactic Civil War. He had the ability to understand and converse in beast languages. [DLS, FNU, TOJ, TSW]

Doole, Moruth

A Rybet, he was kingpin of the Kessel spice-smuggling business. He was a vile, double-crossing being who would murder his own allies to get what he wanted. He was an official at the Imperial prison on Kessel, using his position to increase his own business holdings. It was Doole who tipped off tariff authorities to the route Han Solo's *Millennium Falcon* was taking during a spice run for Jabba the Hutt, leading Solo to dump his cargo. The Hutt didn't trust Doole completely, however, and sent a bounty hunter to kill him. Doole lost only an eye, as his trusted aide Skynxnex came to his rescue.

Moruth Doole eventually took complete control of the Kessel operations. Seven years after the Battle of Endor, Han Solo and Chewbacca returned to the prison planet on a diplomatic mission for the New Republic. Doole imprisoned them in the deepest spice mine, where they met up with a Force-sensitive human named Kyp Durron. As events played out, much of the planet was destroyed by Admiral Daala's Imperial fleet, and Skynxnex and Doole were killed by the spice-producing giant spiders that live in the mines. [COF, JS, SWCG]

Moruth Doole

doonium

A common heavy metal used to build Imperial war machines. [GDV]

Doornik-207

A planet located in the Farlax sector and the Koornacht Cluster. Twelve years after the Battle of Endor, the alien Yevetha attacked and conquered the planet as part of a series of raids known as the Great Purge. [SOL]

Doornik-319

See Morning Bell.

Doornik-628E

See J't'p'tan.

Doornik-1142

A brown dwarf star orbited by four gaseous planets, located on the edge of the Koornacht Cluster. Twelve years after the Battle of Endor, the New Republic astrographic survey ship *Astrolabe* was destroyed by a Yevethan battle cruiser in an effort to conceal the Black Eleven Fleet that was hiding there. [BTS]

Dorja, Captain

The captain of the Imperial Star Destroyer *Relentless* was in charge of that ship since before the Battle of Endor. His vessel had the distinction of not suffering a single casualty during that conflict. His cautious command style and unwillingness to engage an enemy in direct combat could be considered the reason, though he believed his holding tactics were prudent. He was born into a rich family with a long tradition in the Old Republic and Imperial fleets. He was appalled when a junior officer named Gilad Pellaeon announced that he was taking charge of the fleet when the battle turned bad, though Dorja agreed with Pallaeon's order to retreat. Dorja tried unsuccessfully to wrest control from Pellaeon in the five years that followed, though he came very close on a few occasions. Dorja didn't like the alien Grand Admiral Thrawn, and *Relentless* was not included in Thrawn's personal armada. [DFR, DFRSB]

Dornea

Homeworld of the Dorneans. Though the planet never joined the Alliance, its inhabitants fought against the Empire and were able to successfully resist them in several battles. [BTS]

Dornean

A tall humanoid with purplish leathery skin, he was from the planet Dornea. [BTS]

Dorsk 81

An olive-skinned humanoid from the planet Khomm, he was the eighty-first-generation clone, with the same set of genetic attributes as his predecessors, who was still somehow different from all who had come before. Dorsk 81 was Force-sensitive, and he sought out Luke Skywalker to become one of the first twelve Jedi students. He helped deal with the evil spirit of the long-dead dark Jedi Exar Kun, and he died a hero after joining with the other trainees to create a Force storm that repelled an attacking fleet of Imperial Star Destroyers. [DA, DS]

Dorsk 82

The eighty-second-generation clone with the same Force potential as his predecessor, he came to Yavin 4 to find out if he could follow in the footsteps of Jedi trainee Dorsk 81. He succeeded, and became a Jedi. [JAL]

Doruggan, Captain Conn

A native of Alderaan who served the Empire well and always blamed Princess Leia for his homeworld's destruction. The tall, muscular, dark-haired Doruggan was assigned to Bakura, where he was chiefly concerned with the security of the planet's governmental offices. [TAB, TBSB]

Dosin

An Imperial engineer in charge of high-energy concepts and implementation at the secret Maw Installation weapons facility. Dosin died aboard the prototype Death Star when it fell into a black hole. [COF]

dovin basal

A gravity-focusing creature used to propel Yuuzhan Vong worldships and other craft. One was dropped onto the planet Sernpidal, where it focused one beam to latch onto the planet's core and the other to grab one of the circling moons, causing the moon to crash into the world and destroy it. [VP]

Dowager Queen

This ancient, wrecked spacecraft sits in the middle of Mos Eisley. A tangled heap of girders and twisted hull plates—it's all that remains of the first colony ship to arrive on Tatooine. [GG7, ISWU, TMEC]

Drackmarian

A humanoid species of methane-breathers with blue scales, sharp talons, and snouts filled with sharp teeth. Members of this species don't sleep. They are known for generosity and independent natures. Once fierce opponents of the Empire, they loosely allied themselves with the New Republic. [CPL]

Drackmar system

This multiple-sun system is home to the Drackmarians. [CPL]

Dracmus

A Selonian female, she was captured by Thrackan Sal-Solo in the Corellian capital Coronet. Dracmus was forced to fight Sal-Solo's cousin, Han Solo, and then placed in the same cell in hopes she would finish him off. Instead, she helped Han determine that Sal-Solo was the Hidden Leader of the alien-hating Human League. A Selonian rescue team freed them both. [AS]

D'rag

A starship builder from the planet Oslumpex V. [HSR]

dragon pearl

Valuable pearls found in the gizzards of krayt dragons. [TJP]

dragonsnake

A large predator that inhabits the water channels of Dagobah. [ISWU]

Drall

One of five inhabited worlds in the Corellian system, it is a pleasant, temperate planet with light gravity and serves as home to short, furred creatures also called Drall. This species is cautious, honest, and meticulous. A vast planetary repulsor, located beneath Drall's equator, was presumably used in ancient times to move the planet into its current orbit. [AC, AS, HLL, RS, SAC]

Drang

One of two domesticated vornskrs that Talon Karrde employed as pets and guards. [DFR, HE, HESB, LC]

Dravis

A pilot in Talon Karrde's smuggling operation. [DFR, HE, LC]

Drayson, Admiral Hiram

A high-ranking officer in the New Republic military, he did not begin his career as either an Old Republic or Imperial officer. He was in charge of the Chandrila system defense forces, serving as admiral of the Chandrila Defense Fleet for many years. During this time, he came to know Senator Mon Mothma, Chandrila's representative to the Old Republic—and later Imperial—Senate. Mothma was impressed with his efforts, which caused a dramatic decrease in pirate and smuggling activity in Chandrila space. Years later, Mon Mothma asked Drayson to command her headquarters ship in the Alliance. When the New Republic was formed, he was given the rank of admiral and put in charge of the fleet attached to the Provisional Council and the capital system of Coruscant. He later headed up a covert intelligence group within the New Republic's military and security hierarchy—the mysterious Alpha Blue. [BTS, DFR, DFRSB]

Dreadnaught

At one time, this was the largest heavy star cruiser in service. Measuring 600 meters long, the Dreadnaught was first introduced before the start of the Clone Wars. While slow, poorly

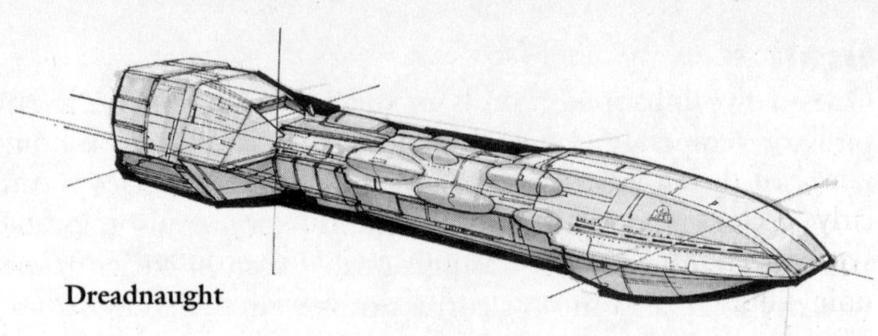

Dreadnaught

shielded, and lightly armed, a number of these ships were refitted for Imperial and Alliance service. It required massive crews to operate a Dreadnaught, as they made little or no use of droid assistants. [DFR, DFRSB, HE, HESB, ISB, RSB]

Dreebo

The pilot of a ship used in Great Bogga the Hutt's pay-for-protection racket. The pirate ship *Starjacker* destroyed his ship. [TOJ]

Dressellian

This wrinkly faced humanoid species from the planet Dressel joined the Alliance just before the Battle of Endor. After fighting the Empire on their homeworld for a long time, they were brought into the larger conflict by the Bothans. [GG12]

droch

Small, sentient insects that bury themselves in flesh and cause the always-fatal Death Seed plague. These tiny domes of purple-brown chitin infested the planet Nam Chorios. A single droch consists of a centimeter-long abdomen that ends in a hard head and a ring of tiny thorn-tipped legs. Larger drochs are called captain drochs. [POT]

droid

The automatons of the galaxy, typically fashioned in the likeness of their creators or in a utilitarian design that stresses function over appearance. Droids are equipped with artificial intelligence, though naturally some are created smarter than others, depending on the function they are designed to perform. Many droids are programmed to understand Basic or the native language of their masters. Only those whose function is to regularly interact with organic beings are provided with a speech synthesizer. All others communicate via a program language unintelligible to most organic beings. Some people who spend a lot of time working with or around droids do pick up the language—at least well enough to understand it. Power is provided by rechargeable cells stored within a droid's body. Many organic cultures, including the Empire, treat droids as property and slaves, and many public areas are considered off limits to droids. The Yuuzhan Vong consider droids an abomination.

There are five droid classifications, each assigned according to a particular droid's primary function. First-degree droids are skilled in physical, mathematical, and medical sciences. Second-degree droids are programmed in engineering and technical sciences. The social sciences and service areas, such as translations, spaceport control, diplomatic assistants, and tutors, are considered the domain of third-degree droids. Fourth-degree droids are skilled in security and military applications. Menial labor and non-intelligence-intensive jobs, such as mining, salvage, transportation, and sanitation, are handled by fifth-degree droids. Most droids, regardless of their classification, have the capabilities of locomotion, logic, self-aware intelligence, communication, manipulation, and sensory reception. [SW, SWSB]

Drome, Captain

The captain hired to transport the Hammertong device from its laboratory to the Death Star. Mistryl Shadow Guards hijacked his ship. [TMEC]

drone barge

A type of large space vessel used to ferry cargo or other supplies. Droids or sophisticated computers control drone barges. These vessels carry no organic crews. [HSE]

Droon, Admiral

An Imperial officer, he attempted to become the governor of Corulag by betraying the then-current governor, Torlock. Darth Vader killed Droon because of his ambitions. [SS]

Droon, Igpek

A small-time trader, he lived on Nam Chorios. [POT]

drop shaft

See lift tube.

drop ship

A fast-moving spacecraft used to transport crew, cargo, or troops from huge capital warships to a planet's surface. Using powerful but short-burst drive units, drop ships plummet from orbit in barely controlled falls. [DFRSB, DSTC, ISB]

Drovian system

This system in the Meridian sector contains the planet Nim Drovis. [POT]

Drudonna

One of the two largest moons orbiting the planet Bespin. With the moon H'gaard, the two are known as the Twins. Shirmar Base, a staging area and processing center for Ugnaught expeditions into Velser's Ring, is located on this small, icy moon. [GG2]

Dryanta

A Wookiee, he accompanied his cousin Chewbacca, and Wookiees Jowdrrl, Shoran, and Lumpawarrump on a mission to rescue Han Solo during the Yevethan crisis. [TT]

Drysso, Joak

Onetime commander of the *Virulence*, he was given command of the Super Star Destroyer *Lusankya* after Ysanne Isard seized control of Thyferra's Bacta Cartel. After a heated battle with Rogue Squadron and other Alliance forces, *Lusankya* was defenseless, locked in a decaying orbit above Thyferra. Drysso refused to surrender, so his crew mutinied and took control of the ship. [BW]

DS-61-2

The Imperial TIE pilot who flew Black Two, Darth Vader's left wing mate, during the Battle of Yavin. Specially trained, his real name was Mauler Mithel, and he was held in reserve to fly missions with Vader. Mithel's son, Rejlii, became a tractor-beam operator aboard Grand Admiral Thrawn's *Chimaera*. [LC, LCSB]

Dubrillion

This planet was the site of Lando Calrissian's mining operations twenty-one years after the Battle of Endor. Dubrillion boasted a major city full of tall towers and starports despite its location so close to the galactic rim. Along with interests on Dubrillion's sister planet, Destrillion, and an asteroid belt known as Lando's Folly, Calrissian had a sweet setup far from the Core Worlds. Luke Skywalker and his companions used the world as their base of operations during the first invasion by the Yuuzhan Vong. [VP]

Duinuogwuin

A member of a huge snakelike species possessing gossamer wings and averaging about ten meters long. This rare, ancient species, sometimes called Star Dragons, has a deep-rooted sense of morality and honor, and most have at least some sensitivity to the Force. Tales are told of an ancient time when Duinuogwuin served as Jedi Knights. [DFRSB, GG4]

D'ukal, Shada

The deceptively decorative-looking mercenary from a mysterious militaristic order of female warriors known as the Mistryl Shadow Guards. She and her friend Karoly D'ulin posed as the Tonnika sisters after botching a mission to transport the

Hammertong device. Shada also served as bodyguard for the smuggler chief Mazzic. In this job, she appeared with plaited hair and a blank expression—until trouble started. Then she was all business, throwing enameled zenji needles with lethal accuracy and using her more-than-capable combat skills to protect the smuggler chief.

Sixteen years after the Battle of Endor, Shada stopped Karoly from performing an assassination and came under punishment from the Eleven who led the Mistryl. She left Mazzic's employment to avoid the Mistryl hunter teams, seeking to join up with the New Republic. Instead, Leia Organa Solo offered Shada's services to Talon Karrde, who was heading into the Kathol sector to locate a copy of the Caamas Document. Shada accompanied him, and the two grew fond of each other. When Karrde located information that revealed the truth about the fake Grand Admiral Thrawn, Shada was there to stop the cloned Major Grodin Tierce from killing Gilad Pellaeon and the Mistryl leader, Paloma D'asima. As a result the hunter teams were called off, and Shada officially joined Karrde's new joint intelligence organization. [LC, LCSB, SP, TMEC, VF]

dukha

A large, cylindrical building with a cone-shaped roof found at the center of every Noghri village. The interior is a single open room that contains the clan high seat, used by the dynast, or clan leader, when he or she holds an audience. [DFR, DFRSB]

D'ulin, Karoly

A Mistryl Shadow Guard involved in the transport of the Hammertong device for the Death Star. Sixteen years after the Battle of Endor, the Eleven who ruled the Mistryl sent her to kill Shada D'akul. She failed and was eventually saved by Shada when Major Grodin Tierce attempted to kill Karoly, one of the Eleven, and Admiral Gilad Pellaeon. [SP, TMEC, VF]

D'ulin, Manda

A Mistryl Shadow Guard and team leader for the mission to transport the Hammertong device to the Empire. She was killed in an Imperial raid after the mission went bad. [TMEC]

Dulok

This lanky, unkempt, bug-infested species is distantly related to the Ewoks. In general, Duloks are nasty, bad-tempered, and untrustworthy. A large Dulok tribe lives in a village in the marshlands of Endor's forest moon. [ETV]

Dune Sea

A vast desert that stretches across Tatooine's wastes and was once a large inland sea. This area is inhospitable due to extreme temperature variations and a lack of water. Ben Kenobi lived in the western portion of the Dune Sea. [SW]

dungeon ship

A gigantic capital ship used to transport prisoners from one system to another via hyperspace. These massive vessels were originally designed during the Clone Wars to hold Jedi Knights. [DE]

Dunhausen, Grand Moff

This lean and crafty human always wore his trademark laser-pistol-shaped earrings. [GDV]

Dunwell, Captain

The crazed human commander of the Whaladon hunting submarine that operated below the waves of Mon Calamari. With his blue uniform, gaudy medals, and neatly trimmed white beard, Captain Dunwell was almost dashing. His obsession destroyed this illusion, however. His main goal was to capture Leviathor, leader of the Whaladon. [GDV]

dura-armor

Industrial-strength military armor capable of diverting and absorbing blaster fire. It is constructed by compressing and binding neutronium, lommite, and zersium molecules together through the process of matrix acceleration. [HSE]

durasheet

A paperlike material used to write on. The writing fades after a short period of time, allowing the material to be reused. [HSR]

durasteel

Ultralightweight metal, it can withstand radical temperature extremes and severe stress due to mechanical operations. Durasteel is used to build everything from aircraft and space vehicles to dwellings and machinery. [SW]

Durga the Hutt

A Hutt crimelord and Black Sun Vigo, or top lieutenant, who was considered to be almost as crafty and deceptive as Prince Xizor himself. He secretly worked toward rallying the Vigos to overthrow Xizor but was unable to gather much support in this effort. Later, he masterminded the top secret Darksaber Project. The effort to build a new superweapon failed, and Durga was killed. [DS, SESB, SOTE]

durkii

A hideous, three-meter-tall creature with the face of a baboon and the body of a reptilian kangaroo. [DTV]

Duro

A planet in the Duro system and the homeworld of the Duros species. The star system contains vast orbiting cities and shipyards. It is governed by a group of starship corporations whose stockholders tried to remain neutral throughout the Galactic Civil War. The planet is covered with uninhabited, automated farms that produce food for the people living in the space cities.

Han Solo's ancestor Korol Solo, a pretender to the throne of Corellia, married and had a son on Duro. [CPL, DA, GG4, KT]

Duroon

This planet within the Corporate Sector was the site of a major Corporate Sector Authority installation that used slave labor. The planet boasts three moons that hang above a surface dotted with lush jungles located between volcanic vents and fissures. Prior to his involvement with the Rebellion, Han Solo took on a job to deliver weapons to the disgruntled migrant workers who were in the midst of revolting against the Corporate Sector Authority. [CSSB, HSE]

Duros

Tall, thin humanoids with large eyes, a thin slit for mouths, and no nose. Members of this species hail from the planet Duro and have traveled the space lanes for thousands of years. [GG4]

Durren

A planet located in a system of the same name, in the Meridian sector. It is the site of the Durren Orbital Station, a major New Republic fleet installation. The New Republic agreed to protect the system in exchange for the establishment of the naval base. [POT]

Durron, Kyp

This human grew up in the Imperial Correctional Facility on Kessel, where he mined the glitterstim spice drug. His parents were executed and his older brother, Zeth, was sent to the Imperial Academy on Carida. An old woman named Vima-Da-Boda arrived at the prison some years after Kyp. She was a Jedi Knight from the days of the Old Republic, and she sensed Kyp's connection to the Force. She trained him until she was removed from the prison.

Seven years after the Battle of Endor, Han Solo and Chewbacca met Kyp when they were mistakenly imprisoned in the mine. Kyp used his Force powers to help Han and

Chewbacca escape, and Luke Skywalker invited him to become a student at his Jedi academy on Yavin 4. There, the spirit of the long-dead Sith Lord Exar Kun, which was trapped within a Yavin temple, showed Kyp the ways of the dark side and convinced him to release the Sun Crusher—a major Imperial weapon—from its resting place in the heart of the gas giant Yavin. When Luke tried to stop them, Kyp and Kun trapped Luke's spirit outside his body, placing the Jedi in a deathlike state.

Kyp Durron

With the Sun Crusher, Kyp almost destroyed Admiral Daala when she was about to launch an attack on Coruscant. He tried to find his brother, but accidentally incinerated Zeth along with the planet Carida. Other Jedi trainees eventually destroyed Kun's spirit and freed Kyp from his influence. Luke agreed to continue Kyp's training, and the two teamed up to destroy both the Sun Crusher and a prototype Death Star.

Twenty-one years after the Battle of Endor, Jedi Knight Kyp Durron led a starfighter squadron he called the Dozen-and-Two Avengers. It featured twelve of the best pilots he could find, as well as two Jedi—himself and his apprentice, Miko Reglia. After a brief rest at Dubrillion, Kyp took his squadron to investigate strange happenings at the planet Helska 4. There, the squadron was engaged by the coralskippers of the invading Yuuzhan Vong. The entire squadron was lost. Only Kyp escaped, to be rescued by Han Solo. Later, Kyp helped defeat the Yuuzhan Vong's first invasion force, fighting alongside Luke Skywalker and the Solo children—Jacen, Jaina, and Anakin. [DS, JAL, JS, SWCG, VP]

Durron, Zeth

Kyp Durron's older brother, he was separated from the family during a stormtrooper raid of their home on the Deyer Colony and sent to the Imperial military training center on Carida. Many years later, Kyp tried to rescue Zeth using the Sun Crusher, but instead killed his brother and destroyed the planet. [DS, JS]

Dusat, Jord

A native of the planet Ingo, he learned to race landspeeders over desolate, crater-studded acid salt flats. He was the best friend and main race competitor of Thall Joben. Jord was a bit of a rebel and a troublemaker, though he dreamed of becoming a professional speeder racer. R2-D2 and C-3PO encountered him in the early days of the Empire. [DTV]

Duskhan League

A federation of colonies and worlds in the Koornacht Cluster, under the control of the Yevetha species from the planet N'zoth. Nil Spaar led the League and pushed his xenophobic people into a campaign to conquer and exterminate non-Yevetha throughout the region. [BTS, SOL, TT]

Dustangle

An archaeologist who hid in the underground caverns of Duro after the Empire subjugated the world. His cousin was Dustini. [MMY]

Dustini

An archaeologist from the planet Duro, he appealed to the Alliance for help for his subjugated world. His cousin was Dustangle. [MMY]

Dutch

The lead pilot of Gold Squadron, a Y-wing starfighter squadron that participated in the Battle of Yavin. [SW]

Duull, Vor

Proctor of information science on the Yevethan Duskhan League's embassy ship *Aramadia.* [BTS]

Duvel, Mayth

A sublieutenant in the Black Sun criminal organization. [SOTE]

D-V9 (DEEVEE)

This research droid belonged to anthropologist Mammon Hoole. It watched over his niece and nephew, Zak and Tash Arranda, whenever Hoole was busy—which was most of the time. D-V9 was badly damaged in a fight on Kova and retired to the Galactic Research Academy on Koaan. [GF]

D'vouran

This planet apparently appeared out of nowhere. Created as part of the first experiment in Project Starscream, it was a living planet that devoured living beings and could travel through hyperspace. The planet apparently devoured itself and was destroyed after swallowing a pendant with an Imperial energy field designed to protect the wearer from D'vouran. [GF]

Dxo'ln, Kid

Han Solo accompanied this smuggler on one of his first runs to Kessel. Years later, Dxo'ln helped Solo free Lando Calrissian from the crimelord Nandreeson. [NR]

Dxun

One of four moons that orbit the planet Onderon. Also known as the Demon Moon because of the monstrous creatures that fill its thick jungles, it is the site of a Mandalorian iron tomb built some 4,000 years before the Galactic Civil War to hold the remains of Queen Amanoa and Freedon Nadd. Exar Kun visited the tomb, and the spirit of Nadd helped him locate hidden Sith scrolls. [DLS, FNU, TOJ, TSW]

Dying Slowly
This town, later known as Death, was the hub of smuggling on the planet Jubilar. [TBH]

Dymurra
Chief executive for the Core systems for Loronar Corporation, he provided the weapons so that factions in the Chorios systems could revolt. This split the attention of New Republic peacekeeping forces and allowed Imperial Moff Getelles to move in. [POT]

Dzym
Appearing as a small brown-skinned man, he was ostensibly Seti Ashgad's secretary. In reality, he was an insectoid captain droch who was altered, mutated, and grown well past his natural size. He was the mastermind behind the Nam Chorios crisis, controlling both Ashgad and Beldorian the Hutt by keeping them alive and young. Dzym himself was about 250 years old. He attempted to escape the planet, but Luke Skywalker destroyed his ship. [POT]

8D8 (Atedeate)
A thin-faced, white-colored droid who worked in Jabba the Hutt's robot operations center as a subordinate to EV-9D9 (Eve-Ninedenine). [RJ]

E522 Assassin
This assassin droid had a narrow waist, huge shoulders, and a flat head. Jabba covered the droid in meat and fed it to a rancor, but the beast spit it out. The droid was later repaired and reprogrammed to serve Lady Valarian. [TMEC]

Ean
A Mon Calamari and member of Wedge Antilles's command crew aboard the New Republic cruiser *Yavin*. [NR]

Eba

Jaina Solo's Wookiee doll. [CS]

Ebrihim

An elderly male Drall who was hired to tutor and guide Leia and Han Solo's children while they visited Corellia. [AC]

Ebsuk, Zubindi

This Kubaz was Beldorian the Hutt's chef on Nam Chorios. His quest to create the perfect designer food and his insect-preparation methods led to the mutation of the droch, Dzym, who fed off Ebsuk until he was powerful enough to enslave Beldorian. [POT]

Echo Base

The comm-unit designation for the secret Alliance command headquarters under the command of General Carlist Rieekan on the ice planet Hoth. The Alliance was forced to abandon Echo Base during an Imperial attack. [ESB]

Echo Station Three-Eight

An isolated Alliance outpost located on the planet Hoth. Each sentry outpost used the comm-unit designation "Echo Station" when transmitting and receiving communications from Echo Base. This particular outpost was destroyed by an Imperial probe droid as a prelude to the full-scale invasion, the Battle of Hoth. [ESB]

Eckels, Dr. Joto

A field researcher and archaeologist for the Obroan Institute, Dr. Joto Eckels headed up the excavation at Maltha Obex. [BTS, SOL, TT]

Eclipse

The reborn Emperor ordered the construction of a seventeen-and-a-half-kilometer-long Super Star Destroyer to serve as his personal flagship. The huge solid-black vessel was designed to inspire dread and hopelessness in every opponent. Luke Skywalker and Leia Organa Solo combined their Force energy to stun the Emperor long enough for his own Force storms to consume the vessel. [DE, DESB, SWVG]

Edict

Admiral Daala's Imperial shuttle. [DA, JS]

Eelysa

A young woman from Coruscant, born after the Emperor's death, she was one of Luke Skywalker's most promising students at the Jedi academy on Yavin 4. [NR]

effrikim worm

This two-headed worm is a favorite snack food of Hutts. [TJP]

Eiattu VI

This planet, covered with light forests and murky swamps, is home to dinosaurlike beasts of burden with bright-colored feathers. The capital is a port city, built out over and below a bay. Quarren live in the underwater zones. [XW]

Eicroth, Dr. Joi

An archaeologist, she examined Qellan remains from Maltha Obex. [TT]

Eistern

Once a member of the Black Sword Command, he betrayed Nil Spaar at the Battle of N'zoth. This led to the New Republic victory over the Yevethan forces. [TT]

Ekibo

A Trianii colony world located within the disputed border of the Corporate Sector. [CSSB]

Elarles

A waiter at a bar on Circarpous V. [SME]

electrobinoculars

A handheld viewing device used to observe distant objects in most lighting conditions. The device's internal display provides the user with information regarding an object's range, relative and true azimuths, and elevation. While sometimes mistaken for macrobinoculars, electrobinoculars are superior instruments because they offer computer-enhanced imaging capabilities. [ESB, SW]

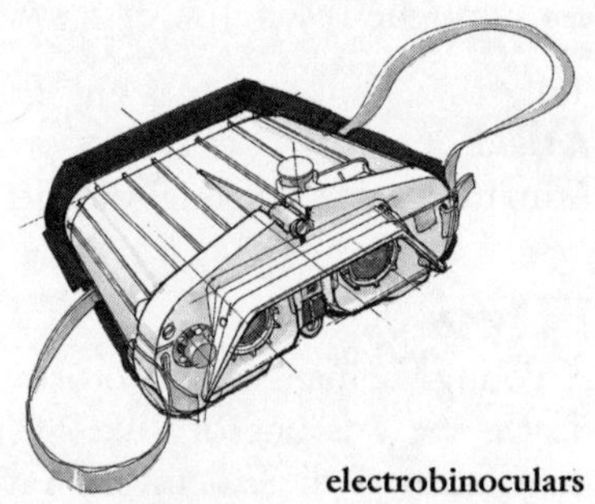
electrobinoculars

electro-jabber

A high-voltage prod used for crowd control or torture. These devices are also called force pikes. [RJ]

electrorangefinder

A device that calculates the distance between itself and a target object. These devices are incorporated into electrobinoculars and macrobinoculars and are essential components in the targeting and fire-control computers used by artillery and ship-mounted weapons systems. [ESB, GG3]

elite stormtroopers

See Coruscant Guards.

Elom

A cold, barren world that joined the Rebellion to combat the tyranny of the Empire and free itself from enslavement. The planet's principal export is lommite ore. Because of the world's location in the Borderland Regions, the Elomin feared reprisals from the reorganized Imperial forces under Grand Admiral Thrawn's command. [HE, HESB, SOL, TT]

Elomin

Tall, thin humanoids from the planet Elom. They sport tusked noses, wide-set eyes, pointed ears, and four hornlike protrusions emerging from the tops of their heads. Elomin admire order. During the last years of the Galactic Civil War and well into the period of the New Republic, the Elomin have tended to serve in units made up exclusively of their own species. During the height of the Empire, the Elomin and their world were placed under martial law. They were forced to labor for the Imperial effort, mining lommite for their Imperial masters. After the Battle of Endor, the Elomin took a place among the member worlds of the New Republic. [HE, HESB]

Eloms

Short, stocky humanoids that dwell in caves on Elom. This primitive species is generally peaceful and quiet, easily coexisting with the more advanced Elomin. [GG12]

Eloy, Dr.

Senior scientist for the Hammertong project. [TMEC]

Elrood

A planet orbited by two moons, it is the site of a commercial colony and trade center. The capital city, Elrooden, is home to the famous Elrood Bazaar. [COJ, POG]

Elshandruu Pica

A planet in the Elshandruu system, it has two white moons and one red moon. The capital city is Picavil, the site of Margath's hotel and casino complex. Pirates use a nearby asteroid belt as a staging area. [BW, GG9]

Emancipator

Originally known as the *Accuser*, this was one of two Imperial Star Destroyers captured by the Alliance during the Battle of Endor. Admiral Ragab commanded the renamed vessel during the raids on Borleias and the conquest of Coruscant. Lando Calrissian and Wedge Antilles commanded it during the Battle of Calamari. It was destroyed by *Silencer-7*, an Imperial World Devastator. [BW, DE, DESB]

Emperor

See Palpatine, Emperor.

Emperor's Citadel

A great black tower at the center of the throne city that served as the reborn clone Emperor's fortified palace on the planet Byss. [DE]

Emperor's Hand

The code name used by Mara Jade when she served as one of the Emperor's elite operatives. Her job was to act as the Emperor's eyes and ears throughout the galaxy, communicating with him at great distances through the Force. She carried out his orders, accomplishing missions that were beyond his other agents. Grand Admiral Thrawn's comments to Mara years later suggested that she was but one of several such operatives. [DFR, HE, LC]

Emperor's Inner Circle

Ministers and governors close to the Emperor at the time of the Battle of Endor. After the Emperor's death, this group unsuccessfully attempted to take control of the Empire. [DE]

Emperor's Royal Guard

Elite Imperial soldiers, they served as the Emperor's personal guards. Only the most promising stormtroopers—selected for their size, strength, intelligence, and loyalty—were chosen for this duty. They were trained in the use of a wide range of weapons and unarmed combat styles, and conditioned to obey the Emperor's will and protect him with their very lives. Royal Guards wore flowing red robes, helmets, and full body armor.

No one knew how many Royal Guards there were, though guesses ranged from as low as fifty to as many as tens of thousands. They reported only to Palpatine, and a handful was always near the Emperor. They were whatever the Emperor wished them to be—soldiers, assassins, bodyguards. They utilized two-meter-long force pikes and heavy blaster pistols.

The best members became Imperial Sovereign Protectors, charged with guarding Palpatine's palaces and monasteries, as well as the special clone vat on Byss. They wore a more ornate and ceremonial version of the red armor and were taught minor dark-side techniques by senior Dark Side Adepts in the Emperor's service. After the Battle of Endor, the Sovereign Protectors remained in place on Byss until the cloned Emperor returned six years later.

When the Emperor died at the Battle of Endor, some of the Royal Guard returned to Imperial Center to serve the Imperial vizier, Sate Pestage. Some remained with the stormtrooper units they had been rotated into, seeking to go down fighting for the Empire. Others remained aloof, following the Emperor's true ideals in secret. After the cloned Emperors fell, the traitorous Carnor Jax ordered Imperial stormtroopers to eliminate all of the Royal Guard, claiming that they were traitors to the Empire. Only one guardsman survived: Kir Kanos. [CE, DE, DESB, RJ, SWSB]

Emperor's skyhook

This orbiting structure tethered to the ground hung above the capital on Imperial Center. Its wide terrace overlooked a park of evergreen and deciduous trees. [SOTE]

Emperor's throne room

Every *Imperial*-class or *Super*-class Star Destroyer, both Death Star battle stations, and every other Imperial location maintained a special throne room set aside for the Emperor's use.

From each throne room, the Emperor could monitor all activity, take control of his fleet, and contemplate the dark side of the Force. [DSTC, RJ]

Empire, the

It lasted for decades, a regime that was transformed from republic to absolute monarchy. The Empire reigned supreme from the time Senator Palpatine donned the Emperor's cowl to his presumed death at the Battle of Endor. The Emperor's regime originally was supposed to eradicate corruption and social injustices, but it quickly became evident that it had no intention of returning the galaxy to a state of peace and justice. This government corrected the many mistakes that made the Old Republic ineffective and unwieldy, but it also installed programs designed to subjugate as many planetary governments as possible, for the personal glory and benefit of the Emperor. The Empire was a regime of tyranny and evil, bolstered by a vast war machine and the scheming of millions who found personal gain in subjugating the inhabitants of the galaxy.

After the Battle of Endor, the Empire was reduced to a quarter of the size it boasted at the height of the Emperor's power. While it continued to rule a small portion of the galaxy and waged battles against the New Republic government, it was nothing more than a remnant. In many ways, the Empire that existed after the Battle of Endor was much like the Rebel Alliance it had once fought—disorganized, lacking in firepower, and engaged in a hit-and-run style of warfare. It showed some signs of its old glory under Grand Admiral Thrawn and the reborn Emperor, but the New Republic was able to win out against both of these threats. [DE, DFR, ESB, HE, LC, RJ, SW, SWSB, etc.]

Empire Reborn

A movement aimed at undermining the New Republic. It was led by Lord Hethrir. [CS]

Empress' Diadem

A modified Corellian light freighter used by Melina Carniss when she worked for Talon Karrde. [BW]

Empress Teta system
See Teta system, Empress.

Em Teedee
A tiny translator droid built by Chewbacca to convert Wookiee speech into Basic. C-3PO programmed the droid, which tended to talk more than it had to. Chewbacca made it for his nephew, Lowbacca, who was a trainee at Luke Skywalker's Jedi academy. [YJK]

Emtrey (Emtreypio)
An M-3PO military protocol droid designed to handle requisitions, duty assignments, and other administrative tasks for Rogue Squadron. Its programming included fluency in more than six million languages and familiarity with a similar number of military doctrines, regulations, codes of honor, and protocols. [BW]

Enara
A Fallanassi female who helped free Han Solo from the Yevethan ship *Pride of Yevetha*. She utilized her illusory powers to trick Nil Spaar into believing that his prisoners were still aboard the ship. She decided to remain aboard the ship herself, declining to escape with the others. [TT]

e'Naso, Bracha
A smuggler, he sold supplies to Chewbacca during the Yevethan crisis. The supplies were used to rescue Han Solo. [TT]

Endor (Sanctuary Moon)
Located in the remote Endor system in the Moddell sector, the silvery gas giant planet Endor was orbited by nine moons. The Endor star system was selected as the construction site of the second Death Star battle station. It became famous as the system in which the Alliance finally won the Galactic Civil War by destroying the Death Star, killing the Emperor, and scattering the remnants of the Imperial fleet.

The largest moon was itself the size of a small planet and was known as the forest moon, the Sanctuary Moon, and simply Endor. The system was difficult to reach, as the uncharted territory and the massive gravitational shadow of the gas giant required several complicated hyperspace jumps to navigate. The moon has a temperate climate, with forests, savannas, and mountains. It is home to many forms of life, including boarwolves, Wisties, Teeks, Yootaks, Gorax, Marauders, and Ewoks.

A cloud of dark-side energy left over from the Emperor's death orbited the moon at the site of the Death Star's destruction. [COJ, DA, DESB, DFR, ETV, ISWU, JS, RJ, RJN, SWSB, XW]

Endor, Battle of

The Battle of Endor was the most decisive engagement of the Galactic Civil War. The Alliance to Restore the Republic and the Galactic Empire clashed near the forest moon of Endor in a battle that saw the deaths of both Emperor Palpatine and Lord Darth Vader.

The Empire had selected the forest moon as the construction site for its second Death Star battle station. Bothan spies intercepted information that named the secret construction site, and provided its location to the Rebels. In addition, those same spies learned that the Emperor himself was heading to Endor in order to supervise the final stages of construction. The Alliance decided that this would be its best opportunity to strike a blow at the Imperial war machine and to get at the Emperor outside of his impenetrable Imperial City fortress.

As Admiral Ackbar gathered the Rebel Alliance fleet around the planet Sullust, a special strike team was sent ahead to sabotage the shield generator protecting the unfinished Death Star. The strike team, led by Han Solo and including Luke Skywalker, Leia Organa, Chewbacca, the droids R2-D2 and C-3PO, and a squad of Rebel commandos, used a stolen Imperial shuttle to get through the Empire's forces and down to the moon's surface. The strike team had to disable or destroy the shield generator by the time the Rebel fleet emerged from hyperspace so that the surprise attack could begin.

Unfortunately, the information, which many Bothans died to deliver to Alliance High Command, turned out to be a deception planned by the Emperor himself. The unfinished Death Star was not as helpless as it appeared, for its superlaser was fully operational. As for the strike team, a full legion of stormtroopers and other Imperial soldiers were waiting to defend the shield generator and capture the Rebel commandos. While the strike team battled on Endor's moon, the Rebel fleet arrived to find the protective shield still in place. The battle, it seemed, was over before it had begun.

The Emperor's plan called for the Imperial fleet to remain in reserve on the far side of the moon while swarms of TIE fighters engaged the outnumbered Rebel ships. Alliance starfighters met their Imperial counterparts in dramatic dogfights as the Emperor looked on. The TIE onslaught was but the first stage of the Emperor's trap. The second stage involved turning the Death Star's prime weapon upon the Alliance's capital ships—vaporizing each one in its path.

Lando Calrissian, leading the Alliance starfighters from the command seat of the *Millennium Falcon*, convinced Ackbar of a new course of action. By engaging the poised but as yet docile Star Destroyers in ship-to-ship combat, the Rebel ships would be using the Empire's own vessels as protection from the Death Star's weapon. The Star Destroyers were more powerful than the Rebel ships, but not by the magnitude of the Death Star. The Alliance bought itself some time through this tactic, but it still needed the strike team to succeed if it was going to have a chance at winning the day.

On the forest moon, the native Ewoks became the key to victory. The primitive natives had been dismissed as inconsequential by the Imperial troops. This mistake was to prove the Empire's undoing. The same Ewoks who had befriended the strike team helped free them, allowing Solo and his companions to carry out the sabotage mission. When the shield generators were destroyed, the protective shield surrounding the Death Star disappeared.

As soon as the opening presented itself, Lando Calrissian and his starfighters moved to attack. The *Falcon* and Wedge Antilles's X-wing flew into the unfinished Death Star's superstructure and fired proton torpedoes at the battle station's power regulator. Simultaneously, Lando Calrissian fired concussion missiles at the main reactor. The resulting explosions destroyed the Death Star with the Emperor on board.

Without the Emperor, the dark side became diffused, and Imperial forces were plunged into confusion. What remained of the Imperial fleet scattered, and this phase of the Galactic Civil War came to an end. [RJ]

Endurance

A carrier in the New Republic's Fifth Fleet. A Super Star Destroyer destroyed the *Endurance* at Orinda. [BTS]

energy gate

A static, preset force field operated from a distance and used to regulate access routes in detention centers and other high-security areas. [SWN]

Engh, First Administrator Nanaod

A New Republic minister who urged Chief of State Leia Organa Solo to utilize public relations techniques to improve her public image. [BTS, SOL]

Engret

This boy was one of the infiltrators who sought the Corporate Sector Authority Data Center on Orron III to learn the location of political prisoners. [HSE]

enhanced human

A human who has been surgically and biologically altered to be larger and stronger than normal. Members of the Empire Reborn movement were enhanced by Lord Hethrir's experiments. [CS]

entechment

This Ssi-ruuk technology is the process of converting the life energy of sentient creatures into a power source. The life energy is absorbed into specialized battery coils to power battle-droid or shipboard circuitry. The process involves the injection of a magnetic solution into a subject's nervous system. This causes external circuitry to become tuned to the internal magnetization, allowing the life energy to leap to storage coils when the electromagnetic field around the coils is activated. The process works on all sentient beings, but the Ssi-ruuk found that humans—especially Force-sensitive humans—provide the most power. [TAB, TBSB]

Enzeen

Natives of the living planet D'vouran, they are blue-skinned humanoids with needlelike spines instead of hair. They are parasites, luring visitors to D'vouran in return for sustenance from the planet itself. Like the planet, they were created by Imperial scientists. None of the Enzeen survived the destruction of D'vouran. [GF]

Eol Sha

This volcanic world was the site of a hundred-year-old mining colony. After the colony failed, the settlers were forgotten for generations until the New Republic relocated their descendants to Dantooine. While they were still establishing the new colony, Admiral Daala's fleet wiped them out. Eol Sha itself was presumed destroyed when the nearby Cauldron Nebula went nova. [DA, JS]

Erg Es 992

A star in the Meridian sector orbited by the planet Cybloc and its inhabited moon, Cybloc XII. [POT]

Eriadu

This polluted factory planet in the Seswenna sector is an Outer Rim trade and government hub. It was the capital world of the territory controlled by Grand Moff Tarkin. Tarkin was traveling from Eriadu to Despayre to view the newly completed Death Star when an Alliance strike force attacked his shuttle. The grand moff was saved by the arrival of a Star Destroyer, but the Alliance rescued Tarkin's servant, the Mon Calamari Ackbar. [COJ, DESB, DS, DSTC]

Errant Venture

The former *Virulence*, this was Booster Terrik's flagship. [BW]

escape pod

A space capsule used by passengers and crew to abandon capital-class starships or small freighters in emergency situations. Escape pods range in size from small capsules barely large enough for two passengers to huge lifeboats capable of carrying many refugees. Most escape pods feature stores of emergency supplies and offer limited life support, navigation, and propulsion units. These pods are not designed for long trips. The basic idea is to provide a safe and stable environment for a limited duration should the main ship have to be abandoned. A pod is designed to float through space until a rescue vessel picks up its distress broadcast and arrives to provide aid. [SW, SWSB]

escape pod station

See lifeboat bay.

escort carrier

A 500-meter-long, boxlike vessel designed to provide Imperial TIE fighter support. Each such inelegant craft carried an entire TIE fighter wing in its cavernous bays and transported the fighters through hyperspace. Smaller bays carried up to six shuttles or other support craft. With only ten twin laser cannons, an escort carrier was not considered a combat vessel. It preferred to stay as far from the battle as possible, serving as a refueling and supply point for the TIEs it carried. [ISB]

escort frigate

The 300-meter-long Nebulon-B escort frigate combat starship was originally built by the Kuat Drive Yards for the Empire. The Empire saw this vessel as the solution to its problems with Rebel raids on supply convoys. The escort frigate proved a great deterrent to Rebel attacks. Fortunately, a significant number of these vessels either defected or were captured by the Rebellion and joined the Alliance fleet. [SWSB]

Espo

Slang term for the private security police employed by the Corporate Sector Authority. Espos are among the worst law-enforcement personnel in the galaxy. They follow no code of law or justice except for the edicts of the Authority. They are unquestioning bullies dressed in brown uniforms, combat armor, and black battle helmets and armed with blaster rifles and riot guns. [HSE, HSR]

Essada, Bin

The Imperial military governor presiding over the Circarpous Major star system. This portly man wore his black hair in a curly fashion, with a spiral orange pattern on top. His eyes had pink pupils, hinting at a not-quite-human origin. [SME]

Estillo, Asrandatha

The son of the royal family on Eiattu VI, he was believed to have been killed along with the rest of his family. Later, Darth Vader sent forth an impostor who claimed to be the royal prince. He was an unwitting dupe who was supposed to lead a phony liberation movement, kill the other nobles who still shared power with the Empire on the planet, and leave the spoils for Eiattu VI's moff. [XW]

Etti IV

A wealthy, hospitable planet on a major stellar trade route within Corporate Sector space. It is home to many of the more affluent and influential Corporate Sector Authority executives. The planet has no exportable resources, so it relies on its natural beauty and prime location to attract visitors and traders. [CSSB, D, HSE]

EV-9D9 (Eve-Ninedenine)

A thin droid with a female voice and sadistic attitude, she was the supervisor of Cyborg Operations in Jabba the Hutt's palace. Prior to working for Jabba, she had destroyed a number of droids on Cloud City. After Jabba's death, she was tracked down and destroyed by the droid 1-2:4C:4-1 (Wuntoo Forcee Forwun). [RJ, TJP]

EV-9D9.2 (Eve-Ninedeninetwo)

Supervisor for Cyborg Operations at the droid manufacturing facility on Telti. After R2-D2 and C-3PO shut down the droids on Telti, R2-D2 dismantled EV-9D9.2's torture instrumentation. [NR]

Evazan, Dr.

An insane doctor who associated with the Aqualish smuggler Ponda Baba and practiced "creative surgery." He disassembled body parts and put them back together in different ways on living creatures. He escaped Imperial institutionalization and used a forged medical license to butcher hundreds of patients in many different star systems. He used a variety of aliases, including Roofoo and Dr. Cornelius.

Doctor Evazan

With the death sentence on his head in more than a dozen star systems, Evazan was eventually tracked down by the bounty hunter Jodo Kast. Evazan's face was badly scarred in the encounter, but Ponda Baba helped him escape. They went on to become partners, smuggling spice for Jabba the Hutt.

The pair assaulted Luke Skywalker in the Mos Eisley cantina on Tatooine. Ben Kenobi was forced to subdue them, slicing Evazan's chest and cutting off Baba's right arm with his lightsaber. After a few misadventures wherein Evazan failed to replace Baba's arm with a cybernetic one but succeeded in transferring the brain of an Ando senator into Baba's body, Boba Fett caught up with the mad doctor and killed him while Evazan was experimenting to bring the dead back to life. [GF, GG1, SW, SWCG, SWR, SWSB]

Eviscerator

An Imperial II Star Destroyer, it patrolled the Mirit, Pyria, and Venjagga systems. [BW]

Evocar

Former homeworld of the Evocii, it was later renamed Nal Hutta. [DESB]

E-wing starfighter

A starfighter introduced to the New Republic fleet during Grand Admiral Thrawn's campaign to reclaim the Empire's glory. A single pilot controls the craft and its advanced armament, and the R7 series astromech droid provides system assistance. Its increased firepower includes triple laser cannons and sixteen proton torpedoes. [DE, SWVG]

Ewok

Curious, primitive, furry humanoids native to Endor's forest moon. About one meter tall, Ewoks possess a tribal culture and society that uses spears, bows, slings, catapults, and similar less-advanced tools and weapons. Through intense teamwork, understanding of their environment, and well-honed survival skills, they flourish on the forest moon. A musical species, Ewoks are overly curious and loyal to both tribe and friends.

Most Ewoks are hunter-gatherers who live in village clusters built high within the moon's giant trees. Easily startled, the Ewoks are nonetheless brave, alert, and loyal, and they can be fierce warriors when necessary. Dismissed as inconsequential by the Empire during the construction of the second Death Star, the Ewoks proved one of the deciding factors in the Battle of Endor. One tribe befriended Leia Organa and her companions in the Rebel strike force. With the help this tribe provided, the strike force was able to complete its mission to disable the shield generator that protected the second Death Star. This allowed the Alliance fleet to engage the battle station directly and win the space battle that raged around the forest moon.

Ewoks

The Ewok language is liquid and expressive, and most humans and other aliens are able to learn to speak it. Ewoks, conversely, can learn Basic, though they often mix in many words from their own language. During the day, Ewoks descend from their tree villages to hunt and forage on the forest floor. At night, the forest belongs to huge carnivores, and even the youngest Ewoks know not to venture out after dark.

The Ewok religion is centered around the giant trees of the forest moon. Legends refer to the trees as guardian spirits and even the parents of the people, which is why the Ewoks believe that the great trees are mighty, intelligent, long-lived beings. The Ewoks' mystical beliefs contain many references to the Force, though it is never named as such. Whenever a baby Ewok is born, the village plants a new seedling and nurtures it as it grows. Each Ewok is linked to his or her totem tree; when they die, it is believed that their spirits go to live in their special trees. [BFE, EA, ETV, ISWU, RJ, SWSB]

Executioners Row

A slum located at the edge of the town Dying Slowly on the planet Jubilar. Boba Fett killed spice trader Hallolar Voors in one of the slum's warehouses. [TBH]

Executor

This *Super*-class Star Destroyer was Darth Vader's personal flagship. It was the first of its class, approximately five times larger than the *Imperial*-class Star Destroyer, measuring 8,000 meters from bow to stern. It was presented to the Dark Lord shortly after the Battle of Yavin and the destruction of the first Death Star. It was constructed at the shipyards on the world Fondor.

Originally under the command of Admiral Ozzel, it was entrusted to Admiral Piett after Ozzel was killed for failing Darth Vader. It was destroyed at the Battle of Endor when it was forced to crash into the second Death Star. [ESB, HE, ISB, MTS, RJ]

EX-F

A weapons and propulsion test bed commandeered by the Yevetha at N'zoth and made part of Nil Spaar's Black Fifteen Fleet. It was renamed *Glory of Yevetha*. [BTS]

ExGal Society

A scientific organization dedicated to watching for signs of extragalactic life. ExGal Society outposts situated on worlds along the galactic rim turn powerful sensors toward the edge of the galaxy to look for communications or actual visitors from beyond the known galaxy. ExGal-4, the ExGal outpost on the planet Belkadan, spotted the Yuuzhan Vong invasion force as it breached the galactic boundary, but all its scientists were killed by a Yuuzhan Vong agent before they could warn ExGal Command. [VP]

Exis Station

An isolated space city in the Teedio system, it was the location of a Jedi convocation called by Nomi Sunrider about ten years after the Sith War. The station was also the repository for artifacts recovered from the planet Ossus. [TOJR]

Exodeen

A former Imperial world located in the center of the old Empire. The planet was considered to be unimportant by the Emperor because its native species was nonhumanoid. [NR]

Exodo II

A planet near Odos and the Spangled Veil Nebula in the Meridian sector, known for its stormy atmosphere and plains of hard, black lava. [POT]

Exozone

An insectoid bounty hunter, he often worked with Boba Fett and Dengar. He helped the pair chase Han Solo and Leia Organa Solo through the streets of Nar Shaddaa. [DE]

Expansion Region

Once a center of manufacturing and heavy industry, it was started as an experiment in corporate-controlled space. When the residents demanded more freedom and change, the Old Republic turned control over to freely elected governments and sent the corporations elsewhere. Years later, the Empire allowed for the creation of the Corporate Sector. As much of the area's natural resources had been depleted, the region sought to pull itself out of an economic slump by maintaining trade routes and portraying itself as an alternative to the crowded and expensive Core Worlds and Colonies regions. [SWRPG2]

Expeditious

An Imperial *Carrack*-class light cruiser under the command of Captain Rojahn. [BW]

Eye of Palpatine

An Imperial battlemoon built eighteen years before the Battle of Yavin, under orders from Emperor Palpatine. The heavily armed space station was automated and designed to wipe out a Jedi enclave on the planet Belsavis. It never reached the planet, disappearing for thirty years thanks to the actions of the Jedi Callista and Geith. Luke Skywalker and his students Cray Mingla and Nichos Marr discovered the battlemoon in the Moonflower Nebula. The super artificial intelligence, known as the Will, that controlled the space station resumed its mission after being reawakened by the son of one of Palpatine's mistresses. In the end, Luke's students gave their lives to destroy the ship. The spirit of Callista passed into Cray's body at the last moment, allowing Callista to live again. [COJ]

4-LOM

A late-model protocol droid who worked aboard the passenger liner *Kuari Princess.* 4-LOM and the ship's computer helped each other alter their programming. 4-LOM became a master thief who garnered the attention of Jabba the Hutt. The crimelord further altered the droid's programming so it could respond to threats of violence. It became a bounty hunter for Jabba and was paired with the Gand tracker Zuckuss. The partners were part of the hunt for Han Solo, but during that time 4-LOM was reconsidering its place in the galaxy. 4-LOM and Zuckuss helped evacuate Rebel soldiers from Hoth, then unsuccessfully attempted to save the carbonite-encased Han Solo from Boba Fett. Later, 4-LOM joined the Rebellion and became a member of the Alliance Special Forces. [ESB, GG3, SOTE, SWCG, TBH]

5P8

A prowler ship in the New Republic's Fifth Fleet that located Plat Mallar's TIE interceptor near the Koornacht Cluster. [BTS]

F8GN (Eight-Gee-Enn)

This tall, spindly, copper-colored droid was programmed by Garris Shrike to teach children to beg, steal, and pick pockets. [PS]

Fadoop

Pilot and owner of the ship *Skybarge*, the green-furred, bandy-legged female was a member of the Saheelindeeli, an intelligent primate species of the Tion Hegemony. She had an intense liking for chak-root, and she once smuggled parts for Han Solo and Chewbacca in and around Corporate Sector space. [HLL]

Falanthas, Minister Mokka

New Republic minister of state at the time of the war with the Yevetha, this cautious individual took his time before officially allowing the Republic to get involved in that war. [SOL]

Fallanassi

A religious order whose members follow the White Current and whose skills are similar to the Jedi use of the Force. The sect members had to go into hiding when they refused the Emperor's offer of protection—in exchange for loyalty. [BTS, TT]

Falleen

Reptilian-humanoid aliens from a planet and star system of the same name, the Falleen are widely regarded as one of the more aesthetically pleasing species in the galaxy. With green-scaled hides, a pronounced spiny ridge running down their backs, powerful mood-altering pheromones, and the ability to change color, the Falleen are considered to be quite exotic. They are a long-lived species, averaging 250 standard years. The criminal Prince Xizor was a member of this species. [SESB, SOTE]

Falleen's Fist

This palatial skyhook was the personal property of Prince Xizor. The orbital installation floated above the surface of Coruscant. It served as Xizor's "country estate" and was filled with every exotic luxury the prince desired. During a final showdown with Xizor, the Dark Lord Darth Vader ordered a Star Destroyer to annihilate the skyhook. [SESB, SOTE]

Fall of the Sith Empire

The Sith were driven to near extinction in a battle that allied the armies of the Old Republic and Jedi Knights against the dark-side minions of Dark Lord Naga Sadow. That conflict occurred 4,000 years before the Galactic Civil War. [TSW]

Fandar

A brilliant Chadra-Fan scientist, he was the leader of Project Decoy. Fandar created a lifelike human replica droid for the Alliance. The prototype resembled Princess Leia. [QE]

Fandomar

The wife of Momaw Nadon, she was left behind on Ithor when Momaw was banished. [TMEC]

Fane, Captain

Captain of the *Tellivar Lady*, a transport ship that made regular runs to and from Tatooine. [TMEC]

Farana

A region of space located on the far side of the Corporate Sector. [SOL]

Fardreamer, Cole

A young boy from Tatooine who became a maintenance worker on Coruscant. His hero was Luke Skywalker, and he dreamed of attending the Jedi academy. His real talent was as a mechanic and engineer, however, and he became a hero when he helped uncover the threat posed by the dark-sider Kueller. [NR]

Farlax sector

An Imperially controlled region at the center of the Empire's Rim Territories that contain the Koornacht Cluster. After the Battle of Endor, Imperial forces abandoned the region and retreated to the Core. Twelve years later, eighteen planets in the sector petitioned to join the New Republic in a move designed to protect themselves against the growing aggression of the alien Yevetha. The New Republic's Fifth Fleet was sent to maintain the peace. [BTS, SOL]

Farlight

A New Republic ship sent to the planet Wehttam in anticipation of a Yevethan attack. [SOL]

Farng

A carbonite trader in the Empress Teta system. His imminent public execution led to a revolt in Cinnagar. [DLS]

Farnym

An alien species identified by their roundness, close-cut orange fur, and small snouts. Tchiery, copilot of the *Alderaan*, was a Farnym. [NR]

Farr, Samoc

A gifted Rebel snowspeeder pilot, she was badly injured during the Battle of Hoth. She escaped aboard the transport carrier *Bright Hope*, along with her sister, Toryn. [TBH]

Farr, Toryn

Chief communications officer of Echo Command, she was among the last to evacuate the command center during the Battle of Hoth. She escaped aboard the transport carrier *Bright Hope*, along with her sister, Samoc. [TBH]

Farrfin sector

One of the targets of Grand Admiral Thrawn's offensive against the New Republic. The sector contains the planet Farrfin and its native sentient species, the Farghul. [LC, LCSB]

FarStar

A Corellian corvette dispatched to hunt down Moff Kentor Sarne four years after the Battle of Endor. The pursuit took the ship deep into the Kathol Outback, to a little-explored region known as the Kathol Rift. [DSC]

Fass, Egome

A Houk with a square jaw and tiny, gleaming eyes set deep beneath his thick, bony brow. He worked for the outlaw twins J'uoch and R'all, and he was known to rival the mighty Chewbacca the Wookiee in both height and strength. [HLL]

Fast Hand

Lando Calrissian's Submersible Mining Environment on *GemDiver Station*. It was a diving bell used to mine Corusca gems from the gas giant Yavin's atmosphere. [YJK]

Faz

This planet in the Koornacht Cluster is one of the primary worlds of the Yevetha species and a member of the Duskhan League. [SOL]

feathers of light

Silver feathers awarded to young Ewoks who completed the journey to the Tree of Light to feed it nourishing light dust. [ETV]

Fef

This planet is home to the insectoid Fefze. [GG4]

Fel, Baron Soontir

Once one of the Empire's top pilots, this Corellian native went from hotshot TIE fighter ace to flight instructor, teaching cadets who would one day become some of the greatest pilots of the Rebel fleet. His students included Tycho Celchu, Biggs Darklighter, and Hobbie Klivian. Fel's career ended after cadets Darklighter and Klivian masterminded a daring mutiny.

While assigned to Imperial Center as a lowly pilot, Fel met and married holodrama star Wynssa Starflare. Starflare was really Syal Antilles, Wedge Antilles's sister. Fel rebuilt his reputation, earning medals, promotions, and a barony along the way. He made an enemy of Imperial Intelligence officer Ysanne Isard. He briefly joined Rogue Squadron after his wife disappeared, believing his ideals would be better served by the New Republic. He was eventually captured by Isard and later served Grand Admiral Thrawn. He became a senior staff member at Thrawn's hidden base, the Hand of Thrawn, and lost an eye in the final battle with the warlords of the Unknown Regions. Sixteen years after the Battle of Endor, he maintained his post at Thrawn's hidden base. [VF, XW]

Femon

Faithful assistant to the dark-sider Kueller, she had long black hair, an unnaturally pale complexion, blackened eyes, and bloodred lips. She withdrew her support of Kueller when she determined that he had the same weakness as the New Republic—he was unwilling to rule with an iron fist and crush his opposition when necessary. Kueller killed her with his Force powers. [NR]

Ferrier, Niles

A large human with dark hair and a beard, he dressed in ornate tunics and smoked long, thin cigarras. This jack-of-all-trades was best known as a starship thief. When Grand Admiral Thrawn placed a bounty of 20 percent over current market value for capital ships, Niles could not pass up the chance to make some quick credits. He worked with a small gang of five humans, a Verpine, and a Defel. Though Lando Calrissian and Luke Skywalker foiled Niles Ferrier's plans to steal a ship from the Sluis Van shipyards, he was able to provide Thrawn with an even greater prize—the location of the legendary *Katana* fleet. [DFR, DFRSB, LC]

ferrocrete

A superstrong building material. Nearly every structure on most Imperial worlds was built with this durable substance. [BW, LCF]

Ferros VI

Site of an Imperial prison camp. [DSTC]

Festival of Hoods

A celebration of the coming of age of young Ewoks. When a young Ewok receives his or her hood, it is a symbol that the young one has made the transition from wokling to preadolescent. [ETV]

Fett, Boba

The exploits of this infamous bounty hunter are known throughout the galaxy. Though his past is shrouded in mystery, some reports indicate that Boba Fett was born Jaster Mereel, who became a young journeyman protector, or law enforcement officer, on the planet Concord Dawn. When he supposedly killed a corrupt protector, he was tried, stripped of his possessions, and exiled. Later, after the Clone Wars, the man who came to be known as Boba Fett worked as a mercenary, a soldier, a personal guard, an assassin, and a bounty hunter—the role he was best known for.

Fett wears Mandalorian battle armor, the same used by a group of fearsome warriors whose exploits date back to ancient times. Some claim these warriors battled the Jedi Knights during the Clone Wars, but many of the records from that period are incomplete at best. Fett's armor is a weapon-covered spacesuit with armaments that include wrist lasers, a jet pack, rocket darts, a fibercord grappling device, and a miniature flame projector. His helmet features a macrobinocular viewplate, motion and sound sensors, infrared targeting, an internal comlink to his ship, and a broadband antenna for intercepting and decoding transmissions. He wears braided Wookiee scalps over his right shoulder.

Boba Fett

The bounty hunter works for whoever can pay his exorbitant rates, including Jabba the Hutt and the Empire. He was on retainer to Jabba for a good portion of his career, as well as to other Hutts, and he often claimed some of the largest bounties ever offered in the galaxy.

Over the years, Fett has had several encounters with the droids R2-D2 and C-3PO. He has also met both Han Solo and Luke Skywalker on various occasions, including encounters in the Panna system and on the frozen world Ota.

During the height of the Galactic Civil War, Fett accepted the same commission from both Jabba the Hutt and Darth Vader, agreeing to hunt down and capture Han Solo after the smuggler escaped from the Hoth system. He missed capturing Solo on Ord Mantell, but succeeded in tracking the smuggler to Bespin's Cloud City. There, Vader had Solo encased in carbonite, then Fett had the frozen smuggler placed aboard his ship, *Slave I,* for transport to Jabba's headquarters on Tatooine. During the resulting rescue carried out by Luke Skywalker, Fett was lost in the Great Pit of Carkoon.

Boba Fett escaped from the pit and was discovered by Dengar, another bounty hunter who had come searching for Jabba the Hutt's remains. Six years later, on Nar Shaddaa, Fett was once again on Han Solo's trail. Fett's contract this time belonged to the Hutts, who wanted Solo and Princess Leia captured alive so that they could be executed for what they did to Jabba. Han and Leia escaped, but Fett has continued to watch for opportunities to once again test his skills against Han Solo and his companions. [BF, DE, ESB, RJ, SWCG, SWSB, TBH]

Fey'lya, Borsk

A master diplomat and a political opportunist, he has served on the New Republic's Provisional and Inner Councils. He brought his Bothan faction into the Alliance after the Battle of Yavin, cutting deals with everyone to achieve a position of power in the galactic union to come. The Bothan spies who discovered the location of the second Death Star were from Borsk's faction, and even though that turned out to be a trap set by the Emperor, the Bothans were hailed as heroes. Fey'lya became one of Mon Mothma's most trusted advisers and a political opponent of military leader Admiral Ackbar.

Borsk Fey'lya

Fey'lya grew up on the Bothan colony world Kothlis. He sometimes appears to be a greedy, self-serving politician, but he has a Bothan's lust for power and is a master of politics. He funded Garm Bel Iblis's private war against the Empire in the hopes of gaining an ally once Garm agreed to join the New Republic. Like most Bothans, Fey'lya sees everything in terms of political and persuasive influence. He believes that everyone is playing the same game as he, and so he bases many of his decisions on prestige rather than the best course of action.

Five years after the Battle of Endor, Fey'lya implicated

Ackbar in a plot of treason and embezzlement. Neither accusation proved true, but Fey'lya's power plays almost led to the destruction of the New Republic. Though pardoned by the Provisional Council for his actions during the retrieval of the long-lost *Katana* fleet, he lost face and much support. During the Yevethan crisis, Fey'lya supported the petition of no confidence in Chief of State Leia Organa Solo. Twenty-one years after the Battle of Endor, Fey'lya became the chief of state of the New Republic. [DFR, HE, LC, TT, VP]

Fidge

A ten-year-old Biituian, he met R2-D2 and C-3PO during the early days of the Empire. Fidge had a pet reptile named Chubb, and he often traveled through the burrows Chubb liked to dig. [TGH]

fifth moon of Da Soocha

The location of the secret New Republic Command Center designated as Pinnacle Base. The intelligent species called Ixlls are native to Da Soocha V. [DE]

Figg, Ecclessis

Lord Figg constructed the first floating settlement of Bespin, near the gas giant's equator. This floating workstation eventually evolved into Cloud City. [GG2]

Filve

A planet targeted by the Star Destroyer *Judicator* in Grand Admiral Thrawn's multipronged attack designed to draw New Republic forces away from the planet Ukio. [LC]

Final Jump

Spacer slang for death. [HSR]

findsmen

Gand bounty hunters who use meditation to locate their prey. [TBH]

Fiolla of Lorrd

An aspiring assistant auditor general for the Corporate Sector Authority. During an undercover assignment to expose top Authority executives and Espo officials who were involved with an illegal slavery ring, Hart-and-Parn Gorra-Fiolla of Lorrd found herself unexpectedly teamed with Han Solo. [HSR]

firefolk

See Wistie.

fire rings of Fornax

One of the unique wonders of the galaxy, in which the planet Fornax appears to be encircled by five rings of intense fire. They are actually solar prominences attracted to the planet due to its close proximity to its sun. [SWN]

Firestorm

An Imperial Star Destroyer. [DS]

Firrerre

All life on this world was destroyed by an Imperial biological weapon. The humanoid natives of Firrerre were believed to have been wiped out until Leia Organa Solo discovered a passenger freighter carrying many of them in suspended animation. [CS]

Firwirrung

A reptilian Ssi-ruuk, he was the personal master of the human Dev Sibwarra and the head of entechment operations aboard the battle cruiser *Shriwirr*. He developed the method to conduct Ssi-ruuk entechment at unlimited distances through the use of a subdued Force-strong individual. [TAB]

Fixer

One of Luke Skywalker's companions on Tatooine, he was an overbearing mechanic employed at the Tosche Station in Anchorhead. He was also the boyfriend of the young woman named Camie. [SWN]

Flarestar

This cantina located aboard the space station at Yag'Dhul was frequented by Rogue Squadron pilots during the Bacta War. [BW]

Flautis

A greasy-looking Corellian, he was a member of the antialien Human League. [AC]

Flax

This planet in the Ptera system is home to the insectoid Flakax species. [GG4]

flechette canister

A weapon that contains clusters of tiny darts. Fired from a shoulder-mounted launcher, when it strikes its target, the canister explodes and releases its cloud of deadly darts. [HSR]

flechette missile

A dart-shaped projectile about 110 millimeters in length. These missiles come in two power levels: antipersonnel and armor-piercing antivehicle. [HLL, HSE]

fleethund

Slang used by X-wing pilots, it describes a dangerous decoy maneuver in which one pilot draws fire to his ship and away from the main convoy. [BW]

Flim

A highly talented con artist, he joined forces with Moff Disra and Major Grodin Tierce sixteen years after the Battle of Endor to perpetuate the false impression that Grand Admiral Thrawn had returned from the dead. It was Flim's job to impersonate the grand admiral, and with Tierce's direction he did a masterful job, until Talon Karrde helped Admiral Gilad Pellaeon uncover the truth. [SP, VF]

floater

See landspeeder.

floating cities of Calamari

These huge, anchored metropolises rest atop the oceans of the water planet Mon Calamari and extend deep below the waves. These cities are home to the amphibious Mon Calamari and the Quarren. [DE, SWSB]

floating fortress

An Imperial repulsorlift combat vehicle designed to augment ground assault and planetary occupation forces. With its distinctive twin-turret heavy blaster cannon, well-armored body, and powerful repulsorlift engines, the roughly cylindrical floating fortress was especially suitable for urban terrain. This war machine was equipped with a sophisticated surveillance system that projected a thirty-meter-radius sensor probe around the vehicle, forming a target identification field. This field could be used to single out a specific target or to lock onto a large number of targets for elimination by the two top-mounted heavy blasters. A floating fortress required a pilot, two gunners, and a sensor chief. It could also carry up to ten troopers. [ISB]

Flurry

Once a simple *Quasar Fire*–class bulk cruiser designed to ferry foodstuffs and other trade goods between settled worlds, it was converted to carry starfighters and served admirably in the Battle of Endor. Later, it was the lead ship in the Alliance task

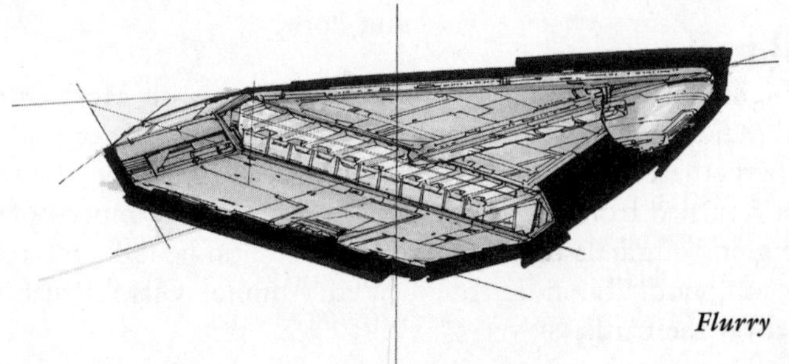

Flurry

force sent to Bakura. The *Flurry* carried twenty X-wings, three A-wings, and four heavy-assault B-wing starfighters in its modified docking bay. The Imperial warship *Dominant* destroyed the *Flurry* over the planet Bakura. [TAB, TBSB]

Fnnbu

Four thousand years before the Galactic Civil War, this Zexx was a companion of the space pirate Finhead Stonebone. [TOJ]

Foamwander City

One of the floating cities of Mon Calamari. [DA]

Foerost shipyards

These vast Republic shipyards orbit the uninhabited planet Foerost and are among the oldest and most successful in the galaxy. Raw materials are collected from the planet below and shipped into high orbit where they are assembled into warships for the Republic navy. The shipyards were attacked during the Sith War, and dark-sider Ulic Qel-Droma captured the operations codes for 300 of the newest Republic vessels. [TSW]

Folna

A New Republic picket ship. [TT]

Folor

The largest moon orbiting the planet Commenor, this craggy gray satellite was the site of an Alliance starfighter training center. The base was built within a network of underground tunnels that had served as a mining complex and a smugglers' hideout in the past. [RS]

Fondor

An industrial planet in a system of the same name, famous for its huge orbital starship construction facilities. After the Battle of Yavin, Darth Vader began work on his personal flagship, *Executor*, at these starship yards. [CSSB, CSW, HSE]

Forbidden

An Imperial shuttle captured by the Alliance and used on numerous missions. It was usually flown on these missions by Tycho Celchu. [RS, WG]

Force, the

A natural yet mystical presence, it is an energy field generated by all living things, sometimes attributed to microscopic organisms known as midi-chlorians. It surrounds and penetrates everything, binding the galaxy together. Like most forms of energy, the Force can be manipulated. Knowledge of these manipulation techniques gives the Jedi Knights their powers. The Force has two sides—light and dark. The light side bestows great knowledge, peace, and serenity. The dark side is filled with anger, fear, and aggression. Both sides of the Force are a part of the natural order; one side life affirming, the other destructive. Through the force, a Jedi Knight might see far-off places, perform amazing feats, and accomplish what would otherwise be considered impossible. A Jedi's strength flows from the Force, but a true Jedi uses it for knowledge and defense, never to attack. It is a powerful ally, regardless of how it is used.

Only Force-sensitive living beings can master Jedi skills. There are three major Force skills: control, sense, and alter. The control skill allows a Jedi to control his or her own inner Force. With this skill a Jedi learns to master the functions of his or her own body. The sense skill helps a Jedi sense the Force in things beyond and outside of himself or herself. With it, a Jedi learns to feel the bonds that connect all things. The alter skill allows a Jedi to change the distribution and nature of the Force in order to create illusions, move objects, and change perceptions.

A dark Jedi is one who has given in to his or her anger and embraced the dark side of the Force. [ESB, RJ, SW, SWRPG, SWRPG2, etc.]

"Forceflow"

The alias used by Borborygmus Gog to contact Tash Arranda on the HoloNet. While trying to find Force-sensitive subjects to use in his experiments, Gog introduced Tash to legends of the Jedi. [GF]

Force lightning

This Force ability was used by the Emperor aboard the second Death Star against Luke Skywalker. This corruption of the Force utilized by those who follow the dark side produces white or blue bolts of energy that flow from the user's fingertips toward a target. Force lightning flows into a target, causing great pain as it siphons off the living energy and eventually kills its victim. [DFR, HE, HESB, LC, RJ]

force pike

A pole tipped with vibro-edged heads that can kill or stun with a single touch. The setting controls and power generators are located within the pike's grip. These weapons were particular favorites of the Emperor's Royal Guard. [HSE, SWSB]

force sabacc

A variation of the electronic card game in which randomness is provided by the other players instead of a separate randomizer. [CPL]

Force-sensitive

An individual who is more keenly attuned to the Force, able to sense its presence and the presence of other Force-sensitives. [SME, SWRPG2]

Force storm

A tornado of energy created by great disturbances in the Force. Dark Side Adepts demonstrate limited control over the creation of these storms, while the reborn clone Emperor was able to create and control Force storms at will. Light-side practitioners can also join to create Force storms. [DE]

Foreign Intruder Defense Organism (FIDO)

A defense droid suggested by Admiral Ackbar and modeled on the krakana, a dreaded sea creature on Mon Calamari. It protected Anakin Solo on Anoth. [COF]

Forge, Inyri

Sister of Rogue Squadron member Lujayne Forge, Inyri was the lover of smuggler and Black Sun terrorist Zekka Thyne. She was with Thyne when he tried to kill Rogue pilot Corran Horn. Horn rescued Inyri twice during two different engagements with Imperial forces. She finally realized that Thyne was just using her to get close to Horn, and when the terrorist tried to kill Horn again, she killed Thyne instead. She helped Rogue Squadron when they brought down Coruscant's shields, and was later made a member of the squadron. [BW, KT, WG]

Forge, Kassar

Father of Inyri and Lujayne Forge, he was a teacher at the Kessel prison camp. [WG]

Forge, Lujayne

A member of Rogue Squadron from the planet Kessel, she was killed in her sleep by Imperial stormtroopers when they made a midnight raid against the base at Talasea. [RS]

Forge, Myda

A Kessel prisoner who married Kassar Forge, one of the instructors charged with rehabilitating the inmates. She stayed with Kassar on Kessel after her sentence ended, and the couple had two daughters—Lujayne and Inyri. [WG]

Forger

An Imperial Star Destroyer sent to suppress a rebellion on Gra Ploven. [SOL]

Formayj

A smuggler and information broker who provided Chewbacca with maps and data that aided in the successful rescue of Han Solo from the Yevetha. Formayj was a Yao who was more than one hundred years old at the time. [TT]

Forno, Jace

A female Corellian gun-for-hire who worked as a pilot for smuggling kingpin Olag Greck and criminal mastermind Movo Brattakin, among others. [D]

Fortress of Tawntoom

A city built into the interior walls of a volcanic crater in the Tawntoom colony of Roon. The seething lava pit powered the city, which served as the base of operations for Governor Koong. [DTV]

Fortuna, Bib

A Twi'lek from the planet Ryloth. Bib Fortuna left his homeworld to seek opportunities in the larger galaxy, eventually joining up with Jabba the Hutt and advancing to the top of the crimelord's court. He served as the Hutt's chief lieutenant and majordomo, overseeing the daily operations in the crimelord's desert palace.

Bib Fortuna

A smuggler and slaver of his own people, Fortuna had been sentenced to death on Ryloth for exporting the drug ryll. He escaped, making his way to Tatooine and Jabba's organization. When Luke Skywalker and company staged the rescue of Han Solo, Fortuna escaped in his private skiff, moments before Jabba's sail barge exploded.

The B'omarr monks who lived in the catacombs below Jabba's palace decided that Fortuna's brain deserved to be preserved in a nutrient jar, and they arranged for it to be removed.

However, the crafty Fortuna discovered a way to transfer his consciousness into Firith Olan, a Twi'lek crook, and carried on his criminal activities from inside a new body. [GG5, RJ, SWCG, SWSB, TJP, XW]

forward gun pod

A concealed antipersonnel blaster emplacement that is installed in the front section of some starfighters and transports. The forward gun pod on the *Millennium Falcon*, for example, extends from a hidden compartment in the ship's lower hull when the ship's anti-intruder system is triggered or when the pilot activates it. [ESBR]

Fossyr, Irin

A false name used by Alliance Intelligence agent Iella Wessiri during an undercover mission to Coruscant. [WG]

Fraan, Tal

An ambitious proctor working with Yevethan viceroy Nil Spaar, he was in charge of the Yevethan attack at Preza. His success led to his promotion to personal adviser and assistant to Spaar. He advised Spaar to kill a Republic hostage to force Chief of State Leia Organa Solo to give in to their demands. The killing only made the Republic leader more determined, and Spaar eventually killed Fraan. [BTS, SOL, TT]

Freebird

A gypsy freighter owned by Captain Stanz. [BTS]

Freedom's Sons

A group of insurgent patriots who battled against tyrannical occupation forces that threatened the Republic during the Clone Wars. These freedom fighters from the conquered star systems helped the Jedi Knights reestablish law and order at the end of this war-torn period. [HSE]

Freedon Nadd Uprising

This conflict on Onderon about 4,000 years before the Galactic Civil War was instigated by the Naddists, a dissident group that followed the spirit of dark Jedi Freedon Nadd. The uprising ended with the death of Onderon's King Ommin. [FNU]

Free Flight Dance Dome

This first-class nightclub on the planet Etti IV is known for its variable-gravity-field dance floors that accommodate not only fun-seekers, but also aliens who need gravity alterations for maximum comfort. [HSR]

freerunner

An armored repulsorlift speeder, or compact assault vehicle (CAV), primarily used by the Alliance and private mercenary bands. Its name was inspired by the free-rotating gun platforms mounted atop them. With two antivehicle laser cannons and two anti-infantry blaster batteries, these speeders pack a powerful offensive punch. [DFR, DFRSB, RSB]

Frenzied River clan

One of the witch clans of the planet Dathomir. [CPL]

Freyrr

A Wookiee, he was second cousin to Chewbacca. [TT]

Frija

A human replica droid, she rescued Luke Skywalker and C-3PO when they crash-landed on Hoth. Imperial technicians created human replica droids of the real Frija and her father, the Imperial Governor Lexhannen, to serve as decoys while the humans escaped a Rebel attack. Unfortunately for the true Frija, the technicians programmed strong survival instincts into the replicas, and when the fighting began, they escaped and hid themselves on Hoth. [CSW]

Fromm, Sise

An old yet powerful crime boss, he operated out of a stronghold on the planet Annoo during the early days of the Empire. This member of the Annoo-dat species considered himself to be the "crown king of crime." His legitimate import-export business was actually a front for extortion, kidnapping, and blaster running. He had a son, Tig, who was also in the business. [DTV]

Fromm, Tig

An Annoo-dat who also went by the names of Baby-Face Fromm and Junior Fromm, he was the son of Sise Fromm. Like his father, he was a gangster of some repute. He led a gang of outlaws, though he often worked in cooperation with his father. Unlike his father, Tig was fascinated by modern technology. He was based on the planet Ingo. During the early days of the Empire, his project to build the weapons satellite called *Trigon One* was shut down by R2-D2, C-3PO, and Kea Moll. [DTV]

Froz

Home planet of the tall, furry, melancholy Frozians. [AC]

Fugo

A Chadra-Fan, he was a colleague of the brilliant scientist named Fandar. After Fandar suffered grievous injuries, Fugo carried on the work of the Alliance's Project Decoy. [QE]

Furgan, Ambassador

Ambassador from the planet Carida to the New Republic, he was actually an Imperial agent. He almost succeeded in killing Republic leader Mon Mothma with a slow-acting poison. He later attempted to kidnap Anakin Solo, but was challenged by Terpfen, a Mon Calamari. The two battled, each utilizing his own MT-AT. Furgan's fell to the rocks below the Anoth fortress. He was presumed dead. [COF, DA, JS]

fusioncutter

An industrial tool that produces wide-dispersion laser beams for use in construction, mining, and metalworking. [SWN, SWSB]

fusion furnace

A power-generating device that produces heat and light and recharges energy cells for vehicles, droids, and weapons. [ESB]

Fuzzum

A primitive species whose members look like balls of fuzz with long, thin legs. [DTV]

Fw'Sen picket ship

A small Ssi-ruuk combat ship used to disable enemy vessels and guard the perimeter of Ssi-ruuvi fleets. Less than fifty meters long, the ships are fragile and require energy-draining shields to ward off attacks. They are crewed by droids and the subjugated species, P'w'eck, leading Ssi-ruuvi commanders to consider the ships disposable and good for suicide missions. [SWVG, TAB]

FX-7

A cylindrical, multiarmed medical assistant droid that used its sophisticated appendages and specialized medical diagnostic and procedural programming to aid both droid and organic surgeons. Considered antiquated by the time of the Galactic Civil War, this droid model was mostly found far from the galaxy's Core Worlds and in the service of the Rebel Alliance. [ESB]

FX-7

Fyre, Commander Silver

A former smuggling colleague of Han Solo's and leader of one of the biggest mercenary gangs in the galaxy, the Aquaris Freeholders. Silver Fyre and her Freeholders joined the Alliance during the Conference of Uncommitted Worlds held on Kabal shortly after the Battle of Yavin. [CSW]

gaderffii

A traditional weapon of Tatooine's Sand People, or Tusken Raiders, this double-edged axlike weapon is fashioned from metal scavenged from wrecked or abandoned vehicles and spaceships found in the Tatooine wastes. Also called a gaffi stick. [SW, SWSB]

gaderffii

Gaff

The aide-de-camp of Governor Koong during the early days of the Empire. Gaff was a Kobok, a green, fuzzy insectoid with deadly stingers on his forearms, and three eyes, one of which was located in the back of his head. [DTV]

Galactic Civil War

The Rebellion started the instant Senator Palpatine declared himself Emperor. His Empire replaced the Old Republic, and tyranny gripped the worlds of the galaxy. It took many years, but scattered Rebels eventually organized into the Alliance to Restore the Republic, and the galaxy shuddered on the edge of civil war. The exact moment when the Galactic Civil War began cannot be pinpointed, but by the time of the Battle of Yavin it was in full swing.

Star system after star system slipped through the Empire's clenched fist to join the Alliance, and civil war rocked the galaxy from the settlements of the Outer Rim Territories to the majestic spires of Imperial City. The Battle of Endor marked the end of the civil war as the Alliance destroyed the second Death Star and routed the Imperial fleet, and the New Republic was born. The war was slow to grind to a halt, though, and for decades the remnants of the Empire continued to struggle with the emerging New Republic. [DE, DFR, ESB, HE, LC, RJ, SW, etc.]

Galactic Constitution

The ancient foundation document of the democratic Old Republic. [DE]

Galactic Core

The heavily inhabited central region of the galaxy and the original location of the ruling nexus of the Republic and, later, the Empire. With Coruscant, or Imperial Center, at the middle, the pathways of the galactic government spread outward like the spokes of a wheel. [DE, HESB, SWRPG2, SWSB]

Galactic HoloNet

An extensive news and information network accessible throughout the galaxy. [SWSB, TBH]

Galactic Republic

See Old Republic.

Galactic Research Academy

This Imperial scientific institute was located on the planet Koaan. Mammon Hoole maintained an office there. [GF]

Galactic Voyager

One of the largest and most powerful Mon Calamari star cruisers in the New Republic fleet. [DS]

Galantos

This planet located in the Farlax sector is the home of the Fia species. [BTS, SOL]

Galaxy Gun

The ultimate weapon developed by the second cloned Emperor. It fired "intelligent" lightspeed torpedoes into hyperspace that would exit at precise coordinates, find their targets, and destroy them. The torpedoes carried particle disintegrators that neutralized all security shields. R2-D2 caused the Emperor's flagship to slam into the weapon, resulting in the destruction of the ship, the weapon, and the planet Byss. [DE2]

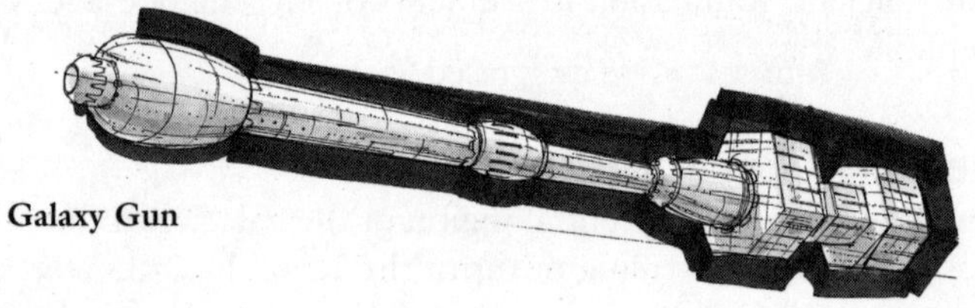

Galaxy Gun

Galia

Daughter of King Ommin and Queen Amanoa, she was heir to the throne of the planet Onderon 4,000 years before the Galactic Civil War. She married Oron Kira and ascended to the throne when her mother died. [FNU, TOJ]

Gall

A moon that circles the gas giant Zhar, located in the Outer Rim Territories. Known for its violent atmospheric and planetary storms, it was home to an Imperial enclave of naval powers. Several Star Destroyers and a force of TIE fighters were stationed around the moon. Boba Fett stopped at this location with his cargo of carbonite containing Han Solo. Princess Leia led an unsuccessful rescue attempt while Fett's *Slave I* was still on the turbulent moon. [RS, SOTE]

Gallandro

An amoral blaster-for-hire, he was lightning fast and uncannily accurate. In his last years, he was one of the most trusted operatives working for the Corporate Sector Authority. His orders came directly from the regional administrator, Odumin. Tall and lean, Gallandro always wore expensive, impeccable clothing. He had a long mustache decorated with golden beads.

Han Solo crossed the gunman's path twice in the years prior to Solo's involvement in the Rebellion. The first time, Solo won their duel by tricking Gallandro into grabbing hold of a rigged security case that sent a bolt of paralyzing energy through both men's right arms. Faced with drawing against the ambidextrous Solo, the right-handed Gallandro opted for surrender.

The second time, the two faced each other in the lost vaults of Xim the Despot. To Solo's credit, he came closer to beating Gallandro in a fair fight than anyone else in a long time. But Gallandro's blaster bolts struck Solo's shoulder and forearm before Solo's own blaster could finish its ascent. The anti-weapon defenses of Xim's treasure vaults zeroed in on Gallandro, however, and a dozen lethal blasts reduced him to a blackened corpse. [HLL, HSR, SWCG]

Gallandro

Gallandro, Anja

Daughter of the blaster-for-hire Gallandro, she was a battle-hungry young woman who became friends with Jacen and Jaina Solo and the other young Jedi Knights at Luke Skywalker's academy. She originally hoped to get revenge against Han Solo for her father's death, but after the twins helped her through her spice addiction she changed her mind. Lando Calrissian offered her a job as a pilot and she accepted. [YJK]

Gallant

A New Republic cruiser, part of the Fifth Fleet. [BTS]

Gallinore

This planet in the Hapes Cluster is the point of origin of the extremely valuable rainbow gems. [CPL]

Galvoni III

This planet housed an Imperial military and communications complex. Alliance historian Voren Na'al infiltrated the base after the Battle of Yavin to learn more about the Death Star project. [GG1, MTS]

Gama system

Home to the Gama-Senn, a species that pledged its allegiance to the second cloned Emperor after witnessing a demonstration of the Galaxy Gun. [EE]

gameboard

A holographic projection table used primarily for amusement purposes. On the gameboard's surface, three-dimensional holograms compete at the directions of the players. Players control the holograms by tapping commands into one of four or more attached keypads. The game dejarik is played on a gameboard. [FT, SW]

Gamorr

The home planet of the Gamorrean species. Its terrain ranges from frozen tundra to deep forests. The planet's history is marked by almost constant warfare between the Gamorrean males. The furry, bloodsucking parasites known as morrts are also native to the world. When traders discovered the planet, they lost seven trading vessels before they sent a heavily armed ship to "finish" negotiations, and the Gamorreans were turned into slaves. [COJ, SWSB]

Gamorrean

A brutish, porcine species, its members are known for their great strength and violent tendencies. Green skinned, with piglike snouts, small horns, and tusks, Gamorreans average approximately 1.8 meters in height. Their size and temperament make them excellent heavy laborers and mercenaries. A number of Gamorreans served as guards in Jabba the Hutt's desert palace.

While Gamorreans understand most alien tongues, they can't produce the sounds necessary to converse in other languages. In Gamorrean culture, females handle all of the productive work. They farm, hunt, manufacture items, and run businesses. The males spend all their time training for and fighting wars.

Gamorreans live in clans headed by matrons. The matrons order the males to battle at the beginning of the campaign season. Wielding primitive melee weapons with expert savagery, the males fight from early spring to late fall. While they adapted to technological weapons, they do not use blasters and power arms in planet-bound campaigns. Technological weapons are saved for off-planet use.

Besides serving as slaves, some Gamorreans sell their contracts on the open market and find employment as guards, mercenaries, professional soldiers, and even bounty hunters. Unfortunately, Gamorreans do not consider a deal binding unless it has been sealed in blood. They would not work for anyone who could not best them in hand-to-hand combat. [RJ, SWSB]

Gamorreans

Gamor Run

A legendary long-haul smuggling route plagued by hijackers and pirates. [DE]

Ganath system

A star system hidden in the radioactive gas cloud near Nal Hutta and completely cut off from the rest of galactic civilization. [DE2]

Gand

This planet is home to the intelligent species of the same name. The mist-shrouded world gave rise to Gand findsmen, bounty hunters that worship the thick gases and use religious rituals to locate targets. A Gand is covered with a hard carapace and possesses remarkable regenerative capabilities that enable them even to regrow lost limbs. [BW, GG3, MTS, RS]

Gank

A species known for its bodyguards and hired assassins, often employed by Hutt crimelords on the streets of Nar Shaddaa and elsewhere. They are also called Gank Killers. [DE, DE2]

Gann, Grand Moff

A governor of one of the Core sectors. [BTS]

Gant

The third adviser selected by the dark-sider Kueller. Kueller believed that his second adviser wouldn't last long, so he began training Gant early. [NR]

Gant, Colonel Trenn

A leader of New Republic Intelligence. [TT]

Gantoris

A leader on the planet Eol Sha, he became one of Luke Skywalker's students at the Jedi academy on Yavin 4. Gantoris often dreamed of a dark man who would tempt him with power and then destroy him. He thought this nightmare pointed toward Skywalker, but it actually referred to the spirit of Exar Kun. The Dark Lord began to seduce Gantoris toward the dark side, but the young man turned on the spirit and tried to destroy it. Instead, Kun burned Gantoris from the inside out, killing him. [DA, JS]

Garch, Commander

Captain of the *Glorious*, command ship for the New Republic chase armada and Colonel Pakkpekatt's command cruiser during the Yevethan crisis. [BTS]

Gardens of Talla

This hillside park overlooked the Great Jedi Library on Ossus some 4,000 years before the Galactic Civil War. [TSW]

Gargan, Yarna d'al'

Yarna d'al' Gargan was the daughter of a tribal chief on the desert planet Askaj. The six-breasted Gargan was kidnapped by slavers and brought to Jabba the Hutt. Her cublings were sold off, and her mate was fed to the rancor. She became a dancing girl and supervisor of the palace housekeeping crew. After Jabba's death she escaped the palace, bought back her children, and left Tatooine with the bounty hunter Doallyn. The two became free traders in textiles and gemstones. [RJ, TJP]

Garindan

A long-snouted Kubaz spy, he trailed Luke Skywalker and Ben Kenobi to Docking Bay 94 in Mos Eisley. He worked for the highest bidder—usually the Empire or Jabba the Hutt. [GG1, SW, SWCG]

Garnoo

An ancient Neti master to Oss Wilum and others some 4,000 years before the Galactic Civil War. [DLS]

Garowyn

Referred to as Captain by some, she was one of the most accomplished of the new breed of younger dark-side Nightsisters on Dathomir. Petite with refined features and creamy brown skin, she wore tight-fitting red lizard-skin armor and a knee-length black cape. During a fight with Chewbacca and Tenel Ka in the treetops of Kashyyyk, she slipped and fell to her death. [YJK]

Gate

The name Wedge Antilles gave to his new R5-G8 astromech droid after it was upgraded and modified. [BW]

GaTir system

This star system located near the Pyria system contains the planet Mrisst. [WG]

Gavrisom, Ponc

A Calibop, he took over the leadership of the New Republic while Leia Organa Solo took a much-needed leave of absence. [SP, VF]

Gbu

This high-gravity planet is home to the Veubgri species. [CS]

GemDiver Station

Lando Calrissian's gem-mining platform that orbited in the fringe of Yavin's outer atmosphere about twenty years after the Battle of Endor. The *Fast Hand* diving bell was lowered from the station into the gaseous levels to catch Corusca gems. [YJK]

Gentes

Homeworld of the Ugnaughts, located in the remote Anoat system. [GG3, MTS]

Gepta, Rokur

The last of the Sorcerers of Tund, he was a heartless, arrogant being with a lust for power. In his quest to rule the Tund sector and beyond, he eliminated the sorcerers who taught him. He appeared in different guises to different people. Some saw him as a malevolent dwarf, others as a three-meter-tall giant. Lando Calrissian discovered that the sorcerer was actually a Croke, a small, snail-like being that used illusions to mask its true form. Lando squeezed the life out of Gepta, ending the evil sorcerer's campaign. [LCS]

Geran

A planet in the Mneon system that was home to a near-human, blue-skinned species and flying reptiles called shell-bats. [TJP]

Getelles, Moff

The Imperial military governor of the Antemeridian sector who struck a deal with Seti Ashgad. He also made a deal with the Loronar Corporation to build synthdroids and new Needles smart missiles. [POT]

Gethzerion

One of the Witches of Dathomir, she was the leader of the dark-side Nightsisters clan. It was Gethzerion's hope to turn all the witches to the dark side. She terrorized the other clans and took command of the stormtroopers who had been abandoned at the planet's Imperial prison colony. It was because of her growing powers in the dark side that the Emperor ordered the planet cut off from the rest of galactic society. Warlord Zsinj promised to provide Gethzerion with a ship if she turned over Han Solo and Princess Leia, who had crash-landed on the planet. When the ship took off, the warlord's men opened fire and destroyed it and Gethzerion. [CPL, SWCG]

Gethzerion

Ghent

The chief slicer for Talon Karrde's smuggling operation. Besides maintaining computer and droid programming, Ghent could break most encrypted codes and computer security measures with relative ease. He got the job when he was barely out of his teens, and only computers and their software could hold his attention. Ghent helped the New Republic break a number of Imperial encrypted codes, including the ones that led to false accusations against Ackbar and those transmitting intelligence information out of Coruscant for the Imperial spynet called Delta Source. He also helped Han Solo, Lando Calrissian, and Mara Jade liberate the Imperial prison facility on Kessel. [COF, DFR, DFRSB, HE, HESB, LC]

Ghorman

A planet in the Sern sector, near the Core Worlds, it was the site of the infamous Ghorman Massacre, an early atrocity committed by the Empire. During a peaceful antitax demonstration, an Imperial warship commanded by Tarkin landed on the crowd, killing or injuring hundreds. Tarkin was promoted to moff for his action, but the event also convinced Bail Organa of Alderaan to support the Rebellion. Years later, an Alliance attack on a vital supply convoy delayed the expansion of the planet's Imperial base by more than a year. [DA, JS, RSB]

Ghostling

Faunlike humanoids, ethereally beautiful and extremely fragile. [CS]

Giat Nor

A city on the planet N'zoth, home to Nil Spaar. [SOL]

Gillespee, Samuel Tomas

A smuggler, he retired from the trade to set up house on the planet Ukio. When Grand Admiral Thrawn took control of the world, Gillespee left in search of a smuggling operation willing to employ him and his men. He signed on with Talon Karrde to indirectly—and for a profit—help the New Republic against the Empire. His ship was *Kern's Pride.* [LC]

gimer stick

An edible twig from plants that grow throughout the swamps of Dagobah, it produces a succulent juice that gathers in sacs on the bark. The sticks are chewed for their flavor and to quench thirst. Yoda, the Jedi Master, enjoyed chewing gimer sticks. [ESB]

Ginbotham

A Hig, this slender, blue-skinned humanoid possessed great piloting skills and was a member of the command crew aboard the *Yavin*. [NR]

Givin

Looking much like animated skeletons, this species wears its bones on the outside of their bodies. Large, triangular eye sockets dominate their skull-like faces, giving them a perpetual expression of sadness. The Givin originated on the planet Yag'Dhul. They are expert mathematicians with a phobia concerning exposed flesh, often going to great lengths to avoid the sight of it in other species. [GG4]

Gizz, Big

A wild-haired bully, he led Jabba the Hutt's swoop troops on the planet Tatooine. The swoopers under Gizz's command were a ragtag gang of ruffians culled from the streets of Mos Eisley. Gizz loved to ride fast, play hard, and hurt any weak and frightened beings who got in his way. [SESB, SOTE]

gladiator droid

A droid designed for close-quarters combat and used in the declining days of the Old Republic in violent sporting events against other droids or living creatures. [HSE]

Glayyd, Mor

The patriarch of the Glayyd family on the planet Ammuud. *Mor* is a title of respect bestowed upon the current clan patriarch. When Han Solo visited the planet, prior to his involvement in the Galactic Civil War, the given name of the Mor Glayyd was Ewwen. [HSR]

glitterstim

A potent spice mined on the planet Kessel, it provides a brief but pleasurable telepathic boost and heightened mental state. This valuable commodity was tightly controlled by the Empire and worth a fortune to smugglers brave enough to transport it. This spice is highly addictive to many species. [JS, NR, TJP, XW]

Glorious

Colonel Pakkpekatt's command cruiser during the Yevethan crisis. [BTS]

Glory of Yevetha

Once the *EX-F*, this weapons and propulsion test bed was captured and turned into a major vessel in Nil Spaar's Black Fifteen Fleet. [BTS, SOL]

Glott

A notorious bounty hunter from Antar 4. [GG4]

Glottal

Homeworld of the Glottalphib species, this hot, humid world consists of swamps and dark forests. [NR]

Glottalphib

Also known as 'Phibs, this species sports scaly yellow-green skin and long, teeth-filled snouts. They have gills, enabling them to live in water and air. The 'Phibs are able to breathe fire, shooting it from their mouths as a weapon. They are also known to carry snub-nosed hand weapons called swamp-stunners. Their hides are resistant to blaster fire, so the best way to hurt a 'Phib is to shoot it in the mouth. [NR]

glow rod

Any device designed to provide a portable light source. Most are long, thin tubes that cast bright light through chemical phosphorescents. Glow rods can be carried, clamped to clothing or equipment, or placed on a stable surface. [HESB, HLL, SWSB]

Gmar Askilon

A star near the site of the fourth documented sighting of the mysterious ghost ship called the Teljkon vagabond. A New Republic task force intercepted the ship and placed a team aboard it before it entered hyperspace, taking the team with it. The team consisted of Lando Calrissian, Lobot, R2-D2, and C-3PO. [BTS]

gnarltree

A bizarre tree found in the swamps of Dagobah. As it grows over the course of centuries, its huge roots rise out of the bog and create a shelter in the hollow spaces. A knobby white spider that appears to live in the tree is actually a mobile root that hunts and devours animals until it builds up enough strength to make a clearing and plant its eight sharp legs. These legs become the roots of a new gnarltree. [ISWU]

Gniev, Jal Te

This Rebel pilot was ill during the Battle of Yavin, leading Luke Skywalker to fly his X-wing. He became extremely jealous of Skywalker and was reassigned to a recruiting station on Dubrava. Later, he performed a suicide run and destroyed an Interdictor cruiser, allowing Skywalker to escape from Darth Vader. [VQ]

Gnisnal

An *Imperial*-class Star Destroyer that was sabotaged during the evacuation of Narth and Ihopek. An intact memory core found in the wreck contained a complete Imperial Order of Battle. [BTS]

Gog, Borborygmus

An evil Shi'ido scientist working for the Empire, he was in charge of Project Starscream. Under great pressure from Lord Darth Vader and the Emperor to succeed, he was especially interested in developing a weapon capable of defeating the Force. He was eventually killed by the Kivan wraiths in revenge for conducting the experiments that transformed them. [GF]

Golanda

In charge of the artillery innovations and tactical deployments sections of the Maw Installation, she complained throughout her ten-year tenure about how pointless it was to test artillery in the middle of a black-hole cluster. [COF]

Golden Sun

A living, collective intelligence made up of thousands of tiny polyps that inhabit the coral reefs of the planet Sedri. These coral dwellers possess an aptitude for the Force, though they refer to it as the universal energy. Through the Force and the connection of thousands of minds, they produce a nearly limitless supply of energy. This energy is so intense that it affects the gravity readings of the planet, registering it as a small sun and causing hyperdrive safety cutoffs to activate when ships pass nearby. The native Sedrians of the planet worship the Golden Sun, and their Force-sensitive high priests hear the voices of the communal polyps as dreams and visions. [BGS, GG4]

Gold Leader

The comm-unit designation for Rebel pilot Dutch's Y-wing during the Battle of Yavin. During the Battle of Endor, it was the comm-unit designation for Lando Calrissian and the *Millennium Falcon.* [RJ, SW]

Gold Squadron

A Rebel Alliance starfighter squadron assigned to the Massassi base on Yavin 4. It was sent into battle against the Death Star during the Battle of Yavin, and the entire squadron, except for Gold Leader, was destroyed. [SW]

Gold Two

The comm-unit designation for Rebel pilot Tiree's Y-wing during the Battle of Yavin. [SW]

Gold Wing

The Alliance starfighter battle group under the command of Gold Leader during the Battle of Endor. [RJ]

Gol Storn

A New Republic ship deployed for duty at Galantos in response to Yevethan aggression. [SOL]

Golthar's Sky

What looked to be an enormous star freighter was actually an illusion created by the dark-side follower Aleema about 4,000 years before the Galactic Civil War. [TSW]

Gopso'o

Ancient enemies of the Drovian species. [POT]

Gorath

A Prakith light cruiser commanded by Captain Voba Dokrett. It attempted to capture the Teljkon vagabond but was instead destroyed by the ghost ship. [TT]

Gorax

A giant creature more than thirty meters high that lives in underground caverns on Endor's forest moon. Covered with thick, matted fur, it has pointy ears and a jutting lower jaw filled with nasty teeth. One such Gorax captured Jeremitt and Catarine Towani. It was killed when their children Mace and Cindel, along with a few Ewok friends, braved the giant's lair to free them. [EA, ISWU]

Gorga the Hutt

Jabba the Hutt's nephew, he expected to inherit Jabba's fortune. The crimelord left him nothing, however. [JT]

Gorgon

This Imperial Star Destroyer was Admiral Daala's flagship. [COF, DA, DS, JS]

Gorm the Dissolver

A huge, droid bounty hunter, he wore heavy plated armor and a full helmet. He seemed to have been destroyed by the young

Rodian bounty hunter Greedo in Nar Shaddaa, the vertical city, but was later repaired and ended up in Mos Eisley. [DE, TMEC]

gorm-worm

A poisonous creature used by pirates to kill Jedi trainee Andur Sunrider about 4,000 years before the Galactic Civil War. [TOJ]

Gornash, Prophet

A Prophet of the Dark Side, he coordinated espionage activities from Space Station Scardia, the headquarters of the Prophets of the Dark Side. [PDS]

Gorneesh, King

The sly, foul-tempered king of the Duloks, he led the inhabitants of the swamps of Endor's forest moon. [ETV]

Gosfambling

Delicate furred creatures, intelligent and soft-spoken, from a planet of the same name. Once a loser on Gosfambling, always a loser, since they never elect anyone who has ever lost an election. The planet's representative to the New Republic is Senator C-Gosf. [NR]

Goss, Joreb

Akanah Norand Pell's long-lost father. The two were reunited on Atzerri. Due to extensive drug use, Joreb didn't remember his daughter or anything about her people, the Fallanassi. [SOL]

Gotal

An intelligent, humanoid species from the moon Antar 4. Each member possesses two cone-shaped growths rising from their heads, flat noses, protruding brows, and shaggy gray fur. The head cones serve as additional sensory organs, able to pick up and distinguish different forms of energy waves. Gotals don't like droids due to their high-energy output that tends to overload a Gotal's senses. They have a hard time interpreting the emotions of other alien species, often mistaking affection for love and anger for hatred. They make excellent scouts, bounty hunters, trackers, and mercenaries. [DFRSB, GG4, NR, TMEC]

Governor Tarkin

See Tarkin, Grand Moff.

Graf, Admiral

A New Republic officer in charge of Fleet Intelligence during the Yevethan crisis. [TT]

Grake

A large, tentacled, gentle Veubgri from the planet Gbu, he was a cook for Lord Hethrir. [CS]

Grammel, Captain-Supervisor

The square-jawed human who commanded the Imperial military garrison on Circarpous V. This mustached, black-and-white-haired administrator was ruthless, routinely torturing prisoners whether he needed information from them or not. [SME]

Gran

A goatlike humanoid species native to the planet Kinyen, exhibiting three eyes atop independent stalks. Ree-Yees, a Gran, was a member of Jabba the Hutt's court. [GG5, GG12, RJ]

Grand Admiral Thrawn

See Thrawn, Grand Admiral.

Gra Ploven

A planet, home to the aquatic Ploven species. When the Ploven refused to pay protection money to Grand Moff Dureya during the waning days of the Empire, the Star Destroyer *Forger* killed 200,000 beings in three coastal cities by creating superhot steam clouds. [SOL]

Grappa the Hutt

A ruthless crimelord with ties to the Black Sun organization, he wanted to take control of the galaxy. Black Sun provided Grappa with Imperial cloning technology and captured members of the Imperial Interim Ruling Council so that they could be replaced with clones under Black Sun's control. He also made a deal with the alien Zanibar, providing them with beings they could sacrifice in their ceremonial rituals. In the end, Grappa's plans unraveled and the Zanibar used the Hutt as a sacrifice. [CE]

Graveyard of Alderaan

This asteroid field is all that remains of the planet Alderaan after it was destroyed by the first Death Star. Spacers and free traders gave it this name and told tales of Jedi artifacts and ghost ships hidden among its ruins. The Empire tried to lure Princess Leia here by spreading rumors that the Royal Palace had been found intact within a huge asteroid.

Survivors who had been off planet when Alderaan was destroyed developed a ritual known as the Returning. As part of the ritual, Returnees fill memorial capsules with gifts for departed friends and relatives and jettison them into the Graveyard. [BW, GA]

gravity-well projector

A device that, by simulating the presence of a large body in space, prevents nearby ships from engaging their hyperdrives and forces ships traveling through hyperspace to drop back into realspace. The projector has to be connected to a massive gravity-well generator aboard a large ship. [ISB, SH]

Gray Leader

The comm-unit designation for the commander of Gray Wing, one of the four main Rebel starfighter battle groups active during the Battle of Endor. Gray Leader and his Gray Wing fell during the early moments of the battle. [RJ]

Gray Wing

One of four Rebel starfighter battle groups participating in the Battle of Endor. [RJ]

Great Bogga the Hutt

A wealthy Hutt crimelord, he ruled the Stenness underworld some 4,000 years before the Galactic Civil War. [TOJ]

Great Dome of the Je'har

An architectural wonder on the planet Almania. Dark-sider Kueller turned it into his command center. [NR]

Great Droid Revolution

A droid revolt on Coruscant some 4,000 years before the Galactic Civil War. [DLS]

Great Heep

An enormous, grotesque droid employed by the Empire to mine fuel ore on the planet Biitu. With a body composed of various droid parts and tubing, the Great Heep operated a huge processing plant during the early days of the Empire. One side of the Great Heep was filled with visible pistons that bounced up and down in terrible rhythm. Grinder blades filled his awful maw, and tiny droids lived on his hull like mechanical parasites. Two crazed humans were always near the Great Heep, busy shoveling fuel into his massive boilers. [TGH]

Great Hyperspace War

An ancient conflict between agents of the light and dark sides of the Force. [DLS]

Great Leader of the Second Imperium

About twenty years after the Battle of Endor, another clone of the Emperor seemed to head a coalition seeking to reestablish the Empire. Brakiss, leader of the Shadow Academy, eventually learned that the Great Leader wasn't a clone of Palpatine—it was a series of recordings and props used by four of the Emperor's most loyal guards to trick the galaxy into believing the Emperor had returned. [YJK]

Great Sith War

A conflict that occurred some 4,000 years before the Galactic Civil War and pitted the evil Brotherhood of the Sith against the Jedi Knights and the Galactic Republic. [DA]

Greck, Olag

A criminal, he kept crossing paths with R2-D2 and C-3PO during the early days of the Empire. [D]

Greedo

Greedo

A Rodian bounty hunter, he had large multifaceted eyes, skull-ridge spines, and a tapirlike snout. He learned the noble profession of bounty hunting from Spurch "Warhog" Goa and became one of Jabba the Hutt's henchmen. He caught up with Han Solo at a cantina in Mos Eisley on Tatooine and attempted to collect the bounty offered by Jabba. Solo was forced to dispose of Greedo. [SW, SWCG, SWSB]

Greelanx, Admiral Winstel

This Imperial officer commanded Moff Sarn Shild's fleet sent to assault Nar Shaddaa a few years before the start of the Galactic Civil War. The Hutts sent Han Solo to meet with Greelanx and figure out if the admiral could be bribed to throw the battle. He agreed to sell the Hutts the battle plan and withdraw at the first justifiable opportunity, but warned that he would fight to the best of his ability before leaving. Darth Vader killed Greelanx for his treachery. [HG]

Green

The only human Vigo in the service of Black Sun, his ambition was to usurp Prince Xizor and take control of the crime syndicate. Unfortunately, he was unaware that Xizor watched his every move. To Xizor, Green was further proof that humans were prone to treachery and could rarely be trusted. Green's activities were concentrated among the Core Worlds, where his vast spynet specialized in blackmail and racketeering. Green had the appearance of an old man, though he was barely middle-aged. [SESB, SOTE]

Greenies

See Mimban.

Green Leader

The comm-unit designation for the commander of Green Wing, one of four Rebel starfighter battle groups active during the Battle of Endor. Green Leader and his group fired the last blaster salvo that caused the disabled Super Star Destroyer *Executor* to crash into the unfinished Death Star. Green Leader died in this assault. [RJ, RJN]

Green Squadron

The B-wings and Y-wings of this starfighter battle group fought in the Battle of Calamari. [DE]

Green Wing

One of four Rebel starfighter battle groups participating in the Battle of Endor. This was also the comm-unit designation for Green Leader's second in command. Green Wing accompanied Red Leader Wedge Antilles, Gold Leader Lando Calrissian, and Blue Leader on an assault of an Imperial communications ship. Green Wing lost his life in the effort, but gave the others the opportunity to destroy the enemy vessel. [RJ, RJN]

Grendu

A Bothan trader in rare antiques who originally sent the rancor that ended up in Jabba's palace on Tatooine. [GG5, TJP]

G'rho

The planet where Dev Sibwarra grew up, it was the first outpost attacked by the Ssi-ruuk. [TAB]

Gribbet

A small froglike alien bounty hunter, he worked with Skorr. The pair almost captured Han Solo on the planet Ord Mantell. [CSW]

Griff, Admiral

The fleet admiral who supervised the construction of Darth Vader's *Super*-class Star Destroyer, *Executor*. He also commanded the Imperial blockade of Yavin 4 after the destruction of the first Death Star. Griff and his ship were destroyed when, in an attempt to intercept the fleeing Rebel fleet, Griff miscalculated a hyperspace jump and dropped out of hyperspace, nearly landing on the *Executor*. [CSW]

Griggs, Kane

A navigator aboard the liberated New Republic Star Destroyer *Emancipator* during the Battle of Calamari. [DE]

Grigmin

A stunt pilot and rumored aerial combat champion who made a living by displaying his talents to paying customers on backwater worlds. He employed Han Solo and Chewbacca for a brief time before the pair became involved in the Galactic Civil War. [HLL]

Grimorg

A Weequay, he was the palace enforcer for Great Bogga the Hutt. [TOJ]

Grimpen, Brother

This B'omarr monk performed illegal brain transfers for Jabba the Hutt. When his crimes were discovered, the monks removed his own brain as punishment. [GF]

Grizmallt

A heavily populated Core world, it was one of the many planets to surrender to Admiral Ackbar and the Alliance fleet in the years following the Battle of Endor. [DESB]

Grizzid

The captain of the ship that carried a rancor to Tatooine, he and his crew were killed when the creature broke out of its cage. [GG5, SWSB, TJP]

Groznik

A Wookiee, he followed Rogue Squadron pilot Elscol Loro after her husband, Throm, died. Groznik owed a life debt to Throm and transferred it to Elscol. Groznik was killed by numerous stormtrooper blaster bolts, but his actions allowed the Rogues to escape from Loka Hask's Imperial forces. Groznik was immortalized with a statue near the site of the ghost Jedi memorial on the Mrlsst Academy campus. [XW]

grutchin

Yuuzhan Vong–bred insectoid creatures, they are irrational beasts. These instruments of destruction, once released, cannot be controlled or recalled. A swarm of the aggressive creatures was used against Kyp Durron's Dozen-and-Two Avengers starfighter squadron in the early days of the first Yuuzhan Vong invasion. [VP]

Guardian-class patrol ship

This addition to the Imperial fleet came into service after the Battle of Endor. Two common models were the XL-3 and XL-5. [DE]

Gudb

This gangster worked for Great Bogga the Hutt. He led the conspiracy to kill Jedi trainee Andur Sunrider 4,000 years before the Galactic Civil War, carrying out the deed with his poisonous pet gorm-worm, Skritch. [TOJ]

Guldi, Drom

The muscular baron administrator of the Kelrodo-Ai gelatin mines, he participated in a big-game hunting expedition to Hoth. The prey, wampa ice creatures, turned on the hunters and killed them all. [DS]

gundark

A wild, four-armed anthropoid about 1.5 meters tall, known for its fearlessness and amazing strength. This animal species inspired the phrase for someone who looked healthy and strong: "You look like you could pull the ears off a gundark." [ESB]

Gungan

A warlike amphibious species living in cities beneath the deep waters of the planet Naboo. For much of their history, the Gungans were at odds with the land-dwelling Naboo, but the two species became allies during the Naboo blockade and have remained at peace ever since. [SWTPM]

Gun of Command

A powerful weapon used by Hapan troops, it releases an electromagnetic wave field that neutralizes an enemy's thought processes. Those shot with the gun tend to stand around and follow any orders given to them. [CPL]

Gupin

A small, elflike species, they live in a large volcanic structure on the forest moon of Endor. The structure sits in the center of a vast grassland and is filled with flowers, waterfalls, and terraced plants. The Gupin can change into other forms, though this ability is dependent on the beliefs of others. [ETV]

Guri

The lovely chief lieutenant and bodyguard for Prince Xizor. She was assumed to be the underlord of the Black Sun crime syndicate. This misperception was actually encouraged by Xizor, and Guri served as the organization's public face. Though Guri appeared to be an attractive woman in her early twenties, she was really a rare human replica droid. Programmed for assassination and designed to serve as a living weapon, the droid has blue eyes, golden hair, and the trim figure of a professional dancer. Xizor paid nine million credits to have Guri built, and he considered her to be one of his most prized possessions.

After Xizor's presumed death, Guri could have taken total control of Black Sun. Instead, she decided to find a way to clear her programming and start over with a new life. With the help of her original creator, Massad Thrumble, and the droid A-OIC, Guri underwent a dangerous neural restructuring that erased her criminal memories but allowed her to retain her martial skills. [SEE, SESB, SOTE]

Gus Treta

A large spaceport located in the Corellian system. Wedge Antilles's parents managed a fueling depot here until pirates murdered them. [GG1, MTS]

Gwig

A young Ewok, he sought to join older Ewoks on their many adventures. [ETV]

Gyndine

An Imperial territorial administrative world ruled by Governor Bin Essada, it had jurisdiction over the nearby Circarpous system. [DESB, SME]

gyro-balance circuitry

This circuitry provides machines three-dimensional direction-sensing capabilities. These devices are found in vehicles and droids, helping the machines achieve stability in all three planes whether at rest or in motion. [HSE]

Hakassi

A planet famous for its shipyards. Twelve years after the Battle of Endor, the New Republic fleet carrier *Intrepid* was constructed here. [BTS]

Halcyon, Keiran

A Corellian Jedi and ancestor of Corran Horn. Horn used his name when he trained at Luke Skywalker's Jedi academy on Yavin 4. [IJ]

Halcyon, Nejaa

A Corellian Jedi Master killed during the Clone Wars, he left behind a wife and son. He was a close friend of Rostek Horn, his liaison with the Corellian Security Force. [BW]

Halkans, Minister

A wealthy carbonite smelter, the last to be executed by a small band of dark-siders who overthrew the Empress Teta government some 4,000 years before the Galactic Civil War. [DLS]

Halla

This old woman with a limited use of the Force lived on the planet Mimban. Shortly after the Battle of Yavin, Halla enlisted Leia Organa and Luke Skywalker to help her find the ancient Kaiburr Crystal. [SME]

Halowan

This planet was the location of a top secret Imperial data storage network and a transsystem data storage library. Voren Na'al, an Alliance historian, infiltrated the data net by posing as an agent of Moff Lorin of the Fakir sector. [MTS]

Halpat

This planet was the location of a New Republic field supply and logistics center. [SOL]

Hammax, Captain Bijo

Courageous and intelligent, this foray commander for Colonel Pakkpekatt's New Republic armada helped pursue the Telijkon vagabond ghost ship. [BTS]

Hammerhead

See Ithorian.

Hammertong

Code name for one of the long, cylindrical sections of the second Death Star's superlaser. [TMEC]

hanadak

A ferocious beast, like a cross between a grizzly bear and a baboon, that lives on the forest moon of Endor. [ETV]

Hand of Thrawn

A hidden base beyond the Outer Rim Territories, established by Grand Admiral Thrawn. It contained a secret chamber where Thrawn was growing a clone of himself. The base was under the command of Captain Voss Parck and Baron Soontir Fel, and included a contingent of Chiss warriors and starfighters that combined TIE components with Chiss technology. The base gathered signals from across the galaxy, feeding information into extensive data banks. The command center oversaw all of the planets and resources Thrawn had gathered under his control—enough to tip the balance of power to whichever side Parck and Fel decided to support. Sixteen years after the Battle of Endor, Luke Skywalker and Mara Jade destroyed the cloning chamber and severely damaged the base. [SP, VF]

Hannser, Captain

A human, he commanded the New Republic gunship *Marauder*. His vessel accompanied the *Glorious* and the D-89 on the original mission to intercept the Teljkon vagabond ghost ship. [BTS]

Hapan

A humanoid species native to the Hapes Cluster. [CPL]

Hapan Battle Dragon

A huge saucer-shaped starship about 500 meters in diameter, recognizable by its double saucers that extend from the main hull. Each carries three squadrons of fighters and 500 ground-assault troops in its docking bays. A fleet of Battle Dragons helped the New Republic defeat Warlord Zsinj at the Battle of Dathomir. [CPL, SWVG]

Hapes Consortium

A cluster of sixty-three inhabited planets, this old and wealthy society was first settled thousands of years ago by the pirates known as Lorell Raiders. Eventually, the Jedi Knights decimated the male pirates, allowing women to take control of the Consortium. Four years after the Battle of Endor, Queen Mother Ta'a Chume of the Royal House of Hapes abandoned the Consortium's long isolation and made contact with the New Republic. [CPL]

Hapes *Nova*-class battle cruiser

A fast, 400-meter-long combat ship, one of many that patrol the outer regions of the Hapes Cluster. Hapan Prince Isolder offered one of these vessels to Han Solo if Solo would cease his efforts to win Princess Leia's hand, so that Isolder could marry her. [CPL, SWVG]

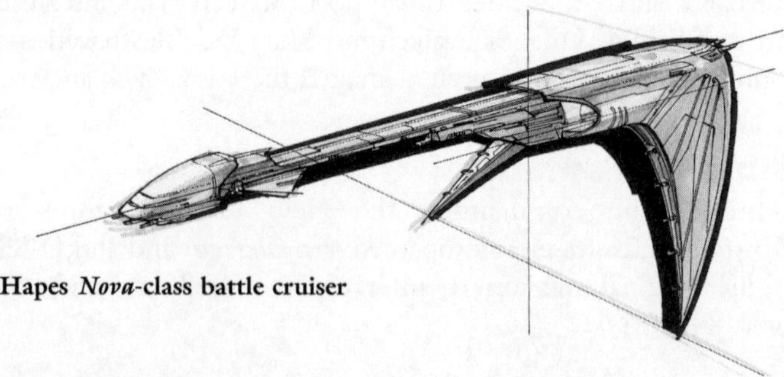

Hapes *Nova*-class battle cruiser

Hariz

A spaceport on the planet N'zoth. [SOL]

Harkul

A vast desert plain located on the planet Kuar. About 4,000 years prior to the Galactic Civil War, it was the site of a battle between Jedi Ulic Qel-Droma and the warrior Mandalore. [TSW]

Harona, Lieutenant Ijix

An officer aboard the *Glorious*, command ship for the New Republic's chase armada sent to find the Teljkon vagabond ghost ship. Harona joined Intelligence agents Pleck and Taisden in an unauthorized mission to recover Lando Calrissian and his companions after the vagabond jumped to hyperspace with them aboard. [BTS, SOL]

Harridan

A *Victory*-class Star Destroyer assigned to protect the Imperial shipyard at N'zoth. It was later sent to join Imperial forces at Notak, and therefore wasn't at the facility to defend it against the Yevethan attack. [BTS]

Harrsk, Grand Admiral

An Imperial warlord, he rose to prominence after the Emperor's death and controlled a number of star systems with a fleet of twelve Star Destroyers. He attended a meeting with a dozen other warlords to discuss unification plans with Admiral Daala. When no agreement could be reached, Daala filled the meeting room with nerve gas, killing Harrsk and the others. [DS]

Hartzig

An Almanian officer under the command of the dark-sider Kueller, he oversaw the holocaust on the planet Pydyr. [NR]

Hask, Loka

Captain of the Dreadnaught *Dominator*. He was among the pirate crew that killed Wedge Antilles's parents at Gus Treta. While enacting his revenge, Wedge destroyed much of the left side of Hask's face. Later, Hask framed Wedge and imprisoned him, but Antilles managed to escape. Hask and his Imperial forces were swallowed by an artificially created wormhole. [XW]

Hatawa sector

A sector defended by the Black Sword Command during the reign of the Emperor, it contained more than 200 inhabited worlds. [BTS]

Hathrox III

A plague weapon devastated this planet some twelve centuries before the Galactic Civil War. By the time of the New Republic, it was still listed as a standing hazard in the galactic registry. [POT]

haul jets

A spacer expression for a quick departure. [SWR]

HC-100

A homework-correction droid with a human shape, silver skin, and glowing blue photoreceptor eyes. Built by DJ-88, its primary function was to correct and grade Jedi Prince Ken's educational assignments. [LCJ, PDS]

Headquarters

A seedy bar located in the Invisec alien zone on Coruscant. [BW]

Headquarters Frigate, the

See *Home One*.

heads-up display

A holographic projector that displays tactical and diagnostic information to starfighter pilots as transparent holograms and holographs, projected at eye level, so that pilots stay focused on the space in front of them without looking down at instrumentation panels. [HSE, SWSB]

Heater

A gunman, he was one of Jabba the Hutt's lieutenants. [SWR]

Hefi

The site of a secret retreat where Death Star designer Bevel Lemelisk was reported to have hidden after the first battle station's destruction. [DS, MTS]

Helska system

This star system near the galactic rim contains seven planets. The fourth planet, an ice world, was where the Yuuzhan Vong invasion force settled after breaching the galactic boundary. The yammosk, or war coordinator, burrowed beneath the ice and established the Yuuzhan Vong base there. To defeat the invasion force, Anakin Solo had the idea to heat the planet and steal the yammosk's energy through evaporation. He used Lando Calrissian's shieldships to reflect energy back to the planet and the evaporation took on a life of its own—the ice planet shattered, destroying the yammosk and the entire Yuuzhan Vong base. [VP]

Hendanyn death mask

A ceremonial mask that molds itself to the wearer's skin. It hides the signs of aging and also stores memories before the wearer dies, allowing the information to be retained after death. Dark-sider Kueller wore one of these masks; his was white with black accents and had tiny jewels in the corners of both eye slits. [NR]

Hensara system

A star system located in the Rachuk sector. The third planet, a jungle world, was the site of the Rout of Hensara three years after the Battle of Endor, in which Rogue Squadron rescued Dirk Harkness and his Black Curs from Imperials without suffering any casualties. [RS]

herd ship

Ithorian vessels that travel the space lanes like great caravans, selling unusual merchandise from one end of the galaxy to the other. Designed for Ithorian comfort, they duplicate the tropical environment of Ithor, full of indoor jungles, artificial storms, wildlife, and vast expanses of lush vegetation. On Ithor, the great herd ships are used as floating cities, harmlessly sweeping over the sacred forests and plains. [GA, SWSB, TMEC]

Herglic

Large bipeds from the planet Giju, they average about 1.9 meters tall and have extremely wide bodies and smooth, hairless skin. Herglic apparently evolved from water-dwelling mammals, though their fins and flukes were replaced by arms and legs, and they breathe through blowholes in the tops of their heads. This species is known for its explorers and merchants, who were among the first members of the Old Republic. The manufacturing centers of Giju were the earliest captured by the Empire, and after a brief and bloody struggle the pragmatic species surrendered completely to the Empire's will. Many species considered them to be traitors to the rest of the galaxy. [DFR, DRFSB]

Hesperidium

A resort moon in the Coruscant system that features luxurious accommodations. Emperor Palpatine maintained a home here for his concubines, and the New Republic has kept villas for the use of visiting diplomats. [POT]

Hethrir, Lord

A Firrerreon, he had gold-, copper-, and cinnamon-striped hair, pale skin, and double-lidded black eyes. He studied the dark side of the Force under Darth Vader and served as an Imperial Procurator of Justice. He destroyed his homeworld and turned his own son into a slave. After the death of Emperor Palpatine, he started the Empire Reborn movement. Later, he kidnapped children, enslaving those without Force abilities and training those with Force powers in the ways of the dark side. With the help of the creature known as the Waru, Hethrir hoped to attain greater access to the Force. He appeased the Waru and cajoled its assistance by giving it Force-sensitive children. Hethrir kidnapped Anakin Solo and planned to give the child to the Waru, but Hethrir's son Tigris helped Anakin escape. The enraged and dying Waru grabbed Hethrir and pulled him into its energy field, destroying them both. [CS, SWCG]

Hextrophon, Arhul

Executive secretary and master historian for the Alliance High Command. [GG1, SWSB]

H'gaard

One of the two largest moons orbiting the planet Bespin. With the smaller, Drudonna, these two moons are known as the Twins. H'gaard appears as a large green sphere in Bespin's night sky. [GG2]

hibernation sickness

A common disorder that affects those awakened from suspended animation, characterized by temporary blindness, disorientation, muscle stiffness and weakness, hypersensitivity, and occasionally madness. Han Solo suffered a mild case of hibernation sickness after he was released from his carbonite prison by Princess Leia. [RJ]

Hig

A slender, blue-skinned alien species. [NR]

High Council of Alderaan

The legislative body that governed Alderaan's planetary government. [SWR]

High Court of Alderaan

The royal house that presided over Alderaan's High Council. [SWR]

Hija, Lieutenant

The Imperial chief gunnery officer aboard the Star Destroyer *Devastator*, he was at his post when the vessel overtook and captured the *Tantive IV* in the Tatooine star system. Years earlier, Hija fired the shots that destroyed the Empire's Falleen biological warfare installation to cover up a mishap. The devastation led to the death of Prince Xizor's family. [SESB, SWN]

Hijarna

This deserted, battle-scarred planet was the location of an ancient fortress where Talon Karrde and other smugglers met to plan against Grand Admiral Thrawn. [LC]

Hin

The Yuzzem miner who helped Luke Skywalker and Princess Leia Organa escape from Captain-Supervisor Grammel's prison on Mimban (Circarpous V). Later, Hin rescued Luke at the Temple of Pomojema. [SME]

Hirf, Qlaern

This Vratix was a member of the Ashern Circle, which was considered to be a terrorist group by the human leaders of the planet Thyferra. Hirf alerted New Republic Intelligence to hidden bacta stores, then secretly made his way to Coruscant to find a cure for the Krytos virus. For security reasons, his experiments and research were transferred to the Alderaan Biotics hydroponics facility on Borleias. [BW]

Hirken, Viceprex Mirkovig

The administrator of the Corporate Sector Authority's installation on Mytus VII, otherwise known as Stars' End. He was a tall, handsome patriarchal figure who always wore impeccable attire. [HSE]

Hissa, Grand Moff

Obviously possessing a bit of alien blood, Hissa had slightly pointed ears and teeth. Of all the grand moffs active after the Battle of Endor, Hissa was the one Emperor Trioculus trusted the most. He was eventually given command of the Empire's Central Committee of Grand Moffs. Due to a mishap with toxic waste on the planet Duro, Hissa lost his arms and legs. He moved around in a repulsorlift chair, and his arms were replaced with limbs taken from an assassin droid. [GDV, MMY, PDS]

Hissal

A scholar and academician from the University of Rudrig, Hissal brought guidance and aid to his home planet, Brigia. The tall, purple-skinned humanoid employed Han Solo and Chewbacca prior to the pair's involvement in the Galactic Civil War. [HLL]

H'kig

A religious leader on the Core world Galand several centuries before the Galactic Civil War, he preached a message of strict morals and goodness. This angered the royal families of Galand, and the viceroy of Galand put H'kig to death. However, H'kig's death served to launch a new religion, and the H'kig faithful purchased two colony ships and fled the religious persecution of Galand's decadent society. They settled on Rishi, establishing a theocratic government whose laws were based on the teachings of H'kig and toleration of other faiths. H'kig dissidents, leaving Rishi over a doctrinal dispute, built a temple on J't'p'tan. [DFRSB, TT]

H'nemthe

This planet with three moons is home to a species of the same name. The H'nemthe have blue-gray skin, double rows of cheekbones, a gently curved nose, four conelets on the skull, and three fingers on each hand. [TMEC]

Hobbie

See Klivian, Derek "Hobbie."

Ho'Din

A gentle humanoid species from the planet Moltok, they prefer natural processes to technology, and their natural-medicine techniques are recognized throughout the galaxy. Their name translates as "walking flower." A typical Ho'Din has a lanky three-meter frame, with thick, snakelike tresses sprouting from his or her head. [GG4, HESB, LC, LCJ]

Hoff, Colby

A business rival of Prince Xizor, leader of the Black Sun criminal organization. After Xizor had Colby killed, Colby's son attacked Xizor in retaliation, ambushing him deep inside the supposedly well-protected core of Imperial Center. Xizor easily defeated the younger Hoff, but he never was able to determine who had granted his attacker access. He suspected it was Darth Vader. [SOTE]

Hoggon

This down-on-his-luck spacer met Ulic Qel-Droma about ten years after the Sith War. Ulic hired Hoggon to take him to an out-of-the-way location where he could isolate himself from the galaxy. Hoggon took Ulic to the ice planet Rhen Var, then decided to make a name for himself by killing the infamous dark Jedi. [TOJR]

Hokuum station

A station within many bars and casinos throughout the galaxy that caters to those who prefer nonliquid stimulants, including glitterstim and other spices. [NR]

Hollowtown

Once, this area at the core of Centerpoint Station was rich in vegetation and other life. When Centerpoint became active and charged with star-destroying energy, Hollowtown was reduced to a burned-out hulk. [SAC]

holocam

Video surveillance devices used throughout the galaxy for espionage and security. [RSB]

holocomm

A HoloNet comm unit, it allows users to transmit and receive messages over a holographic-based transmission network. [DFRSB, ISB]

Holocron

See Jedi Holocron; Sith Holocron.

holocube

A hand-sized, six-sided object designed to hold three-dimensional holo images. By moving around the cube, a person can see all aspects of a displayed image. [HSE]

hologram

A moving three-dimensional image that can be broadcast in real time as part of a comm unit communication or via the galaxywide HoloNet. [SW]

Hologram Fun World

A theme park located inside a glowing, transparent dome that floats inside a blue cloud of gas suspended in outer space. The promotions declare that the park is "a world of dreams come true." Lando Calrissian served as baron administrator of Hologram Fun World for a time after the Battle of Endor. The park was used by the evil scientist Borborygmus Gog as a testing ground for his Nightmare Machine. [GF, PDS, QE]

holograph

A static three-dimensional image. [SWR]

holographic recording mode

A recording process for capturing images and sounds in a three-dimensional format. Devices featuring holographic recording modes store high-resolution images as both holograms and holographs. R2 astromech droids possess this capability. [SWR]

holomonster

Animated holograms of fantastic creatures taken from the myths and legends of the galactic community. These three-dimensional images are projected onto hologameboards for use as playing pieces in various hologames. [SW]

HoloNet

The Old Republic Senate commissioned the construction of this galaxywide, near-instantaneous communication network to provide a free flow of information between the member worlds. The HoloNet uses hundreds of thousands of nonmass transceivers connected through a vast matrix of coordinated hyperspace simutunnels and routed through massive computer sorters and decoders. When the Emperor came to power, he shut down large portions of the HoloNet. It remained active in the Core Worlds and was used as a military communications medium for the Imperial fleet, but all of the outer systems were cut off to isolate them and keep news of the Emperor's atrocities from spreading. [DFRSB, ISB]

holoprojector

A device that uses modulasers to broadcast real-time or recorded holograms. [DFRSB, HSE]

holoshroud

A holographic projection used to mask the operator in covert missions. [TMEC]

Holowan Laboratories

The company commissioned by Imperial Supervisor Gurdun to build the IG series of assassin droids. [TBH]

Home One

This Mon Calamari starship served as Admiral Ackbar's personal flagship during the Battle of Endor. The vessel, also referred to as the Headquarters Frigate, was cylindrical and organically artistic, with no hard angles to mar its fluid surface. The vessel also served as the Alliance command center during the reconquest of Coruscant. [BW, RJ]

Honoghr

The fourth planet in the Honoghr system, it was the homeworld of the fierce Noghri. The planet was devastated when a starship crashed into it during the Clone Wars, releasing toxic chemicals into the atmosphere. Afterwards, Honoghr appeared as a uniformly brown, mostly dead world, with only an occasional blue lake and the green region called the Clean Land. The major city of Nystao and various clusters of small villages were located throughout the Clean Land. It was in this Clean Land that Darth Vader found the Noghri. He provided medicine, food, tools, and decon droids to clean the land. The Noghri bowed down to this black-clad savior, and Vader became their master. This was all part of a grand deception. Vader and the Empire were not repairing the land—they were keeping the world in such a state that the Noghri would always be dependent on them. Princess Leia uncovered the deception and told the Noghri that their world should have been cleansed years ago. She restored their freedom and released them from Imperial bondage after Grand Admiral Thrawn's defeat.

A decade later, hopes for bringing the world back to life had mostly faded. Instead, most of the Noghri had moved to the planet Wayland. [DFR, DFRSB, HE, LC, SP]

Hoole, Mammon

A Shi'ido anthropologist, he was Zak and Tash Arranda's uncle by marriage and took the children in after their parents died in the destruction of Alderaan. Hoole was a geneticist who worked alongside Borborygmus Gog for the Empire. He was tricked into believing their experiments were safe, but they actually destroyed the Kivans. When Hoole realized his error, he fled and helped his niece and nephew seek revenge against the Empire. [GF]

Hoom

A massive Phlog youngster on the forest moon of Endor, he was the son of Zut and Dobah, and the brother of Nahkee. [ETV]

Hoona

An adolescent Phlog female on the forest moon of Endor who once fell in love with the Ewok Wicket W. Warrick because of a magic potion administered by a Dulok shaman. [ETV]

Hoover

A quadruped alien with a long, disproportionate snout and large eyes, he was a member of Jabba the Hutt's court until the crimelord was killed and his organization shattered by Princess Leia Organa and Luke Skywalker. [RJ]

Horm, Threkin

The president of the powerful Alderaanian Council, this grossly overweight human needed a repulsor chair to move around. C-3PO discovered that the illegitimate daughter of the infamous pirate Dalla Suul, who was possibly related to Han Solo, was Horm's mother. [CPL]

Horn, Corran

A Rogue Squadron pilot whose grandfather fought in the Clone Wars alongside Jedi Knights and whose father was a Corellian Security Force (CorSec) officer. When his mother died and his father was murdered, Corran left CorSec and joined the Alliance. He participated in some of Rogue Squadron's most dangerous missions, including the raids on Vladet and Borleias. Later, he served in the advance party during the Alliance's bid to take control of Coruscant. After being imprisoned in and escaping from the buried Super Star Destroyer, *Lusankya*, he learned important information from Luke Skywalker. Luke revealed that Horn's true grandfather was the Jedi Master Nejaa Halcyon. Skywalker presented Horn with Nejaa's lightsaber and offered to train him in the ways of the Jedi. Corran declined the offer in order to make good on his promise to free the rest of the prisoners from the *Lusankya*.

Corran Horn

Later, seven years after the Battle of Endor, Horn's wife, Mirax Terrik, disappeared while on an undercover mission for General Airen Cracken. Horn needed to hone his Force skills to find her, so he agreed to become one of Luke Skywalker's first students at his new Jedi academy. He helped defeat the menace of Exar Kun's evil spirit, but suffered injuries that required extensive bacta treatments. When he healed, he left the academy because he did not agree with many of Skywalker's methods. He infiltrated the pirate Invids in hopes of locating his wife. He constructed his own lightsaber while serving the Invids' leader, Leonia Tavira. With Luke Skywalker's help, Horn rescued Mirax and brought her out of the hibernation trance she had been placed in. [BW, IJ, KT, RS, WG]

Horn, Hal

Corran Horn's father, he was a member of the Corellian Security Force (CorSec). The bounty hunter Bossk killed him. [RS]

Horn, Rostek

During the Clone Wars, this member of the Corellian Security Force befriended the Jedi Master Nejaa Halcyon. After Halcyon was killed, Rostek supported the Jedi's widow and son, later marrying her and adopting the boy. He used his position to alter records, effectively hiding Halcyon's family from the Emperor and saving them from the Jedi Purge that rocked the galaxy. [RS]

Hornet Interceptor

A sleek air-and-space fighter built by black marketeers and used by smugglers, pirates, and other criminals. [GG11, JS]

Horuz system

Located in an isolated region of the Outer Rim Territories, this system contained the prison planet Despayre. The first Death Star battle station was secretly constructed here. Upon completion, it destroyed Despayre. [DSTC, LC, MTS]

Hosk Station

A major trading port and space station in the Kalarba system. [D, SWVG]

Hoth

The sixth planet in a star system of the same name, this frozen world of wind, snow, and ice was the location of the primary Rebel Alliance base three years after the Battle of Yavin. While daytime temperatures across the planet are tolerable for humans wearing proper clothing, the night brings such cold that to travel or even leave protected shelters is tantamount to suicide. Hoth's native life-forms include the tauntaun and the wampa ice creature. The Empire discovered the secret Echo Base, and the ice planet became the site of a terrible engagement known as the Battle of Hoth. After Darth Vader's forces defeated the Rebels here, an Imperial garrison and detention center were placed on the planet. Eight years after the Battle of Hoth, Luke Skywalker and Callista attempted to rescue an expedition of wampa hunters. The ice creatures killed everyone in the expedition, and Skywalker and Callista barely escaped. [DS, ESB, ESBN, ISWU, MTS, PDS]

Hoth, Battle of

One of the worst defeats the Rebel Alliance suffered during the Galactic Civil War. After winning a major victory at the Battle of Yavin, the Alliance spent the next three years running from the Imperial fleet. The Alliance evacuated and relocated its command center—Echo Base—many times during this period to avoid a confrontation with the Imperial armada. The Alliance thought it had finally found the perfect location for its secret base at Hoth. The base was just nearing completion when one of the many Imperial probe droids searching the galaxy happened to discover the Rebels.

Admiral Ozzel's mistake—bringing the Imperial fleet out of hyperspace close enough to alert the Rebels of their arrival—gave the Rebels time to evacuate, though they still suffered grave losses. The Rebels were able to activate the shields protecting the base, making a bombardment from space impossible. As the Rebels prepared to escape, Imperial Star Destroyers moved into position around the planet and Imperial ground forces dropped to the surface beyond the range of the planetary shields. Once on the ground, a squadron of AT-AT walkers and several legions of snowtroopers advanced on the Rebel base.

Alliance High Command ordered the most important staff and materiel loaded into transports and blasted off planet, while Rebel soldiers moved to engage the Imperials in conventional warfare. Heavy casualties ensued. The holding action delayed the Imperials long enough to get the command personnel away, but the Imperials won a major tactical victory—their first in over three years. This dark event influenced the Rebels to try an all-or-nothing attack at Endor one year later. [ESB]

Hoth asteroid belt

A storm of rocks in the Hoth system, the asteroid belt was formed billions of years ago when two planets collided. A pure platinum asteroid, Kerane's Folly, is rumored to exist within the belt. The notorious pirate Clabburn built bases in the larger asteroids and used huge space slugs to guard these hideouts. Eight years after the Battle of Endor, Durga the Hutt began mining raw materials from the asteroids to use in the construction of his Darksaber weapon. [DS, ESB, ISWU]

Hoth system

A remote system located in the Ison Corridor. Notable locations in the system include a dangerous asteroid belt and the sixth planet, Hoth. [ESB, ISWU]

Hound's Tooth

The modified Corellian light freighter used by the bounty hunter Bossk, purchased after Han Solo and Chewbacca destroyed his previous vessel. The ship carried a smaller scout ship, the *Nashtah Pup*, for emergencies. [MTS, TBH]

House Glayyd

See Ammuud clans.

House Reesbon

See Ammuud clans.

hoverscout

A craft that combines hover engines with repulsorlifts to handle most terrain types. The Empire's primary model was the Mekuun Swift Assault Five, which operated effectively as a small unit reconnaissance craft, an offensive point vehicle, and even an infantry and armor support craft. In this capacity, hoverscouts sometimes worked in conjunction with AT-AT walkers. It was armed with a heavy blaster cannon, a light laser cannon, and a concussion missile launcher. [DFRSB, ISB]

Howler Tree People

A species from the planet Bendone, they speak an ultrasonic language. [YJK]

howlrunner

A wild, omnivorous canine that inhabits the planet Kamar. Their heads resemble human skulls. [HSR]

Howzmin

A human, he was chief of security and operations within Prince Xizor's palace on Coruscant. In addition to his duties as captain of the guard, Howzmin worked to uncover spies in the palace and watched all activities occurring within Xizor's sanctum. The bald, squat man was rarely seen without his gray jumpsuit and hip-strapped blaster. His black-chromed teeth gave him an unnerving smile, and he had infrared visual enhancers and cybernetic implants that allowed Xizor to summon him. [SESB, SOTE]

Hrasskis

Homeworld to a species of the same name. Hrasskis are notable for the large, veined air sacs on their backs. [BTS, SOL]

hrrtayyk

A coming-of-age ritual for Wookiees. [TT]

hssiss

Thousands of years before the Galactic Civil War, these ferocious dark-side dragons lived in Lake Natth on the planet Ambria. [TOJ]

Hui, Andoorni

A Rodian member of Rogue Squadron, she was seriously injured during a night raid at Talasea and later killed during the first raid on Borleias. [BW]

hulgren

A forty-meter-long snakelike creature that inhabits the lower levels of Hosk Station. [D]

human-droid relations specialist

A classification identifying those droids programmed to provide an interface between humans and other droids or other self-aware mechanicals, such as ship computers. Language interpretation and diplomatic programming are this classification's primary functions. [SW]

Human League

The most powerful private militia on Corellia, it was opposed to any nonhumans in the Corellian sector. The league, commanded by the mysterious Hidden Leader, was in favor of self-rule and opposed to any interference from the New Republic. [AC]

human replica droid

Lifelike droids constructed from biomechanical, electronic, and synthetic materials. Most beings, and most sensors, can't tell the difference between these mimics and real humans. The ultimate replica droid was Guri, the bodyguard and top aide of Prince Xizor. [PDS, QUE, SESB, SOTE]

human replica droid

hunter-killer probot

A capital-ship-sized droid modeled after the Imperial probe droid and designed for pursuit and police actions against isolated quarries. The fully automated droid ship has offensive and defensive weapons and an interior holding bay for detaining captured freighters. [DE, DESB]

Hurcha

The eighth planet in the Churba star system, so far from the sun that it remains too cold to support life. [DFR, DFRSB]

Hutt

Large sluglike creatures from the planet Varl, with great bulbous heads, wide blubbery bodies, short stubby arms, and tapering muscular tails. They grow to lengths of up to five meters but have no legs. They move by slithering or by ferrying themselves on hoversleds. The Hutts escaped disaster on their homeworld and migrated to the planet Nal Hutta many millennia ago. The planet and its moon, Nar Shaddaa, became the center for smuggling in the galaxy.

Throughout history Hutts have been thoroughly immoral, taking and exercising power over others. They are long-lived creatures, some even claiming to be nearly 1,000 standard years old. Many Hutts became criminal underlords, following a business philosophy of kajidic, which roughly translates as "Somebody's going to have it, so why not us?" [DS, GG4, SWCG]

Hutt caravel
A short-range space transport used by Hutt crimelords to travel between Nal Hutta and its spaceport moon, Nar Shaddaa. [DE]

Hutt floater
Repulsorlift platforms used by members of the Hutt species to move their bloated, nearly limbless bodies from place to place. [DE]

Hutt Haven
This bar was the site of a meeting between Imperial agent Kirtan Loor and Nawara Ven of Rogue Squadron. [BW]

Huwla, Xarrce
A Tunroth, she joined Rogue Squadron just before the Battle of Brentaal. She asked to be transferred out due to the squadron's high casualty rate, but decided to stick with the Rogues after battling Baron Soontir Fel's 181st Imperial fighter group. [XW]

Hydra
One of the four Star Destroyers in Admiral Daala's fleet, it was destroyed when Han Solo piloted the Sun Crusher through its command center. [DA, JS]

hydrospanner
A powered wrench. [ESB]

Hyllyard City

The major population center on the planet Myrkr, this frontier town consists of ship landing pits and a close-packed collection of makeshift structures. A few settlers live in this haven for smugglers and fugitives from other worlds. [HE, HESB]

Hyos, Dr.

A Codru-Ji doctor, she has long, gold fingers. [CS]

hyperbaric medical chamber

A supermedicated and superoxygenated cubicle used to heal burned tissue. Darth Vader spent time in his personal hyperbaric chamber as it allowed him to breathe without his helmet or body armor for short periods of time. [SOTE]

hyperdrive

The starship engine and its interrelated systems that propel space vessels to superlight speeds and into hyperspace. Powered by incredibly efficient fusion generators, hyperdrive engines work with astrogation computers to assure safe and dependable hyperspace travel. To protect ships from hyperspace gravity shadows, most hyperdrives are equipped with an automatic cutoff. If a gravity shadow is scanned along the route ahead, the cutoff dumps the ship back into realspace. Even with cutoffs, ships that fly too close to gravity shadows while traveling through hyperspace could sustain massive—and sometime fatal—amounts of damage. [ESB, HESB, SWSB]

hyperdrive motivator

The primary lightspeed thrust initiator in the hyperdrive engine system, connected to a vessel's main computer system to monitor and collect sensor and navigation data in order to determine jump thrusts, adjust engine performance in hyperspace, and calibrate safe returns to realspace. [ESBR]

hyperspace

A dimension of space-time that can be reached only by traveling at light speed and using a hyperdrive engine. Hyperspace converges with realspace, so that every point in realspace is associated with a unique point in hyperspace. If a ship travels in a specific direction in realspace prior to jumping to hyperspace, then it continues to travel in that direction through hyperspace. Objects in realspace cast gravity shadows into hyperspace that have to be plotted to avoid collision. [SW, SWRPG, SWSB]

Hyperspace

A restaurant on the Yag'Dhul space station and a favorite hangout of Rogue Squadron between missions. [BW, KT]

hyperspace compass

A device used by starships to navigate by orienting on the center of the galaxy. It can be used in realspace and hyperspace. [DE]

Hyperspace Marauder

A starship owned and operated by the smuggler Lo Khan. [DE, DESB]

hyperspace transponder

The heart of all hyperspace communications systems, it produces the weak signals that send comm messages through hyperspace. Since it is not always reliable or effective, the New Republic poured a huge amount of resources into designing and building a more effective hyperspace communication system. [DE]

hyperspace wormhole

An unpredictable natural phenomenon, it suddenly connects distant points of the galaxy by creating hyperspace tunnels. These wormholes produce vast amounts of energy in the form of violent storms. Great disturbances in the Force sometimes trigger a wormhole. [DE]

hyperwave inertial momentum sustainer

(HIMS)
Invented by the Bakurans, this device was able to defeat an interdiction gravity field. [AS]

hyperwave warning

A mechanism that detects ships about to emerge from hyperspace and sounds an alert. [TBH]

I-7 (Howlrunner)

An Imperial starfighter introduced during the period marked by the appearance of the clone Emperor. Pilots nicknamed the craft Howlrunner, after the wild omnivores from the planet Kamar. [DE, DESB]

Ialtra

The former village of the Fallanassi religious order on Lucazec, it was desecrated by neighbors who feared the Fallanassi's powers. [BTS]

I'att, Tinian

This armaments heiress lost everything when the Empire took control of her family's business and killed her parents. Thereafter, she dedicated her life to fighting the Empire and became an apprentice bounty hunter to the Wookiee Chenlambec. She eventually became Chenlambec's partner, and the pair often helped people defect to join the Rebel Alliance. [TBH]

Ibtisam

A Mon Calamari, she was a member of Rogue Squadron who had been part of the first B-wing squadron. Haughty and arrogant, she was both attracted to and repulsed by fellow Rogue Nrin Vakil, a Quarren. She also felt disappointed to be assigned to fly an X-wing, a starfighter she felt was far inferior to her beloved B-wing. [XW]

Icarii

These green-skinned humanoids are extremely difficult to kill, as their limbs continue to fight even after being cut off. [BFEE]

ice worm

Creatures that tunnel through Hoth glaciers, leaving behind honeycombed shafts. [ISWU]

ID profile

A ship's identification, broadcast from its transponder. This electronic signal contains information about the ship, including its name, registration number, current owner, home port, classification, armament and power plant ratings, and any restrictions that apply to it, its cargo, and its owner. The transponder is activated when queried by interrogator modules such as those aboard military vessels and spaceport control towers. ID profiles can be altered, but the process is difficult and illegal. [HSE]

IG-72

One of the original series of IG assassin droids, it refused to accept sentience programming from IG-88 in order to keep its independence. It self-destructed in an attempt to capture Republic hero Adar Tallon, killing Tatooine prefect Orun Depp in the process. [TBH, TM]

IG-88

An infamous assassin droid, he went on to become a feared bounty hunter. Tall and slender, the droid was given sentience and independence by programmers at Holowan Laboratories

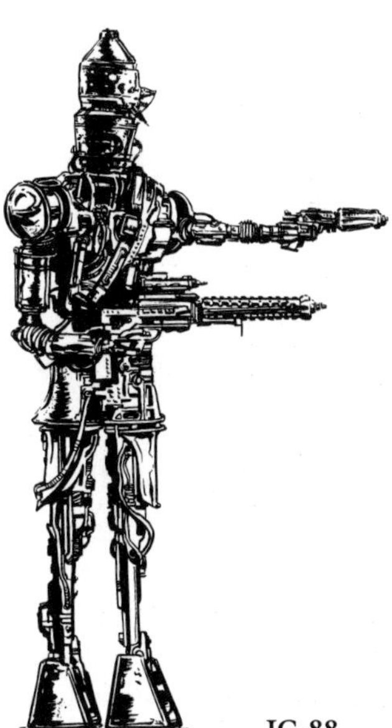

IG-88

as part of Project Phlutdroid. IG-88 and three other similar droids murdered the programmers. With a bounty on his own head, IG-88 nevertheless took on contracts and killed with cold efficiency. A built-in arsenal of weapons and an array of sensors made him extremely formidable. He was among the six bounty hunters hired by Darth Vader to find the *Millennium Falcon*. [ESB, GG3, MTS, TBH]

IG-2000

An assault starfighter owned and operated by the assassin droid IG-88. The twenty-meter-long vessel was fast, built for combat, and could carry up to eight captives in its prisoner hold. The starfighter was destroyed over Tatooine in a battle with Boba Fett. [MTS, SOTE, SWVG, TBH]

IG series prototype

An experimental line of assassin droids commissioned by Imperial Supervisor Gurdun and designed by Chief Technician Loruss of Holowan Laboratories as part of Project Phlutdroid. IG-88 was created as a result of this project. [GG3, TBH]

Ihopek

A planet the Empire was forced to evacuate after the Battle of Hoth. [BTS]

Iillor, Uwilla

The human captain of the *Black Asp*, she served under Colonel Thrawn as part of the elite NhM squad. Later, she and her staff defected to the Alliance. Her ship was renamed *Corusca Rainbow*, and it led the Alliance Invasion fleet during the conquest of Coruscant. [WG]

Ikon

A red dwarf star orbited by an asteroid belt. Princess Leia helped Rebel sympathizers install a turbolaser here after the Battle of Yavin. [ROC]

Ikrit

An ancient Jedi Master, he could not free the spirits from the golden globe, so he remained at the Palace of the Woolamander on Yavin 4 to watch over it. Anakin Solo and his friend Tahiri found him at the Palace. [JJK]

ILC-905

This star system in the Koornacht Cluster was the location of the Black Nine orbital shipyard until the Imperial installation was destroyed by New Republic forces. [TT]

Ilic

One of eight walled cities clustered in the jungles of New Cov, where biomolecule-producing plants are harvested. Ships and shuttles enter the city through vents near the top of its silver-skinned dome. Bothan leader Borsk Fey'lya had numerous business interests in Ilic, and it was here that he often contacted Garm Bel Iblis. While the city and corporate-controlled planetary government considered themselves to be part of the New Republic five years after the Battle of Endor, they still paid periodic tributes to the Imperial remnants. [DFR, DFRSB]

ILKO

One of the master encrypt codes the Empire used for transferring data between Coruscant and the original Death Star construction facility at Horuz. An Alliance team needed a month to break the code; Ghent, a twelve-year-old slicer working for Talon Karrde, took two months to crack the code without any help. [LC]

Illodia

A planet located in a sector of the same name. It and its colony worlds are home to the Illodian species. [TT]

Illustrious

A cruiser in the New Republic's Fifth Fleet. [SOL]

Ilo, Plourr

A Rebel pilot, she served aboard *Home One* during the Battle of Endor, then transferred to Rogue Squadron. Her true name was Isplourrdacartha Estillo, and she was heir to the throne of the planet Eiattu VI. With the help of Rogue Squadron, she unseated an impostor who claimed to be her brother from the Eiattu throne, and squashed a plot by Moff Leonia Tavira. Her world was then invited to join the New Republic, and despite her royal duties she continued to fly with Rogue Squadron. [XW]

Ilthmar Gambit

A hologram board-game move used to gain a tactical advantage over an opponent's guarded position. The player employing the Ilthmar Gambit uses a single playing piece as bait to draw out his opponent's defended pieces. After capturing the piece, the rest of the opponent's forces are left open to the player's follow-up attack. [HSR]

Ilum crystals

See Adegan crystals.

Imperial Academy, the

See Academy, the.

Imperial Center

During Palpatine's reign, the name the Empire used for the planet Coruscant. [SOTE]

Imperial Charter

A document containing the rules and agreements set forth by the Empire to govern the rights and responsibilities of all Imperial worlds and star systems. The charter granted to each member system featured provisions concerning resource usage, rights of passage, military protection, tributes, and colonization. [SME]

Imperial City

The capital of the planet Coruscant, it has changed allegiance a few times in its long history. During the Old Republic, it was called Galactic City, and it served as the capital of the galactic union and the permanent headquarters of the Republic Senate. When Emperor Palpatine came to power, he named it Imperial City, and the planet Imperial Center, and it became the ruling seat of the New Order. After the Battle of Endor, Imperial City was declared the capital of the New Republic. A cosmopolitan city, it has always been crowded. During the Old Republic, millions of species were drawn to the bright lights of this beautiful city. The Emperor later closed the city to nearly all nonhumans.

The ancient, gigantic Senate Hall filled part of the city. The massive Imperial Palace looms over the hall, its tapered spires and fragile-looking towers jutting from every surface. These glowing towers stretch out to blend with the rest of the city's architecture, giving the impression of one endless structure.

The city remained unscathed during the Galactic Civil War, but suffered extensive damage later when it was attacked by the remnants of the Empire. Under the New Republic, the city underwent a painstaking reconstruction program. [DE, DFR, HE, JS, LC]

Imperial code cylinder

A device, issued to Imperial officers, that allowed its user to access computer information via scomp links or gain entry to restricted areas of a ship or installation. A cylinder was coded to its officer's personal security clearance. [DSTC, ISB]

Imperial customs vessel

Light corvettes about 180 meters long, these ships patrolled Imperial space and performed spot inspections on merchant vessels to look for contraband or undeclared cargo. [GG6]

Imperial drone ship

Cylindrical, pilotless ships about nine meters long, they were used to carry messages. [TAB]

Imperial Freight Complex

This huge docking tower and spaceport orbited the planet Byss. Licensed independent haulers brought cargo to this facility for unloading. [DE]

Imperial garrison

Dark, ominous, prefabricated structures that could be set up quickly on nearly any terrain, Imperial garrisons served a number of functions. These bases were scientific, diplomatic, and military strongholds for the Empire that were carried aboard Star Destroyers for immediate deployment by Imperials charged with the subjugation and protection of planets within the Empire. Garrisons were employed to enforce martial law, squelch uprisings, support local governments loyal to the Empire, and deter piracy. Typical personnel included 800 stormtroopers and various support personnel, assorted ground-assault vehicles, and forty TIE fighters. [SWSB]

Imperial gunner

Highly trained weapons masters with keen eyesight, superior reflexes, and a familiarity with gunnery weapons, they were part of a special subunit of the Imperial pilot corps. Gunners wore specialized computer helmets equipped with macrobinocular viewplates and sensor arrays to assist with targeting fast-moving fighter craft. [ISB]

Imperial Hyperspace Security Net

Remnants of the Empire utilized this technology to continuously monitor any unauthorized space traffic in the hyperspace lanes connected to Imperial systems in the Deep Galactic Core. [DE]

Imperial Information Center

The huge computer database on Imperial Center (Coruscant). [DS]

Imperial Intelligence

The military counterpart of the civilian-controlled Imperial Security Bureau (ISB), it consisted of four distinct divisions:

The Ubiqtorate, the Internal Organization Bureau, the Analysis Bureau, and the Bureau of Operations. One of the best-trained and most-professional portions of the Empire to survive the Battle of Endor, it gladly gave its full support to Grand Admiral Thrawn's war effort. [DFRSB, ISB]

Imperial Interim Ruling Council

An assembly of political, military, and business leaders, it took control of the Empire after its members conspired to assassinate the cloned Emperor Palpatine. When the last surviving member of the Emperor's Royal Guard killed its leader, Carnor Jax, the council was thrown into chaos. After a series of murders of various council members, Xandel Carivus took control. He disbanded the council and declared himself emperor. Kir Kanos killed Carivus, and New Republic forces captured the remaining members of the council. [CE]

Imperialization

The process of galactic conquest as set forth by Emperor Palpatine. It focused on the conquest of star systems, the regulation of commerce, and the taxation and appropriation of goods and services for the benefit of the Empire. [SWN]

Imperial Redesign teams

COMPNOR units, they were charged with brainwashing and surgically altering citizens to make them loyal servants of the Empire. [ISB, TBH]

Imperial Security Bureau

A civilian-controlled Imperial agency, it handled espionage and other intelligence work. The Emperor created it as a rival to the military's Imperial Intelligence and to keep him informed of political events. [ISB, SWRPG]

Imperial Senate

The last holdover from the days of the Old Republic, this body was titled "Imperial" after the Empire was established. All member worlds of the Empire sent elected politicians to the senate to create laws, pacts, and treaties to govern the galactic union. In an Empire that was becoming more and more dictatorial and tyrannical, the democratically elected members of the senate were an anomaly. It was the Imperial Senate's job to steer the course of the galactic government and administer to the many member systems. The leader was the chancellor of the senate, who was elected by the other senators to serve as a roving ambassador, arbiter, policymaker, and planner. Once the Death Star battle station was declared operational, the Emperor "suspended" the senate for the "duration of the galactic emergency," instituting his doctrine of rule through fear. [SW]

Imperial Sleeper Cell Jenth-44

A collective of clones on the planet Pakrik Minor, they were cloned by Grand Admiral Thrawn from the genetic material of Baron Soontir Fel. The impostor Thrawn activated this sleeper group, along with others, sixteen years after the Battle of Endor. This group refused to fight for the Empire. Instead, they threw in with the New Republic and helped expose the fake Thrawn. [SP, VF]

Imperial Sovereign Protectors

The highest-ranking members of the Imperial Royal Guard, they served as the Emperor's personal bodyguards. At least one Sovereign Protector was at the Emperor's side at all times. These warriors were rumored to be empowered by the dark side of the Force. After the Emperor's rebirth, the Sovereign Protectors guarded the clone vats on Byss. [DE]

Imperial Star Destroyer

See Star Destroyer.

Imperial stormtroopers

See stormtrooper.

Imperial walker

See All Terrain Armored Transport.

Inadi, Captain

Commander of the New Republic ship *Vanguard.* His vessel was destroyed by Yevethan thrustships and he was killed at ILC-905. [TT]

Incom T-16 skyhopper

See T-16 skyhopper.

Incom T-65

See X-wing starfighter.

Indexer

An octopuslike creature native to Chalcedon, it supplied information about the slave trade and other illegal practices—for a price. [CS]

Indomitable

A cruiser in the New Republic's Fifth Fleet, it was under the command of Commander Brand and served as the battle operations center for Task Force Aster. [SOL]

Industrial Automaton

One of the largest droid manufacturing corporations in the galaxy, it produces various models including the MD series of medical droids and the R series of astromech droids. [SWSB]

Infinity

The ship piloted by BoShek, which he used to beat Han Solo's record for the Kessel Run. [TMEC]

Ingey

The cherished pet of young Prince Coby of Tammuz-an, this small, rare creature was a tessellated arboreal binjinphant—a sort of cross between a kangaroo and a ferret. [DTV]

Ingo

A desolate world of salt flats and craters, its inhabitants are mostly human colonists who work hard and have little to show for it. [DTV]

I'ngre, Herian

A Bith in Rogue Squadron, she was fascinated by emotions and studied heroism. She sacrificed herself on Malrev Four, flying her X-wing into a Sith temple and destroying it. [XW]

Inner Council

The ruling body of the New Republic's Provisional Council, its original members included Mon Mothma, Admiral Ackbar, Leia Organa Solo, and Borsk Fey'lya. It was led by the chief of state. [HE, HESB]

Inner Rim Territories

Originally known as the Rim, the area was once thought to mark the end of galactic expansion. This diverse region is nearly as civilized as the Core Worlds, though it benefits from being less crowded. As the Empire made more and more demands of this region, disgruntled colonists struck out to find better lives in the Outer Rim Territories. [SWRPG2]

insignia of the New Republic

The seal adopted by the Provisional Council was based upon the symbol of the Alliance that preceded it. The blue crest of the Alliance, itself taken from the seal of the Old Republic, was set within a circle of stars that represented the galactic community. The circle was trimmed in gold, symbolizing the right of the people to govern themselves. [HESB]

interdiction field

A field generated by a ship, it produces a gravity well that prevents hyperspace maneuvers in its vicinity. Ships inside an interdiction field cannot jump to light speed, and ships passing through it are abruptly pulled into realspace. [AC]

Interdictor-class cruiser

This 600-meter-long Imperial heavy star cruiser was designed to prevent ships from escaping into hyperspace. A massive gravity-well generator and four gravity-well projectors provide the core of this vessel. The projectors emit waves of energy that disrupt the mass lines of realspace, simulating the presence of a true stellar body. This displacement of mass lines serves two purposes: First, ships within the sphere of influence of a gravity well cannot engage their hyperdrives; and second, ships traveling through hyperspace that come in contact with the resulting gravity shadow have to drop back into realspace. [DFR, HE, HESB, ISB, SWVG]

Internal Organization Bureau

A division of Imperial Intelligence, the Internal Organization Bureau (IntOrg) protected the rest of Intelligence from both internal and external threats. Its agents policed other divisions to verify loyalty and reliability. [ISB]

interrogator

A device that emits an electronic high-frequency signal in order to activate a starship's ID profile transponder. All military ships and spaceports are equipped with interrogators so that authorities can identify and screen approaching vessels. [HSE]

interrogator droid

Terrifying mechanicals designed by the Empire to question prisoners through a variety of techniques, including torture and chemical injection. These black globe-shaped droids possess multiple appendages tipped with pain-inducing tools and are equipped with repulsorlift engines for movement. [SW]

interrogator droid

interruptor template

Metal panels on ships such as the *Millennium Falcon* that help prevent accidental damage from the ship's own weapons. These panels automatically slide into position to keep the ship's lower quad-laser battery from shooting the landing gear or entry ramp when the ship has landed. [HSE]

Intimidator

An Imperial Super Star Destroyer, its crew was killed and the vessel was captured by Nil Spaar during the Yevethan attack on the N'zoth shipyards. It was renamed *Pride of Yevetha* and made part of the Black Fifteen Fleet. [SOL]

Intrepid

A fleet carrier and the flagship of the New Republic's Fifth Fleet, it was under the command of Captain Morano. [SOL]

Intruder

A light cruiser, the flagship of the Bakuran fleet. [AS]

Intuci

This planet was raided by the armies of war criminal Sonopo Bomoor. [JAB]

Invids

Pirate crews working with the ex-Imperial Star Destroyer *Invidious*, they were loyal to ex-Moff Leonia Tavira. [IJ]

Invisec

A huge area of Imperial Center (Coruscant), it was also called the Invisible Sector or the Alien Protection Zone. [KT, WG]

ion beamer

A Ssi-ruuk medical instrument that can also be used as a weapon, it fires a thin silver beam that disables the nervous system but does not penetrate nonliving tissue. [TAB]

ion cannon

A weapon that fires bursts of ionized energy that inflict damage on a target's mechanical and computer systems by overloading and fusing circuitry. Unlike blaster bolts, ion bursts cause no structural damage. They do, however, neutralize ship weapons, shields, engines, and other vital systems. Planetary ion cannons are mounted in multistory spherical towers that hurl devastating bursts of ionized energy into space to ward off hostile vessels. [ESB]

ion cannon

ion engine

The most common sublight drive, it hurls charged particles through an exhaust port to produce thrust. [SW]

IRD

Starfighters used by Corporate Sector Authority police, extremely fast but not very maneuverable. [HSE]

Irenez

A Corellian soldier, she was a member of Senator Garm Bel Iblis's private army at Peregrine's Nest. She served as chief of security, intelligence coordinator, pilot, and bodyguard for Bel Iblis and his chief adviser, Sena Leikvold Midanyl. [DFR, DFRSB]

Iridium

This planet was home to space pirates who preyed on merchant vessels in the Old Republic until the Jedi Knights wiped them out. The pirates used unique Iridium power gems to break through starship shields. Han Solo exhausted the last of these gems following the Battle of Yavin. [CSW]

Iron Citadel

The ancient fortress of the Krath sect, it was located in Cinnagar, the largest city of the seven worlds that comprised the Empress Teta star system. [DLS]

Iron Fist

This Super Star Destroyer was Warlord Zsinj's flagship and the primary vessel in his fleet. [CPL, IF]

Isard, Ysanne

Director of Imperial Intelligence on Imperial Center (Coruscant), she was nicknamed Iceheart. She was the daughter of Emperor Palpatine's last internal security director, and she killed her father in order to replace him. Following the Emperor's death, she rose in power and held the Empire together.

Isard captured Mara Jade while Jade was still reeling from the Emperor's death. Isard believed that Jade was a traitor, and hated her because she could never learn anything about her. She considered Rogue Squadron to be a significant threat to the Empire, so she commissioned Agent Kirtan Loor to destroy them. Meanwhile, she went about trying to crush the Alliance by bankrupting it. She had the Krytos virus developed to infect Coruscant's alien population. None of her schemes succeeded, and she was eventually forced to flee Imperial Center. During the final moments of the Bacta War, her shuttle was destroyed when she tried to escape.

But that wasn't the end for Isard. Two years later, two Isards showed up to harass Rogue Squadron—the real Isard and her clone. Wedge Antilles destroyed the clone, while New Republic Intelligence officer Iella Wessiri confronted the real Isard and killed her aboard the *Lusankya*. [BW, IR, KT, MJ, RS, WG, XW]

Ishi Tib

A bulbous-eyed humanoid with a beaklike mouth, this alien was one of Jabba the Hutt's subordinates. Ishi Tib was the name of his species. They come from the planet Tibrin, where they live in cities built atop carefully cultivated coral reefs. They are meticulous planners, and many intergalactic corporations seek them out as managers and technicians. [GG4, RJ]

Ismaren, Roganda and Irek

The mistress and rumored son of Emperor Palpatine, this pair hid on the planet Belsavis until Leia Organa Solo arrived to follow up on rumors that the planet had housed a large group of Jedi children. Leia discovered that, at fifteen, Irek was becoming strong in the dark side of the Force. He wanted to bring the powerful *Eye of Palpatine* ship to the planet, but it was destroyed before it could reach Belsavis. The Ismarens escaped into the planet's dense jungle. [COJ, SWCG]

Roganda and Irek Ismaren

Isolder, Prince

Prince Isolder

The heir to the Royal House of Hapes and one of the handsomest humans in the galaxy, he nevertheless had a rough life. A pirate named Haravan murdered Isolder's older brother, and his first love, Lady Ellian, drowned in a reflecting pool. Both deaths were arranged by his mother, Queen Mother Ta'a Chume, for political purposes. He eventually discovered this, thanks to his bodyguard, Captain Astarta.

Isolder fell in love with Princess Leia and presented her with gifts from the sixty-three planets of the Hapes Consortium. To compete with the prince, Han Solo kidnapped Leia and took her to the planet Dathomir. There, Isolder met Teneniel Djo, one of the Witches of Dathomir. He fell in love with her, and the two married and had a daughter, Tenel Ka, who was later accepted into Luke Skywalker's Jedi academy. [CPL, SWCG]

Ison Corridor

This region of space is located next to the Corellian Trade Spine and contains the Bespin, Anoat, Hoth, and Ison systems. [DFR, GG2]

Ithor

The fourth planet in the Ottega star system, located deep in the Lesser Plooriod Cluster, it is home to the nature-loving Ithorians, or Hammerheads. This lush, tropical world teems with plant and animal life, and its unspoiled rain forests are considered beautiful to behold.

The Ithorians have tamed some of the planet, but large regions remain wild and undeveloped. Nature and technology coexist on this world and work together to support the Ithorians' peaceful, ecology-based civilization. Ithorians live in great floating cities that hover above the surface and migrate around the planet's three developed continents. Each city is a several-levels-high, disk-shaped repulsorlift complex that serves as a center of industry, commerce, and culture. Each herd city was built to mimic the planet's surface, complete with indoor jungles, artificial storms, examples of Ithorian wildlife, and vast corridors of lush vegetation. The *Tree of Tarintha*, the *Cloud-Mother*, and the grand herd ship *Tafanda Bay* are such floating cities. Ithorian starships are herd cities equipped with hyperdrives that serve as traveling bazaars and marketplaces.

The great jungle that covers much of the planet is considered to be sacred by the Ithorians. To them it is the Mother Jungle, and they believe that it sometimes calls certain Ithorians to the surface to live as ecological priests. [COJ, DA, MTS, SWSB, TMEC]

Ithorian

The proper name for the species commonly referred to as Hammerheads. Their nickname originates with their T-shaped heads that rest atop long, curved necks. Ithorians speak with a strange twist because of their two mouths, each located on opposite sides of their necks. This generates a stereo effect that produces one of the most beautiful and difficult to learn languages in the galaxy. Their homeworld, Ithor, is a jungle planet that the Ithorians have learned to respect and even worship. Herbivores, Ithorians never

Ithorian

take more than they need from their planet, and they are bound by the Law of Life that requires them to plant two trees for every one they are required to take from the jungles. Every five years, Ithorians gather at their planet for the Meet. The herd cities link through an intricate and graceful network of bridges and platforms, and decisions regarding Ithorian society are discussed and agreed upon. [SWSB]

Ithor Lady

One of two New Republic cruisers sent to deal with a pirate fleet in the Chorios systems. [POT]

Ithull

Homeworld of the Ithullan species. About 4,000 years before the Galactic Civil War, the exoskeletons of the planet's colossus wasps were used as the hulls of cargo ships, called Ithullan ore haulers, or Nessies. Several hundred years before the Battle of Yavin, the warlike Ithullans were attacked and exterminated by the fierce Mandalorians. [TMEC, TOJ]

IT-O

A prisoner interrogator droid, it uses probes and needles to dispense truth drugs and torture a subject. [GG1, MTS]

Ivak

An Imperial officer that Ysanne Isard sent to talk to the imprisoned Mara Jade in the months following the Emperor's death. He tried to convince Jade to be honest with Isard. Mara used the Force to manipulate Ivak so she could escape. [MJ]

IX-26

A New Republic Intelligence Service ferret ship. [SOL]

IX-44F

This New Republic Intelligence Service ferret ship trailed the mysterious Teljkon vagabond. [BTS]

Ixll

Small, intelligent flying creatures that inhabit the fifth moon of Da Soocha. Their language consists of chirps and whistles similar to the language of R series astromech droids. Ixlls have developed a friendly relationship with the New Republic's Pinnacle Base personnel and often guide New Republic ships through the dangerous peaks of the moon. [DE]

Iziz

An ancient walled city on the planet Onderon, it was once governed by the dark Jedi Freedon Nadd. [DLS, FNU, TOJ]

Izrina

The queen of the Wisties, glowing, flying creatures that live on Endor's forest moon. [EA, ETV]

Jabba's Throne Room

A club on the planet Atzerri, it was almost an exact replica of Jabba the Hutt's throne room on Tatooine, complete with a carbonite-block imitation Han Solo hanging on the wall. [SOL]

Jabba the Hutt

Jabba the Hutt, the notorious crimelord who ran his organization from the planet Tatooine, was one of the major criminal kingpins in the Outer Rim Territories. His organization was involved in a wide variety of illegal activities, including smuggling, spice dealing, slave trading, assassination, loan sharking, protection, and piracy. Born Jabba Desilijic Tiure, he was raised and trained by his father, Zorba, on a private estate on Nal Hutta. By the time he was 600 years old, Jabba had surpassed his father. His desert palace on Tatooine, built around the ancient B'omarr monastery, was full of decadent luxuries, an army of alien and human criminals, droid slaves, and fawning servants. Every smuggler, bounty hunter, pirate, and thief in the Outer Rim Territories eventually took on a job for Jabba, including Han Solo and his partner, Chewbacca. In fact, it was because of a job Solo botched that Jabba ultimately met his end. After Solo dumped a shipment of spice to avoid an Imperial blockade, Jabba gave the smuggler a limited time to make good on the shipment's worth. When Solo failed to return to Tatooine to pay off his debt—he was off helping the Rebellion—Jabba put a price on his head. Boba Fett eventually collected the bounty, but Solo's Rebel companions, including Luke Skywalker, came to rescue the Corellian. Although Skywalker's Jedi "mind tricks" did not work against Jabba, his other abilities made short work of the crimelord's army. It was Princess Leia, however, who killed Jabba, strangling him with the very chains he had used to imprison her. [DS, ESB, GG3, MTS, RJ, SOTE, SW, SWCG]

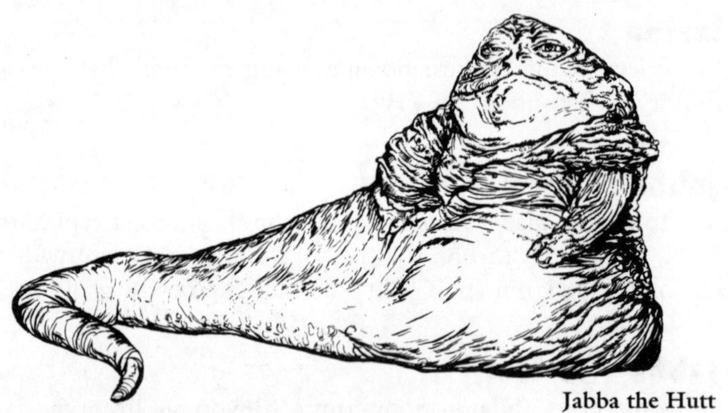

Jabba the Hutt

Jace, Bror

A human pilot from Thyferra, he made twenty-two kills on his first five missions for Rogue Squadron. Hailing from a wealthy family, Jace owned a major share of Zaltin Corporation stock, a bacta-producing company. He was apparently killed while returning to his homeworld, but that was part of an elaborate plan by the Ashern rebels working within the corporation. He helped plan the civil war against Xucphra Corporation and the Imperial, Ysanne Isard. Later, he fought alongside Rogue Squadron in the final battle to defeat Isard. He was then given the task of forming the Thyferran Aerospace Defense Forces. [BW, RS, WG]

Jacques

A family of moisture farmers on Tatooine, they supported Ariq Joanson in his plans to make peace with the Jawas and the Sand People. [TMEC]

Jade, Mara

See Skywalker, Mara Jade.

Jade Sabre

A shuttle Luke Skywalker built especially for his wife, Mara Jade Skywalker. [VP]

Jade's Fire

Mara Jade's personal starship and her most prized possession. It represented freedom, the ability to pick up and leave at a moment's notice. She sacrificed it to help Luke Skywalker disable the hidden Imperial base known as the Hand of Thrawn. [VF]

Jagga-Two

This planet located in the Venjagga system was the site of an Imperial base that made concussion missiles and supported the Imperial II Star Destroyer *Eviscerator.* [RS]

Jagg Island Detention Center

This prison was where former Imperial Navy officer Davith Sconn was held. He provided vital information concerning the Yevetha to Chief of State Leia Organa Solo and Admiral Ackbar. [SOL]

Jamer, Captain Dren

This Imperial Navy officer was repeatedly disciplined for a lack of enthusiasm and ambition. His record showed long stretches of mediocrity broken by brief moments of excellence. He eventually was offered the position of second in command aboard the *Carrack*-class cruiser *Dominant*. The short, pudgy Jamer was on the *Dominant* during the events leading to the truce at Bakura. When the Imperial forces at Bakura surrendered to the Alliance, Jamer refused to defect. [TAB, TBSB]

Jandi, Aellyn

The wife of the Imperial moff on Elshandruu Pica, Riit Jandi, she was forty years younger than her husband and having an affair with Captain Sair Yonka. [BW]

Jandi, Riit

An Imperial moff, his base of operations was the planet Elshandruu Pica. [BW]

Jandur

A planet that, along with Cortina, petitioned for membership in the New Republic and was eventually accepted. [BTS]

Janson, Lieutenant Wes

A Rebel Alliance snowspeeder gunner during the Battle of Hoth, he served in the craft piloted by Wedge Antilles. Later, he became a member of Rogue Squadron, eventually becoming one of the New Republic's brightest flight instructors. [ESBR, GG3, XW]

Jantol

This New Republic ship was deployed at Wehttam in anticipation of a Yevethan attack. [SOL]

Jarril

A small man with narrow shoulders and a scarred face, he was an old smuggling contact of Han Solo and Chewbacca. He was involved in the sale of Imperial equipment to the dark-sider Kueller in the asteroid belt known as Smuggler's Run. He invited Solo to meet with him on Coruscant to provide information and was killed for his trouble. [NR]

Jawa

Meter-tall rodentlike scavengers, they are intelligent, smelly natives of Tatooine who constantly jabber away in their own language. To protect themselves from Tatooine's fierce double suns, they wear coarse cloaks with hoods that leave only their glowing eyes visible. Jawas travel in bands, utilizing huge, treaded sandcrawlers for shelter and mobility. They scavenge droids and other machinery, cleaning and repairing it to sell to moisture farmers and others. [ISWU, SW, SWCG, SWR, SWSB]

Jawa

Jawaswag

The name of Rogue Squadron pilot Gavin Darklighter's astromech droid. Also known as Toughcatch or Catch. [BW]

Jax, Carnor

A member of the Emperor's Royal Guard, he bribed the Emperor's personal physician into sabotaging Palpatine's clone bodies. He then ordered the elimination of the Royal Guard, massacring all but one: Kir Kanos. Jax took control of the Imperial Interim Ruling Council, but Kanos eventually caught up to him and engaged him in a fierce battle. Jax died in the fight, and the council was thrown into chaos. [CE]

Jedcred

Slang for Jedi credit. This Corellian coin commemorated a Jedi Master from the planet, but it became very rare and valuable following Imperial persecution of all things related to the Jedi. Corran Horn wore one around his neck as a good luck charm. The coin was passed down to the Rogue Squadron pilot from his grandfather. [RS]

Jedgar, High Prophet

A tall, bald-headed, bearded member of the mysterious order of the Prophets of the Dark Side, he assisted Supreme Prophet Kadann in his attempt to gain control of the Empire. [MMY, PDS]

Jedi battle meditation

A powerful Jedi technique, it was used to influence the outcome of a battle by visualizing the desired result. [DLS, TOJ, TSW]

Jedi Code, the

The philosophy that sums up the beliefs of the Jedi Knights, it is embodied in this credo: There is no emotion; there is peace. There is no ignorance; there is knowledge. There is no passion; there is serenity. There is no death; there is the Force.

A Jedi does not act for personal power or wealth but seeks knowledge and enlightenment. A true Jedi never acts from hatred, anger, fear, or aggression but instead acts when calm and at peace with the Force. [SWRPG, SWRPG2]

Jedi Explorer

A two-person ship used by Luke Skywalker, it was designed to navigate uncharted hyperspace routes. The ship was destroyed when the cloned Emperor's dark-side aides attacked the secret New Alderaan settlement. [DE2]

Jedi Holocron

A repository of Jedi knowledge and teaching, these legendary artifacts were palm-sized glowing cubes of crystal that combined primitive holographic technology with the Force to provide an interactive learning device that could be activated only by a Jedi. [DE]

Jedi Knights

Protectors of the Old Republic from its earliest days some 25,000 years before the Galactic Civil War, they were the guardians of justice and freedom, the most respected and powerful force for good for more than a thousand generations. While the Jedi were known for their uncanny abilities and supernatural skills with lightsabers, their real power came from the ability to tap into and manipulate the Force.

Jedi Knights defended the Old Republic from all threats, including the proponents of the Clone Wars, but there was one threat they could not stand against—internal corruption. The Republic itself fell to the corruption of its leaders, and the Empire was born. Then, before the Jedi could move against him, the Emperor used one of their own to destroy the Jedi. Through treachery, deception, and the actions of the corrupted Jedi Knight called Darth Vader, the Jedi Knighthood was exterminated. Only a few remained.

One of the survivors, a Jedi Master named Yoda, trained Luke Skywalker as the first of a new line of Jedi Knights. After the Battle of Endor, Luke began searching the galaxy for other Force users and started an academy to train those strong in the Force. [COF, DA, ESB, JS, RJ, SW]

Jedi Master

A title bestowed upon the greatest of the Jedi Knights, those who were strong enough in the Force and patient enough to pass on their skills by teaching a new generation. [ESB]

Jedi reader

A device used by the Emperor's minions to hunt down Jedi, it revealed those who were Force-sensitive. [JS]

Je'har

The inhabitants of the planet Almania. During a raid against the moon Pydyr, the Je'har killed the parents of a young man named Dolph. Later, after Dolph became the dark-sider Kueller, he returned to Almania and destroyed the Je'har. [NR]

Jenet

A scavenging species from the planet Garban in the Tau Sakar system, they were known for their incredible memories and their quarrelsome nature. After developing starships, they quickly colonized the other worlds in their star system. During the Galactic Civil War, the Empire turned the Jenet colonies into labor camps. [GG4, ZHR]

Jensaarai

Force users from the Suarbi system, they wore armor constructed of cortosis ore fibers and used lightsabers. They were forced to serve ex-Moff Leonia Tavira and her Invids pirates. They believed themselves to be the true Jedi, and their name was a Sith word for "the hidden followers of truth." They were taught the Jedi way by people who had accepted Sith thoughts and philosophies but who were not sufficiently developed to be initiated into the dark ways. Luke Skywalker offered them a place in his new Jedi tradition, if they were willing to turn away from Tavira. [IJ]

Jensens

A family of moisture farmers on Tatooine, they opposed efforts to make peace with the Jawas and the Sand People. [TMEC]

Jerjerrod, Moff

The commander in charge of overseeing the construction of the second Death Star battle station. [RJ]

Jessa

The daughter of Doc, leader of a band of outlaw techs operating in and around Corporate Sector space, she was her father's second in command and an accomplished technician herself. Called Jess by her friends, she was a tall, shapely woman with curly blond hair and freckles. [HSE]

Jeth, Jedi Master Arca

This Jedi Master lived some 4,000 years before the Galactic Civil War. He trained as many as twenty students at a time in his compound on Arkania. His apprentices included Ulic and

Cay Qel-Droma. Jeth died fighting renegade droids directed by the evil Krath sorcerers on the planet Deneba. [DLS, TOJ]

Jevanche, Amber

A holostar, she was very popular on Coruscant. [POT]

Jewel of Churba

A Dairkan Starliner, it transported disguised Rogue Squadron members to Coruscant for an undercover mission. [WG]

Jhoff, Controller

An expert in space traffic control, he served aboard the Super Star Destroyer *Executor*. During the construction of the second Death Star, Jhoff was responsible for clearing, directing, and tracking space traffic into and within the restricted space surrounding Endor's forest moon. [RJN]

Jinn, Qui-Gon

A Jedi Master who tended to follow his own ideals and instincts rather than the orders of the Jedi Council, Qui-Gon Jinn was sixty years old at the time of the Naboo blockade. Jinn was a tall, powerfully built man, his long hair streaked with white and tied in a ponytail. He and his apprentice, Obi-Wan Kenobi, were assigned to negotiate a peaceful end to the Naboo blockade, but they were targeted for death by the Trade Federation acting under the influence of the Sith Lord Darth Sidious. Against the judgment of the Jedi Council, Qui-Gon adopted young Anakin Skywalker as his apprentice, but when the Jedi was killed by Darth Maul, Obi-Wan Kenobi took on the task of training Skywalker. [SWTPM]

Jixton, Wrenga

A former combat trainer at the Imperial Academy, Jix was ordered by Darth Vader to assassinate Governor Torlock of Corulag before the governor could defect to the Rebel Alliance. [SS]

jizz

A popular style of free-form wailing music. [TMEC]

jizz-wailer

A musician who plays a fast, contemporary, upbeat style of music. [RJ]

Joanson, Ariq

A Tatooine moisture farmer, he tried to negotiate land rights with the Jawas and the Sand People to create a lasting peace. During the meeting with the Sand People, the Empire ambushed them to assure a continuance of the antagonistic relationship between the humans and the Sand People. Because of this, Joanson eventually joined the Rebellion. [TMEC]

Jobath

A councilor of the Fia, he was from the planet Galantos. [SOL]

Joben, Thall

A native of the planet Ingo, he grew up with his best friend and rival, Jord Dusat. Thall had a passion for building and racing landspeeders. When he was seventeen years old, during the Empire's early days, he encountered the droids R2-D2 and C-3PO. [DTV]

Jojo

A pilot with the New Republic's Fifth Fleet, he was killed during a battle with Yevethan forces at Doornik-319. [SOL]

Jomark

An isolated, watery planet, it was ruled by the insane cloned Jedi Joruus C'baoth. The planet came to prominence when rumors circulated that a Jedi Master had been hiding on the world since before the rise of the Emperor. It is the second of six worlds in the system and the only one capable of supporting life. The planet has one small continent, Kalish, and thousands of islands. Joruus C'baoth ruled from a structure called High Castle, built by a long-vanished species. It was on this world that C'baoth tried to take Luke Skywalker prisoner. [DFR, DFRSB, HE, HESB]

Joruna

A New Republic planet located near the Koornacht Cluster. [BTS]

Jospro sector

A remote sector that contains the Dar'Or system, it is the source of the tiny creatures called ix dbukrii that were used by Imperial forces on Bakura to suppress the memories of Eppie Belden. [GG4, TAB]

Jovan Station

The command center for the Imperial fleet blockading Yavin 4 following the destruction of the first Death Star. [CSW]

Jowdrrl

A Wookiee, she was the cousin of Chewbacca. She accompanied him on a mission to rescue Han Solo during the Yevethan crisis. [TT]

J'Quille

A gold-furred Whiphid, he was a spy and former lover of Lady Valarian who kept an eye on Jabba the Hutt's palace. J'Quille eventually had his brain removed by the B'omarr monks so that he could escape Tatooine's unbearable heat. [TJP]

J't'p'tan (Doornik-628E)

This quiet world of garden cities is located in the heart of the Koornacht Cluster. The Fallanassi religious community settled here. After the Battle of N'zoth, the Fallanassi departed aboard the liner *Star Morning* in search of a new home. [BTS, SOL, TT]

Jubilar

A penal colony world, it is orbited by a single moon. The city Dying Slowly, later renamed Death, can be found on this world. [TBH]

Jubnuk

A Gamorrean, he served as a guard in Jabba's palace until he fell into the rancor pit along with Luke Skywalker. Jubnuk was quickly eaten by the rancor. [TJP]

Judicator

This Imperial Star Destroyer was under the command of Captain Brandei and served in Grand Admiral Thrawn's armada. [DFR, HE, LC]

juggernaut

A hulking, cumbersome heavy-assault vehicle that can cross most terrain types on its five sets of drive wheels. With a scanning tower, thick armor, and powerful weapons, the fifteen-meter-tall vehicle first saw action during the waning days of the Old Republic. [ISB]

Julpa, Mon

The crown prince of the planet Tammuz-an during the early days of the Empire, he was stripped of his title and memory by the evil vizier Zatec-Cha, and for a time Mon Julpa wandered the planet as the tall, frail, simple-minded Kez-Iban. [DTV]

jump beacon

A stationary structure, also called a hyperspace beacon or safe point, it was erected in space by pioneers of faster-than-light travel to mark the safe, proven coordinates for jumping to and from hyperspace. [DLS, FNU, TOJ]

Jundland Wastes

This rocky, dry, and extremely hot canyon and mesa region on the planet Tatooine borders the Dune Sea and is inhabited by the nomadic Sand People. [SW]

Junkfort Station

This spaceport is known as a place where ships can be modified and fitted with illegal equipment. [CSW]

J'uoch

An unscrupulous, evil woman, she and her twin brother R'all owned and operated a mine on the planet Dellalt. The pair competed with Han Solo to be the first to discover the lost treasures of Xim the Despot just before Solo became involved with the Rebellion. [HLL]

Juvex sector

A region of space near the Senex sector and the Ninth quadrant, it was run by groups of Ancient Houses, including House Streethyn. [COJ]

K749 system

Located in the Outer Rim near the Moonflower Nebula, it contains the planet Pzob. [COJ]

K8-LR

This protocol droid worked in Jabba the Hutt's Mos Eisley town house. When Muftak and Kabe removed the droid's restraining bolt, it helped the pair rob the town house and escape. [TMEC]

Ka, Tenel

The daughter of Prince Isolder of Hapes and Teneniel Djo of the Witches of Dathomir, she grew up to be a somewhat humorless, impatient, but hard-driven teenager with a strong connection to the Force. She preferred to rely on her athletic prowess, though, believing that using the Force was a sign of weakness. She joined Luke Skywalker's Jedi academy and became friends with Jacen and Jaina Solo and the Wookiee Lowbacca. When it came time to build her own lightsaber, Tenel took a few shortcuts and didn't give the task her full attention. During a practice session with Jacen, her lightsaber blade sputtered out and her left arm was severed at the elbow. This didn't stop her from helping her friends and Luke Skywalker thwart the plans of the Shadow Academy, however. [SWCG, YJK]

Tenel Ka

Ka'aa
An ancient species whose members wander the galaxy. [BTS]

Kabal
This neutral world was the site of the Conference of Uncommitted Worlds held just after the destruction of the first Death Star. [CSW]

Kabe
A Chadra-Fan pickpocket abandoned by slavers on Tatooine when she was very young, she survived by learning the ways of the street and honing her skills at breaking into security systems and gambling. The large, furry Muftak, a Talz, also protected her, and the two became partners. [GG1, SWCG, TMEC]

Kadann

The Supreme Prophet of the Dark Side, he was a human dwarf with a black beard who assumed leadership of the Empire for a brief time after the Battle of Endor. [LCJ, PDS]

Kadann

Ka'Dedus

This ultraviolet supergiant star is orbited by the planet Af'El, home to the Defels. [GG4]

Kaell 116

A clone leader of the spaceport city on the planet Khomm, he ignored warnings and his planet was nearly destroyed by Admiral Daala's Imperial forces. [DS]

Kahorr, Ssk

A Cha'a merchant lord, he lived some 5,000 years before the Galactic Civil War. [FSE, GAS]

Kai, Tamith

A member of the dark-side Nightsisters from Dathomir, she helped train Force-sensitive youths at the Shadow Academy. She was killed in a battle on Yavin 4 during an attempt to destroy Luke Skywalker's Jedi academy. [YJK]

Kaiburr Crystal

A deep crimson gem, it rested within the Temple of Pomojema on Circarpous V, also known as Mimban. Legends described the crystal as a Force-enhancing artifact, capable of strengthening the abilities of those who wield the Force. The priests of the temple were rumored to have mysterious healing powers, perhaps enhanced by the crystal's natural properties. [SME]

Kaikielius system

Near the Coruscant system, it was one of the first systems that the revived Imperial forces conquered six years after the Battle of Endor. [DESB]

Kail

This planet in the Corporate Sector was controlled by the family of Torm Dadeferron, an associate of Han Solo. It featured a large area known as the Kail Ranges. [CSSB, HSE]

Kaink

An elderly Ewok priestess, she served as guardian of the Soul Trees and was the village legend-keeper. [ETV]

Kalarba

A planet in the system of the same name, it is orbited by the moons Hosk and Indobok. [D]

Kalenda, Belindi

An operative of New Republic Intelligence, she warned Han Solo of possible trouble awaiting him and his family on their trip to Corellia. She went into hiding on the planet to covertly watch over and guard the Solo family. [AC]

Kalior V

This planet was the site of an Imperial aquarium. [GG4]

Kalist VI

This planet was the site of an Imperial labor colony for political prisoners. [GG3, MTS]

Kalla

This planet is located within the Corporate Sector. The planet is the site of a university for the education of Corporate Sector Authority members' children. Rekkon was an instructor there, and Fiolla of Lorrd attended the school. [CSSB, HSE, RS]

Kamar

This hot, desert planet orbits a white sun in a star system just outside Corporate Sector space. [CSSB, HSR]

Kamarian

A native of the planet Kamar, these insectoids have two sets of arms, spherical skulls, thick, segmented prehensile tails, and lightly colored exterior chitin. Han Solo ran a brief business venture for the Kamarians who lived in the arid Badlands region of the planet. These Badlanders were smaller in size and had lighter chitin than typical Kamarians. After the Badlanders turned Solo's holovid theater into a religious experience, the smuggler was forced to pack up and leave the planet in due haste. [HSR]

Kamparas

This planet was the site of a Jedi training center attended by Jedi Master Jorus C'baoth. [DFR]

Kanos, Kir

The last surviving member of the Emperor's Royal Guard, he sought vengeance against those who betrayed the Emperor and his ideals. Scarred by Darth Vader's lightsaber during his final test before the Emperor, he tried to live up to Palpatine's ideals on his own after the bitter loss at the Battle of Endor. When another guardsman, the ambitious Carnor Jax, betrayed the cloned Emperor, Kanos went into hiding. He eventually caught up with Jax at the barren training world where all guardsmen started out, Yinchorr. He won the deadly duel, killing Jax with a vibroblade. Then he went after the Imperial Interim Ruling Council, whose members conspired with Jax against the Emperor. He killed Xandel Carivus and helped capture the remaining council members for the New Republic. [CE]

Kanz Disorders

This series of violent uprisings in the time of the Old Republic lasted for 300 years. During this period, the Lorrdian people were held captive. Eventually, Old Republic forces and the Jedi Knights liberated these people. [CSSB, HSR]

Karda, Abal

A human, he was colonel of the Imperial Lightning Battalion just prior to the start of the Galactic Civil War. He was declared an enemy of the Empire for shooting his commanding officer. Lord Darth Vader hired bounty hunter Boba Fett to track him down and kill him. Fett succeeded. [BFEE]

Kardue'sai'Malloc

A Devaronian spy, he indiscriminately shelled the city Montellian Serat, an act that earned him the title Butcher of Montellian Serat. He changed his name to Labria and became an information broker on Tatooine. Boba Fett eventually captured him, claiming the five-million-credit bounty and returning him to Montellian Serat. There, Kardue'sai'Malloc was publicly executed by being thrown to a vicious pack of quarra. [GG1, SWCG, TBH, TM]

Karfeddion

This planet in the Senex sector was the site of several slave farms run by House Vandron. Lady Theala Vandron was summoned to the High Court of Coruscant to defend the presence of slave farms on her homeworld. [COJ]

Kark, Kith

A Jedi and a Gotal, he was killed during the Freedon Nadd Uprising some 4,000 years before the Galactic Civil War. [FNU]

Karnak Alpha

A planet located beyond the Hapes Consortium near the Deep Galactic Core, it is home to the fur-covered Karnak Alphans. [YJK]

Karrde, Talon

A smuggler, information broker, and one of the top operators in the galaxy's fringe community, Karrde remained neutral throughout the Galactic Civil War. Later, when the New

Republic was established, he began to side with the government more and more as the galactic battle waged on against Imperial remnants and other threats. He believed such a course was just good business.

Talon Karrde

A slender, thin-faced human with short, dark hair, pale blue eyes, and a long mustache and goatee, he was a man of his word, but he could be cold and calculating. His main vessel was the *Wild Karrde*, and his space yacht was the *Uwana Buyer*. For years his base of operations was the planet Myrkr, home to the ysalamiri, creatures with the natural ability to dampen the Force.

During the war against Ysanne Isard and her Bacta Cartel, Karrde provided Rogue Squadron with most of its weapons and munitions. When his top aide, Quelev Tapper, was killed, he hired a hyperdrive mechanic named Celina Marniss—who turned out to be Mara Jade, the Emperor's Hand. During the events surrounding the return of Grand Admiral Thrawn, Karrde was unwillingly dragged into the struggle between the Empire and New Republic. He decided to support the New Republic and helped earn the victory over Thrawn's forces at Bilbringi. Later, he and Jade helped form the Smugglers' Alliance, after which he temporarily retired.

Sixteen years after the Battle of Endor, Karrde agreed to try to acquire a copy of the Caamas Document from his past associate Jorj Car'das. It was hoped that the document could put an end to the brewing civil war that threatened to destroy the New Republic. With the Mistryl Shadow Guard Shada D'akul at his side, he traveled deep into the Kathol sector. He returned without the Caamas Document, but he did acquire data that helped Admiral Gilad Pellaeon uncover the truth of the impostor Grand Admiral Thrawn. This led to the start of peace between the New Republic and the Empire. Karrde then accepted a post as head of a joint intelligence service that reported to both governments. Shada agreed to stay with him, as their fondness for each other continued to grow. [BW, DFR, DFRSB, HE, HESB, LC, NR, SP, VF]

Karreio

A woman devoted to Emperor Palpatine's New Order, she was engaged to Imperial officer Crix Madine. Madine defected to the Rebel Alliance without telling Karreio, fearing that any knowledge she possessed could put her life in danger. Later, he learned that Karreio had been killed during a battle between Rebel and Imperial forces. [DS]

Karsk, Amil

A former X-wing pilot, he was on a mission to Alderaan when the Death Star destroyed the planet. [BW]

Kasarax

A Sauropteroid on the planet Dellalt, he provided aid to Han Solo and his companions during the quest to find the lost treasures of Xim the Despot. [HLL]

Kashyyyk

A green jungle planet covered with kilometers-high wroshyr trees, it is the homeworld of the Wookiee species. The huge trees form an extensive ecosystem that is divided into several horizontal levels. The Wookiees and various flying creatures live in the uppermost levels. Increasingly more hostile lifeforms, such as the dangerous webweavers, live in the lower ecosystems nearer the planet's surface.

The massive Wookiee cities, such as Rwookrrorro, are built hundreds of meters above the ground, in the highest branches of the jungle trees. The cities combine modern technology with natural beauty to create some of the true wonders of the galaxy. Under the Empire, a fleet of ships and numerous garrisons guarded Kashyyyk and its inhabitants. The Wookiees were enslaved, forced to use their great strength to serve the Empire. By Imperial decree, free Wookiees were illegal. Those found off planet or outside Imperial work camps were considered outlaws. After the Battle of Endor, Kashyyyk was liberated and became a full member world of the New Republic.

Nineteen years after the Battle of Endor, a Second Imperium assault team led by the Dark Jedi Zekk and the Nightsister Tamith Kai raided Kashyyyk to obtain New Republic guidance and recognition codes. During the assault, TIE bombers attacked the Wookiee cities. [HE, HESB, HLL, SWSB, SWWS, TBH, YJK]

Kast, Jodo

A ruthless, cunning bounty hunter, he wore the same type of battle armor favored by Boba Fett and didn't mind being mistaken for the more famous bounty hunter. He often worked with the alien Puggles Trodd and Zardra. Fett eventually hunted Kast and killed him in a final confrontation. [TBH, TM]

Katana fleet

This fleet, also called the Dark Force, consisted of 200 Dreadnaught heavy star cruisers. The fleet's flagship, the *Katana*, was considered to be the finest starship of its time. The entire fleet was fitted with full-rig slave circuits to significantly lower the size of the crews needed to run the ships. The fleet's unofficial name came from the dark gray hull surface on each Dreadnaught. With the Clone Wars still years away, the *Katana* fleet was launched to a massive Old Republic public relations drive. Unfortunately, the crews were infected with a hive virus that drove them all mad. In their insanity, they slaved the ships together and the whole fleet jumped to light speed—to disappear for decades. Grand Admiral Thrawn located the dormant fleet and turned them against the New Republic five years after the Battle of Endor. [DFR, DFRSB]

katarn

A predator native to the planet Kashyyyk. [HESB]

Katarn, Kyle

A Rebel Alliance agent, he infiltrated the top secret Imperial installation on Danuta and acquired the technical plans for the Empire's first Death Star battle station. Later, these plans were beamed to Princess Leia Organa's consular ship, the *Tantive IV*. In the aftermath of the Battle of Yavin, Katarn captured Imperial weapons specialist Moff Rebus from his hidden stronghold in Anoat City. From there, Katarn discovered that the Empire was arming new Dark Troopers, and he destroyed the mining facility supplying the phrik alloy. [DF]

Katarn Commandos

See Page's Commandos.

Kathol sector

A remote sector on the fringes of the populated galaxy, it contains thirty colonies, the cluster of stars known as the Kathol Outback, and the difficult-to-navigate Kathol Rift. [DSC]

Kavil's Corsairs

A Blazing Claw cadre, these pirates were brazen, fearless, and talented. Rogue Squadron flew against them during an undercover operation on Axxila. The corsairs were another pawn of Moff Leonia Tavira in her quest for power and wealth. [XW]

Kee

A Yuzzem miner on the planet Mimban, he helped Luke Skywalker, Princess Leia, and the old woman Halla retrieve the legendary Kaiburr Crystal from the Temple of Pomojema. [SME]

Keeheen

A Trianii, he was a prisoner at Stars' End. His mate Atuarre and her cub Pakka accompanied Han Solo to the Corporate Sector Authority penal colony to rescue him. [HSE]

Keek, Inspector
The chief of the planet Brigia's Internal Security Police, he was a pompous, quasimilitaristic individual who wore numerous decorations on his oversize uniform. [HLL]

Keeper (GRODON LAKKY)
Tormentor and slave master of the Wookiees on Maw Installation, he was killed when Chewbacca freed the Wookiee slaves. [COF, JASB]

Kei
First mate of Yevethan strongman Nil Spaar and mother of three, she succumbed to the "gray death." [SOL]

Kellering, Dr.
A scientist at Imperial Prime University, he worked on the Hammertong weapons project and hired the Mistryl Shadow Guards to safely transport it to the Empire. [TMEC]

Kelrodo-Ai
This planet is the site of the gelatin mines once operated by Baron Administrator Drom Guldi. [DS]

kelsh
A bronze-colored metal. [TJP]

Kemplex Nine
A strategic jump station in the Auril sector and the Cron system some 4,000 years before the Galactic Civil War, it played a role in the Sith War. When dark-side practitioners Aleema and Crado activated a Sith weapon, they inadvertently ignited all ten stars in the Cron Cluster and wiped out Kemplex Nine, the surrounding area of space, and their own ship. [TSW]

Ken

The son of the three-eyed mutant Triclops and the princess Kendalina, and the grandson of Emperor Palpatine, he grew up locked away from the world and most other living creatures. A Jedi Master placed the baby Ken in the underground Lost City of the Jedi on Yavin 4, where the boy was raised by droids—DJ-88, caretaker of the Jedi library and Ken's teacher; HC-100, who oversaw Ken's homework; and the small Microchip, or Chip, who was Ken's friend. He also had a pet, a small feathered mooka named Zeebo.

Kadann, the Supreme Prophet of the Dark Side who was backing Trioculous as the successor to Palpatine, found Ken and tried to kill him. When he finally captured the boy, he decided to steal the secrets of the Lost City and then destroy it. But Luke Skywalker and Ken combined their Force powers to defeat the Supreme Prophet. [LCJ, PDS, ZHR]

Kendalina

A princess, she was forced to serve as a nurse in an Imperial insane asylum on Kessel. There she met and fell in love with the son of Emperor Palpatine, Triclops, and bore him a son, Ken. She was killed after giving birth to the boy. [PDS]

Kenlin, Bors

Captain of the *Xucphra Rose*, a Thyferran bacta tanker. [BW]

Kenobi, Ben (Obi-Wan)

Jedi Knight, general in the Clone Wars, protector and mentor of Luke Skywalker. To the people of Tatooine, he appeared to be a hermit and recluse who lived in the Jundland Wastes by the western Dune Sea. The locals considered him a crazy old man, but in reality he was Obi-Wan, servant of the Old Republic.

Kenobi had studied under the Jedi Masters Yoda and Qui-Gon Jinn, learning the ways of the Force. When the Clone Wars erupted, Kenobi became a general, fighting alongside Bail Organa of Alderaan and his young apprentice Jedi Anakin

Skywalker. Obi-Wan and Anakin became good friends, sharing many adventures as they battled to protect the galaxy. Kenobi took Anakin as his Padawan learner when his own master died. But Kenobi wasn't an experienced teacher, and Anakin was lured to the dark side.

Ben Kenobi

Much to Kenobi's horror, his friend and pupil was so corrupted by the dark side of the Force that he became essentially a new person—the Dark Lord Darth Vader. When Kenobi saw what had become of Anakin, he tried to dissuade him and draw him back from the dark side. According to tales told later, discussion turned to battle and the two fought fiercely. The fight ended when the man who had been Anakin Skywalker fell into a pit of molten lava. Kenobi helped hide Anakin's children to protect them from the Emperor, and then Vader.

In the years that followed, as Vader and the Emperor systematically hunted down and destroyed the Jedi Knights, Kenobi remained in hiding. He stayed on Tatooine near Anakin's son, young Luke Skywalker, watching over him and waiting for the moment when he would step in and reveal the young man's destiny to him. The event that triggered the beginning of this revelation was inspired by Anakin's other child, Princess Leia Organa. Leia's foster father told her to seek out Kenobi and convince him to join the Rebellion. That was what she was doing when the Empire captured her over Tatooine. Kenobi became Luke's mentor and protector, starting the young man's training in the ways of the Force as the pair went off to rescue the princess.

On the Death Star, while Luke and Han Solo worked to rescue Princess Leia, Kenobi faced Darth Vader for a final time. He sacrificed his life to help Luke and advance the cause of the

Rebellion, but his sacrifice was not the end. He became one with the Force, a being of light who was much more than the crude matter of flesh and bone. He continued to guide Luke even in death, giving him support in desperate times. It was Kenobi who instructed Luke to "use the Force" to destroy the original Death Star, who directed him to seek out the Jedi Master Yoda on Dagobah, and who helped him prepare for his final confrontation with Vader.

Obi-Wan appeared to Luke on several other occasions after the Battle of Endor. On Coruscant, Kenobi explained that the distances between them were becoming too great, and this would be their final meeting for a long time. "I loved you as a son, and as a student, and as a friend," Obi-Wan told Luke. "You are not the last of the Jedi, but the first of the new." [ESB, RJ, SW, SWCG, SWSB]

Kessel

A planet located near the worlds of Fwillsving and Honoghr, it is the only source of the telepathy-inducing glitterstim spice, and it was the site of a brutal Imperial prison and spice-mining facility. The Kessel system is adjacent to a cluster of black holes known as the Maw. This made navigation in the area difficult and gave rise to the smugglers' Kessel Run. [COF, COJ, HLL, JS, LC, SW, XW]

Kestic Station

A free-trader outpost near the Bestine system, it saw more than its share of smugglers, pirates, and outlaws. It was annihilated by the Star Destroyer *Merciless.* [GG3, MTS]

Kestrel Nova

A freighter that operated some 4,000 years before the Galactic Civil War, it was captured by Republic forces in a battle with pirates near Taanab. [DLS]

Ketaris

This trade center was one of Grand Admiral Thrawn's targets during his battles with the New Republic. [LC]

kete

A large winged creature that looks like a giant dragonfly, it lives in spiral mounds made out of a sticky, marshmallowlike substance on the forest moon of Endor. [ETV]

Keto, Lord

This leader ruled the Empress Teta system about 4,000 years prior to the Galactic Civil War. He and his wife, Magda, were killed when his son, Satal, and niece, Aleema, staged a rebellion. [DLS]

Keto, Satal

An heir to the throne of the Empress Teta system, he staged a rebellion some 4,000 years before the Galactic Civil War and became coleader of the dark-side Krath cult. Along with his cousin, Aleema, he received powers from the spirit of the dark Jedi Freedon Nadd. Jedi Ulic Qel-Droma eventually killed him. [DLS]

Kez-Iban

See Julpa, Mon.

Khabarakh

The Noghri Khabarakh was a member of the Death Commando squad sent to capture Princess Leia Organa Solo on the Wookiee planet Kashyyyk. He was the only member of his squad to survive. Khabarakh recognized Leia as the daughter of Lord Darth Vader. He became a member of Leia's Noghri honor guard and aided the Republic in its attack on Mount Tantiss. Khabarakh later became caretaker of the lush Hidden Valley on the Noghri homeworld, Honoghr. [DFR, HE, HESB, LC]

Khan, Lo

A smuggler, he was the owner and operator of the *Hyperspace Marauder*. He assisted Salla Zend and Shug Ninx during their visit to Byss. His partner and first mate was Luwingo, a Yaka cyborg. [DE]

kholm-grass

A plant that once grew across the Noghri homeworld of Honoghr, it was destroyed by the Empire's deliberate contamination of the planet. The Empire replaced it with a bioengineered version that secretly killed other forms of plant life and kept the planet from recovering. Only animals capable of eating the kholm-grass survived outside a small area of the Clean Land, so the Noghri were forced to rely on imported food supplies, thus keeping them in the Empire's debt. [DFR, HE, LC]

Khomm

A moonless world near the Deep Galactic Core, it remained neutral throughout the Galactic Civil War. Populated by genderless clones of previous generations, the world and its inhabitants kept to their own affairs. One clone, Dorsk 81, showed an unusual connection to the Force and joined Luke Skywalker's Jedi academy. Eight years after the Battle of Endor, Dorsk 81 returned to Khomm to warn of an imminent Imperial attack. His warnings were ignored, and Colonel Cronus's fleet of *Victory*-class Star Destroyers devastated the planet. [DA, DS]

Khuiumin

This system was the base of operations for the notorious Eyttyrmin Batiiv pirates until the Empire made a concerted effort to destroy the group during the early days of the New Order. Two *Victory*-class Star Destroyers, *Bombard* and *Crusader*, employed superior tactics to outfight the pirates. They eventually destroyed the pirate armada and its base. [SWSB]

Kil, Kenix

A false identity Kir Kanos assumed after he killed Carnor Jax. [KK]

Kile

One of many moons orbiting the planet Zhar, Kile was the site of the temporary Rogue Squadron base from which the elite starfighter unit launched a raid on the neighboring moon Gall.

The purpose of the raid was to free Han Solo from the clutches of Boba Fett. The raid failed. [SOTE]

Kimanan

Home to the animals known as furballs—tiny, clownish marsupials that make wonderful pets. Sabodor's pet shop on Etti IV sold them. [HSE]

Kimm systems

Systems known for trafficking in Senex sector slaves. [COJ]

King's Galquek

A planet in the Meridian sector, it is sometimes referred to as K-G. Nine years after the Battle of Endor, the Loronar Corporation secretly supported a palace coup on K-G. [POT]

Kintan

The Nikto homeworld, it was conquered by the Hutts long before the Old Republic was established. [GG12]

Kiph, Dmaynel

A Devaronian and the leader of the Alien Combine, he passed judgment on Gavin Darklighter and other members of Rogue Squadron. Before he could kill them, however, Imperial forces attacked the Combine's hideout. Kiph was seriously wounded, but the Rogues helped him escape. Later, he helped the Alliance liberate Coruscant. [WG]

Kir

A planet deep within the heart of the Corporate Sector, where crystals are mined and refined for use as crystalline vertex, the Corporate Sector currency. [HSE]

Kira, Drokko

Father of Modon Kira, he was also known as Drokko the Elder. He was cast out of Iziz for challenging the legacy of Freedon Nadd four millennia before the Galactic Civil War. [TOJ]

Kira, Modon

A Beast-Lord of Onderon and the father of Oron Kira, he lived some 4,000 years before the Galactic Civil War. [TOJ]

Kira, Oron

Son of Modon Kira, he and his fellow Onderonians joined the Jedi in their battle against the dark-side Krath cultists some 4,000 years before the Galactic Civil War. [DLS, FNU, TOJ]

Kirdo III

This planet in the Outer Rim is the homeworld of the Kitonak species. Eight years after the Battle of Endor, the planet was visited by the Imperial battlemoon *Eye of Palpatine.* [COJ, GG4]

Kirl

A province of Munto Codru and a Kirlian ambassador shared this name. The ambassador was an attractive, flirtatious male. [CS]

Kirrek

One of seven planets in the Empress Teta system, it was one of the last to bow to the authority of Satal Keto and Aleema some 4,000 years before the Galactic Civil War. Three Kirrek cities were destroyed due to its resistance. [DLS]

Kithra

A Mistryl Shadow Guard, she accompanied Mara Jade in the liberation of Kessel. [COF]

Kitonak

A species of pudgy, yeast-colored beings with tough, leathery hides, they are natives of Kirdo III. Their ability to draw in upon themselves and seal vulnerable body openings in folds of flesh protects them from the world's harsh desert environment. Droopy McCool, a member of Max Rebo's jizz-wailer band, is a Kitonak. [GG4]

Kiva

This planet was the location of Project Starscream. Its native citizens, the Kivans, were transformed into shadowy wraiths by Imperial experiments led by scientists Borborygmus Gog and Mammon Hoole. [GF]

Kkak, Hrar

A Jawa, he lived on Tatooine and provided the blaster rifle that Jawa Het Nkik used to attack Imperial stormtroopers. [TMEC]

Kktkt

A planet in the Farlax sector near the Koornacht Cluster. [SOL]

Klaatu

One of the Nikto skiff guards employed by Jabba the Hutt. Like other members of his species, Klaatu had olive-colored reptilian skin and small horns around his face. [RJ]

Klatooine

This planet is home to the Klatooinian species. The Hutts conquered this world long before the Old Republic was established. Barada, Jabba the Hutt's repulsor pool chief, was a member of this species. [MTS, TJP]

kleex

Large, flealike parasites that infest the tails of the huge creatures called durkii. Though the durkii was normally a docile beast, it could become a raging monster due to the discomfort caused by kleex infestation. [DTV]

Klev, Commander Titus

An Imperial officer, he commanded *Silencer-7*, one of the Imperial World Devastators that fought in the Battle of Calamari. Titus Klev died when Luke Skywalker tampered with the master control signal and caused *Silencer-7* to crash into the Calamari ocean. [DE, DESB]

Kleyvits

A female Selonian who spoke for the Overden, Selonia's central power. She assumed responsibility for Han Solo, Leia Organa Solo, and Mara Jade after the Hunchuzuc Den was won over to the Overden cause. [SAC]

klick

Slang used by X-wing pilots, it means *kilometer.* [RS]

Klivian, Derek "Hobbie"

Shipmate of Biggs Darklighter on the Imperial ship *Rand Ecliptic*, he defected to the Rebellion at Darklighter's side. He joined Rogue Squadron at Hoth and was assigned the comm-unit designation Rogue Four at the Battle of Hoth. He later fought in the battles of Endor and Bakura. [ESB, GG3, XW]

kloo horn

A musical instrument. Figrin D'an played this type of instrument at the Mos Eisley cantina. [GG1, TMEC]

Kloper

This planet is the homeworld of the Kloperian species. [NR]

Kneesaa, Princess

The daughter of Chief Chirpa, this brave Ewok had many adventures on the forest moon of Endor. She was a hero, battling the fierce Duloks, the evil witch Morag, and the giant Phlogs, among others, from an early age. Wicket W. Warrick was her best friend. [ETV, SWCG, TRG]

knobby white spider

Not a real spider, but a detachable mobile root from the gnarltree that grows on Dagobah. The spiderlike root roams the swamps, hunting and devouring animals to collect enough energy to plant itself and transform into another gnarltree. [ISWU]

Knolstee

This planet in the Corporate Sector is one of the stops for the luxury liner *Lady of Mindor* during trips from Roonadan to Ammuud. [CSSB]

Knossa Spaceport

This spaceport is located on the planet Ossus. [DLS]

knytix

Creatures that resemble Thyferran Vratix but are smaller, less elegant, and used as either work animals, pets, or food by the Vratix. [BW]

Koh'shak

The master of the Kala'uun Spaceport on Ryloth, he was also the head of all merchant clans that operated from this location. [BW, PSG]

Kojash

A planet in the Farlax sector and the Koornacht Cluster, it was the site of a Morath mining operation. Twelve years after the Battle of Endor, the Yevetha conquered it in a series of raids called the Great Purge. [SOL]

Kokash sector

This region of space in the Rim Territories was never properly surveyed. During the Empire's reign, the Black Sword Command defended this and other neighboring sectors. After the Battle of Endor, Imperial forces abandoned this sector and retreated into the Core. [BTS]

Komad, Koyi

A Twi'lek, she was a student at the Mrlsst Academy when she met members of Rogue Squadron. She later joined the Rogues as their chief mechanic and became a trusted friend and confidante to many of the pilots. [XW]

Koong, Governor

A burly, unshaven human, he led a band of criminals in the Tawntoom region of Roon during the early days of the Empire. He used political intrigue, theft, and hijacking to increase his personal power in the Roon system. [DTV]

Koornacht, Aitro

A palace guard of Emperor Preedu III on Tamban prior to the rise of the Empire, he performed a favor for the First Observer of the Court of the Emperor. To honor this favor, the Koornacht Cluster was named after Aitro. [BTS]

Koornacht Cluster

An area within the Farlax sector, it consists of 2,000 stars and 20,000 planets, though less than a hundred of these are habitable. The Yevetha species controlled and colonized eleven planets in the cluster, but were brutally subjugated by the Empire. Twelve years after the Battle of Endor, the Yevetha started the Great Purge to rid the cluster of "inferior" species. [BTS, SOL, TT]

kor

The rarest grade of the addictive spice ryll. [BW]

Koros Major

One of seven planets in the Empress Teta system, it was one of the last to resist the dark-side Krath some 4,000 years before the Galactic Civil War. A joint Republic-Jedi space fleet battled with Krath ships in the planet's orbit, but were badly defeated and forced to retreat. [DLS]

Koros system

A star system with seven worlds, it became the Empress Teta system after the empress united the planets under her rule. [FSE, GAS]

Korrda the Hutt

A small, sickly, often scorned Hutt, he was a special envoy and servant to Lord Durga the Hutt. [DS]

Korriban

This planet was the long-hidden repository for the mummified remains of Sith Lords. The remains were stored within great temples in the Valley of the Dark Lords. The temples were designed to focus and amplify the abundant dark-side energy of the area and were guarded by human skeletons activated through a combination of machinery and Sith magic. [DLS, EE]

Korus

The tutor of Satal Keto and Aleema, the heirs to the throne of the Empress Teta system, he was one of their first victims when they made their play to take control of the system. [DLS]

Kothlis

A colony world of the Bothan species, it was the home of New Republic Councilor Borsk Fey'lya. It was here that Bothan spies captured secret data about the second Death Star battle station. [DFR, SOTE]

Kowakian monkey-lizard

Rare animals from the planet Kowak, they are semi-intelligent and known for their mimicry and constant laughter. Salacious Crumb, of Jabba the Hutt's court, was of this species. [RJ]

Kraaken, Deputy Commander

A humanoid with long pointed ears, he was Commander Silver Fyre's second in command. Kraaken was a traitor who attempted to kill Luke Skywalker and steal a data card carrying secret information vital to the Alliance. [CSW]

Kratas, Commander

An Imperial officer, he commanded Admiral Daala's flagship, the *Gorgon*. [COF, JS]

Krath

A secret society founded by dark-siders Satal Keto and Aleema some 4,000 years before the Galactic Civil War, it was named after a demon from the stories of their youth. This magical sect ruled the Empress Teta system for a time. Princess Leia Organa Solo learned their story while accessing the knowledge stored in the Jedi Holocron. [DE, DLS]

Krath Enchanter

The royal Tetan space yacht of Satal Keto and Aleema. [FNU]

krayt dragon

Large carnivorous reptiles that live in the mountains surrounding Tatooine's Jundland Wastes. These creatures continue to grow throughout their lifetimes and show no sign of becoming weaker with age. Beautiful and valuable dragon pearls are contained within their gizzards. [DS, ISWU, SW, TJP]

Kreet'ah

A Black Sun Vigo, he inherited his position from his mother. Kreet'ah was a Kian'thar, a species with the ability to sense the emotions and intentions of others. Using a vast network of spies to infiltrate the megacorporations that served the Empire, Kreet'ah provided much vital information to Prince Xizor about such companies as the SoroSuub Corporation, Sienar Fleet Systems, and Dynamic Automata. Stern and businesslike, Kreet'ah's place in Black Sun was assured; and his daughter was in line to inherit his title. [SESB, SOTE]

Kre'fey, General Laryn

A Bothan general and a celebrated military leader, he led the raid on Borleias that was actually a trap that almost destroyed Rogue Squadron. [RS]

Kre'fey, Karka

Grandson of Bothan General Laryn Kre'fey, he attempted to goad Gavin Darklighter into a duel. Darklighter refused. [KT]

Krenher sector

Home to a New Republic station. Twelve years after the Battle of Endor, the *Marauder* was ordered to abandon its search for the Teljkon vagabond and report to the station's commodore. [SOL]

Krenn, Josala

An Obroan Institute archaeologist, she was buried in an avalanche while searching the planet Maltha Obex for clues to the origin of the Qella civilization. [SOL]

Kressh, Ludo

A powerful Sith Lord, he competed with Naga Sadow for the position of Dark Lord of the Sith after the death of the previous Dark Lord, Marka Ragnos, some 5,000 years before the Galactic Civil War. He died during a battle for leadership of the Sith after Sadow's failed invasion attempt. [FSE, GAS]

Kritkeen, General Sinick

A tyrannical COMPNOR officer on the planet Aruza, he was assassinated by the bounty hunter Dengar on a contract from the Aruzan people. [TBH]

kroyie

A species of bird native to the Wookiee planet Kashyyyk. They are hunted for food by the Wookiees. These huge birds inhabit the upper branches of the planet's giant trees. [HE, HESB]

Krytos

A virus developed by Imperial General Evir Derricote at the request of Ysanne Isard, director of Imperial Intelligence. It was the central element in a plot to bankrupt the New Republic. The virus could be cured by bacta, and it was deadly to alien species but would not harm humans. [KT]

KT-10

An R2 unit with a female personality program, she and R2-D2 became friendly while both were in the Great Heep's droid harem during the early days of the Empire. [TGH]

KT-18 (KATE)

A pearl-colored housekeeping mechanical with a female personality program. Luke Skywalker purchased KT-18 from Tatooine Jawas as a gift for Han Solo. [ZHR]

Ktriss

A pet of Great Bogga the Hutt, this dark-side hssiss emanated a sinister force that paralyzed the minds of its victims. [TOJ]

Kuar

This planet is located near the Empress Teta system. Its ruined underground cities were used as a base by Mandalore and his warrior clans some 4,000 years before the Galactic Civil War. [TSW]

Kuari Princess

A Mon Calamari luxury space liner famous for its staterooms, bazaar deck, and recreational slafcourses. The droid 4-LOM started his career as a thief on this vessel. [RM, TBH]

Kuat

A star system in the Kuat sector, it is the site of the massive Kuat Drive Yards starship construction facility. It had been one of the Empire's primary producers of warships, including the *Imperial*-class Star Destroyer. [BW, ISWU, PSG, RS, SWSB, WG]

Ku'Bakai system

A system named for its blue giant star, it contains the planet Kubindi, homeworld of the Kubaz. [MTS]

Kubaz

A humanoid species from the planet Kubindi whose members average 1.8 meters in height and have short, prehensile trunks instead of noses. They have rough-textured, green-black skin and large, sensitive eyes. On many worlds, Kubaz are required to wear special goggles to protect their eyes from harsh light. They are a cultured species who place a high value on tradition, art, and music. [CPL, GG1, GG4, MTS]

Kubindi

The fifth planet in the Ku'Bakai system, it is the homeworld of the Kubaz species. [CPL, GG4, MTS]

Kueller

Once called Dolph, this extremely talented student of Luke Skywalker's eventually left the Jedi academy and turned to the dark side. He wore a Hendanyn death mask to hide his boyish features. Luke Skywalker and Leia Organa Solo confronted Kueller on the planet Almania. When Han Solo curtailed Kueller's powers with several ysalamiri, Leia killed the dark-sider with a blaster shot to the head. [NR]

Kun, Exar

A Dark Lord of the Sith, he was responsible for the deaths of millions 4,000 years before the Galactic Civil War. Jedi Knights killed him in the bloody Sith War, but not before he drained the life force from every Massassi on Yavin 4. This act kept his spirit alive, though it remained trapped in the Yavin temples until the time of Luke Skywalker's Jedi academy. Kun tempted Skywalker's students and seduced Kyp Durron into helping him, but Skywalker and his other students prevailed and destroyed Kun's spirit. [COF, DA, DLS, SWCG, TSW]

Exar Kun

Kurp, Kosh

A bomb expert. Jabba the Hutt gave him Gaar Suppoon's holdings after Suppoon's death. [JAB]

Kurtzen

A soft-spoken, peaceful species that make up about 5 percent of Bakura's population. They appear as white-skinned humanoids with corrugated leathery scalps instead of hair. [TAB, TBSB]

Kwenn Space Station

See, Space Station Kwenn.

Kwerve, Bidlo

A scar-faced Corellian with white-streaked black hair, he was Bib Fortuna's rival for the post of Jabba the Hutt's majordomo. Bidlo helped Fortuna acquire Jabba's rancor and was then "honored" by being the first person fed to Jabba's new pet. [SWSB, TJP]

Kybacca

The senior Wookiee New Republic senator, she opposed allowing former Imperials to serve in the senate. [NR]

Laakteen Depot

The Rebel Alliance outpost closest to Fondor around the time of the Battle of Endor, it was destroyed by Darth Vader on the maiden voyage of his Super Star Destroyer, *Executor.* [CSW]

Laboi

A carnivorous, aggressive species, its members have the appearance of fur-covered snakes. They make up for a lack of limbs with a limited telekinetic ability, possibly linked to the Force. [GG4]

Laboi II

This planet is home to the carnivorous, aggressive Laboi species. [GG4]

labor droid

Mechanicals that perform duties that do not require high levels of artificial intelligence. Labor droids work in mines, operate simple transports, and handle sanitation duties, among other menial tasks. [HSE]

labor pool overseer

A sentient being or droid, the overseer coordinates the work assignments of all droids on a vessel. [SWR]

Labria

See Kardue'sai'Malloc.

Lady Luck

Lando Calrissian purchased this modified space yacht from an Orthellin royal mistress about the time he set up his mining operation, Nomad City, on the planet Nkllon. The fifty-meter-long space yacht was equipped with a hyperdrive engine, smuggler compartments, a sophisticated sensor package, combat shields, and a laser cannon. [DFRSB, HE, HESB]

Lady of Mindor

A commercial starship, it travels throughout Corporate Sector space to ferry passengers from star system to star system. Han Solo and Fiolla of Lorrd once booked passage on the starship to travel from Bonadan to Ammuud in order to evade Espos—members of the Corporate Sector's private security force—and slavers who were searching for them. [HSR]

Lafra

This planet near Corporate Sector space is home to intelligent, gray-skinned humanoids called Lafrarians. While their ancestors once soared through the air on great wings, all that is left to the Lafrarians are vestigial soaring membranes, feathery growths on their heads, and innate piloting skills. [COJ, CSSB, HSE]

Lake Natth

A lake on the planet Ambria, it was the place where dark-side forces congregated some 4,000 years before the Galactic Civil War. Jedi Master Thon drove them to the lake and kept them there. [TOJ]

lake spirit of Mimban

An amorphous, translucent, and phosphorescent creature, it inhabits the subterranean waterways of the planet Mimban. [SME]

lamb

Slang used by Rebel pilots to refer to Imperial *Lambda*-class shuttles. [RS]

Lambda-class shuttle

An Imperial cargo and passenger shuttle, its three wings make it resemble an inverted *Y* in flight. The two lower wings fold up upon landing. The shuttle can carry up to twenty passengers and their gear, or the equivalent amount of cargo, plus the command crew. [HESB, RJ, SWSB]

Lancer-class frigate

A 250-meter-long Imperial combat starship, it was designed as a countermeasure against Rebel starfighters after the destruction of the first Death Star. Armed with twenty quad antistarfighter laser cannons mounted on towers, it has few defenses against other capital ships. [DFRSB, ISB]

landing claw

Magnetic or mechanical grips on space vehicles, they adhere to nearly any surface for landing or docking. [ESB]

Landing Zone

This popular bar on the planet Bonadan is located in the planet's Alien Quarter. [HSR]

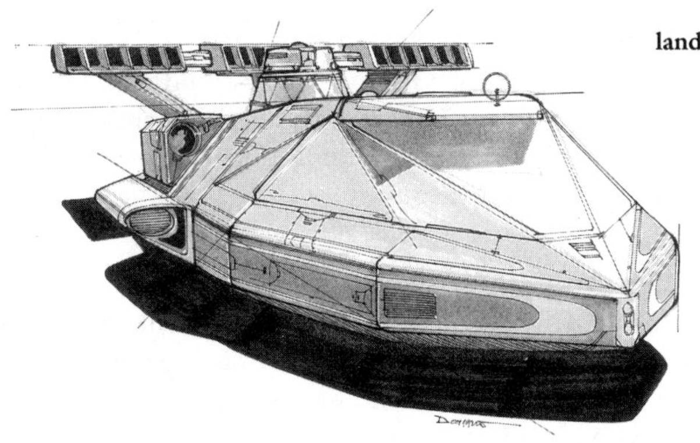
landspeeder

landspeeder
Any type of surface transport vehicle that employs repulsorlift propulsion engines. [SW, SWSB, SWVG]

lantern bird
A large, beautiful flying creature with incandescent tail feathers, it lives in shimmering nests high in the trees of Endor's forest moon. Ewoks use the tail feathers to create medicinal potions. [ETV]

lantern of sacred light
An Ewok holy item. It is believed that as long as its flame remains lit, the Ewok villages are safe from the Night Spirit and its worshippers. [ETV]

Lanthrym
This planet in the Elrood sector is the site of outlaw stations that will service any ship. [POG]

Larkhess
A Rebel escort frigate commanded by Captain Afyon. [HE, HESB]

Larm, Admiral
The main military aide to Moff Getelles of the Antemeridian sector, he was killed in a battle above Nam Chorios. [POT]

Lars, Beru

Wife of moisture farmer Owen Lars, she and her husband raised Luke Skywalker on Tatooine. Luke called her Aunt Beru. Imperial stormtroopers killed Beru and Owen after tracking R2-D2 and C-3PO to their moisture farm. [SW]

Lars, Owen

Husband of Beru Lars, he and his wife raised Luke Skywalker on Tatooine. Luke called him Uncle Owen. Imperial stormtroopers killed Beru and Owen after tracking R2-D2 and C-3PO to their moisture farm. [SW]

laser cannon

A more powerful version of a blaster, it is usually mounted on a ship or vehicle and fires visible bolts of coherent light. Laser cannons are prone to overheating and rely on internal cooling systems to keep them functioning throughout an extended battle. [SWSB]

Latara

A pretty, mischievous young female Ewok who loves to play pranks. She also loves to play her flute and is Princess Kneesaa's best friend. [ETV]

LE-BO2D9 (LEEBO)

Dash Rendar's trusty droid and copilot, nicknamed Leebo, was a skeletal droid composed of both new and old parts. [SOTE]

Leebo

See LE-BO2D9.

Legorburu, Ixidro

A Cornish intelligence officer, she served as Colonel Pakkpekatt's tactical aide aboard the *Glorious.* [SOL]

Leia
See Solo, Princess Leia Organa.

Leiger, Vin
A false identity used by Gavin Darklighter during Rogue Squadron's undercover mission to Coruscant. [WG]

lekku
The highly sensitive dual head-tails of a Twi'lek. [TJP]

Lelmra
This planet served as a temporary base for Senator Garm Bel Iblis's private army. [DFR, LC]

Lemelisk, Bevel
A human, he was one of the main designers and chief engineer of the Imperial Death Star project. [CCC, DS, DSTC, GG5, JS, SF, SWSB]

Leria Kerlsil
This planet is home to life-witches, or life-bearers, beings that can sustain another in perfect health for years. When they withdraw their support, their beneficiary dies. [AC]

Lesser Plooriod Cluster
A region comprised of twelve star systems far from the hub of Imperial activity. The Ottega system, site of the planet Ithor, is in the cluster. After leaving Corporate Sector space, Han Solo and Chewbacca attempted a military-scrip exchange scam in the cluster. [HLL, SWSB]

Leth, Umak
An Imperial engineer, he created the Leth universal energy cage and the World Devastators, among other destructive items. [DE]

Leth universal energy cage

A floating confinement cell designed to hold the most powerful prisoners and able to block Force energies. [DE]

Leviathor

The ancient leader of the Whaladon, he was known as a great and wise ruler. He helped many of his species remain free by outsmarting those who would hunt them. He was believed to be the last great living white Whaladon. [GDV]

Lianna

An industrial world in the heart of the Allied Tion sector, it was home to Santhe/Sienar Technologies, the parent company of Sienar Fleet Systems and manufacturer of the Imperial TIE fighter. [DESB, ML]

Liberator

One of two Imperial Star Destroyers captured by the Alliance during the Battle of Endor, the former *Adjudicator* was placed under the command of Luke Skywalker. After the Empire recaptured Coruscant, *Liberator* crashed into the Imperial City. Luke's skillful deployment of the Star Destroyer's shields and repulsorlifts prevented the death of the crew. [DE, DESB]

Liberty

An Alliance star cruiser, it was the first Rebel casualty in the Battle of Endor. The second Death Star vaporized the ship and its crew. A second *Liberty* was part of the New Republic's Fifth Fleet during the Yevethan crisis. [BTS, RJ]

Lifath

A proctor of information, he served on the flagship *Pride of Yevetha.* [BTS]

life-bearer

Also referred to as life-witches, these beings born on the planet Leria Kerlsil can link their own body chemistry to that of another—usually someone old, sick, or dying—and keep the other healthy and alive. [AC]

lifeboat
See escape pod.

lifeboat bay
A special enclosure on starships, it contains emergency escape pods and their jettisoning systems. [HSR]

life debt
See Wookiee life debt.

life pod
See escape pod.

life-witch
See life-bearer.

lift
A lift moves people and objects from one level to another within multidecked ships, buildings, and space stations. These elevators are either mechanical or antigravitational in nature. [SWR]

lift tube
A cylindrical shaft, it moves people in a variety of directions through buildings, ships, and space stations. Repulsor fields are the most frequently used method of movement. [SW]

light dust
A sacred powder that Ewoks use to nourish the Tree of Light on Endor's forest moon. [ETV]

Light Festival
An Ewok celebration on Endor's forest moon, it honors the periodic rejuvenation of the Tree of Light. [ETV]

Lightning

A converted Prinawe racer in Colonel Pakkpekatt's chase armada. [BTS]

Light of Reason

A spacecraft used by Nam Chorios strongman Seti Ashgad. [POT]

Lightrunner

A cruiser owned and operated by Mammon Hoole, it was destroyed by the living planet D'vouran. [GF]

lightsaber

The powerful yet elegant weapon of the Jedi Knights for thousands of years, these power swords project blades of pure energy capable of cutting through most materials—except for the blade of another lightsaber. By tradition, most lightsabers are built by their users as part of their Jedi training. Seemingly simple in design, a lightsaber has a handle about twenty-four to thirty centimeters long. Inside, power cells and multifaceted Adegan crystals (jewels) produce a narrow beam of meter-long light that emerges from a concave disk atop the handle. When activated, a lightsaber hums with power. Considered archaic when compared to blasters and other modern weapons, lightsabers are nonetheless impressive and powerful personal weapons that require extensive training to use effectively.

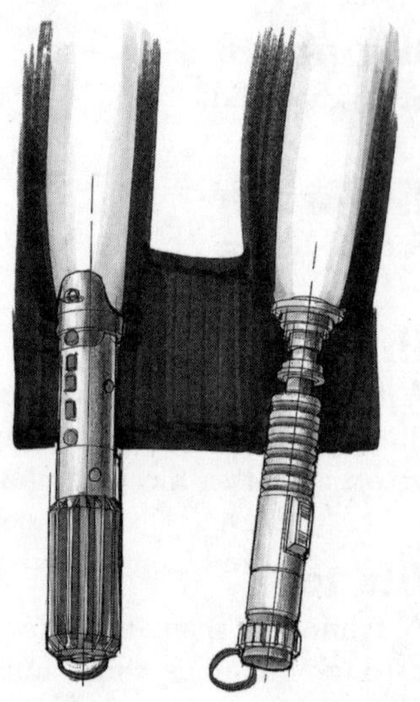

lightsaber

A saber with a single jewel has a fixed amplitude and blade length. Those with multiple jewels—usually no more than three—allow the user to alter the amplitude and change the length of the light blade or blades. This is accomplished by rotating an exterior control that varies the distance between the jewels. The emitted beam is arced back from its positively charged continuous energy lens to a negatively charged high-energy flux aperture set in the disk atop the handle. The power amplitude determines the point at which the beam arcs back, thus setting the blade's length. [ESB, HESB, RJ, SOTE, SW, SWSB, TOJ]

Lightside Explorer

A spacecraft that Andur and Nomi Sunrider owned about 4,000 years before the Galactic Civil War. [TOJ, TSW]

lightspeed engine

See hyperdrive.

Light Spirit

A benign entity worshipped by the Ewoks. They believe that it protects and guides them through every activity. [ETV]

light table

A holoprojector array, it displays both holograms and holographs through a parabolic holoprojector at the center of the table's top. Data displays surround the projector, and they can be manipulated from touchboards around the table's edge. [RJ]

Linuri

Site of a confrontation between Senator Garm Bel Iblis's private army and the forces of Grand Admiral Thrawn. [DFR]

Lisstik

The leader of the Kamarian Badlanders, he traded with Han Solo and Chewbacca during their stay on the planet Kamar. [HSR]

"Little Lost Bantha Cub, The"

Young Anakin Solo's favorite bedtime story, it was usually presented to him by C-3PO. [JS, NR]

L'lahsh

A food dish from the planet Alderaan. [SWR]

Llewebum

A species whose members have large bumps on their bodies, including a secondary series of bumps below the arms. [NR]

Lobot

Son of a slaver, then a slave himself, he eventually escaped from his pirate captors and arrived on Bespin's Cloud City. Forced to steal to survive, he was caught and sentenced. Cloud City's baroness administrator suggested an alternative to a lengthy prison term—he could become indentured to the city as its first cyborg liaison officer. Fitted with advanced cyborg components, his intelligence was greatly enhanced and he was able to communicate directly with the city's central computer. He retained this position even after his sentence had run its course, helping Lando Calrissian win control of the city from a draconian administrator in a sabacc game. When Calrissian fled the city with Princess Leia and other members of the Rebel Alliance, Lobot remained behind.

During the Yevethan crisis, Calrissian sought Lobot's help to solve the mystery of the Teljkon vagabond ghost ship. Years later, he served as Calrissian's aide on the *GemDiver Station* that orbited Yavin. [BTS, ESB, GG2, GG3, SWCG, TT]

locomotor

A servomechanism that gives droids and other automatons the ability to move. [SW]

Loctob, Cycy

One of Nar Shaddaa's alien denizens, he made a living by selling contraband to any and all interested parties. [DE]

Logray
An Ewok medicine man for the tribe that befriended Princess Leia and her companions, he was a tan-striped Ewok who wore the half skull of a great forest bird atop his head. He carried a staff of power, decorated with the spine of a great enemy. In his youth he was a great warrior, but as time passed he was revered for his great wisdom. He could also be a bully, and after the Battle of Endor, Chief Chirpa replaced him as medicine man with Paploo. [EA, ETV, GG5, RJ]

Lomabu III
One of six planets in the Lomabu system, it was the site of a trap set by Imperial Governor Io Desnand for Alliance agents. Using several hundred Wookiee females and cubs as bait, he planned to kill them all to attract Rebel rescuers. The bounty hunters Chenlambec and Tinian I'att successfully rescued the Wookiees before any harm befell them. [TBH]

Lomin-ale
A favorite beverage of many members of Rogue Squadron, it has a bitter, spicy flavor. [RS]

lommite
This mineral from the planet Elom is a major raw material used to manufacture transparisteel. [HESB]

Lonay
A clever but cowardly Twi'lek, he was one of the Black Sun Vigos who served Prince Xizor. [SESB, SOTE]

Long, Gee
A member of Auren Yomm's famous racing team that competed in the Roon Colonial Games. [DTV]

Long Snoot
See Garindan.

Loor, Kirtan

Once an Imperial liaison to the Corellian Security Force (CorSec) and an Imperial Intelligence agent on Imperial Center, he was assigned the mission to destroy Rogue Squadron by Ysanne Isard, director of Imperial Intelligence. Later, he became leader of the terrorist Palpatine Counterinsurgency Front, challenging the New Republic with the same tactics its agents had used on the Empire. When he saw that his service to Isard was coming to an end, he offered to reveal the identities of Imperial agents on Coruscant and the spy within Rogue Squadron in exchange for immunity and a new identity. Before he could testify, he was assassinated by one of Isard's sleeper agents. [KT, RS, WG]

Lord of the Sith

See Dark Lord of the Sith.

Loro, Elscol

The leader of the resistance against the Empire on the planet Cilpar, she took over the organization after her husband Throm died. She later accepted a position in Rogue Squadron. The Wookiee Groznik transferred his life debt from Throm to Elscol and watched over her. When her actions turned reckless, Wedge Antilles discharged her from the squadron. She then became an insurgency fighter in the New Republic's attempt to overthrow the Thyferran government. [BW, XW]

Loronar

This planet was the site of the facilities used by the Emperor to build his largest warships and special weapons platforms. [ISB, ISWU]

Loronar Corporation

A nearly galaxywide conglomerate that manufactures many products, including synthdroids and advanced spacecraft. [ISB, POT]

Loronar Strike cruiser

A large star cruiser employed by the Empire. One of these vessels was hollowed out and used to transport the Hammertong device. [ISB, TMEC]

Lorrd

A planet in the Kanz sector. [CSSB, HSR]

Lorrdian

The human inhabitants of the planet Lorrd. They are renowned throughout the galaxy as the best mimes and mimics. [HSR]

Loruss, Chief Technician

An employee of Holowan Laboratories, she was the manager of the IG series assassin droid prototype project. She was killed by IG-88 when the droid became self-aware and staged a bloody escape. [TBH]

Lost City of the Jedi

An ancient city built long ago by Jedi Knights, it is located deep below the surface of Yavin 4. Droids cared for the city and its hidden secrets for ages. Ken, the grandson of Emperor Palpatine, was raised in the city by the droid DJ-88. [LCJ, PDS]

Lost Ones, the

A youth gang that prowled the lower levels of Coruscant some twenty years after the Battle of Endor. Their symbol was a cross inside a triangle. A teenage boy named Norys was their leader. [YJK]

lotiramine

A drug used to counteract the drug skirtopanol, a truth serum. However, mixing these two drugs could cause chemical amnesia or even death. [BW]

Lowbacca

The nephew of Chewbacca, he was the first Wookiee to train at Luke Skywalker's Jedi academy. Nicknamed Lowie, he became friends with Jacen and Jaina Solo. He wore a belt that held a small translator droid, Em Teedee, that interpreted the Wookiee language into Basic. [SWCG, YJK]

Lowbacca

L'toth, Kiles

A Dornean, he was the associate director of the Astrographic Survey Institute. His old friend General Etahn A'baht asked him to assemble a survey team and do some undercover scouting for the New Republic in the Koornacht Cluster. A secret Yevethan fleet destroyed the survey team's vessel, *Astrolabe*, at Doornik-1142. [BTS]

Lucazec

This planet is the former home of the Fallanassi religious sect. [BTS, TT]

Luka, Zona

A Jedi apprentice of Master Dominis some 4,000 years before the Galactic Civil War. [TSW]

lum

This fermented, fiery ale is a favorite beverage of many members of Rogue Squadron. [TM, XW]

Lumat

An Ewok warrior, he also served as the tribe's woodcutter. Married to Zephee, he was the father of Latara, Nippett, and Wiley. [ETV]

lumni-spice

The rarest form of spice in the galaxy, it grows deep in the caverns on Hoth. It is fiercely protected by a dragon-slug that feeds on the spice. [CSW]

Lumpawarrump

A Wookiee, he is Chewbacca's son. Nicknamed Lumpy, he accompanied his father on a mission to rescue Han Solo. This mission served as Lumpy's coming-of-age ritual, the hrrtayyk. After the mission, he changed his name to Lumpawaroo, or Waroo for short. [SWWS, TT]

Lur

This planet is constantly pummeled by turbulent winds, rain, sleet, and snow. The world, which lies in a star system close to the Corporate Sector, is partially covered by huge glacial fields. The intelligent inhabitants of the planet are called Lurrians. These small, bipedal hominids have fine white fur and large blue-green eyes. They are peaceful and sociable but are constantly threatened by slavers. [CSSB, HSR]

Lusa

From the planet Chiron, she has four legs and a horselike body and a humanoid torso. She is a friend of Jaina Solo, and she loves to run fast and jump high. [CS, YJK]

Lusankya

This Super Star Destroyer was buried beneath Imperial Center to serve as an emergency evacuation vehicle for Emperor Palpatine. Ysanne Isard, director of Imperial Intelligence, used it as her private prison and sanctuary. Prisoners that survived the torture and experiments emerged as sleeper agents who would do the Empire's bidding when a command was issued. When Isard was forced to abandon Imperial Center, she used *Lusankya*, thereby destroying more than one hundred square kilometers of Imperial City and killing millions of inhabitants. [BW, KT]

Luure, M'yet

A powerful New Republic senator, he was an Exodeenian with six arms and legs and rows of uneven teeth. He died in an explosion in Senate Hall and was replaced by the junior Exodeenian representative, R'yet Coome. [NR]

Luwingo

First mate on the *Hyperspace Marauder*, he was partner to Lo Khan, the ship's owner. He was a Yaka cyborg, possessing brain implants like other members of his race. Though he appeared brutish, Luwingo could beat the L7 logician droid in hologames on a regular basis. [DE]

Lwhekk

This planet is the homeworld of the Ssi-ruuk. [TAB]

Lycoming

A New Republic quarantine enforcement cruiser. [POT]

Lyric

A Melodie from Yavin 8, she was a student at Luke Skywalker's Jedi academy. She returned to Yavin 8 to undergo her metamorphosis. [JJK]

M3-D2

A housekeeping droid that worked in Jabba the Hutt's palace and served as a contact for many of Lady Valarian's spies. [TJP]

M-3PO

See Emtrey (Emtreypio).

macrobinoculars

A handheld viewing device that magnifies distant objects and allows for both day and night vision through built-in light and dark scopes. Readouts within the viewplate provide information on the viewed object's true and relative azimuth, elevation, and range. It can also be mounted in a helmet. [SW, SWSB]

macrofuser

A miniature welding tool designed and calibrated for heavy-duty repairs of complex metals, such as those found in starships. [ESB]

Madine, General Crix

General Crix Madine

A Corellian who was a highly decorated Imperial officer, he defected to the Rebel Alliance after the Emperor personally ordered him on a top secret mission to subjugate the planet Dentaal. He found the mission to be so vile and criminal that he defected shortly after the Battle of Yavin. The Alliance was initially suspicious of Madine, but he quickly proved himself and became one of Mon Mothma's most important military advisers. He developed Rebel ground tactics and strategies while Admiral Ackbar concentrated on space-combat tactics. When the Alliance learned that the Empire was building a second Death Star above the forest moon of Endor, Madine executed the procurement of an Imperial shuttle. Then he trained and assembled the strike team that accompanied Han Solo to Endor's moon to destroy the shield generators protecting the new Death Star.

After the Battle of Endor, Mon Mothma offered him a seat on the Provisional Council. "I'm a warrior, not a politician," he replied, declining the offer. Instead, he became head of covert operations as supreme allied commander for Intelligence. He helped plan the battle against Grand Admiral Thrawn and the Imperial World Devastators. He even joined the commando team that located Durga the Hutt's new superweapon. Durga killed Madine with a laser shot through the heart. [DFR, DFRSB, DS, GG5, RJ, SWCG]

Madis, Captain

A New Republic officer, he commanded the picket ship *Folna* during the Yevethan crisis. [TT]

Mageye the Hutt

A crimelord, he was accidentally killed by the bounty hunter Zardra. [TMEC]

Magg

A slave trader, he posed as Fiolla of Lorrd's personal assistant in order to keep tabs on her investigations in Corporate Sector space. [HSR]

main drive

A starship's primary propulsion unit and most powerful onboard engine. [SWR]

maintenance hauler

A star tug for towing disabled spacecraft to the nearest spaceport. [HLL]

Maires

This ocean planet in the Hapes Cluster is the homeworld of the water-breathing Mairans. [YJK]

maitrakh

A Noghri word referring to the female ruler of a clan. The word is used as a title of reverence and respect. A maitrakh from clan Kihm'bar helped Princess Leia and was influential in convincing the Noghri to turn away from the Empire. [DFR, DFRSB, LC]

Maizor

A onetime rival of Jabba the Hutt. Jabba had Maizor's brain placed in a nutrient-filled jar and attached to metal legs by the B'omarr monks. [DS]

makant

Large, playful insects that appear to be a combination of a mantis and a cricket, they live on the forest moon of Endor. [ETV]

maker, the

A droid phrase that refers to their creator and is often said in a worshipful, almost religious manner. [SW]

Makki

A member of the crew of the New Republic survey ship *Steadfast.* [BTS]

Mala Mala

A crippled bounty hunter, she rode a droid called Fordee. Mala learned the name of the Rebel pilot who destroyed the original Death Star—Luke Skywalker. She escaped from Darth Vader and took the name to the Emperor. [VQ]

Malakili

A professional beast trainer from the Corellian system, he left the Circus Horrificus to work for Jabba the Hutt as a rancor handler. After Jabba's death, he opened a restaurant in Mos Eisley with funds looted from the Hutt's palace. [GG5, TJP]

Malani

A young Ewok from the forest moon of Endor, she is Teebo's little sister. She had a huge crush on Wicket W. Warrick when they were growing up. [ETV]

Mal'ary'ush

The Noghri title applied to Leia Organa Solo, it identifies her as the daughter of Lord Darth Vader and heir to the debt the Noghri believe they owed to him. [DFR, HE, LC]

Malkite Poisoner

An elite assassin in a secret order of killers, he or she learns the deadly craft on the planet Malkii. These assassins carry small vials of lethal toxins in specialized kits hidden within their clothing. By the group's code, no assassin could be captured alive. [HSR]

Mallar, Plat

A young Grannan, he took one of six operational TIE interceptors during the Yevethan attack on his homeworld Polneye and destroyed a Yevethan scout fighter. Later, New Republic forces found him, and he alerted them to the Yevethan threat. He eventually became a New Republic pilot. [BTS, SOL]

Mallatobuck

A female Wookiee, she was Chewbacca's wife. [SWWS]

Malorm Family

An infamous group of human psychopathic killers, they hijacked the luxury spaceliner *Galaxy Wanderer* as it passed through the Corporate Sector. The Corporate Sector Authority Counterterrorist Security Team apprehended the three men and two women who comprised the group on Matra VI. [HLL]

Manaroo

A tattooed dancing girl and empath, she was able to alter her performance to play off her audience's emotions. She eventually escaped from Jabba the Hutt and rescued Dengar the bounty hunter after Jabba had left him to die in the desert. Later, she and Dengar were married. [TBH]

Manchisco, Captain Tessa

A brash young captain, she helped bring the Virgillian Free Alignment Starfleet into the Rebel Alliance in time for the Battle of Endor. Her vessel, the *Flurry*, served as Luke Skywalker's command ship during the crisis at Bakura. She was killed when the Imperial warship *Dominant* destroyed the *Flurry* in a surprise attack. [TAB, TBSB]

Mandalore

A mercenary warlord, he conquered a planet that later took his name about 4,000 years before the Galactic Civil War. He wore a full-face metal mask and was the model for the Mandalore supercommandos of later generations. [TSW]

Mandalore system

This star system was home to fierce masked warrior clans some 4,000 years before the Galactic Civil War. These deadly but honorable crusaders were led by the mysterious warlord Mandalore and were considered to be the best warriors in the galaxy. The mask and title of Mandalore were passed down from one leader to the next upon the death of the former. During the Sith War, Mandalore and his armies swore allegiance to the mystical Krath sect. During the Clone Wars, the Jedi Knights defeated a group of Mandalorian warriors. The bounty hunter Boba Fett wore blaster-resistant armor and used ships and weaponry based on Mandalorian design. Mandalorians even designed Imperial dungeon ships, introduced during the Jedi Purge to contain dangerous Force users. [D, DE, DESB, DLS, MTS, SWSB, TMEC, TSW]

Manticore

This Star Destroyer was one of four in Admiral Daala's fleet. [JS]

mantigrue

A hideous, dragonlike creature with leathery wings, sharp claws, and a long, pointed beak. It lives on Endor's forest moon. One of these creatures was the slave of Morag, the Tulgah witch. [ETV]

Marauder
A species of tall, barbaric humanoids, they prey upon the more peaceful inhabitants of Endor's forest moon. The Marauders, under the command of their king, Terak, built a dark fortress on a desolate plain. [BFE, ISWU]

Marauder
This New Republic gunship accompanied the *Glorious* to intercept the Teljkon vagabond. [BTS]

Marauder-class corvette
A staple of the Corporate Sector Authority's picket fleet and popular with planetary navies, large corporations, and smugglers, it is a light cruiser streamlined for atmospheric combat. [CSSB, HSE, SWVG]

Marauder Starjacker
An ore raider commanded by pirate captain Finhead Stonebone some 4,000 years before the Galactic Civil War. This ship resembled a hundred-meter-long insect. [SWVG, TOJ]

Marcha, Duchess of Mastigophorous
A Drall female and Ebrihim's aunt, she provided help and information to Chewbacca and the Solo children when they were forced to flee Corellia. [AS]

Marcopious, Yeoman
A member of Chief of State Leia Organa Solo's honor guard, he helped R2-D2 and C-3PO escape in a scout boat after Leia was kidnapped. Shortly thereafter, he died from the Death Seed plague. [POT]

Margath, Kina
The owner of Margath's, a luxury hotel on Elshandruu Pica. She was also a Rebel agent. [BW, GG9]

Mark II reactor drone

A utility droid built and programmed for menial labor. Its outer casing is heavily shielded to protect its internal circuitry. [SWR]

Mark X executioner

A gladiator droid designed to participate in combat sports. It is equipped with flame projectors, flechette missile launchers, blasters, and two crawler threads for mobility. [HSE]

Marook, Senator Cion

A belligerent senator from Hrasskis, he was a member of the New Republic Senate Defense Council. [BTS, SOL]

Marr, Nichos

A Jedi student of Luke Skywalker, he came to the Jedi academy with his fiancée, the scientist Cray Mingla. When he was struck with the fatal Quannot's syndrome, Mingla transferred Marr's intelligence into a near-human artificial body. He later accompanied Luke Skywalker on a mission to destroy the *Eye of Palpatine* battle station. Marr volunteered to remain on the station to make sure it was destroyed. Mingla, realizing she couldn't live without Marr, stayed behind, too. Her body then served as a receptacle for the essence of the Jedi woman Callista, who had been trapped within the station's computer core. [COJ, SWCG]

Marso

The leader of a group of mercenary pilots called the Demons. [HLL]

Masposhani

This planet is the site of subterranean caves where Jedi Knights once trained—at least according to Beldorian the Hutt. [POT]

Massassi

This ancient species of fierce warriors lived on the fourth moon of Yavin some 4,000 years before the Galactic Civil War. Naga

Sadow purposely mutated these half-civilized beings. Sadow and Exar Kun used the Massassi to build and guard huge temples. Sith Lord Kun killed the Massassi in a final sacrifice. [CSW, DA, DLS, SW, TSW]

master control signal

A transmission beamed through hyperspace, the signal guides and controls automated vessels such as the Empire's World Devastators. [DE]

Mattri asteroids

Site of a temporary base for the private army of Garm Bel Iblis during its attacks on the Empire. [DFR]

Mauit'ta, Colonel

A New Republic officer, he served as General Etahn A'baht's staff intelligence officer for the Fifth Fleet. [TT]

Maul, Darth

One of two Sith Lords in existence at the time of the Naboo blockade, he was the apprentice to the Sith Lord Darth Sidious. Born with hornlike bones growing out of his head, Maul had his face tattooed in a terrifying mask of jagged red and black stripes. He was sent by Sidious to stop Jedi Master Qui-Gon Jinn and his apprentice Obi-Wan Kenobi in their mission to protect Naboo's Queen Amidala and end the blockade. Maul killed Qui-Gon with his double-bladed lightsaber and was in turn killed by Obi-Wan. [SWTPM]

Darth Maul

Maw

A cluster of black holes near the planet Kessel. It served as the hiding place for the Maw Installation. [JS]

Maw Installation

This top secret weapons-development facility was located on a cluster of planetoids crammed together at a gravitational island at the center of the black-hole cluster near Kessel. Weapons such as the Death Star, World Devastators, and the Sun Crusher were developed there. New Republic forces destroyed the installation. [COF, JS]

Max Rebo Band

An odd collection of jizz-wailers from a variety of worlds, the band often performed exclusive engagements for the crimelord Jabba the Hutt of Tatooine. The original band consisted of Max Rebo, Droopy McCool, and the singer Sy Snootles. Later, it expanded to include the Yuzzum singer Joh Yowza, the amphibian Rappertunie, the Rodian horn player Doda Bondonawieedo, the Bith Barquin D'an, and the drummers Weequay Ak-Rev and Klatooinian Umpass-Stay. Max also hired three backup singers and dancers: Greeata, a Rodian; Lyn Me, a Twi'lek; and the exotic red-spotted Rystáll. [RJ]

Mayro

A resort world located in the Corporate Sector. [CSSB]

Mazzic

A militaristic smuggler chief whose fleet consisted of freighters of all descriptions and a number of customized combat starships, including the *Skyclaw* and the *Raptor*. He traveled in his personal transport, the *Distant Rainbow*. The woman named Shada D'akul, his deceptively decorative bodyguard, was never far from his side. Mazzic was among the smuggler chiefs that Talon Karrde convinced to join forces to aid the New Republic in its fight against Grand Admiral Thrawn. [LC]

McCool, Droopy

A Kitonak musician, he was a member of the Max Rebo Band. The chubby musician originally named Snit played a variety of wind instruments. Droopy was "owned" by Evar Orbus and forced to play in the band for a variety of clients, including Jabba the Hutt. After Jabba died, Droopy left the band and walked into Tatooine's desert in search of others of his kind. [GG5, RJ, SWCG, TJP]

McPhersons

A family of moisture farmers on Tatooine, they supported Ariq Joanson in his plans to make peace with the Jawas and the Sand People. [TMEC]

MD-model droid

Medical droids manufactured by Industrial Automaton are among the most commonly used medical droids in the galaxy. From the MD-0 (Emdee-Oh) diagnostic droids that assist physicians with patient examinations, to the MD-5 (Emdee-Five) general practitioner droids that are considered the "country doctors" of space, the MD series is versatile, competent, and affordable. When the MD-10 model was developed, it revolutionized the manufacture of medical droids. [NR, SWSB]

mechanical

A colloquialism for droids, often used in a derogatory manner. [SWN]

Mechis III

A polluted world covered with sprawling droid factories and considered the most important in the industry. Prior to the Battle of Hoth, the planet was taken over by IG-88 and his duplicates. IG-88 hoped to use the factories to trigger a droid revolution. [TBH]

medical cocoon

A portable enclosure that can sustain sick or injured patients while transporting them to a medical facility. A medical cocoon is totally self-sufficient, equipped with a miniature power generator, regulators, and monitoring banks. [SME]

medical droid

A droid whose primary function is to diagnose and treat illnesses and injuries and can also perform or assist with surgeries. Medical droids are found in hospitals and clinics throughout the galaxy. Many models are stationary, tethered to huge diagnostic and treatment analysis computers. The MD series of medical droids are the most common models. The older 2-1B and FX series droids were used by the Alliance and on frontier worlds. [ESBR, SWSB]

medical frigate

Any small star cruiser devoted exclusively to the transportation and care of the wounded and convalescent, and staffed primarily by medical personnel. [ESB]

meditation chamber

A personal inner sanctum, the best known of which was perhaps Darth Vader's personal chamber aboard the Super Star Destroyer *Executor*. This spherical enclosure split open to permit exit and entry, its top and bottom halves separating like jaws. The interior consisted of a comfortable reclining chair, a comlink and visual display, and a mechanical device for quickly removing and replacing Vader's helmet and breath mask. The pressurized sphere kept Vader comfortable even when his helmet was off. [ESB]

medpac

A compact first-aid kit that contains a synthflesh dispenser, vibroscalpel, flexclamp, painkillers, disinfectant pads, and precious fluid and gas cartridges. [HLL, HSE, HSR, SWRPG2]

meewit

A screeching animal native to Tatooine. [TJP]

Megadeath

See Nataz, Dyyz.

Meido

A New Republic senator from the planet Adin, he was a former Imperial. He called for the no-confidence vote that led to Chief of State Leia Organa Solo's temporary resignation, and he supported the idea that Han Solo was involved in the bombing of Senate Hall. [NR]

Melan, Koth

A Bothan who used his official job as assistant consul general for the Bothan Trade Mission to mask his true role as spymaster for the Bothan spynet. He was instrumental in uncovering the truth about the Emperor's plans to build a second Death Star, and accompanied Dash Rendar on the raid against the *Suprosa*. Later, while staying at a Bothan safe house on the planet Kothlis, Melan was killed by a team of bounty hunters charged with kidnapping Luke Skywalker. [SESB, SOTE]

melding, the

An intimate process of sharing the same mind, practiced by Aruzans. The Aruzans use a device called the Attanni to cybernetically link the thoughts of two people. [TBH]

Melihat

This planet manufactures dome fisheyes, a type of optical transducer. [TT]

Melodie

A humanoid species from the moon Yavin 8. They start life much like human infants but metamorphose into aquatic beings with webbed tails instead of legs. [JJK]

Meltdown Café

A restaurant located on the spaceport moon Nar Shaddaa. [DE2, TMEC]

memory flush
A memory wipe used to erase all of the accumulated data stored in a computer system or droid data bank. Most droids dread this procedure. [SW]

Mendicat
A scrap mining and recycling station. It was destroyed when Imperial General Sulamar incorrectly programmed the station's orbital computers. [DS]

Mereel, Journeyman Protector Jaster
See Fett, Boba.

Merenzane Gold
A golden liquor popular throughout the galaxy. [TBH]

Meridian sector
This lightly populated area near the Outer Rim contains several New Republic planets, including Nim Drovis and Budpock, as well as the fleet bases at Durren and Cybloc XII. Much of the rest of the area is neutral, including the Chorios systems. [POT]

Meridias
This planet in the Meridian sector is a lifeless world. [POT]

Merisee Hope
A slave-running ship for a brothel in Coruscant's Invisec. Its transponder code was used by the smuggler Mirax Terrik to secretly transport members of Rogue Squadron to Imperial Center on her ship, *Pulsar Skate*. [WG]

metal-crystal phase shifter (MCPS)
A weapon constructed at Maw Installation, it produced an energy field that altered the crystalline structure of metals. It

could penetrate conventional shielding and turn hull plates, for example, into powder. [COF]

Meteor Way

An area in Coronet, capital of the planet Corellia. [AC]

M'haeli

This agrarian planet serves as a refueling point for several nearby systems. The population consists of human colonists and native H'drachi. [ROC, SOL]

Micamberlecto

A governor-general of Corellia, he was a Frozian. [AC]

Midanyl, Sena Leikvold

Senator Garm Bel Iblis's chief aide and adviser, she once served as his unofficial ambassador-at-large for Peregrine's Nest—headquarters for Bel Iblis's private army. [DFR]

midi-chlorian

Microscopic life-forms that reside as symbionts within all living cells and communicate with the Force. [SWTPM]

Mid Rim

This huge expanse of space between the Inner Rim and Outer Rim Territories is less wealthy and less populated than the regions around it. As an undeveloped area with few natural resources, much of the Mid Rim remains either unexplored or is controlled by smugglers and pirates. [SWRPG2]

Millennium Falcon

A Corellian stock light freighter that has been accused of looking like a piece of junk but is one of the fastest, best-equipped vessels in the galaxy, despite its tendency to break down or malfunction. For years, it has been Han Solo's ship, copiloted and maintained by his partner Chewbacca the Wookiee. In the past, it has belonged to a number of owners before Lando Calrissian

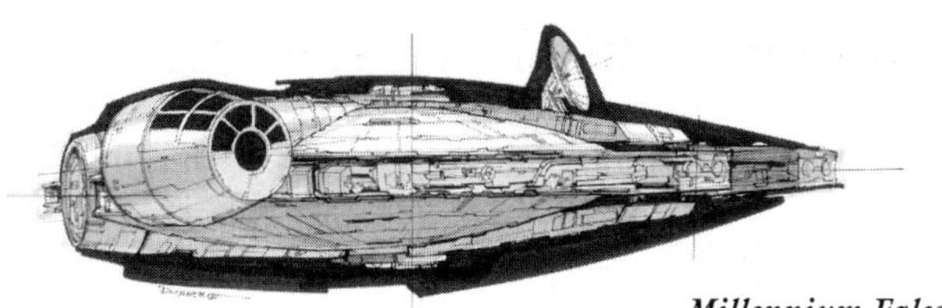
Millennium Falcon

took possession of it. Lando lost the ship to Solo in a game of sabacc. Lando won it back twice, but eventually returned the ship to Solo.

Under Solo's guidance and Chewbacca's careful and loving administration, the *Falcon* has undergone major overhauls, refittings, and modifications that make it vastly different from the manufacturer's specifications. The outside has been left deliberately dilapidated to hide the ship's true abilities. This Corellian Engineering YT-1300 is twenty-seven meters long and sports a hyperdrive that is nearly twice as fast as most Imperial warships'. Both the hyperdrive and sublight engine can be finicky, though, due to all the modifications.

The *Falcon* has a heavily armored hull, custom security mechanisms, computer-assisted targeting consoles, boosted deflector shields, and a more powerful weapons system than a ship of its class, size, and designation is allowed to carry. It has a powerful—and illegal—sensor suite, shielded smuggling compartments, two quad laser cannons, two concussion missile launchers, and a retractable light laser cannon.

During much of the Galactic Civil War, the *Falcon* suffered from a rash of minor problems that required almost constant periods of repair. Still, it was one of the best ships in service to the Alliance. It participated in the destruction of both Death Star battle stations, ran Imperial blockades with apparent ease, and ferried Princess Leia Organa on many of her most important missions during those dark years. Solo was still flying the *Falcon* as of the launch of the Yuuzhan Vong incursion, though without the aid of his longtime copilot, Chewbacca, who died in a rescue mission to a moon of Sernpidal. [DA, DFR, ESB, LCM, RJ, SW, SWSB]

Mimban (Circarpous V)

A swampy world covered by a perpetual cloud of rainstorms and mostly unexplored and uncolonized. It had a secret

Imperial mining operation. There are three intelligent species: Mimbanites (large-eyed beings called greenies), Coway (thin, gray beings), and an unnamed furry species with four arms and four legs. In addition, the long-extinct Thrella built hundreds of temples, cities, and near-bottomless Thrella Wells. [SME]

Mimban Cloudrider

This Thyferran bacta tanker was captured by Rogue Squadron during a raid against Ysanne Isard's Bacta Cartel. It was then used in a mission to Thyferra to bring aid to the Ashern rebels. [BW]

Mingla, Cray

A student at Luke Skywalker's Jedi academy, she was a scientist who was on the cutting edge of artificial intelligence. When her fiancé, fellow student Nichos Marr, was overcome by a fatal disease, she transferred his mind and intelligence into a near-human artificial body. During the *Eye of Palpatine* crisis Mingla and Marr sacrificed their lives to destroy the battle station. However, at the last possible moment, she enabled the essence of the Jedi Callista—whose spirit had been trapped in the battle station's computers—to occupy Mingla's body so that Callista could be united with her new love, Luke Skywalker. [COJ]

mining remote

Designed by Death Star engineer Bevel Lemelisk for crimelord Durga the Hutt, these automated spacecraft move through asteroid belts to seek out and extract metals from the rocks. [DS]

Minos Cluster

Located on the edge of the known galaxy, beyond which there are no star charts, the worlds of the Minos Cluster have only recently been colonized. The isolated region is home to smugglers, pirates, and outlaws. Mara Jade and Talon Karrde traveled to the cluster thirteen years after the Battle of Endor on an errand. [GG6, NR]

Mirage
A ship used by the Mistryl Shadow Guards. [TMEC]

Miraluka
A humanoid species from Alpheridies, they are born without eyes. Many of them can see using the Force, and many became Jedi in ancient times. [FNU]

Miranda
An X-wing pilot for Blue Flight in the New Republic's Fifth Fleet, she died during the failed blockade of Doornik-319. [SOL]

Mirit system
Located at the edge of the Galactic Core, it contains the planet Ord Mirit, site of a former Imperial base. [RS]

Miser
The innermost planet in the Bespin system, this small world is rich in valuable metals. [GG2, HE, IC]

mistmaker
A creature from the planet Msst. It resembles a giant pink bubble with teeth. [NR]

Mistryl
A humanoid species whose world was ravaged by the Empire. Few Mistryls survived. [TMEC]

Mistryl Shadow Guards
This cult of warrior women who once fought the injustices of the Empire became mercenaries to earn money to help their suffering people. [COF, TMEC]

Moddell sector
The region of space that contains the planet Endor and its moons. [SWSB]

moff

A title given to Imperial military commanders who ruled certain sectors of the Empire. Moffs reported to grand moffs, who controlled groups of sectors. [ISB, SWN]

mogo

A massive, black-furred creature with a camel-like head and an undulating body. It is used for transportation on the planet Roon. [DTV]

moisture farm

A usually rural, privately held operation to extract water from the atmosphere for profitable use on dry, desert worlds. The moisture farms of Tatooine, for example, use vaporators to squeeze water from the air to irrigate subterranean produce farms and for human consumption. [SW]

mole miner

This utility craft, designed to operate in space, on asteroids, and on worlds with hostile environments, digs ore from places that are normally impossible to mine. Mole miners operate from a base or headquarters ship, returning at the end of a work shift. A mole miner can be operated by a crew or by remote control. Using its bottom-mounted plasma jets to slice through solid rock, the mole miner gathers minerals and ores into storage bins through a series of vacuum shafts and grinders. Though once in widespread use, mole miners have been mostly replaced by mining droids.

Lando Calrissian employed mole miners at his operation on the planet Nkllon until Grand Admiral Thrawn stole many of the craft. The Empire used the mole miners at the Battle of Sluis Van to burrow into capital ships so that Imperial crews could hijack the vessels. [HE, HESB]

Moll, Demma

This reserved, attractive woman owned a farm on the planet Annoo. During the early days of the Empire, the Fromm gang wanted Demma's farm and gave her and her daughter, Kea, all kinds of trouble. Demma secretly led a band of freedom fighters working to destroy Fromm's weapons satellite, the *Trigon One*. [DTV]

Moll, Kea

A beautiful seventeen-year-old when R2-D2 and C-3PO first met her during the early days of the Empire, she lived on her mother's farm on the planet Annoo. She was brave and athletic, able to handle both spacecraft and landspeeders with an expert's touch. [DTV]

Moltok

This planet in the Dartibek system is the homeworld of the Ho'Din species. [COJ, GG4, LCJ]

Mon, Ephant

A pachydermoid Chevin from the planet Vinsoth, he was not an official member of Jabba the Hutt's organization, but he was the closest thing to a friend the crimelord admitted into his inner court. Once a mercenary of some repute, he turned to weapons running after concluding that it was safer and more profitable to sell arms than to use them. He sold weapons to anyone, from pirates to outlaws to Rebels, though his most profitable ventures were with Jabba the Hutt. After the two survived a raid on an Imperial weapons depot, Jabba made Ephant Mon his secret internal security officer. He tried to convince Jabba to believe Luke Skywalker and let the Jedi and Hans Solo go free. Jabba refused, and Ephant Mon decided not to ride out on the sail barge that day. He returned to his homeworld and founded a sect of Force worshippers. [GG5, RJ, SWCG, TJP]

Monarch

An Imperial Star Destroyer. Its commander, Captain Averen, surrendered it to the Alliance rather than see it destroyed in the invasion of Coruscant. [WG]

Mon Calamari

This planet is nearly completely covered by water and serves as home to two species: the peace-loving Mon Calamari and the cautious Quarren. The surface features small marshy islands and enormous floating cities that extend above and below the water, including Reef Home, Coral Depths, Kee-Piru, and Coral City. The architecture and design used throughout the planet maintains an organic appearance, demonstrating the inhabitants' love for the world.

The Mon Calamari had already constructed space vessels and were beginning to explore the galaxy beyond their star system when the Empire arrived. The Imperials destroyed three floating cities to convince the inhabitants to stop resisting enslavement. A Quarren, Seggor Tels, was believed to have deliberately lowered Calamari's defenses to allow the Empire's attack. This led to tension between the two species on Mon Calamari. With the help of the Rebel Alliance, the planet threw off the yoke of Imperial oppression and converted its ships and space docks to aid the Rebellion.

Six years after the Battle of Endor, as the New Republic was solidifying its position in the galaxy, the Empire began a new campaign to reassert its power and dominance. The water world was the first planet attacked by the clone Emperor's World Devastators, in the Battle of Calamari. The planet suffered great damage, but the new Imperial war machines were stopped thanks to the actions of Luke Skywalker.

A year after that attack, Leia Organa Solo visited Calamari Admiral Ackbar at his home to convince him to return to the Republic. A subsequent attack by Admiral Daala's Star Destroyers led to the destruction of the floating city, Reef Home. [AS, DA, DE, DESB, DS, GG4, POT, RJ, SWSB, TJP, YJK]

Mon Calamari

A species of humanoid amphibians from the planet of the same name. These gentle beings became powerful members of the Rebel Alliance after the Empire invaded their world. Used as slave labor to build the Imperial war machine, the Mon Calamari eventually became a formidable fighting force for the Alliance, contributing badly needed capital starships and the military leadership of Admiral Ackbar. [GG3, GG4, RJ]

Mon Calamari star cruiser

The primary capital ships in the Alliance and New Republic's battle fleet, these organic-looking vessels were originally designed for pleasure, colonization, and exploration efforts. Each Mon Calamari star cruiser is handcrafted by dedicated technicians and engineers and treated as works of art. These vessels are built with many redundant systems, making them difficult to service but extremely reliable in combat situations. [DESB, MTS, RJ, RSB, SWSB]

Money Lane

A nickname for the overlapping field of fire between the *Millennium Falcon*'s upper and lower quad laser batteries. Whenever Han Solo and Chewbacca were forced into a battle, they wagered on who could hit more enemy targets. Those targets hit in the Money Lane were worth double, as both gunners had an equal chance at them. [HSE]

Mon Remonda

An interim MC-80B Mon Calamari star cruiser delivered to the New Republic about eighteen months after the Battle of Endor. It participated in the invasion of Coruscant, served as the flagship of the fleet sent to repel Warlord Zsinj's offensive, and was eventually destroyed by the World Devastator *Silencer-7* at the Second Battle of Calamari. [CPL, DA, DESB, HE, SWVG]

Montellian Serat

This city on the planet Devaron was the site of a massacre when Kardue'sai'Malloc ordered the area shelled. [GG1, TBH]

Mon Valle

This Rebel ship was the base of operations for General Horton Salm's Defender Wing squadron of Y-wings. The *Mon Valle* was destroyed during the raid on Borleias. [RS]

Mookiee

A baby Ewok, or wokling, she lived on the forest moon of Endor. [ETV]

Moon Dash

This shuttle, piloted by Captain Narek-Ag and copiloted by Trebor, ran into the cloaked Shadow Academy space station and was destroyed. [YJK]

Moonflower Nebula

This large nebula in the Outer Rim contains several stars and a vast asteroid field where the Imperial battle station *Eye of Palpatine* drifted for thirty years. [COJ]

Mooth

An elderly trader, he operated a trading post on Endor's forest moon. This fast-talker resembled a humanoid anteater and wore a primitive gambler's visor on his head and an abacus strapped across his chest. [ETV]

Mora

A human female, she was rescued as a baby by Ch'no, an H'drachi soothsayer. The only survivor in an attack that led to the Empire taking control of the planet M'haeli, Mora was the heir to M'haeli's ruling house. [ROC]

Morag

A powerful Tulgah witch, she lives on the forest moon of Endor. With a shriveled, stooped body and a mandrill's face, she is thoroughly evil. Her skills in magic and medicine rival even Logray's. She lives in a castlelike formation set into the side of the active volcano called Mount Thunderstone. Spear-wielding Yuzzums patrol her home atop rakazzak beasts. [ETV]

Morano, Captain

A human, he was the commander of the New Republic's Fifth Fleet flagship, the *Intrepid.* [SOL]

Morath Nebula

A mysterious formation that was never properly surveyed by the New Republic, it is located in either the Kokash or Farlax sector. [BTS]

Morning Bell

A planet in the Koornacht Cluster and site of a Kubaz colony, it is listed as Doornik-319 on New Republic astrogation charts. The Yevetha called it Preza. The Yevetha destroyed the Kubaz colony twelve years after the Battle of Endor. [BTS, SOL, TT]

morrt

Parasites about the size of field mice, these creatures are native to the planet Gamorr. These bloodsuckers feed on living organisms, staying with a single host throughout their long lives. Gamorreans consider morrts to be friendly, cuddly, and loyal. They keep these parasites as pets and status symbols, and the morrts are the only creatures that Gamorreans display open signs of affection to. The more morrts attached to a Gamorrean, the more status the Gamorrean has in the eyes of his peers. Matrons and clan warlords regularly have in excess of twenty morrts covering their bodies. [SWSB]

Mos Eisley

A spaceport city on the Outer Rim world Tatooine, it attracts interstellar commerce as well as all sorts of spacers looking for rest and relaxation after a long haul. The vast number of aliens and humans constantly moving through the spaceport, and its distance from the centers of galactic activity, have made Mos Eisley a haven for all types of thieves, pirates, and smugglers. Even after the influence of Jabba the Hutt was ended, the city remained a "hive of scum and villainy." The city's old central section is laid out like a wheel, while the newer sections are formed into straight blocks of half-buried buildings designed to protect them from the heat of the twin suns. The entire city acts as a spaceport, with craterlike docking bays scattered throughout. [GG7, SW, TM]

Mos Eisley cantina

A popular spot in the spaceport city Mos Eisley, located on the desert planet Tatooine. It is sometimes called Chalmun's cantina after its Wookiee owner. Everyone and everything is welcome in the cantina except droids. For many years, a grouchy man named Wuher served drinks at the cantina, and Figrin D'an and the Modal Nodes entertained patrons with their famous brand of jizz-wailing music. Luke Skywalker and Ben Kenobi met Han Solo and Chewbacca in this cantina. [SW, TM, TMEC]

Mos Espa

A large and sprawling spaceport on Tatooine, on the lip of the Dune Sea. [SWTPM]

Motexx

This planet is separated from the planet Arat Fraca by the Black Nebula in Parfadi. [SOL]

Mothma, Mon

Committed to the cause of freedom in the galaxy, the senator from the planet Chandrila became the leader of the Rebel Alliance and the founder and first chief of state of the New Republic. Mon Mothma's family background prepared her for her role in galactic politics. Her father was an arbiter-general for the Old Republic who was called upon to settle disputes between the various member species. Her mother was a planetary governor who taught her daughter how to administer, to organize, and to lead. Mon Mothma remained the youngest person to serve in the Old Republic Senate, until the election of Princess Leia Organa of Alderaan.

Mon Mothma served with vigor and integrity, even through the troubles the Old Republic fought. She led the factions that opposed the growing power of the evil Senator Palpatine, who worked behind the scenes to have himself elected supreme chancellor of the senate. She was the last to hold the position of senior senator prior to the disbanding of the senate.

Mon Mothma

With the support of Bail Organa of Alderaan, Garm Bel Iblis of Corellia, and others, she became increasingly vocal in her opposition to Palpatine. When he anointed himself Emperor and founded his New Order, Mon Mothma secretly started helping the fledgling Rebellion. When her involvement with the Rebels was discovered, she barely escaped Coruscant ahead of the Imperial secret police.

In the Corellian system, Mon Mothma participated in a secret meeting to draft the Declaration of Rebellion and the Corellian Treaty. Unimpressed, Palpatine formally disbanded the senate and declared Mon Mothma a traitor.

She was elected as the Alliance's chief of state and worked hard to turn the ragtag resistance into a force to be reckoned with. Thanks to central leadership, the Rebellion began to make strides against the Empire, culminating in the destruction of the Death Star at the Battle of Yavin. Once the Empire's tyranny and weaknesses were exposed, many planets and groups joined the Rebellion. Having gained strong military leaders and constantly improving supplies, Mon Mothma gave the order for an all-out offensive that became the Battle of Endor.

Following the victory at Endor and the deaths of the Emperor and Darth Vader, Mon Mothma began the task of creating the New Republic. With ambassadors working throughout the galaxy and keeping a watchful eye on the remnants of the Empire, she established the new government's seat of power on Coruscant—the capital world that had served the same function for the Old Republic and the Empire. Later, as she succumbed to a terrible wasting disease, Mon Mothma assigned her duties to Princess Leia Organa Solo and resigned. Her life was eventually saved by Cilghal, one of Luke Skywalker's Jedi students. She decided to remain retired so Leia could continue to govern, although she temporarily resumed her role while Leia battled a vote of no confidence and charges brought against her husband, Han Solo. When the crisis ended, Mon Mothma gladly returned the reins of government to Leia. [DA, DFR, GG5, HE, JS, LC, NR, RJ, RSB, SWSB]

motivator

A droid's main internal mechanism, it converts energy into mechanical motion. [SW]

Motti, Admiral

The senior Imperial commander in charge of operations on the original Death Star battle station who believed that Darth Vader's methods were outdated and archaic. He died when the station was destroyed. [SW]

Mountain Terrain Armored Transport (MT-AT)

Nicknamed the spider walker, this Imperial machine was designed to navigate steep inclines with independently articulated legs and clawed footpads. The MT-AT was first used on the planet Anoth in an attack on a New Republic facility. [COF, DA, SWVG]

Mount Meru

On the planet Deneba, it was the site of a huge assembly of Jedi prior to the Sith War that occurred some 4,000 years before the Galactic Civil War. [DLS]

Mount Tantiss

This mountain on the planet Wayland was used by the Emperor as a private storehouse for those items he deemed important to his long-range plans. The storehouse was a combination trophy room and equipment dump, built within the hollowed-out mountain. The multiple levels included vast chambers of art, captured souvenirs, and experimental devices, as well as royal suites and a throne room for the Emperor. Among the treasures hidden within Mount Tantiss's vaults were a working prototype for a cloaking device and tiers upon tiers of Spaarti cloning cylinders. [DFR, DFRSB, HE, HESB, LC, LCSB]

Mount Yoda

This mountain on the planet Dagobah was named in honor of the famed Jedi Master after the Battle of Endor. The Alliance established a base on the mountain. [MMY, PDS]

Mrisst

A planet in the New Republic. Grand Admiral Thrawn planned an assault on the world as a lure to defeat the New Republic fleet. [LC]

Mrlssi

Natives of the planet Mrlsst, they appear to be humanoid birds whose bodies are covered in feathers, although they are incapable of flight. [XW]

Mrlsst

This planet in the Mennaalii system is a sanctuary for scholars and scientists and is known as a university planet. [XW]

Mrrov

A Togorian and the promised mate of Muuurgh, she left Togoria to explore the galaxy. She wound up on Ylesia, discovered that the religion was a sham, and would have left except that the Ylesian priests threatened to kill Muuurgh if she did. [PB]

MSE-6 mouse droid

This small droid delivers orders and sensitive data throughout a vessel or installation, as well as handling other tasks such as cleaning and patrolling. [DSTC, ISB, SW]

Msst

A small planet located near the Rim worlds, it is the site of a former Imperial installation and the world where the Dark Jedi Brakiss hid after failing to infiltrate Luke Skywalker's Jedi academy. [NR]

mudman

A creature made entirely of mud that lives on the planet Roon. Mudmen explode into small blobs if they are sprayed with water, though they then regenerate into more mudmen. [DTV]

Muftak

A Talz who grew up in the streets of Mos Eisley, he made a living doing odd jobs and even begging. Kabe, a Chadra-Fan, was his constant companion. Muftak eventually helped Kabe rob Jabba the Hutt's town-house and later did espionage work for the Alliance before he set out for Alzoc III to learn more about his past. [GG1, TMEC]

Mulako Corporation Primordial Water Quarry

A comet that becomes warm enough to support life in its hollowed-out interior whenever it gets close to its sun—an event that happens for a few months every one hundred years. During this period, it serves as a tourist destination. Luke Skywalker and Callista visited the comet eight years after the Battle of Endor in an attempt to help Callista regain her Jedi powers. [DS]

Mullinore, Captain

An Imperial officer, he was the commander of the Star Destroyer *Basilisk*. [DA]

multitool

A multipurpose tool that contains a lens, a drill, and other useful implements. [CS]

Munto Codru

A planet orbited by several moons and home to the four-armed beings known as Codru-Ji. Leia Organa Solo's three children were abducted while she was on a diplomatic mission to the planet. [CS]

Murgoob, the Great

Also known as Murgoob the Cranky, he was the ancient and unpleasant oracle of the Duloks on the forest moon of Endor. [ETV]

Muskov, Chief

Chief of the Cloud Police, the force that protects Bespin's Cloud City. [MMY]

Muuurgh

A Togorian, he was assigned to Han Solo as a "bodyguard" during Solo's piloting job on Ylesia. Muuurgh gave his word of honor to accompany Han everywhere he went, as a safeguard by the Ylesian priests to prevent Solo from abandoning his job. Muuurgh was a highly honorable being who valued his sworn word above all. The Togorian came to Ylesia looking for his promised mate, Mrrov. He took a job as a guard for the priests in order to earn enough credits to continue his search. When Han revealed that the Ylesians had lied, Muuurgh agreed to help Bria Tharen and Han escape with Mrrov. [PS]

Muzzer, Grand Moff

Plump and round-faced, he was a member of the Central Committee of Grand Moffs that declared the pretender Trioculus to be the rightful successor of Emperor Palpatine after the Battle of Endor. [GDV]

MX

A laser cannon that uses ion flow as an energy source. [TSW]

Myneyrsh

Tall, thin humanoids with four arms and a smooth layer of blue crystal flesh that makes a Myneyrsh appear as a being of glass. They average about 1.9 meters tall and inhabit the planet Wayland. Like the Psadans, the Myneyrshi were present on the world when the first human colonists arrived centuries ago. The Myneyrshi use bows and arrows and animals instead of blasters and repulsors. They reached an uneasy peace with the other inhabitants of Wayland after years of warfare. [HE, HESB, LC, LCSB]

mynock

This leathery black flying creature is a silicon-based life-form that evolved in the vacuum of space. Mynocks are nourished by stellar radiation, and they absorb silicon and other minerals from asteroids and space debris. When they absorbed enough material, they reproduce by dividing in two. As they are extremely energy-tropic, they often attach themselves to passing starships not only for the energy spillage these ships give off, but to absorb the minerals from the hulls in order to reproduce. Although they once came from a single system, mynocks have migrated throughout the galaxy as unwanted passengers aboard unsuspecting starships. [ESB, SWSB]

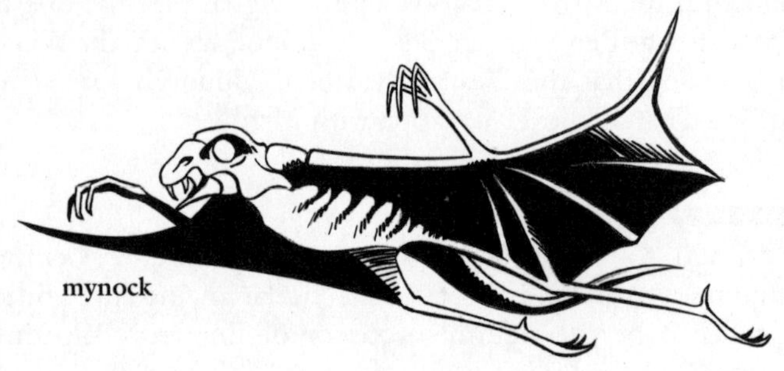
mynock

Mynock

Wedge Antilles's R5-D2 astromech droid. Its memory was later wiped, and it was reprogrammed and renamed Gate. [BW, KT, RS, WG]

Myrkr

An isolated world located within the Borderland Regions of space that separate the New Republic from the remnants of the Empire. The temperate planet once served as the private base of operations for Talon Karrde's smuggling ring. He was forced to abandon the base after Grand Admiral Thrawn invaded the planet in search of Luke Skywalker. Myrkr's tall trees have a high metal content that blocks sensor sweeps. One of its native species, the creatures called ysalamiri, have the ability to push back the Force. While Luke Skywalker was visiting the planet, he recalled stories from his youth that invoked frightening images of fortresses inhabited by evil beings that had trees growing through them. His memories of the dark tales were incomplete, and all he could remember were feelings of danger, helplessness, and fear. [DE2, DFR, HE, HESB, TOJ]

Mystra

A professional killer, she carried a wrist blaster and wore a cybervision helmet that gave her perfect aim at any target. [CSW]

Mytus VII

A planet located deep within Corporate Sector space, it was the site of the Authority's secret prison facility called Stars' End. Prisoners were kept in suspended animation between interrogations. This rocky, airless planet orbits at the edge of its solar system and has two small moons. Han Solo destroyed the prison during a jailbreak. [CSSB, HSE]

Na'al, Voren

A researcher and historian, he was responsible for recording much of the history and adventures of the heroes of the Battle of Yavin, especially Luke Skywalker, Han Solo, and Princess Leia Organa Solo. He started as an assistant historian under Arhul Hextrophon and eventually became director of council research for the New Republic. [DFRSB, GG1]

Naberrie, Padmé

See Amidala, Queen.

Naboo

A small planet in the Mid Rim, known for its vast uninhabited regions that offer sweeping vistas and striking scenery. An ancient planet, Naboo has no molten core. Naboo is home to two dominant species, the land-dwelling Naboo and the water-dwelling Gungans. The Trade Federation blockade of the planet led the Naboo ruler, Queen Amidala, to seek assistance from the Republic, and when the senate became mired in endless political discussions, Amidala initiated the vote of no confidence against the senate chancellor. This led to the election of Naboo's own Senator Palpatine as the new chancellor. [SWTPM]

Nadd, Freedon

This Jedi was seduced by the dark side of the Force and apprenticed himself to a Dark Lord of the Sith some 4,000 years prior to the Galactic Civil War. He ruled the planet Onderon for many years. When he died, he was entombed within the walled city Iziz. His crypt became a site of concentrated dark-side power. Jedi Knights eventually moved his sarcophagus to the secure moon Dxun. Later, Exar Kun reawakened Nadd's spirit, which helped him locate the hidden Sith scrolls. Nadd forced Kun to accept the dark side of the Force, though Kun used a powerful amulet to later destroy Nadd's spirit forever. [DLS, FNU, TOJ]

Naddists

A group of dissidents from the planet Onderon, they proclaimed their allegiance to the spirit of the dark Jedi Freedon Nadd and staged an uprising some 4,000 years before the Galactic Civil War. [DLS, FNU]

Nadon, Momaw

An Ithorian, or Hammerhead, he lived on the planet Tatooine after being exiled from his native Ithor for turning over Ithor's agricultural secrets to the Empire. He had been a high priest, or herd leader, of the *Tafanda Bay*, one of the huge floating cities that hover above the jungles of Ithor. When the Empire's

Captain Alima threatened to destroy the floating city, Nadon relented and handed over the data. On Tatooine, Nadon provided aid to the Alliance, including information and shelter for Rebel agents. He returned to his world after the Battle of Endor. [GG1, SWCG, TMEC]

Nahkee

A baby Phlog, or phlogling, he stood more than two meters tall. Despite his great size, he displayed all of the trust, innocence, and curiosity of children his age. [ETV]

Nailati, Evilo

A B'omarr monk, he was often consulted by Bubo. [TJP]

Nal Hutta

A planet whose name means "Glorious Jewel" in Huttese. It was one of the main planets colonized by the Hutts after they left their ancestral home Varl. Once a pleasant world, Nal Hutta and its moon Nar Shaddaa were transformed into gloomy, industrial centers that lay flat at the heart of Hutt space. The planet is ruled by a council of the eldest members of the Clans of the Ancients, the oldest Hutt families. [DE, DE2, DESB, DS, GG4]

Nam Chorios

A barren world in the Chorios systems of the Meridian sector, the planet became a political prison for the Grissmath Dynasty, who seeded it with the insectlike drochs—carriers of the Death Seed plague—some 750 years before the Battle of Yavin. Around the time of the New Republic, Beldorian the Hutt and Seti Ashgad held power on Nam Chorios. Dzym, a mutated droch, kept Ashgad alive and young. Beldorian imprisoned Callista when she arrived on the planet, and Ashgad took Leia Organa Solo prisoner when she came to meet with him about nine years after the Battle of Endor. Eventually, Leia and Callista teamed up; Leia killed Beldorian, and the drochs were destroyed. [POT]

Nampi, Princess

A giant purple sluglike being from the planet Orooturoo, she trapped Jabba the Hutt and his crew aboard her ship. She ate Jabba's top aide, Scuppa, but Jabba killed her when he used a remote control to release a vial of acid that was implanted in Scuppa's head. [JAB]

Nandreeson

A Glottalphib, he is one of the most powerful crimelords in the galaxy. He is the undisputed kingpin of Smuggler's Run and long ago put a price on Lando Calrissian's head. [NR]

nano-destroyer

These artificially created viruses dismantle an infected person one cell at a time. Nano-destroyers were the basis of the disease infecting Mon Mothma seven years after the Battle of Endor. [COF]

NaQuoit Bandits

An outlaw group that operates in the Ottega system, where they prey upon local space traffic. [DE]

Narra, Commander

After the death of Red Leader at the Battle of Yavin, Commander Narra was put in charge of the X-wing fighter group that Luke Skywalker belonged to. The pilots of the squadron called Narra, the Boss. Prior to the events at Hoth, Commander Narra was killed in an Imperial ambush near Derra IV. Several TIE fighter squadrons attacked the Rebel convoy that Narra and his squadron were escorting. In the wake of this tragedy, Luke Skywalker was promoted to the rank of commander and placed in charge of the fighter group. Under Luke's command, the fighter group evolved into the legendary Rogue Squadron. [ESBR, GG3]

Nar Shaddaa

This spaceport moon orbits the planet Nal Hutta and is controlled by the Hutts and assorted smuggling guilds. An untold number of smuggling operations are based on Nar Shaddaa, and many Corellian pirates use the place as a refuge. In addition, all manner of galactic dregs, both aliens and humans, fill the streets of the vertical city. [D, DE, DE2, DESB, DF, TMEC]

Narth

This Imperial planet was evacuated following the Battle of Endor, and in doing so, the Imperial Star Destroyer *Gnisnal* was incapacitated by internal explosions. The New Republic was able to attain a complete copy of the Imperial Order of Battle from the Star Destroyer's wreckage. [BTS]

Nartlo

A black marketeer, he provided both Kirtan Loor and Fliry Vorru with the location of the New Republic's bacta storage facilities. [BW]

Nashira

The name of Luke Skywalker's mother, at least according to Akanah Norand Pell, who told him that his mother had lived with the Fallanassi religious order on Lucazec and had perhaps escaped with them when they fled the planet. This turned out to be a lie. [BTS]

nashtah

A six-legged hunting creature native to the planet Dra III. These bloodthirsty reptilians are vicious and tenacious. With triple rows of jagged teeth and diamond-hard claws, nashtahs are green in color with sleek hides and long, barbed tails. [HSR]

Nashtah Pup

A scout ship aboard the bounty hunter Bossk's vessel, the *Hound's Tooth*. [TBH]

Nass, Boss

The leader of the Gungan species on the planet Naboo. When Queen Amidala bowed before him, he joined his forces with those of the Naboo in the effort to free the planet from the Trade Federation blockade. This ended a long-standing rivalry between the Gungans and the Naboo. [SWTPM]

Nataz, Dyyz

A bounty hunter, also known as Megadeath, who is a denizen of Nar Shaddaa. He wears full Ithullan armor. Nataz trained the Rodian bounty hunter Greedo. Afterwards, he betrayed Greedo to Thuku, who was sent to kill the Rodian. [DE, TMEC]

nav computer

A specialized processing unit that calculates lightspeed jumps, plots hyperspace and realspace trajectories, and suggests routes based upon available time and energy fuel. Nav computers also display astrogation charts and work in conjunction with a ship's navigational sensors. [SWRPG, SWSB]

Navik the Red

A Rodian, he was the leader of the warlike Chattza clan. Identifiable by the enormous red birthmark on his face, Navik was the Rodian grand protector during the Galactic Civil War. [TMEC]

Nawruun

An old, gray-furred Wookiee, he was a slave at the Maw Installation until Chewbacca rescued him. [COF]

Nazzar

A bipedal species with equine features. The Jedi Qrrl Toq, who lived some 4,000 years before the Galactic Civil War, was a Nazzar prince. [FNU]

Nebo

A Naddist street philosopher in the walled city Iziz, he and his fellow zealot Rask unsuccessfully tried to protect the sarcophagi of King Ommin, Queen Amanoa, and Freedon Nadd from the dark Jedi Exar Kun some 4,000 years before the Galactic Civil War. [DLS]

Nebulon Ranger

This large courier ship was used by the Jedi brothers Ulic and Cay Qel-Droma and the Twi'lek Jedi Tott Doneeta some 4,000 years before the Galactic Civil War. The ship had retractable wings that could be extended for atmospheric flight. [SWVG, TOJ]

Necropolis

A planet whose traditions revere the dead. Not long after the Battle of Yavin, Dr. Evazan conducted experiments in regeneration here in hopes of creating an undead army. [GF]

Needa, Captain Lorth

An Imperial officer, he was commander of the *Imperial*-class Star Destroyer, *Avenger*, part of Lord Darth Vader's task force prior to the Battle of Hoth. It was Needa's ship that took the point during the subsequent search for the *Millennium Falcon.* When Han Solo's vessel escaped, Captain Needa's personal apology to Vader was met with acceptance and a quick death through the powers of the Force's dark side. [ESB, GG3]

Needa, Virar

An Imperial lieutenant and a cousin of Lorth Needa, he was commander of OSETS 2711, an Orbital Solar Energy Transfer Satellite above Imperial Center. [WG]

Needle

A long-distance smart missile with nearly infinite range and capable of hyperspace travel. [POT]

Neela

A Rodian, she was the mother of the bounty hunter Greedo. [TMEC]

Neema

The daughter of the Jedi Vima-Da-Boda. [DE]

nek

A battle dog bred in the Cyborrea system for sale on the galactic black market. These vicious creatures are fitted with armor and attack stimulators. [DE]

nek battle dog

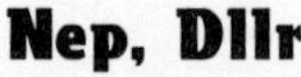

Nep, Dllr

A Sullustan member of Rogue Squadron, he thrived on the freedom of being out from under the rules of his highly regulated society. He was a scrounger for the Rogues and was adept at retrofitting parts to serve new purposes. Nep was also Force-sensitive. He made the ultimate sacrifice, absorbing Sith magic and leading fellow Rogue Herian I'ngre into a Sith temple on Malrev Four to destroy it. [XW]

Nereus, Wilek

The Imperial governor assigned to Bakura, he ruled and maintained order by instilling fear and terror in the population. The tall, dark-haired Nereus had heavy features and thick eyebrows. He was cunning, ruthless, and extremely ambitious. When the Ssi-ruuk fleet was defeated, the Alliance helped the Bakuran people overthrow Nereus's regime. The governor refused to surrender, however. He tried to shoot Luke Skywalker with a blaster pistol, but Skywalker deflected the bolt with his lightsaber and sent it back to Nereus. The resulting wound proved fatal; Governor Nereus died as Bakura became free. [TAB, TBSB]

nerf

A rangy, supple creature with curving, dull horns and long fur, this domesticated herbivore is temperamental and cantankerous. Cared for by tenders called nerf herders, these animals are grown as a meat source, and their pelts are used for a variety of applications. [ESB, ISWU]

nergon 14

An unstable, explosive element, it was one of the primary components in Imperial-made proton torpedoes. A pulsating blue color when inert, nergon 14 changes to bright red and then white before it explodes. [DTV]

Nespis VIII

A derelict space city located at the center of the six remaining Auril systems near the Cron drift, it was abandoned long before the start of the Clone Wars. Originally built by the Jedi, it contained a library of Jedi texts and was supposedly haunted by the ghost of a dark Jedi. Darth Vader found and destroyed the library, and afterwards the evil scientist Borborygmus Gog created a false library to trap the essence of the first Jedi to attempt to access it.

Six years after the Battle of Endor, Luke Skywalker freed Kam Solusar from the dark side of the Force while visiting this site. Later that year, the New Republic established a base at the remote space city, and Leia Organa Solo's third child was born there. The cloned Emperor destroyed Nespis VIII with the Galaxy Gun. [DE2, EE, GF]

Neva, Captain

The Sullustan commander of the New Republic escort frigate *Rebel Star*. [DE]

New Alderaan

A planet settled as an Alliance safe world, it was renamed New Alderaan to serve as a home for the refugees from the destroyed world Alderaan. Following the Battle of Endor, General Jan Dodonna retired to the planet until he was called back into service to fight the Empire. Warlord Zsinj discovered the world and forced its inhabitants to temporarily evacuate. During the cloned Emperor's reappearance six years after the Battle of Endor, Mon Mothma's disabled daughter convalesced on the planet. Jacen and Jaina Solo were hidden on New Alderaan, but the cloned Emperor attacked their location with seven dark-side warriors and a phalanx of advanced AT-ATs. [CPL, DE, DE2, DESB, RSB]

New Brigia

A colony within the borders of the Koornacht Cluster, it was once the site of a struggling chromite mining operation. Twelve years after the Battle of Endor, the Yevetha eliminated the entire colony as part of their Great Purge. [BTS]

New Cov

The third planet in the Churba star system, it has no indigenous intelligent life, but its vast jungles teem with abundant natural resources. Eight walled cities, including the city Ilic, were built on New Cov by the New Cov Biomolecule Company to serve as work colonies. The sentient plants of the world are a great source of biomolecules. These biomolecules are used to create medicines and other items. The armored city walls were designed to keep out the carnivorous plants and their spores. The planet was allied with the New Republic, but it made periodic tributes to the Empire in the form of sanctioned Imperial raids in which the Empire took all the refined biomolecules it needed. In this way, the Covies remained on good terms with both governments. [DFR, DFRSB]

New Order

The phrase that Emperor Palpatine used to describe his new regime. [SW]

New Republic

The name of the democratic government established after the Battle of Endor by the Alliance to Restore the Republic, sometimes called the Alliance of Free Planets. It was based on the tenets and principles of the Old Republic. [DE, DFR, HE, LC, TBSB]

New Republic Insignia

New Republic Intelligence (NRI)

This organization was the successor to the old network of Rebel spies. [AC]

Next Chance

This casino on Rodia is where Princess Leia Organa first met Guri, the human replica droid who served Prince Xizor. [SOTE]

Nezriti organization

A criminal group that did business with Prince Xizor's Black Sun organization. [SOTE]

Nha, Mnor

A Gotal in the Azure Dianoga cantina, he sensed Gavin Darklighter's fear at the approach of Imperial stormtroopers, as well as Asyr Sei'lar. He assumed the Rogue Squadron pilot was bigoted, so he took Darklighter before the Alien Combine to be judged. [KT]

night beast

A fierce creature left as a guardian by the Massassi on Yavin 4 to protect their sacred temples. When an Imperial TIE fighter crashed into the Massassi ruins, the night beast emerged and ravaged the Rebel base. With the aid of the Force and R2-D2, Luke Skywalker was able to lure the night beast into a Rebel supply ship and send it off world. [CSW]

night beast

Night Hammer

This Super Star Destroyer was taken over by Admiral Daala and became her flagship. She later renamed the vessel *Knight Hammer* prior to its assault on the Jedi academy at Yavin 4. Callista, who had lost her Jedi powers, entered the Star Destroyer and sabotaged it. It then hurtled into the gas giant Yavin. [DS]

Nightmare Machine

A genetically mutated creature, it was able to enter a victim's nightmares and use the victim's own fears against him or her. It was killed by Lando Calrissian. [GF]

Nightsisters

A group of witches on the planet Dathomir whose members turned to the dark side of the Force. Four years after the Battle of Endor, they enslaved Imperial guards at a Dathomir prison and attempted to escape from the planet. Luke Skywalker, Leia Organa, and Han Solo stopped them, but fifteen years later the group returned. The new Nightsisters were younger, stronger, and allied with Imperial forces seeking to regain control of the galaxy. [CPL, YJK]

Night Spirit

An evil entity on the forest moon of Endor, the Ewoks feared it and the Duloks worshipped it. It sometimes manifested as a ghostly apparition. [ETV]

Nikto

A humanoid species with a flat face and multiple nostrils, they originated on the planet Kintan in the Si'klaata Cluster. Jabba the Hutt employed several Nikto as skiff guards and hired muscle. [GG5, GG12, RJ]

Nim Drovis

A planet located in the Meridian sector. A sector medical facility and research base is on this planet, as well as a small New Republic outpost. [POT]

Ninedenine

See EV-9D9.

Ninth quadrant

This area of space near the Senex and Juvex sectors contains the Greeb-Streebling Cluster and the planet Belsavis. [COJ]

Ninx, Shug

A master mechanic whose father was Corellian and mother was Theelin. He set up his own shop on the smugglers' moon Nar Shaddaa. His spacebarn became a hangout, and he became friendly with the likes of Han Solo, Chewbacca, and Lando Calrissian. Later, Han Solo's onetime lover Salla Zend became Ninx's employee and then business partner. When Solo and his wife Leia were betrayed to bounty hunters on Nar Shaddaa, Ninx and Zend saved them. It wouldn't be the last time, as the pair became embroiled in Alliance affairs—including helping out at the Battle of Calamari and saving Leia and her children from an attack on New Alderaan. [DE, DE2, DESB]

Nippett

An Ewok on Endor's forest moon, he was an infant at the time of the Battle of Endor. [RJ]

Nkllon

This planet in the Athega system is a superhot world rich in ores and other raw materials. Nkllon is very close to its sun, and ships that approach without the protection of accompanying shieldships risk having their hulls melted away. The planet has a very slow rotation, however, and this allowed Lando Calrissian to set up a mining operation on the planet. As the dark side of the world is relatively safe to work on, Calrissian built a moving city to serve as a base and processing plant. Called Nomad City, the base moves to always stay on the planet's dark side. [HE, HESB, LC, YJK]

Noa

An old man who had been stranded on Endor's forest moon for many years, he arrived by star cruiser while conducting a surveying expedition, but his ship crashed. He has a gruff exterior but a kind heart. He befriended Cindel Towani and Wicket W. Warrick the Ewok mostly at the urging of his companion, Teek. [BFE]

Nodon and Nonak

These brothers were Cathar, felinelike humanoids. They joined Burrk, a former stormtrooper, in setting up big-game hunting expeditions to Hoth in order to attain wampa ice creature pelts. The three, as well as the hunters they guided, were killed by the wampas. Luke Skywalker and Callista barely escaped from the creatures. [DS]

Noghri

Lord Darth Vader discovered the Noghri species on the planet Honoghr sometime before the formation of the Rebel Alliance. The Empire tended to ignore nonhuman primitives unless they could somehow be exploited, and the Noghri were ripe for exploitation. Through a massive deception and planet-toxification program, Vader convinced the Noghri that they were indebted to him and the Empire. They became the Emperor's personal Death Commandos, serving as Imperial assassins until Princess Leia revealed the deception during the events instigated by Grand Admiral Thrawn.

Noghri

Noghri are small, compact killing machines with large eyes, protruding teeth-filled jaws, gray skin, and thin, powerful muscles. With their enhanced sense of smell, they can identify individuals by scent alone. They have a strong code of honor, not unlike that displayed by the Wookiees of Kashyyyk. With long arms and sharp claws, they developed an unarmed combat style that is among the deadliest in the galaxy.

The Emperor kept the Noghri a secret, using them as clandestine warriors. They bowed to Lord Vader as their savior, extending the same respect to Princess Leia when she eventually met them and convinced them of her identity as Vader's daughter. Grand Admiral Thrawn kept a Noghri as his personal bodyguard and sent squads of the Death Commandos to capture Leia and her unborn twins. After Thrawn's defeat, the Noghri left the service of the Empire and joined the New Republic. [DFR, DFRSB, HE, HESB, LC, LCSB]

Noimm, Senator Cair Tok

A New Republic senator, he was a member of the Security Council. [SOL]

Nok

A Rodian, he was the uncle of the bounty hunter Greedo. [TMEC]

Nomad City

A mobile mining base on the planet Nkllon that Lando Calrissian established following the Battle of Endor. Built from scavenged vessels such as an old Dreadnaught cruiser and over forty captured AT-AT walkers, the huge, humpbacked structure used the planet's shadow to protect itself from the intense heat of the system's sun. Lando designed Nomad City using plans for a rolling mining center he found among the personal belongings of Cloud City's founder, Ecclessis Figg. [HE, HESB, LC, YJK]

Nooch

A New Republic Fifth Fleet pilot, he was killed during the failed blockade of Doornik-319. [SOL]

Noorr, Vol

Primate of the Yevethan battle cruiser *Purity*, he ordered the destruction of the New Republic astrographic ship at Doornik-1142. [BTS]

Nootka, Lai

A Duros, he was the captain of the freighter *Star's Delight.* He was killed by the Empire to keep him from testifying at Tycho Celchu's trial. [KT, WG]

Noquivzor

This planet served as the staging area for an attack by Rogue Squadron on Borleias. After Borleias was conquered, Borsk Fey'lya arranged for the New Republic Provisional Council to meet on the planet to discuss using Black Sun extremists to disrupt the Imperial government prior to the invasion of Coruscant. Later, Warlord Zsinj attacked the base, but Rogue Squadron's underground hangars survived the barrage. [KT, RS, WG]

Norgor

An aide to dark-side Krath cultist Satal Keto some 4,000 years before the Galactic Civil War, he was sent to assassinate the Jedi Ulic Qel-Droma. He failed. [DLS]

normal space

See realspace.

Norulac

This planet was home to a bandit gang that raided Taanab every year. Lando Calrissian wiped out the bandits in the famous Battle of Taanab. [RJN]

Norval II

This planet is the homeworld of General Horton Salm, commander of the New Republic's starfighter training center on Folor. Norval II sent a detachment of fighters to battle the reborn cloned Emperor six years after the Battle of Endor. [DE, RS]

Norvanian grog

An expensive and potent intoxicant from the planet Ban-Satir II. It is produced and marketed from the isle of N'van in the planet's northern hemisphere. [HSE]

Norys

A teenage street tough on Coruscant, he was the leader of the Lost Ones gang. He was trained as a stormtrooper after the

Shadow Academy determined he had no Force sensitivity. His trainer, a former TIE pilot named Qorl, found Norys's attacks against the young Jedi Knights at Yavin 4 to be so ruthless that he shot down Norys's TIE fighter, killing him. [YJK]

Nothos, Commander Bane

The Imperial district commander Bane Nothos was in charge of the operation to locate and destroy Admiral Ackbar's Shantipole Project. Nothos failed, and the Alliance was able to finish work on the new B-wing starfighter. This led to his demotion, and he was placed in charge of an Outer Rim Territories patrol fleet. He was subsequently captured by the Alliance, placed aboard a Rebel ship for transport to a hidden outpost, and lost in the mysterious dimension called otherspace when a problem developed with the ship's hyperdrive. [OS, OS2, SFS]

Nova Demons

See swoop gang.

Novar

Minister of state and aide to King Ommin and Queen Amanoa of Onderon about 4,000 years before the Galactic Civil War. He was a minor dark-side wizard. [TOJ]

Null, Warb

Leader of the dissident Naddists on Onderon 4,000 years before the Galactic Civil War, he combined physical prowess with mastery of the dark side of the Force. He was killed by Jedi Ulic Qel-Droma. [FNU]

Nunb, Aril

Sister to Nien Nunb, she became a Rogue Squadron pilot after serving time as its executive officer (XO). She was injured and left behind during the undercover mission to Coruscant. She was captured and used as a test subject by Imperial General Evir Derricote for the Krytos virus project. After the conquest of Coruscant, Aril was found alive and well in Invisec. [KT, RS, WG]

Nunb, Nien

A Rebel pilot from the planet Sullust, he served as Lando Calrissian's copilot aboard the *Millennium Falcon* during the Battle of Endor. After that famous battle, Nunb went on to fly missions with Han Solo and Chewbacca and eventually went to work for Calrissian as manager of the spice mines of Kessel. At Kessel, he employed droids instead of slave labor. [GG5, RJ, SWCG]

Nunurra

This city on the planet Roon is the site of the Roon Colonial Games. [DTV]

Nuum, Cabrool

A longtime business associate of Jabba the Hutt who went insane, he ordered Jabba to kill Vu Chusker. Jabba refused and was imprisoned, but he eventually killed Nuum with help from Nuum's own son. [JAB]

Nuum, Norba

Cabrool Nuum's daughter. She double-crossed Jabba and was eaten by him. [JAB]

Nuum, Rusk

Cabrool Nuum's son. Jabba the Hutt killed him when Rusk double-crossed the crimelord. [JAB]

Nyiestra

An Alderaanian, she was to become Tycho Celchu's wife. She waited for him to graduate from the Imperial Academy and serve his first year of duty, but she died when the Death Star destroyed the planet. [BW]

Nylykerka, Ayddar

A Tammarian who served as chief analyst of the Asset Tracking office of Fleet Intelligence, he was the first Rebel to acquire the data files from the damaged Imperial Star Destroyer

Gnisnal. He delivered them personally to Admiral Ackbar when he realized they contained a complete Imperial Order of Battle. [BTS, SOL]

Nynie

A 9-A9 child-care droid, she took care of Plourr Ilo, Rogue Squadron pilot and heir to the throne of Eiattu VI, when Plourr was a child. [XW]

N'zoth

This planet is the homeworld of the Yevethan species. [BTS, SOL, TT]

Obah, Jyn

A tall humanoid, he was first mate to the pirate captain Kybo Ren in the early days of the Empire. He wore the upper portion of a stormtrooper's helmet on his head, as well as a stormtrooper's chest plate for protection and as a fashion statement. [DTV]

Obica

This planet was the site of a rendezvous between Alliance leaders and Sullustan Captain Syub Snunb just prior to the Battle of Endor. [DESB]

Obroan

An inhabitant of the planet Obroa-skai. [HE, HESB]

Obroa-skai

A planet in a system of the same name located in the Borderland Regions. In the years following the Battle of Endor, the system occupied a strategic position between these portions of space controlled by the remnants of the Empire and the New Republic. It was a neutral star system, though its inhabitants showed some favoritism toward the New Republic. The planet is renowned for its massive library computers that supposedly contain the complete knowledge of the galaxy. It was from these library computers that Grand Admiral Thrawn pulled the astrogation coordinates for the planet Wayland. Later, Luke Skywalker sent R2-D2 and C-3PO to search the library computers for information about his mother. [BTS, HE, HESB, SOL]

Observer

An experimental, quasi-official part of the New Republic created about sixteen years after the Battle of Endor. An Observer's job is to move freely about an assigned sector and report directly to the High Council and senate about whatever is seen and heard. An Observer is especially entrusted with watching for improper governmental activities. Only strongly ethical beings willing to work far from their home systems are selected for this service. [SP, VF]

Ocheron

A member of the Nightsisters clan of the Witches of Dathomir, she was skilled at deception. [CPL]

Odan-Urr

A young Jedi who lived about 5,000 years before the Galactic Civil War, he was fascinated by the history of the Sith. He saw a vision of the Sith invasion and warned Empress Teta of the coming conflict. After the invasion, he built a Jedi academy on the planet Ossus.

As a Jedi Master, he presided over six centuries of Jedi assemblies up to the time of the massive gathering at Mount Meru 4,000 years before the Galactic Civil War. As the Keeper of Antiquities, he was entrusted with the Sith Holocron. He was killed by Exar Kun. [DLS, FSE, GAS, TSW]

Odik II

This planet was the site of a political detention ward where Palpatine imprisoned many of his opponents from the Old Republic. [DSTC]

Odle, Hermi

One of the aliens in Jabba the Hutt's desert palace. He served the crimelord faithfully until the organization was toppled by Luke Skywalker and his companions. A huge bipedal of unknown origin, Hermi wore a tattered robe. [RJ]

Odos

A planet located in the Meridian sector. [POT]

Odosk, General

An Imperial officer, he served in Admiral Daala's fleet. [DA]

Odumin

See Spray of Tynna.

Off Chance

An old Blockade Runner that Lando Calrissian won in a game of sabacc. Lando lent the ship to Luke Skywalker and Tenel Ka so they could search for the villains who kidnapped Jaina and Jacen Solo and Lowbacca. [YJK]

Offen

A species. Offens were relatively new to space travel at the time of the New Republic. [NR]

Ohann

A gas giant in the Tatooine system. It has three moons. [GG7]

Okeefe, Platt

A smuggler who grew up on Brentaal but left home as a cabin steward aboard a Sullustan starliner. She eventually acquired her own freighter, the *Last Chance*, and often passed on advice to less-experienced traders. [PSG]

Okins, Admiral

A trusted and loyal servant of the Emperor, he was often dispatched to rout pirates or subjugate unruly worlds. During the period immediately following the Battle of Hoth, Okins was assigned to Lord Darth Vader to ensure that the Emperor's wishes were carried out. [SESB, SOTE]

Okko, Great

A shaman chief, he led the Ysanna of the planet Ossus. [DE2]

Oko E

A planet whose rivers overflow with sulfur ice. Lobot visited the world for a wild-water rafting vacation, then used the skills he acquired to save Lando Calrissian's life aboard the Teljkon vagabond ghost ship. [SOL]

Okor, Feldrall

A pirate. Boba Fett earned 150,000 credits for capturing him. [TJP]

Olabrian trichoid

A parasite from the Olabria system. It eats its host's internal organs. Governor Wilek Nereus of Bakura tried to kill Luke Skywalker by using these parasites. [TAB]

Olan, Firith

A Twi'lek, he came to Tatooine to help Bib Fortuna overthrow Jabba the Hutt. He arrived too late; Jabba was dead and the B'omarr monks had placed Fortuna's brain within a robot spider. Olan drove off the monks and took over Jabba's palace. Fortuna eventually exchanged their brains and stole Olan's body. [TJP, XW]

Old Republic

A democratic galactic government that lasted nearly 25,000 standard years, it grew as a direct result of the development of hyperspace travel and communications, and spread justice and freedom from star system to star system, encompassing millions of inhabited worlds. Elected senators and administrators from all the member worlds participated in the Republic's governing process, while the Jedi Knights served as its protectors and defenders. Starting about a century before the Galactic Civil War, corruption, greed, and internal strife began to destroy the Old Republic from within. Special interest groups and power-hungry individuals accomplished what no outside threat ever could—they weakened the galactic government and gave rise to apathy, social injustice, ineffectiveness, and chaos. This destructive trend allowed Naboo Senator Palpatine to rise to power. He eventually named himself Emperor, abolished the Republic, and began a reign of terror and social injustice based upon his dark vision of a New Order. The Old Republic passed away, and the Empire was born. [DLS, FNU, SW, SWN, SWSB, TOJ, TSW]

Omega signal

A code used by the Rebel Alliance, it was an order to completely disengage from combat and retreat. At the Battle of Hoth, the code was "K-one-zero, all troops disengage." [ESBR]

Ommin

King of the planet Onderon, husband of Queen Amanoa, and father of Queen Galia, he ruled more than 4,000 years before the Galactic Civil War. He was a direct descendant of dark Jedi Freedon Nadd, and he initiated Satal Keto and Aleema in ancient dark-side Sith magic. He was killed during the Freedon Nadd Uprising. [DLS, FNU, TOJ]

Omogg

A Drackmarian warlord who had incredible wealth. Four years after the Battle of Endor, she lost the deed to the planet Dathomir to Han Solo in a game of sabacc. [CPL]

Omwat

This planet in the Outer Rim Territories is the homeworld of Qwi Xux, a scientist and weapons designer at the Maw Installation. [COJ, JS]

Onderon

A planet located in a system of the same name. More than 4,000 years before the Galactic Civil War, dark Jedi Freedon Nadd brought dark-side Sith magic to the planet. Four hundred years later, Jedi, including Ulic Qel-Droma, negotiated a peace between the beast-riders and Queen Amanoa of Iziz, and later put down an uprising by the followers of Freedon Nadd.

Millennia later, six years after the Battle of Endor, Princess Leia Organa Solo and her newborn son Anakin landed the *Millennium Falcon* on this world to make repairs. The reborn clone of the Emperor stalked them and tried to possess the child's body. He was stopped by Jedi Empatojayos Brand. Later, Mon Mothma and Leia Organa Solo gathered the leaders of the New Republic in the fortress of Modon Kira to reestablish their galactic government. [DLS, EE, FNU, TOJ, TSW]

Onderon, Beast Wars of

A centuries-long conflict fought between the citizens of the walled city Iziz and the beast-riders of the planet Onderon more than 4,000 years before the Galactic Civil War. The Jedi Knights eventually intervened to resolve the dispute. [TOJ]

Onoma, Captain

A Calamarian officer, he served aboard the star cruiser *Mon Remonda*. [CPL]

Oodoc

A species whose members have great size and strength but are not extremely intelligent. They have spiked arms and massive torsos. [NR]

Oola

A beautiful Twi'lek dancer, she performed her last dance for crimelord Jabba the Hutt. Oola grew up on Ryloth until Jabba's majordomo, Bib Fortuna, kidnapped her and trained her in seductive dancing. When Oola refused to obey one of Jabba's orders, the crimelord fed her to his pet rancor. [GG5, RJ, SWCG]

Oolas, Captain
A New Republic officer, he commanded the *Steadfast.* [BTS]

Oolidi
This planet is the homeworld of New Republic Senator Tolik Yar. [SOL]

Oolos, Ism
A Ho'Din physician, he practiced at the port of Bagsho on Nim Drovis. [POT]

orbital gun platform
Any vessel or fortification that can launch attacks from space to the planet it orbits, or against enemy vessels approaching the planet. [SWR]

orbit dock
An orbital landing and maintenance facility. It also provides other services to spacers and their ships. Large orbit docks with multiple docking facilities operate like small space stations, providing hotel, food, and entertainment facilities. Sluis Van has an extensive collection of orbit docks in its shipyard facilities. [HE, HESB]

Orbiting Shipyard Alpha
A spaceship repair dock high above the planet Duro. [MMY]

Orbus, Evar
The Letaki leader of a jizz-wailer band, he died on Tatooine from a stray blaster bolt. The other members of his band, Max Rebo, Sy Snootles, and Snit (later called Droopy McCool), were left to fend for themselves. [TJP]

Ord Mantell
A planet. Han Solo and his companions outwitted and escaped from bounty hunters twice while visiting this world. Five years after the Battle of Endor, Grand Admiral Thrawn's forces

assaulted Ord Mantell to create fear in the surrounding systems and ease the pressure being asserted by the New Republic on his shipyard supply lines. [COJ, CSW, ESB, LC, MTS]

Ord Mirit

A planet that once housed an Imperial base. [RS]

Ord Pardron

This planet is the site of a major New Republic military base that defends the Abrion and Dufilvian sectors. Grand Admiral Thrawn's forces hit several targets in the region at once, reducing Ord Pardron's own defenses to the bare minimum as it sent assistance to the beleaguered worlds. The base was subsequently unable to assist the planet Ukio—Thrawn's true target all along. [LC]

Ord Trasi

This planet was the site of a major Imperial shipyard. [LC]

Orelon

This star is one of sixty-three in the Hapes Cluster. [CPL]

Organa, Bail Prestor

The foster father of Princess Leia Organa, he was a strong defender of the Old Republic and one of the founders of the Rebel Alliance. He fought in the Clone Wars, battling beside Obi-Wan Kenobi and other heroes of the period. He served as viceroy and first chairman of his native Alderaan until he died when the original Death Star battle station destroyed the planet. [RJ, SW, SWCG, SWR]

Organa, Princess Leia

See Solo, Princess Leia Organa.

Orin

A volcanic planet located in the Bespin system. [GG2]

Orinackra

This planet was the site of a high-security Imperial detention center. Shortly after the Battle of Yavin, Rebel agent Kyle Katarn rescued Crix Madine from this facility. [DF]

Orko SkyMine

A fake corporation set up by Durga the Hutt to hide huge amounts of credits. It was supposed to be a commercial venture to exploit the riches of the Hoth asteroid belt. The money was actually being diverted to the top secret Darksaber Project. [DS]

Orlok, Commander

An Imperial officer, he was in charge of the Imperial training center on Daluuj. [CSW]

Orn, Kalebb

A worker on the droid production world Mechis III, he was the first human killed by IG-88 when the assassin droid and its counterparts took over the planet. [TBH]

Orooturoo

This planet is the homeworld of Princess Nampi. [JAB]

Ororo Transportation

A competitor to Xizor Transport Systems. Crimelord Prince Xizor ordered his aide Guri to murder Ororo's top executives while he convinced Emperor Palpatine to destroy an Ororo shipyard by telling the Emperor that it was a Rebel base. [SOTE]

Orrimaarko

The true name of the Dressellian called Prune Face. He was a noted Rebel agent during the Galactic Civil War. [GG12]

Orron III

An agricultural world in Corporate Sector space. An Authority Data Center is located there. [HSE]

Orto
This planet is the homeworld of the blue-furred Ortolans. [GG4]

Ortola
A New Republic officer, he was captain of a corvette used in the assault on the Maw Installation. [COF]

Ortolan
Heavy, squat bipeds from the planet Orto, with long trunks and dark, beady eyes. Ortolans have floppy ears, small mouths, short, chubby fingers, and thick, baggy, blue-furred hides. Max Rebo, the jizz-wailer who played Jabba's palace, was an Ortolan. [GG4]

Ortugg
A Gamorrean, he was the leader of Jabba the Hutt's nine Gamorrean guards. [SWSB, TJP]

Orus sector
A region of space that includes the planets Chazwa and Poderis. It was incorrectly believed that Grand Admiral Thrawn's clone traffic was passing through the area. [LC]

Orvak, Commander
An Imperial officer, he led a TIE fighter attack on Luke Skywalker's Jedi academy on Yavin 4. [YJK]

Oseon 2795
This asteroid in the Oseon system is the site of a mining colony. [LCM]

Oseon 5792
This asteroid in the Oseon system is the private estate of Bohhuah Mutdah, a retired industrialist and the wealthiest person in the system. [LCF]

Oseon 6845

This asteroid is the largest in the Oseon system. Nightclubs and resorts, including the Hotel Drofo, cover the surface. [LCF]

Oseon system

A star system filled with nothing but thousands of asteroids, it is famous for its wealthy inhabitants and booming tourist trade. [LCF]

OSETS

An acronym for Orbital Solar Energy Transfer Satellite, an orbital energy system used on Coruscant for gathering and delivering sunlight to cold regions of the planet. [WG]

Oslumpex V

This planet is the site of Vinda and D'rag's Starshipwrights and Aerospace Engineers Incorporated. [HSR]

Ossel II

This planet is the swampy homeworld of the Ossan. [COJ, GG4]

Ossilege, Admiral Hortel

A Bakuran naval officer, he was the leader of the Bakuran fleet that was loaned to the Alliance. He died in the conflict at Centerpoint Station. [AC, SAC]

Ossus

This planet in the Adega system was the site of an important Jedi stronghold and learning center in ancient times. Some scholars have speculated that the order of the Jedi Knights started here, but that was never proven. Many cities once covered the world, and sites of interest such as the Great Jedi Library and the peaceful Gardens of Talla once drew visitors from far and wide. The planet was scorched and wiped clean about 4,000 years before the Galactic Civil War when the nearby Cron

Cluster went nova. The few Jedi that remained on the planet and survived grew into the Ysanna, a tribe of primitive warrior-shamans who use the Force. [DE, DE2, DLS, EE, FNU, TSW, YJK]

Oswaft

A species of intelligent manta ray or jellyfishlike beings, they inhabit the sack-shaped interstellar nebula called ThonBoka. Broad and streamlined, the Oswaft have powerful wings and sleek, muscle-covered dorsal surfaces. Their bodies have a glasslike transparency with hints and flashes of inner color. They are a long-lived species, with a patient and conservative outlook on life. [LCS]

otherspace

A dimension beyond realspace and hyperspace, full of dead, lifeless planets. A void, it appears as a storm-gray expanse of nothingness with some small swirls of colored gases and stars that look like shining holes of darkness. A few biologically engineered Charon ships roam this dead void, seeking any vestiges of life to sacrifice to their cult of death. [OS]

Otoh Gunga

The underwater city on Naboo that serves as the capital for the water-dwelling species known as the Gungans. [SWTPM]

Otranto

This planet was the site of the headquarters of the Church of the First Frequency before the headquarters was closed by Imperial Grand Inquisitor Torbin. [CSSB]

Ottega system

This star system in the Lesser Plooriod Cluster has an unusual number of inhabited worlds and moons. The 75 planets and 622 moons combine to make the entire system a popular tourist region. Its notable planets include Ithor and Ottega. [DE, EE, SWSB]

Ottethan system

This star system is where Neema, daughter of Jedi Vima-Da-Boda, was executed for attempting to use the dark side of the Force against her warlord husband. [DE]

Ourn, Belezaboth

Consul of the Paqwepori delegation on Coruscant, he was also a spy for Yevethan leader Nil Spaar. He provided Spaar with information about the mobilization of the New Republic's Fifth Fleet, allowing the Yevethan forces to prepare for its arrival. [BTS, SOL, TT]

Outbound Flight Project

An expensive project funded by the Old Republic Senate at the urging of Jedi Master Jorus C'baoth. Its goal was to search for and contact intelligent life outside the known galaxy. C'baoth was one of six Jedi Masters attached to the project, which launched from Yaga Minor. The ship, its crew, and the six Jedi Masters disappeared and were never heard from again. It was later revealed that Senator Palpatine and Grand Admiral Thrawn were behind the foul play that resulted in the loss of the project and those participating in it. [DFR, HE, LC]

Outer Rim Territories

This group of star systems located on the farthest edge of the galaxy includes the desert world of Tatooine. This region has been considered the galaxy's frontier since it was originally opened for settlement during the time of the Old Republic. When the Empire controlled all of known space, it was considered a backwater area good for nothing but exploitation. The worlds of the Rim were pillaged by the Empire, for it was from this region that the Empire got most of its slaves and resources. Because the Emperor was free to conduct his most terrible atrocities here, away from the eyes of the Core Worlds, the planets and species of the Rim Territories tended to support the Rebellion. [HESB, SW, SWRPG2]

outlaw tech

A member of a band of well-equipped and highly trained technicians who operate in Corporate Sector space, making a living by illegally modifying and repairing space vessels. Their clients have included criminal organizations, fugitives, the Rebellion, and other groups politically opposed to the Corporate Sector Authority. [HSE]

Outlier

Small star systems in the Corellian sector, far from central Corellia. [AC]

Outpost Beta

This isolated sentry station served as an advance lookout point for the Rebel Alliance base on Hoth. The soldiers assigned to this station were the first to spot the Imperial invaders at the start of the Battle of Hoth, and their warning alerted the base before the devastating attack began. [ESBR]

Outrider

A heavily modified YT-2400 belonging to Dash Rendar, it was originally a stock cargo hauler. Rendar added improvements to make it a state-of-the-art vessel specifically designed to match his dangerous lifestyle. [SESB, SOTE, SWVG]

Outrider

owriss

A large, harmless bloblike creature that inhabits Endor's forest moon. [ETV]

Ozzel, Admiral

This Imperial officer commanded Lord Darth Vader's task force during the events leading up to the Battle of Hoth. The Imperial Death Squadron, as the task force was dubbed, consisted of Vader's flagship *Executor* and five Imperial Star Destroyers. Ozzel's contempt for the Rebels and his unwillingness to see the Alliance as a credible threat led to his downfall. When he brought the task force out of hyperspace within Hoth's sensor range, Vader eliminated the admiral for prematurely alerting the Rebels and for "being as clumsy as he is stupid."

Years before, Ozzel presided at the ceremony in which Han Solo was dishonorably discharged from the Imperial Navy. [ESB, GG3, HG]

Pa'aal

The primary moon of the fifth planet in the N'zoth system. It was the site of a Yevethan prisoner-of-war and slave-labor camp. The former headquarters of the Imperial Black Sword Command was also located here. [SOL, TT]

Pacci

A New Republic pilot, he was killed during the failed blockade of Doornik-319. [SOL]

Padmé

See Amidala, Queen.

Page, Lieutenant

A top New Republic officer and undercover operative, he grew up as the pampered son of a corrupt Imperial senator from Corulag. He idolized the ancient Jedi Knights and dedicated himself to their ideals. He was forced into the Imperial

Academy, and upon graduation he was assigned to General Maximilian Veers's ground-assault command. While on leave, he heard Senator Leia Organa speak on the subject of galactic rights. She inspired him to defect and join the Alliance. He became part of General Crix Madine's and Major Bren Derlin's commando units and was eventually offered command of his own squad. He decided to keep the rank of lieutenant as a sign of humility. [HE, HESB]

Page's Commandos

A special-missions team officially called the Katarn Commandos, the unit consisted of twelve of the best-trained soldiers serving the Republic. Officially, the special-forces unit was attached to the office of the commander in chief, but in practice it often operated independently for weeks or months at a time. It was a rogue team, like Wedge Antilles's Rogue Squadron, with no set mission profile but designed to handle most assignments. It operated either as a single unit or broken up into smaller elements; all members were trained to work in any environment. Each soldier was a jack-of-all-trades as well as a specialist in a single field. The team included Lilla Dade, the pathfinder or scout; Gottu and Idow, urban combat specialists; Frorral the Wookiee, wilderness fighter; Mian Hoob of Sullust and Korren of Alderaan, team technicians; the Bothan Kasck, infiltrator and shadow; Vandro, heavy weapons and repulsorlift specialist; Syla Tors, ex-Corellian pirate and pilot; and Jortan and Bri'vin, medical technicians. The assault squad participated in the offensive against the Maw Installation. [COF, HE, HESB]

Paiq

A planet where five Fallanassi children were sent for safekeeping after the religious sect was persecuted on Lucazec. [BTS]

Pakka

A young Trianii, he was the son of Atuarre and Keeheen. He helped Han Solo infiltrate the Corporate Sector Authority's prison facility at Stars' End. [HSE]

Pakkpekatt, Colonel

A semitelepathic Hortek, he was a veteran intelligence officer who led a New Republic chase team charged with unraveling the mystery of the Teljkon vagabond ghost ship. Tough, cautious, and a man who played by the rules, he was disappointed when the gambler Lando Calrissian was assigned to the mission. Pakkpekatt lost his command after the vagabond departed with Calrissian, Lobot, and the droids R2-D2 and C-3PO aboard, but he convinced General Carlist Rieekan to let him pursue the ghost ship on his own. Using Calrissian's own *Lady Luck*, Pakkpekatt and a small team rescued Calrissian and his companions. [BTS, SOL, TT]

Pakrik Minor

This planet was the location of Imperial Sleeper Cell Jenth-44, a community of clones established by Grand Admiral Thrawn. [SP, VF]

Palace of the Woolamander

One of the Massassi temples on Yavin 4. It was named for a blue and gold animal of the moon's jungle. A golden globe within the temple contained the spirits of Massassi children. Anakin Solo and his friend Tahiri were able to break the globe and free the spirits. [JJK]

Palanhi

This planet remained neutral during the Galactic Civil War in an effort to profit from both sides. Grand Admiral Thrawn had funds transferred through the planet's central bank into Admiral Ackbar's account to discredit the Mon Calamarian. [DFR]

Palle, Lieutenant Eri

The first attaché, or personal aide, to Yevethan strongman Nil Spaar. [BTS, TT]

palmgun

A small blaster pistol designed for close combat and easy to conceal. These weapons are also called holdout blasters. [HSR]

Palpatine, Emperor

The Emperor ruled the galaxy for years as the malevolent dictator of the Empire. As the Naboo senator named Palpatine, he carved his Empire from the dying corpse of the Old Republic, employing guile, fraud, and astute political manipulations.

As a senator in the Old Republic, Palpatine was an unassuming man. It was a time of widespread corruption and social injustice. The massive bureaucracy of the Republic had grown twisted and sickly over the span of generations. Like an immense tree with decaying roots, the Republic appeared strong but was slowly dying from within. When a trade dispute caused a vote of no confidence in the Republic's supreme chancellor, Palpatine stepped forward as a candidate for change. He won the election.

Palpatine exceeded everyone's expectations after he was elected as supreme chancellor of the Republic. He positioned himself as a great leader who inspired trust and commitment. During the time of jubilation, promise, and hope that followed his election, he slowly introduced the New Order and declared himself Emperor. The period of hope and light quickly turned dark as tyranny spread across the galaxy. The Empire was born.

Emperor Palpatine

It was an Empire based on tyranny, hatred of nonhumans, brutal force, and constant fear. Members of the senate who had once tried to legally oppose Palpatine turned to rebellion, putting their support behind the Alliance to Restore the Republic. The Emperor was unconcerned by this development. In fact, he welcomed it. A rebellion and the threat it represented gave him a motive to wipe away the last remnant of the Old

Republic. He disbanded the Imperial Senate and instituted the crowning policy of his New Order—rule by fear.

How the Emperor achieved his mastery of the dark side of the Force remained a secret. Through his dark will, Anakin Skywalker became Darth Vader, the Jedi Knights were destroyed, the Old Republic was swept away, the Empire was forged, and the greatest military force ever assembled was unleashed upon the galaxy. He worked on levels few could comprehend, forming plans within plans and manipulating his Empire the way a master gamer manipulates the pieces on a holoboard. His grand schemes continued until a new player stepped to the table—Luke Skywalker.

From the moment the Emperor learned of Skywalker's existence, he knew he had to bring the young man into his fold. Like his father before him, Luke possessed nearly unlimited strength in the Force. The Emperor wanted that strength in his camp, under his tutelage. He wanted Luke turned to the dark side. In fact, the massive trap the Emperor set up in the Endor system was designed specifically to lure young Skywalker into the open. For Skywalker had to be turned to evil like his father before him, or he had to be destroyed. In the end, it was the Emperor who was destroyed, however, refusing to believe that good could actually find a way to triumph over evil. He was thrown into the Death Star's power core by a redeemed Darth Vader.

Six years after his death over Endor's forest moon, the Emperor returned in a new clone body. He revealed that he had cloned himself many times before, discarding decaying, used-up bodies in favor of new, youthful clone bodies whenever the need arose. For a brief period, Luke Skywalker accepted the cloned Emperor's dark-side training, but eventually the Emperor's second reign of terror was stopped by the actions of Luke Skywalker and Leia Organa Solo.

A few months later, a final clone appeared. He planned to kidnap Leia and turn her unborn child to the dark side. He also brought forth a new superweapon, the Galaxy Gun, and planned to use it to destroy the top Alliance leaders. The second cloned Emperor failed, and he was reduced to ashes and his weapon was sabotaged—wiping out the Imperial throneworld Byss. [DE, DE2, EE, ESB, ISB, RJ, SWCG, SWN]

Palpatine Counterinsurgency Front (PCF)

A terrorist organization formed by Ysanne Isard, director of Imperial Intelligence, shortly after the New Republic took control of Coruscant. [KT]

Panib, Captain Grell

This short, stiff-backed human had close-cropped red hair and a thick mustache. A rough-and-tumble sort known for his temper and his lack of social graces, Panib served the Imperial commander at Bakura. When the Imperial forces surrendered, he defected along with Commander Pter Thanas. Later, he helped rebuild the Bakuran military defenses. [TAB, TBSB]

Pantolomin

The primary planet in the Panto star system, it is a tropical ocean world. Its three continents and five major islands are jungle paradises, and the underwater coral reefs are renowned for their great beauty. A popular attraction is the subocean cruise ships, like the *Coral Vanda*, which take leisurely tours through the ocean depths. The amphibious Lomins are the planet's inhabitants. [DFR, DFRSB]

Paploo

A scout in the Ewok tribe that befriended Princess Leia and the Rebel strike team sent to the forest moon at the start of the Battle of Endor. He was known for his brazen actions and near-

Paploo

ly foolhardy bravery. He stole a speeder bike and distracted the attention of the guards watching over the secret Imperial facility on Endor's forest moon, providing the Rebel strike team the opportunity to penetrate the Imperial base. [GG5, RJ]

Paqwepori

An autonomous territory represented by Belezaboth Ourn. Its inhabitants are short, wide, yellow-green beings called Paqwe. Paqwepori society forbade its citizens from joining the New Republic military. [BTS, SOL, TT]

Paradise system

This massive star system had been turned into a space junkyard, controlled and operated by the Ugors. The scavenger Squibs compete with the Ugors over the system and its "glorious treasures." [GG4, SH]

paralight system

A combination of mechanical and opto-electronic subsystems found in a hyperdrive. It is responsible for translating a pilot's manual commands into a set of corresponding reactions within the hyperdrive power plants. [ESB]

Parck, Admiral Voss

The Imperial captain who found Thrawn on a deserted planet at the edge of the Unknown Regions and brought him to the Emperor. Parck subsequently joined Thrawn in his shame and supposed exile from the Empire. Sixteen years after the Battle of Endor, Parck was in command of the Hand of Thrawn, a secret base beyond the Outer Rim. He was waiting for Thrawn's promised return, safeguarding a storehouse of information and a wealth of resources located throughout the Unknown Regions. [SP, VF]

Paret, Jian

The commander of the Imperial garrison at N'zoth, he was brutally murdered by Yevethan strongman Nil Spaar. [BTS]

Parfadi

This region of space contains the unnavigable Black Nebula. [SOL]

Parq, Colonel

An Imperial officer on Tatooine, he captured the Mistryl Shadow Guards Shada D'akul and Karoly D'ulin after mistaking them for the notorious Tonnika sisters. [TMEC]

Par'tah

A Ho'Din, she controls a smuggling operation in the Borderland Regions. It is a marginal operation, though Par'tah puts on airs of wealth and success. She collects technological items, often rummaging through her clients' cargo for new additions before completing a delivery. She dislikes her competitor Brasck, but enjoys a good relationship with Talon Karrde. She prefers to deal with the New Republic, but needs the large payoffs the Imperials offer to make ends meet. [HE, HESB, LC]

particle shielding

A defensive force field that repels any form of matter. This type of deflector shield is usually used in conjunction with ray shielding to provide full protection to starships and planetary installations. [SWSB]

particle vapor trail

A signature left behind by most ships, which, if detected, can be used to track a vessel. [TBH]

passenger liner

Also called spaceliners, these ships are the basic mode of transport used by most galactic travelers. These vessels range in size from small in-system ships to giant interstellar luxury liners complete with multiple entertainment decks. [SWSB]

Payback

The name bounty hunter Dengar is known by throughout the galactic underworld. [TBH]

Peckhum

A supply courier and message runner, he operates the battered *Lightning Rod* supply ship. [YJK]

Pedducis Chorios

This planet is a hotbed of smuggling and piracy in the Chorios systems. [POT]

Pell, Akanah Norand

The widow of Andras Pell and a member of the Fallanassi religious order. She was traumatized as a young woman when her people fled Imperial persecution. She urged Luke Skywalker to help her find her people, claiming that his mother was Nashira, another Fallanassi. Akanah lied. Nashira wasn't Luke's mother, and Akanah's own mother had betrayed the Fallanassi and reported them to the Empire. [BTS, SOL, TT]

Pell, Andras

The late husband of Akanah Norand Pell. He left her the ship *Mud Sloth* when he died. [SOL]

Pellaeon, Admiral Gilad

A dedicated officer, he has served in the Imperial fleet, and the Old Republic before it, for nearly fifty years. Gilad Pellaeon is always loyal, always professional. At the Battle of Endor, after his commander was killed, Captain Pellaeon took control of the Star Destroyer *Chimaera* and saved it from certain destruction. He took command of the remnants of the fleet that day, bitterly ordering the ships to retreat instead of remaining to fall to the victorious Rebellion. He did his best to fight back in the five years that followed, but he was only a simple captain, not a powerful leader like the Emperor or Darth Vader or Grand Admiral Thrawn. It was Pellaeon who received Thrawn's call announcing that a grand admiral had returned. He offered his ship to serve as Thrawn's flagship and remained at the grand admiral's side throughout the campaign to destroy the New Republic once and for all.

Years after Thrawn's death, Pellaeon was promoted to the rank of vice admiral and commanded the fleet of the Imperial warlord High Admiral Teradoc. He then switched his loyalty to Admiral Daala and joined her in a campaign to destroy the Jedi academy on Yavin 4. When Daala's plan failed, Pellaeon again took control of the Imperial remnants.

Sixteen years after the Battle of Endor, Pellaeon was the supreme commander of the Imperial fleet. He looked at the dwindling resources of the Empire and convinced the eight remaining moffs that the only way to survive was to reach a peace accord with the New Republic. He met with Leia Organa Solo aboard the *Millennium Falcon* to begin negotiations, then met with Talon Karrde to gain the proof he needed to expose the impostor Grand Admiral Thrawn. [DFR, DFRSB, DS, HE, HESB, LC, SP, VF]

Admiral Gilad Pellaeon

Penga Rift

This Obroan Institute research transport was the command vessel for the excavation of Maltha Obex. [TT]

People's Liberation Battalion (PLB)

A socialist-oriented group dedicated to bringing down all nobles and eliminating the vestiges of the Empire. Asran, who promised to establish a government where everyone shared the wealth, led the group. [XW]

Peramis, Senator Tig

A human, he was a New Republic senator from the planet Walalla and a member of the Senate Defense Council. His distrust of Chief of State Leia Organa Solo led to his betrayal of the New Republic. He leaked top secret information concerning the deployment of the Fifth Fleet to Yevethan strongman Nil Spaar. [BTS, SOL]

Peregrine

One of six Dreadnaughts from the legendary *Katana* fleet that made up Garm Bel Iblis's private strike force. It was his flagship. [DFR]

Peregrine's Nest

Garm Bel Iblis's last hidden base before his strike force joined the New Republic. The base was constructed of bistate memory plastic for quick breakdown and setup. It was protected by anti-infantry, antivehicle, and antiorbital artillery and featured a large cache of personal armaments. [DFR]

Perit

A Mon Calamari, he was a Vigo of the Black Sun crime syndicate. Perit's operatives specialized in crimes related to computers and technology. He had his hands in credit laundering, bank fraud, data theft, and corporate espionage, among other high-tech crimes. [SESB, SOTE]

Permondiri Explorer

A survey starship that was sent on a mission to explore and chart a new star system, it was never heard from again. Several expeditions were organized to locate the *Explorer* in the years after its disappearance, but none ever discovered what happened to her. [HSR]

Pernon, Count Rial

A tall, strong human, he was betrothed to Princess Isplourrdacartha Estillo (Plourr Ilo) as a child and considered the vow binding even as an adult. Plourr, a member of Rogue Squadron, resented Rial due to the actions of his father, but her feelings toward Rial eventually softened and she did marry him. [XW]

Pernon, Grand Duke Gror

A human male, he would have been the heir to the throne of Eiattu VI if Plourr Ilo, the daughter of the crown prince, hadn't survived the execution of the rest of the family. He believed the coup had been vital because Ilo's father was too weak to withstand the Empire, but he didn't advocate the murder of the entire family. [XW]

Pestage, Sate

Emperor Palpatine's grand vizier. [DESB, ESB]

Phalanx

This cruiser in the New Republic's Fifth Fleet was severely damaged during the blockade of Doornik-319. [SOL]

Phenaru Prime

This mythical planet was used in a training simulation for Rogue Squadron prior to the return mission to Borleias. [RS]

Phlog

This giant, brutish species lives in the desert land Simoom on Endor's forest moon. The Phlogs are usually calm and peaceful, but they can become dangerous when disturbed. [ETV]

Phlutdroid

See IG-88.

phobium

A metal alloy used to coat the power core of both Death Star battle stations. [GDV]

Phonstrom, Lady Lapema

A resident of Kabal, she was one of Lando Calrissian's marriage candidates. [AC]

Pho Ph'eah

This planet is home to the Pho Ph'eahians, an intelligent humanoid species with four arms and blue fur. [HSR]

Phorliss

Site of a cantina where Mara Jade once worked as a serving girl, using the name Karrinna Jansih. [DFR]

photoreceptor

A device that captures light rays and converts them into electronic signals for processing by video computers. Among their many uses, these devices serve as eyes for most droid models. [SWSB]

phototropic shielding

A process that turns transparent materials into light filters while retaining their transparency. [SWSB]

Phracas

This planet in sector 151 of the Galactic Core was the destination of the mysterious Teljkon vagabond ship after Lando Calrissian and his companions stowed away on board. [SOL]

Piett, Captain

The first officer on Darth Vader's flagship *Executor*, he assisted Admiral Ozzel in overseeing the crew and helped direct the entire fleet assigned to the flagship. He was promoted to admiral and given command of the flagship and the fleet after Admiral Ozzel made a fatal mistake during the assault on the Rebel base on Hoth. Piett remained in command of *Executor* through the Battle of Endor, where the Super Star Destroyer was lost in combat with the Rebel fleet. [ESB, RJ]

Pike sisters

Zan and Zu Pike were twins trained in the art of teräs käsi—"steel hands." This martial arts discipline served them well in both their public and private lives. In public, the Pike sisters were professional fighters beginning to make a name for themselves in galactic circles. In private, they were operatives secretly employed by Prince Xizor's Black Sun organization. The sisters were as beautiful as they were deadly, dressing in formfitting tunics that were functional but also showed off their lithe, powerful bodies. It was a point of pride that the sisters refused to carry weapons. They considered their skills more than a match for any opponent. After Prince Xizor's death, the Pike sisters changed their name to the Pikkel sisters. [SEE, SESB, SOTE]

Pikkel sisters

See Pike sisters.

Pilgrim 921

The name given to Bria Tharen by the Ylesian priests. [PS]

pinnace

Small ships carried aboard large space vessels for defensive purposes. Built for speed, heavily armed, and highly maneuverable, pinnaces come close to combat starfighters in terms of performance and utility. They are sometimes called battle boats. [HSR]

Pinnacle Base

The New Republic High Command Center on Da Soocha's fifth moon. High Command was transferred to this location after Imperial forces invaded Coruscant. [DE]

Pirol-5

This planet is located in the Koornacht Cluster and was the site of a former Imperial factory farm operated by droids. The Yevetha seized the planet twelve years after the Battle of Endor during the Great Purge. [BTS]

Pitareeze

A family on the planet Kalarba. The droids R2-D2 and C-3PO agreed to work for the family for a time after they escaped from bounty hunter IG-88 prior to the start of the Galactic Civil War. [D]

Platform 327

The landing pad on Bespin's Cloud City where the *Millennium Falcon* was moored on its visit to the outpost after the Battle of Hoth. [ESB]

Ploovo Two-For-One

One of the galaxy's infamous crimelords, he was an unscrupulous and portly humanoid from the Cron drift. Ploovo was a con man, a loan shark, a thief, a smash-and-grab man, and a bunco artist. Han Solo sometimes worked for Ploovo, and for a time he owed the crimelord a good amount of credits. As Solo also caused Ploovo to lose face on a number of occasions, the crimelord ordered Solo's termination back in the days before the smuggler became involved in the Galactic Civil War. [HSE]

pocket cruiser

An obsolete class of capital ships that saw extensive service during the end phase of the Clone Wars. Small compared to modern capital ships, the pocket cruiser was easy to manufacture and was on par with most of the other warships of its day. They could be found as training platforms, pirate ships, and in local military forces well into the Galactic Civil War. [HLL]

pocket patrol boat

A small single-pilot ship with high speed but limited firepower. [AC]

Poderis

A planet located in the Orus sector. Luke Skywalker visited the planet in an attempt to learn more about the Empire's clone-trafficking network, and he narrowly escaped a trap set for him by Grand Admiral Thrawn. [LC]

Podrace

A high-speed, adrenaline-packed contest involving pilots who fly small, fragile cockpits pulled by twin high-powered engines. Each of these Podracer's is heavily customized by the pilot and his crew, and quick reflexes are required to successfully navigate the grueling racecourses. Spectators wager large sums on the competition. Almost all of the pilots, also known as Podracers, are nonhuman, though one of the most famous was young Anakin Skywalker, who competed at the Mos Espa Arena presided over by Jabba the Hutt. [SWTPM]

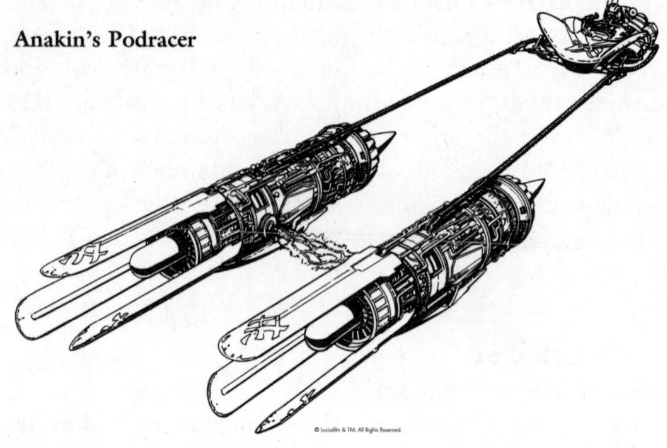

Anakin's Podracer

Poe

A silver protocol droid with one black metal peg leg, he was assigned to Rogue Squadron. [XW]

Point 5

A game of chance played in many casinos throughout the galaxy. [HSR]

Polneye

A planet located on the far side of the Koornacht Cluster from Coruscant. The site of an Imperial military supply depot, it was abandoned by the Empire after the Battle of Endor. Twelve years later, it suffered a brutal assault by the Yevethan military. Admiral Ackbar pushed through an emergency petition for membership in the New Republic for the planet, which Chief of State Leia Organa Solo approved. [BTS]

Pops
A veteran human pilot, he was the wing mate for Gold Leader and was Gold Five at the Battle of Yavin, where he died. [SW]

Poqua, Commodore
A New Republic task force commander during the Yevethan crisis, he was a friend of General Etahn A'baht. [TT]

Porcellus
Jabba the Hutt's personal chef. He opened a restaurant in Mos Eisley with Malakili the rancor-keeper after Jabba died. [TJP]

Porkins, Jek
An Alliance X-wing pilot from Bestine IV, he was Red Six at the Battle of Yavin. He died when his X-wing was hit by a Death Star turbolaser. [GG1, SW]

Porus Vida
A planet famous for its ancient cultural museums. Imperial Admiral Daala targeted the Porus Vida treasures for destruction as a psychological blow against the New Republic. [DS]

Post, Avan
A Jedi Master from Chandrila, he served during the Clone Wars. [KT]

power converter
The ignition system for a starship, it routes energy from a ship's primary power source, or furnace, to its propulsion units to achieve thrust. [ESB, SWN]

power coupling
A starship device that directs large amounts of energy to the hyperdrive motivator, which then activates the hyperdrive engine to achieve the jump to light speed. [ESBN]

power droid

An ambulatory power generator, this box-shaped GNK droid walks on two thick, articulated legs and carries a generator in its body. The primary function of this service droid is to provide energy to other droids, ships, vehicles, and other mechanical devices. [SWR]

power gem

A rare mineral that radiated a magnetic disruption aura that could render defensive shields useless. Vrad Dodonna used the last gem to penetrate the shields and crash into the *Executor.* [CSW]

Pqweeduk

A Rodian, he was the younger brother of the bounty hunter Greedo. [TMEC]

Praesitlyn

This planet is the site of a major communications station in the Sluis sector. [HE, SOL]

Praget, Chairman Krall

The chairman of the New Republic Senate Council on Security and Intelligence, he was from the planet Edatha. He attempted to overthrow Chief of State Leia Organa Solo by bringing a petition to the Senate Ruling Council seeking her removal. [SOL]

Prakith

This planet in the Galactic Core is the ruling world of the Constitutional Protectorate controlled by the Imperial warlord Foga Brill. [SOL, TT]

praxeum

A name Luke Skywalker applied to his Jedi academy on Yavin 4, it means a place for the learning of action. There, using every resource available, Skywalker teaches his students to fight and to think. [JAL]

preducor

A ferocious night hunter on the forest moon of Endor, it has four powerful, clawed legs and grows as high as four meters and as long as five meters. A mane of razor-sharp hair surrounds its head, and a long, spiked tail stretches behind it. Its protruding maw is full of fearsome teeth, and its eyes glow as it hunts at night. Large folds of skin on its back are vestiges of wings. [DFRSB]

Preedu III, Emperor

The ruler of Tamban, he reigned before the rise of the Empire. [BTS]

pressor

Small repulsor projectors used to control and induce pitch in a starship. Pilots activate them via their control sticks. [SWN]

Prevaro

A Rodian, he was an information dealer who believed that the Falleen antique dealer Azool was Prince Xizor in disguise. When Azool turned out to be Xizor's niece, she offered Prevaro a spot in the Black Sun criminal organization—as soon as she took control of it. [SEE]

Priamsta

On the planet Eiattu VI, this group was composed of native nobles who wanted to restore local rule. [XW]

Pride of Yevetha

Formerly the Super Star Destroyer *Intimidator*, it was seized by the forces of Nil Spaar during a raid on the Imperial shipyard at N'zoth. [SOL]

Priests of Ninn

A religious order that inhabits the planet Ninn. Its members normally dress in green vestments and practice formalistic abstinence. [HSR]

Princess Leia Organa

See Solo, Princess Leia Organa.

probe droid, probot

probe droid

A droid designed to perform reconnaissance missions, gathering data and transmitting it back to its master. As sophisticated surveillance and tracking droids, probots have a wide variety of scientific and military applications. Tenacious hunters and searchers, probots are equipped with an array of sensors, including electromagnetic, motive, acoustic, seismic, and olfactory measuring devices. Military probots typically receive offensive and defensive ordnance. Naturally designed to withstand the rigors of space and hostile planetary environments, these droids are extremely tough and durable. They possess a variety of specialized tools connected to many mechanical appendages. The Empire employed a large number of these droids to search for the hidden Rebel base after the Battle of Yavin. One finally tracked the Rebels to the ice planet Hoth. After broadcasting its findings back to its command ship, the probot self-destructed to avoid capture. [AC, ESB, MTS, SWSB]

proctors

Assistants to Lord Hethrir. They wore light blue jumpsuits. [CS]

Procurator of Justice

The head of the Empire's criminal justice system, Lord Hethrir was a shadowy figure who persecuted political prisoners. It was only after the Battle of Endor that the name of the Procurator became public. [CS]

Proi, Lieutenant Norda

The commanding officer of the fleet hauler and junker *Steadfast*. Her ship discovered the wreckage of the Imperial Star Destroyer *Gnisnal*. [BTS]

Project Decoy

A secret Alliance program headed by the Chadra-Fan scientist Fandar. Its goal was to create a human replica droid. [QE]

Project Starscream

An Imperial program on the planet Kiva that led to the development of the living planet D'vouran. It was led by the scientist Borborygmus Gog, who reported directly to the Emperor. [GF]

Prophets of the Dark Side

A group of Imperial operatives that posed as great mystics strong in the Force's dark side, they were actually an investigation bureau with a vast network of spies. Led by the Supreme Prophet Kadann, these false mystics wielded much power in the Empire. They retained control by making their prophecies come true through any means necessary—including bribery, force, and even murder. [LCJ]

prosthetic replacement

After the Clone Wars, medical science made great advancements in the field of prosthetic replacements. By the time of the Galactic Civil War, doctors could replace lost limbs and organs with effective and lifelike prosthetic parts. Most prosthetics do not enhance normal physical abilities. They employ synthenet neural interfaces to give recipients full control of replaced limbs. Synthflesh covers biomechanical replacement parts, giving them the look and feel of natural body parts. As there is a natural prejudice against droids and cybernetics, those with replacement parts usually keep the fact to themselves. Luke Skywalker has a prosthetic hand that replaces the one he lost in his first battle with Darth Vader. [ESB, HESB]

protocol droid

A droid whose primary programming includes languages, interpretation, cultures, and diplomacy, all geared toward helping it fulfill its usual function as an administrative assistant, diplomatic aide, and companion for high-level individuals. C-3PO is a protocol droid. [SW]

proton grenade

A small concussion weapon capable of damaging a starfighter. [CSW]

proton torpedo

A projectile weapon launched from a specialized delivery system, it is standard ordnance for both starfighters and capital ships. There is even a smaller version that can be fired from a shoulder- or back-mounted launcher. These concussion weapons carry a proton-scattering energy warhead. Proton torpedoes were used to destroy both Death Star battle stations. [RJ, SW, SWSB]

Provisional Council

A temporary body established by the Provisional Government of the New Republic. Its main jobs were to provide leadership and direction for the new government and to work toward the formal reestablishment of the principles and laws of the Old Republic. Its ruling body, the Inner Council, included Mon Mothma, Admiral Ackbar, and Leia Organa Solo. [HE, HESB]

Prune Face

See Orrimaarko.

Psadan

A short, stocky humanoid species, they live on the planet Wayland. Thick, stonelike scales cover their bodies, forming irregular, lumpy shells over each Psadan's back. These shells start over the ridge of the brow, sweep across the head, and fall down the back. Smaller, closer-packed plates cover the rest of their bodies. The Psadans share their world with the Myneyrshi and human colonists. All three have engaged in open hostilities at various times in the planet's history. Like the Myneyrshi, the Psadans have a primitive society. Bows and arrows are their primary weapons, and animals serve as transportation and beasts of burden. [HE, HESB, LC]

Ptaa, Eet

The leader of a clan of Jawas. His clan was attacked and driven off by Sand People. [TMEC]

pubtrans flitter

A public transportation system mainly used by the poorer inhabitants of heavily developed planets such as Coruscant. [SOTE]

Pui-ui

These small, sentient beings are natives of the planet Kyryll's World. A Pui-ui measures about 1.25 meters tall and appears as two spherical bodies connected by a short neck. Cilia projections growing out of the base of the bottom sphere provide these beings with locomotive capabilities. The Pui-ui language consists of a wide range of shrill sounds. [HLL]

Pulsar Skate

This modified *Baudo*-class star yacht is commanded by Mirax Terrik, who inherited it from her father, Booster. It is used to carry on the family tradition of smuggling black-market goods. The ship carried a team of Rogue Squadron pilots to Coruscant on a covert mission. [KT, RS, WG]

Punishing One

A Corellian Jumpmaster 5000 owned and piloted by the bounty hunter Dengar. [TBH]

Purity

A Yevethan battle cruiser commanded by Vol Noorr. This ship destroyed the New Republic astrographic probe *Astrolabe*. [BTS]

P'w'eck

A sentient saurian species native to the planet Lwhekk, they were enslaved by the reptilian Ssi-ruuk. The P'w'eck are brown-scaled miniature versions of the Ssi-ruuk, growing no taller than 1.5 meters from head to tail. They are considered by the Ssi-ruuk to possess no souls and are often enteched to provide energy for the Ssi-ruuk. [TAB, TBSB]

Pydyr

One of the moons of Almania. The dark-sider Kueller killed more than one million people there during his first bombing campaign against the New Republic. [NR]

Pypin

A Trianii colony world within the disputed border of the Corporate Sector. [CSSB]

Pzob

This planet was colonized by a group of Gamorreans years before the Galactic Civil War. Eighteen years before the Battle of Yavin, a company of stormtroopers were ordered to await pickup by the *Eye of Palpatine* battlemoon at an Imperial base on Pzob. The battlemoon never arrived. [COJ]

Q9-X2

A jet-black droid, it looks like a taller, thinner version of R2-D2. Han Solo ordered the droid to protect his family. [AC]

Qalita Prime

This planet located in the Seventh Security Zone is a member of the New Republic. [BTS]

Qaqquqqu, Lord

One of the followers of Lord Hethrir, he was a slave trader. [CS]

Qat Chrystac

This planet was the site of a battle between the forces of Garm Bel Iblis and Grand Admiral Thrawn. [LC]

Q-E, 2-E, and U-E

Three small droids who were forced to assemble illegal blasters for Master Vuldo. [D]

Qel-Droma, Cay

A Jedi, he trained under Master Arca Jeth some 4,000 years before the Galactic Civil War. He and his brother Ulic were born on Alderaan. Cay was a gifted mechanic who lost his left arm during the Beast Wars of Onderon. He replaced the limb himself with an arm made from parts of an XT-6 service droid. When Ulic turned to the dark side, Cay never stopped trying to bring him back to the light. In a final confrontation, Ulic murdered Cay. [DLS, TOJ, TSW]

Qel-Droma, Ulic

A Jedi who lived 4,000 years before the Galactic Civil War, he thought he could learn the ways of the dark side and then return with his knowledge to the light. His disastrous failure began when he was named watchman for the Empress Teta system, where the cult of dark-side magicians called the Krath was gaining power. Ulic decided that the only way to defeat the Krath was to infiltrate them and learn their secrets. The Krath leaders, Satal Keto and Aleema, played along with Ulic while plotting his destruction. In anger, Ulic killed Satal. Aleema then gave Ulic half of a Sith amulet that had been given to Satal by the spirit of Freedon Nadd.

Exar Kun, another fallen Jedi, confronted Ulic, and the two engaged in a fierce lightsaber battle. Both men wore Sith amulets, and when these were activated, the two were visited by the spirits of ancient Sith Lords. The spirits proclaimed that Kun was the new Dark Lord of the Sith, and Ulic was his first apprentice. Exar and Ulic raised an army, and the subsequent battles became known as the Sith War. In the end, Ulic betrayed Kun and led a force of Jedi against the Sith Lord's base on Yavin 4. Ulic was blinded to the Force and robbed of his powers by the Jedi Knight Nomi Sunrider.

For ten years Ulic wandered the galaxy, trying to hide and forget his past. Eventually, he hired a down-on-his-luck spacer named Hoggon to take him to an out-of-the-way place. He settled on Rhen Var, an ice-covered world, to isolate himself from the galaxy. However, Vima Sunrider, Nomi's daughter, sought him out. She convinced Ulic to train her, and through that training he found his own redemption. He was killed by Hoggon, who hoped to make a name for himself by killing the infamous dark Jedi. In death, Ulic vanished, joining the Force as a forgiven Jedi Master. [DLS, TOJ, TOJR, TSW]

Ulic Qel-Droma

Qella (MALTHA OBEX)

A dead planet. Luke Skywalker helped the organic starship known as the Teljkon vagabond begin the process of thawing the planet and restoring Qellan society. [BTS, SOL, TT]

Qom Jha

Natives of a planet in the Nirauan system, these winged beings look like a cross between a mynock and a praying makthier. Marginally Force-sensitive, each clan is led by a bargainer. The Qom Jha are cave dwellers. A contingent of Qom Jha and Qom

Qae helped Luke Skywalker and Mara Jade infiltrate the secret base called the Hand of Thrawn. [VF]

Qom Qae

Natives of a planet in the Nirauan system, these winged beings look like a cross between a mynock and a praying makthier. Marginally Force-sensitive, each clan is led by a bargainer. The Qom Qae live in the open air. A contingent of Qom Qae and Qom Jha helped Luke Skywalker and Mara Jade infiltrate the secret base called the Hand of Thrawn. [VF]

Qorl

A TIE fighter pilot during the Battle of Yavin, he crash-landed on Yavin 4, where he remained for over twenty years. Lowbacca, a Jedi trainee at Luke Skywalker's Jedi academy, discovered the craft and restored it to working order. Then Qorl appeared and kidnapped Lowbacca's friends Jaina and Jacen Solo. The twins were eventually rescued, but Qorl escaped in the restored TIE fighter. He then joined the Dark Jedi Brakiss and the Shadow Academy, where he was put in charge of training those youths who weren't Force-sensitive. After the Shadow Academy was destroyed, Qorl was shot down over Yavin 4 again. He decided to live out his life in the planet's jungles. [YJK]

Qretu-Five

This planet is the site of a bacta-producing colony with strong ties to Thyferra. [BW]

Qrygg, Ooryl

A Gand, he was a member of Rogue Squadron. [RS, WG]

Quamar Messenger

A luxury spaceliner. It carries up to 600 passengers and is serviced by a crew of forty-five. It was hijacked on its maiden voyage by Gallandro. [HLL]

Quanto

A henchman of Great Bogga the Hutt, he helped murder Jedi Andur Sunrider some 4,000 years before the Galactic Civil War. Andur's wife, Nomi, killed Quanto in self-defense with her husband's lightsaber. [TOJ]

quarrel

Energy projectiles fired by Wookiee bowcasters, they explode upon impact. [RJN, SWSB]

Quarren

These amphibious beings, sometimes called Squid Heads, share the world Mon Calamari with the Mon Calamari species. Quarren prefer the depths of the floating cities to the upper reaches the Mon Cals call home. They are more practical and conservative than their idealistic worldmates. Whereas the Mon Calamari adopted Basic as their language of choice, the Quarren kept their oceanic tongue. The Quarren are sea dwellers, able to live out of the water but preferring the security of the ocean depths. These pragmatic people are unwilling to trust new ideas. They became dependent on the Mon Calamari, and this dependency led to resentment and even outright hatred. Rumors persist that it was a small number of Quarren who helped the Empire originally invade the planet. In the face of invading forces, the Quarren cooperated with the Mon Calamari to repel the Imperials. But since that day, many Quarren have fled the planet to seek a life elsewhere in the galaxy. They seem to have purposely remained apart from both the Alliance and the Empire, preferring to find a place among the fringe society. Quarren can be found working with pirates, slavers, crimelords, smugglers, and other unsavory sorts. [SWSB]

Quee, Danni

This scientist joined the ExGal Society when she was only fifteen. From an overcrowded Core planet, independent Danni wasn't a fan of any government and believed that the "ordering" of the galaxy stifled excitement and buried cultures beneath the blanket of common civilization. The thought of something undiscovered, of life beyond the galaxy, excited her. Born the year of the Battle of Endor, she was twenty-one when her outpost, the ExGal-4 facility on Belkadan, discovered the first sign of a galactic breach.

Danni and the other scientists thought the object was a comet. When it struck but didn't vaporize the fourth planet of the Helska system, they decided to investigate. Using a lumbering Spacecaster shuttle, Danni and two other ExGal scientists traveled to the ice planet and were captured by the invading forces of the Yuuzhan Vong. Da'Gara, prefect of the invaders, hoped to convert her to their cause. She alone of her companions was allowed to live. She was imprisoned with captured Jedi Knight Miko Reglia, and the two underwent a series of ordeals at the hands of the Yuuzhan Vong, designed to break Miko and convert Danni.

Jacen Solo, on a mission to discern the strength of the invaders, received a telepathic call for help. It came from Danni, though she had exhibited no Force abilities prior to her captivity. With help from Danni and Miko, Jacen rescued Danni. He realized that, while she wasn't a Jedi Knight, she *could* be. Perhaps a great one. [VP]

Queen of Ranroon

This cargo vessel carried the spoils gathered during the interstellar conquests of Xim the Despot. The legendary ship never reached port on its last run. It was lost with its cargo stored deep in its many holds and bays, and it became the subject of wild spacer stories. To spacers, the name symbolizes wealth beyond measure, and many have tried to discover its whereabouts over the centuries. Even Han Solo participated in a quest for the vessel prior to his involvement in the Galactic Civil War. [HLL, HSR]

Quelii sector

A region of space containing the planet Dathomir. It was once controlled by Imperial Warlord Zsinj. [CPL]

Quill-Face, Hideaz

A massive, three-meter-tall smuggler and a member of an unidentified alien species. He works with Spog, his partner. The pair can often be found in the Byss Bistro. [DE]

Quin, Sixtus

A former Special Intelligence operative, he conducted several missions for the Empire. He was betrayed by his commander and defected to the Rebel Alliance. He applied for an assignment with Rogue Squadron to help topple Ysanne Isard's puppet government on Thyferra. He went to the planet to organize an uprising, training members of the Ashern rebels and the Zaltin Corporation. While Rogue Squadron led the orbital battle against the planet, Quin and his operatives quickly took command of Isard's headquarters with very little loss of life. [BW, XW]

Q-Varx, Senator

This New Republic senator led the Rationalist Party on his homeworld Mon Calamari. He accepted a bribe to arrange a secret meeting between Chief of State Leia Organa Solo and Nam Chorios strongman Seti Ashgad. [POT]

R2-D2 (Artoo-Detoo)

This three-legged R2 series astromech utility droid is one of the most famous automatons in the galaxy. Usually teamed with the golden protocol droid C-3PO, the squat, barrel-shaped astromech speaks in beeps and whistles and has evolved his programming to a near-human personality that is brash, bold, and brave. R2-D2 was designed to operate in deep space, making repairs on the outer surface of a starship or interfacing with the computers of a starfighter. When plugged into a starfighter socket, he can augment the capabilities of the ship and its pilot.

R2-D2 understands most sentient languages, but his own information-dense electronic language has to be interpreted by C-3PO or by a ship's computer that turns the electronic data into written words on a display screen. R2-D2's fully rotational domed head contains infrared receptors, electromagnetic-field sensors, a register readout and logic dispenser, dedicated energy receptors, a radar eye, heat and motion detectors, and a holographic recorder and projector. Doors in his cylindrical body open to reveal a variety of hidden instruments including a storage/retrieval jack for computer linkup, auditory receivers, flame-retardant foam dispenser, electric shock prod, high-powered spotlight, grasping claws, laser welder, circular saw, and a cybot acoustic signaler.

R2-D2

One of R2-D2's earliest posts was aboard the Naboo Royal Starship, where he demonstrated his bravery and starship repair skills. Just after that time, R2-D2 first met a half-assembled C-3PO and the young Anakin Skywalker on Tatooine. After the two droids hooked up again, they had a number of masters. These have included Thall Joben, Jann Tosh, Mungo Baobab, the Pitareeze family, and the Royal House of Alderaan. Both droids were aboard the Alderaan consular ship *Tantive IV* when the Star Destroyer *Devastator* captured it over Tatooine. Princess Leia Organa placed stolen technical readouts for the Death Star battle station into R2-D2's memory banks, then sent him to find Obi-Wan Kenobi in the Tatooine desert.

It was through these events that the droids fell into the possession of Luke Skywalker and became deeply involved in the Galactic Civil War. R2-D2 rode with Luke Skywalker when Luke fired the shot that destroyed the first Death Star. He accompanied Luke to Dagobah and witnessed Luke's Jedi training. The droid played a prominent role in the rescue of Han Solo from Jabba the Hutt and participated in Han Solo's strike team during the Battle of Endor. After the New Republic was established, R2-D2 has remained mainly at Luke Skywalker's side, though he did take on a few missions without his master, including saving the New Republic from a sabotage scheme set up by the darksider Kueller. [D, DTV, ESB, GG1, GG3, GG5, NR, RJ, SW, SWSB]

R2 unit

One of the most popular astromech droid models, this utility droid was designed to operate in hostile environments, especially deep space. By plugging into terminals or ship-interface sockets, R2 units augment and enhance the computer capabilities of starships, assist with piloting and navigation, and serve as onboard repair and maintenance technicians. About one meter tall, R2 units are built by Industrial Automaton. [ESB, RJ, SW, SWSB]

R5-D4

An inexpensive astromech droid commonly referred to as Red, it allowed R2-D2 to program its motivator to blow up after it learned of R2-D2's mission. The motivator malfunction allowed R2-D2 and C-3PO to remain together. Red was later repaired and sold to a moisture farm. [GG1, SWR]

R5 unit

This astromech droid performs the same function as the R2 series but is less expensive. R5 units are skilled mechanics but can not match the other skills of the R2 droids. [SWR]

R7-T1

An R7 series astromech droid assigned to Luke Skywalker's E-wing starfighter. [BTS]

R7 unit

A newer series of astromech droids, specifically designed to interface with E-wing starfighters. [DE]

Ra, Vonnda

An evil Nightsister from Dathomir, she helped the Second Imperium recruit trainees from the various witch clans. A syren plant killed her on Kashyyyk. [YJK]

Raabakyysh

A Wookiee, she admired Lowbacca and was his younger sister's best friend. She wanted to impress Lowbacca by performing her Wookiee Rite of Passage alone. She never returned. All that was found of her was her bloodstained backpack. [YJK]

Raalk, Proctor Ton

A civic leader, he led the government of N'zoth's capital city, Giat Nor. [SOL]

rakazzak beast

A three-meter-tall spiderlike creature that inhabits Endor's forest moon. Yuzzum warriors often ride rakazzak mounts. [ETV]

Rakrir

This planet is the homeworld of a sentient insectoid species whose members are wealthy and highly cultured. [CSSB, HSE]

Ra-Lee

A pretty, tan-furred Ewok, she was the wife of Chief Chirpa. She died defending her daughters, Kneesaa and Asha. [ETV]

R'all

The fraternal twin of J'uoch, he ran a mining concern on the planet Dellalt with his sister. A human, he had pale skin offset by black-iris eyes. Along with his sister, R'all competed with Han Solo to be the first to find the lost treasures of the legendary ship, *Queen of Ranroon.* [HLL]

Ralls, Agent

A New Republic Intelligence agent, he questioned prisoner Davith Sconn for information on the Yevethan military fleet. [SOL]

Ralltiir

A high-technology planet known for its banking industry. When the Ralltiir High Council tried to oppose the Empire prior to the Battle of Yavin, the Emperor decided to make the planet an example to other worlds that would defy his will. He sent a brutal Imperial force, led by Lord Tion, to invade and devastate the planet.

Princess Leia Organa was permitted to deliver medical supplies during a mercy mission. She rescued a wounded Rebel soldier who informed her of the Death Star project. Years later, Inath of Ralltiir became a New Republic senator. [GG2, MTS, POT, SWR, SWSB]

Ralrra

A tall, powerfully built Wookiee whose full name is Ralrracheen. He wears a gold-threaded tan baldric. A speech impediment allows Ralrra to speak Basic. Before the Empire, he was an ambassador to the Old Republic. As a slave to the Empire, he was used by his Imperial masters to communicate with the rest of his species. He originally attempted to resist the Imperial occupation forces, but forced himself to comply after they executed a dozen women and children from his family unit. Afterwards, his proximity to Imperial officers provided him with information vital to the Alliance's effort to free Kashyyyk. When Chewbacca brought Princess Leia to Kashyyyk to keep her safe from Grand Admiral Thrawn's Noghri Death Commandos, Ralrra was one of two Wookiees assigned to protect her. [HE, HESB]

Ralter, Dack

A young Rebel soldier assigned to the Alliance forces on the ice planet Hoth. He served as gunner on Luke Skywalker's snowspeeder. Dack died when Skywalker's snowspeeder took a hit from an Imperial walker. [ESB, GG3]

Rana, Queen

Queen Rana was the ruler of the planet Duro in ancient times. A huge monument dedicated to the queen fills the Valley of Royalty on Duro. [MMY]

Ranat

A ratlike species whose members are small and cunning, with sharp teeth and long tails. They call themselves Con Queecon, or "the conquerors." They are savage killers with a taste for other intelligent beings. Since Jabba the Hutt's death, a group of these aliens have taken over the crimelord's desert palace. [GG4, TBH, TMEC, ZHR]

rancor

This terrible beast is a five-meter-tall carnivore that walks on two legs and is reptilian in appearance. With long, out-of-proportion arms, huge fangs, and long, sharp claws, the rancor is a fearsome sight. One rancor was kept in a special pit in Jabba the Hutt's desert palace on Tatooine. The crimelord used the creature as a source of entertainment and as a method for getting rid of employees and others that failed him. Semisentient rancors are common on the planet Dathomir, and they can also be found in the Ottethan system. [CPL, DE, RJ, SWSB]

Rand Ecliptic

This space freighter was Biggs Darklighter's first assignment after he graduated from the Academy. He served as first mate until he jumped ship to join the Rebellion. [SWN]

Random, Sarl

Security chief on Cloud City, she was in charge during the droid EV-9D9's revolt and escape. [TMEC]

Raort, Romort

An Irith spice-jacker based on Nar Shaddaa, he is unpopular even among his underworld cohorts because he steals from many of them. His gang is swift to take vengeance on those who cross them, and they have a deal with the Hutts that allows them to operate along many major galactic spice routes. [DE]

Rask

A street philosopher in the city Iziz, he was a Naddist, a follower of the Sith apprentice Freedon Nadd. [DLS]

Raskar

A former space pirate and the owner of the last power gem, he staged arena fights for those seeking the gem and made a fortune betting on the fights. Chewbacca beat the best fighter, and he and Han Solo left with the gem. Later, Raskar captured Solo and Luke Skywalker above Hoth. Solo unknowingly led Raskar to a deep cavern containing a huge deposit of lumni-spice, but the dragon-slug that guarded the cave forced them to leave. Raskar redeemed himself on Ord Mantell when he rescued Han Solo and Luke Skywalker from the bounty hunter Skorr. [CSW]

Rathalay

A planet known for its gray basalt beaches. Twelve years after the Battle of Endor, Han Solo, Leia Organa Solo, and their children relaxed on a Rathalay beach as the Yevethan crisis began. [SOL]

Rattagagech

Chairman of the New Republic Senate Science Council and a senator from Elom, he voted to remove Chief of State Leia Organa Solo from office. [SOL]

Ravager

This Imperial *Lancer*-class frigate was destroyed by Rogue Squadron at Vladet. [RS]

Raynar

A Jedi student, he was good-looking, spoiled, and troublesome. [YJK]

ray shielding

A force field designed to block and absorb energy fire. It is an essential part of every starfighter's and capital ship's defensive system. [SWN, SWSB]

reactivate switch

A droid's master circuit breaker, used to turn a droid on and off. [SWR]

realspace

Normal space, the dimension in which all residents of the galaxy live. Travel within realspace is slow compared to traveling through the shadow-dimension called hyperspace. [SWRPG, SWRPG2]

Rebel Alliance

Rebel Alliance Insignia

The common name for the Alliance to Restore the Republic. The Alliance opposed the tyranny of the Empire and its New Order. Star systems, single worlds, and even factions and individuals from otherwise neutral or Empire-aligned planets united to bring justice and freedom back to the galaxy. Opposition took forms that ranged from subversive activities to military actions, culminating in the massive Battle of Endor. The Empire used the term *Rebel*, never *Alliance*. [ESB, RJ, SW, SWSB]

Rebel Dream

Princess Leia's flagship for a short time. It was a Star Destroyer captured from the Imperial Navy. [CPL]

Rebellion

Another name for the war to topple the Empire that was carried on by the Alliance to Restore the Republic. It was especially used by the Imperials. [ESB, RJ, SW]

Rebels

A term applied by the Empire to supporters and members of the Alliance to Restore the Republic. [ESB, RJ, SW]

Rebel Star

This New Republic escort frigate was one of the ships that participated in the rescue of the downed *Liberator* and its crew. [DE]

Rebo, Max

An Ortolan musician, he is the leader of a jizz-wailer band. He plays keyboards on his Red Ball Jett organ. His band was signed to a lifetime contract to entertain Jabba the Hutt, but Max and his associates were able to escape when Luke Skywalker and company destroyed Jabba's sail barge. After a short stint working for Lady Valarian, Max joined the Rebellion. [GG5, RJ, SWCG, TJP]

Reboam

A sparsely populated planet located in the Hapes Cluster. [CPL]

recording rod

A long, clear, cylindrical tube used to record and play back audio and visual images. Recorded material appears as two-dimensional images on a rod's surface. Activation switches are located on each end of the rod. [SME]

Redemption scenario

Also known as the Requiem scenario, this X-wing pilot simulation training exercise is built around a no-win situation featuring the *Redemption* hospital ship and an attacking force of TIE bombers and fighters. [RS]

Redesign

An Imperial COMPNOR program, it was designed to culturally edify the galaxy's citizens so that they would function more efficiently within the Empire. [ISB, TBH]

Red Five

The comm-unit designation for Rebel pilot Luke Skywalker's X-wing fighter during the Battle of Yavin. [SW]

Red Four

The comm-unit designation for Rebel pilot John D's X-wing fighter during the Battle of Yavin. [SW]

Red Hills clan

One of the clans of the Witches of Dathomir. [CPL]

Red Leader

The comm-unit designation for veteran pilot Garven Dreis during the Battle of Yavin. When he was young, he met Anakin Skywalker and was very impressed with his skills as a pilot. Dreis was killed during the Yavin conflict.

During the Battle of Endor, Red Leader was the comm-unit designation for Rebel pilot Wedge Antilles's X-wing. He commanded the Red Wing attack element that took on the Imperial fleet and the second Death Star battle station. [RJ, SW, SWR]

Redoubtable

A Star Destroyer captured by Yevethan strongman Nil Spaar and renamed *Destiny of Yevetha*. [SOL]

Red Shadow

A bistro on the planet Taboon. The bounty hunter Zardra accidentally killed Mageye the Hutt there. [TMEC]

Red Six

The comm-unit designation for Rebel pilot Jek Porkins's X-wing fighter during the Battle of Yavin. Porkins died in the battle. [SW]

Red Squadron

One of the Alliance's X-wing fighter squadrons. Luke Skywalker was assigned to Red Squadron during the Battle of Yavin. It evolved into Rogue Squadron. [ESB, SW]

Red Terror

An elite guard of about 500 gladiator droids scattered throughout the droid-manufacturing facilities on the planet Telti. [NR]

Red Three

The comm-unit designation for Rebel pilot Biggs Darklighter's X-wing fighter during the Battle of Yavin. He was killed in the battle. [SW]

Red Two

The comm-unit designation for Rebel pilot Wedge Antilles's X-wing fighter during the Battle of Yavin. [SW]

Red Wing

One of the four main Rebel starfighter battle groups participating in the Battle of Endor. It was also the comm-unit designation for Red Leader's second in command. [RJ]

Reef Home

This Mon Calamarian floating city was destroyed in Admiral Daala's attack on Mon Calamari. [COF]

Ree-Yees

A three-eyed, goat-faced Gran from the planet Kinyen, he was a member of Jabba the Hutt's court. He was aboard the crimelord's sail barge when it exploded. [GG5, RJ, SWCG, TJP]

Reezen, Corporal

An Imperial officer, he was slightly Force-sensitive. He alerted Warlord Zsinj of Han Solo's trip to the planet Dathomir. [CPL]

Reglia, Miko

Apprentice to Jedi Knight Kyp Durron, he was a quiet and unassuming type who spent most of his time training with his lightsaber or sitting alone looking up at the stars. Twenty-one years after the Battle of Endor, he was a member of Durron's doomed starfighter squadron, the Dozen-and-Two Avengers. He was captured by the Yuuzhan Vong, invaders from beyond the edge of the galaxy, and imprisoned on the fourth planet of the Helska system. Prefect Da'Gara wanted to break Miko, to measure his willpower and discover the limits of the Jedi. Though Miko suffered greatly, when Jacen Solo arrived to rescue him and fellow prisoner Danni Quee, Miko sacrificed himself so that Jacen and Danni could escape. [VP]

Rek

A gangster who worked for Great Bogga the Hutt some 4,000 years before the Galactic Civil War. He participated in the murder of Jedi Andur Sunrider and was killed in turn by Sunrider's wife, Nomi. [TOJ]

Rekkon

A university professor from the planet Kalla, he left his post to find his nephew, a suspected activist who supposedly opposed the Corporate Sector Authority. Rekkon gathered a group of others who were searching for missing friends, relatives, and loved ones who had somehow run afoul of the Authority. As their leader, Rekkon enlisted the aid of Han Solo in the search that eventually led to a prison called Stars' End. Rekkon was killed by Torm Dadeferron. [HSE]

Relentless

This Imperial Star Destroyer was under the command of Captain Parlan following the Battle of Yavin. One of his major missions was to locate and capture the brilliant Old Republic naval officer Adar Tallon on Tatooine before Tallon could be recruited by the Rebellion. Parlan failed and was summarily executed by Lord Darth Vader. The ship was then turned over to Captain Westen, who commanded it for a time until he, too, disappointed Lord Vader. Later, under the command of Captain Dorja, the *Relentless* failed to capture Han Solo and Luke Skywalker at New Cov five years after the Battle of Endor. [DFR, OS, TM]

Reliance

This Republic command ship was helmed by Captain Vanicus some 4,000 years before the Galactic Civil War. It carried Jedi Ulic Qel-Droma on a mission to protect the Empress Teta system from the Krath offensive. [DLS]

Rell, Mother

The leader of the Singing Mountain clan of the Witches of Dathomir, she was nearly 300 years old four years after the Battle of Endor and claimed to know Jedi Master Yoda. [CPL]

Relstad, Minor

Personal assistant to Imperial Supervisor Gurdun, he skimmed funds to create the IG series of assassin droids. [TBH]

remote

An owner-programmable automaton, it can perform its primary functions without supervision but possesses no capability for independent initiative. Luke Skywalker used a remote to practice his lightsaber skills aboard the *Millennium Falcon*. [SWN]

Ren, Kybo

A pirate captain whose full name was Gir Kybo Ren-Cha, he was a short, overweight human who was distinguished by his long, dangling mustache and a small goatee. [DTV]

Rendar, Dash

A promising young student at the Imperial Academy who had a bright career ahead of him until his brother Stanton's fateful freighter accident that resulted in the destruction of the Emperor's private museum. The Empire seized all Rendar family holdings and banished all who bore the name from Coruscant and the Core Worlds. So, Dash became a mercenary. He traveled the galaxy for fun and profit, with only his state-of-the-art vessel, *Outrider*, and his droid copilot LE-BO2D9—called Leebo for short.

Tall and lean, Dash had red hair and striking green eyes. Though a rogue and a scoundrel, Dash's dazzling skills and piloting expertise often brought him into contact with the Rebel Alliance. While bringing supplies to the secret Alliance base on Hoth, Dash was forced to fight alongside the Rebels when the Imperial fleet showed up. Dash distinguished himself by flying a snowspeeder in the AT-AT attack and helping Alliance personnel escape.

After that, Dash flew with Luke Skywalker and the Bothan Blue Squad in the battle to acquire the plans for the new Death Star. Later, blaming himself for the lives lost in that mission, Dash helped Luke rescue Princess Leia from Prince Xizor's palace. A furious aerial battle over Imperial Center, involving the *Outrider*, Xizor's fighters, TIE fighters, and Rogue Squadron, ended with the destruction of Xizor's skyhook—and the apparent death of Dash Rendar and the death of Prince Xizor. [SESB, SOTE]

Rendili

This planet was the site of a space construction center where the Empire built some of its largest warships. [ISWU, SWSB]

renegade

Onetime law-abiding citizens, they turned to pillaging and thievery to survive following the collapse of social order on Coruscant. They lived among the ruins of Imperial City, competing with the Scavs for survival. [DE]

Renegade Flight

This code name referred to the Rebel pilots charged with escorting and protecting an Alliance supply convoy that carried needed supplies for the Rebel base on the planet Hoth. [ESBR]

Renegade Leader

The comm-unit designation for Commander Narra, the Alliance starfighter pilot in charge of Renegade Flight. [ESBR]

Reprieve

This Imperial Nebulon-B frigate was seized and used by Rogue Squadron as a temporary headquarters after the loss of the base at Talasea. [RS]

Republic
See Old Republic.

Republic City
This huge, sprawling metropolis, also known for a time as Galactic City, was the capital of the Old Republic on Coruscant. It was renamed Imperial City when the Empire was established. [FNU, TSW]

Repulse
This assault carrier was part of the New Republic Fifth Fleet deployed to blockade Doornik-319. [SOL]

repulsor
An antigravitational propulsion unit, also called a repulsorlift engine. It is the most widely used propulsion system in land and atmospheric vehicles. The engine produces a repulsor field that pushes against a planet's gravity, providing the thrust that makes landspeeders, airspeeders, and speeder bikes move. Repulsorlift engines are also used in starfighters and small starships as supplementary propulsion systems, for docking, and for atmospheric flight. [ESB, RJ, SW, SWSB]

repulsorlift engine
See repulsor.

Resh, Shaalir
A name used by X-wing pilot Riv Shiel on Coruscant during Rogue Squadron's undercover mission. [WG]

Resolve
This New Republic Star Destroyer was under the command of Captain Syub Snunb. [BTS]

resonance torpedo
The primary weapon used by the Sun Crusher. [COF]

restraining bolt

This small, cylindrical device fits into a special socket on the exterior of a droid to keep the droid from wandering off. It also forces the droid to respond immediately to signals produced by a handheld summoning device, a caller, keyed to a specific bolt. [SW]

Rethin Sea

The liquid metal core of the gas giant Bespin. [GG2, ZHR]

retinal print

A security device used to identify individuals by comparing retinal patterns with the prints stored in a computer database. [SME]

Return

A ritual among the survivors of Alderaan, it holds deep spiritual significance. The survivors purchase gifts for loved ones they lost when Alderaan was destroyed, then try to visit the site called the Graveyard of Alderaan to set the gifts adrift in the remains of the planet. [BW]

reversion

The act of returning to realspace from hyperspace. [SWR]

Rieekan, General Carlist

The Alliance officer in command of all Rebel ground and fleet forces in the Hoth star system. Years later, Rieekan was Chief of State Leia Organa Solo's second in command. He normally took over in her absence. He eventually became the New Republic Intelligence director. [ESB, GG3, SOL]

Rillao

A beautiful, golden-skinned Firrerreon with black-and-silver-striped hair, she had strong Force abilities and was trained by Darth Vader. She met another student of Vader's, Hethrir, fell in love with him, and became pregnant. While Hethrir embraced the dark side, Rillao remained a healer and a follower of the light side. When Hethrir destroyed her homeworld, she fled with her unborn child. She named him Tigris and raised him in solitude.

Years later, Hethrir found Rillao and Tigris. He imprisoned her on an abandoned slave freighter and made Tigris his personal slave—never revealing Tigris was his son. Rillao was rescued by Leia Organa Solo while Leia was searching for her children, who had been kidnapped by Hethrir. Leia and Rillao tracked Hethrir to the Crseih Research Station, where Rillao told Tigris the truth. Tigris saved Anakin Solo from Hethrir, and then Tigris and his mother went to Coruscant. [CS]

Rim Territories

See Inner Rim Territories; Outer Rim Territories.

Risant, Tendra

A minor functionary on Sacorria, she warned the New Republic of a threat from a huge Sacorrian fleet. Rich, tall, and strong, she was one of Lando Calrissian's marriage candidates. Her ship was the *Gentleman Caller*. [AC]

Rishi

This planet orbits the sun called Rish and is a hot, moist world of mountains, valleys, and swamps. Human and alien colonists live in the deep valleys. The native Rishii live in the high mountains. The colonists are part of a fundamentalist religious sect called the H'kig. They follow strict standards of propriety concerning clothing, length of hair, and social mores. As long as visitors do not break any of the religious laws or disturb the colonists, they are free to come and go as they please. Many underworld organizations have established bases in Rishi's cityvales, including Talon Karrde. The colonists export minerals, ores, primitive fuels, and H'kig missionaries from the planet to spread the tenets of the faith in spaceports throughout the galaxy. [BTS, BW, DFR, DFRSB, TT]

Rishii

These small avians live in tribal clusters atop the mountains of the planet Rishi. Rishii have feathered wings that allow them to fly and humanlike hands that helped them develop into primitive tool users. Each tribal cluster, or nest, is composed of a number of family groups. These nests live in peace with the neighboring nests and even with the human colonists who live in the city-vales. The Rishii have a knack for languages, which they learn by mimicking the sounds made by newcomers. They use slings to hunt and have very little interest in advanced technology. [DFRSB]

Ristel, Darsk

A name used by Corran Horn during Rogue Squadron's undercover mission to Coruscant. [WG]

Rivan, Dix

A quiet member of Rogue Squadron, he was affectionately called Dixie. He served as Rogue Five, the unit's rear guard, always watching out for his friends and ready to provide whatever aid was needed. [SESB, SOTE]

Roa

A former smuggler and blockade runner, he gave Han Solo one of his first fringe jobs and gave him his first pair of pilot's gloves. In those days Roa was a shepherd to young smugglers, teaching them the ropes with "Roa's Rules." He taught Han how to make the Kessel Run, then managed a spaceship lot for Lando Calrissian after suffering injuries in a battle at Nar Shaddaa. He later became a respectable and successful entrepreneur, owning one of the largest import-export firms serving the systems of Roonadan and Bonadan. [HG, HSR]

Roat, Antar

A name used by Wedge Antilles during Rogue Squadron's undercover mission to Coruscant. [WG]

Robida Colossus

This Ganathan steam-powered battleship towed the badly damaged *Millennium Falcon* into port after the *Falcon* barely escaped from Boba Fett. [DE2]

robot starfighter

An Imperial-designed ship introduced seven years after the Battle of Endor, the fully robotic TIE/D fighter was operated by remote computer control or onboard droid brains. [DE, DESB]

Roche system

This star system contains the Roche asteroid field. This cluster of rocks has a relatively stable configuration. The Verpine species lives among these asteroids. It was here, at the asteroid designated Research Station Shantipole, that the Verpine techs helped Admiral Ackbar design and build the B-wing starfighter. After the Battle of Endor, New Republic forces were sent here to prevent a war between the Verpine and the Barabels. [CPL, GG4, LC, RS, SFS]

rocket-jumper

Members of the Republic armed forces some 4,000 years before the Galactic Civil War who used rocket packs to make aerial attacks. [FNU]

Rodia

A planet located in the Tyrius system halfway between Gall and Coruscant. It is an industrial planet that is home to the violent Rodian species. The society is tightly controlled by the Rodian grand protector, and only the most accomplished hunters are allowed to leave the planet. [GG1, GG4, RS, SOTE, SWSB, TMEC]

Rodian

A species with multifaceted eyes, tapirlike snouts, rough, green skin, a ridge of skull spines, and long, flexible fingers that end in suction cups. These beings are natural bounty hunters. On their homeworld Rodia, they learn to hunt for sport. They accept contracts as part of grand games and contests, caring nothing for the concept of law enforcement. The bounty hunter Greedo was a Rodian. [GG1, GG4, TMEC]

Rogua

A Gamorrean, he worked as a guard for Jabba the Hutt and was often posted at the palace's main entrance beside the guard leader, Ortugg. [GG5, TJP]

Rogue Five

The comm-unit designation for Rebel pilot Dix "Dixie" Rivan's X-wing fighter after the Battle of Hoth. [SESB, SOTE]

Rogue Flight

The code name for the Rebel starfighter pilots charged with protecting evacuating forces during the Imperial assault on Hoth. [ESBR]

Rogue Four

The comm-unit designation for Rebel pilot Derek "Hobbie" Klivian's snowspeeder during the Battle of Hoth. [ESB]

Rogue Leader

The comm-unit designation for Rebel pilot Luke Skywalker's snowspeeder during the Battle of Hoth. [ESB]

Rogue Six

The comm-unit designation for Rebel pilot Wes Janson's X-wing fighter after the Battle of Hoth. [SESB, SOTE]

Rogue Squadron

The X-wing starfighter squadron that took on the original Death Star and has included such pilots as Luke Skywalker, Biggs Darklighter, and Wedge Antilles eventually became known as Rogue Squadron. It was Luke who originated the concept of a squadron without a set mission profile. Without standing orders, his "Rogue Squadron" could take on any and all missions that came its way. He combined the best pilots with the best fighters and taught them to work as a single unit.

When Luke finally resigned to spend more time with his Jedi studies, Wedge took charge of the squadron. Twelve X-wings, their pilots and astromech droids, and varied support personnel comprised Rogue Squadron.

After the Battle of Endor, the Provisional Council sent Wedge on a goodwill tour of the galaxy. Every world seeking to join the New Republic sent its best pilots and expected them to become members of Rogue Squadron. Wedge had to carefully select the twelve best-qualified candidates for his team. After a series of missions, the Rogues took part in the liberation of Coruscant. [BW, DFR, GG3, HE, HESB, KT, LC, RS, WG, XW, etc.]

Rogue Three

The comm-unit designation for Rebel pilot Wedge Antilles's snowspeeder during the Battle of Hoth. [ESB]

Rogue Two

The comm-unit designation for Rebel pilot Zev Senesca's snowspeeder during the Battle of Hoth. Later, Will Scotian took on the designation Rogue Two. [ESB, SESB, SOTE]

Roke, Boss

A human, he was in charge of prison crews in the spice mines of Kessel. [JS]

ronto

A huge but gentle pack animal used as a beast of burden by Jawas on Tatooine. Averaging about 4.25 meters tall, they can carry hundreds of kilograms of cargo but are skittish and easily frightened. [SWSE]

Roofoo

See Evazan, Dr.

Roon

A mysterious planet surrounded by a belt of moonlets, asteroids, and other cosmic debris. Spacer legends claim that the star system is filled with treasures. [DTV]

Roonadan

The fifth planet in the Bonadan system of the Corporate Sector, it is the world from which Han Solo and Fiolla of Lorrd boarded the spaceliner *Lady of Mindor.* [CSSB, HSR]

Royal Guard

See Emperor's Royal Guard.

Royal Protectors

This elite warrior group on Onderon about 4,000 years before the Galactic Civil War protected Satal Keto and Aleema. [TOJ]

Rudd, Jerris

A pilot, he was hired by Bib Fortuna to transport the Twi'lek dancers Oola and Sienn'rha from Ryloth to Tatooine. [TJP]

Rudrig

A planet in the Tion Hegemony, it contains the worldwide University of Rudrig. By the time of the New Republic, it was represented by Senator Nyxy. [BTS, HLL, NR]

ruetsavii

In Gand society, those sent to observe, examine, criticize, and chronicle the life of an individual to determine if they are worthy of individuality. [BW]

Rukh

A Noghri, he once served as one of the Emperor's Death Commandos. When Grand Admiral Thrawn returned from the Unknown Regions, he took charge of the Noghri and selected Rukh to be his personal bodyguard. Rukh was never far from the grand admiral's side, hiding in the shadows until his particular talents were called for. When the truth of how the Empire kept the Noghri in line was revealed by Princess Leia, Rukh waited for the best opportunity to take his revenge on Thrawn and assassinated him. [DFR, HE, HESB, LC]

Rula, Captain

The commander of a small fleet, she was with Han Solo when Solo first encountered a Hapan warship. [CPL]

Ruluwoor, Chertyl

A Selonian sent to the Corellian Security Force, or CorSec, for training as part of a cultural exchange program. She developed a relationship with Corran Horn that ended when they became allergic to one another. [WG]

Ruuria

This planet is home to the insectoid species called Ruurians. The world's society is made up of 143 colonies, and every Ruurian belongs to a single colony for life. [CSSB, HLL]

Ruurian

An insectoid species from the planet Ruuria, they are slightly longer than one meter. Bands of reddish brown decorate their woolly coats. Eight pairs of short limbs jut from their bodies, and each limb ends in four digits. Feathery antennae emerge from a Ruurian's head, protruding above multifaceted red eyes, a tiny mouth, and small nostrils. This alien species has three main life cycles: larva, chrysalis, and chroma-wing stages. With their great natural linguistic abilities, Ruurians often go into diplomatic and scholarly fields. [HLL]

Rwookrrorro

This Wookiee city, nestled high atop a tight ring of giant wroshyr trees, is considered one of Kashyyyk's most beautiful metropolitan centers. The city covers more than a square kilometer, with wide, straight avenues and multilevel buildings. The branches of the trees grow together to form the foundation of the city. Houses and shops are built directly into the tree trunks, with many entrances open to empty space. Only the natural climbing abilities of the Wookiees allow them to get into and out of these openings. This city served as a hiding place for Princess Leia Organa Solo while she was pregnant with the twins Jacen and Jaina. Chewbacca and other Wookiees defended the princess from a Noghri commando squad. [HE, HESB]

Rybet

A froglike species, they have large lanternlike eyes with vertical slits and long fingers with vestigal suction cups. Moruth Doole, an official of the Imperial prison on Kessel, was a Rybet. [JS]

rycrit

A cowlike animal raised by the Twi'leks on the planet Ryloth. [SWSB]

rylca

A medication created by Qlaern Hirf to combat the Krytos virus. It was synthesized from bacta components and ryll spice. [KT]

ryll

Mined on the planet Ryloth, this relatively weak form of spice is used to create a number of medicines. It is also smuggled into the Corporate Sector for illegal sale to the workers. As a recreational substance, ryll can be addictive and extremely dangerous. [SWSB]

Ryloth

A planet in the Outer Rim near Tatooine, it is home to the Twi'lek species. This dry, rocky world of shadowy valleys and mist-covered peaks has a thin but breathable atmosphere. The planet rotates in such a way that one side of the world bakes under perpetual daylight, while the other side is locked in a constant night. Most of the world's inhabitants live in this darkness. The dark side would be nothing more than frozen rock if not for the swirling currents of hot air that blow in from the sun-swept regions. These heat storms are dry twisters that provide the warmth necessary to support the dark side's ecology. The Twi'leks live within massive catacombs built directly into the rocky outcroppings and cliff sides that cover the planet's dark side. A primitive industrial world, Ryloth's inhabitants use windmills and air-spun turbines to convert the hot winds into power for the city complexes. The Twi'leks' chief export is the medicinal mineral known as ryll, which has illegal uses in addition to its legitimate ones. Twi'lek government is organized around a five-member head clan that makes all community decisions. When one member of the head clan dies, the remaining four are exiled to the day-side desert, called the Bright Lands, and a new head clan is selected. Bib Fortuna and the Jedi Knight Tott Doneeta were natives of Ryloth. [SWSB]

ryshcate

A dark brown Corellian cake that is shared as a celebration of life and is traditionally served for birthdays, anniversaries, and other momentous occasions. [RS]

sabacc

A popular electronic card game played using a deck of seventy-six chip-cards with values that change randomly in response to electronic impulses. The deck's four suits are sabers, staves, flasks, and coins. Each suit consists of cards numbered one to eleven and four ranked cards numbered twelve to fifteen. The ranked cards are the Commander, the Mistress, the Master, and the Ace. There are also sixteen face cards. A hand is dealt when the dealer presses a button on the sabacc table to send out a series of random pulses that shift the values and pictures shown on the card-chips. Through several rounds of bluffing and betting, players watch and wait for their card-chips to shift. They can lock any or all of their card-chip values by placing them in the table's interference field, which blocks the pulses and stops the card-chips from changing. To win at sabacc, a player needs a "pure sabacc" that totals exactly twenty-three, or an "idiot's array" that consists of an idiot face card (value zero), a two-value card and a three-value card—a literal twenty-three. Some players cheat by using a skifter, a card-chip rigged to change its value when the player presses the corner of the card.

Lando Calrissian and Han Solo are both fond of sabacc. In fact, they traded the *Millennium Falcon* back and forth several times over games of sabacc, and each has won and lost control of cities and planets in this manner. [CCC, ESB, HESB]

Sabodor

The owner of an exotic pet store on the planet Etti IV, he was born on the planet Rakrir. Sabodor had a short, segmented, tubular body, five pairs of limbs, two eyestalks, an olfactory cluster, and a vocal organ located in the center of his midsection. [HSE]

Sacorria

A planet located in one of the Outlier systems of the Corellian sector. It is a pleasant but secretive world with strict regulations. The Triad, a secretive council of dictators consisting of a human, a Drall, and a Selonian, ruled the planet. Fourteen years after the Battle of Endor, the Triad set in motion a plan to force the New Republic to acknowledge the Corellian sector as an independent state. The Triad was eventually stopped by the New Republic and a Bakuran task force. [AC, AS, SAC]

Sadow, Naga

A Dark Lord of the Sith, he lived 5,000 years before the Galactic Civil War. He was a member of an elite priesthood of pure Sith blood, a group that practiced the dark magic of the Sith. From his private stronghold on the moon Khar Shian, he planned to expand the Sith empire and become the new Dark Lord. He led a Sith fleet attack on Republic worlds, using illusions to boost the strength and apparent size of his fleet. Afterwards, Sadow was exiled from his homeworld for rebelling against the reigning Dark Lord and was marked as a criminal by the Republic. He eventually ended up on Yavin 4, where he conducted genetic experiments that caused the primitive Massassi warriors to mutate into horrific creatures. [DLS, FSE, GAS, TSW]

Saelt-Marae

This mysterious being, also called Yak Face, was a member of Jabba the Hutt's court. He sold information concerning Jabba's henchmen to the Hutt himself. Saelt-Marae might have been a Yarkora, a species of similar appearance that has been sighted in the Outer Rim Territories. [GG5, RJ]

Saheelindeel

A planet in the Tion Hegemony, it is home to an intelligent simianlike species. The world is technologically slow and backward, ruled by a queen who seeks to modernize her society. [HLL]

sail barge

A huge repulsorlift vehicle that operates over any flat terrain, including water, sand, and ice. [RJ, SWSB, SWVG]

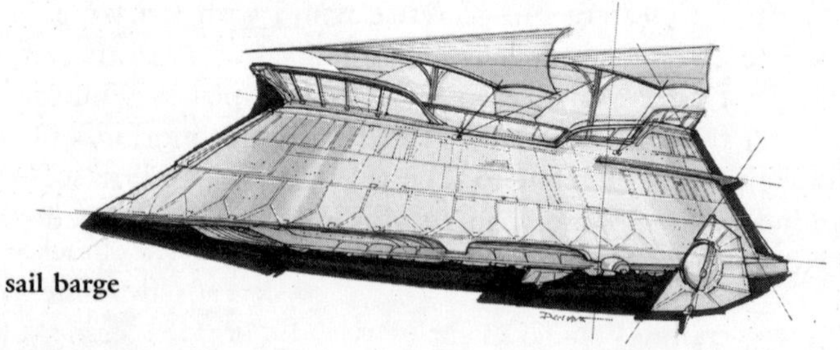

sail barge

Salculd

A Selonian, she was a member of the Hunchuzuc Den. The rebel group opposed the Overden, Selonia's central power. She jury-rigged a ship to transport Han Solo from Corellia to Selonia. [AS]

Salis D'aar

The capital city of the planet Bakura. [TAB]

Salm, Horton

A human general from Norval II, he was charged with rebuilding Rogue Squadron. Although often at odds with Rogue Leader Wedge Antilles, Salm was honorable. [RS]

Salporin

Chewbacca's childhood friend, he was one of two Wookiees charged with protecting Princess Leia Organa Solo during her stay on Kashyyyk while Grand Admiral Thrawn's Noghri Death Commandos were searching for her. He was a master of the ryyyk blade, often wielding two of the wicked-looking knives simultaneously. Salporin remained on Kashyyyk after the wanderlust gripped Chewbacca and sent him traveling across the stars. Salporin fell in love with the Wookiee maiden Gorrlyn, and the two started a life together high in Kashyyyk's trees. Unfortunately, this left him on the planet when the Imperial troops arrived. He was forced into slavery, toiling for many long years until Alliance special forces set up secret bases in the lower jungles. Salporin escaped his chains and joined the freedom fighters. With his help, and the help of other escaped Wookiees, the Alliance was able to set Kashyyyk free. Salporin died protecting Princess Leia during a Noghri attack. [HE, HESB]

Sal-Solo, Thrackan

Han Solo's first cousin, he is about six years older than Han and looks a lot like him except for his beard. Thrackan is a demanding, vindictive, and sadistic individual. When Han escaped from the *Trader's Luck* as a teenager, Thrackan returned Han to Garris Shrike. Presumed dead by the time of the New Republic, Thrackan surfaced as the Hidden Leader of the antialien Human League. He declared the Corellian sector an independent region. He was captured by a New Republic–Bakuran task force, and his Human League was defeated. [AC, PS]

Sanctuary Moon

One of the names given to the forest moon of Endor. [RJ]

sandcrawler

A huge, multistoried land vehicle that travels on giant treads. Sandcrawlers were originally brought to Tatooine long ago. When the mining venture that owned them failed, the sandcrawlers were abandoned. The Jawas, scavengers who collect all

sandcrawler

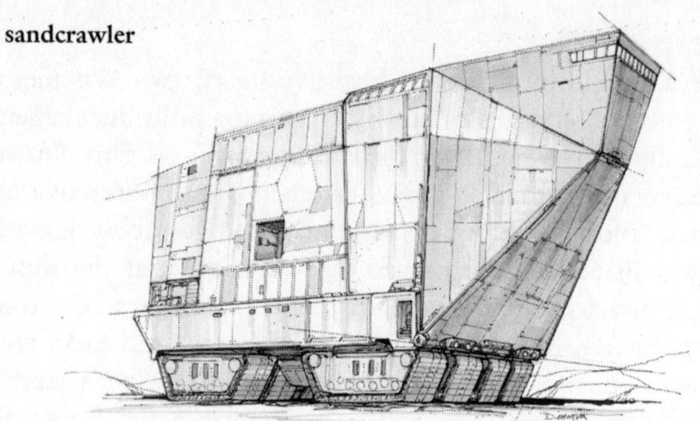

kinds of mechanical equipment and specialize in rebuilding droids, quickly claimed the vehicles.

Nearly twenty meters high, each sandcrawler houses a full Jawa clan numbering as many as several hundred individuals. The interior of each is warrenlike, a maze of sleeping and eating alcoves otherwise filled with salvaged junk, machinery, spare parts, and droids. [GG7, MTS, SWN, SWSB]

Sand People

See Tusken Raider.

sand skimmer

A one-person repulsorlift vehicle that consists of a disk to stand on and a large sail that extends from the rear. [DTV]

sandtrooper

A stormtrooper trained in desert tactics and outfitted with desert equipment. [GG1, ISB]

sandwhirl

A type of desert storm that occasionally ravages Tatooine. [SWN]

Sarcophagus

The moon of Sacorria, it is a vast graveyard. Only those burying their dead ever visit the moon. [AC]

Sarlacc

An omnivorous, multitentacled beast with needle-sharp teeth and a large beak. It lives at the bottom of a deep sand pit called the Great Pit of Carkoon, in the wastes of Tatooine's Dune Sea. It prefers live food, using its tentacles to snatch passing creatures and drag them into its mucus-coated maw. Local belief states that victims caught in the Sarlacc's gut die slow, painful deaths, as the digestive juices require one thousand years to break down food. Jabba the Hutt often used the Sarlacc as a means of eliminating opponents. The bounty hunter Boba Fett, along with a few of Jabba's henchmen, fell into the Sarlacc's pit while attempting to feed Han Solo and Luke Skywalker to the creature. Boba Fett escaped from the Great Pit of Carkoon to show up on Nar Shaddaa six years after the Battle of Endor. He claimed that the Sarlacc found him to be "somewhat indigestible." [DE, GG5, RJ, SWCG]

Sauropteroid

These intelligent aquatic reptiles from the planet Dellalt range in size from ten to fifteen meters long. They constantly swim Dellalt's oceans, keeping their heads held above the water on long, muscular necks. Their humanoid heads feature blowholes, and their hides range from light gray in color to greenish black. [HLL]

scan grid

A device used to measure and analyze the magnetic and thermal properties of metals by applying electrical surges to the metal and examining the effects with specialized sensors. Darth Vader used a scan grid to torture Han Solo on Cloud City. [ESBN]

scarab droid

A small, beetlelike droid that can be used to poison an enemy. The cloned Emperor attempted to kill Luke Skywalker with scarab droids while his dark-side knights went to New Alderaan to kidnap Jaina and Jacen Solo. [DE2]

Scardia

See Space Station Scardia.

Scardia Voyager

A golden starship used exclusively by the Prophets of the Dark Side. [MMY, PDS]

Scav

A junk trader who gathered wares from battlefields, often looting while the combat was in progress. Scavs employed armored, wheeled transports, nek battle dogs, and weapons droids to protect themselves. [DE]

Scimitar assault bomber

One of the first ships constructed under the orders of Grand Admiral Thrawn, it combined the best features of the TIE interceptor, the TIE bomber, and Alliance starfighters to create a dedicated assault bomber. With an ion-thrust sublight engine and two interlocked repulsorlift generators, the Scimitar is a very fast, very maneuverable atmospheric craft. It carries twin racks of concussion missiles beneath its wings and has two laser cannons for additional defense. [DFR, DFRSB, SWVG]

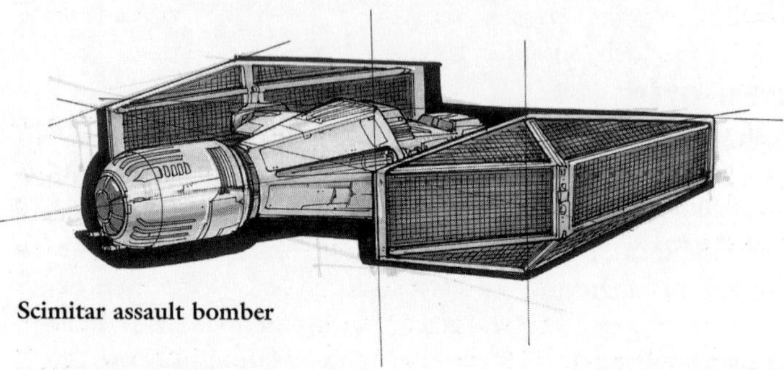

Scimitar assault bomber

scomp link access

A computer connection access port used mainly by droids to plug into database networks and locate information or perform diagnostics and maintenance. [DSTC]

Sconn, Lieutenant Davith

An Imperial officer aboard the Star Destroyer *Forger*, he was captured by the New Republic and imprisoned at the Jagg Island Detention Center. He provided Chief of State Leia Organa Solo with crucial information concerning the Yevetha. [SOL]

scout trooper

See stormtrooper.

scout walker

See All Terrain Scout Transport.

Scraf, Arvid

A human about six years younger than Luke Skywalker, he was the first inhabitant of Nam Chorios that Skywalker met when he landed on the planet. [POT]

Screed, Admiral

This Imperial officer was the Emperor's right-hand man during the early days of the Empire. He was a no-nonsense military man, easily recognizable due to the electronic patch he wore over his left eye. The droids R2-D2 and C-3PO had various encounters with Screed during this period. [DTV]

Scuppa

A starship pilot who worked for Jabba the Hutt. Scuppa betrayed his boss when they were both trapped aboard Princess Nampi's ship. He played up to the princess, agreeing to become her mate, but instead she ate him. Jabba then detonated an implant he had placed within Scuppa years before, releasing super acid that dissolved the revolting princess. [JAB]

scurrier

Scavengers found in Mos Eisley and other settlements, they scuttle from one pile of garbage to another in search of food.

Small creatures, scurriers are good at finding hiding places aboard starships and can thus be found in most spaceports. [SW, SWSE]

Scy'rrep, Evet

A legendary space bandit reputed to have robbed fifteen luxury starliners over the course of his fanciful career. Supposedly, Scy'rrep garnered millions of credits in jewels and money before he was eventually apprehended. He reportedly claimed to rob luxury ships because "that's where the credits are." Luke Skywalker's dreams of adventures among the stars were fired, in part, by an old holofilm of Scy'rrep's infamous deeds—*Galactic Bandits.* [SOTE]

seafah jewel

The source of great wealth on the planet Pydyr. Seafah jewels are formed deep in the ocean within the shells of microscopic creatures. [NR]

Second Imperium

The name given to an attempt to reestablish control of the Empire some nineteen years after the Battle of Endor. The attempt was led by four of Emperor Palpatine's most loyal personal guards. They set up a Shadow Academy wherein Dark Jedi Brakiss trained new legions of Dark Jedi and stormtroopers. They tricked many into believing that a clone of the Emperor was the Great Leader of the Second Imperium. [YJK]

sector

A cluster of star systems banded together for economic and political reasons. The Old Republic originally began the practice of combining linked star systems into sectors. At first, a sector was made up of as many star systems as it took to give it approximately fifty habitable, or already inhabited, planets. This definition became less binding as the Republic continued, and in its later days most sectors were vast and unmanageable. When the Emperor introduced his New Order, he reinvented sectors to better control and administer to his Empire. Under the Empire, a moff controlled a sector. All of the planetary governors within the sector answered to the moff, who also served as a governor of a favorite world. Each moff had a military sector group under his command, using these forces to secure the hundreds of systems within his sector. To deal with rebellious or otherwise difficult systems, the Emperor appointed grand moffs to oversee priority sectors. [ISB]

Secura, Nat

The last descendant of the planet Ryloth's great Twi'lek house, he sold many of his own people into slavery. He was controlled by Bib Fortuna, who eventually brought him to Tatooine and had his brain removed by B'omarr monks. [TJP]

Sedri

This planet covered by warm, shallow seas is home to the aquatic Sedrians and a communal intelligence of tiny polyps known as Golden Sun. Golden Sun is attuned to the Force and provides power, healing, and other benefits to the Sedrians. The Sedrians worship Golden Sun as the center of their society. Golden Sun's use of the Force creates gravitational disturbances that interfere with hyperspace travel through the region. [BGS, GG4]

Sedrian

Sleek aquatic mammals about three meters in length with a fine slick fur that covers them from head to fluke. These humanoid seals inhabit the water planet Sedri. While they can breathe air and live outside of water for brief periods of time, they prefer the water and live in underwater cities. These peaceful, reflective beings worship the living coral called Golden Sun, which also provides them with a unique source of power. [BGS, GG4]

Sedriss

Emperor Palpatine's dark-side executor, he commanded the dark-side elite warriors after the death of the first clone of the

Emperor. On the planet Byss, he discovered that the Emperor had been reborn into another clone body. He was ordered to go to Ossus to capture Luke Skywalker, but the executor was destroyed by the power of an ancient Jedi, Ood Bnar. [DE2]

See-Threepio

See C-3PO.

Sei'lar, Asyr

A graduate of the Bothan Martial Academy, she was on a mission to Coruscant when she first encountered Gavin Darklighter and Rogue Squadron. She was working with the Alien Combine, and she believed that Darklighter's nervousness and his refusal to dance with her were signs that he was bigoted. Darklighter and the Rogues were brought before the Combine, but during an attack by Imperials the Rogues demonstrated that they were no friends of the Empire. Sei'lar helped them escape. She later joined forces with the Rogues and helped them disable Coruscant's defense shield system. After the liberation of the planet, she accepted a position in Rogue Squadron and developed a serious relationship with Darklighter. [BW, KT, WG]

Selab

This planet in the Hapes Cluster is home to the trees of wisdom. The fruit of the trees is believed to greatly enhance the intelligence of those in their old age. [CPL]

Selaggis

A planet whose colony was obliterated by Warlord Zsinj's Super Star Destroyer *Iron Fist.* [CPL]

Selestrine

Leader of the Icarii, she had the gift of prophecy. Abal Karda had her decapitated for foretelling he would die in agony, then carried her head in a jeweled box. Boba Fett and Darth Vader fought over possession of her head, and Vader emerged victorious. She foretold the possible futures that stretched before the Dark Lord, then he had her totally destroyed so that the Emperor could not use her gift. [BFEE]

Selonia

One of the five inhabited worlds of the Corellian system, it is home to a hive species with thick tails, sleek fur, long faces, and needle-sharp teeth. An ancient planetary repulsor is located deep beneath the world's surface. It was used in ancient times to move the planet to its current location. [AC, AS, SAC]

Seluss

A Sullustan, he often teamed with the smuggler Jarril aboard the ship *Spicy Lady*. [NR]

Semtin, Captain Marl

An Imperial officer, he commanded the *Harrow*, a *Victory*-class Star Destroyer. He was vaporized by his own troops for acts of cowardice. [XW]

Sendo, General Harid

An aging Imperial Intelligence officer, he agreed to betray the Empire for the lucrative credits offered by the Black Sun criminal organization. He was but one of hundreds of bureaucrats on Prince Xizor's payroll. [SESB, SOTE]

Senesca, Zev

A Rebel Alliance snowspeeder pilot, he was among the defenders of Echo Base on the ice planet Hoth. He rescued Luke Skywalker and Han Solo after they spent a night on the frozen tundra. His comm-unit designation was Rogue Two. He was killed when his snowspeeder was shot down during the Battle of Hoth. [ESB, GG3]

Senex sector

A region of space ruled by an elite group of aristocratic Ancient Houses. It was mostly left alone by Palpatine's Empire, and the New Republic has had very little success influencing its leaders. [COJ]

sensor

A device that analyzes an area, gathers information, and displays its findings. Passive-mode sensors gather information from the immediate area around a ship. Scan-mode sensors send out pulses in all directions, actively gathering information in a much wider range. Search-mode sensors actively seek out information in a specific direction. Focus-mode sensors closely examine a specific portion of space. [SWRPG2]

sensor suite

All of the major systems and subsystems, both hardware and software, associated with complex sensor arrays. [HSE]

sensory plug-in

Devices that allow astromechs and other droids to interface with computers, sensors, monitors, and data systems via a direct connection. They are similar to scomp links. [SME]

sentient tank

See tank droid.

Sentinel

A cruiser in the Bakuran task force. [AS]

Sentinel

A massive guard employed to protect the reborn Emperor's citadel on the planet Byss. Their origin is unknown, but some believe that they were giant cyborgs or droids. [DE, DESB]

Serenity, Celestial

An enhanced human gambler on Crseih Research Station. [CS]

Sernpidal

The third planet in the Julevian system and the most heavily populated world of the sector. The Yuuzhan Vong destroyed the world through the use of a dovin basal, a living creature capable of focusing gravity. It pulled the smaller of the planet's two moons out of orbit and sent it crashing into the surface. Chewbacca died on this world, saving Anakin Solo and hurling him into the *Millennium Falcon* just before the moon struck. [VP]

Serpent Masters

These slavers rode winged serpents controlled by ultrasonic signals emitted from a medallion worn by the Supreme Master. R2-D2 was able to duplicate the ultrasonic signals so that Luke Skywalker could ride a serpent and defeat the Serpent Masters, freeing Tanith Shire's people from slavery. [CSW]

Serpent Master

servodriver

A powered hand tool used to tighten and loosen bolts, screws, and fasteners. It produces motion when it receives signals from a controller. [SWN]

Seswenna sector

This region of space contains the planet Eriadu. Grand Moff Tarkin developed the Tarkin Doctrine of rule by fear while he governed the Outer Rim Territories from the Seswenna sector. [DSTC, MTS]

Sette, Urlor

A large man, he helped Rogue Squadron pilot Corran Horn escape from the top secret prison *Lusankya*. [KT]

S-foil

The wing-section assembly of an X-wing starfighter. The double-layered wings spread apart for attack, forming the X that gives the craft its name. Each wing section is connected to the diagonal wing section opposite it. [RJ, SW, SWSB]

Shadow Academy

This torus-shaped space station located near the Galactic Core was built by the Second Imperium to house a training center for Dark Jedi. Covered with weaponry and concealed by a powerful cloaking device, the Shadow Academy was capable of hyperspace travel. Luke Skywalker's former student Brakiss led the academy, with help from the Nightsister Tamith Kai. When the leaders of the Second Imperium grew displeased with Brakiss's progress, they destroyed the station and killed the academy's leader. [YJK]

Shadow Chaser

A spacecraft owned by the Nightsister Garowyn, it was covered in powerful quantum armor. Luke Skywalker used the ship to escape from the Shadow Academy after he rescued Jaina and Jacen Solo and Lowbacca. [YJK]

shadow droid

Imperial attack fighters built by the reborn cloned Emperor, they were constructed around the brains of fallen Imperial fighter aces. The brains were hardwired to tactical computers and empowered by the dark side of the Force. [DE2]

Shallamar

A Barabel, she tried to kill Han Solo after accusing him of cheating at sabacc. Chewbacca stopped her. [HG]

Shana

A Mistryl Shadow Guard, she accompanied Mara Jade to Kessel to liberate the planet. [COF]

Shannador's Revenge

This *Invincible*-class capital ship operated under the banner of the Corporate Sector Authority. [HSE]

Shayoto

A Jedi, he attended the great Jedi assembly at Mount Meru some 4,000 years before the Galactic Civil War. [DLS]

Shazeen

A Sauropteroid, he helped Han Solo and his party on the planet Dellalt during their quest for the lost treasures of Xim the Despot. A veteran of many conflicts, Shazeen has a nearly black hide, notched and bitten flippers, and only one eye. [HLL]

Shiel, Riv

A Shistavanen from Uvena III, he was a member of Rogue Squadron. While on a mission to hijack a bacta convoy during the Bacta War, he was killed when his ship was destroyed by the *Corrupter*. [BW, KT, RS, WG]

Shield

This assault carrier in the New Republic's Fifth Fleet participated in the blockade of Doornik-319. [SOL]

shield

See deflector shield.

shield generator

A device that produces the power needed to create and maintain deflector shields. These shields can be focused around almost any object—a ship, building, or even parts of an entire planet—to protect it from attack. [RJ]

shieldship

This custom-designed escort vessel was built to protect ships traveling to Nkllon in the Athega system from the heat of the system's superhot sun. The mining operation Lando Calrissian set up on the planet Nkllon, the closest world to Athega's sun, required transports to bring in supplies and take mined ore off to market. He presented his design for the shieldship to the newly created Republic Engineering Corporation and commissioned it to build the vessels he envisioned.

A shieldship resembles a massive flying umbrella. A curved, 800-meter-wide dish provides protection against Athega's intense rays, while its underside contains tubes, fins, and cooling apparatus to keep the dish from melting during the trip in-system. A cylindrical, 400-meter-long pylon stretches beneath the dish. A tug at its center drives the massive shieldship. Shield-

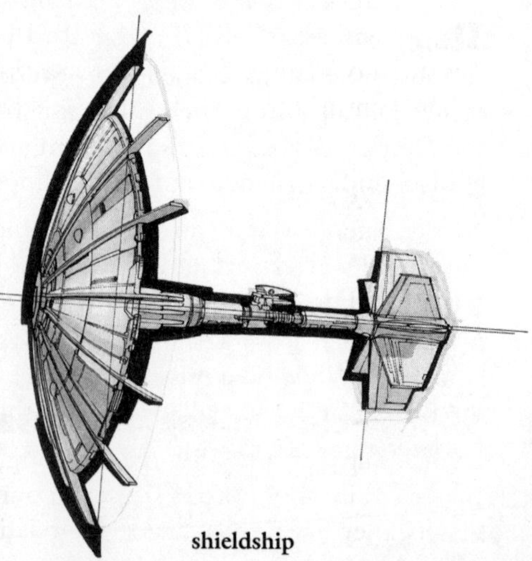

shieldship

ships require constant maintenance, and coolant and cooling gear must be replaced after every trip. [HE, HESB, LC]

Shi'ido

A humanoid species from the planet Sh'shuun. Its members have light gray skin and extremely long fingers. They are shapeshifters, capable of transforming into other creatures. [GF]

Shild, Sarn

A tall, pale sector moff before the start of the Galactic Civil War. The Hutts of Nar Shaddaa paid him to ignore their illegal operations. Bria Tharen, working for the fledgling Rebellion, traveled with him as his supposed concubine, but Shild's sexual preferences did not extend to human females. He had a secret ambition to break away from the Empire and form his own independent sector. When the ill-fated attack on the Y'Toub system failed, he was called back to face the Emperor at Imperial Center. Instead of facing Palpatine's punishment, Shild decided to escape by committing suicide. [HG]

Shire, Tanith

A supply tug operator at the starship yards of Fondor, she stole drone barges and sent them crashing to the planet's surface. The stolen barges were then salvaged by the Serpent Masters, slavers who controlled Shire's people. Luke Skywalker defeated the Serpent Masters and freed Shire's people. [CSW]

Shistavanen

An intelligent, violent species whose members are fur-covered humanoid wolves with powerful claws, sharp teeth, and glowing eyes. Hunters by nature, they are popularly called the Shistavanen Wolfmen. [GG1, GG2]

Sh'ner-class planetary assault carrier

Ovoid ships nearly 750 meters long, they carry Ssi-ruuvi Imperium invasion forces. Closer to transports than to combat vessels, they have weak shields, are relatively slow, and have little weaponry. They depend on Fw'Sen picket ships to protect them. When a target city is neutralized, the carrier lands to gather subjects for its entechment labs. The invasion fleet at Bakura contained three Sh'ner carriers. [SWVG, TAB]

shock-ball

An outdoor team sport whose object is for one team to stun the other into unconsciousness by employing a charged orb. Team members use insulated mitts to handle the orb, and scoops to fling and catch it. After the specified game length expires, the team with the most conscious members wins the match. [HLL]

Shooting Star

An Alliance frigate destroyed in a collision with another Alliance frigate, the *Endor.* [BTS]

Shoran

A Wookiee, he was a cousin of Chewbacca who died during the rescue of Han Solo from the *Pride of Yevetha.* [TT]

short-term memory enhancement

Through the use of this Force control technique, a Jedi Knight can replay recent events in his or her mind to carefully examine images and peripheral happenings. This allows the Jedi to recall a particular detail that was observed but not consciously remembered. [DFRSB]

Showolter, Captain

A member of New Republic Intelligence, he greeted Luke Skywalker and Lando Calrissian when they returned to Coruscant with disturbing news from the Corellian sector. [AS]

Shreeftut, His Potency the

The supreme leader of the Ssi-ruuvi Imperium. [TAB]

Shrike, Garris

The leader of a nomadic band of space criminals who traveled the Corellian sector aboard the *Trader's Luck*, he was a strict taskmaster. He started as a bounty hunter but wasn't patient enough for the job. He had a warped sense of humor, enjoyed gambling, and was fast on the draw. He collected orphans and trained them to steal, beg, and pick pockets to pay their way. Han Solo was one such orphan who was raised aboard the *Trader's Luck*. [PS]

Shriwirr

One of the largest of the Ssi-ruuvi customized battle cruisers, it was the lead ship in the assault on the planet Bakura. The 900-meter-long ovoid ship was under the command of Admiral Ivpikkis. Luke Skywalker single-handedly captured the vessel after the Ssi-ruuk evacuated rather than face his Force abilities in battle. [SWVG, TAB, TBSB]

Shroud

This ship once belonged to Dr. Evazan. Mammon Hoole purchased it to replace his lost *Lightrunner*. [GF]

Sh'tk'ith, Elder (Bluescale)

The leader of the Ssi-ruuvi invasion force at Bakura, he was nicknamed Bluescale as an honorific reference to his unusual bright-blue coloration. Young Dev Sibwarra killed the Elder, but he was mortally wounded in the fight. [TAB, TBSB]

Shyriiwook

The Wookiee language. It translates as "tongue of the tree people." [TBH]

Sibwarra, Dev

The young man used by the Ssi-ruuk to locate humans. While still a young boy, Dev Sibwarra and his mother fled their homeworld Chandrila to escape the Emperor's frequent Jedi purges.

Dev's mother was an apprentice Jedi, and Dev himself inherited her sensitivity to the Force. While hiding on the planet G'rho, Dev and his mother were caught up in a Ssi-ruuk raid. His mother was killed in the raid, but Dev was captured and taken to Lwhekk to serve the warlike Ssi-ruuk. When his latent Force powers began to manifest, Dev was brainwashed into helping the Ssi-ruuk; he scouted the galaxy for humans—especially Force-sensitive humans—to use in the Ssi-ruuk entechment process.

Dev was placed in the service of Firwirrung, an entechment master, who cajoled the youth into assisting in raids on human settlements. Firwirrung promised to personally entech Dev as a reward for his service, freeing him from fear and pain. Luke Skywalker released Dev from his servitude and broke the Ssi-ruuk hold on his mind. Later, Dev returned the favor by helping Luke escape from the Ssi-ruuk. Dev was mortally wounded in the final battle with the Ssi-ruuk over the planet Bakura. [TAB, TBSB]

Sidious, Darth

A robed Dark Lord of the Sith during the time of the Naboo blockade, he was the influence behind the Trade Federation assault on that planet and their attempt to kill the Jedi Knights who had been sent to end the hostilities. When the Jedi eluded him, he sent his apprentice, Darth Maul, to hunt them down. He often communicated with his Trade Federation pawns, Nute Gunray and Rune Haako, by means of an advanced holographic projector. [SWTPM]

Sidrona

The leader of the Old Republic Senate at the time of the Sith War some 4,000 years before the Galactic Civil War. [TSW]

Sienar Fleet Systems

The company that manufactured the Empire's various TIE fighters and other craft. It was once Republic Sienar Systems. [SWSB]

Sienn'rha

A young Twi'lek, she was stolen from her family by Bib Fortuna, instructed in the art of dance, and then presented as a gift to Jabba the Hutt along with Oola. In gratitude for being rescued and returned to her family by Luke Skywalker, she gave a spectacular performance for Rogue Squadron when they visited Ryloth. She offered Wedge Antilles a private dance, but he declined. [BW]

Sileen

A Mistryl Shadow Guard, she was involved in the failed transport of the Hammertong device to the Empire. [TMEC]

Silencer-7

One of the reborn cloned Emperor's Imperial World Devastators, it led the attack on Mon Calamari. It was 3,200 meters long, 1,500 meters tall, and had a crew of 25,000. The Emperor had a system built into the Devastators that allowed him to seize control of the ships. Luke Skywalker gave the control codes to R2-D2, and the droid shut down the ships during the Battle of Calamari so that New Republic forces could destroy them. [DE, DESB]

Silver Egg

Smuggling kingpin Nandreeson's private ship, it was specially outfitted for an amphibian species' needs. [NR]

Silver Speeder

The sleek racing landspeeder once owned by the bounty hunter Boba Fett. The speeder was loaded with nasty gadgets for eliminating opponents—cutting lasers, magnetic harpoons, and a terrible chain-saw shredder. [DTV]

Simoom

A great desert land on the far side of Endor's forest moon. It is inhabited by the Phlogs. [ETV]

Singing Mountain clan

A group of the Witches of Dathomir. Its members follow the light side of the Force. [CPL]

Sinidic

An aide to Drom Guldi, baron administrator of the Kelrodo-Ai gelatin mines. Sinidic was a small, nervous man with wrinkled skin. He was with his boss on a big-game hunting expedition on Hoth when the entire party was killed by the creatures they were hunting—wampa ice creatures. [DS]

Sinn, Mirith

A New Republic commander. The day the Imperials killed her husband for refusing to provide them with supplies, she swore she would fight the Empire until she died. She led the Rebel cell on Phaeda and offered Kir Kanos sanctuary with her troops. She hoped to capture Carnor Jax before Kanos could kill him, but instead she watched as Kanos killed the Imperial warlord and her second in command. She vowed to hunt Kanos down and destroy him. Soon after, she infiltrated Grappa the Hutt's organization to find evidence that he was hijacking New Republic supply ships. Her mission was discovered and Grappa gave her to the Zanibar. She was taken to their homeworld as a sacrifice, but Kanos rescued her. She later returned the favor, then joined him in a raid on the Imperial Interim Ruling Council headquarters. She was attracted to the ex-guardsman and hoped to turn him from his vengeance quest. Only time will tell if she succeeded. [CE]

Sirrakuk

A Wookiee, she is Chewbacca's niece and Lowbacca's younger sister. [YJK]

Sith

An ancient people, they were conquered by powerful dark-side magic. Over their 100,000-year history they came close to vanquishing the Jedi several times. Some 4,000 years before the

Galactic Civil War, they battled the Jedi in a conflict that was known as the Sith War. They maintained an unbroken line of chief practitioners known as Dark Lords of the Sith. Since an internal conflict 2,000 years before the Battle of Yavin, the Sith were reduced to just two members—a master and an apprentice. [DLS, TSW]

Sith Holocron

The Dark Holocron, it contains the teachings and histories of the Sith Dark Lords. Only a Dark Lord of the Sith can access the information. [DLS, TSW]

Sith War

A great conflict that occurred some 4,000 years before the Galactic Civil War, it pitted Jedi Knights against Exar Kun's dark-side forces. It ended when Kun's spirit was trapped in the ruins of Yavin 4. [TSW]

Sivrak, Lak

A hunter and scout for the Empire, he was a Shistavanen Wolfman who refused to reveal the location of a colony of Rebel sympathizers and was in turn targeted for elimination. He fled to Mos Eisley spaceport on Tatooine and eventually joined the Alliance. He died when his X-wing crashed onto the surface of Endor's forest moon during the battle against the second Death Star. [GG1, TMEC]

Sivron, Tol

One of the members of a Twi'lek head clan that was sent into the desert to die, he killed the other members of his clan and went to work for Moff Tarkin. He was set up as chief scientist and director of the Maw Installation. [COF, JS]

Skahtul

A Barabel, she led the bounty hunters who captured Luke Skywalker on the planet Kothlis. [SOTE]

Skidder, Wurth

A Jedi, he is a stubborn and fun-loving pilot with a hotshot attitude. Leia Organa Solo believes that Skidder is a hair trigger, a Jedi who only wants to add kill markers to the side of his X-wing. His intervention against the Osarians twenty-one years after the Battle of Endor cost the New Republic a year of diplomatic missions to repair the damage. [VP]

skiff

A surface utility vehicle that uses repulsors to float and move about. A single driver operates a skiff, guiding it through the use of two directional steering vanes. [RJ, SWSB]

skiff

skimmer

See landspeeder.

Skipray blastboat

Assault gunships used by the Empire. The most popular model was the Sienar Fleet Systems GAT series. Blastboats operate equally well in atmosphere and deep space. While it was designed for point missions and patrol assignments for the Imperial fleet, it never replaced the TIE fighter. Consequently, the blastboats were dumped on the open market and found their way into local defense fleets, smuggler camps, and mercenary forces. With hyperdrives and power-boosted armaments, blastboats are formidable ships. They are considered to be capital ships not because of their size, a mere twenty-five meters long, but because of the power rating of their weapons systems. Its weapons include three medium ion cannons, one twin laser cannon turret, one proton torpedo launcher, and one concussion missile launcher. [HE, HESB, ISB]

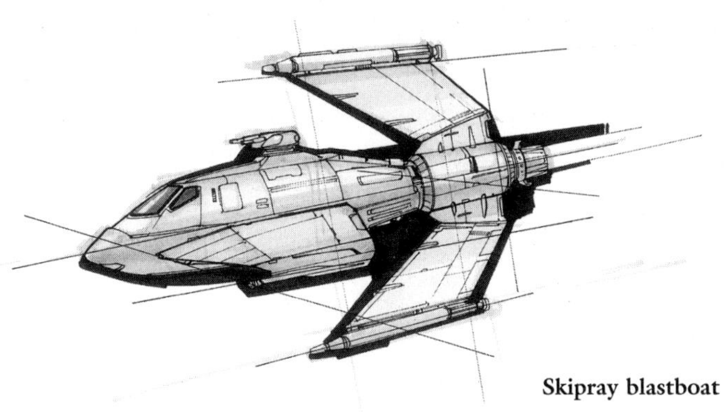

Skipray blastboat

skirtopanol

A truth serum used to interrogate prisoners. [RS]

Skorr

A bounty hunter, he nearly captured Han Solo on the planet Ord Mantell shortly after the Battle of Yavin. He died in a final battle with Han Solo when he fatally shot himself during their struggle. [CSW]

Skreej, Tamtel

The name Lando Calrissian assumed when he worked undercover in Jabba's palace as part of the plan to free Han Solo. [TJP]

Skritch

A gorm-worm, it was used to kill Jedi Andur Sunrider about 4,000 years before the Galactic Civil War. [TOJ]

Skyclaw

A ship used by the Mistryl Shadow Guards during the Hammertong mission. [TMEC]

Skyhook

The code name used to identify the secret Alliance operation that sent the *Tantive IV* to retrieve the technical readouts of the original Death Star battle station. [SWR]

skyhook

A space station in low orbit, tethered to a planetary surface. The tether is used to ferry supplies and passengers to and from the station via transport tubes. Skyhooks became a symbol of wealth and power in the skies over Imperial Center during Emperor Palpatine's reign. [SOTE]

skyhopper

See T-16 skyhopper.

Skynx

An insectoid scholar from the planet Ruuria, he accompanied Han Solo on the quest to find the lost treasures of the *Queen of Ranroon.* [HLL]

Skywalker, Anakin

Son of a slave named Shmi Skywalker, Anakin would father Luke Skywalker and Leia Organa, and become a hero of the Clone Wars and one of its youngest warriors. When the Jedi Master known as Qui-Gon Jinn first encountered the young boy on Tatooine, Anakin demonstrated an unusually high level of flying and fighting talent due to his innate ability to tap the Force. Later, as a student of Obi-Wan Kenobi, Anakin honed his use of the Force to near perfection, fighting alongside Kenobi and Bail Organa, among others. Unfortunately, the young Jedi Knight was lured to the dark side by the Emperor and transformed into the evil Darth Vader. At the end of his life he reclaimed his original identity to save his son's life. He then became one with the Force. [RJ, RJN]

Anakin Skywalker

Skywalker, Luke

Raised on the backwater world Tatooine by Owen and Beru Lars, Luke Skywalker was in his late teens when he discovered that he was the son of Anakin Skywalker, the man who became Darth Vader, that Princess Leia was his twin sister, and that a crazy old man named Ben Kenobi was really a Jedi Knight.

Obi-Wan Kenobi had taken Luke as an infant and given him to Owen and Beru Lars to raise. Kenobi was fearful that Luke's innate Force powers would be corrupted by the boy's father. But Luke passed through a mostly uneventful childhood, working on his foster parents' moisture farm and becoming a skilled T-16 skyhopper pilot. He raced through the canyons and shot womp rats with good friends such as Biggs Darklighter. He hoped to enter the Academy with Biggs, but Owen kept asking him to stay "for just one more season." When Luke was eighteen, everything changed with the arrival of two droids—R2-D2 and C-3PO.

R2-D2 had come to Tatooine to locate Obi-Wan Kenobi and present him with an important message, a hologram of a beautiful princess from Alderaan who appeared to be in terrible trouble. Luke knew Obi-Wan as Old Ben, but at Ben's house Luke learned some astounding secrets—that Obi-Wan and Luke's father had been Jedi Knights, and Luke's father had been betrayed and murdered by Darth Vader. Ben gave Luke his father's lightsaber and explained to him the basic concepts of the Force. This seemed all too much for Luke, and he was ready to abandon the old man and the princess to whatever trouble they were in. But when Luke returned home to find his aunt and uncle dead, murdered by Imperial stormtroopers, he vowed to become a Jedi Knight. With the help of Han Solo and Chewbacca the Wookiee, Luke, Obi-Wan, and the droids escaped from Tatooine and rescued Princess Leia from the Death Star, though Obi-Wan was killed by Darth Vader during the campaign. With the help of technical readouts that had been hidden within R2-D2, Luke Skywalker used the Force and fired the shot that destroyed the Death Star and ended the Battle of Yavin.

Over the next three years, Luke became a prominent member of the Rebel Alliance. He achieved the rank of commander and took charge of the X-wing Rogue Squadron. He helped stave off an Imperial attack on Hoth long enough for the base personnel to escape, then followed a vision of Obi-Wan Kenobi to the swamp planet Dagobah. There, he met a Jedi Master named Yoda. Luke learned much from the wizened old Yoda, but he cut his training short to help Leia and Han at Cloud City. This was the site of Luke's first confrontation with Darth Vader. He lost three things in this meeting: his right hand, lost to Vader's lightsaber; his own lightsaber, which had followed the severed hand into the bowels of Cloud City; and his innocence. For Vader told him that Kenobi had lied. Vader had not killed Luke's father—he *was* Luke's father. With the help of Princess Leia and Lando Calrissian, Luke barely escaped with his life.

After being fitted for a prosthetic hand, Luke had to fend off assassination attempts by Prince Xizor, head of the Black Sun criminal organization. Once Xizor was defeated, Luke traveled to Tatooine to rescue Han Solo from Jabba the Hutt. Jabba refused to hand over Solo and let them all go free, so Luke was forced to destroy the crimelord and his entire operation. He then returned to Dagobah to finish his training and discover the truth of Vader's words. He found a dying Yoda, who con-

Luke Skywalker

firmed his worst fears. "Your father he is," Yoda explained. The Jedi Master told Luke that his training was complete. All he had to do to become a full Jedi was to confront Vader a second time. Luke also learned, from Ben Kenobi's spirit form, that Leia was his sister. At Endor, Luke decided to meet Vader not in battle, but to free the good in his father and return him from the dark side. Even as the Emperor worked to corrupt Luke, Luke managed to reach the small spark of good buried deep within the armor of Vader. Anakin reemerged and sacrificed his own life to save Luke. Both Vader and the Emperor died aboard the second Death Star.

Luke Skywalker went on to play a major role in forging the New Republic from the Rebel Alliance. He helped fight the Ssi-ruuk invaders at Bakura right after the Battle of Endor. Five years later, Luke was instrumental in putting a stop to Grand Admiral Thrawn's campaign to destroy the New Republic through the use of cloned warriors and the mad Jedi Master Joruus C'baoth. During this period, Luke withstood the threats of Mara Jade and eventually convinced her to join the New Republic and allow him to help her learn to use her Force abilities. One year later, Luke decided that the best way to defeat the reborn Emperor and resolve the latest galactic conflict was by learning the Emperor's darkest secrets as his protégé. In the end, Luke was forced to fight a young clone of the Emperor, filled with the undying evil of the ancient Palpatine. The Emperor defeated Luke in lightsaber combat, but Leia came to her brother's aid. Together they destroyed the clone.

As time went on, Luke discovered others who were strong in the Force. He founded a new Jedi academy in the Great Temple of the Massassi on Yavin 4. This led to a confrontation with the spirit of an ancient Dark Lord of the Sith, Exar Kun, who killed one trainee and corrupted another before he was defeated by the combined powers of Luke's students. More than ever, Luke Skywalker dedicated himself to the ideals of the New Republic and the rebirth of the Jedi Knights.

Fifteen years after the Battle of Endor, Luke Skywalker went to the Nirauan system to rescue Mara Jade. The two discovered a secret base on a planet in the system that turned out to be Grand Admiral Thrawn's hidden headquarters—the

Hand of Thrawn. While on the planet, Jade helped Skywalker come to a realization: The Force isn't just about power, it is also about guidance. The more Skywalker tapped into it for raw power, the less he was able to hear its guidance over the noise of his own activity. It was all part of the lingering effects of his brush with the dark side. He also discovered the true feelings they shared for one another. Not only did they make a good team, they loved each other. Luke asked Mara to marry him, and she said yes. They planned to slowly turn the Jedi academy into a pre-Jedi school, from which students would graduate to train in personal one-on-one relationships with more experienced Jedi. Luke and Mara planned to travel around the New Republic with their more advanced students, teaching, mediating, and helping where they were needed.

Six years later, Luke considered reestablishing the Jedi Council to help him collect the scattering of Jedi Knights and coordinate their activities. He is one of only a few Jedi with two apprentices—he has continued instructing Jacen and Anakin Solo in the ways of the Force. [DE, DFR, ESB, HE, LC, RJ, SP, SW, VF, VP, etc.]

Skywalker, Luuke

A clone of Luke Skywalker created from cells taken from the hand Luke lost in his lightsaber duel with Darth Vader at Cloud City. The Jedi Master Joruus C'baoth, himself a clone, ordered the creation of Luuke from the Emperor's prized souvenir: sample B-2332-54. He wanted a Jedi student of his own, and if it could not be the real Skywalker, he would settle for the specially created clone. Using Luke's lost lightsaber, the one Obi-Wan Kenobi gave him back on Tatooine, which Luke lost along with his hand, the clone nearly destroyed the true Skywalker during their confrontation on Wayland. Mara Jade killed Luuke Skywalker during the fray, fulfilling the powerful last command thrust upon her years before by the dying Emperor. [LC]

Skywalker, Mara Jade

Once the Emperor's Hand, an extension of the Emperor's will who could go anywhere in the galaxy to advance his evil, this beautiful woman with the dancer's figure, green eyes, and red-gold hair was consumed by deep hatred for Luke Skywalker and bound by a blood oath to assassinate him. Ironically, she was destined to become one of the New Republic's ablest friends.

Mara Jade Skywalker

Palpatine, learning of Darth Vader's invitation to Skywalker to join him in ruling the Empire, secretly ordered Jade to kill Skywalker. As "Arica," she went undercover in Jabba's palace but was unable to complete her mission, and Skywalker went on to help destroy the Emperor. Nonetheless, she vowed to carry out the Emperor's last command.

She possessed limited Force abilities that diminished after the Emperor's death. Captured and interrogated by Ysanne Isard, director of Imperial Intelligence, she eventually escaped. For a time she hid on Phorliss where she worked as a waitress and bouncer. When bar owner Gorb Drig was killed by enforcers for Dequc and the Black Nebula, Mara decided to fulfill an earlier mission and kill Dequc.

She became an outcast, eventually ending up in the employ of smuggler Talon Karrde and rising to a post as his second in command. She and Karrde were drawn into the New Republic's battle with Grand Admiral Thrawn. When the mad Jedi clone Joruus C'baoth called Skywalker and Jade to his side, Jade killed Skywalker's clone, Luuke, and C'baoth himself, with help from Luke Skywalker and Leia Organa Solo. Thus she freed herself from the Emperor's will.

In the years that followed, Jade helped Karrde form the Smugglers' Alliance guild. She ran Karrde's operations for a time and even briefly attended Luke's Jedi academy. She left to go back to the guild and to challenge the threat posed by Imperial Admiral Daala. While undertaking daring missions with Han Solo and Lando Calrissian, it seemed that she had become romantically involved with Calrissian. This was just part of the scam, as the pair were actually on a long-term mission for Talon Karrde. During the battle with the dark-sider Kueller, she and Karrde brought several Force-inhibiting ysalamiri to the planet Almania to help Luke and Leia defeat the dark-sider.

Fifteen years after the Battle of Endor, she helped Luke Skywalker find the hidden base Hand of Thrawn. During that mission, Jade became a Jedi and the two settled their past differences, discovering that they had true feelings for one another. Skywalker proposed marriage, and Jade accepted. Six years later, she had adopted the role of Jaina Solo's master, instructing her in the ways of the Jedi. She also contracted a mysterious disease secretly created by Nom Anor's genetically manipulated spores. Though it weakened her, the disease did not stop Mara from fighting and defeating the Yuuzhan Vong warrior Yomin Carr. [DA, DFR, DFRSB, DS, HE, HESB, LC, MJ, NR, SP, SWCG, VF, VP]

Skywalker, Shmi

A slave on Tatooine, owned by the merchant Watto, she was the mother of young Anakin Skywalker. When the Jedi Master Qui-Gon Jinn was able to bargain for Anakin's freedom, he sought to do the same for Shmi, but did not succeed. [SWTPM]

Slave I

A modified *Firespray*-class patrol and attack ship owned and operated by the feared bounty hunter Boba Fett. The ship is equipped with several hidden weapons systems, interior prisoner cages, and reinforced armor plating. [DE2, DESB, ESB, MTS, SWSB]

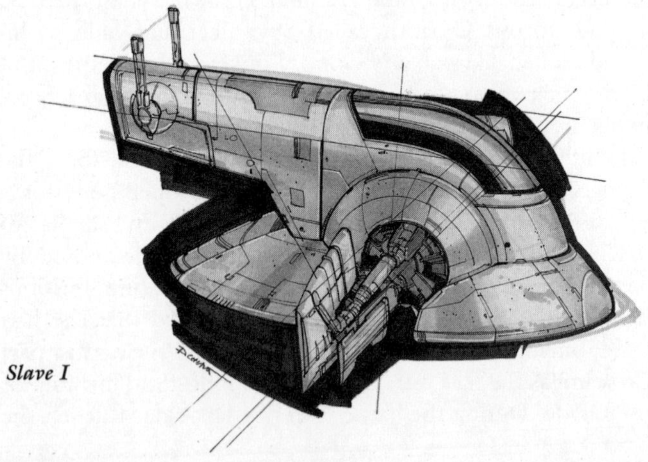

Slave I

Slave II

When Boba Fett escaped from the Sarlacc and discovered his vessel had been impounded, he selected a *Pursuer*-class patrol ship used by the Mandalorian police. *Slave II* was severely damaged above the planet Byss when Fett tried to follow the *Millennium Falcon* and smashed into a planetary shield. He left the heavy patrol cruiser in dry dock and reclaimed his original *Slave I.* [DE, DESB]

slave circuit

A mechanism that allows remote control of a starship, usually by a spaceport control tower to assist with landing, or by the ship's owner to remotely power up the ship. Fully rigged slave circuits create totally controlled vessels that require few crew members and sometimes only a single pilot. [DFR, HE, LC]

slicer

A computer hacker. [DFR, HE, LC]

Sliven

A Tusken Raider leader. His tribe raised the young Force-sensitive human named Tahiri. [JJK]

Sluis sector

This region of space contains the planets Dagobah, Bpfassh, Praesitlyn, and Sluis Van. [HE, ISWU]

Sluissi

A technologically advanced species from the planet Sluis Van, its members appear as humanoids from the waist up, though their lower bodies end in a snakelike tail. They are renowned for their expertise with starships, and the Sluis Van shipyards are considered one of the best places to go for repairs or maintenance. A longtime member of the Old Republic, the Sluissi people readily joined the New Republic after the Battle of Endor. Nothing ever seems to excite or disturb a Sluissi, for they are even-tempered and very calm. They consider themselves to be mechanical artists, and they believe that great art should not be rushed. [DFRSB]

Sluis Van

The primary planet and central star system in the Sluis sector, it contains an extensive deep-space shipyard facility considered to be the best and largest in the area. The facilities consist of dozens upon dozens of orbit docks. Shuttles constantly travel from the docks to Sluis Van and back again, ferrying spacers throughout the shipyards and to the planet it orbits. Huge armored defense platforms protect the shipyards from pirate raids and smugglers, but larger forces require the intervention of the New Republic fleet.

Grand Admiral Thrawn's first real strike against the New Republic occurred in the Sluis Van shipyards. In response to the Empire's attack on the Bpfassh system and its neighbors in the Sluis sector, the New Republic was forced to send combat starships to the area to help with relief efforts. As the ships gathered around Sluis Van, Thrawn and his armada arrived. The grand admiral hoped to capture the warships intact to increase the size of his fleet. The plan would have worked if not for the intervention of Luke Skywalker, Han Solo, and Lando Calrissian. [HE, HESB]

Smarteel

This planet was the home of Cabrool Nuum, a business associate of Jabba the Hutt. Jabba visited Nuum to sell him a captured freighter but wound up killing the crime boss, his son, and his daughter. [JAB]

smokies

These crystals, sometimes called spooks, are illegally exported from Nam Chorios to the Loronar Corporation. The Force-sensitive crystals are used as receivers in synthdroids and Needle missiles. [POT]

Smuggler's Run

This asteroid belt located near the planet Wrea serves as a hideout for hundreds of smugglers. Han Solo and Lando Calrissian spent time in Smuggler's Run early in their careers. [NR]

Snit

See McCool, Droopy.

Snitkin, Pote

A Nikto, he worked as a helmsman for Jabba the Hutt. He piloted one of Jabba's skiffs and was among those killed during Luke Skywalker's rescue of Han Solo and Princess Leia from the Hutt's vile clutches. [GG12, RJ]

Snootles, Sy

The lead singer for Max Rebo's jizz-wailing band, she has long, spindly limbs and a mouth that protrudes on a snout from her face. She and the band performed for Jabba the Hutt's court just before the crimelord died. [GG5, RJ, TJP]

Sy Snootles

Snoova

Perhaps the most vicious of the few Wookiees practicing the bounty hunter trade, he carries a death mark from his own people due to his tendency to use his climbing claws in combat. Snoova often takes on Imperial contracts and performs services for various underworld organizations. In addition to his legendary anger and bloodthirsty rage, the Wookiee is easily recognized due to the patches of black in his fur and the spacer's short flattop haircut. Chewbacca took on the identity of the infamous

Wookiee bounty hunter to avoid arrest while in Imperial City as part of a plan to rescue Princess Leia Organa from Prince Xizor. [SESB, SOTE]

snowspeeder

Incom T-47 airspeeders specially adapted to the hostile environment of the ice planet Hoth. These small, wedge-shaped airspeeders are heavily armored and highly maneuverable, redesigned to provide air protection to the Rebel base on Hoth. A forward-sitting pilot and rear-facing gunner crew each snowspeeder, employing two forward heavy laser cannons and a rear-mounted harpoon cannon. [ESB, ESBN, RSB, SWSB]

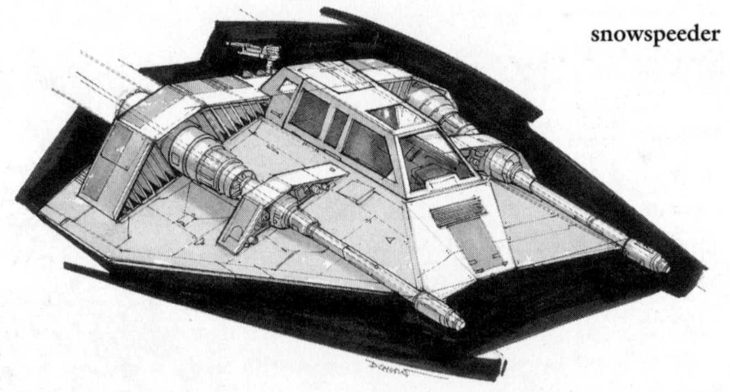

snowspeeder

snowtrooper

A specialized stormtrooper trained and equipped to operate in frozen conditions. [SWSB]

snubfighter

See X-wing starfighter.

Snunb, Captain Syub

The Sullustan commander of the New Republic escort frigate *Antares Six.* [DE]

Solo, Anakin

Anakin Solo

The youngest son of Han Solo and Leia Organa Solo. Like his mother, siblings, and uncle Luke Skywalker, Anakin is strong in the Force. He was born approximately six years after the Battle of Endor, during the events surrounding the rebirth of the Emperor. Anakin grew up on Coruscant with his older brother and sister, the twins Jacen and Jaina. Leia's assistant Winter, C-3PO, or Chewbacca watched over the children whenever the business of the New Republic called their parents away. Anakin has always been more intense and quieter than the twins. At the age of five he began to demonstrate a gift for mechanics when he took apart and reassembled computers. He started attending Luke Skywalker's Jedi academy when he was only eleven years old.

Twenty-one years after the Battle of Endor, when Anakin was fifteen years old, he became one of Luke Skywalker's two apprentices (the other is Jacen). During the Yuuzhan Vong attack on Dubrillion, Anakin served as the focal point for a complete mental joining that allowed him and his siblings, Jaina and Jacen, to act as one within the Force. This proved to be the key to defeating the extragalactic invaders in that battle. Later, he came up with the idea that also destroyed the Yuuzhan Vong's primary base on Helska 4. [CS, DE, DE2, JJK, SWCG, VP, YJK]

Solo, Berethon

A Corellian, he introduced democracy to Corellia some 300 years before the Galactic Civil War. [PS]

Solo, Dalla

A Corellian who was also known as Dalla Suul or Dalla the Black, he was an infamous murderer, kidnapper, and pirate. [PS]

Solo, Han

Many tags can be applied to the Corellian-born Han Solo: starship pilot, smuggler, pirate, Rebel hero, and "first husband" of the New Republic.

Han grew up in the Corellian star system aboard Garris Shrike's *Trader's Luck*, where he was befriended by the Wookiee known as Dewlanna. Han enrolled in the Imperial Academy, graduated with honors, became a lieutenant, and was on his way to a brilliant career in the Imperial Navy when his conscience got in the way. He was disillusioned with the Empire's treatment of nonhumans, and when he witnessed an Imperial officer use a force whip on a Wookiee, Han decided to rescue the Wookiee before he could be hurt or before he killed the officer. This earned Han a dishonorable discharge, a ban from piloting ships on Coruscant, and the lifelong gratitude of the Wookiee. After being discharged, Solo wandered the galaxy. He took on a number of unsavory jobs, and Chewbacca remained at his side—even though Han tried repeatedly to get him to leave. A Wookiee's life debt is not something taken lightly, and Chewbacca stayed until Han finally accepted his presence. They became partners and then fast friends. Han participated in a high-stakes sabacc game on Cloud City, where he won a stock light freighter, the *Millennium Falcon*, from Lando Calrissian. He went on to modify the vessel, adding armor plating, hidden compartments, and more.

Han Solo

Han became involved in the Galactic Civil War when he took on a simple transport job for two strangers in a cantina in Tatooine's Mos Eisley spaceport. Han needed to raise enough credits to repay a debt owed the crimelord Jabba the Hutt. For 17,000 credits, he agreed to ferry Ben Kenobi, Luke Skywalker, and two droids to Alderaan in the *Millennium Falcon.* In the adventures that followed, Solo helped rescue Princess Leia Organa from the depths of the Death Star and then provided covering fire for Luke's shot that destroyed the huge battle station. He became one of the heroes of Yavin and spent the next three years helping the Alliance avoid the growing number of Imperial hunters searching for the Rebel leaders.

Solo received more than enough credits from Princess Leia to pay off Jabba, but he and his longtime partner, Chewbacca, became embroiled in the Rebellion, and the debt to Jabba remained unpaid. When Solo finally decided the time was right to return to Tatooine, Jabba had already put a death mark on the Corellian's head. Bounty hunters from all over the galaxy were stalking Solo, his ship, and his Wookiee companion. On Ord Mantell, a pair of hunters came close to collecting the bounty, but Solo managed to evade them. As the finishing touches were being made to the new Rebel base on Hoth, Solo made ready to depart, but before he could get away, the Empire again caught up with the Rebels.

One notorious hunter, Boba Fett, tracked Solo to Bespin and led the Empire right to him. Encasing Solo in carbonite, Darth Vader turned the frozen hero over to Boba Fett for delivery to Jabba. Solo's friends would not give him up so easily, however, and they launched a rescue mission that destroyed Jabba and his criminal organization, and Boba Fett was lost to the Sarlacc. On his return, Solo agreed to lead the Alliance strike team to Endor's forest moon as the prelude to the Battle of Endor.

Solo possesses great skills as a pilot and sharpshooter. His reputation among other smugglers is almost as large as his own ego, and he loves to add his own boastful tales to those already in circulation. He is arrogant, extremely lucky, and graced with a sharp wit and biting sense of humor. A natural gambler, Solo is brave to a fault, impulsive, and willing to risk everything to win. Before Tatooine, Chewbacca and the *Millennium Falcon* were the only constants in his life, but he found he had gained a group to belong to, and a cause worthy of his talents. Luke Skywalker became the younger brother he never had. Princess Leia Organa became the love of his life, and their affection for each other grew over the course of their adventures. Lando Calrissian, his old friend and business associate, returned to round out the group.

During the six years following the Battle of Endor, Han Solo married Princess Leia and became the father of three children who are powerful in the Force—the twins Jacen and Jaina, and Anakin. He continued to take on missions for the New Republic in the years beyond that time. He accepted the rank of commodore and remained at the center of the action as the New Republic grew and matured. More recent events, however, have challenged Han's resolve—perhaps more than anything he has experienced in his colorful career. Chewbacca was killed in the Yuuzhan Vong assault on Sernpidal, and his death has left a void in Han's life. It remains to be seen how he will deal with his loss. [CPL, DE, DFR, ESB, HE, HG, HLL, HSE, HSR, LC, NR, PS, RD, RJ, SW, SWSB, etc.]

Solo, Jacen

The elder son of Han Solo and Leia Organa Solo, he is strong in the Force—like his mother and uncle, Luke Skywalker. He and his twin sister Jaina were born approximately five years after the Battle of Endor, during the events surrounding the return of the Empire's Grand Admiral Thrawn. He was raised in hiding, first on New Alderaan and then on the planet Anoth under the guidance of Leia's trusted aide Winter. When the twins were two, they were brought back to their parents to live on Coruscant and were cared for mostly by C-3PO and Chewbacca.

Jacen Solo

Jacen loves nature and has kept a variety of pets and plants. His Force powers manifested in strong communication abilities, particularly with other Jedi and animals. He became a student at Luke Skywalker's Jedi academy on Yavin 4 when he entered his teenage years. There, he became friends with Chewbacca's nephew, Lowbacca, and Tenel Ka, daughter of a Dathomir Witch and the prince of Hapes.

Twenty-one years after the Battle of Endor, when Jacen was sixteen years old, he became one of Luke Skywalker's two apprentices. The other is Jacen's brother, Anakin, and the two have often found themselves strongly disagreeing on the role they envision for the Jedi. Jacen helped turn the tide of the Yuuzhan Vong extragalactic invasion, going so far as to infiltrate the enemy base on Helska 4, and rescue Danni Quee. [COF, DFR, HE, JS, LC, NR, VP, YJK, etc.]

Solo, Jaina

The daughter of Han Solo and Leia Organa Solo, she is older than her twin brother Jacen by five minutes. Like her brother, she is strong in the Force. Jaina takes after her father and demonstrated a mechanical aptitude at an early age. By the time she was nine, she was helping her father repair the *Millennium Falcon*. Her impulsiveness, spirit, and self-confidence often get her into trouble—much like her father.

Jaina Solo

Jaina and her brother Jacen became students at Luke Skywalker's Jedi academy when they entered their teenage years. Along with her brother and their friends, Lowbacca and Tenel Ka, Jaina participated in many adventures as she studied to become a Jedi Knight. When she was sixteen, she requested to become Mara Jade Skywalker's apprentice and was accepted by the older woman. She helped turn the tide of the Yuuzhan Vong invasion, using her considerable piloting skills and Jedi powers to help defeat the first waves of the extragalactic menace. [COF, DFR, HE, JS, LC, NR, VP, YJK, etc.]

Solo, Princess Leia Organa

While she retains some memories of her natural mother, Leia Organa Solo was raised by viceroy and first chairman of the planet Alderaan, Bail Organa. She grew up to become a princess of Alderaan's Royal House, the youngest senator in galactic history, a Jedi Knight, chief of state of the New Republic, and a loving mother. Raised as Bail Organa's daughter, she only found out many years later that she was in fact the twin sister of Luke Skywalker and the daughter of Darth Vader.

In her days as an Imperial senator, she publicly fought for reforms and privately performed secret missions for the Rebel Alliance. On one such mission, she was sent to Tatooine to recruit Jedi Obi-Wan Kenobi to the Rebellion's cause and to deliver an important cargo. The Star Destroyer *Devastator* captured Leia and her ship, *Tantive IV,* but not before she stored the stolen technical plans for the Death Star battle station in R2-D2 and sent the droid in search of Kenobi.

As a prisoner of Vader, Leia underwent terrible interrogation sessions as the Imperials sought to discover the location of the main Rebel base and the whereabouts of the stolen technical plans. She withstood every torture they used, and when Grand Moff Tarkin threatened to destroy Alderaan if she didn't reveal the base's location, she named an abandoned base, Dantooine. But Tarkin ordered the destruction of Alderaan anyway. Leia watched in horror as the Death Star destroyed her adopted planet. Shortly thereafter, Luke Skywalker and Han Solo rescued her from the battle station and ferried her—and the technical plans—to the real Rebel base on Yavin 4. Through Leia's efforts and the help of her new companions, the first Death Star was destroyed. But the victory included losses—Obi-Wan Kenobi was killed while fighting Darth Vader.

With Alderaan gone, Luke, Han, and Chewbacca became Leia's new family, and she threw herself into her work with the Alliance. During the three years that followed the Battle of Yavin, Leia grew to love her companions. The group had numerous adventures, becoming heroes and the source of inspiration for the struggling Alliance. When Han Solo was captured and turned over to the bounty hunter Boba Fett, Leia was among the small team that went to rescue him. To facilitate the rescue attempt,

Leia contacted Prince Xizor, head of the Black Sun criminal organization, but Xizor proved more enemy than ally, and Leia and her companions had to battle and defeat him. Months later, she pretended to be the Ubese bounty hunter Boushh in order to infiltrate Jabba the Hutt's stronghold. Her identity was discovered, however, and Leia had to endure the humiliation of becoming Jabba's slave for a time. But she paid back the crimelord, strangling him with the very chain that held her captive. Han was rescued and Jabba's organization was ruined.

Leia and Han led the strike team that went to the forest moon of Endor to destroy the shield generator that protected the second Death Star. Her diplomatic skills helped her convince the native Ewoks to aid the Rebellion, thus speeding the end to the Galactic Civil War. During the Battle of Endor, Luke Skywalker revealed to Leia that she was his twin sister. The two had been separated at birth and placed in hiding by Obi-Wan Kenobi to keep them safe. It was believed that the twins, with their latent abilities in the Force, would be the last hope for the galaxy, provided they could be kept secret from the Emperor and Vader long enough to realize their potential.

Princess Leia Organa Solo

Leia became the Alliance's—and then the New Republic's—foremost ambassador. The day after the victory at Endor, she accompanied a force sent to the besieged planet Bakura. She became a member of the Provisional Council formed to establish a second Galactic Republic, and she served on the smaller Inner Council that ran the government on a day-to-day basis. Leia had to resolve her relationship with Han Solo when Prince Isolder of Hapes proposed marriage. She decided that she truly loved Han, and the two were married. While pregnant with twins, she helped foil the plans of Grand Admiral Thrawn and convinced the Noghri to renounce the Empire and join the New Republic. Between the battles, she gave birth to Jacen and Jaina, both of whom proved strong in the Force.

Shortly thereafter, pregnant again, Leia faced the crisis of the cloned Emperor and Luke's slide toward the dark side. Leia and Luke were able to overcome the clone's dark-side powers, and they gained the Jedi Holocron in the process. Leia's third child was born, and she named him Anakin. When Luke left to start his Jedi academy, Leia agreed to become minister of state for the New Republic. Then, when Mon Mothma grew increasingly ill, she urged Leia to replace her as chief of state. Even after Mon Mothma was healed, Leia remained in place as leader of the New Republic, a position she held until she could no longer deal with the political infighting. Even after leaving office, though, Leia continued to act as one of the New Republic's most influential representatives, a position that led her to encounter the charismatic Yuuzhan Vong leader Nom Anor and continues to place her on the front lines of conflict. [CPL, DE, DFR, ESB, HE, LC, RJ, SOTE, SW, TAB, etc.]

Solusar, Kam

Apprenticed to his father, the great Jedi Master Ranik Solusar, Kam Solusar was a hard-edged man who fled the Empire after his father was slaughtered in Darth Vader's Jedi Purge. When Kam returned from his period of isolation, he was captured by dark-side Jedi and turned to the dark side of the Force. Luke Skywalker met Solusar on Nespis VIII and persuaded him to renounce the dark side. Solusar then joined Skywalker's Jedi students in defeating the spirit of Exar Kun. [DA, DE2, DS]

Song of War

Prince Isolder's Hapan Battle Dragon spacecraft. [CPL]

Sonniod

A former smuggler and bootlegger, he was an acquaintance of Han Solo and Chewbacca the Wookiee. When Solo last met up with the compact, gray-haired little man, Sonniod was running a legitimate holofeature loan service. [HSR]

Sonsen, Jenica

The chief operations officer at Centerpoint Station, she was left in command after the chief executive ordered a complete evacuation. [SAC]

Sookcool, Avaro

A Rodian, he was Lando Calrissian's contact in the Black Sun criminal organization. He manages the modest Flip of the Credit Casino in Equator City on the planet Rodia. The casino is a front for Black Sun. Sookcool coordinates most Black Sun operations on the planet. He reported directly to Vigo Clezo, but he also maintained direct ties to Prince Xizor. Sookcool, the uncle of the late bounty hunter Greedo, agreed to set up a meeting between Princess Leia and Black Sun—despite the fact that it was Han Solo who put an end to his nephew. [SESB, SOTE]

Sorannan, Major Sil

A former officer in the Imperial Black Sword Command, he betrayed Nil Spaar and the Yevethan fleet, helping the New Republic emerge victorious. [TT]

Soul Tree

Special trees planted at the time an Ewok baby is born. Ewoks feel a great kinship toward their individual Soul Tree. They care for it throughout their lives. When an Ewok dies, a hood is tied around the trunk of his or her Soul Tree to signify the sad event. [ETV]

Sovereign

A Star Destroyer in Warlord Zsinj's fleet. [CPL]

Sovereign Protectors

See Imperial Sovereign Protectors.

Spaar, Nil

A tall, slender humanoid with a mandrill-like face and concealed claws on each wrist, he was a bigoted Yevethan and the viceroy of the Duskhan League. He pretended to engage in diplomatic relations with Chief of State Leia Organa Solo, but all the while he planned to declare war on the New Republic. Xenophobic, he began the Yevethan purge to wipe out alien "vermin" and secure new places to start Yevethan colonies. He destroyed the Koornacht Cluster settlements of New Brigia and Polneye, slaughtering their inhabitants. Spaar attacked New Republic forces when they attempted to blockade the Yevethan staging area of Doornik-319. Spaar kidnapped Han Solo when he arrived to take command of the New Republic's Fifth Fleet and almost killed him. After the Yevethan defeat at the Battle of N'zoth, Spaar was killed by former members of the Black Sword Command. They sabotaged his ships and helped the New Republic's fleet defeat the Yevethan forces. [BTS, SOL, TT]

Spaarti cloning cylinder

A device used to grow human clones, it was a remnant of the terrible Clone Wars. Clones grown in less than a year's time usually suffered from clone madness. The Emperor kept a large number of Spaarti cloning cylinders hidden in his private storehouses scattered around the galaxy. Grand Admiral Thrawn discovered one storehouse on the planet Wayland, and he used the cylinders to grow clone soldiers and crews to fill his forces. By using the ysalamiri to form bubbles devoid of the Force around the Spaarti cylinders, Thrawn was able to grow perfect clones in as little as twenty days. [DFR, HE, LC]

space barge

A heavy-duty short-range vessel with a powerful engine and large cargo bays. Space barges move goods quickly and efficiently among larger hyperdrive-equipped cargo ships, orbiting storage holds, and planetary spaceports. They are also used to unload massive container ships that cannot make planetary landings. [SWSB]

spacer
Someone who makes a living by traveling the space lanes. [SWN]

Spacers' Garage
A huge starship repair facility on Nar Shaddaa, owned and operated by Shug Ninx, an old friend of Han Solo. [DE]

space slug
A colossal wormlike creature that lives within asteroids. Its metabolism allows it to survive in airless vacuums and subsist on minerals. This strange creature grows to lengths as great as 900 meters. Like mynocks, space slugs are silicon-based life-forms. They prey upon mynocks, as well as anything else moving around asteroids. Space slug flesh has a number of commercial uses, and some spacers make a living hunting these creatures. They reproduce through fission, splitting into two separate creatures. [ESB, ISWU, SWSB]

Space Station Kwenn
Considered to be the last fuel and supply stop before entering the Outer Rim Territories, the citylike station features everything the weary spacer might need after a long voyage. The station was built atop an extensive docking platform consisting of scores of modular space docks and docking bays. Still farther below the station is the massive dry-dock gridwork, used for parking, overhauling, refitting, or otherwise repairing capital-class starships. Jabba the Hutt acquired Salacious Crumb at the station's Royal K Casino. [SF, TM]

Space Station Scardia
The cube-shaped headquarters for the Prophets of the Dark Side. [LCJ, PDS]

spacing
A form of execution that consists of casting the victim into space without any protective gear. [HLL]

speeder

See airspeeder; landspeeder; snowspeeder.

speeder bike

A small, one-person repulsor land vehicle. Speeder bikes move at incredible rates of speed, making them perfect for use as scout and reconnaissance craft. Four directional steering vanes extend from the front of a speeder bike on twin outriggers, providing a high degree of maneuverability. The pilot directs the bike with elevation and maneuver controls located in the handgrips. Two rocker-pivoted foot pads regulate speed, while controls at the forward end of the saddle handle parking, weaponry, communications, and energy recharging. Military speeder bikes, like those used by the Empire's scout troopers, have armor plating and are armed with blaster cannons. [ISB, RJ, SWSB, SWVG]

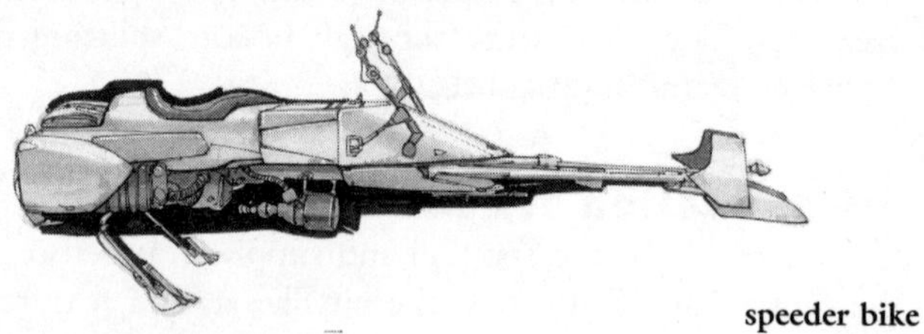

speeder bike

speeder transport

Large shuttlecraft used by the New Republic to move V-wing airspeeders from capital ships to launch points in a planet's atmosphere. [DE]

Spero

Once the chief gardener of the Royal House of Alderaan and a friend of Princess Leia Organa, this ancient Ho'Din supplied her with information about Black Sun and Prince Xizor. Spero owned a plant shop in the Southern Underground section of Imperial Center. He earned the title of master gardener for developing a strain of yellow fungus used throughout the galaxy as a decoration and to convert noxious fumes into oxygen. [SESB, SOTE]

spice

Any of a variety of drugs, in particular the glitterstim spice mined on the planet Kessel. It is a highly taxed and controlled substance, and a popular commodity for smugglers. Spice has a number of legitimate applications, but it is also dangerous and highly addictive. [JS, SW, SWSB, TBH]

Spicy Lady

This distinctive ship is a cross between a stock light freighter and an A-wing fighter. It was owned by the smuggler Jarril. Lando Calrissian found Jarril murdered aboard the drifting vessel. [NR]

Spince, Mako

A grizzled Corellian smuggler about ten years older than Han Solo. He met Han at the Imperial Academy at Carida. The son of an Imperial senator, Spince just wanted to have fun at the Academy. He was expelled after accidentally blowing up Carida's moon when a prank got out of hand. He prospered for a while as a smuggler, but eventually settled down as a traffic controller at the spaceport moon Nar Shaddaa. [DE, HG]

Spirit Tree

Considered to be the original tree of the forest on Endor's forest moon. The Ewoks believe that all life started with this tree, and that all life must eventually return to it. [ETV]

Spore

A gene-spliced sentient creation of the Ithorians, it was made from vesuvague and bafforr trees. The creature turned evil, and the Ithorians buried it in an asteroid belt. It was able to possess bodies and send out tentacles from a possessed body to take control of even more. It was stopped when the Star Destroyer carrying it was exposed to vacuum by space slugs. [GF]

Sprax

A Nalroni Vigo, he controlled a number of criminal businesses dealing with galactic trade for the Black Sun organization. His shipping network stretched from the Outer Rim Territories to the Core Worlds and consisted of loosely connected bands of smugglers, black-market dealers, and shipjackers. During the time of the Galactic Civil War, Sprax made a small fortune trading in weapons, medical supplies, and much-needed spare parts, often favoring the Alliance over the Empire—on Prince Xizor's orders. [SESB, SOTE]

Spray of Tynna

The name used by a short, bipedal skip tracer employed by Interstellar Collections Ltd. A member of a species of intelligent sea otters, Spray was actually Odumin, a powerful and influential territorial sector manager for the Corporate Sector Authority. [HSR]

Spuma

This planet is where New Republic Intelligence first noticed increased trooper recruitment by Imperial warlord Grand Admiral Harrsk's fleet about eight years after the Battle of Endor. [COJ]

Squab

The star orbited by Skor II, home planet of the Squibs. [GG4]

Squeak

A Tin-Tin Dwarf, he worked for Big Bunji as a messenger and gofer. [HSE]

Squib

Small, furry bipeds with tufted ears, large eyes, short muzzles, and black noses. Their fur ranges in color from deep red to brilliant blue. From the world of Skor II, these fearless nomads roam the galaxy in reclamation ships, using tractor beams to salvage junk—which they consider treasure. The Squibs have an intense rivalry with the Ugors, as both try to claim salvage before the other. Squibs are overconfident and curious, sometimes even overbearing and uppity. They love to haggle, a practice that they have turned into an art form. The more complicated and convoluted a deal a Squib can strike, the better they like it. [GG4, SH]

Squid Head

See Quarren.

Ssi-ruuk

A species of warm-blooded saurians from beyond the Empire's borders. Adult Ssi-ruuk average about two meters tall. Huge, muscular tails extend from their massive bodies, and short, well-muscled upper limbs end in three-clawed, prehensile digits that allow them to make use of tools and weapons. Their beaked muzzles contain knife-sharp teeth.

The patterns and colors of scales differ greatly from individual to individual, though one color often dominates a single Ssi-ruuk's body. The Ssi-ruuk wear no clothing—they find the concept amusing—but do wear pouches and belts to carry necessary equipment. Their language consists of a complex series of honks, whistles, and musical notes. The Bakurans call the saurians Fluties because of the musical sounds they emit.

A rigid code of honor helped shape Ssi-ruuk society. An ancient pictograph known as the G'nnoch described the Ssi-ruuk's place in the universe. It stressed that they were superior to all other beings. Others were considered little better than cattle: useful, but not equal to the Ssi-ruuk.

Even among the Ssi-ruuk, not all are created equal. A caste system determines the status of each Ssi-ruuk clan. Those with sapphire-blue scales are of the highest caste, holding the most positions on the Elders' Council. Gold-scaled Ssi-ruuk make up the religious caste. Those with russet scales comprise the bulk of the military caste. The emerald-green scales denote the lowest caste in Ssi-ruuk society—the lowest level to still possess any measure of honor and prestige. Dark-brown Ssi-ruuk are considered soiled and are thus shunned, while the rare black-scaled saurians are trained as assassins and bodyguards for the Ssi-ruuk leaders.

Ssi-ruuk

As resources dwindled on the Ssi-ruuk home-world Lwhekk, the saurians developed a process called entechment to tap the life energy of the P'w'eck as a power source. The P'w'eck, another saurian species that also developed on Lwhekk, were dominated by the Ssi-ruuk and turned into "energy slaves." Some years before the Battle of Endor the Ssi-ruuk began an expansionist policy and eventually reached the limits of Imperial space.

Emperor Palpatine made contact with the Ssi-ruuk during a Force meditation exercise. He craved their entechment technology and was willing to sacrifice his subjects to possess it. So when the Ssi-ruuk began to raid human settlements for energy slaves, the Emperor blamed the raids on the Rebels.

As the Battle of Endor drew to a close, the Ssi-ruuk attacked the Empire-controlled world Bakura. The Imperial forces stationed in the region were able to repel the invaders' initial assault, but they knew they could not hold off the aliens forever. A distress call was sent out, and the Alliance decided to send help. The Alliance task force, under the command of Luke Skywalker, established a truce with the Imperial representatives and eventually helped defeat the invaders. [TAB, TBSB]

ST 321

The comm unit designation for Darth Vader's personal *Lambda*-class shuttle. [RJ]

Stalwart

This New Republic cruiser was part of the Fifth Fleet that blockaded Doornik-319. [SOL]

Standard Time Part

The basic unit used to measure time throughout the Empire. [SWN]

stang

An Alderaanian expletive. [SME]

Stanz, Captain

A Bothan, he owned and operated the freighter *Freebird*. [BTS]

star cruiser

A class of capital ship. [ESB, RJ, SW]

Star Destroyer

This colossal, wedge-shaped capital starship was the core of the Imperial Navy. There are four classes of Star Destroyers: the *Victory*-class that appeared near the end of the Clone Wars, the versatile *Imperial*-class, the *Super*-class, and the *Eclipse*-class.

The *Imperial*-class Star Destroyer is 1.6 kilometers long and bristles with offensive weaponry. Turbolasers and ion cannon batteries create wide-ranging fields of fire around the wedge, and a full wing of seventy-two TIE starfighters are carried within its docking bays. Defensive shield generators, tractor beam projectors, and sophisticated sensor arrays are standard, and they carry drop ships, landing barges, shuttles, repair vessels, deep-space probes, an assortment of specialized droids, field artillery weapons, walkers, ground assault vehicles, modular building units, soldiers, and Imperial stormtroopers. Lira Wessex, daughter of famed engineer Walex Blissex, was the designer of the Imperial model.

The *Super*-class Star Destroyer is eight kilometers long and is primarily used as a command ship, guiding fleets and serving as headquarters from which to conduct planetary assaults and

Imperial-class Star Destroyer

space battles. The more powerful *Eclipse*-class Star Destroyer was built to serve as the reborn Emperor's flagship six years after the Battle of Endor. This solid-black model is sixteen kilometers long and covered with weapons and defenses.

The Empire built more than 25,000 Star Destroyers. Half of them were kept in reserve in the Galactic Core to protect key military and industrial sites, though they could be deployed anywhere at short notice. [DE, DESB, ISB, SWN, SWSB, SWVG]

Starflare, Wynssa

A holodrama star on Imperial Center, her true name was Syal Antilles, sister to Rogue Squadron member Wedge Antilles. She met and fell in love with Soontir Fel, and the two were married. When she disappeared, Fel joined the New Republic in a belief that Rogue Squadron could help him find her. [XW]

Star Galleon

A 300-meter-long Imperial vessel designed to combine the cargo space of a bulk freighter with the armament of a combat starship. The interior hampers boarding parties, with fortress-like emplacements in the corridors, 300 troopers, force fields, and heavy blast doors, and it takes a much larger force to physically take over the ship. The cargo hold pod, located in the very center of the ship, has an added level of protection. It can be jettisoned from the vessel, its computers automatically activating a small hyperdrive to send it on a prearranged lightspeed jump. [DFRSB, ISB]

Star Home

A unique transport vessel designed more than 4,000 years before the Galactic Civil War for the queen mother of the Hapes Cluster. It was a duplicate of the queen mother's castle on the planet Hapes. This spaceworthy vessel featured towers capped with crystal domes that looked out into space, and great gardens filled the upper courtyard levels. [CPL, SWVG]

Starlight Intruder

A hot-rod transport built for smuggling runs by Salla Zend and equipped with a hyperdrive and immense cargo holds. [DE, DESB, SWVG]

Star Runner

A star cruiser owned and operated by Kea Moll. [DTV]

Starry Ice

This freighter owned by Talon Karrde was used to carry weapons and munitions for Rogue Squadron to a rendezvous point at the Graveyard of Alderaan. [BW]

Star Saber

An experimental attack vessel built 4,000 years before the Galactic Civil War. It was equipped with wing cannons. [DLS]

Stars' End

A secret Corporate Sector Authority penal colony on the planet Mytus VII. Its name refers to the location of the Mytus star system, which sits at the end of a faint wisp of stars at the edge of Corporate Sector space. [HSE]

Starstorm I

The starship that Dark Lord of the Sith Exar Kun used to escape with ancient scrolls given to him by the spirit of Freedon Nadd some 4,000 years before the Galactic Civil War. [DLS, TOJ, TSW]

Startide

A Mon Calamari battle cruiser. [DA]

Steadfast

A New Republic vessel commanded by Captain Oolas. It surveyed the wreckage of the Imperial Star Destroyer *Gnisnal.* [BTS]

Stenness Node

A group of three star systems containing seven mining worlds. They were discovered 4,000 years before the Galactic Civil War. Twenty-five humanoid species collectively referred to as Nessies inhabit the region. At the time of the Sith War, the node was controlled by Great Bogga the Hutt. Mageye the Hutt controlled the area during the Galactic Civil War until he was killed by the bounty hunter Zardra. [DE, TMEC, TOJ]

stim-shot

A major component of a medpac, it is a stimulant administered by a pneumatic dispenser. [ESBR]

Stinger

This modified Surronian assault ship was a sleek craft given to Guri by her master, Prince Xizor. The vessel featured powerful engines and impressive weapon emplacements both fore and amidships. [SESB, SOTE, SWVG]

stock light freighter

This Corellian-built vessel is among the most common small trading ships operating in the known galaxy. At one time, this class of ship was the backbone of intergalactic trade, but many companies turned to larger bulk freighters and container ships to move their wares. While these vessels come in a variety of shapes and sizes, all are built around the basic design of a command pod, storage holds, and engines. The *Millennium Falcon* is a modified stock light freighter, a model YT-1300 Corellian transport. [SWSB]

Stokhli spray stick

This long-range stun weapon was developed by the Stokhli species of the planet Manress. It releases a fine, electrically charged mist up to 200 meters from the nozzle atop the stick. Originally developed as a tool for hunters, Stokhli spray sticks gained popularity as both defensive and offensive personal weapons. [HE, HESB]

Stone Needle

A rocky spire in Beggar's Canyon on Tatooine. It has an oval hole near the top and serves as an obstacle during speeder and swoop races. [SWR, TJP]

Stonn, Li

A name used by Luke Skywalker during his travels on Teyr and Atzerri. [SOL]

Stopa, Kroddok

An Obroan Institute archaeologist, he headed up the expedition to Qella to recover biological samples. He was killed in an avalanche on Maltha Obex. [SOL]

Storm

The personal starfighter of Prince Isolder of Hapes. It was just over seven meters long. [CPL, SWVG]

stormtrooper

A member of the Imperial shock troops totally loyal to the Emperor. Stormtroopers wore white-and-black armored spacesuits over black body gloves. The armored spacesuits provided limited protection against blaster fire. The eighteen pieces that made up the outer shell created an enclosed, self-sustaining environment. Stormtroopers deployed to neutralize resistance to the New Order rode aboard Imperial vessels to serve as first-strike forces and to make sure lower officers remained loyal to the Emperor. Stormtroopers could not be bribed, seduced, or blackmailed into betraying their Emperor.

They lived in a totally disciplined, totally militaristic world where obedience was paramount and the will of the Emperor was absolute.

stormtrooper

In addition to the main stormtrooper legions, a number of special units were assembled to operate on the varied worlds of the Empire. To deal with problems on ice-covered worlds, cold assault troopers, or snowtroopers, were equipped with terrain-grip boots and breath masks. Second only to the Royal Guard, the elite zero-g stormtroopers, or spacetroopers, were trained to operate exclusively in outer space. These troopers wore full body armor capable of withstanding the rigors of hard vacuum. This armor functioned as a personal spacecraft and attack vehicle, complete with sensor arrays, magnetic couplers for adhering to ships, repulsor-lift propulsion units, and a wide assortment of weaponry. Lightly armored, highly mobile scout troopers used speeder bikes to patrol perimeters, perform reconnaissance missions, and scout enemy locations. To assist them when traveling at high speeds, scout troopers wore specialized helmets equipped with built-in macrobinocular viewplates and sensor arrays. These fed into computers that analyzed terrain features instantaneously.

Other stormtrooper types included aquatic assault troopers (seatroopers), storm commandos, radtroopers, and self-contained weapons platforms called Dark Troopers. [DF, ESB, HE, HESB, ISB, RJ, SW, SWSB]

Streen

A hermit and cloud prospector, he lived in the abandoned city Tibannopolis on Bespin. Force-sensitive, he could predict gas eruptions within the planet's cloud layers and hear the thoughts of those around him. Luke Skywalker located him and invited him to join his Jedi academy. Streen was influenced by the spirit of dark Jedi Exar Kun, but later helped the other Jedi students destroy Kun's spirit forever. Luke taught him to overcome his need for isolation. His Force affinity is with the wind and weather. [COF, DA, JAL, JS]

Strike-class medium cruiser

Introduced near the end of the Galactic Civil War, this 450-meter-long Imperial star cruiser served an important role in Grand Admiral Thrawn's fleet. Thanks to its modular design, the interior can be configured to accommodate specific mission profiles. Some have room to carry a ground assault company; others have been modified to transport a squadron of TIE fighters. Other configurations include prefab garrison deployers, troop transports, and planet assault cruisers. [HESB, ISB]

Sturm

One of two domesticated vornskrs used by smuggler Talon Karrde as pets and guards. [DFR, HE, HESB, LC]

Subjugator

This *Victory*-class Star Destroyer under the command of Captain Kolaff was targeted by a Rebel Mon Calamari strike force code-named Task Force Starfall. The task force, made up of Mon Cal star cruisers, engaged the Star Destroyer and managed to destroy it. [SF]

sublight drive

An engine that moves starships through realspace by producing charged particles through a fusion reaction that hurls ships forward when released. Starships with sunlight drives use repulsorlifts for travel within a planet's atmosphere. [SWSB]

Sulamar, General

An Imperial officer, he plotted with Durga the Hutt to unleash a new superweapon on the New Republic. He and Durga died when the weapon failed. [DS]

Sullust

A volcanic world in a star system of the same name. Its vast network of underground caves provide the only habitable areas. The native Sullustans are jowled, mouse-eared humanoids with large round eyes. They built beautiful underground cities and are highly valued as pilots and navigators due to their instinctive ability to remember any path previously traveled. The planet is the headquarters of the vast intergalactic conglomerate SoroSuub Corporation. This leading mineral-processing company has subdivisions that handle energy, space mining, food packaging, and technological products. During the height of the Galactic Civil War, SoroSuub Corporation dissolved the planetary government and proclaimed the tenets of the New Order as the ruling authority for the world.

Late in the war, Sullust leaders voted to secede from the Empire and join the Alliance. The Rebel fleet gathered near Sullust just prior to the Battle of Endor. The Sullustan Nien Nunb became Lando Calrissian's copilot aboard the *Millennium Falcon* for the battle. Nunb's sister, Aril, later served as the executive officer for Rogue Squadron. [COJ, DESB, RJ, RJN, RS, SWSB]

Sulon

The moon of the planet Sullust. It was the home of Alliance agent Kyle Katarn. [DF]

Sun Crusher

An Imperial superweapon prototype designed at the Maw Installation. Slightly larger than a starfighter, its resonance torpedoes were powerful enough to destroy a star. The slender, cone-shaped vessel was equipped with laser cannons and shimmering quantum-crystalline armor that made it nearly impervious to damage. Han Solo and his companions, imprisoned at the Maw Installation, managed to break free and escape with the vessel, delivering it to Coruscant. Kyp Durron stole the Sun Crusher and demolished several Imperial worlds before the superweapon was destroyed at the Battle of the Maw in a black hole. [COF, DA, JS]

Sunfighter Franchise

One of the false names used by Han Solo to register the *Millennium Falcon* during adventures in the Corporate Sector Authority. [HSE]

SunGem

A courier ship that Jedi Master Arca Jeth owned some 4,000 years before the Galactic Civil War. The ship contained a training facility for his Jedi students. [TOJ]

sungwa

Massive doglike creatures, these wolf-weasels are native to the bog moon Bodgen. [DTV]

Sunrider, Andur

A Jedi Knight, he was killed some 4,000 years before the Galactic Civil War in a senseless battle with petty gangsters at the Stenness hyperspace terminal. He was survived by his wife, Nomi, and their daughter, Vima. [TOJ]

Sunrider, Nomi

The wife of Jedi Andur Sunrider, she lived some 4,000 years before the Galactic Civil War and became one of the great Jedi Knights of her time. When her husband was killed by Great Bogga the Hutt's henchmen, she used his lightsaber to defend herself and defeat the gangsters. Jedi Master Thon convinced her to undergo Jedi training, and she apprenticed under Master Vodo-Siosk Baas. She joined a team of Jedi on a mission to Onderon to rescue Master Arca Jeth and his students from dark-siders. She developed feelings for the Jedi Ulic Qel-Droma and helped him lead a joint peacekeeping force of the Galactic Republic and Jedi Knights to defeat the dark-side Krath cult. She had to blind Ulic to the Force after he killed his own brother. Later, she became a spokesperson for the Jedi and a great Jedi leader. [DA, DLS, FNU, TOJ, TOJR, TSW]

Sunrider, Vima

The daughter of Nomi and Andur Sunrider, she lived some 4,000 years before the Galactic Civil War. Ten years after the Sith War, she sought out Ulic Qel-Droma at his hiding place on the ice planet Rhen Var. She convinced the now-powerless Ulic to train her, as her mother was too busy with Jedi affairs to help her. Through that training she helped Ulic finally find redemption in the Force. [TOJ, TOJR, TSW]

Super-class Star Destroyer

See Star Destroyer.

Suppoon, Gaar

An alien criminal, he was visited by Jabba the Hutt for business purposes. He tried to make sure Jabba didn't leave his planet alive, but the Hutt reversed the situation and Suppoon died. [JAB]

Supreme Prophet

See Kadann.

Suprosa

This unescorted but heavily armed freighter was under contract to Xizor Transport Systems, the transportation company owned by Prince Xizor. It carried fertilizer to the planet Bothawui, but it also contained an Imperial computer full of information concerning the top secret second Death Star project at Endor. The Bothan Blue Squad, led by Luke Skywalker, sustained heavy losses in an attack on the freighter but eventually escaped with the Imperial computer core. [SOTE]

Survivors

These descendants of the spacers marooned when the legendary starship *Queen of Ranroon* crashed on the planet Dellalt are extreme isolationists who hate other Dellaltians. As generations passed, they forgot their true origins and turned the customs and technology of their ancestors into myths and legends. The technological artifacts salvaged from the crash became sacred talismans and implements for use in their religious practices. A major ritual is based upon the actions undertaken by marooned spacers—setting up an emergency beacon and calling for rescue. Powered by sacrifices, the Survivors hope that the "signals" of their prayers will be "received" and lead to their "deliverance." [HLL]

Susejo of Choi

One of the oldest residents of the Sarlacc's stomach, he had been in the process of being digested for hundreds of years when Boba Fett entered the Great Pit of Carkoon. He taunted the bounty hunter endlessly until Boba Fett escaped. [TJP]

swamp crawler

A land vehicle used for traveling across marshy terrain. A swamp crawler features a multiwheel transmission system, six balloon tires, and a central spherical wheel that can execute quick turns of up to 180 degrees. [SME]

swoop

Basically an engine with a seat, these fast and highly maneuverable speeder vehicles are difficult to control. Swoop racing is a very popular sport in the Galactic Core and throughout the civilized regions of the galaxy. The sport requires huge domed arenas called swoop tracks. These arenas hold tens of thousands of viewers, circular flight paths, obstacle courses, and massive concession booths. Han Solo was a top swoop racer in his youth. [DFRSB, HSR, SWSB, SWVG]

swoop gang

Some outlaw bands scattered throughout the galaxy use swoops, and swoop gangs like the Nova Demons and Dark Star Hellions have gained infamy for their crimes. Swoop gangs run spice, smuggle weapons, and serve as muscle for underworld factions. [SOTE, SWSB]

S'ybll

A mind witch who could change shapes, she tried to entice Luke Skywalker to abandon his friends and stay with her. [CSW]

Sylvar

A Cathar Jedi, she was apprenticed to Master Vodo-Siosk Baas about 4,000 years before the Galactic Civil War. When her lover Crado turned to the dark side, she felt she had to kill him. [DLS, TSW]

synthflesh

This translucent gel derived from the cellular regeneration medium called bacta seals wounds and promotes rapid healing of damaged tissue. [HSE]

system patrol craft

A type of vessel that operates within star systems as the first line of defense against pirates, smugglers, and hostile alien forces. They are equipped with powerful sublight engines but have no hyperdrives. They also perform custom inspection duties and watch for disabled ships. [DFRSB, ISB]

2-1B (Too-Onebee)

This medical droid in service to the Rebel Alliance was a skilled surgeon and field medic. The droid treated Luke Skywalker twice during the time of the Battle of Hoth, including performing an operation to replace Luke's severed hand with a mechanical replacement. [ESB]

T-12

A service droid in a Jedi outpost on the planet Ossus some 4,000 years before the Galactic Civil War. It packed Sith artifacts for shipment to the Jedi archives. [DLS]

T-16 skyhopper

This high-speed pleasure craft has a distinctive tri-wing design that makes it amazingly maneuverable. Luke Skywalker owned a T-16 and often raced his friends through Beggar's Canyon on Tatooine. [SWN, SWSB, SWVG]

T-47

See snowspeeder.

Ta'a Chume, Queen Mother

Ruler of the sixty-three worlds of the Hapes Cluster. Her beauty matches her ruthlessness. She lacked a female heir and her first son seemed so weak that she secretly had him assassinated. She demanded that her second son, Prince Isolder, take a superior wife to continue the Hapes dynasty. She murdered his first choice, then tried to have his second choice, Princess Leia Organa, killed as well. She eventually accepted Isolder's choice of Teneniel Djo of Dathomir.

Years later, Ta'a Chume tried to stop her granddaughter, Tenel Ka, from enrolling in Luke Skywalker's Jedi academy. Despite Ta'a Chume's opinions, Tenel Ka and other young Jedi Knights saved the queen mother from Bartokk assassins. [CPL, YJK]

Taanab

This agrarian planet was the site of a small but significant battle against space pirates that earned gambler Lando Calrissian a reputation as a good military strategist. Pirates bothered the peaceful farmers of Taanab for millennia. Before Calrissian joined the Rebellion against the Empire or served as baron administrator of Cloud City, he was at Taanab's Pandath spaceport. Pirates from the planet Norulac seasonally raided Taanab for spoils. Lando Calrissian was refueling his ship when a Norulackian raid took place. Lando decided to aid the Taanabians because the pirates had damaged his ship, because they were taking advantage of defenseless farmers, but mostly because someone bet him he couldn't beat the Norulackians. With superior tactics, amazing flying, the help of the farmers, and a lot of luck, Lando managed to destroy the attacking space pirates and foil the raid. [DLS, RJ, RJN]

Tafanda Bay

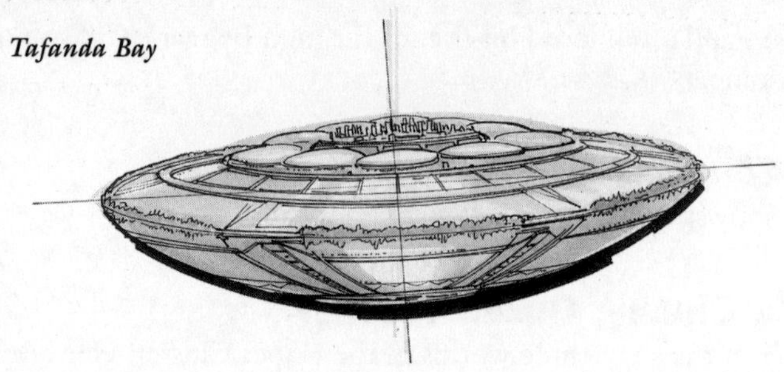

Tafanda Bay

An Ithorian herd ship. It floats above the jungles of Ithor and is commanded by Momaw Nadon. [DA, GA, MTS, SWSB, SWVG, TMEC]

Taggar, Lieutenant Rone

A member of the New Republic's 21st Recon Group, he piloted the recon-X fighter *Jennie Lee.* He revealed the size of the Yevethan fleet and then committed suicide as he was about to be taken captive by Yevethan forces. [SOL]

Tagge, General

One of the senior Imperial officers serving under Grand Moff Tarkin on the original Death Star battle station. [SW]

Tahiri

A Force-sensitive human, she was orphaned and raised by a tribe of Tusken Raiders on Tatooine. She was found by Jedi Tionne and brought to Luke Skywalker's Jedi academy on Yavin 4. There, she became fast friends with young Anakin Solo, who saved her from drowning in a river—just as she foresaw in a prophetic dream. [JJK]

Taisden

A New Republic Intelligence officer, he accompanied Colonel Pakkpekatt on his private mission to rescue Lando Calrissian from the Teljkon vagabond. [SOL]

Talasea
This planet located in the Morobe system was used as a staging area for Rogue Squadron's assault on Coruscant about three years after the Battle of Endor. [RS]

Tal'dira
A giant Twi'lek warrior, he challenged Wedge Antilles to a vibroblade duel during Rogue Squadron's visit to Ryloth. He offered his squadron of Chir'daki fighters to help the Republic cause during the Bacta War and later accepted a position in Rogue Squadron. [BW]

Tallon, Adar
A brilliant naval commander and military strategist of the Old Republic. Many of the space combat tactics he developed were still in use by both the Empire and the Alliance during the time of the Galactic Civil War. When the Old Republic gave way to the Empire, Tallon faked his own death and settled on Tatooine to hide. A group of Rebel agents found Tallon and convinced him to join the Alliance. [TM]

Talsava
Akanah Norand Pell's real mother, she abandoned her fifteen-year-old child on Carratos. [SOL]

Talus
One of five habitable planets in the Corellian system. It is the same size as its sister planet Tralus. [AC, AS, SAC]

Talz
A large, strong species from Alzoc III, these white-furred beings stand about two meters tall and have four eyes. While they appear fierce, they have gentle personalities. [GG4]

Tamban
This planet was once home to Emperor Preedu III. [BTS]

Tampion

This New Republic shuttle was carrying Han Solo to his new command of the Fifth Fleet when it was captured by Yevethan forces. [TT]

tank droid

This advanced Imperial combat droid (Arakyd XR-85), or sentient tank, combines the properties of an armored vehicle weapon with the intelligence and programming of a droid. These weapons played a significant role in the Imperial invasion to reclaim Imperial City that occurred six years after the Battle of Endor. [DE, DESB, SWVG]

Tannath

A member of the Singing Mountain clan of the Witches of Dathomir. [CPL]

Tantive IV

Princess Leia Organa's consular ship. It was owned by the Royal House of Alderaan and was used for Imperial Senate business, as well as covert Rebel Alliance activities. It was captured in the Tatooine star system after intercepting the technical plans for the original Death Star battle station. [SWN, SWR]

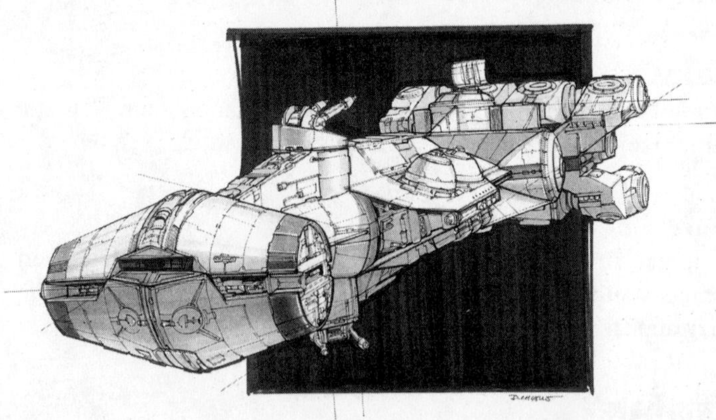

Tantive IV

Targeter

Code name for Princess Leia Organa's top aide and friend Winter during her time of service with Alliance Procurement and Supply. Her mission profile was to enter Imperial installations, use her perfect memory to gather intelligence and create detailed maps, then pass the information along to Rebel agents so that they could procure supplies for the Rebellion from Imperial stockpiles. [DFRSB, LC]

targeting computer

A sophisticated device that acquires hostile targets for a ship's weapons systems. By calculating trajectories and attack and intercept courses, targeting computers help pilots and gunners track and fire at fast-moving enemy ships. [SWN]

target remote

See remote.

Tarkin, Grand Moff

The Imperial governor charged with overseeing a large section of the Outer Rim Territories. As one of the Emperor's most loyal administrators, Tarkin devised and implemented the construction of the first Death Star battle station. His concepts led to the Empire's doctrine of rule by fear and helped thc Emperor disband the Imperial Senate. He was as ruthless as he was evil, and as the young governor of the Seswenna sector he fully supported Senator Palpatine's takeover of the Old Republic. He became the first grand moff.

Although married, he took Daala as his mistress and put her in charge of the top secret weapons development project, the Maw Installation.

Grand Moff Tarkin

He named her the first female admiral in the Imperial navy, and she helped oversee the construction of the Death Star. He took command of the Death Star on its maiden voyage, personally giving the order to destroy Alderaan when the captured Princess Leia refused to cooperate. He died in the Battle of Yavin after refusing to evacuate the Death Star prior to its destruction by Rebel forces. [COF, DSTC, GG1, SW, SWCG]

Tarlen, Bentu Pall

Chief of the Imperial Center Construction Contracts Division, the ministry responsible for planning public works, military facilities, and other Imperial building projects on Coruscant. Tarlen used his position to help the Black Sun crime syndicate by providing information about competing contract bids to three of the syndicate's fronts: Core Construction, Durasteel Corporation, and Hightower Conglomerate. In addition to leaking bidding information, Tarlen supplements his income by passing along secret military and government construction plans and by allowing Black Sun to install surveillance devices during the construction process. [SESB, SOTE]

Tarrik

One of Bail Organa's most trusted aides on the planet Alderaan, he later became an aide to Princess Leia. [SOL, SWR]

Tascil, Moff Boren

The governor of Cilpar, he earned his post as reward for leading a TIE-fighter wing at the Battle of Derra IV. He was negotiating to turn his world over to the Alliance when word of the Emperor's death reached him and the Emperor's grand vizier, Sate Pestage, contacted him. Seeing more opportunity in the collapsing Empire, he threw in with Pestage. [XW]

Taselda

Dirty and unkempt, she was rumored to be a Jedi living in the Ruby Gulch on Nam Chorios. Long ago, she competed with Beldorian the Hutt to rule the city Hweg Shul. Luke Skywalker revealed this insane woman to be a fraud, though she did manage to capture Callista for a brief period. [POT]

Tatoo I, Tatoo II

The twin suns of the Tatooine system. They are binary stars. [SWN]

Tatooine

This harsh desert planet in the Outer Rim was the childhood home of Luke Skywalker. The surface is littered with ancient starship wrecks, most half-buried by the fierce sandstorms that rage across the planet. Jawas and Tusken Raiders are native to Tatooine, and many life-forms live in the deserts, including banthas, dewbacks, womp rats, krayt dragons, rontos, and the terrible Sarlacc. Moisture-farm colonists have settled parts of the planet, though they struggle with both the Tusken Raiders and the elements in order to survive.

Points of interest include the Dune Sea, the Jundland Wastes, Anchorhead, Motesta, Tosche Station, Bestine, Beggar's Canyon, and the Mos Eisley spaceport. The spaceport attracts all kinds of scum and villainy, from smugglers to pirates to underworld types of all descriptions. A number of religious orders have found their way to Tatooine, such as the Dim-U monks, who worship the bantha, and the B'omarr order, seeking enlightenment once they have been freed from the distractions of the flesh. Crimelord Jabba the Hutt controlled his vast criminal empire from the Tatooine deserts until Princess Leia Organa killed him.

Jedi Knight Obi-Wan Kenobi brought the infant Luke Skywalker to the planet and placed him in the care of Owen and Beru Lars. Years later, a message from Princess Leia made Kenobi give up his life of hiding and reveal to Skywalker his heritage as a Jedi. [GG7, ISWU, MTS, RJ, SW]

Tatooine

A New Republic cruiser destroyed in the Battle of Almania. [NR]

tauntaun

This easily domesticated creature is also called a snow lizard. Wild tauntauns roam the frozen wastes of Hoth, while the Alliance used trained tauntauns as mounts and pack animals during its stay on the ice planet. Thick gray fur protects tauntauns from the extreme temperatures, though they cannot survive Hoth's brutal nights without shelter. Herds of these swift and surefooted creatures can be seen running across the plains of snow and ice during the daylight hours. [ESB, ISWU, SWSB]

Tavira, Moff Leonia

A human, she was sixteen when she began an affair with the Imperial governor of Eiattu VI. She was as ambitious as she was beautiful, arranging the "accidental" death of the moff's wife and marrying him herself. She assumed his title and duties when he suffered from a stroke and then apparently killed himself, although she was eventually forced to flee the planet by Rogue Squadron. Seven years after the Battle of Endor, she turned up as the head of the Invids pirate crews. Using the ex–Imperial Star Destroyer *Invidious* as a base, she caused all kinds of trouble for the New Republic until Luke Skywalker and Corran Horn deprived her of her secret weapon—the *Jensaarai* Force users. [IJ, XW]

Tchiery

A Farnym, he was Leia Organa Solo's copilot aboard the *Alderaan.* [NR]

TDL3.5

A nanny droid sent to replace C-3PO as the caretaker of the three Solo children as part of a prank played by young Anakin Solo. [NR]

Teebo

An Ewok with gray-striped fur, he was a leader in the tribe that befriended Princess Leia Organa on the forest moon of Endor.

He wore a horned half skull decorated with feathers atop his head, and carried a stone hatchet. He was a dreamer and a poet who had a mystical ability to communicate with nature. [ETV, RJ]

Teek

A scruffy, furry being with close-set eyes and buck teeth, he is very mischievous. His lightning-quick speed allows him to dart from place to place in the blink of an eye. He lives on Endor's forest moon. [BFE, ISWU]

telesponder

A shipboard device that automatically broadcasts a ship's identification profile in response to signals sent by spaceports and military authorities. [HSE]

Teljkon system

The star system where the second documented sighting of the ghost ship called the Teljkon vagabond occurred, giving the mysterious vessel its name. [BTS]

Teljkon vagabond

A mysterious ghost ship, it kept jumping into hyperspace as other ships approached to investigate it. It was actually a key instrument in rebuilding the long-dead Qellan homeworld, a planet renamed Maltha Obex. The organic starship was programmed to return, thaw out the planet, and restore the Qella to life. Luke Skywalker discovered how to use the ship for its intended purpose. [TT]

Tels, Seggor

A Quarren, he admitted to betraying his homeworld Mon Calamari by lowering the shields when the Empire invaded. He also helped organize his people to stand with the Calamarians to try to repel the invaders. Jealous of the Calamarians, he was also ashamed of his actions. He remained on his homeworld even while many of his fellow Quarren fled. [SWSB]

Telti

This moon was the site of a collection of droid factories operated by failed Jedi academy student Brakiss. The droids were fitted with bombs and detonators at the behest of dark-sider Kueller to use in a campaign of terror against the New Republic. [NR]

Temple of Fire

A Massassi temple on Yavin 4. [DLS]

Temple of Pomojema

This temple on the planet Mimban is a shrine to the Mimbanite god Pomojema. The legendary Kaiburr Crystal was kept in this structure. [SME]

Teradoc, High Admiral

One of thirteen squabbling warlords, he was poisoned by Admiral Daala after they refused to join her in her campaign against the New Republic. [DS]

Terak

A cruel and evil king, he led the Marauders who preyed upon the inhabitants of Endor's forest moon. [BFE, ISWU]

teräs käsi

The Bunduki martial arts discipline known as teräs käsi, or steel hands, is the art of combat without weapons. It is taught by the Followers of Palawa on Bunduki, a world in the Pacanth Reach. [SESB, SOTE]

Termagant

This Imperial Strike cruiser allied with Warlord Zsinj was reconfigured into a TIE-fighter carrier. Rogue Squadron tore the ship in half with a volley of proton torpedoes for its part in the destruction of a bacta convoy. [BW]

Teroenza

A t'landa Til, he was the Most Exalted High Priest of Ylesia. He enjoyed collecting rare and expensive items from all over the galaxy. He was eventually killed by the bounty hunter Boba Fett. [PS, RD]

Terpfen

A Mon Calamarian, he was Admiral Ackbar's chief mechanic. While an Imperial prisoner, part of his brain was replaced to compel him to carry out secret orders and report back to Imperial forces. He sabotaged Ackbar's B-wing fighter and provided Imperial Ambassador Furgan with the secret location of Anakin Solo. He eventually overcame his programming and helped defeat Furgan. [COF, DA]

Terrik, Booster

A retired Corellian smuggler, he was a negotiator for Rogue Squadron and their manager of operations at the Yag'Dhul space station. [BW]

Terrik, Mirax

The beautiful daughter of Booster Terrik, she took over her father's smuggling business when he retired. From her ship *Pulsar Skate* she maintained contacts throughout the galaxy. Wedge Antilles regarded Mirax as a sister. Although not officially allied with Rogue Squadron, she provides the team with help now and then. She ferried the squad to Coruscant for the covert mission prior to the Alliance invasion. She eventually married Corran Horn. [BW, KT, RS, WG]

Tessek

A Quarren, he fled his homeworld Mon Calamari after the Imperial invasion and wound up as an accountant for Jabba the Hutt. Tessek escaped the destruction of Jabba's sail barge but was ambushed at Jabba's palace by B'omarr monks, who placed his brain into a nutrient jar atop a spider droid. [RJ, SWCG, TJP]

Teta, Empress

A long-lived warlord who lived millennia before the Galactic Civil War, she conquered and united the seven planets that became the Empress Teta system. [DLS]

Teta system, Empress

This star system, named for the woman warlord who conquered it in the distant past, is located near the Kuar system. The system contains seven carbonite-mining worlds, including Kirrek and Koros Major. It was long ruled by the descendants of Empress Teta, who shared power with the leaders of the carbonite guild. According to the Jedi Holocron, terrible events involving the dark side of the Force occurred in this system approximately 4,000 years before the Galactic Civil War. [DE, DLS, ISWU, TSW]

Teyr

A crowded bureaucratic world located at the crossroads of three highly traveled hyperspace routes. [BTS, SOL]

Thanas, Commander Pter

A native of Coruscant, he rose to the rank of commander in the Imperial military. He was stationed at Bakura, in charge of the Imperial forces there when the Ssi-ruuk attacked. During the initial invasion, Thanas demonstrated masterful starship tactics that held off the alien fleet until help could arrive. The tall, thin Thanas has a narrow face and a sharp, angular nose. His sense of honor and duty is tempered by ruthlessness; despite the truce, he destroyed the Alliance carrier *Flurry* after the alien threat was averted. Later, he surrendered his ship *Dominant* and defected to the Alliance. He was then placed in command of the newly formed Bakuran Defense Militia. He married Gaeriel Captison, and they had a daughter named Malinza. [SWCG, TAB, TBSB]

Tharen, Bria

A Corellian, she was one of the pilgrims on Ylesia who was forced to work in the spice processing plant. She was skilled at processing glitterstim, but had been an archaeology student before arriving on Ylesia. Han Solo met her during his time on the planet, which occurred when he was about nineteen. Han convinced the priest Teroenza to let Bria organize his art collection, getting her out of the glitterstim mines. She was Han Solo's first love.

Bria Tharen

After leaving the Ylesian religion, she started working with the Rebellion, making contacts and leading new Rebels to the growing organization. After participating in a raid to free Ylesian pilgrims, she transferred to Rebel Intelligence and was assigned to work at the largest Imperial base on Corellia. First as a spy and later as Moff Sarn Shild's consort, she helped the fledgling Rebellion greatly.

Bria eventually became a commander in the Corellian resistance. On Cloud City, she met with Alderaanian resistance leaders to urge them to form a Rebel Alliance. The year before, she had met with the Wookiee underground, the Quarrr-tellerrra, on Kashyyyk. Bria was killed during an attack on an Imperial comm center that was used to transmit the technical readouts of the Death Star battle station to Princess Leia Organa's consular ship. Han Solo learned of Bria's death the day before he met Obi-Wan Kenobi and Luke Skywalker in the Mos Eisley cantina. Boba Fett told Solo because he had promised Bria he would make sure her father learned of her death. [HG, PS, RD]

Tharen Wayfarer

A ship owned by the Pitareeze family. [D]

Theed

This large, elegant city on Naboo serves as the capital for the land-dwelling species also known as the Naboo. [SWTPM]

Theelin

An extinct, near-human species. Shug Ninx of Nar Shaddaa has Theelin blood. His mother was one of the last of that species. [DE]

thermal cape

A lightweight poncho made of a metal-foil and spider-silk composite. It retains the wearer's body heat to provide protection from the cold. [SME]

thermal detonator

This small, metal ball is a powerful explosive that is activated when pressure is removed from the trigger. When activated, a fusion reaction causes an explosion. Princess Leia Organa, disguised as the bounty hunter Boushh, threatened Jabba the Hutt's court with a thermal detonator to demonstrate Boushh's nerve and impress the crimelord. [ISB, RJ]

Thistleborn, Grand Moff

This authoritative grand moff had bushy eyebrows that framed his dark, penetrating eyes. His loyalty to the Empire's Central Committee of Grand Moffs was absolute and above question. [GDV]

Thon, Master

A Jedi Master who trained students on the planet Ambria, he was a fearsome, armor-plated quadruped who lived approximately 4,000 years before the Galactic Civil War. As the teachings of the Krath sect were gaining prominence, Master Thon addressed a great assembly of 10,000 Jedi who had gathered on Mount Meru on the desert world Deneba. He spoke eloquently against straying from the light side, hoping to convince his peers about the dangers of the Krath philosophy. [DE]

Thpffftht

A Bith consular ship. [CPL]

Thrawn, Grand Admiral

A Chiss, he was the only nonhuman to be named one of the twelve grand admirals who served as the Emperor's military commanders. Thrawn was a tall man of regal bearing with shimmering blue-black hair, pale blue skin, and glowing red eyes. His real name was Mitth'raw'nuruodo, and he was discovered by Victory Star Destroyer Captain Voss Parck alone on an uninhabited world on the edge of Imperial space. After a time in the Emperor's court, Thrawn was supposedly exiled to the Unknown Regions, but he was actually sent there on a mission for the Emperor. He spent much of his career in the Unknown Regions, earning the right to wear the white uniform of a grand admiral.

Like the other grand admirals, Thrawn was a military genius. He had a habit of pulling stunning victories out of certain defeat. His passion for art was more than a simple diversion, for he believed that by studying an opponent's art he could discover a way to defeat him.

Five years after the Battle of Endor, at a time when the New Republic thought that all of these leaders were destroyed, Thrawn returned from his extended mission in the Unknown Regions to discover that the Emperor was dead and the Imperial fleet was in ruins. He rallied the remnants of the empire and set in motion a plan to destroy the New Republic, which he refused to call anything other than the Rebellion. The plan included the use of Force-inhibiting ysalamiri, a dark Jedi Master, and two items from the Emperor's hidden storehouse in Mount Tantiss—a working cloaking device and a set of Spaarti cloning cylinders. Through the use of hit-and-run attacks, political schemes, spies, and superior planning, Thrawn almost destroyed the New Republic. But its heroes rallied, and Thrawn's personal bodyguard Rukh betrayed him, ending the grand admiral's threat.

Grand Admiral Thrawn

Ten years later, an impostor tried to convince the galaxy that Thrawn had returned. The impostor was eventually revealed by Admiral Gilad Pellaeon. However, at a secret base called the Hand of Thrawn in the Nirauan system, the grand admiral's clone was almost ready to step out of its Spaarti cylinder. Luke Skywalker and Mara Jade destroyed the cloning chamber while they were trying to escape from the secret base, forever ending any hope of Thrawn's return from the dead. [DFR, DFRSB, HE, HESB, LC, SP, VF]

Thrella Well

Any of a series of shafts that lead from the surface of Circarpous V to the network of caverns deep within the planet's crust. These wells are located all over the planet's surface and are believed to be the work of the legendary species, the Thrella. [SME]

Thrumble, Massad

A onetime Imperial captain, he worked in a droid production center and was the creator of the human replica droid Guri. After the Battle of Endor, he operated a small cantina on Hurd's Moon in the Qont system. Guri sought him out, and he helped perform the neural restructuring needed to remove her criminal programming while leaving her martial skills intact. [SEE]

Thyferra

This planet is homeworld to the mantislike Vratix and the center of the galaxy's bacta industry. [BW, KT, RS, WG]

Thyfonian

A *Lambda*-class shuttle destroyed by Rogue Squadron as it attempted to flee into hyperspace during the Bacta War. Ysanne Isard was believed to be on board. [BW]

Ti, Kirana

One of the Witches of Dathomir, she helped Luke Skywalker uncover an ancient wrecked space station that held records of Jedi training. Later, she joined Skywalker's Jedi academy and aided other students in the defeat of the spirit of Dark Lord

Exar Kun. She was a skilled warrior and an expert in the physical aspects of the Force. [COF, DA, JAL]

Tibanna gas

A rare gas extracted from Bespin's atmosphere and processed at Cloud City. Hot air sucked through Cloud City's unipod captures a variety of gases, including Tibanna gas. It is processed and spin-sealed in carbonite for transport off planet. Tibanna gas produces four times the energy output when cohesive light passes through it. In this way, blasters and other energy weapons produce greater energy yields—and therefore greater amounts of damage—when Tibanna gas is used as a conducting agent. Personal weapons cannot tolerate this extra power, but ship-mounted blasters benefit greatly from the use of Tibanna gas. [GG2, ISWU]

Tibannopolis

The abandoned city on Bespin where Luke Skywalker found Streen, one of his Jedi candidates. [ISWU, JS]

Tibor

A vicious Barabel bounty hunter, he frequented the Mos Eisley cantina and was an employee of Zorba the Hutt. [ZHR]

Tibrin

This planet is the home of the alien Ishi Tib species. The planet's cities are built atop carefully cultivated coral reefs. [GG2, GG4, POT]

TIE/Advanced fighter

The prototype used by Darth Vader during the Battle of Yavin. Its best designs were later incorporated into the TIE interceptor and TIE Advanced. [HE, SWSB, SWVG]

TIE bomber

An Imperial assault bomber. It has a double pod to hold ordnance and targeting systems. [ISB, SWSB, SWVG]

TIE crawler

A cheap, expendable ground-assault vehicle modeled after the TIE fighter. It has huge tread wheels instead of solar-panel wings. [DE, SWVG]

TIE defender

A prototype Imperial fighter developed shortly before the Battle of Endor. It featured three sets of solar collector panels and multiple heavy-weapons systems. [SWVG, TT]

TIE fighter

The standard starfighter used by the Empire. It was named for the twin ion engines that propel it through space. With a single-pilot command pod housed between a pair of hexagonal solar array wings, it is a maneuverable, fast, short-range ship. It has no hyperdrive, operating out of cruisers or from a planetary base. Sienar Fleet Systems produced a series of different TIEs to handle different Imperial missions, including the TIE/rc, a sensor and communications reconnaissance fighter; the TIE/fc, which provided fire control for long-range navy artillery; and the fully robotic TIE/D fighter, introduced six years after the Battle of Endor. [ESB, RJ, SW, SWSB, SWVG]

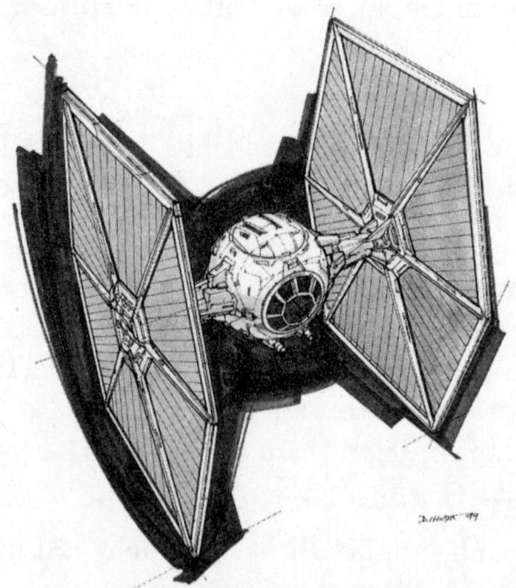

TIE fighter

TIE interceptor

Faster and more maneuverable than the standard TIE fighter, it was developed from Darth Vader's TIE/Advanced prototype. The dagger-shaped solar panels made the interceptor more intimidating, and it was almost as fast as the A-wing starfighter. Grand Admiral Thrawn began arming some interceptors with shields to better protect these exceptional starfighters. [HESB, SWSB, SWVG]

Tierce, Major Grodin

A Royal Guardsman, he appeared sixteen years after the Battle of Endor to help Moff Disra and the con artist Flim pull off the illusion of Grand Admiral Thrawn's return. Tierce was actually a clone of one of the finest combat stormtroopers ever to serve the Empire. The real Tierce died in combat in Thrawn's campaign against Generis. The cloned Tierce was the first of what was to be a new breed of warlords—combining the loyalty and combat abilities of a stormtrooper with the tactical genius of Thrawn. The experiment was a failure, however. While Thrawn believed in order and stability, the cloned Tierce wanted only vengeance. Thrawn wanted a tactically brilliant leader. What he got was a tactically brilliant stormtrooper—a manipulator with no vision, just a thirst for revenge. The Mistryl Shadow Guard Shada D'akul killed him when he was revealed and attacked Admiral Gilad Pellaeon. [SP, VF]

Tigris

The son of two parents who were both strong in the Force, he has no Force powers of his own. He is the son of Lord Hethrir and the healer Rillao, students of Lord Darth Vader. When Rillao rejected the dark side, she fled her planet's destruction with her unborn child. Tigris grew up on a remote planet with no knowledge of his father. When Hethrir found them, he imprisoned Rillao and made Tigris his personal slave.

Hethrir led the Empire Reborn organization and convinced Tigris to despise his mother. Hethrir, meanwhile, kidnapped children from dozens of worlds and imprisoned them aboard his worldcraft. If the children showed Force talents, he tried to corrupt them to the dark side. If not, he sold them to slavers. Tigris, gentle and compassionate, sneaked food to the captives and tried to comfort them.

When the Solo children were kidnapped, Tigris grew especially fond of Anakin. Tigris eventually learned the truth about his father and helped save Anakin from the Waru, which instead swallowed Hethrir. Tigris and his mother then left to start a new life on Coruscant. [CS]

time-stream

A method used by the H'drachi, a species whose homeworld is M'haeli, to interpret the Force, especially to foresee events. [ROC]

Tin-Tin Dwarf

An intelligent rodentlike species whose members are bipedal and stand less than a meter tall. [SWR]

Tion, Lord

An Imperial noble and soldier, he served the Emperor as a task force commander. He was charged with identifying and eradicating all Alliance personnel and Rebel sympathizers on the planet Ralltiir. Lord Tion played an instrumental role in providing the location of the plans for the original Death Star battle station to Bail Organa. He was killed in a scuffle with Princess Leia. [SWR]

Tion Hegemony

A remote cluster of twenty-seven star systems near Corporate Sector space, far from the heavily populated Core Worlds. [HLL, HSR]

Tionne

One of Luke Skywalker's first Jedi students, she found her true calling in teaching other Jedi initiates. She also loves to turn Jedi history into haunting and evocative ballads. Her studies of history provided the other students with an edge when they battled the spirit of Exar Kun. Years later, Skywalker entrusted the academy to Tionne when he left for a mission. She used parables and songs to communicate even more effectively than Skywalker and became a regular instructor, specializing in helping students find their own skills in the Force. She gives Luke the perspective he needs to understand the challenges facing his Jedi Knights in the context of thousands of years of Jedi history. [COF, DA, DS, JAL, JASB, SWCG, YJK]

Tiree

See Gold Two.

t'landa Til

A long-lived species native to Nal Hutta and related to Hutts. Its members are large with broad faces and bulbous, protruding eyes. They have leathery gray-tan skin, a large blunt horn above nostril slits, a wide lipless mouth, and a head attached to a short, humped neck. They walk on four tree-trunk-like legs. They possess the unique ability to create physical and emotional pleasure in others by humming. The effect is addictive, and only those with the strongest willpower can resist. The t'landa Til used this low-grade empathy to form the Ylesian religion. [PS]

Toda, Lord

Ruler of a major portion of the planet Tammuz-an during the early days of the Empire. He called himself the "overlord of the outer territories." He was gruff and surly. He dressed like his warrior tribesmates, wearing a combination of rough canvas and organic armor. [DTV]

Togorian

A humanoid feline species from the planet Togoria in the Thanos star system. These tall, slender beings are covered with fur and have long, thin muscles of great strength. To outsiders, they appear aloof and very suspicious. [GG4]

Toklar

A Mon Calamari philosopher, he was an inspiration to Admiral Ackbar. [SOL]

Tokmia

This planet was one of three where Imperial probe droids searched for the new Rebel Alliance base after the Battle of Yavin. The other planets were Allyuen and Hoth. [ESBR]

Tonnika, Brea and Senni

Identical twins and con artists, they used their natural charms to manipulate people and earn credits. Often, only one sister would appear at a time, using the name Bresenni to pull off intrigues. Han Solo convinced them to pull such a trick on Lando Calrissian once long before the two sisters joined the Alliance. [GG1, SWCG, TMEC]

Toprawa

This planet served as the Alliance's initial hiding place for the Death Star's technical readouts. From the Toprawa Relay Station, the plans were transmitted to Princess Leia Organa's ship, the *Tantive IV*. [DS, RS, SWR]

Toq, Qrrl

A Nazzar prince, he lived some 4,000 years before the Galactic Civil War. He was a fearless Jedi who designed and built Jedi armor. [DLS, FNU, TSW]

Torlock, Frija

Daughter of Governor Torlock of Corulag, she worked with Admiral Droon to frame her father, accusing him of preparing to defect to the Rebel Alliance, so they could take control of the planet. [SS]

torpedo sphere

A dedicated siege platform designed to knock out planetary shields prior to an Imperial attack. The massive 1,900-meter-diameter torpedo sphere was the forerunner to the Death Star battle station. It was covered with thousands of dedicated energy receptors designed to analyze shield emissions to find weak points in the shields. With 500 proton torpedo tubes arranged in an inverted conical formation, the torpedo sphere could rain a massive salvo onto a weak point. The resulting hole that opened for a few microseconds provided a window through which the sphere's turbolasers could target the shield generators. [ISB]

Torve, Fynn

A human member of Talon Karrde's smuggling organization, he was among the best of Karrde's freighter pilots. While not as flashy as Han Solo or as sophisticated as Lando Calrissian, Torve usually handled the most important and difficult runs for his boss. [DFR, HE, LC]

Tos, Ganar

An old Zisian, and Teroenza's majordomo, he wanted to marry Bria Tharen. [PS]

Tosche Station

A power and distribution station located near the town Anchorhead on the planet Tatooine. It serves as a gathering place for Anchorhead's young people. Luke Skywalker and his friends frequented the place during his youth. [SWN]

Towani, Catarine

The mother of Mace and Cindel Towani, she and her family were marooned on Endor's forest moon for a time. Wicket W. Warrick and his Ewok tribe befriended them. [BFE, EA]

Towani, Cindel

The youngest of the Towani children, she and her family were marooned on the forest moon of Endor. After her parents, Jeremitt and Catarine, were captured by a creature called a Borra and imprisoned in the lair of the giant Gorax, Cindel and her brother, Mace, were forced to forage for food. When Cindel became ill, the pair were rescued by Deej the Ewok, who took them back to his village. After she recovered, Cindel became friends with Deej's son, Wicket W. Warrick. The Ewoks helped rescue Cindel's parents from the Gorax.

Several months later, humanoid Marauders who had also been stranded on Endor's forest moon attacked the Ewok village. Cindel's mother and brother were killed, but Cindel escaped. Her father was then killed by the Marauder king Terak and the witch Charal. With the help of Teek and his human master Noa, Cindel and Wicket helped neutralize the Marauders. She left Endor's forest moon with Noa, promising to someday return to visit Wicket.

Cindel grew up to become an idealistic journalist on Coruscant. She received the Plat Mallar tapes from Admiral Hiram Drayson and leaked a story designed to gain sympathy from the public and the senate. [BFE, EA, TT]

Towani, Jeremitt

Husband of Catarine and father of Mace and Cindel, he and his family were shipwrecked on Endor's forest moon. [BFE, EA]

Towani, Mace

A young teenage boy, he was among a human family that became shipwrecked on Endor's forest moon. His sister, Cindel, watched as Marauders killed Mace and their mother, Catarine. [BFE, EA]

tractor beam

A modified force field that immobilizes and moves objects caught within its influence. An emitting tower, called a tractor beam projector, produces the beams, though range and strength are determined by the power source. Tractor beams serve a number of important functions. In spaceports and docking bays, tractor beams help guide ships to a safe landing. Salvage vessels, cargo haulers, emergency craft, and engineering ventures all employ tractor beams to assist in their jobs. On military ships, tractor beams are used to capture enemy vessels or simply hold them in place while offensive weaponry is brought to bear. [ESB, RJ, SW]

Trade Federation

A commercial organization headed by the species known as the Neimoidians. In the pursuit of profit, the Trade Federation maintained a large droid army, making it capable of attaining by force that which it could not buy. About thirty-two years before the start of the Galactic Civil War, the Trade Federation blockaded the planet Naboo. The blockade, led by Nute Gunray and his lieutenant, Rune Haako, was subtly arranged by the Sith Lord Darth Sidious. Though the blockade was ultimately dispersed, it first drove Naboo's queen—Amidala—to seek aid from the Republic Senate on Coruscant. When the senate became mired in endless political discussions, Amidala initiated a vote of no confidence against the supreme chancellor, allowing Naboo's Senator Palpatine to ascend to the chancellorship. [SWTPM]

Trader's Luck

This ancient troopship, formerly called the *Guardian of the Republic*, was a relic of the Clone Wars. Garris Shrike turned this *Liberator*-class vessel into the headquarters for his nomadic band of space criminals that operated in the Corellian sector. Han Solo grew up on this vessel, a virtual slave to the cruel Shrike. [PS]

Trade Spine

Also called the Corellian Trade Spine, this region of space is located near the Ison Corridor. [DA, GG2, LC]

Tragett, Bogo

Leader of excavation Team Alpha, he was assigned to Maltha Obex by the Obroan Institute for Archaeology. [TT]

Tralus

One of five habitable planets in the Corellian system, it is the same size as its sister world Talus. A planetary repulsor located deep within the world was used in ancient times to move Tralus to its current orbit. [AC, AS, SAC]

Trandoshan

Large humanoid reptiles from the planet Trandosha. This warlike species allied early with the Empire. Trandoshans value hunting above all else and worship a deity known as the Scorekeeper. The bounty hunter Bossk was a member of this species. [COF, GG3, TBH]

transfer register

An electro-optical device that records the sale or trade of merchandise and property. [SWR]

transparisteel

A malleable metal that can be pressed and formed into thin, transparent sheets that retain nearly all of the metal's strength and durability. This see-through metal is used in place of glass on starships and other structures that require both visibility and protection. [HSE]

transport, Rebel

The Rebel Alliance used a number of different types of ships to supply food, ammunition, and other ordnance to its troops. Converted passenger liners, small freighters, and other older ships were used as transports. The transports used in the evacuation of Hoth were Gallofree Yards Medium Transports. About 90 meters long, they could carry 19,000 metric tons. An outer hull protected the cargo containers and passenger pods that were fastened to the inner hull. These vessels carried little or no armament, relying instead upon escort ships and starfighters to protect them. They were equipped with hyperdrives, however. The command crew of a Rebel transport operated out of a small, cramped pod located toward the rear of the vessel and atop the outer hull. [ESB, RSB, SWSB, SWVG]

treadwell robot

A multipurpose, six-limbed wheeled droid. It can be programmed to perform many menial tasks. [SWN]

Tree of Light

A mystical tree on Endor's forest moon. It is surrounded by a bright, beautiful glow that keeps the Night Spirit from using its powers during the day. According to tradition, a group of young Ewoks must periodically travel to the tree and feed it the sacred dust that rejuvenates its strength. [ETV]

Tregga

An old acquaintance of Han Solo and Chewbacca the Wookiee, he was captured in the act of smuggling contraband and sentenced to life imprisonment in the planet Akrit'tar's penal colony. [HSR]

Trell, Poas

The executive aide to New Republic First Administrator Nanaod Engh. [BTS]

Tremayne

The Imperial high inquisitor, he hunted down those who displayed any Force aptitude. He wore cybernetic reconstruction components on the right side of his face due to an old lightsaber wound. [GG9]

Trianii

This intelligent, spacefaring species of humanoid felines from the planet Trian established many off-world colonies. The Corporate Sector Authority claimed many of the older Trianii colony worlds even before its charter over that sector of space was granted. The Trianii on these worlds were forced to leave, though some were retained to labor for the Authority. [HSE]

Trianii Ranger

An elite member of Trian's law enforcement legion. [HSE]

Triclops

The true son of Emperor Palpatine, he was a three-eyed mutant. The Empire considered Triclops insane, and most officials feared that disaster would result should he become Emperor. Few outside the Imperial leaders knew of Triclops's existence, as he spent most of his life hidden in an Imperial insane asylum. Despite the shock-treatment scars that marred his temples, Triclops always looked serene and peaceful. He possessed a quiet, iron determination. Though he professed to believe in peace, his subconscious mind invented terrible weapons of destruction while he slept. Triclops was the father of the Jedi Prince Ken. [LCJ, MMY, PDS, QE, SWCG]

Triclops

tri-fighter

A custom-designed starfighter used by the Invids pirate crews. It is constructed around the ball cockpit and ion engine assembly of Sienar Fleet System's basic TIE fighter and married to a trio of angular blades set 120 degrees apart. Tri-fighters are equipped with basic shields and have side viewports cut into them to give the pilots more visibility. [IJ]

Trioculus

The supreme slavelord of the spice mines of Kessel. He came forward after the Emperor's death to claim that he was Palpatine's banished son. He was a handsome human with a third eye on his forehead. He became Emperor for a time due to the support of the Central Committee of Grand Moffs, though his claim was false. [GDV, MMY, PDS, ZHR]

Trodd, Puggles

A one-meter-tall rodentlike alien, he is a bounty hunter who often teams up with Jodo Kast and Zardra to complete difficult contracts. He fears the other bounty hunters, but he realizes that together they can make more credits than if they work alone. Pessimistic, unpleasant, and brooding, he loves to watch things explode. [TM]

Troujow, Hasti

A young, beautiful ex-mining-camp laborer, she helped Han Solo and Badure reach the secret treasure vaults of Xim the Despot. This expedition took place shortly before Solo became involved in the Galactic Civil War. [HLL]

Troujow, Lanni

The sister of Hasti Troujow, she was killed after she discovered a log recorder from the legendary starship *Queen of Ranroon.* With the information stored in the recorder, and the help of Han Solo and Chewbacca the Wookiee, Hasti was able to locate the ancient ship's lost treasures. [HLL]

Tsayv, Liat

A Sullustan, he was a crew member aboard Mirax Terrik's *Pulsar Skate.* [RS]

Tschel, Lieutenant

A young officer aboard the Imperial Star Destroyer *Chimaera*, he served as a member of the bridge crew under Captain Gilad Pellaeon and Grand Admiral Thrawn during Thrawn's campaign to destroy the New Republic five years after the Battle of Endor. [DFR, HE, LC]

tsil

This crystal formation on the planet Nam Chorios is a sentient creature and the source of Force-sensitivity on the planet. Tsils prevented the drochs from spreading the Death Seed plague throughout the galaxy. [POT]

Tsoss Beacon

An automated beacon station built by droids and suicide crews, located on a desolate planetoid in the Deep Galactic Core. Imperial Admiral Daala met with and murdered the remaining Imperial warlords here eight years after the Battle of Endor. [DS]

Tulgah

A rare species of troll-like beings on the forest moon of Endor. They have an extensive knowledge of magic. Some Tulgah are great healers. Others, like Morag, twist their knowledge to evil and wield powers of black magic. [ETV]

tumnor

A flying creature that lives in the upper atmosphere of Da Soocha and its moons. These predators stalk Ixlls, hunting the intelligent species for food. [DE]

Tund

A remote planet, rumored to be the home of the powerful Sorcerers of Tund. Rokur Gepta, a snail-like Croke, learned the secrets of the Sorcerers and then murdered his teachers and turned the lush paradise into a blasted wasteland. [LCS]

Tuomi, Senator

A New Republic senator from Drannik, he opposed Chief of State Leia Organa Solo during the Yevethan crisis. He challenged her by attacking her credentials, claiming that the destruction of Alderaan had disqualified her from senate membership since there was no legitimate territory for her to represent. [SOL]

turbolaser

A weapon that fires supercharged bolts of energy, usually from the deck of a capital ship or a surface-based defense installation. Turbolasers are more powerful than regular laser cannons, discharging hotter and more concentrated energy bolts. [SW, SWSB]

Tusken Raider

Also called the Sand People of Tatooine, Tusken Raiders are nomadic marauders. To protect themselves from the harsh desert environment, Sand People wear heavy robes and strips of cloth, breath masks, and eye protectors. Very aggressive, they hold an uneasy peace with Tatooine's moisture farmers. They have been known to attack settlements from time to time. Traveling atop their banthas, these nomads are experts at desert survival. Their traditional weapon is the gaderffii stick. [ISWU, SW, SWSB]

Tusken Raider

twi'janii

The Rylothan grant of hospitality to travelers. When twi'janii is invoked, the people of Ryloth are obliged to offer their guests sustenance and entertainment. [BW]

Twi'lek

This humanoid species with twin head tentacles, called lekku, comes from the planet Ryloth in the Outer Rim. The Twi'lek language combines verbal components with subtle head-tail movements. With the undercurrents provided by the head-tail movements, Twi'leks can carry on private conversations in the midst of other species. Twi'leks are omnivorous. On their homeworld, they cultivate edible molds and fungi, and raise cowlike rycrits for meat and hides. These beings are nonviolent, preferring to use cunning and slyness instead of force.

Twi'leks live in vast city complexes located on their planet's dark side. Each complex is autonomous, governed by a head clan of five Twi'leks who jointly control production, trade, and other endeavors. These leaders are born into their positions, and they serve until one of their number dies. At this time, the remaining members of the head clan are driven from their complex to die in the Bright Lands of the planet's light side. This makes room for the head clan of the next generation. As the technology level of Ryloth does not support spacefaring capabilities, the Twi'leks depend on neighboring systems, such as Tatooine, and on pirates, smugglers, and merchants for their contact with the rest of the galaxy. They attract these ships with their chief export, ryll. The mineral ryll has legitimate medicinal uses, but it is also a popular and dangerously addictive spice used in the Corporate Sector. One hazard that the Twi'leks face on a regular basis is slavers, who come to their world to fill their ships with Twi'lek slaves. Bib Fortuna and the dancing girl Oola were Twi'leks. [SWSB]

Tydirium

This *Lambda*-class Imperial shuttle was used by Han Solo's Rebel strike team to covertly reach the surface of Endor's forest moon. The shuttle had been captured by the Alliance prior to the mission. [RJ]

Tymmo

The consort of the Duchess Mistal of Dargul. His real name was Dack. [JS]

Tynna

This cold, arboreal world was the home planet of the skip tracer named Spray. [HSR]

Tyrann

The Supreme Master of the Serpent Masters. [CSW]

U-33

A class of orbital space boats. These sublightspeed loadlifters are used to shuttle personnel and material between planetary spaceports and orbiting space stations. [HLL]

Ubese

A species from the Uba system. Their planet was ravaged by a preemptive Old Republic strike due to their aggressive weapons development program. The bounty hunter Boushh was an Ubese. Their language is typified by its metallic sounds. [RJ, TJP]

Ubiqtorate

This division of Imperial Intelligence oversaw all of the activities of the agency at the highest levels. It was considered the true center of Imperial Intelligence, and it formulated strategies for the entire agency. Ubiqtorate members were anonymous, often unknown even to their subordinates. [ISB]

Ubrikkian

A manufacturer of vehicles, including landspeeders, sail barges, and weapons platforms such as the HAVr A9 floating fortress. [SWSB]

Ucce, Lady

A slave trader, she was a follower of Lord Hethrir. [CS]

Ugmush, Captain

A Gamorrean, she was the captain of the *Zicreex*, the ship that C-3PO and R2-D2 used to leave Nam Chorios. [POT]

Ugnaught

A species of small porcine humanoids that live and work on Bespin's Cloud City. Ugnaughts are usually found in the Tibanna gas processing plants, or as general laborers in the bowels of the floating city. [ESB, MTS]

Ugor

A species of intelligent unicellular protozoans. Ugors grow as large as one meter in diameter. They can extrude up to thirty pseudopodia at a time, some of which contain visual and other sensory growths, or even openings and membranes that allow them to speak. Ugors move by oozing from place to place or by controlling specialized environment suits built with two arms and legs. They come from a star system called Paradise, a junk-filled asteroid field that they administer. To them, garbage is holy. Every piece of junk is a religious relic. They had an exclusive contract with the Empire to collect garbage jettisoned from Imperial fleet ships and store it in their garbage-dump system. Gambling, bargaining, and cheating are the high moral standards the Ugors live by. Other scavenger species, like the Squib, are considered business rivals to be crushed and eliminated. [GG4, SH]

Ukio

This agricultural world is one of the top five producers of foodstuffs for the New Republic. During Grand Admiral Thrawn's military campaign against the New Republic, Ukio was forced to surrender to the Empire after Thrawn demonstrated a powerful new weapon. To those on the planet's surface, it appeared that the Empire had developed turbolasers capable of firing through planetary shields. This was actually accomplished by an elaborate illusion. While Thrawn's Star Destroyer fired bolts of energy at the shield, cloaked Dreadnaughts hiding invisibly beneath the shield fired matching bolts with uncanny timing.

The Ukian overliege, fearing the destructive power of such a weapon, surrendered to the Empire. For the rest of Thrawn's campaign, the Ukian food distribution and processing facilities, with its vast farming and livestock grazing regions, were under Imperial control. [LC]

Umboo

This colony in the Roon star system is the home of Auren Yomm and her parents. A lightstation in space guides ships through the treacherous dust cloud that surrounds the system. [DTV]

Umgul

This planet is a center for gambling and sports attractions. Tourists visit the world mainly to watch the famous blob races. [JS]

Umwak

The true name of the Dulok shaman. He often traveled in disguise to trick the Ewoks of Endor's forest moon. [ETV]

Unknown Regions

A name given to any parts of the galaxy that remain unexplored. Certain regions within the borders of known space are also called Unknown because they appear on no official astrogation charts. Some of these places were known to the Empire, the Rebellion, and even fringe society groups, but they remained hidden from the galaxy at large. [HE, HESB, SWRPG2]

Uplands, the

A pastoral region on the Thon continent located on the planet Alderaan. [SWR]

Urdur

This planet is the site of one of the secret bases used by the outlaw techs operating in and around Corporate Sector space. [HSE]

Uteen

An eel-like species. Uteens are members of the New Republic. [NR]

Uul-Rha-Shan

The bodyguard of Viceprex Mirkovig Hirken of the Corporate Sector Authority, he was a member of an intelligent reptilian species with red-and-white-patterned green scales, black eyes, a darting tongue, and sinister-looking fangs. [HSE]

Vader, Darth

The personification of the fear and evil the Emperor used to rule the galaxy, in the end Vader showed that the light side of the Force remained within him.

Born Anakin Skywalker, a spirited and talented child who exhibited great potential in the Force, he became an expert pilot and was one of the heroes of the Clone Wars. But he felt that the methods taught by his mentor, Obi-Wan Kenobi, were too slow. He was impatient to unlock the powers he glimpsed in the Force, seeking a quicker, less difficult path to the vast power he sensed all around him. Senator Palpatine offered him just such a path—the dark side. All Anakin had to do was give in to his anger, fear, and aggression. Ambitious and headstrong, he stepped into the dark side's embrace and became a servant of evil.

When Kenobi saw what had become of his friend and student, he tried to draw Anakin back from the dark side. But Anakin wanted none of that. The two fought, and Anakin fell into a molten pit. Though Kenobi thought him dead, Anakin emerged from the pit as Darth Vader. Vader's shattered body, however, had to be sustained by life-supporting armor and periodic stints in a hyperbaric medical chamber. When Kenobi learned that Vader lived, he helped Anakin's wife and newborn twins—whom Vader was not aware of—escape into hiding. Luke was taken to Tatooine, and Leia to Alderaan.

As a new Dark Lord of the Sith, Vader helped the self-proclaimed Emperor Palpatine hunt down and exterminate the Jedi Knights during the last days of the Old Republic. Later, he was sent to help Governor Tarkin develop the original Death Star battle station. When the Rebellion stole the plans for the Death Star, Vader was sent to retrieve them. Events conspired to bring Kenobi and Vader once more into battle, and in this fateful lightsaber duel aboard the Death Star, Kenobi allowed himself to be struck down. His corporeal body disappeared as he became one with the Force.

During the subsequent Rebel attack on the Death Star, Vader joined the battle in his own TIE interceptor. He concentrated his efforts on a lone X-wing from which Vader felt strong Force emanations. An unexpected blast caught Vader's ship and sent it spinning into space, allowing the pilot of the X-wing to target the battle station's weak spot and destroy it.

Vader survived the battle and a second encounter with the Force user on Mimban, though he lost his right arm in the resulting lightsaber duel. He soon discovered that the Force user was the son he never knew he had. Both the Emperor and Vader wanted to convert young Skywalker to the dark side, but Vader had his own agenda. He wanted to rule the galaxy with Luke at his side. Because of this development and because the Rebellion was proving to be more dangerous than previously suspected, Vader was put in charge of the Imperial fleet assigned to find and destroy the Alliance leaders.

Darth Vader

The next time that father and son met was on Cloud City, after Imperial probe droids and bounty hunters tracked down Princess Leia and Han Solo. Luke's friends were used as bait, and during a furious lightsaber battle

Vader revealed his true identity to the young Jedi. "I am your father," Vader said. Luke rejected Vader's claims and offers, losing his right hand to his father's lightsaber and barely escaping from Cloud City with his life.

Over the next few months, Vader oversaw a galaxywide effort to locate the elusive Luke Skywalker and his Rebel associates. Vader's plans to turn young Skywalker to the dark side were jeopardized by a new threat—Prince Xizor, head of the Black Sun criminal organization. Xizor attempted to usurp Vader's position with the Emperor and assassinate Luke. He failed in both endeavors.

The last meeting between father and son occurred on the forest moon of Endor after Luke surrendered to Vader's troops. This time the younger Skywalker did not arrive as a half-trained apprentice Jedi, but as a full-fledged Jedi Knight. Luke's faith in his father's innate goodness won the day, bringing Anakin out of the darkness of Darth Vader and back into the light. Vader saved Luke and destroyed the Emperor, but at the cost of his own life. Vader's final act—as Anakin and not as the Dark Lord of the Sith—was to look upon Luke and tell him that he was right: there was still a spark of light trapped deep within the dark side, and Luke had helped set it free. [DSTC, ESB, RJ, SME, SOTE, SW, SWSB]

Vakil, Nrin

A Quarren, he was a member of Rogue Squadron. [XW]

Valarian, Lady

A Whiphid, she was a crimelord on Tatooine who competed with Jabba the Hutt. After Jabba's death, she set out to take over much of the Hutt's empire. [GG7, SWCG, TJP]

Valiant

This Alderaanian *Thranta*-class war cruiser was one of three ships modified with robotic controls and slaved to accept commands from *Another Chance*. The *Valiant* and its companions defended the armory ship from pirates and smugglers. It came to the aid of Rogue Squadron when the pilots were ambushed at the Graveyard of Alderaan. Later, it was refitted and placed under the command of New Republic officer Aril Nunb. [BW]

Valley of Royalty

Located on the planet Duro, this valley is famous for its massive monuments to ancient rulers, including Queen Rana. [MMY]

vaporator

This device used on arid planets, such as Tatooine, consists of three-to-five-meter-tall refrigeration cylinders that condense water vapor and store the resulting liquid in large underground tanks. The water is kept for later consumption or sold for profit. [ISWU, SW]

Varn

The chief scout for Tyrann, the Supreme Master of the Serpent Masters. [CSW]

Veers, General Maximilian

Commander of the Imperial ground troops assigned to Lord Darth Vader's special armada during the Galactic Civil War. He was ordered by Vader to personally lead his troops into battle on the planet Hoth. His force consisted of AT-AT walkers and waves of Imperial snowtroopers. He was later betrayed by his son, Zev, who joined the Alliance. [ESB, GG3, SWSB]

Veers, Zev

Son of the Imperial general who commanded the ground assault against the Rebel base on Hoth. He disowned his father and went against his wishes when he joined the Alliance. During the Battle of Calamari, Zev was the chief gunner aboard the New Republic Star Destroyer *Emancipator*. [DE]

Vek

A handpicked survivor of the dark-sider Kueller's pogroms on Almania, he was a young man who served the dark-sider as best he could. Even so, Kueller could never remember why he spared the boy's life in the first place. [NR]

Vekker

A Quarren, he was a Vigo in the Black Sun criminal organization. He controlled a small empire of casinos and entertainment-based industries. Some of these were legal establishments, but many served as fronts for illegal Black Sun ventures. [SESB, SOTE]

Ven, Nawara

A Twi'lek, he was a member of Rogue Squadron. [BW, KT, RS, WG]

Verdanth

A jungle planet where R2-D2 and C-3PO were stranded after they were sent to investigate an Imperial messenger drone prior to the Battle of Hoth. [CSW]

Vergere

A Jedi Knight during the time of Palpatine's chancellorship, Vergere was a member of the rare, nearly extinct Fosh species. Sent by Jedi Master Mace Windu to investigate the mysterious planet Zonama Sekot, she disappeared and was presumed lost, then reappeared fifty-four years later during the Yuuzhan Vong invasion. [CHR, HT, RP]

Verpine

An advanced species of humanoid insectoids. Verpine possess thin, sticklike bodies with awkwardly articulated joints and chitinous shells. The Verpine live in the Roche asteroid field, using great repulsor shells to keep inhabited asteroids from crashing into each other and to deflect other bits of space debris. They hollowed out the asteroids for use as colonies, sealing them against space and filling them with technological wonders. They have innate expertise in most fields of technology, and their childlike fascination with machinery serves them well.

The Verpine are expert starship builders. The Slayn & Korpil Corporation, named for two neighboring Verpine colonies, has been well known and respected since the days of the Old Republic. The Verpine helped Admiral Ackbar design and build the B-wing starfighter. [BW, CPL, DFRSB, GG4, SFS]

Ver Seryan, Karia

A life-bearer on Leria Kerlsil, she was about 300 years old when Lando Calrissian investigated her as a possible marriage candidate. [AC]

vibro-ax

A handheld melee weapon with a broad blade. An ultrasonic generator located in the ax handle produces the vibrations that allow the blade to cut with only the slightest touch. [HSR, SWSB]

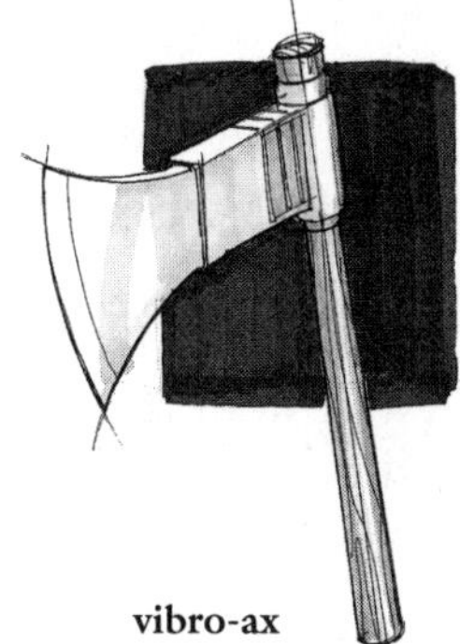

vibro-ax

vibroblade

This ultrasonic-vibration weapon is a powered knife or dagger with a reverberating blade edge that produces great cutting power with only the slightest touch. [HSE, HSR, SWSB]

Victory-class Star Destroyer

The earliest version of the Imperial Star Destroyer, this smaller vessel measures 900 meters long. It was designed by Republic engineer Walex Blissex near the end of the Clone Wars. As the *Imperial*-class vessels came to prominence, more and more *Victory*-class vessels were relegated to planetary defense roles. A number were decommissioned and sold to planetary defense forces, including the Corporate Sector Authority. [HSR, ISB, SWSB, SWVG]

Vidkun, Benedict

A henpecked engineer with a sallow complexion and emaciated form. He agreed to help Luke Skywalker and company rescue Princess Leia Organa from her prison in Prince Xizor's palace.

Vidkun not only provided maps of the sewer conduits beneath the palace, he also led Luke, Lando Calrissian, Dash Rendar, and Chewbacca through the labyrinthine passages. In the end, Vidkun revealed his true nature and shot Dash in the hip with his blaster. Unfortunately for the traitor, Dash returned fire with a direct hit from his own blaster pistol. [SESB, SOTE]

Vigo

The title granted to Prince Xizor's most powerful lieutenants. Each was entrusted with a portion of the Black Sun crime syndicate. They controlled all activities within their sphere of influence and reported back to Xizor on a regular basis. [SESB, SOTE]

Vilas

A male from Dathomir, he was the Force-sensitive companion and apprentice of Nightsister Vonnda Ra. She wanted him to lead a new order of Dark Jedi, but his competition for that spot was Zekk. The two battled in the Shadow Academy space station, where Zekk sliced Vilas in half with his lightsaber. [YJK]

Vima-Da-Boda

A powerful Jedi, she was directly related to Vima Sunrider, daughter of Nomi Sunrider. Vima-Da-Boda lost her powers after giving free reign to her anger and hatred, then finally succumbed to despair after her daughter's death. Her retreat from the world saved her from the Jedi Purge. She was imprisoned in the spice mines of Kessel for a time, where she provided elementary training to Kyp Durron. She eventually found a hiding place on the streets of Nar Shaddaa, where the old

Vima-Da-Boda

woman lived as a beggar. Six years after the Battle of Endor, the 200-year-old Vima met Princess Leia Organa Solo and gave her a gift—her ancient lightsaber. Months later, she took a post in Luke Skywalker's Jedi academy and helped him train new Jedi. [DE, DE2, JS]

Vinda

Co-owner, with D'rag, of Starshipwrights and Aerospace Engineers Incorporated, he was once owed credits for the work his company performed on Han Solo's *Millennium Falcon.* [HSR]

Virago

Prince Xizor's personal transport and assault ship. It was the first of the extremely fast *StarViper*-class assault fighters. [SOTE, SWVG]

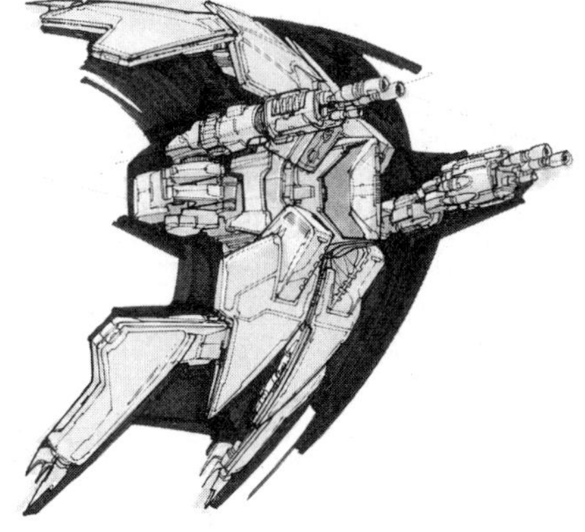

Virago

Virgilio, Captain

New Republic officer in command of the escort frigate *Quenfis*, one of the ships in Admiral Hiram Drayson's Home Guard Fleet assigned to protect Coruscant. Virgilio had long been a supporter of the Bothans, for he was among the crew of the Alliance ship that helped the Bothan spies return with the plans for the second Death Star battle station. At the time, Virgilio was a young third officer on a Corellian gunship. The ship picked up a distress call whose code identified its senders as members of a large team of Bothan intelligence agents operating in the outer regions. Of that team, only six survived—but they carried with them the plans and secret location of the second Death Star. They also intercepted the Emperor's private schedule, indicating when he would be visiting the site. [DFR, DFRSB]

Vjun

The planet where Darth Vader built his remote private refuge, Bast Castle. It was later the headquarters of dark-side executor Sedriss and the Emperor's elite force of Dark Jedi. [DE2, EE]

Vlee, Ussar

One of the three famous Gand ruetsavii who were sent to observe Ooryl Qrygg's life and determine his worthiness to become janwuine. [BW]

vocabulator

A device that allows a droid to produce sounds. It is usually visible as a grille or orifice. Protocol droids use the most sophisticated vocabulators. [SWN, SWSB]

voice manipulation

One of the most frequently used manifestations of the Force by Jedi Knights, it allows a Jedi to verbally implant suggestions into the minds of others and cause the appropriate responses. The Jedi employ voice manipulation to peacefully achieve their objectives. [RJN, SWN]

Voice Override: Epsilon Actual

A verbal command that immediately supersedes a droid's primary programming. This override function is activated by a verbal code, usually delivered in the form of a word or phrase. [SWR]

Vontor, Third Battle of

The last in a series of major conflicts directed against the pre-Republic tyrant known as Xim the Despot. In this battle, the forces that opposed his rule finally defeated him. [HLL]

Vorn, Liegeus Sarpaetius

Seti Ashgad's pilot, he was a master holo-forger and a competent designer of artificial intelligence systems for spacecraft. He was a captive of the droch Dzym, who wanted the pilot to transport him safely off Nam Chorios. Later, Vorn was reunited with his lost love, Admiral Daala. [POT]

vornskr

A violent, long-legged quadruped with a doglike muzzle, sharp teeth, and a whiplike tail. It lives on the planet Myrkr. During the day, vornskrs are sedate and inactive. At night, they are nocturnal hunters. The vornskr's tail is covered with a mild poison that inflicts painful welts and has the capability to stun prey. Vornskrs display an unnatural hatred of Jedi, often going out of their way to hunt and attack Force users. Talon Karrde has two domestic vornskrs, his pets Sturm and Drang. These guard animals had their tails clipped to reduce their normally aggressive nature. [HE, HESB]

Vorru, Fliry

The onetime administrator of the Corellian sector for the Old Republic, he always turned a blind eye to the smuggling activities all around him. He was sent to the Kessel spice mines by Palpatine and was eventually freed by Rogue Squadron. He later joined up with Imperial Intelligence Director Ysanne Isard and was named her minister of trade on Thyferra. He was eventually left behind by Isard and captured by Rebel forces. [BW, KT, WG]

Vri'syk, Peshk

A Bothan, he was a member of Rogue Squadron. He was killed during the raid on Borleias. [RS]

Vuffi Raa

This astrogation/pilot droid traveled with Lando Calrissian for at least a year shortly after the young gambler won the *Millennium Falcon*. The droid was technically Lando's property, as the gambler had won him in a game of sabacc, but after a few adventures he came to regard the droid as his friend. Vuffi Raa stood a meter tall, with five multijointed tentacle limbs that he could move at various angles and even prop himself up on to achieve more height. Vuffi was the shape of an attenuated starfish with sinuous manipulators that served both as arms and legs. These were connected to a dinner-plate-sized pentagonal torso with a single, softly glowing deep red vision crystal. Vuffi's entire body was covered in highly polished chromium. In reality, Vuffi Raa was a "baby starship," a member of a sentient droid-ship species. [LCF, LCM, LCS, RD]

V-wing airspeeder

An atmospheric attack craft deployed from orbit into a planet's air space by huge speeder transports. The New Republic used these airspeeder fighters during the Battle of Calamari. [DE]

Wadda

A humanoid employee of the slaver Zlarb. He was distinguished by his great strength and height, standing nearly 2.2 meters tall. He had a jutting forehead, protruding vestigial horns, and glossy brown skin. [HSR]

Waivers List

A Corporate Sector Authority register that lists ships exempt from the multitude of vessel requirements usually imposed on vessels entering Authority-controlled space. [HSE]

walker

See All Terrain Armored Transport; All Terrain Scout Transport.

wampa ice creature

A terrible carnivorous beast that fearlessly hunts the snow-packed tundra of Hoth. It is more than two meters tall, with white fur, yellow eyes, and sharp claws and teeth. Wampas carve lairs out of the ice, forming huge caves in which to nest. When they hunt, they often surprise prey due to the natural camouflage provided by their white fur. Wampas never hunt when they are hungry. Instead, they capture living prey and store it in their ice caves for later consumption. [ESB, GG3, ISWU]

war droid

Older mechanicals designed for combat, they were also called war robots. Less refined in appearance than newer droids, they had heavy armor plating, inefficient power delivery systems, and generally less intelligence and self-awareness than their more sophisticated descendants. War droids could be found in isolated and remote sections of the galaxy even during the Galactic Civil War and later. [DE, HLL]

Warlug

A Gamorrean, he was a guard for Jabba the Hutt. [SWSB, TJP]

Warrick, Erpham

This legendary Ewok warrior built the great Ewok battle wagon. His great-grandson was the Ewok hero Wicket W. Warrick. [ETV]

Warrick, Wicket W.

An Ewok hero, he was the first of his tribe to find and befriend Princess Leia Organa after she crashed a speeder bike and became lost on Endor's forest moon. Wicket was influential in convincing the rest of his tribe to aid the Rebel strike team that sought to disable the Imperial shield generator located on the forest moon. When Leia and the Rebels attacked the Imperial installation, Wicket fought at their side, helping them gain access to and destroy the guarded facility. [BFE, ETV, RJ, RJN]

Wicket W. Warrick

Waru

A powerful being from a parallel universe, it was drawn through a split in the space-time continuum created by a black hole and a quantum crystal star. The Waru appeared to be a complex construct of gold shields covering a slab of raw tissue.

It was able to heal others by encasing them in its ichor, but it sometimes killed a being brought to it for healing by sucking away its strength. Lord Hethrir planned to offer Anakin Solo to the Waru in return for great Force powers. Hethrir was taken into the Waru instead, which then closed in on itself and disappeared. [CS]

Watchkeeper

A destroyer in the Bakuran task force. It was vaporized by a Selonian planet repulsor. [AS]

watchman

A title given to the Jedi Master with the responsibility of maintaining harmony and justice in a particular star system or segment of the galaxy, as arranged through agreement with the Old Republic. [DLS, TOJ]

wave walker

An Imperial light attack vehicle designed to operate above the surface of water. During the Battle of Calamari, wave walkers were constructed aboard the World Devastators and unleashed upon the Mon Calamari and their New Republic allies. [DE]

Wayland

This planet was the site of one of the Emperor's private storehouses and figured prominently in Grand Admiral Thrawn's plan to destroy the New Republic and reestablish the Empire. On Wayland, Thrawn found what he needed deep inside Mount Tantiss—a working cloaking shield and plenty of Spaarti cloning cylinders. He also found the dark Jedi Master Joruus C'baoth.

The planet was originally discovered during the Old Republic's second wave of expansion. A colony ship crashed on the planet, and due to an improper entry in the official astrogation charts, the colonists were left on their own. Besides the human colonists, Wayland was inhabited by two intelligent species, the Psadans and the Myneyrshi. With only bow-and-arrow technology, the two species were no match for the blasters and repulsors the colonists brought with them. However, power cells eventually failed, and the colonists were forced to take up the technology of the natives. Centuries later, the Empire rediscovered the planet. The Emperor himself ordered the planet's location stricken from all records, then had a special storehouse built within a hollowed-out mountain. [HE, HESB, LC, LCSB]

webweaver

A large, deadly arachnid. Webweavers live on one of the lower ecolevels of the planet Kashyyyk. [HLL]

Weequay

A humanoid species with coarse leathery skin and bald heads. They wear a traditional single braided topknot on one side of their heads. Jabba the Hutt employed two Weequays as skiff guards. [GG5, RJ, SWCG]

Wermyn

A huge, one-armed brute, he was in charge of plant operations at Maw Installation. [COF]

Whaladon

A species of intelligent, whalelike mammals that inhabit the deep oceans of the planet Mon Calamari. [GDV]

Whiphid

A species of hulking, fur-covered bipeds about 2.5 meters tall with a prominent forehead, long, bowed cheekbones, and two upturned tusks rising from their jaws. The bitterly cold planet Toola in the Kaelta system is their homeworld. These ferocious predators love the hunt, enjoying the whole process of tracking something down and killing it. They also appreciate the luxuries of advanced technology, often accepting lucrative bounty-hunting contracts from law enforcement agencies, criminal organizations, and the Empire. [GG4]

Whistler

Corran Horn's R2 series astromech droid. It is equipped with a special criminal investigation and forensics circuitry package provided by CorSec, the Corellian Security Force. [BW, RS]

Whistler's Whirlpool

This tapcafe on the planet Trogan is situated on the coast of Trogan's most densely populated continent and built around a natural formation called the Drinking Cup. This bowl-shaped rock pit is open to the sea at its base, and six times every day the tidal shift causes the water level to rise and fall. At these times, the bowl fills with a violent white-water maelstrom. The tapcafe's tables are arranged in concentric circles around the bowl, striking a nice balance between luxury and spectacular natural drama. Unfortunately, the noise made by the water striking the natural breakers within the bowl is quite uncomfortable for most of the clientele, and the Whistler's Whirlpool isn't very popular. Talon Karrde held a meeting for his fellow smuggling chiefs at the Whirlpool to discuss how Grand Admiral Thrawn's campaign against the New Republic might affect their businesses. [LC]

Wialu

A member of the Fallanassi religious order. Luke Skywalker convinced her to help in the New Republic's war on the Yevetha. She used her gift of immersion meditation to create a "phantom" fleet of New Republic ships. [TT]

Wiamdi, Vviir

One of three famous Gand ruetsavii sent to observe Ooryl Qrygg's life and determine his worthiness to become janwuine. [BW]

Wicket

See Warrick, Wicket W.

Wild Karrde

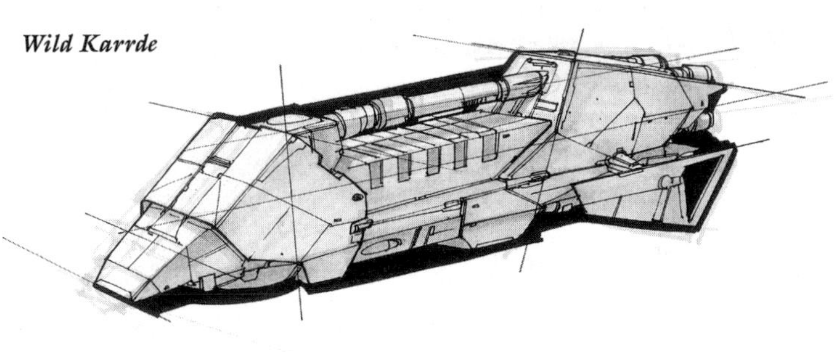

Wild Karrde

Talon Karrde's personal space vessel. This dilapidated-looking bulk freighter looks like any of a thousand Corellian Action VI transports plying the space lanes. But Karrde extensively modified the 125-meter-long vessel, making it faster and more powerful than it appears. The freighter serves as Karrde's base of operations when he is on board. It has combat-rated shields and three turbolasers. Its warship-class sensor package and armor-reinforced hull are definitely not standard issue, and its sensor stealth travel mode rivals the best Imperial spy ship in the fleet. The interior underwent modifications, as well. A large portion of the forward hold was converted into living quarters and offices, and a permanent kennel was installed in the main hold for Karrde's pet vornskrs. [DFRSB, HE, HESB]

Wild Space

The galaxy's true frontier, it was once considered part of the Unknown Regions until it was opened to exploration and settlement as one of the Emperor's last acts. Grand Admiral Thrawn was charged with taming this wilderness, and he declared it part of the Empire. However, as the Empire was too busy to enforce its subjugation, much of Wild Space remained free. [HESB, SWRPG2]

Wiley

An Ewok on Endor's forest moon. [ETV, RJ]

Willard, Commander Vanden

An Alliance officer serving under General Jan Dodonna at the Rebel base on Yavin 4. In the years prior to the dissolution of the senate, he was a spy for Princess Leia and Viceroy Bail Organa of Alderaan. [GG1, SWN]

Windy

One of Luke Skywalker's childhood friends. Windom Starkiller grew up with Luke on the planet Tatooine. [SWN]

Winter

A tall, regal, and beautiful woman with silky white hair and an aura of confidence, she is Princess Leia Organa Solo's aide and companion. She grew up with Leia on Alderaan. As children, Winter was often mistaken for the true princess because she always looked the part. The two became close friends, and when Leia entered the senate, Winter went along as her royal aide and executive assistant.

In addition to her normal organizational skills, Winter has a perfect memory. Everything she sees, hears, or otherwise senses is recorded in her memory. She forgets nothing, even if she wants to. She was off planet when Alderaan was destroyed. Bail Organa had sent her to help Rebel agents, temporarily sending her away from Leia's side. This separation lasted throughout the Galactic Civil War, as Winter was assigned to Alliance Procurement and Supply where her perfect memory was used to create maps and gather intelligence for the agents charged with

Winter

gathering supplies for the Alliance. Her reputation became so well known in intelligence circles that the Imperials began to call her Targeter. Her perfect memory has bad points. Where other Alderaan survivors are able to let the pain of the planet's destruction fade with time, Winter's memories are clear and bright even years later. She serves as Leia's aide in the New Republic, and was nursemaid to Leia's children for a time. She eventually became quite friendly with Admiral Ackbar. [BW, COF, DFR, DFRSB, HE, LC, NR, SWCG]

Wistie

A tiny, giggly, pixielike being also known as firefolk, that glows brightly and can fly. Wisties live on Endor's forest moon. [EA, ETV]

Witches of Dathomir

This group of Force-sensitive women lives on the planet Dathomir and is organized into nine clans. Their main foes are the Nightsisters, a group of witches who were cast out for embracing the dark side. The Witches' society is completely matriarchal where men are used as slaves and breeders. [CPL]

womp rat

A carnivorous creature that inhabits the canyons of Tatooine. Womp rats are vicious, hair-covered rodents that grow as large as three meters. They travel in packs and use their claws and teeth to bring down prey. Luke Skywalker used to hunt womp rats in Beggar's Canyon, targeting them at high speeds from the cockpit of his T-16 skyhopper. [SW, SWN, SWR]

Wookiee

A tall, strong, fur-covered species native to the planet Kashyyyk. They have a reputation as ferocious opponents and loyal allies. The average Wookiee stands over two meters in height and lives much longer than a human. On Kashyyyk, Wookiees live in cities situated high within giant trees. Though they appear to be primitive, they combine a love of nature with modern technology. The Wookiee language consists of grunts and growls. They understand other languages, but their limited vocal ability makes it impossible for them to speak anything other than their own tongue. A Wookiee also has amazing regenerative powers that let them heal more in a day than a human would in two weeks.

As tree dwellers, Wookiees have wickedly curved claws that pop from hidden fingertip sheaths with the flex of a muscle. With the aid of these claws and their strong limbs, Wookiees travel through the upper reaches of the great wroshyr trees of their homeworld, clinging to vines and branches with ease. Wookiees never use their claws in combat, however, as that is considered a serious breach of the Wookiee code of honor.

From the earliest days of the Empire, the Wookiees, their world, and their colonies were placed under martial law and enslaved. It wasn't until after the Battle of Endor that the Alliance was able to finally set the Wookiees free.

Chewbacca, Han Solo's copilot and partner, was a Wookiee. [CPL, ESB, HE, HESB, RJ, SW, SWHS, SWSB, SWWS]

Wookiee honor family

A special bond of friendship that joins one Wookiee with a group of other Wookiees, or even with members of other species. An honor family comprises a Wookiee's true friends. Chewbacca the Wookiee considered his companions Han Solo, Princess Leia Organa Solo, Luke Skywalker, and the droids R2-D2 and C-3PO to be part of his honor family. [HESB, HLL, SWSB]

Wookiee life debt

A sacred Wookiee custom pledged to anyone who saves a Wookiee life. Not slavery, a life debt is a sacred act of honor to repay that which is without measure. Chewbacca pledged a life debt to Han Solo for acts Solo performed when the pair first met. [HESB, HLL, SWSB]

Wookiee Rite of Passage

A test that calls for an adolescent Wookiee to perform a feat that is dangerous and difficult. A Wookiee can attempt the feat alone or with friends. If successful, the Wookiee emerges with physical proof of bravery that can be worn or carried as a trophy. [YJK]

worldcraft

A planetoid-sized starship created by command of the Emperor and given to a few of his cruelest officers. One was used by Lord Hethrir. [CS]

World Devastator

A great Imperial war machine even more terrible than the Death Star. World Devastators could inflict massive amounts of destruction, then salvage and use the destroyed material to create new warships to bolster the Imperial fleet. These machines were also referred to as World Sweepers, World Smashers, and City Eaters. Designed by Imperial engineer Umak Leth, these massive machines were powered by gigantic ion engines and repulsorlift gravity transformers. The open maws contained raging molecular furnaces that were powered by microscopic black holes. Whole cities were pulled into these furnaces, where the raging power disassembled the material into simple molecules. These molecules, in turn, were reassembled within the onboard factories as new Imperial warships.

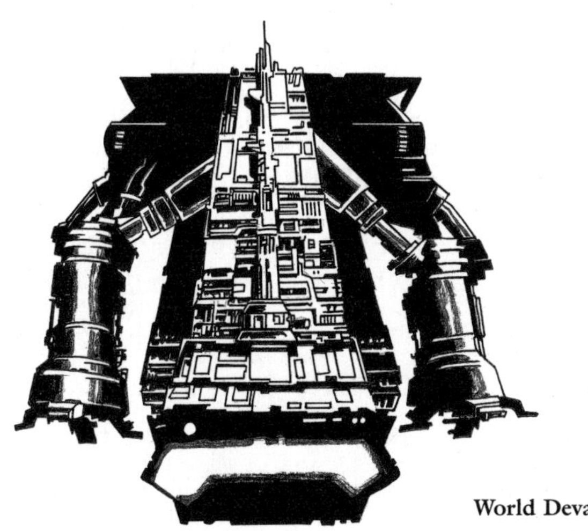

World Devastator

Within a Devastator's core were processing plants—blast furnaces, testing laboratories, foundries, metalworks, stamping mills, and chemical vats. The machine didn't always use everything a Devastator destroyed. Some raw materials were stored for transport to specialized industrial planets. The upper decks of a Devastator housed control towers, command stations, living areas, and docking bays. The outer surface was covered with gun towers and missile launch ports. Shield generators cloaked the entire vessel, though selected portions of the shields could be raised and lowered by the command personnel.

World Devastators contained complex computer and guidance systems that were regulated from the planet Byss by means of a hyperspace-transmitted master control signal. This signal led to their eventual downfall, thanks to Luke Skywalker and R2-D2. [DE, DESB, SWVG]

Wormie

A nickname given to Luke Skywalker by his childhood friends Camie and Fixer. [SWN, SWR]

wroshyr tree

A giant tree native to the jungle world Kashyyyk. The separate branches of the wroshyr trees meet to form one interlocked branch, which then sprouts new branches of its own. These reach out in all directions to find other branches to join with. This tendency toward unity makes wroshyr trees strong, and it is a natural symbol of the Wookiee concepts of honor and family. The wroshyr trees in the Rwookrrorro city grouping are actually a single giant plant with a unified root system. [HE, HESB]

Wuher

A human, he was a shift bartender at the Mos Eisley spaceport cantina. [TMEC]

Wwebyls

A tiny humanoid from the planet Yn, he was a New Republic senator. [NR]

Wynni

A Wookiee smuggler, she tried to seduce Chewbacca on his first visit to Skip 1. [NR]

X-1 Viper Automadon

A war droid manufactured on the factory world Balmorra. It is equipped with molecular shielding, which absorbs energy from an attack and redirects it to the droid's own turbolasers. [DE2]

X-222

A sleek high-altitude atmospheric fighter craft, commonly called a triple-deuce. [HLL]

Xaverri

A friend of Han Solo's from his smuggling days, she was an accomplished stage magician and con artist whose husband and children had been murdered by the Empire. Considered to be one of the best illusionists in the galaxy, she had golden skin and heavy black hair. She hated the Empire with a passion. Han Solo spent about six months traveling with Xaverri, working as her assistant and helping her pull off scams on Imperial officials. She eventually abandoned Han because she believed she couldn't afford to get too close to anyone. [CS, HG]

xenoarchaeology

The scientific study of ancient alien cultures through the artifacts they left behind. [SME]

Xim the Despot

A tyrant, he conquered a vast region of space long before the Old Republic was established. Some historians claim that he ruled thousands of star systems. His armies reportedly plundered and subjugated world after world, filling Xim's coffers with wealth beyond imagining. Xim's royal guard consisted of war droids programmed to guard him and his treasures. Ruthless and unscrupulous, Xim committed atrocities against those he conquered, including mass spacings. Xim ruled for thirty standard years before the conquered star systems were finally able to overthrow him and end his reign of terror. [HLL]

Xizor, Prince

This Falleen prince, a tall humanoid of reptile stock, sat at the center of the shadows that formed the Black Sun criminal organization, which he secretly commanded. He watched and manipulated events to pit the Empire against the Rebel Alliance. With a powerful personal charisma and a brilliant grasp of strategy, he was publicly known as the owner and president of Xizor Transport Systems (XTS).

Prince Xizor

Xizor often indulged his luxurious tastes. He lived in an immense palace in Imperial Center, delighted in fine food from around the galaxy, and had an eye for females of all species. Like all Falleen males, he produced powerful pheromones to entice humanoid women.

Xizor was more than a century old during the time of the Galactic Civil War. He wore his hair in an elaborate topknot, with a second, smaller ponytail at the base of his skull. He possessed regal stature and the cool, calculating manner of a man who was used to getting his own way.

The son of the king of Falleen, Xizor was not on his homeworld when Darth Vader ordered the eradication of 200,000 Falleen nearly a decade before the Battle of Hoth. Xizor hated Vader and sought to destroy the Dark Lord even as he strove to improve his own standing with the Emperor. Prince Xizor died in a final confrontation with Darth Vader when the Dark Lord ordered the destruction of Xizor's skyhook retreat. [SESB, SOTE]

Xizor Transport Systems (XTS)

An immense shipping megacorporation owned and operated by Prince Xizor. The megacorp maintained fleets of container ships and bulk freighters, making billions of credits by hauling cargo throughout the galaxy. In addition, XTS offered high-paying clients the services of fast courier ships and light freighters. The megacorp served as a front for the Black Sun crime syndicate and provided substantial funds to Xizor's criminal enterprises. [SESB, SOTE]

XP-38

This landspeeder was one of the newer models to hit the market about the time of the Galactic Civil War. [SW, SWSB]

XT-6

A service droid used by Jedi Cay Qel-Droma to replace the arm he lost in battle. [TOJ]

Xucphra

This Thyferran corporation was a leader in bacta production and distribution. The company promoted civil war on Thyferra, seeking complete control of the Bacta Cartel. Former Imperial Intelligence Director Ysanne Isard helped and was eventually awarded control of the corporation. Rogue Squadron defeated them after a long and bloody war. [BW]

Xux, Qwi

A blue-skinned humanoid from Omwat, she was taken from her home at an early age and sent to work in Grand Moff Tarkin's secret weapons development lab—the Maw Installation. Under the tutelage of Imperial designer Bevel Lemelisk, she helped develop the first Death Star and the World Devastators. Her most powerful design was the indestructible Sun Crusher. She helped Han Solo and his companions escape from the Maw Installation, but had her memory erased by the Force powers of Kyp Durron. General Wedge Antilles helped her start her own healing process. [COF, JS]

X-wing starfighter

This starfighter played a significant role in the first major Alliance victory of the Galactic Civil War—the Battle of Yavin. The T-65 was the last design produced by Incom Corporation

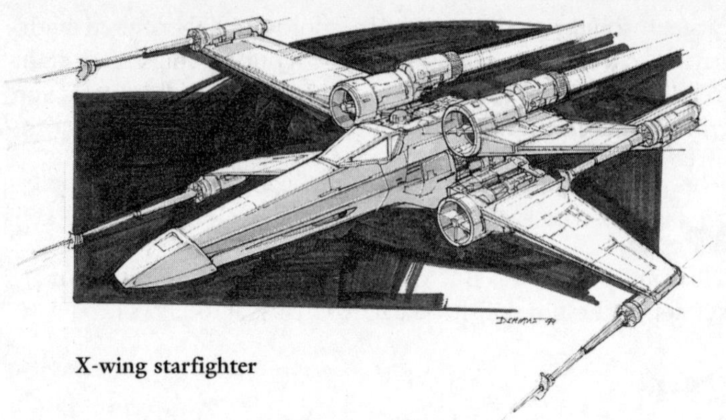
X-wing starfighter

prior to its nationalization by the Empire. An Alliance commando team helped Incom's senior design staff defect with plans and prototypes of the X-wing.

Named for its double-layered wings that split open for atmospheric flight and during attack runs, this small, single-pilot starfighter measures 12.5 meters from nose to engine block. With powerful sublight ion engines, a targeting computer, defensive shields, four wingtip laser cannons, and a pair of proton torpedo launchers, the X-wing is fast, highly maneuverable, and extremely well armed. These starfighters are also equipped with hyperdrives for lightspeed travel.

A recessed socket, situated on the outer hull behind the cockpit, was designed as an interface for an R2 astromech droid. An R2 unit assists the pilot by monitoring onboard systems, performing routine and emergency maintenance, and even flies the craft when circumstances warrant. Astromechs also augment the craft's computer capabilities, aiding with astrogation and holding preset hyperspace jump coordinates. [ESB, RJ, SW, SWSB, SWVG]

Y-4 Raptor transport

A military transport shuttle used by Warlord Zsinj's elite commandos. Just under thirty meters long, it ferries troops between starships and bases, and can carry a number of compact assault vehicles for combat missions. [CPL, SWSB]

Yaga Minor

This planet is the site of a major Imperial shipyard. [DFR, LC, LCSB]

Yag'Dhul

This planet is the homeworld of the Givin. The system contains an *Empress*-class space station that was loyal to Warlord Zsinj. [BW, GG4, KT]

Yaka

A species of near-human cyborgs transformed by superintelligent invaders from the planet Arkania. The Arkanians implanted cyborg brain enhancers into the Yakas, increasing the species' intelligence to genius level. One side effect was a twisted sense of humor that all Yakas possess. [DE]

Yak Face

See Saelt-Marae.

yammosk

This living creature was the war coordinator of the first Yuuzhan Vong invasion force, the Praetorite Vong. The extragalactic invasion force was unified by the telepathic willpower of the great yammosk, which connected all of the Yuuzhan Vong warriors so they acted in unison and were therefore vastly more effective. They were joined by something that was like the Force, but was not the Force.

The great creature established a base on the fourth planet of the Helska system and prepared its defenses for an all-out assault on the New Republic. It was even preparing to spawn when Luke Skywalker and his companions led an attack on Helska 4. The yammosk died when the planet was destroyed, thus ending the first Yuuzhan Vong invasion. [VP]

Yang, Kar

Considered by some to be the second most skilled bounty hunter in the galaxy, this vulture-headed humanoid was hired by Azool to track down the human replica droid Guri after Prince Xizor's presumed death. When Yang found her, Guri killed him. [SEE]

Yar, Senator Tolik

An Oolid, he was a member of the New Republic Senate Defense Council and one of Chief of State Leia Organa Solo's champions during the Yevethan crisis. [BTS]

Yavin

A gas giant planet located in a system of the same name in the Outer Rim Territories. Of its dozens of moons, three are capable of supporting humanoid life. These are designated Yavin 4, 8, and 13. Several kinds of creatures live within the gas giant, including floating gasbag creatures in the upper atmosphere and nearly two-dimensional crawlers in the frozen liquids that surround the planet's metallic core. The pressures near the core compress carbon and metallic hydrogen together to form quantum crystals called Corusca gems. Nineteen years after the Battle of Endor, Lando Calrissian established *GemDiver Station* in Yavin's atmosphere to mine Corusca gems. [GG2, SW, SWN, YJK]

Yavin, Battle of

The first major engagement of the Galactic Civil War was also the first major tactical victory for the Rebel Alliance. The battle occurred in the shadow of Yavin, near its fourth moon. This was not a planned engagement. Instead, it was the result of the actions of Rebel spies, the capture of Princess Leia Organa, and her eventual escape from the original Death Star battle station.

Rebel spies stole the plans for the Death Star, the Empire's newest weapon of mass destruction, barely escaping with their lives. They were chased across the galaxy, finally transferring the stolen data to the consular ship carrying Princess Leia Organa of Alderaan. The Princess had a twofold mission. She was to receive the stolen data for transport back to Alderaan, where it could then be used by the Alliance to discover the Death Star's vulnerabilities. On the way, she was to seek out the reclusive Jedi Knight Obi-Wan Kenobi from his hiding place on Tatooine and convince him to aid the growing Rebellion in its fight against the Empire. Before she could complete either of these missions, the Empire intercepted her ship as it entered orbit around Tatooine.

The Imperials, under the command of Lord Darth Vader, quickly overwhelmed the small contingent of soldiers aboard the consular ship and began an intensive search for the stolen plans. With time running out, Leia placed the technical readouts into the memory banks of the astromech droid R2-D2. She gave him specific orders to get off the ship and present himself to Obi-Wan Kenobi. The brave droid eluded capture and, along with his counterpart C-3PO, used an escape pod to reach the planet's surface. Through a series of adventures that brought the droids into the possession of Luke Skywalker and led to the dramatic rescue of Princess Leia, the secret plans finally reached the Alliance base on Yavin's fourth moon, with the Death Star close behind.

Rebel technicians and tacticians quickly studied the technical readouts and devised a plan for combating the battle station. The plan utilized the limited number of starfighters the Alliance could muster. The Death Star followed the *Millennium Falcon* to Yavin, and the Alliance quickly threw every vessel it had into space and attacked. The Rebel forces had little time, for once the Death Star cleared Yavin, the moon holding the secret base would be exposed to the full power of the battle station's primary weapon.

There were only two possible outcomes: the survival or total destruction of the Alliance. The success of the Rebel plan depended on the ability of a single starfighter to navigate the trenches in the Death Star's surface while avoiding laser tower fire and TIE fighters. Then the pilot had to target a small thermal exhaust vent and score a direct hit with a proton torpedo. Anything less would fail to cause the chain reaction needed to ignite the power core. After suffering massive losses and demonstrating high levels of skill and bravery, the Rebels seemed to be out of time. One chance remained, and it rested in the hands of the farm boy from Tatooine who was strong in the Force—Luke Skywalker.

Using the power of the Force, and aided by the timely intervention of Han Solo and the *Millennium Falcon*, Luke fired the shot heard around the galaxy. The Death Star, along with its crew of many of the most talented officers in the Empire, was destroyed in spectacular fashion. The Alliance quickly grew because of this impressive victory, and Luke Skywalker and his companions became known as the heroes of Yavin. [SW]

Yavin 4

This moon orbiting the gas giant Yavin is the site of ancient temples and ruins of the Massassi species. A jungle moon teeming with animal and plant life, it once served as the primary base for the Rebel Alliance. Underground tunnels connect almost all of the ruined complexes and lead to the Lost City of the Jedi. More than 4,000 years before the Galactic Civil War the Sith magician Naga Sadow fled to Yavin 4 with his followers. He created the Massassi warrior species, who were later enslaved by the dark Jedi Exar Kun and forced to construct many of the temples. Seven years after the Battle of Endor, Luke Skywalker turned the Great Temple into his Jedi Academy. [COF, CSW, DA, DLS, GG2, ISWU, LCJ, PDS, SW, SWN, TSW, YJK]

Yavin 8

A tundra moon orbiting the gas giant Yavin and inhabited by the intelligent amphibious humanoids called the Melodies. Some eighteen years after the Battle of Endor, Anakin Solo and the Jedi trainee Tahiri brought back a new Melodie child, Sannah, to be trained at the Jedi academy on Yavin 4. [GG2, JJK]

Yavin 13

A desert moon orbiting the gas giant Yavin and inhabited by the two intelligent but primitive species, the rabbitlike Gerbs and the serpentine Slith. [GG2]

Yavin system

This star system did not appear on many astrogation charts until after the Rebel Alliance victory in the Battle of Yavin during the Galactic Civil War. Three planets orbit the orange star: Fiddanl, Stroiketcy, and Yavin. [GG2]

yayax

A fierce, pantherlike beast that lives on Endor's forest moon. [ETV]

Yemm, Yarbolk

A Chadra-Fan, he was a reporter for TriNebulon News stationed on Nim Drovis. He was a controversial figure who had a bounty on his head because of his stories. He rescued C-3PO and R2-D2 while they were on Nim Drovis. [POT]

Yevetha

The dominant species in the Koornacht Cluster. These skeletal humanoids are from the planet N'zoth. Their six-fingered hands have retractable claws beneath their wrists. The Yevetha believe that their world is the center of the universe. They colonized eleven nearby planets into the Duskhan League with nothing more than sublight drive thrustships.

The Koornacht Cluster was restricted during the Empire's reign, and its inhabitants were forced to labor for their Imperial masters. Three years after the Battle of Endor, when the last remnants of the Empire finally fled the region, the Yevetha underwent a Second Birth. They settled a dozen more colony worlds and took command of captured Imperial vessels. Twelve years after the Battle of Endor, the Yevethan fleet eleminated all non-Yevethan colonies in the cluster in a series of brutal attacks known as the Great Purge. This led to a bitter war with the New Republic, in which the Yevethans were defeated. [BTS, SOL, TT]

Yevethan Protectorate

The proper name of the Duskhan League, an alliance of Yevethan worlds in the Koornacht Cluster. [BTS]

Yfra, Ambassador

An ambassador from the Hapes Cluster, she was a traitor who planned to have Queen Mother Ta'a Chume and Tenel Ka assassinated. [YJK]

Ylesia

This planet near Hutt space is the site of a fanatic religious colony whose priests use religion as a cover for their spice processing business. The false religion is based on a belief in the Oneness and the All, but the good feelings associated with it are the result of low-grade empathy provided by the t'landa Til. Pilgrims come to the planet to worship but end up working in the spice processing plants to help fill the Ylesian priests' coffers. [PS]

Ylesian Dream

A droid freighter that Han Solo used to escape *Trader's Luck* when he was about nineteen. Later, he earned a living piloting it for the Ylesian priests. [PS]

Ynr, Rhysati

A gifted pilot from Bespin, she became a member of Rogue Squadron. During training, she became friends with Corran Horn and started a relationship with Nawara Ven. [BW, RS]

Yoda, Jedi Master

A small, long-lived Jedi Master, he trained Jedi Knights for more than 800 years. When the Empire began its Jedi Purge, Yoda went into hiding on the swamp planet Dagobah. He used the Force and the planet's own natural defenses to discourage visitors, but maintained a watch over Luke Skywalker and Leia Organa through the Force. After the Battle of Hoth, visions of Obi-Wan Kenobi sent Luke to Dagobah. There, he encountered Yoda, who was almost 900 years old at the time. The Jedi Master reluctantly agreed to train Skywalker, despite the young man's reckless nature, age, and innate anger.

Against Yoda's protests, Luke cut his training short to go to the aid of his friends on Bespin. He returned to Dagobah after rescuing Han Solo from Tatooine, only to find that Yoda was dying. The Jedi Master revealed that Luke would have to confront Darth Vader and the Emperor to complete his Jedi training. Then Yoda vanished, becoming one with the Force. [ESB, GG5, RJ, SWCG, SWSB]

Jedi Master Yoda

Yomm, Auren

R2-D2 and C-3PO met the then fifteen-year-old girl during the early days of the Empire. She lived in the Umboo colony of Roon, where she demonstrated the skills and talents of an excellent athlete. She often led her competitive team, which included the sleek droid Bix, to victory in the Colonial Games. Her parents were Nilz and Bola Yomm. [DTV]

Yomm, Nilz

The father of Auren Yomm, he ran a trading post during the early days of the Empire and was a very respected physician in the Roon colonies. [DTV]

Yowza, Joh

A Yuzzum, he had a deep, raspy voice and served as the lead male singer for the Max Rebo Band. He performed at the band's last engagement for Jabba the Hutt. [RJSE]

ysalamiri

Indigenous to the planet Myrkr, these small, salamanderlike creatures have the unique ability to push back the Force. Furry snakes with legs, they live in the branches of Myrkr's metal-rich trees. An ysalamiri's claws grow directly into the branches, making it difficult to remove the creature from its perch without killing it. A single ysalamiri creates a ten-meter-radius bubble in which the Force does not exist. Those who have studied the creatures theorize that ysalamiri push the Force away from themselves like a bubble of air pushes away water. Within this bubble, a Force user cannot call on his or her powers or otherwise manipulate the Force.

Grand Admiral Thrawn's plans to destroy the New Republic included the use of the docile ysalamiri. He ordered Imperial engineers to build frames of pipes to support and nourish the creatures so that they could be removed from their branches and transported off planet. The nutrient frames were designed so that Thrawn and others could wear them as a mobile defense against Force users. The creatures also figured prominently in Thrawn's plans to rapidly grow clones in the Spaarti cloning cylinders he retrieved from the Emperor's storehouse on Wayland. [DFR, HE, HESB, LC]

Ysanna

Force-sensitive shaman-warriors that live on the planet Ossus. [DE2]

Yuuzhan Vong

An extragalactic humanoid species. The Yuuzhan Vong despise technology, especially droids. Instead, they utilize living organisms and biological agents to create a kind of living technology. Yorik coral is grown into coralskippers and other fighting vessels. The Yuuzhan Vong even cultivate creatures called dovin basals that can focus gravity.

While most reasoning species understand that death is inevitable, the Yuuzhan Vong culture embraces it. Life is preparation for death, and how one dies is the most important factor. Scars and tattoos mark each Yuuzhan Vong's rise toward godhood, and to die in battle is among their highest honors.

Through advance scouts like Nom Anor, the Yuuzhan Vong breached the galactic boundary—how long ago is unknown—

and learned much about the Empire and the New Republic. Twenty-one years after the Battle of Endor, the Yuuzhan Vong sent a small war force to start their full-scale conquest of the galaxy, planning to establish bases and spawn additional weapon-creatures one planet at a time. Working with Nom Anor and other hidden agents such as Yomin Carr, the Yuuzhan Vong arrived in a living worldship and established a base on the fourth planet of the Helska system for their yammosk, the creature that was their war coordinator.

This first Yuuzhan Vong invasion force was defeated at Helska 4. Nom Anor, however, continues to stir up chaos in the Core, ready to assist when the next invasion force arrives. [VP]

Yuzzem

These humanoids with long snouts, long arms, and heavy fur have great strength and volatile, unpredictable tempers. They were often found as slaves in Imperial labor camps or as hired hands employed to handle physical activities like mining. A pair of Yuzzem aided Princess Leia Organa and Luke Skywalker during their mission to the Circarpous star system. [SME]

Yuzzum

A round, fur-covered being with long, thin legs, and a wide mouth full of sharp, protruding teeth. Yuzzum inhabit the forest moon of Endor and are intelligent though somewhat barbaric. A few have found their way off planet to seek fame and fortune, like Joh Yowza who sang for the Max Rebo Band. [ETV, ISWU, RJSE]

Y-wing starfighter

This twin-engine, sixteen-meter-long starfighter is a multipurpose craft that can be used as an attack vessel or as a bomber. This hyperdrive-equipped starfighter is armed with two forward-mounted laser cannons, a rear-mounted twin ion cannon, twin proton torpedo launchers, and a droid-interface socket. It has combat-rated deflector shields, and its rugged construction allows it to take a considerable amount of damage before its systems fail. [ESB, RJ, SW, SWSB, SWVG]

Z-95 Headhunter

A compact, twin-engine atmospheric fighter craft that can be modified for space travel. A single pilot controls the fighter. These outdated ships were still in service on backwater worlds during the time of the Galactic Civil War, which is a testament to their durability and construction. The Incom Corporation used the Z-95 as the basis for the X-wing starfighter. [HSE, RSB, SWSB, SWVG]

Zaltin

This major Thyferran corporation was a leader in bacta production and distribution. It was brought against its will into the Bacta Cartel by the Empire, primarily to serve as competition to Xucphra. It made a secret alliance with the planet's natives and provided aid to the Ashern Circle rebels during the planet's civil war. [BW]

Zanibar

Natives of the planet Xo, these tall, thin, blue-skinned humanoids joined forces with Grappa the Hutt in the years following the birth of the New Republic. They provided a variety of services in exchange for sacrificial victims to use in their ceremonial rituals. These services included acting as bodyguards, soldiers, and smugglers for the Hutt. When Grappa failed to live up to his end of the bargain, the Zanibar took him for their next ritual. [CE]

Zardra

A tall, dark-haired bounty hunter, she appears strikingly sensual, with more than a hint of danger about her. She carries a force pike and wears a flowing cloak. She has exceptional skill and daring, and she often teams up with Jodo Kast and Puggles

Trodd. She enjoys personal combat and appreciates the fine things that credits can buy, but the hunt is the most important thing in her life. She fears that she will die senselessly—to her, this means naturally and not in combat—so she often tempts disaster by taking huge risks. After she killed Mageye the Hutt, the Hutts placed a huge price on her head. [OS, TM, TMEC]

Zatec-Cha

The grand vizier of the planet Tammuz-an during the early days of Imperial rule. He hoped to usurp the throne of Mon Julpa. [DTV]

Zavval

A Hutt, he oversaw the Ylesian spice operation. He was killed during Han Solo's escape from Ylesia when Han was about nineteen years old. [PS]

Zeebo

A four-eared mooka, he was the furred and feathered pet of Ken the Jedi prince. [LCJ, PDS]

Zekk

A onetime street urchin, he was taken in by old Peckhum, a supply courier and message runner for the New Republic on Coruscant. Zekk became friendly with Jedi academy members during supply runs to Yavin 4. He also had numerous run-ins with Norys, leader of the Lost Ones gang in Coruscant's lower levels. When Tamith Kai of the Shadow Academy discovered that Zekk had Force potential, he was taken before Brakiss and trained as a Dark Jedi. He defeated rival Vilas in a lightsaber duel and was awarded the title of Darkest Knight. Later, he was badly wounded in an explosion that partly destroyed the Great Temple on Yavin 4. He was then taken in by the Jedi academy and cared for there. [YJK]

Zend, Salla

A tough smuggler and the former girlfriend of Han Solo, she built the *Starlight Intruder* transport ship. After an accident almost killed her, she retired from smuggling and set up a starship repair business with Shug Ninx. [DE]

Salla Zend

Zhar

This gas giant located deep in the Outer Rim Territories has two primary moons: Gall and Kile. After Boba Fett's ship *Slave I* suffered damage in a battle with IG-88, the bounty hunter landed at the Imperial enclave on Gall for repairs. From nearby Kile, the Alliance's Rogue Squadron established a temporary base and launched an unsuccessful raid on Fett to rescue the imprisoned Han Solo. [SOTE]

Ziost

This planet was the central world for the Sith Lords and the seat of the Sith Empire some 5,000 years before the Galactic Civil War. [FSE]

Zlarb

A slave trader, he was a tall human with fair skin, white-blond hair and beard, and clear gray eyes. He once commandeered the *Millennium Falcon* and its crew when he needed to deliver contraband to the planet Bonadan. [HLL]

Zorba's Express

An ancient, bell-shaped starship owned by Zorba the Hutt. [ZHR]

Zorba the Hutt

The father of Jabba the Hutt. He did not immediately learn of his son's death because he was imprisoned on the planet Kip. Zorba resembled his son, though he had long, white hair braids and a white beard. All of Jabba's possessions were bequeathed to Zorba, including the desert palace on Tatooine and the Holiday Towers Hotel and Casino on Cloud City. He vowed to kill Princess Leia Organa Solo for the murder of his son. [MMY, PDS, QE, ZHR]

Zraii, Master

A Verpine, he was in charge of repairs and maintenance for Rogue Squadron's fleet of X-wings. [RS]

Zsinj, Warlord

An Imperial warlord, he firmly controlled a third of the galaxy for a time after the Battle of Endor. [RS]

Z'trop

A scenic, romantic tropical world noted for its pleasant volcanic islands, its wide beaches, and its clear waters. Han Solo, Princess Leia, and their companions vacationed on this world. [MMY]

Zuckuss

A Gand bounty hunter, he was among those commissioned by Darth Vader to locate the *Millennium Falcon* and its crew after the ship escaped from Imperial forces during the Battle of Hoth. [ESB, GG3, TBH]

Zuckuss

Zuggs, Commodore

A bald-headed, beady-eyed Imperial officer, he was assigned to Trioculus, serving as the pilot for his Strike cruiser. [LCJ]

Zyggurats

This terrorist group operated on the fringes of the galaxy and was believed to have come from outside known Imperial space shortly after the Clone Wars. The rising Empire quickly suppressed the terrorist group before its activities could cause much damage. [DE]

Zythmar

The temple priest of the Massassi warriors on Yavin 4 some 4,000 years before the Galactic Civil War. Exar Kun used him as a test subject for Naga Sadow's Sith transformation machines. [DLS]

ZZ-4Z (ZEE ZEE)

This housekeeping droid cared for Han Solo's apartment on Nar Shaddaa and was seriously damaged during a battle with Boba Fett. [DE]

About the Author

Bill Slavicsek, professional game designer and *Star Wars* expert, saw the original *Star Wars* movie thirty-eight times in the summer of 1977. It changed his life. Since then, in between countless viewings of the various *Star Wars* films, he has been a columnist for *Marvel Age Magazine*, creative director of West End Games, and director and lead designer of roleplaying games for Wizards of the Coast, Inc. He has written well over a dozen *Star Wars* game products, as well as the hugely successful second edition of *A Guide to the Star Wars Universe* and the new *Star Wars* RPG from Wizards. He lives in Washington with his wife, two cats, and more *Star Wars* "research material" than he ever imagined. And he can imagine a lot.